SEVEN DEGREES

SEVEN DEGREES

LEWIS HASTINGS

This edition published in Great Britain in 2020

by Hobeck Books Limited, Unit 14, Sugnall Business Centre, Sugnall, Stafford, Staffordshire, ST21 6NF

www.hobeck.net

A CIP catalogue for this book is available from the British Library.

ISBN 978-1-913-793-16-6 (pbk)

ISBN 978-1-913-793-15-9 (ebook)

Cover design by Jem Butcher

http://www.jembutcherdesign.co.uk

Printed and bound in Great Britain

Seven Degrees logo © Russell Budden

Poem: 'Imogen' (abridged) by Claire Borlase

❈ Created with Vellum

ARE YOU A THRILLER SEEKER?

Hobeck Books is an independent publisher of crime, thrillers and suspense fiction and we have one aim – to bring you the books you want to read.

For more details about our books, our authors and our future plans, plus the chance to download free novellas, please sign up for our newsletter at **www.hobeck.net**.

You can also find us on Twitter **@hobeckbooks** or on Facebook **www.facebook.com/hobeckbooks10**.

NOTE ON THE SEVENTH WAVE TRILOGY

My most detective-worthy readers will note that the number seven features in my writing; I met 'her' on the seventh and the trilogy is in seven parts. When I started the story there was only one book. Then it grew, and grew, so if you are finding yourself immersed in this book and wondering why there is a Part Three without a Part One or Two... Now you know, you might want to park this one up and start with *Seventh* (Parts One and Two), then finish off with *Seven of Swords* (Parts Four, Five, Six and Seven). Case solved...

Lewis

My past has gone;
Though the storm rages on.
She underestimates me;
Her destructive force threatens;
Intrinsic beauty under her skin.
My senses transcend.
I...fear being alive.

Hungarian author Frigyes Karinthy proposed the six degrees of separation theory in his early twentieth century work *'Chains'*.
Karinthy suggested that everyone and everything is six or fewer steps away, by way of introduction, from any other person on the planet. His concept being that any two people could be connected in a maximum of six steps.

But what if there were seven degrees?

PROLOGUE

I KNEW AS SOON AS I SAW HER, THAT THINGS WERE GOING to be difficult.

With a recently estranged and at times God-awful wife in my wake, I had set out to press the reset button, only a week after a career-altering event with a senior officer. I had friends in high places it seemed. I had earned their respect and in turn, they had gained mine. Take the opportunity and go they said. It wouldn't be the last time I heard that statement, just when I thought things couldn't be any better.

I walked into a regional British airport, a few hours north of London and knew within a few paces that I had made the right decision. You do. Your heart tells you so. Policing does that to you, makes you cynical. But as cynical as I had become, because of the way I had been treated, I knew I had to embrace change and start from scratch. A change, I was told, was as good as a rest.

Day One, a mixture of handshakes and moments of mental chaos, akin to drinking from a fire hose. You know how to do it but it isn't quite as simple as it looks. Looking back now there was really only Day One.

Day Two and Three were a blur. She saw to that, with her incredible eyes, that shock of red hair and a body that would look good in a hessian bag, she had it in spades. And she knew it too. But that was what I fell for – she was sexy and arrogant and beautifully naïve all at once.

Nikolina Petrov drove a stake into my heart and planted a seed deep in my mind that day. Over many hours I interviewed her, checked and cross-checked her account. I allowed her to amble, then pinned her down. Not once did I find fault in her story, because it was true.

She had arrived, under the guise of a normal passenger – albeit she had training, confidence and a false travel document. That apart, yep, she was normal alright, right up until the moment she started to confess and play with my mind.

By the following morning I knew her life story and she knew me as Sergeant Cade.

I had finished my interview with her on a Wednesday morning, it may have been a Thursday, life had a habit of compressing things. As I wrapped the exhibit label around the interview tape, she put her hand across the table and held mine. Her hands were strong but soft, her nails needed cutting but I could sense that this was a lady who had recently experienced the things that only serious money could buy. She held my hand a little too long. It was a deliberate act and something told me to allow it.

As I signed the exhibit labels she carried on with her story – now off the record. She had shredded her life just as they had taught her. I could learn a lot from Niko – as she liked to be called.

She told me her plans were to return to her daughter once it was safe, guide her to Britain and start a new life. Just the two of them. She needed my help, that much was obvious, but she also had the help of someone else, someone in a position of authority. But that, she said, was a strict need to know. As curious as I was, I decided not to ask.

Once she had told me what she knew, she stopped and began to cry. And she cried for hours.

She had tried to kill him and failed, and now, amongst other things he was coming after her.

The sociopath and the rose. But this rose had thorns.

That was all she ever told me. It was as if she had run out of life. My years of instinctive policing offered me two clear choices; believe her, or not.

I believed her of course. Her story was too convincing. And she had gained my complete attention from that moment on. All I needed to do was protect her.

She became my intelligence source; I prevented her removal from Britain – probably bent the rules, at the very least adapted them for the first and only time in my career. I extended her life and gave her hope. John 'Jack' Cade, police officer and defender of the weak. It felt good to be a knight in shining armour once more.

I slept well, for the first time in years. She approached me in a dream that night, the first of many. I could literally feel her next to me. She smelt of vanilla and evening orange groves, her hair shone, her skin radiated pure wellbeing and above all she sensed hope.

Within days, she was dead.

Days later, what she had told me began to happen. Everything, just as she had said it would. Almost to the letter.

Simple, yet brilliantly efficient. A plague of locusts stripping away the goodness, ripping the heart out of the financial sector of the city. Her legacy left me with two decisions, only one of which I knew I could abide by.

Protect the city, or protect my team.

I couldn't do both.

PART FOUR

CHAPTER ONE

New Scotland Yard London 2004

THE TEAM HAD BEEN STOOD DOWN, MANY WERE surviving on adrenaline but typical of teams like them around the world they never knew quite when to give in.

'Another ten minutes guv and I'll be out of here...' which was normally followed with a swift call home. 'It's me. I'll be late.'

Detective Sergeant Jason 'Ginger' Roberts was saying goodbye to them in the car park, it was something he always did, thanking his staff, every day, for their hard work and dedication. He was an exception to the managerial rule.

It was mid-afternoon, most of them had been on the go for thirty-six hours, grabbing disturbed sleep when and wherever they could. One of the small group was walking away from the Yard when he received a text message. He stopped, digested the contents twice then dug deep into his reserves of energy and ran back to the car park.

"Boss, stop the team, I've got some news, and it's not good."

Detective Constable Del Murphy handed his phone to Roberts.

"I've read it three times."

Roberts stared at the words and managed to form them into a cohesive sentence.

"Gather everyone together at The Sanctuary, Del. I'll be there in twenty."

Roberts was walking across the car park when he met an equally weary male walking towards him.

Good looking, in a salt-and-pepper hair, just-awake fresh blue eyes and always smelling of something exotic, it was his partner, and technically his boss, John 'Jack' Cade. Cade had arrived from a small but demanding international airport two hundred miles north of London. His exact reason for being on the team was best described as fate. Or luck, good or bad, hadn't quite been established. Either way, he had impressed the right people and at risk of falling into a stereotypical trap, favoured by crime writers, had taken the offer of a permanent job in the city of London – or technically, according to the locals the City of Westminster. This somehow added to the mystique of the place for a man who was born in the south of England, gravitated north and had never spent any formative time in the capital.

It was either take the opportunity or remain in Nottingham, live separately from his openly adventurous wife and end up before a custody sergeant on a charge of attempted murder – of his boss, not his estranged wife. With any luck, Penelope, for that was the bitch's name, would contract a hideous social disease and simply fade away.

Carrie O'Shea, Roberts' brightest analyst and a female

with a bittersweet relationship with the Metropolitan Police, was two steps behind Cade.

"I know you are both knackered, but I need you to support me at the pub. The team's re-grouping as we speak. We need to meet...to have a drink to..."

"But boss I'm exhausted, Jack needs to get to a doctor to have those wounds looked at, he's struggling to walk for God's sake, this had better be important!"

Roberts spoke quickly. Staccato words, trying to create a sentence. "Clive's dead, Carrie. Took his own life. Hung himself with his regimental tie. His missus got home an hour ago. Found him. A local unit is holding the fort. I'm heading there with the boss after we've toasted his memory. I know you two didn't..."

She cut him off.

"I'll be there, boss. Clive was an arsehole who couldn't keep his hands to himself but he was a bloody good detective and I won't denigrate his professional memory. The team needs to stay strong. I think what we witnessed in the last twenty-four hours was only the start. I will be there."

"Me too. That is if I'm now part of this sorry bunch of misfits you call a team Jason?" Cade shuffled awkwardly, trying to find somewhere comfortable to stand.

Roberts slapped Cade across the backside. "Course you are, you muppet!"

Whilst Cade stifled a cacophonous scream worthy of a Stephen King novel, now was not the time to shed a tear. His injuries were very much in the pre-healing phase, seeping, as raw as the news that had just been delivered about the demise of long-term member of the team, former paratrooper-turned-detective Clive Wood.

How Cade had sustained the injuries was relatively easy to explain – if explained quickly, he found that preferable.

He had leapt from the rear door of an iconic red, double decker London bus during a high-velocity-round-firing pursuit that had ended with a public servant dead, a police officer in hospital, a young, as-yet unidentified male in a mortuary and two more on the run, one with an obvious wound – the work of a single 5.56 mm round unleashed by the leather-wrapped index finger of its tactical operator. It was all in a day's work, if that work happened to involve crime and the people that perpetrated it.

Wood had never been able to get to know his new boss, but the fact that Cade had leapt from what appeared to be a perfectly serviceable bus would have appealed to him greatly.

The fact that the bus was at the time on its side, sliding gracefully along a comparatively quiet city road, was neither here nor there. He had leapt from it and had endured the almost interminable slide along the carriageway, its abrasive surface shredding the clothing, a defiant leather belt and the primary layer of skin from Cade's backside and hip.

Respect indeed. And now, in time-honoured fashion a number of people had gathered to pay their respects to Wood, a man who had more friends than enemies, but like most hardworking police officers had a few of the latter – and one, ironically, in the same office.

O'Shea had stated without hesitation that she hated him since the night when he had taken the liberty that he had. Alone in an office with the 'girl-next-door' that was Carrie O'Shea, in the doyen of British policing – New Scotland Yard.

He thought that things were going well until she tried to take control. Wood, being a full-blooded Welshman and former soldier, felt intimidated, impotent almost, so pushed things just a little too far.

Hindsight would tell O'Shea that ramming a highly sharpened pencil into the back of his hand, into the web between his thumb and forefinger and through to the other side may not have been ideal.

Thoughtfully wiping the condensation off a scotch glass in the dowdy English pub, she reflected upon that night and couldn't help but smile.

Leaving him in the office naked without so much as an excuse as she made good her escape, dumping his clothes in the foyer of New Scotland Yard was, in the Welshman's eyes, unforgiveable.

She smiled again now – for the first time she had found a place in her heart to forgive him, the dirty old bastard.

Roberts was beginning a speech, like he did all of his speeches.

"Team. I assume you know what has happened? Like you, I'm gutted. I'm too tired to bloody cry and too angry to go anywhere right now. So ladies, gentlemen, supporters of Welsh rugby, people who have never leapt from a perfectly serviceable aircraft, or bus for that matter, and the rest of you that simply didn't fit into a category that Clive considered honourable..."

He stopped. Paused and looked around the private bar at The Sanctuary, the adopted, nicotine-stained London pub and default choice of the section. It was a conscious decision to look at every face in the room. That morning and for the first time, for the first time, he began to worry about who might be next and unlike some bosses, he genuinely cared.

Whilst the group that called themselves The First Wave were not directly responsible for Wood's death they had, Roberts felt, somehow played their part in it. Their presence alone meant that he had found himself guarding precious cargo, in the form of a perfectly shaped Bulgarian female, from a long line of beautiful girls, each with a history of survival. He only hoped her value was going to mean more to the team than office eye candy.

The girl in question, Nikolina Petrov, had arrived into the lives of the Metropolitan Police team led by Roberts. Alongside, and guarding, or rather what he referred to as 'nurturing her for intelligence' was Sergeant Jack Cade. They had arrived as a pair, inseparable and yet entirely unconnected.

Cade's professional connection was actually very clear, even though he had repeatedly questioned why this wasn't a task carried out by the Home or Foreign Office, or even the security services.

'Jack. On behalf of the British Home Office, find out what this girl knows. We need a breakthrough in the area of criminal syndicates targeting this country. This is not a job for any of the teams you have alluded to. End of. These are travelling criminals and unless we act, they are here to stay. We need a break, an opening, and this may be the chance we have been looking for. It matters not that you are a 'mere' sergeant, this girl trusts you and you alone must exploit this trust. That is the reason why. Within reason you have our support and we will make whatever you need available.'

When Cade had first met her, a hundred miles north of London at a regional airport near the city of Nottingham, she was broken; both her heart and her body were fractured.

But her mind was as sharp as one of Carrie O'Shea's much-favoured pencils. Petrov had a story to tell and when she had first looked into the azure-blue eyes of her interviewer through her own bloodshot, but equally piercing green eyes she had found him to be both physically attractive and more importantly, trustworthy.

It wasn't what he said that gave her this assurance, but the way he said it.

Petrov had escaped from a relationship that centred exclusively on a male who considered himself, via dubious gypsy folklore, to be her husband. The marriage was self-governed and binding. He had chosen her. And that was the end of the courting phase.

'Do what I ask and your life will be filled with material things. Accept that I will have other women and that occasionally I may respond unfavourably towards you.' This was how she had interpreted their relationship.

'Your bruises will heal in time, my dear...' was how he wrote off his incessant appetite for brutality.

She had met him in a bar, a place called Byzantin, apparently alone, naïve and completely unaware of his status in a part of the city that he arguably ran, practically owned. He certainly owned a number of palatial properties, more vehicles than he could ever drive, and a plethora of local government officials, all too eager to be his friend, were nestled comfortably in his back pocket.

What the male, Alexandru Stefanescu did not realise was that his newfound, lithe yet immature lover was there with a precisely defined goal. Whilst still in her teens she had been groomed, trained and almost indoctrinated by her wonderful father's employers – the Durzhavna Sigurnost – the Bulgarian Intelligence Service.

The aim was simple enough. Kill Stefanescu – who was

also referred to by the self-imposed nickname of the Jack-daw, due in part to his familiar cackling laugh, but equally because the ornithological world considered the inquisitive bird of the same name to be an expert thief.

Stefanescu had embarrassed the Bulgarian government once too often and had taken to mocking them via his well-crafted criminal syndicate, who were as adept at hurting people as the businesses they targeted. Moving high-end vehicles around Europe was enough to keep him on Interpol's radar, the agency having at any one time at least two staff monitoring his progress from their headquarters in Lyon, France.

As far as they could see he had successfully avoided trafficking drugs around Europe and further afield. His reputation had been won by virtue of his love for money, preferably cash, but electronic transactions would often suffice – and as his techniques had been enriched, so had his enviable offshore bank balances.

As skilled as the Interpol staff were, they were always three steps behind him, chasing their own tails, acting upon informant information that more often than not was provided by Stefanescu's own network of people.

His avaricious nature meant that sooner or later someone, somewhere would catch him, but on the rare occasions he was produced to a judge, he would either walk away, having discreetly enhanced the prosecutor's own account or escape using a network of associates. There was simply no denying, he was a very gifted criminal with a network that was growing and potentially viral in nature.

And it appeared that in mainland Europe in 2004 criminal syndicates were beginning to realise that there was more to gain from cooperation than conflict.

. . .

Nikolina's plans had changed. She had probably failed to kill Stefanescu, despite waiting a painfully long time to do so. Contrary to her external feelings, she had grown to love him – Stockholm syndrome had played a part. Her captor had become her lover and in time he had provided for her, in ways she could only have dreamt of in her former home. He had fathered a child too – a child that had become the first person he had ever truly wished to protect.

The issue though was that as compassionate as he was becoming, he still had a ruthless, spiteful streak, and that scared her. She needed to leave, to formulate a plan for the future, one that provided for both her and her daughter Elena.

Until she was able to create that platform she had to go, to leave her safely in another part of Europe and deal with him either to the letter of the mission, or as best as she could.

But in order to carry out the mission, she had to first say goodbye to her little girl – and that would prove to the single hardest decision of her young life.

Stabbing a Ricin-laced mechanism into his thigh and escaping from their opulent Spanish home was supposed to be simple, but the poison had diluted over time, and whether it had done its job remained a worrying unknown. She daren't go back or enquire. She needed to vanish.

Petrov could not look back, she had neither the opportunity nor the courage. She left Spain during the night, having changed her appearance and her identity, praying that he would die a slow and rather exquisitely painful death, or at best leave her alone and continue to love and protect their daughter until the day came that she could reunite with her and allow her to make her own mind up about the truth, about her father and importantly about why she left.

She had put things into place; written Constantin, left messages with a few people. They were selected as they were people she both loved and trusted and hoped that the stories she had told her baby – about their beautiful homeland and her heritage – would act as an umbilical cord for the future.

Whether he knew it or not, for now, Jack Cade *was* her plan. Every minute piece of it.

Roberts stood in the middle of the close-knit team and continued with his eulogy.

"It is my honour to raise a glass to our friend and our colleague, Clive Wood. May his memory live on within the team, and for all the right reasons..."

Roberts paused, beginning to feel emotional at the sudden realisation that for the first time in his career he had lost a staff member. He stopped, took a moment to control himself and then quoted from an anonymous poem, in time reaching the last line.

...Come walk a beat on Heaven's streets, you've done your time in hell.

He let out a profound sigh.

"Team. The Thin Blue Line just got thinner."

He glanced at O'Shea.

She was the first to raise her glass.

"Detective Clive Wood, a proud man, and forgiven for his sins, especially being Welsh. May you always rest in peace."

The team all followed Roberts' lead – even the barman Roger Walsh raised a pint in the officer's honour. It was the least he could do given the amount the team spent in the place.

Roberts took a long glug of his drink before placing the glass on a stained and peeling beer mat and asking for silence once more.

"Guys, forgive me. Be upstanding, I have another toast."

The team stood and held their glasses, ready for the next announcement. They were used to adulation among their close-knit group. To quote their boss, who they adored, 'no other bastard will praise you!'

"To Jack Cade, the Northern Monkey. Part of the team!"

"Jack Cade! Part of the team!"

Cade, unused to such camaraderie, took a long and slow gulp of his drink before placing his glass onto the counter.

"Jason, if I may?"

"Mon pleasure."

"Team, and I've worked with a few... I just wanted to thank you for your hard work, your commitment and for embracing everything I have said, and agreeing to everything I have asked for." He looked around the nicotine-stained room, its walls and ceilings a shade of ochre only reserved for such buildings.

"It's not always easy when a new boss arrives and most of us despise change, but trust me when I say be the best you can be and I will back you all to the hilt. Now, if you would flatter me for a few more seconds, I would like to quote my Shakespearean namesake Jack Cade?"

A few staff raised their eyes to the ceiling. Surely now was not the time to quote the Bard himself?

At his theatrical best, Cade entered the middle of the crowd and climbed onto a bar stool. It wobbled causing a few sharp intakes and then he settled, turned around from his new lofty position and commenced what many thought would be a long, drawn-out and painful adaptation. He waited for silence then adopted a character voice, pretty effective too, at least O'Shea thought so.

'I thank you, good people: there shall be no money; all shall eat and drink on my score.'

It took a few seconds, but what followed was a genuinely appreciative cheer.

Roberts seized the moment.

"Right, you lot take up Jack's most generous offer, then bugger off to your loved ones. Rest well and remember, look after each other. I don't want you back to work until ten o'clock tomorrow, earliest..."

He scanned the room and noticed John Daniel had arrived.

"Guys, guys, I'm sorry. At risk of being lynched – one, last thing." He received a combined moan of disapproval.

"I promise this is the last toast... Our new boss had arrived to buy us all a drink for a job well done before Sergeant Cade's most indecent proposal. Therefore, it would be rude, no outrageous to turn down such a benevolent offer. Everyone meet Detective Chief Inspector John Daniel. JD to his friends, but he assures me I can call him Detective Chief Inspector!"

Daniel moved to the front of the group, leaned on the back of a worn, green velvet upholstered chair and allowing the room to settle spoke from the heart.

"Thank you, Jason. You'll go far, I'm thinking Essex... Listen team, it's always hard when a new boss arrives, you worry about what they will do to the group? What they will change?" The speech was familiar. "Well, let me assure you, having seen what I've seen in the last few days, only a fool would make any substantial changes and I hope you'll quickly realise that whilst I'm many things, a fool, I am not."

There was an approving sound around the bar. He was saying the right things.

Cade looked at a man who he felt he could trust, something tangible told him to.

"Finally, and yes, unlike your boss here, I do mean finally. I'd like to add to the toasts if I may be so bold?"

Nods of endorsement occurred around the bar.

"I never had the pleasure of meeting them, and I hear Detective Wood was a fine man and he will, I know, be sorely missed. But there is someone else, if I may?"

There were signs of encouragement from the group.

"I never met her either, but I heard she was a true warrior, a brave young woman in a foreign land whose life was cut short all too soon. It is incumbent upon every man and woman in this team to ensure her legacy is achieved. We need to find out why she came to Jack and then to us. This young lady left behind all she knew, including her daughter. I want to know what secrets she carried, and I believe you are the people to reveal them. May she please not die in vain? Rest in peace Nikolina Petrov."

The team stood for the last time that day, emptied their glasses, and one by one left the bar after shaking the new boss's hand.

Tomorrow would be another day.

CHAPTER TWO

"Jack, do you have a minute?"

"Of course sir, what do you need?"

Daniel was forthright and honest. He also liked what he saw in Cade.

"Jack, I want you to consider a permanent transfer to this force, see it as a promotional opportunity. Jason is going places and won't be with us forever. Come down here and try something different, we could certainly do with your skills and it seems as though you have been a lone voice on the issue of Eastern European crime, until now. Forget the fact that we are the best force in the country – this stuff is new, developing, unchartered waters and like it or not you have unwittingly become the subject matter expert in a field of probably a dozen people. So?"

Daniel let the offer hang in the musty room, his words clinging to the walls and joining a thousand lost conversations.

Cade pondered the offer.

"Is it as easy as that, sir? Just pick up and come here,

accept a promotion I haven't even applied for? Seems a little passé to me. It just doesn't happen that way. There's stuff to do, things to consider. There's the application process, HR, interviews...referees..."

Daniel held his hand up.

"It is that easy or I wouldn't have asked. And before you ask, yes. I've run it by Malcolm Johnson and he's one hundred percent behind it. I think your circus analogy hurt him a little, but he liked your honesty. We'll have to interview you, of course, but you appear to be the only applicant. We've taken the liberty of speaking to your force for references and they accept on your behalf. It would appear that you have a few notable friends up north. So, what's it to be?"

"Putting it like that boss, I have little option. Besides, there's very little back at home for me these days. If you can accept the overly clichéd movement of a brass-necked, gritty, northern copper into the metropolis, then I accept."

"This is reality old son, not some dog-eared paperback you'd find in a bargain bin. And I'd hardly call you gritty, except for the bits that the doctor has yet to pick carefully out of your arse. Good man, come round to my place for dinner tomorrow night if you are not too tired? Be good for you to meet Lynne, Mrs Daniel, great cook and all round general *bon vivant*."

"Again, an offer one cannot easily turn down. Do you have comfy chairs to sit in? My aforementioned arse feels like a championship dart board."

"We do! Oh, and Jack..."

"Boss?"

"Bring the girl with you too, help balance the numbers a little." He winked, grabbed his jacket and left.

"Girl boss?"

"Oh, come on Jack, you are surrounded by bloody

coppers, do you really think your secret is safe? Everyone knows that you and Carrie are an item. She's a lovely girl, you could do a lot worse and I suspect she will be loyal..." He paused. "Sorry. Too soon?"

"Not anymore, sir. It's evident that my old force let you read all of my personal file. Did the part where I almost knocked out a uniformed inspector not bother you?"

"Hardly. Good call. If he'd done that with Mrs Daniel, his days as a marathon runner would be over."

Cade frowned.

"I meant he'd be competing in a wheel chair Jack."

"But he could still compete..."

"Not if I slashed his tyres."

Cade walked out into a brighter day. O'Shea was waiting for him.

"Come on you, let's head back to my place for some sleep. It's been an incredibly long couple of days."

He smiled and started walking. After a hundred paces he put his left arm out and nodded to it, O'Shea took his lead and linked her own arm through his.

"What if anyone sees us Jack, you a sergeant on the team and all that, aren't you worried about your reputation?"

"Ah, you see that's where you are wrong Carrie, up until ten minutes ago I *was* a sergeant, but I am afraid I am no longer."

"Dear God, man don't tell me you've resigned?"

"No, of course not, do you think I'm mad girl?"

"Sacked?" Her voice was almost pleading him to say no.

"No, Carrie. But thanks for your confidence. I just got promoted, and there's another thing..."

"Do go ahead, Inspector, I'm all ears..."

"And great breasts too, so I recall…"

She pulled her arm back and was about to slap him on the backside, but seeing his eyes widen, she stopped millimetres from her target.

"I hate it when you keep secrets from me. Go on, please, tell me."

"I'm moving to London Carrie, turns out my skills are finally of some use."

She beamed, placed her arm back through his, rested her head on his shoulder and allowed him to pull her closer to him. It was getting chilly, but she felt a sense of genuine warmth for the first time in years.

They got to her flat, kicked the door shut behind them, closed the curtains, undressed and fell into her bed. Within ten minutes O'Shea entwined around her newly promoted man and drifted quickly into a deep sleep. Cade was five ahead of her.

It was later in the day when Cade found himself deliberating, long enough to change his mind twice, possibly more. Should he accept her offer?

They had only been acquainted for such a short amount of time. Yes, there was a tangible sense of chemistry – albeit he didn't quite understand its exact place in his current jumbled 'I just need a few days to myself' and most recent lifestyle.

"It's up to you, boss. If you are not comfortable with the offer, then by all means turn it down. I'm a big girl, I don't make offers like this without thinking through every aspect of risk. I'm a female, you are a male, you are the boss and I'm a subordinate. OK, perhaps an element of risk exists, but really, I suspect the last thing that will be at the forefront on your mind when you arrive home and walk into the apartment will be 'I really must seduce my best analyst, after all the last person to do that became impaled on a piece of sharpened graphite…"

It took the rest of the day for him to accept. Quietly, she shook inside and forced herself not to smile. She looked out of the window. It was her safe haven. Why give away her non-verbals in front of an expert?

"I accept Carrie, but only because I have nowhere else to go other than the shoddy motel that the Met have housed me in, and for now I hear HRH's place across the road is full. When shall I move in my one suitcase and tawdry belongings?"

"Tonight?"

"Tonight it is. I shall cook, my treat, but don't get used to it. My spag bol is one of my three signature dishes."

"And the others?"

"If you are a good girl, you may find out."

The flirting had started.

Cade made good on his promise, his worldly goods were placed onto the bedroom floor of the smaller of the two rooms; he closed the door too behind him and entered the kitchen, forced O'Shea to take a seat at the small breakfast bar, opened a bottle of Pinot Noir and poured two glasses which were clinked together.

"Cheers. And thank you."

"For what? You'll be rewarding me handsomely for a room with a view and in such close proximity to work – I can assure you of that, Mr Cade."

To the uninitiated she was cool, frigid almost, but he sensed something more, a far greater depth that he already wanted to explore. Keep your distance, Jack.

The meal was as described, seasoned perfectly and

complimented by a third glass of the Central Otago classic red. She knew she had to set the tone of this relationship – if indeed that is what it had become – if it was to work.

"Thank you, Jack. Lovely. Unnecessary, but lovely nonetheless. I need to head to bed. We both have an early start and I'm a little drunk if I'm honest." She leaned towards him and stopped herself.

"Goodnight."

He smiled. It would have been all too easy. "Goodnight Carrie and thank you again. I will finish clearing up and head to bed myself. I will make sure I get some money tomorrow as a down payment. You need to let me know what you want each week."

"Why Mr Cade, I can assure you I am far from cheap..."

His eyes gave away his true feelings, bluer than normal, his pupils dilated slightly and he could feel himself responding physically to her.

"Indeed, Miss O'Shea, Indeed. Notwithstanding we have a syndicate of bad buggers to pursue, I will find an ATM – if there are any left in this fine city – and put the money on the worktop this time tomorrow."

O'Shea waved her hand as she entered her room, a failed indication that she wasn't that worried about the money. She closed her door, clicked the handle to ensure it was shut, and started to undress. A minute later, she heard Cade enter his own room.

She sat for ten minutes in an antique white French buttoned-back chair that was positioned at forty-five degrees to her bed. Her curtains were open, and she stared through the window, across the inner-city parkland and smiled as she heard Cade moving around in her guest room. She waited a further ten minutes for him to get into bed.

She got into her own bed, pulling back the immaculate

700 percale thread count Egyptian cotton sheets and enjoying the feeling of their coolness on her body. She lay in the half light of the street lamps and listened to Cade moving around. She tried to remove him from her thoughts, but he returned, again and again. The sheer thought of having him in such close proximity aroused her – she knew it was wrong – but it felt incredibly right.

Cade was wide awake, listening for sounds in a foreign house. She was asleep, a pity, he could spend hours talking to her, perhaps he should knock on her door and ask if she wanted a nightcap. 'No! Far too clichéd Jack and besides, she'd probably kick you out onto the streets and make a complaint first thing in the morning.'

But she continued to invade his thoughts.

Cade had closed his eyes again but soon found himself thinking about her, her eyes, those darting looks that she thought he hadn't observed.

An hour later he was awake. He had woken with an enormous jolt, the type that normally indicates the dreamer has fallen from a great height, and struck the ground. His heart was audibly pounding.

He had found himself on a boat, drifting along a major river system. He was hunting for something or someone, but was unable to steer the dream in a direction that suited him. He was going with the tide. The boat slowed and then stopped.

Cade was the only passenger on board. He looked around for guidance, but he was definitely alone.

The boat became stuck fast on an obstruction.

He knew he somehow needed to free the vessel, but was powerless to move it. He lacked the required skills and couldn't, despite an overwhelming desire, be in two places at once. He walked aimlessly around the deck, peering over the edge into murky brown, fast-flowing, eddy-filled water. All he saw was his own face, a vision of dread.

Stopping at the stern, he found himself drawn to the edge once more. The boat started to rotate, slowly at first, then quicker. He could see the shore, but it was just out of reach.

If he could just lean over a little further, perhaps grab hold of that wooden frame? From there it was a short swim to the steps. Just a short swim. Even with the tide rushing out towards the sea, he felt he could make it.

The boat began to spin faster and faster, reminiscent of a much-worn wooden and iron roundabout from his distant childhood, painted in bottle green, its circular metal bars shining from repeated contact with the hands of long grown-up children. Round and around. And around.

He was nauseous. Out of control and shaking with fear.

Jump.

He abandoned the boat which immediately dislodged from the obstruction and drifted downstream. He was now more alone than ever. Swimming against the tide.

He pushed through the water, for every one stroke towards his goal the river took him two back. Again he pushed...dragged himself through the maelstrom.

Get to the bloody frame, man.

He was shouting in his sleep.

He extended his hand. His arm was shuddering, desperate to take hold of the only obvious form of salvation.

He made it. Breath.

He placed his head beneath the surface. The dark brown water was now crystal clear, he could see everything. The river bed, cluttered with historical artefacts, small fish darting between swirling reeds. A hundred or so paces away he could see the entire outline of the boat, which was now stationary in the water, ambiguous outlines of human figures staring back at him.

He turned, looking around at the incredible sight. He could breathe underwater. He placed his arms outwards, in a crucifix form and began to float, ethereally. It was magnificent.

He gently wafted his right hand, each stroke enabled him to turn effortlessly in the river. He turned and turned. He began to laugh. Mouth open. The water never travelled beyond his lips.

As he turned again, her hand brushed across his face, cold, desperately cold. He instinctively grabbed for it, it grabbed back, holding him in a vice-like grip, almost crushing his fingers, not letting him go.

The euphoria vanished.

He found himself looking at the girl. She was crying, her tears flowing into the river. She pulled him towards her. She was shouting, but he couldn't make out the words. Her naked body, three times its normal size, her face stretched, distorted, hideous. Her eyes were pathetic, shallow and life-less. Disinterested.

She pointed.

He turned.

Another naked female was drifting past them. She was clawing at an imaginary object. Her fingers bleeding. Lost, alone and trapped – as if she were beneath the ice of a frozen lake. She screamed a silent scream and began to swim towards Cade, her fingers lengthening, desperate to reach him. He put his hand out to hers. He was now looking at the hand in minute detail; it was in front of his face, detached from its owner. His own fingers were sinking into her flesh which was rotting, shards of it peeling away and vanishing in the darkness.

He could see straight through her skin, she had become almost translucent. In the shadows he made out more grotesque female forms. They too were beckoning him towards them, screaming, silent, drowning screams.

He looked at his own hand, it too was semi-transparent. He could see the bones, the ligaments and tendons, blood running through his veins, bright red. As he stared at the limb, it began to fall to pieces, each piece washing away downstream.

She was still there, floating. She had a crooked half smile but her eye sockets were now empty, obscure black openings in a snow-white face.

He began to swallow water. He could taste it, it became denser, more acrid. He started to panic, to choke. He tried in vain to swim back up to the surface.

And then she was gone. They were both gone. They were all gone.

She just slipped away.

Cade was alone in a blackened river. Afraid to turn, sinking towards the bottom. Finished. Frigid. Forgotten.

"Morning, I won't ask how you slept." It was O'Shea with freshly brewed Jamaican Blue Mountain coffee. She was sat cross-legged on the edge of the bed, wearing an over-sized shirt. Her hair was a little tousled. She looked great.

"My goodness, that's good. What is it?"

"Expensive. That's what it is!"

With eighty percent of it being exported from the Caribbean to Japan, she considered herself lucky to obtain one of the world's more expensive beverages. Grown at altitudes of over five thousand feet, it had become favoured by the richer set for its distinctive aroma and lack of bitterness.

She had her contacts, this girl, and liked the finer things in life.

"You were dreaming, Jack."

"Sorry." He placed the mug of heady liquid on the bedside cabinet.

"Nikolina?"

"Yep, among others. Terrible images. What they did to her. The way they left her in the river." He closed his eyes. The images had gone for a while. "It was inhuman."

She leant over and kissed him on the forehead.

"You look like you've not slept in weeks. Go back to sleep, Jack."

He already was. The dream would return once more and then it would never visit him again.

CHAPTER THREE

THE TEAM SLOWLY PARADED INTO WORK THE FOLLOWING day. Some were bedraggled, drained and still running on empty. Roberts was only marginally better, having knowingly broken the fabled eight hour rule.

It was apparent that the preceding days had taken it out of the team. Having had staff shot at, almost killed and worked to exhaustion, they had also witnessed the death of their newest collaborator and importantly, the tragic loss of one of their own team – albeit at his own hand.

Daniel, contrary to his own implicit instructions, had arrived earlier, dapper in a dark grey suit and a red, white and blue tie. He was one of those managers who appeared to survive without sleep, in fact he appeared to thrive on it.

Word spread around the office that the new 'guv' had summoned everyone back into the briefing room, and so within ten minutes they had all been rounded up and took up every available seat in the compact room.

"Team, good morning."

A resounding response of 'guv' echoed around the room.

Daniel's impassioned speech the previous day had obviously struck a chord.

"OK everyone, accepting what has happened to you all over the last week, I need to quickly formulate a plan of attack. This is not to say that I do not recognise the physical and mental strain this has put you under, but if we are to strike back at this group – whoever they may be – then we need, in my humble opinion, to do it quickly, decisively, and sadly, within the law. However, we also need help and sleep and as we know an army marches on its stomach."

Everyone continued to nod.

Sensing a mutual bonding, he continued.

"To me, there are three important issues here. One, the scale of the operational capability of the group calling itself The First Wave is unknown. Two, our ability to assimilate their activities and translate them into actionable intelligence is equally, ambiguous. Last, but by no means least, this group are directly and indirectly responsible for the loss of two of our team."

He looked slowly around the packed audience.

"And, let me tell you folks, there will be no more deaths or injuries of any kind on this team. Do I make myself clear?"

He did. Explicitly.

"Lastly, Sergeant Roberts is, as of this moment, an acting inspector. He's going to be working closely with me on this project, as is Inspector Cade. I'm sure I speak for you all when I offer congrats on the various promotions?"

There was an approving rumble around the room which ended with one of the team theatrically coughing the phrase 'first round is on Jason!'

"Indeed," said Daniel, warming to the team. "However, before we get too carried away, we have some serious work to do. Jason will be running the day to day logistical needs of Operation Breaker, Detective Constable Paul Clarke will be acting as Jason's second in command, albeit he didn't know until now. Jack...Inspector Cade will take an oversight of the operation and will be assisted by Carrie who will provide some right hand support."

The latter got a huge and ice-breaking cheer from the team.

Daniel shook his head and couldn't help but smile.

"You despicable bunch of inbreds. Go on, get to it. Start getting into the hearts and minds of an active Eastern European crime cell. Think like they think. Ask yourselves where next? Why? When? How? And make sure you eat."

He then turned to Carrie O'Shea.

"Carrie, I need you to start supporting the analytical aspect of the op. In fact, I want you to take the lead – you are the senior analyst now. Work with Cynthia – she's already plotting the basics and has a lot of source knowledge within the wider financial community. Let's start drilling down on our intelligence holdings, shall we? Start an i2 chart and let's see how quickly we can gain a visual understanding of the group. I need to know what their numbers are..."

O'Shea was rapidly taking notes. She knew the i2 software back to front – it was the go-to of any modern analyst, its maker saying it turned data into intelligence, which was just what the Breaker team needed.

"...I need to know every possible ATM event in the Metropolitan area over the last six months; if you can throw the net out over the Home Counties forces even better. Get the Business Objects system to run a query on *anything* that is related to Eastern Europe, but specifically Romania and definitely anything financial."

O'Shea was liking what she heard. This was more suited to her skill-set than pursuing criminals on a bloody bus!

"Oh, and Carrie, when you've done all that, think about what you might wear tonight."

"You taking me out, boss?" She put on a coy look. "A bit forward for day two."

"Ha ha! No, hardly, I'm far too old for you young lady, delightful on the eye though you are. But I will be feeding you, you are Jack's date at my place. Did he not tell you? I want you to meet Mrs Daniel. Good chance for you and Jack to become acquainted too, as you will be working so closely."

"I look forward to it, boss. Coffee?"

"Good stuff. Seven o'clock, Jack's got the address, and tea would be smashing."

Cade and Roberts were busy brainstorming the last week. They tracked back to Petrov's arrival into East Midlands Airport, the regional hub serving the cities of Midlands' England. They spent time looking at every minor detail.

They needed to examine her departure from Spain. Interpol Madrid would be the liaison for that.

Her arrival, her interview, her confession; was it genuine? They both agreed that yes, given her demise, it must have been. Hindsight is always a wonderful thing in any investigation.

They ruled out a few people, including the hapless but vaguely lovable Geoff Pullen, the faded Ibiza-based club DJ who had provided the first link in the chain that was to become Operation Breaker.

Unwittingly engaged in a police pursuit across two counties, driving his own battered but much-prized Vauxhall,

Pullen had somehow deputised himself as a County Sheriff – and despite his perceived hatred of the police he was actually enjoying it, right up until the point where guns were actually drawn and a Romanian criminal had succumbed to an early death behind the wheel of a white Mercedes Benz.

Somewhat to Cade's relief, it appeared that Pullen had slipped back into a spray-tanned obscurity.

Their radar then locked onto the driver of the Mercedes saloon that had arrived at the airport to pick up Nikolina Petrov. Her misguided decision to get into his car had started the series of events that confirmed her trust in Cade and had led to the unknown driver suffering a hideous injury, caused by his diminutive passenger, almost moments before his demise. She had told Cade she enjoyed the smell of his flesh burning under the searing heat of the car's cigarette lighter.

They needed to liaise with Leicestershire Police to obtain as many details as possible about him. Were his fingerprints recorded anywhere in the British database? If not, could Interpol London get them checked with Interpol sites in Bucharest, Budapest, Belgrade, Chisinau and Sofia?

They still had no idea who the young male was that lay alone in the mortuary with his throat slashed. Perhaps they never would. Days after his discovery in the doorway his fingerprints had failed to draw any positive – or for that matter, negative responses from across Europe. He didn't exist. How was he connected?

Next, the two males who had also died on the streets of London. Shot by police firearms officers or killed in a pursuit. They added their own chaos to an already busy operation in a busier city. Again, who were they? Were they linked by nationality or criminality or both? Were they linked at all? The same enquiries would need to be made.

They carried absolutely no identity documents, therefore it would be critical to use their DNA, 'prints or dental records to identify them. The single greatest problem being that in order to identify them, they had to have a start point in their host nation. If these individuals were criminals, but criminals without a known history, they would effectively be ghosts.

Nikolina had been captured then transferred to a stolen Ford Transit van where a small group of men had stripped her of her dignity and her clothes, taunting her and forcing her to listen to a phone call from her husband– or rather the man who said that Roma folklore had declared them man and wife.

She met her demise in the River Thames. A solitary, frigid way to end a life, strapped to a rudimentary wooden frame and left at low tide to watch the rushing water coming in from the sea, slowly, then more rapidly consuming her.

The group that did this to her, deprived her of a young life in such a violent and cold way, later set fire to the van and left it on an industrial estate as interesting and grey as its paintwork. A few small exhibits were recovered from parts of the vehicle but proved to be worthless.

Any forensic evidence from the van was most likely gone. The almost-obliterated Mondeo would act as a source. Blood deposits, if nothing else, gave them an opportunity. Hair fibres, possibly clothing too. They would try any avenue.

When had these people arrived into the United Kingdom? Last week, the week before, the month before? A year, maybe two? Had they even, possibly, been born there? The latter would at least help, but both Roberts and Cade considered it unlikely.

"A common theme is the tattoo, Jason. I've heard about

it, read about it, seen one up close and it was also present on the two deceased. They had the simple outline of the wave on their right wrist. These were obviously new marks, perhaps an indicator that our boys were freshly badged – you know, trying out for the bigger league by kidnapping Niko? Expendable resources..." Cade's voice petered off as he began to visualise the tattoo.

"And then, of course," said Roberts feverishly chewing the end of someone else's pen, "there's the bastard that got away. Who the hell, and where the hell is *he?*"

Like so many similar days in the rapidly changing world of law enforcement, this one was unravelling and disappearing at a rate of knots.

The newly promoted colleagues visited O'Shea who was sat behind a larger-than-normal screen. She was clearly in her element. Cade considered it a positive that her skills were being used. He chose not to endorse them publicly for fear of being considered patronising and worse still, for fear of being identified as the new man in her life. He wanted to, but couldn't announce that he was also desperate to exploit as many of her hidden talents as he could.

Despite what he had said the evening before, it was not a good look for them to be in a relationship quite so soon. Besides, he rather liked the clandestine approach.

"So, professor, how's it going with the crime science stuff?" Roberts had a broad understanding of the unique ability to extract data from a series of software programmes, extrapolating the sexier bits and then producing a few graphs. Beyond that, like most non-practitioners, he was lost. What he needed was a report, preferably one, that like all quality intelligence recommendations was actionable, which made him look good. It was often said that a great intelligence team was invisible, that its finest work was never publicly discussed – only when they got it wrong.

"Looking good, Carrie. Looking good. So how are we doing with Eastern Euro activity in the Big Smoke then?"

"I've looked at London boss, I've done as you asked too and thrown the net wider. Essex has responded with a negative. Nothing for the last twelve months. Surrey likewise. Kent on the other hand have seen a lot of lower-level activity in the Medway Towns' area."

Cade nodded. He knew the region like the back of his hand.

"So why north Kent?"

O'Shea took a short moment, then offered a considered opinion.

"Boss, I look at it like this. If you want to enter the heart of the greatest financial centre in the world why not go through its arteries?"

Cade nodded. "So you think they enter the UK via the sea port at Dover, set up camp as close to London as they could, hit a few sites and retreat back to a safe haven, before doing it all again and then heading back home with their ill-gotten gains before Old Bill has a chance to lock them up?"

She smiled "Absolutely, Inspector. Look at the other night, the van we all ended up pursuing? It was heading to the A2. Lots of older back roads, with fewer electronic monitoring systems than the motorways. It was heading south alright, straight back to one of the main towns around the Medway area; Gillingham, Strood, Chatham or Rochester."

"OK, get to work with Kent too. I'll get the DCI to start making some higher-level connections with their organised crime teams. We want everything they have on ATM targeting, however small. Let's speak to our colleagues at Port of Dover Police too, see if they have ANPR – pretty sure they do, and CCTV. In fact, give them what we know so far and let them go hunting. We need as many friends as possible. The Channel Tunnel too – they have UK staff on both sides of the channel, build some relationships, you never know when we might need to cash in. As you said the other night, we are missing something. I think this is just the beginning."

He felt positive for the first time in days.

"OK, Jason, starting with the most recent event that we went to. Let's look at available evidence, get something out to the troops, we want to go overt now. Stand by with the media, though. Agreed?"

He didn't wait for affirmation.

"Then we need to commence twice-daily briefings on this and treat every single report of ATM-related crime as our priority – if it's within our boundary let's get our guys to speak to every victim. I want a template of questions to ask each and every one. Oh, and one more thing."

"Go ahead..."

"Let's get someone checking the outgoing international mail. It's dawned on me that they won't just be taking cash from the machines – they are extracting security data too..."

She slapped herself on the head.

"Of course! They post that back to larger cells overseas where it can be sold as a package, all with less..."

They both looked at one another and said in unison: "risk!"

Cade and his colleague spent the next thirty minutes recording what they had so far and drawing up the template. They sent the list of questions out to all stations and reporting lines. Nobody was to miss the opportunity to record the data. Only when they had what they needed could the analysts really conduct a true scan of the criminal environment.

The pair continued throwing ideas around, hypotheses at its best – raw and straight from the mind without critique. Cade had found in his relatively short career that it was often the most productive way of gaining the answer.

"So what?"

Roberts looked temporarily puzzled and replied with exactly the same question.

"So what?"

"Indeed, my thoughts entirely Dr Watson."

"You'll 'ave to stop being so bloody cryptic Jack, I'm a DS, correction, Acting DI, so spare me the rocket science."

"It's a phrase that any good Intelligence Officer uses. It should follow every statement. In our case, we know that a group of what we believe to be entirely Eastern European offenders are targeting the British financial markets via the easiest entry point – ATMs. The risks are relatively low, with the general public writing off the offences as 'victimless'. So what?"

Roberts stood to stretch his legs and gazed out of the window.

"So...we know we are not talking about the whole of Romania coming into Britain and stealing everyone's cash. That would be at best xenophobic and extreme. So what we are looking at is a smaller group, well organised but expendable, as in the case of our boy with his throat hanging out... he didn't make the cut."

He winced at the unintended pun and continued, now riding the crest of the wave.

"...and this group may be living under our noses. Coming

into the city and striking quickly, gathering cash and buggering off before we even have a chance of catching 'em. We should speak to the councils, get their CCTV operators to concentrate on ATMs, we could do the same, let's start gathering some imagery, if nothing else it will show us who we might be dealing with – we could then cross-match that with our colleagues at Dover and see if they have observed similar folk crossing into the UK."

Daniel joined them.

"So gents, what do we know? Anymore new activity in the last twelve or so hours? Have we got someone liaising with the banks? Do we have anything at all? Let's be honest with one another."

"All fair questions boss," said Cade, "since the pursuit and the male escaping we've seen no activity whatsoever. Which tells me that they were a three-man cell. Our thoughts are that they go to ground in a north Kent town, strike out and return – it's possible to do this within thirty minutes at night. I think we need to monitor the trunk roads into the city. Our guess is that each cell, assuming there are indeed more, uses a van, but in truth they could use anything."

"Trains?"

"Planes, or automobiles, boss. I'm sorry, but we are no nearer."

The team spent the rest of that day working through every piece of data they had. Detectives not gainfully employed on the streets were ringing around financial institutions, offering prevention advice and gathering information. Like worker bees, they fed back the intelligence to the Queen Bee – in this case O'Shea. Her confidence was growing by the hour and her newfound status within the team appeared to provide her with additional thinking skills too.

She called over to Roberts.

"Boss, I've been thinking."

"Ooh, this could be interesting. Someone grab me a coffee and some biscuits. I need biscuits but remember, no fucking ginger…they play havoc with my teeth."

"Nuts!" said O'Shea. "We get it, boss. No ginger nuts. Promise. Whilst there won't be any offending biscuits in the tin what I can tell you is I've seen a pattern developing on our patch."

Roberts was now very much alert.

"I'm all ears. Jack, are you all over this like the proverbial rash, my son? Come on, grab a Rosie Lee and join us."

Cade accepted the offer and en route poured himself a strong mug of tea, snatched a handful of biscuits to replenish his ebbing blood sugar and sat down next to O'Shea who, he thought, smelled of freshly peeled lemons and a night of sin.

It was, to say the least, very arousing. He hoped Roberts couldn't detect it.

"My, my, Carrie O'Shea, are you wearing perfume? Not like you. Not at all. You remind me of a night I once had in Santorini among the lemon groves."

"Is that right, boss? I'll remember to wear it more often."

Roberts took a sip of his hot drink. "So what's it called?"

She looked sideways at Cade before answering.

"Lust."

Without flinching, she started to point out the developing patterns on the screen. She had created a map from the previous twelve months' ATM attacks – first starting with all offences. She included filters to show fraud, robberies, theft and miscellaneous offences.

Then she allowed the software to update the map, slowly filtering out the offending that didn't – for this operation – interest them. It meant that robberies went first. Cade had studied this m.o. for long enough to know that his potential offender's favoured crimes that were lucrative, not violent. He recalled however that the group was highly capable of inflicting pain upon their victims, just not on the streets of London.

The map was quite non-descript – as bland as a crime map for one of the biggest cities in the world could be.

Six months had passed. The pattern was irregular with events both north and south of the river, a few in the east and hardly any in the west.

At five months, the pattern altered. Robberies almost stopped. The Metropolitan Police task force set up to target street robberies was having an impact.

The four-month mark saw a shift across the river into the west – within spitting distance of Scotland Yard. O'Shea had drawn a boundary around the crimes. The almost perfect circle covered about ten square miles of prime inner-city territory.

The red icons on the map were changing, slowly, obviously moving from the east into the City of London, Westminster, Kensington and Chelsea, Hammersmith and Fulham and an emerging hotspot in Richmond upon Thames.

Cade was not a native of the city, but he knew the wealthiest suburbs and they were staring back at him from the map. All north of the river and all, united, worth more than the wealth of some small countries.

"This area south of the river, Carrie?" He pointed to the map, brushing her back as his hand glided over her shoulder.

"It's Lambeth, Jack. Another borough with a bank balance to make your eyes bleed."

"But why are these clustered like this? Surely there are plenty more ATMs in the city than just here."

Roberts interjected, "Fair point Jack, fair point. My view is that the majority of the victims won't bother reporting the loss of twenty quid, whereas in the lower-socio-economic areas to the east and south, they will. And trust me, in some of these places on Carrie's map the owners of accounts that have lost twenty quid have plenty more in the bank, and I mean plenty!"

"He's right, Jack."

Daniel leaned over the group. "As an example, that property just...there. How much?"

"Ball park sir? Given the current climate, I'd guess two million." Cade's estimate was reasonable, but stratospherically wrong.

"If only Jack. A flat sold on Green Street recently, two point four million. A flat! A leasehold bloody flat. The one I'm pointing to? Four million. There's an urban legend, which I suspect is true, that if you combined the property values in this borough alone, they'd be worth more than the entire value of all the properties in Wales. As Jason rightly alludes, these folk won't miss twenty quid."

"Don't you remember telling us that the group were likely to target wealthier areas, Jack? You are looking at them right there." Roberts dunked a formidable-looking biscuit into his drink and cursed when its rigidity failed to live up to his expectations.

"So what?" asked Cade, again.

"So I think we should set up an ATM right in the middle of the crime pattern, Jack. Use the crime triangle as a guide."

She explained the concept behind the science. Each

crime had a location, an offender, and a victim. Eradicate one and you were on the way to preventing the offence.

"In the case of Westminster we can't remove the location, we can't yet locate and remove the offender, but we can prevent victimisation at least."

"Agent provocateur?"

"Indeed. I think we should find a way of equipping one of these five ATMs in the hotspot with CCTV or our own device to counter the equipment that the offenders are using. Worst case, we carry out surveillance on the identified target machines and catch them in the act."

O'Shea had planted a seed. All Cade and Roberts needed to do was allow it to germinate – and Daniel was to be the Head Gardener.

Roberts gathered the unit together and conducted a quick-fire tactical briefing. He finished within fifteen minutes.

"OK team, let's wrap it up for today," announced Roberts.

"Everyone except Phil and Mark head home. Tomorrow, my legion of gladiators, is another day. We shall rise at dawn and attack the enemy when and where he least expects it. Phil, Mark, you know where to head. You've got my cell phone number, if the soft brown stuff should collide with the rapidly revolving white blades, ring me."

Cade and Roberts stayed behind, hoping to convince Daniel that their plan was robust.

"It's a sound and well thought-out idea lads, I'm all for it, but the problem I have is a lack of manpower. Each ATM will take two staff to surveil. It means putting teams onto nightshift, and for how long? The Regional Crime Squad is working on something that not even I have a need to know about, apparently. So that counts them out. Flying Squad don't want to know unless it involves shooting people, and all other local CID units are drowning. If we are going to do this, everyone is going to have to dig deep."

"We've started already, boss. Piecemeal I know, but I've got two volunteers watching the identified ATMs within the target location tonight. We've picked out the ones that appear chronic rather than ad hoc."

"Fine, then you have my backing. See you tomorrow, Jason. Jack, see you at seven. Don't be late, I've got a bottle of Macallan Fine Oak that needs investigating."

CHAPTER FOUR

THE FOUR DINERS FINISHED A SENSATIONAL MEAL. SIMPLY roasted Mediterranean vegetables had complimented a perfectly cooked fillet of salmon. Lynne Daniel had drizzled something equally mesmerising upon the plate and had served it all with an accompanying Sauvignon Blanc.

The deeply attractive Daniel smiled across at Cade.

"What do you think of the wine, Jack? It's a Sancerre."

"It's fine Mrs Daniel, be sincere by all means, but, if you want me to be brutally honest, it's a close second to a New Zealand Sav in my humble opinion. The salmon on the other hand was sublime."

O'Shea discreetly rubbed his leg under the table. Both Daniels noticed but said nothing until much later that evening.

"Is that so Jack? Have you been there?"

"Not yet, but I plan to one day. I even have a notion to open a restaurant alongside the Pacific Ocean. Call it the top of my bucket list."

"Bucket?"

Cade laughed. "Bucket list. It's a quote from a book by Patrick Carlisle. I read it somewhere recently, on a train or in a newspaper magazine more like. '...in his querulous twilight years, who doesn't want to go gently into that blacky black night. He wants to cut loose, dance on the razor's edge, pry the lid off his bucket list!'"

"Before we die?" Daniel enquired.

"Before we die."

Spontaneously all four raised their glasses and made the toast.

"Before we die!"

Lynne Daniel took O'Shea, perhaps stereotypically, on a tour of her London home. It was quietly sophisticated, much like its owner.

"He's rather lovely, Carrie. You should pounce whilst you can. John tells me he's available."

It took O'Shea by surprise. But she went with the moment.

"Trust me Lynne, I'm trying. Events keep getting in the way."

Daniel and Cade were doing their level best to wash away the taste of the French wine with something from north of the border. Clashing his glass against Cade's, Daniel spoke.

"I like what I see, Jack. We need you to stay. I've got a God-awful feeling about this operation. What they did to that girl was...bloody terrible, but I can't help wondering what next. Your thoughts?"

What they had done to Nikolina Petrov – foreign intelligence asset or not was as close to pure evil as he had ever seen or read about in a book. To kill her was one thing, to strap her naked graffiti-daubed body to a roughly made wooden frame and sink her into the all-consuming mud of the River Thames was another. Waiting for the tide to slowly and deliberately drown her had stepped over the border of malevolent and into the pit of perdition itself.

"My thoughts echo yours, boss. They really do. I cannot erase what they did to her, ever. But I have to focus on the now. When you have success with twenty quid here and thirty there then you up the ante, all criminals become greedy, and I have the same feeling as you. I just wish I knew what that bloody feeling was."

"Bank job?"

"No, I don't think so sir…"

"Call me John."

"I don't think so…John. It's not their territory. We've seen some local machismo and posturing from the Albanians, but even they stick to what they do best. Again, I think their day is yet to come. Perhaps look at them again in five to ten years. There's a piece of the jigsaw we are missing."

Cade's glass was refilled.

"Do what you can, my friend, it's actually all you can do. Now, tell me about your plans for New Zealand. Lynne and I harbour a desire to retire there, set up a small boutique restaurant on the Pacific coast too. Small world, isn't it? I've only got a few more years to go. Lynne has kiwi heritage – you couldn't have said a finer thing about the wine, you smooth-talking bastard!"

They were joined by the two women, fresh from their overly lengthy tour.

"Join us, Carrie. Grab a glass. Let us raise another toast."

They all stood as Daniel held his again freshly topped up crystal vessel aloft.

"To distant lands and closer relationships!"

. . .

In the taxi back to O'Shea's flat, Cade found himself holding her hand. She was leaning into him. It was all she actually needed. All she really wanted.

In the network of streets in the boroughs, including and surrounding hers, all was quiet.

The taxi pulled up outside the flat, Cade tried to shrug off the effects of the Macallan as he settled the bill and looked across the narrow street to see O'Shea's hand beckoning from the half-opened door. Her index finger was clearly visible, as were her knickers that hung provocatively off her wrist.

The driver couldn't help but grin as he offered the change to Cade's twenty pound note.

"Looks like you are in for a rough night squire. Look after yourself. Don't forget to use protection!"

The doors locked as the quintessential cab turned left and headed back towards the feeding grounds that made 'The Knowledge' such a lucrative trade.

He had barely made it through the door when he was accosted by the intoxicating and intoxicated O'Shea. She was trying, as drunken people do, to suppress her giggles. As naked as the day she was born, she looked wonderful through Cade's rapidly hazy vision. He wished that Daniel had not been quite so generous with the malt.

"Come on, Cade. Tell me it's not what you want? Right here, right now."

"For the love of God woman, keep the noise down, you'll wake the dead and I think you'd sleep with them too right now."

She rammed her palm against her mouth, desperately trying to block her schoolgirl giggles.

"Last one upstairs is a fairy!"

She ran, leaving Cade to pursue her, grabbing her abandoned clothes as he cleared the staircase to heaven. He had the best view in the house.

By the time he reached her flat, the alcohol had impacted upon both of them. Cade would claim altitude as a corroborative factor at a later stage. It felt as if he were climbing the hazardous north-west route of his own sexual Everest.

He was more affected than his female companion, who was clearly ready for anything. Anyone, in fact. It didn't have to be Cade – but it helped.

As he pushed her door closed, she was pulling off his shirt, buttons exploded across the room and his trousers hit the ground as she pulled him on top of her. The roguish driver's words were ringing in his ears, but it was too late. She guided him inside her and was very much in control. There was no heading back to base camp now.

He woke the next morning, his head laying comfortably on her chest.

"Good morning Sir, is there anything you would like me to take down for you as evidence?" She giggled.

Without raising his head he sealed his lips over her breast and contrary to what she expected him to do he blew out, his mouth creating a youthful sound, resonating on her smooth skin.

It shocked her, but she laughed again. Grabbing a pillow, she tried to smother him. He gave in far too easily, she felt, but just as she had the apparent upper-hand he launched his counter-attack.

He grabbed her hips and moved his hands up a notch and began to tickle her vigorously. How did he know? Had someone told him that she was so incredibly sensitive, just there?

She twisted and turned until she was able to sit astride him. She grabbed handfuls of his chest, pulling the hairs as she did so. Her smile was captivating. Although he had nothing to act as a point of reference he felt somehow that she had not been this happy for a very long time.

He didn't resist. Looking into her eyes he found somebody who he could not only trust but also someone who he genuinely found attractive. Penny, the relatively recently estranged Mrs Cade was pretty – that was undeniable and many men could vouch for that. Carrie was striking, smart and intelligent. And the two, he decided, as she sat on top of him, naked and visibly aroused, were entirely different beings.

Her hips were soon moving in time with his.

They stared intently at one another and spoke at exactly the same time.

"We...are going to be...very...late."

They walked into the office together, O'Shea was holding a take away coffee, sipping upon its still-hot contents. They were joined by Roberts.

"All right, you two. You look like you've been up all night."

"Not at all, Jason. I've always been up as early as possible."

The quip wasn't lost on Roberts.

"So, what's happened in the world of Metropolitan crime since we last left this building Jas?"

"Honestly, Jack? Nothing. Zero. Zip. Zilch. Zambala!"

"Zambala?"

"I'm not sure Jack, I might have just made that one up."

He smiled, some light relief was needed all around. It had been such a comparatively short time since the team had been knee-deep in chaos and he was aware of the mid-term effect on them; losing Nikolina was bad enough, but to never see Wood again was for some too much to comprehend. Even the arrogant and vaguely misogynistic Wood was better than none at all. His loss was a huge and impactive factor upon the current mental state of the men and women who had been bound together under Roberts' guidance.

O'Shea spoke next.

"Any news on Nikolina's funeral?"

Roberts offered a non-committal, "Honestly Carrie, I'm not sure. But if there is one, we will of course attend. We've reported her death to the Bulgarian embassy; it's protocol. They say she has no known family, but Jack mentioned that she had a daughter. God only knows where she might be. We know Niko's parents are both dead. As for her 'partner', well, we all know who he is and why we won't be in a hurry to alert him, don't we? Quite where he is, only the man upstairs seems to know."

He had done that thing with the fingers of both hands as he mentioned the word partner.

The team gathered around the briefing room once more. Going over what they knew, and just as importantly, what they didn't. Daniel, looking slightly flaky, had joined them.

"Good morning team, apologies for my tardiness. I had a meeting with a Scotsman last night. Got a bit messy." He need say no more.

"Boss. We are just re-capping."

"Good, but it seems to me that we are doing a lot of re-capping and not a lot of intelligence collection. Let's get a proper plan written up and start examining what ifs, so whats, and wheres?'

They all nodded as Roberts' phone started to rumble on the tabletop.

For nearly ten minutes he appeared to listen more than talk. Occasionally he would add a few words, a couple of questions. And then, after saying goodbye with a furrowed brow, he switched the phone off.

Daniel looked at him quizzically.

"OK?"

"Yes boss, well yes and no. That was the BBC. *Panorama* to be precise. They want to ride along with us to examine the growing impact of attacks upon ATMs – how cyber-crime is affecting the great British public and to get our comment on what they are calling the *Great Trained Robbery*. They are going to air in a few weeks with a documentary about organised crime on the streets of London and how the victim is almost entirely unaware, how the banks are trying to redistribute the cost, and how ultimately this is going to impact upon the nation's financial stability. They say they've already spoken to someone at the Yard."

Daniel winced at the headline. He'd heard worse, but surely they could have come up with something a little more inventive? The tabloids could do better, and he hated them.

Roberts continued. "They say they have some source information to support that what we are seeing is the second wave of attacks, that things are escalating quickly, that what we have been investigating is the twenty percent of the eighty that is actually happening."

Daniel scratched the back of his head – it was an automatic movement, pointless, but it enabled him a second to think.

"But have we really had that many Jason? Aren't we in danger of opening the floodgates here?"

Two questions, one answer. And it was O'Shea who answered them both, handing out some warm photocopies as she spoke.

"I can resolve that boss. We've been doing some background analysis over the last few days and the results are startling. Cynthia can talk to the figures if you need proof. Let them ride along. I don't think it will make any difference to our crime stats. If anything, we might be able to be, dare I say it? Pro-active."

It was one of the many new buzz words floating around the Yard, rumour had it that a lot of the junior staff were already playing 'Management Bingo' – in one meeting a young officer was waiting for 'Blue Sky Thinking' for a full house, but was pipped at the post by a colleague who managed to win the game, silently and to the envy of his colleagues with 'helicopter overview'.

"You do dare say it Miss O'Shea. And by the way, thanks for your company last night."

"Boss, you tiger!" said a passing detective. Earning himself a wry smile and a rainy morning's work as opposed to a size ten in his nether regions.

"I'll leave Miss O'Shea to deal with that remark. Do yourself a favour? Before she puts you in hospital get yourself and the rest of the team out on the streets and start looking into each of these, start close to home and then cascade outwards. I want EVERY one of these branches visiting."

He placed a sheet of A4 into the detective's hand and then threw a few copies of the recent attack statistics across the table to the rest of the group.

Cade picked one up, scanned it slowly, blew an almost silent whistle and then spoke.

"A hundred and thirty occurrences. Is that right, Carrie?"

"If you mean is it too high? No, I suspect it's too low, Jack. These are the local ones that people could be bothered to report. But already I'm picking up some chatter from the banks too. The devices are getting more sophisticated, and the banks are now more scared about their reputations than their losses. The stakes have been raised. Someone has turned up the heat and the losses are far greater than we realised. This is serious stuff, Interpol-type stuff, and it's occurring under our noses."

"Explain their losses, Carrie." Cade was all ears, staring intently at her, purely business-like.

"Remember how you talked us through the Lebanese Loop method a while back? The metal tool that they use to trap cash? Then banks started to report that the odd note was failing to show up? Well, more recently customers are reporting that their cards were remaining in situ and now..."

"Go on..."

"Now the cards are being inserted into the hole in the wall, money is being requested and it is being delivered. The card is being returned and hey presto everyone is happy."

Cade looked confused.

"So why the interest from the banks, the BBC?"

"Remember that kid you and Jason saw at the mortuary?"

He did. Vividly. His blue lips and maroon open wound were tangible.

"A BBC reporter, who ironically had money taken from her savings a few weeks ago, decided to follow up on the story. She was incensed by the theft from her account but more so about the murder which took place in the area that she lives."

"I don't get it."

"Neither did the reporter at first, but the more she delved, the more she found out. She can prove the boy was involved. She had twenty pounds missing in one transaction. She reported it but the bank just refunded her without question. We were never informed. A close source told her over a drink that hers was the fiftieth such transaction – that week!"

"And?"

"And the following week at the same branch, her card took longer to return than normal. Already suspicious, she got down close to the machine and noticed a gap in the surround. A plastic frame had been added. The glue pads were losing their grip. A perfectly matched device had been attached to the machine and to the unwary it was completely legitimate. Until she peeled it back and saw some electronics strapped to the inside. She knew then that she had stumbled across something interesting, took a discreet photo, stuck the device back down and reported it to the bank, who asked politely, but firmly not to discuss it outside the branch. She was offered a complimentary cup of coffee and a free session with a financial advisor."

"But she smelled the proverbial rat? They hadn't got a clue about her work, I guess?"

"Indeed. Within five minutes the device was removed. But the most telling point of all, and she didn't realise at the time, was that she saw him."

"Who?"

"Our mystery boy. As she left the branch, she saw him. She knows now, of course, but what she saw she described as a startled rabbit. A boy in a man's world. Working beyond his limits and to a journalist who had worked in some of the world's worst places, among its worst people – he stood out like a..."

"Bulldog's wedding tackle?"

"Yes, Jason, that. She walked after him, tried to approach him. He started to walk quickly, a man running from a woman. She considered it odd but kept pursuing him. She kept up with him too until a white van intervened, the cargo door opened and he was all but dragged in. It was on stolen plates. Anyway, another week passed and then five thousand disappeared from her savings within twenty-four hours. Now the bank was listening. She was refunded of course, but she also had the makings of a great story. She asked if she should report it to the police and was told it was pointless as we weren't interested in financial crimes of this nature. That's when she walked into the public counter downstairs and asked to speak to someone. I was free, so I did."

It was Roberts, again. "OK, I'm hearing all of this, so what did you tell her?"

"I told her we would be interested in anything she dredged up, but that for now it wasn't a significant problem. I gave her my card, and I took hers. I didn't think she would be in touch. I'm sorry if I've done wrong."

Roberts asked a straight question. "Julia Fleming?"

"Yes."

"Then we've both had the pleasure. Turns out she's been doing more dredging than a Thames silt shifter Carrie. She's identified the young lad, obviously slipped someone some-where some money and managed to trace the kid back to his family in Romania. She just told me that she travelled there to meet them. Turns out he had hope. A rare series of opportunities had fallen unexpectedly at his feet after he had been spending a lot of time surfing the internet. He was offered a chance to travel the world and work in the financial sector. At least that's what he was told. He travelled to England, legitimately, met a girl, all too conveniently in a pub, fell in love and soon became embroiled in her circle of friends and activities."

Cade nodded, adding emphasis to his interest. O'Shea and Daniel were also listening in, the latter sipping on his second black coffee of the morning.

"Educated and from a decent family, the lucky lad had soon been blinded by the appeal of a voracious, slightly older lover who swiftly led him down a path previously unseen. A lamb, if you like, to the slaughter. She even convinced him to have a tattoo. The same one that all of her friends had; blue, inside the right wrist."

"A wave?" It was Cade's voice.

"Naturally. From there the path of the wave twisted and turned and all he could do was surf along on the crest of it. He was given small luxuries, which even with his background of comparative wealth were unfamiliar to him. A Tag-Heuer watch, a wallet, nice shoes. Sadly, the female of the species finished him off I suspect. You know, like a praying mantis?"

Roberts mimicked, in a somewhat comedic manner, the insect attacking its mate before adding a final question.

"But why?"

Cynthia Bell, O'Shea's analytical support officer, walked over to the group and dropped a still-damp, recently printed photograph onto the desk.

"That's your male of the species boss. Just faxed through from the BBC. Miss Fleming provided it. Grainy, but it's very much him."

O'Shea shrugged her shoulders and offered an apologetic grin. The cat was out of the bag and besides, someone needed to take the lead on this. Simple mathematics was all that was required to see why Fleming was better on board than off. Multiply a hundred or so customers by five thousand pounds. In just one week. Daylight robbery – daylight trained robbery. And with none of the normally associated violence, it meant that the authorities were at best likely to ignore the trend. It was like stealing a child's candy, but easier.

The photo had been taken as he was leaving his hometown in the Black Sea town of Constanta, full of promise, a sparkle in his dark brown eyes. Another photo followed, landing gently and partly obscuring the first. This one showed the same hopeful young man. This time he was wearing upmarket clothes, a limited edition wristwatch and a confident smile, borne out of ceaseless hours of lovemaking with a demanding and athletic woman. His life couldn't be any better. His face told the entire story.

The third photo had been taken by Cade months later. The eyes were still dark, darker. His skin was whiter and his smile gone. His prized Swiss watch was missing, now sitting proudly on its new owner's wrist. His feet held onto the equally coveted shoes, brown speckled brogues, barely run-in, the soles still shiny in places. All that was missing was the price tag.

His neck gaped as a result of a single slicing blow, from which, even with a warning and immediate medical care, he was never going to survive. Instead of seeing out his days in his albeit lesser hometown, with its lesser trappings of success, where he would have reached a reasonable retirement age on a sun-drenched coastline, he would instead drop to the floor like a piece of discarded rubbish, his soul left to flutter in the wind, trying unsuccessfully to make its way home.

"Pointless death at the hands of people he respected? Or a misguided youth who couldn't see the writing on the wall? Either way, he shouldn't have died on our streets. So tell me Carrie, what else does our BBC reporter know about this group?" Daniel looked around the team, including them all in his gaze.

"Not much more yet, boss. Her belief is that he was killed because he was too aware. A law-abiding young man lured by his own Siren onto the rocks of his untimely death. He'd served a purpose in placing devices on bank machines around the city, thus reducing the threat of losing a more experienced operator. He was cannon fodder, nothing more. I'm surprised they even left him with his shoes. The more I read, the more I hear..."

"Thank you Carrie." Daniel interrupted in a timely fashion. He could tell things were getting emotive and he needed his team to remain focused.

The day slowly proceeded. Snippets of information here, dead-ends there, until one by one the staff left the building and headed to their respective homes. Like most investigations it was three percent action and ninety-seven percent monotony.

CHAPTER FIVE

Ten hours after Roberts had left his home station the normally manic streets of London had started to quieten. As with most metropolitan cities it never truly slept, just took a moment to recover and shake off the excesses of the day before the sun hopefully rose across the English Channel, its stealthy, lengthening fingers reaching out across the Thames estuary, casting shadows on the northern and southern shores of one of the truly iconic waterways.

Across the mudflats and past the burgeoning industrial networks the sun's pathway had once more illuminated historic and newly constructed buildings, had awoken flocks of starlings, aroused sea birds and had brought early warmth to a city seen by many to be powered by a cold, self-interested and callous heart.

Those that worked through the night knew different. For them, the Old Girl was theirs, a place they identified with, belonged to, and if someone should choose to berate her, they would react. Better still, if another group were to attack her they would close ranks, find a common bond, lose the inhibitions that existed from day to day and actively resist any marauder.

History had shown how the people of London had done this, time and time again, coming together, talking to one another, embracing awkwardly and finally working in union to counter attacks upon their lives.

In a few years they would do it again. It wouldn't be the last time either.

Fortunately, with the odd exception, life in London, whilst chaotic, was comparatively normal in that it was really no different to any other major city. Men, women, rich or poor, black and white, tall, short and everything between, worked in relative harmony to keep the blood pumping through the veins of the place they called home.

For hundreds of years it had survived, a settlement built upon a river, a centre of trade and colonial might. They turned up in all weathers to earn their salary, co-exist and then head home to their loved ones.

Sadly, despite a fierce loyalty to the city, many acts took place which were either unwittingly condoned or deliberately ignored. One could cherish his or her city but there were limits, and no one wanted to push the boundaries too far. With knives being carried by so many there was no longer such a thing as a fair fight. With this came a chance for those that had little to lose to exploit the loopholes, prey on the weak and target victims.

If the victim were a corporation, with even lesser risk of being detected, then all the better.

It was acceptable, wasn't it?

· · ·

Roberts slept soundly, the first time in a week. Ten miles away O'Shea shuddered, woke momentarily and remembered where she was and with whom. She felt around under the duvet before brushing her hand against Cade's equally naked body and for a moment decided that he needed to be woken up too. His breathing was rhythmic and like Roberts he was sleeping soundly for the first time in days. He was mumbling under his breath, words that were indistinct but no doubt important. Against her lustful and better judgement she chose instead to hold his unreceptive fingers, tucked her hips into his, found a cool spot on her pillow and fell back to sleep.

Less than half a mile away a solitary rider steered his expensive and somewhat rare Scott Pro Racing mountain bike along the pavements, hugging the shadows, better not to be seen by intrusive cameras.

If the male heard a vehicle approaching he would keep on riding, never focusing on or acknowledging the traffic. It was normal, even at a few minutes after three in the morning. It was the dead of night, when shift worker's skin started to develop a grey pallor and a vice-like headache ensued. Even a passing police patrol would only consider the rider worthy of a stop if he exuded a good enough reason.

The fact that the cycle was stolen was reason enough, but the two officers who whipped along the main thoroughfare were hungry, their sergeant had called up for them to get him some food after a manic few hours and his order was now sat alongside theirs on the foot well of their vehicle, sweating under the hot downdraft from the heater.

The cyclist didn't even attract a second glance.

With a clear opportunity to operate in the amber glow of

the street lights, the first thing the cyclist did was to place a small piece of paper over the security camera on the bank cash machine – a camera most customers did not even realise was there. His actions were simple and effective and left no obvious evidence trail.

He kept his back to the panning and zooming lens placed higher up on the corner of the building and for all intents appeared to be a customer carrying out a transaction on his way home from work.

The whole act took three minutes. Slipping a grey and green cover from beneath his jacket the male had stuck it into place expertly, allowing just enough time to let the glue to set before adding another new device above it. He was the consummate professional. Practised and paranoid, discovery was his nemesis.

The devices discovered by banks up until this point were relatively unsophisticated, albeit visually giving the impression that they formed part of the machine. Within the framework was a simple cash trap, it was rudimentary, but it worked. With the banks catching up and learning from their costly mistakes the offenders had sought once more to stay in front.

Their next move was to install a device that could read the two lines of magnetic data encoded in the black strip on the rear of the bank card. Having gathered this they needed other operatives, those less expert in technological advances but possessing old-fashioned street skills. The technique became known as shoulder surfing. The customer would approach a high street cash point, shield their personal identification number, carry out the transaction and obtain their hard-earned cash.

Walking away from the site they would be wholly unaware that the device hidden from view had just captured their bank data. All the team needed was the matching PIN.

Women and children were by far the best operators when it came to obtaining these and they would do so either by blatantly watching a customer which was rarely successful or better still, but not without increased risk they would collide with them in the street, using their children as a distraction. Those that were desperate for a simple source of income would even expose their children to arrest. They did whatever was needed to keep a meal on the table. Besides, children were a commodity, they had more.

By the time the victim had realised their purse or wallet had been removed, it was too late. Even with a daily transaction limit of a few hundred of the local currency it was more than worth the risk when multiplied by the sheer number of potential targets in a city of seven and a half million people.

Eventually the wallet would be discarded in a litter bin and most would never be seen again. For many victims the most frustrating aspect was losing valuable data, they could just claim the money from the bank but it might take months to rebuild the contents.

To make matters worse, society soon accepted this as a victimless crime.

This method of offending continued for some time. It was lucrative and spread across the globe when and wherever there was a chance of a victim. There was no honour among thieves and they were even known to prey upon each other. Operating on someone else's patch however was strictly forbidden, rigorously enforced.

Roma gypsies swarmed into some areas of north

London, begging and stealing, brilliant opportunists, they would also work with their more conventional peers, content to take their cut, better still to steal it and a little more when their stupid employers were distracted.

Equally the latter group knew not to step on the toes of their powerful competitors from Albania who had imposed a fearful reputation, using a cellular structure, their mafia had begun to spread across the United Kingdom.

Alexandru was very aware of just how far his reputation could take him should the need arise, however he was no fool and knew that he would be cut down swiftly if he tried to operate in London and more so within the realms of prostitution, illegal people trafficking and the heroin trade. That belonged to the Albanians, the Russians and to a point, syndicates from West Africa.

He had once said mockingly, but enviously, 'They want the money from the drug trade in Britain, let them have it! Plenty more fish in the sea.'

Nearby a song played on a radio. Robbie Williams at his snarling best singing about the devil.

He considered it his anthem.

The second device that twenty-four-year-old Dorin Gabor had placed upon the cash machine was equally well made. This was the next phase. A cell phone was taped inside the housing and its on-board video camera was initiated when a customer carried out a transaction.

Simple, but rather brilliant it allowed a nearby team to monitor the activity, and return later in the guise of a customer who would remove the device, clean the surrounding fascia and leave with enough data to make the risk outweigh the consequences of being caught.

Later, at a safe house the members of the group would download the bank data and using the footage from the cell phone they were able to discover the PIN number. The subsequent ill-gotten goods were either used and traded in London, shipped as pure data on portable memory devices or sold online to the highest bidder. It was a thing of criminal splendour.

As a modus operandi it would eventually be discovered, but not before countless victims had had their accounts attacked, which at best were used to purchase commodities online via the internet or worse still, systematically emptied, the funds never likely to be recovered due to a warren of offenders who would quickly conceal the monies and making them all but disappear.

Gabor would receive the equivalent of a month's wages for a few days' work. He was still woefully under-rewarded, but he had seen what had happened to the boy from the Black Sea. Better to be fed and given cash or drugs than finish his days in an anonymous doorway. Dead.

The new devices were arriving at the safe location in north Kent and from there distributed to the teams. The distributors used a 'shotgun' system, flooding the international mail centres with devices in the hope that many got through the system. As they were made of plastic and didn't fit within the criteria used by border agency search teams, the majority made it to their destination.

Utilising the darkest hours, and often at the weekends they spread their web of financial gain across the city. With luck on their side and the continuing stupidity of the financial world, they could make enough to head home. As long as Jackdaw was happy they could be too, and rumour had it he was more than content. For now.

The greatest asset the team had was mobility. Once the banks had discovered the devices, or by working with the victims had realised that something was wrong, they would begin investigations. But they were often two steps behind; the team had already picked up their simple operation and moved onto Bristol, Leicester, Luton, Manchester and Nottingham.

There were hundreds more targets and when they were exhausted there was the rest of Europe, north America even Australia, but not the Asian countries.

Alexandru had a healthy respect for people in that region and had declared it out of bounds. Fear of reprisal was his key motivator and financial gain was its equal. He would rather allow what the banks described as 'an escalating cancer' to spread independently in financially driven locations such as Malaysia, Singapore and Hong Kong, allowing him to operate in a licentious manner in Europe.

If the twain never met, he was content. He was greedy, but he wasn't a fool.

Spain was an hour behind the United Kingdom. In Madrid, earlier but still the middle of the night a cell phone rang next to the hearth of a traditional log burner whose embers were still glowing; the last remaining indicator of a previously red fire.

The fireplace sat in a traditional home, approximately an hour north of the capital city. Strategically located in the foothills of the Sierra de Guadarrama Mountains it had been purchased, like many of his assets via a career in the criminal underworld where cash was king.

Despite the agreeable climate in Spain the Guadarramas could surprise with their climatic extremes and the owner of the sprawling property, known as *La Najarra,* had long outgrown the desire to be cold.

He looked at the cell phone screen and chose to ignore the call. Somebody wished to discuss business and he no longer cared for such interruptions. His days of having to agree to everything, having to take risks, were a thing of the past, locked within a vault of memories in a country far away to the north east.

He motioned to the girl who walked back into the living room wearing a falsified smile and a short black kimono.

"Put another log on the fire, it is dying down..."

She considered it beneath her but immediately did as she was told, picking up the freshly cut timber and bending provocatively in front of him, placing the wood onto the embers which quickly built to a flame and once more warmed the vaulted room. The nameless girl turned, slipped the dressing gown from her shoulders and strode towards him.

He smiled, a sense of physical excitement building within him. Was there nothing he couldn't have?

In the nearby undergrowth a European wildcat called out to its mate, disinterested in the carnal activity within the homestead a few metres away, visible to anyone foolish enough to be roaming around the mountains on such a cold night. Within seconds the cat was gone, blending skilfully into its environs, hunting for the vulnerable.

The following morning Alex was woken by her again, she was persistent if not a little desperate. She met his needs but as lithe and enthusiastic as she was she would never replace

Nikolina. No one ever would. He had misread her. She had betrayed him, and she deserved what she got.

With luck, their daughter would inherit his genes. He missed her, but she needed to be isolated from him, for now. The risks were too high in a corner of society that used threats and kidnapping as a reward mechanism.

When the time was right, he would get her back from her secure location, once he was somehow able to get back into his mother country. The border police were watching for him constantly, only a complete change of facial appearance would enable him to cross over the invisible dotted line.

So for now, she would stay. But only until her schooling was complete, and she had become a young upwardly mobile female with the world at her feet. Educated, intuitive, smart, proud of her origins, but so far removed from criminality that even a free lunch would offend her.

'You will live well under my legacy, my darling Elena.'

As the sun appeared and started to illuminate the Iberian Peninsula he stared out of his bedroom window at an agreeable vista from within an equally spectacular home. His eyes closed gently, the sun creating a chromatic spectrum on his lashes, filling his blurred vision with colour. He should be happy, yet even surrounded by all the trappings of success and a whore in every port he felt somehow hollow.

He sensed that the girl was still next to him, willing but almost too eager; he brushed her to one side, he might concede to having her again before breakfast, but for now she was an irritant.

"Go and do something, make yourself look attractive.

Go into town, buy whatever you need. Go." He ushered her away with a few brushstrokes of his hand.

He really should ask her what she was called.

She smiled. Her existence had fringe benefits, and it helped support her academic dreams.

"When you come back, bring a friend."

He was bored. And when he became bored, like most domesticated animals, he became destructive. He lit a cigarette, took one long draw of the narcotic contents then crushed it in a nearby ashtray. Waiting for the ember to die he then picked up his cell phone.

In the city of London Roberts and his team were making their way back into work, downtime was rare and each officer acknowledged their good fortunes for having understanding wives or partners. The single ones were drunk on policing, never able to think of or talk about anything else.

They still talked about the loss of Wood. It had quietly impacted upon the team; it had been a mistake to leave him with an attractive girl, in truth they all knew that, but conceded that anyone was capable of making the same mistake he had.

O'Shea woke Cade with a cup of tea, stroking his cheek with her index finger, worried that to do it whilst he was awake might send a message that she had very much fallen for him. How much was too much so soon into a relationship?

The fact that he suddenly moved forward and bit her finger either confirmed that is was fine or proved that she was a nuisance. Grabbing her and pulling her back into bed offered reassurance at a time when she needed it. Her life had previously been a roller coaster of emotions, a free ride on a switchback of positive and negative feelings, controlled by a single incident that led to a series of events she no longer wished to recall.

Cade had arrived into her life; for a reason, for a season or hopefully forever.

"Come on you, we need to get to work or people will talk." Carrie was heading to the en-suite bathroom wearing only a slightly-too-small towel and hoping for company, knowing it was hypocritical as it would make them even later than they currently were, she could hope nonetheless.

When a minute or so later two sets of hands left distinctive shapes on the heavily condensed, tinted glass cubicle it confirmed one thing: He already knew how to read her mind.

Kissing her under the pounding and intensely hot water they struggled at times for breath, which in turn made the whole experience more erotic. She swallowed water, closed her eyes, ran her hands across his smooth back, lower, grabbing at him as he reciprocated, lifting her against the glass, caring not if it would give way.

Her hair was darker, wetter and heavier, he ran his hands through it, pushing his face into it, inhaling the scent of something fruity, mildly exotic which mixed with her natural oils and smelled intoxicating, better than anything else he could recall.

He ran his tongue down her neck, biting her throat before doing the same on her chest, darting from side to side, left to right, pausing momentarily to admire her through the building steam.

She was as aroused as he was.

He dropped onto his knees and felt the sensation of her once more, different, coarser, but equally stimulating. He placed his hands behind her, putting pressure on her lower back, guiding her towards him.

Did she hate herself for not resisting? Hardly.

She opened her legs, then closed them again, open, closed, each time allowing him further and further into her until she gave in to the intense muscular power of his tongue. It was physically impossible to wrap her legs around him, but were it so, she would have, and willingly.

She thrashed around trying to find something to grip onto; she needed to be the centre of attention, his turn would follow, possibly later, even at another time entirely, but for now, this was all about her.

One wet hand grabbed hold of the door handle, the other pushed against the glass. Moments later they would shift again, with both hands now on his head, holding him in abeyance, then releasing him once more.

Her eyes were unable to focus, the water, the steam all doing its best to deprive her of one of her key senses. It all added to the occasion. She couldn't see the person that was sending her into a series of involuntary tremors and she didn't care. It could be anyone, she could fantasise if she chose to, but she knew exactly who it was and that made her so intensely happy she wanted to cry.

What shocked her was how the physical act made her laugh, she was literally laughing. She had read about such a 'release' before, in a much-loved, well-thumbed magazine in a salon or surgery somewhere and now it was happening to her.

What have you done to me Mr Cade?

She wasn't sure. Normally very vocal she could think of only one word.

"Again?"

· · ·

The last part of the walk to work was no different to any other. She didn't flinch when a male, head down and with places to go walked straight into her. He grabbed hold of her arm to steady himself and then nodded and unusually for such a chaotic city apologised and hurried on, just as O'Shea did. Both were eager to go about their business. Cade was a step ahead of her and didn't even register the moment. His mind was on other things and they were a million miles from work-related.

Alone and feeling antagonistic Alexandru pressed speed dial 1 on his phone. It was answered almost immediately.

"Buna dimineata."

"Dimineata."

Having said good morning Alexandru pressed on, there was no point in any more pleasantries. He did not consider them necessary and this morning he felt, unpleasant.

"So, what do you have to tell me, brother? Make sure, whatever it is, it is all good. I am in no mood for apologies."

Stefan Stefanescu spoke quickly and deliberately, afraid perhaps that he was being listened to. As a state of mind, paranoia did not exclusively belong to his older brother.

"We lost a few good men Alexandru. The British pigs killed them, shot them like dogs, for what? For doing their jobs…"

"Move on, as you say, they were doing their jobs, like any employee, they were paid well and are replaceable."

"Indeed. So, we have lost two of our men, we rescued Artur. He had injuries, but we found a friend in a town who could help. He has lost an eye…"

"Again brother, I do not care. Artur is a loyal man, I pay him well, he has another eye, is there anything else?"

"Our plan is working. The money is being collected. The banks are one step behind us my brother, we are laughing at them, every day. When those victims have been bled dry we move onto a new town. The newspapers said we were like rats...vermin..."

"Good. We should be proud of this name. Is it better than *Primul Val?*"

He knew the answer, God help anyone who thought so.

Stefan continued. "There are police watching us everywhere. But we are OK. We will go to ground if we need to. The machine parts keep being delivered. We have trained a new boy to fit them, he is now training others. Soon, we will have a stronger, larger team, then we can really become rich. Rats with money..."

For the older brother it was no longer an issue of finance, it was about power, reputation, presence and above all becoming a criminal icon, held aloft by what the general public saw as the underworld.

Actually, it *was* all about reputation. Having lived in his brother's shadow for so long he was growing to despise him, always covertly for he considered him capable of cruelty towards anyone. Seeing what he had done to their mother, all those years ago had remained with him, an ink stain, dropping onto pure white linen, slowly growing until the original mark had spread like a malignant being.

That summed him up. But for the immediate future he needed to be close. He heard Alex sigh.

"Anything else? I am getting bored."

"The police have a man called Cade. We don't know where he came from but he is the one they all look to. We saw him alone in a car with Nikolina, the first time we tried to kidnap her, he managed to escape. Our friends tell us they were possibly more than work colleagues. Cade is working with another officer called Roberts, their boss is called Daniel. They have women helping them too, one is very close to Cade."

He took a deep breath. "And, Alex...you need to know that Niko is dead. She was dealt with as you asked. They found her the next morning. There is nothing in the newspapers. They are pretending she did not exist. Not even a funeral."

Alex liked the way his brother had refused to acknowledge Nikolina with any more than a few words.

"Good. Very good. I hope she was as cold as she was alone when the end came. Watch out for this Cade and his friends, we do not need any inconvenience. Now, go and make me some more money, make us rich. It looks like I have two girls to play with."

"Only two brother? You are getting old."

He smiled, grabbed a bottle of Johnnie Walker Blue Label and unscrewing the cap walked towards the two eager girls. He took a long swig of the whisky, savouring its multi-layers and feeling its silky heat as it ran down his throat. He handed it to the first girl; she was new and excitable. She had chestnut-coloured hair, what a nice change.

"Drink. And don't stop until I say so."

She did as she was told, struggling at first but willing to oblige. Shaking her head and pulling a disapproving face as the whisky scorched her throat. Her friend had regaled her with tales of wealth and excitement and as such she wanted to appear enthusiastic.

"You still there brother?" As he spoke he placed the older girl's hand on the younger girl's breast and nodded towards it. He loved nothing more than seeing two of the finer species indulging one another. One giggled enthusiastically, the other gasped. It was almost certainly her first time.

"Yes, I am waiting."

"Good. I wanted you to hear what success sounds like. Now leave me to play with girls who I don't even know. I have valuable time to make up. Find the slut that makes Cade smile and cut something off of her body, the choice is yours. Gift wrap it and send it to him by courier, and make sure it is not subtle. Leave an open wound in his mind that bleeds every time he stops to rest. Oh, and Stefan..."

"Yes?"

"Tell the Albanians that Cade is hunting them. That should put the cat among the little birdies. Then turn up the heat a little. They are getting wise to us. Bring some distractions to the pathetic capital of England. As we discussed. Do remember that this but a game...the real fun is yet to come."

"Yes, of course. Do you really think I have forgotten? The new boy Dorin is doing well, he has recruited six of our people already. They have been tried and have passed the test. We will soon move south and then north, away from the financial part of the city. We will still make plenty of money. That is the beauty of our plan."

"My plan actually. But whatever you say dear brother. Like I care anymore. I have money, what I want now is something else, something more powerful than money. I want people to respect me. And they will. The boy from Pazardzhik Prison; where they left me to rot in my own filth."

He took a moment to recall the occasionally torrid, often freezing nature of his existence in a miniscule cell that was never cleaned, chained to a bed, lying in his own waste. Bastards.

"The authorities will come for me one day Stefan and when that happens you will have to take over the organisation. I had someone else in mind but she betrayed me after everything I gave her, she is lucky she is only dead. The mastery of my long-term plan is simplicity itself. One day I will be notoriously wealthy and it will come to me as a result of good fortune and a moment of genius. Who would have thought a few pieces of paper could be so valuable? Go away now, you are annoying me."

He left the phone line open so his brother could listen then pulled the fair-haired girl towards him leaving her with no doubt what he wanted. When he was satisfied, the other one could have her turn. Look at them, filthy whores; everyone had a price, a pity theirs was so cheap. But then everyone he dealt with was as much of a whore.

Stefan stared at the display on his phone, despising the name that lingered on the liquid crystal display.

"One day brother."

"OK, boy's heads up! We've got some new footage. This lad on the mountain bike? Local branch of National Westminster reckon he's been seen at other branches of theirs over the river. He's a creature of habit, same clothes every time. Let's get his ugly mug out there on the system, see if we can't try out that new photo recognition software, I want every wooden top to know what he looks like, the last bastard escaped from under our noses because of them. I want this one banged up and in my cells so I can talk to him personally."

Roberts was in an unusually miserable mood, throwing out derogatory terms about the uniform branch as if they worked for a separate organisation.

He turned to see Cade and O'Shea arriving.

"Late again? Teacher will have to keep you behind after school. You look like you've been up all night Jack."

It was salacious, and he knew it.

"Hardly Jas, I got an hour at least and besides I'm always in bed early. I'm an early riser."

"I bet you are my son, I bet you are."

O'Shea stared at them both before marching to her work station, logging on and trying to make sense of the abundance of emails that sat on her desktop. She hit the delete key over and over again until she found something of interest.

"Carrie, can you see if you and your team can dig out any footage from the previous attacks, match the individual on the mountain bike to them? If we find him we've cracked it. I think he might be working alone."

Cade shook his head. "Never."

Daniel walked into the room, he'd been eavesdropping in his office.

"Jason, sorry but I agree with Jack. This cell is bigger than we realise. Although they've taken thousands they are most likely taking a whole lot more from somewhere. They have to work to saturation point then pull out and disappear. And our European colleagues say that is exactly what they will do."

"I think it's a matter of time before this little business venture diversifies boss." Cade looked at Daniel who was busy biting the frame of his Hugo Boss spectacles.

"As negative as it sounds I am inclined to agree Jack. The greedy bugger at the helm isn't going to be happy with twenty thousand a fortnight for long."

"Hello, yes this is Dorin. Who is this?"

"You never ask. Ever! I have spoken to the person in charge. He is pleased with your work. But now we must work harder. Meet me in an hour. You know the vehicle? Same place. If you see a police unit, keep driving. By the way do you like your new car?"

He did. Very much.

"Good. Get this wrong and we will burn you alive in it my friend. OK?"

"OK. But I have a question..."

The caller had already cleared the line, obsessed and distrustful, he too wanted to make enough money and head home to what was left of his family. Everything came with a risk, but why increase it?

Dorin opened the cheap Nokia, pulled out the SIM card, tossed the phone onto the nearby road and waited for the first large vehicle to crush it. He then fished in his pocket for his new phone and inserted a new SIM having snapped the previous card in half, dropping each half down consecutive drains before walking quickly to his car.

An hour later he met the two males in a quieter part of south London, took possession of four cardboard boxes and left without acknowledging either of them. Later that day he would assemble the devices and distribute them to his team, none of whom knew each other – like layers of an onion. They worked together for a common purpose but would never meet. His instructions were clear. His life was worth more than theirs, he had already worked out what true value was to members of his newfound and elite club.

"Boss, this will interest you."

"Fire away, mademoiselle." Roberts was more upbeat, putting on an affected French accent; a few strong and over-brewed coffees always pulled him back from the abyss. He was strutting now, Jagger-esque and optimistic.

"We've run through about a hundred sets of CCTV footage. This guy here?"

"Go on…"

"He's new. This one too. And this one…" O'Shea kept pointing to the screenshots as she identified each new member of the team.

"And we're happy that they are working together, not lone operators?"

"I think we have to be. The m.o. is too similar for it not to be linked."

"OK, how much has gone from each of those ATMs?"

"Right now I don't know, but when Del and Terry get back we'll know."

"Del and Tel, The A Team, excellent. Carrie, let me know ASAP." He slapped his fingers together in a style that indicated his pleasure.

"Will do. Oh, and boss?"

"Go ahead."

"You know about me and Jack don't you?"

He sipped on his acrid beverage.

"That you are working together like a well-oiled machine Carrie, yes absolutely."

He winked, brushed her shoulder and walked to Daniel's office where he found the DCI talking to Cade.

"Good girl that one Jack, wouldn't you say?"

"Cut to the chase…Jas."

"You erm…you know, you…as it were…how shall we put it?"

"Sleeping with her?"

"Yep, that'll be it."

"Yes."

It was easier than they both thought.

"That was easier than I thought Jack."

"You only had to ask Jason. It won't get in the way." The latter was directed at Daniel who had already given his seal of approval at their evening.

Daniel continued the conversation.

"So we know that the group have increased their activities, that they are using the same m.o., that they are goal-driven and that above all they are adaptable."

"And making money." Cade added.

"Yes, Jack, and making a lot of money. But I think there is more to this. Are they funding something else?"

"Terrorism? I don't think so boss, not their thing. I've run them through the standalone databases upstairs, negative I think it's all about greed. Nothing else."

They all nodded and threw a few ideas around about how they could target the group.

It was Roberts who pushed the conversation forward this time.

"Our team is only so big boss. I know the Commissioner likes what we are doing but up against community policing and knife-point robberies on the streets of London this op is only ever going to gain so much ground politically. We need to engage the rank and file, somehow get them on board. A league table with sponsorship by the banks would be my suggestion, a prize for the most detections."

It was fraught with danger and Roberts knew it. They all did.

"Can't be done Jason. We both know that. Great plan but we need to engage the troops in another way. We need their attention attracted."

"Isn't Clive's death enough?" asked Roberts.

"Fair point, I apologise. But you know what the job is

like. When you are surrounded by mayhem, it can quickly become BAU."

"BAU boss?"

"Business as usual."

Roberts filed that one away for the next round of Management bingo.

"Once we have the thin blue line on board, we can really hunt these buggers. Without becoming xenophobes we need to point out how ruthless this group is, that they will do pretty much anything to gain money and a reputation throughout Europe. What do you think Jack?"

Daniel could see that Cade had switched off.

"Sorry sir. Jason is correct, even though they've harmed some of our own this is not sexy enough yet. We need our guys to become victims. Once their wives or girlfriends or mothers lose money at the hole in the wall, then they'll be on side, not until."

"Actually, my wife had her credit card stolen last week Jack." Roberts had his attention now.

Cade sat up in the chair, "Do go on."

"It was awful. But I didn't report it to the authorities."

"Jason, why the hell not, given all that we are doing to try to stop this type of offending..."

Hook. Line. Sinker.

"Because the thief is spending less than my missus Jack!"

Cade snorted. He'd been played but the brief moment of levity was needed. He looked up at his colleague. "Twat."

Four days passed without any obvious activity until O'Shea called out one morning from her desk.

"Everyone, we've got a new hit. HSBC branch in Hammersmith report that they've lost about three thousand overnight. East Acton the same. There's even a branch near Wormwood Scrubs nick that has been targeted.

Her analytical side-kick Cynthia Bell was busy noting the new occurrences on a whiteboard, it was conventional but effective.

"An ATM outside a prison? That's taking the piss." It was Detective Constable Del Murphy. "We've been bang at it for a bloody fortnight now guv. I'm getting sick of being one step behind all the time."

"Derek my son just be patient. The early bird catches the monkey."

It was his long-time partner Terry Campbell, equally famed for his detection clear-up rate and appalling mixed metaphors.

"Criminals are like eels, slippery as a fish and just when you think you've lost 'em, three come at once."

Murphy shook his head.

"See what I have to put up with guvnor?"

Cade offered a sympathetic smile.

"It's not unlike the blind man and the elephant Del. You can lead a horse to water but you should never judge a book by its cover."

O'Shea was suppressing a giggle, and Daniel had to walk back out of the room.

"Inspector Cade – my office, please."

"You wanted to see me, sir?"

"Sort of Jack. Two things, stop winding my detectives up, and this."

He handed over a letter. Whilst it was addressed to Daniel, the subject was Cade.

The letter bore a crest which was instantly familiar to Cade. A picture of a globe at its centre, flanked by two olive branches to symbolise peace. A vertical sword ran through the globe, indicating action. Either side of the sword were the letters OIPC and ICPO, one French the other English but both meant the same thing, this was an organisation that pooled the strength of many units into one.

Beneath the sword a contraction of the term International Police combined the abbreviations into one simple word and one which was familiar to many: Interpol.

"What the hell is this boss?" Cade was genuinely surprised.

"Seems as though you've ruffled the right cages Jack if I may use a Campbell-ism?"

"This says they want me to go to Lyon to join up with other 'like-minded officers' to form a team whose sole purpose is to target the growth in cyber and financial crime?"

"I know, Jack, I read the letter too."

"But..."

"But what Jack? This is one hell of an opportunity, and in my book, and it's a well-thumbed bloody book too, you take these chances when they are offered."

"OK, fair point sir, but where have they got my name from?"

"A mutual acquaintance has proffered your details during one of his most recent European tours. You have friends in low places Jack."

"But I don't know anyone in France John."

"You do now. John Hewett has paved the way for you. He likes what you've done so far and so do I. The managers here are impressed. Jack, for God's sake take the opportunity. You were a sergeant only months ago, now an acting inspector. The move will cement your promotion, I can almost guarantee it. It's about who you know. Nepotism rules and all that. Hewett wants to meet with you as soon as possible. Keep him on side Jack and you'll go far."

"I get that sir, but what about Operation Breaker? Is Hewett trying to get rid of me? Who will keep that going?"

"Come on Jack, I suspect on the contrary, Hewett likes what he sees. There are plenty of people here to keep that ticking over, there's Jason and his team and if he starts to slacken off, I'm sure a certain Miss O'Shea will crack the whip."

As soon as Daniel had finished the sentence the excitement of a move to the heart of international policing abated – and it was one name that did it. O'Shea. Carrie bloody O'Shea. Obsessive Compulsive border-line nymphomaniac is what Wood had called her, or something like that.

Had she made him equally compulsive? The reality was after spending intimate time with her all he saw was positive, slightly keen on detail, but far from obsessive.

Cade was about to consider carrying out a selfish and compulsive act by leaving London and heading to France where his skills could really be utilised, where he could carve out his future. He knew he needed to do it, wanted to do it in fact. Had to do it.

He was replaying Daniel's words as he took a moment to think, 'for God's sake take the opportunity'...

'But could I do it without her?'

CHAPTER SIX

He walked back to her flat, taking the long way around and rarely raising his head to look where he was going. His mind was in three different places. Things had travelled at a stellar pace since he'd been given the chance to leave his old force and work at East Midlands Airport. One event, one woman, had now changed the course of his career and possibly his life.

He laughed, one woman had ruined his life, and another had changed it, the third had altered his perceptions of women entirely. And somewhere between them was a drop-dead gorgeous Irish girl who had exploited him as much as he had her on a moonlit night in the Peak District.

Despite all the 'Met' jokes he'd swiftly grown to admire the team at the Yard. They worked hard, played hard and took things very seriously, too seriously in Clive Wood's case. And for Cade that was the difficulty he faced.

How could he leave such a well-ordered team to travel to a foreign country – surely it was madness? He'd only been there on a few day trips to top up his duty-free collection. But this was Interpol. Every police officer's secret dream.

He made up his mind he would take the offer. All he had to do now was break it gently to the new girl in his life. If she adored him as much as he did her she'd go with him. Wouldn't she?

He arrived at the flat to find it empty.

He reminded himself that she had a life too. She was probably picking up some food or seeing a friend, or had gone to a nearby gym. Yes, whatever it was she was doing it was normal. She wasn't strapped to a wooden frame and slowly drowning, praying for salvation.

But hang on. She didn't go to a gym, ever. And she had few friends outside work. So, he surmised, she must be at a nearby shop buying something great to eat, or possibly something even nicer to wear. 'Calm down. This may be a massive metropolis but the percentage of good far outweighed evil. Relax will you?'

He smiled, catching a reflection of himself in a nearby glass cabinet.

'You're a bad man Jack Cade so you are.'

Another half hour passed before he heard footsteps approaching the door. It opened, and he instantly saw that he was right. Of course she was fine. 'Why the need for paranoia Jack?'

She looked at him, quizzically. "Hi you. You OK, you look worried?"

"No, I'm fine. Just...missed you."

"You soppy old Hector, you were worried about me weren't you? I'm a big girl Jack, I'm fine." She berated him but quietly adored the fact that someone cared enough to be worried.

They ate and ended up watching television, a comedy

about a failed television chat show host which made Cade laugh. Whilst she didn't find it anywhere near as amusing she loved to see him relax. Things had quickly become 'conventional' and she hoped they would remain so. As long as things were never conventional in the other rooms in the house she would start to enjoy life again.

"How have you explained not needing accommodation to the job?" It was a fair and overdue point.

"Easy. I told John Daniel I had moved in here and to be grateful for how much money I was saving the Metropolitan Police."

"And that was that?"

He repeated the question, shaping it into an answer.

"Come on let's get to bed, I suspect it will be another long day tomorrow. Last one there turns the light off."

They ran through the flat with Cade finishing a narrow second. This girl was competitive as well as attractive.

They laid in the dark, her breathing slowly becoming more regular.

"Carrie."

She didn't reply.

"Carrie, thank you for everything you've done for me, I..."

He couldn't bring himself to say he loved her, partly in fear of sending out the wrong message and mostly because of his former wife and how she had damaged his ability to ever truly love someone again.

Despite the internal dialogue, he could not stop himself from thinking of her constantly. Each thought was positive, warm, loving even. Surely this was a start?

She lay very still on the left side of the large double bed, next to the bedroom door and grinned from ear to ear in the almost complete darkness. She knew it wouldn't be long before he was able to complete the sentence.

Within minutes they were both asleep.

Two hours later a darkly clothed figure entered the ground floor of the Old Queen Street property. Having carried out a number of reconnaissance dry-runs the male knew the street and the property well.

Dressed as a tradesman he had been able to walk up to the front door and gain access to the building when another occupant had seen him trying to enter awkwardly with what appeared to be decorating equipment.

He'd feigned a London-based accent which was enough to convince the dweller that he was not a threat. Pathetic at best it was indicative of the trend of many residents in the area; head down, arse up and get on with life, never taking the opportunity to talk to a stranger, or worse still, look them in the eye.

Once inside the dark hallway he had checked the letter boxes, confirming O'Shea's presence. He opened the front door again, looked up the street and ran his blank data card over the card reader. Bingo! It had worked.

A few days before he had picked her out in the street, near her workplace.

A little too close but it added to the thrill. He was highly trained and they would never identify him. He was just too good.

Valentin Iliescu involuntarily licked his lips. It was good to be back in business, he could almost taste success. He was being paid what he considered an obscene amount for a few days of what he did not even consider to be work. For him it was as if he were stepping back onto a conveyor belt, working for the Romanian Intelligence Service, the SRI.

He had learned his field craft during the early Nineties when the government had seen fit to respond to an uprising of a group of students and intellectuals, each of whom were opposed to communists being able to vote in government elections. Student numbers had built to a point that concerned the then government and their intelligence services were deployed to collect information. The subsequent riots saw the deaths of at least seven people. Iliescu had earned his reputation as a formidable covert operative, who legend had it could obtain intelligence so easily he made it look like child's play. Hence his nickname 'Copilul' – The Child.

Iliescu's loyalty had waned in 1997, the second that his wife was imprisoned for divulging state secrets. She was innocent; she knew this, her husband knew this and the state too, but despite all of this they continued to hold her in a cold and isolated detention facility where the food was the highlight of her day, infested though it was. The abuse, both physical and mental, by both her captors and her peers made it a living hell.

The truth was, he had outlived his purpose; he had a monetary value now and that, simply, was not convenient. Raised by the state. Trained by the state. And now despised by the state.

The problem was the state were anxious about punishing Iliescu; fearful of how he could wreak vengeance, instead they punished him by depriving him of his one true love: Ana.

Copilul wrote to Ana every day despite not one letter ever reaching her, burned before she even had a chance to gain strength from its contents. With each lost opportunity adding to the cancer that consumed him, he turned evermore towards the darker side of his field craft.

He lived on a pittance, stashing away his earnings, day after day, month after month, until he was able to live a comparatively comfortable lifestyle. Then, when he was ready, mentally prepared and physically able, he would travel back to his motherland from mainland Europe and having judiciously selected a target within the government, would kill them.

His tally to date was seven. All were lower-level servants, easily replaced, but their passing caused the government a headache for which they appeared to have no cure. Seven dead. One for every year those bastards held her in captivity until the day she had died.

Seven years later and his reputation, his urban folklore as an operative had grown exponentially and his name had changed subtly but changed nonetheless to *Copil de umbra*. Child of the shadows.

It fascinated him that adults associated a child-like name with mischief, with evil. Who was he to downplay the fear? He liked to live up to the reputation too. Falling short of leaving a calling card, his modus operandi was always brilliantly researched, carefully rehearsed and technically beautiful. He would always do something that provided an indication of his capabilities, which in itself tended to strike fear into the heart of his enemy, leaving investigators to question who he was and when he would be caught.

At the very worst he had an alibi, at best a reason for his alibis. Always cautious about leaving a footprint, of being caught, he lived a life of vigilance which he skilfully blended with the need to relax and enjoy the spoils of his own individual war.

The brief phone call he had received from a British-registered cell phone had made his tasking quite clear. It had outlined the location, the target and the mission.

Child's play indeed.

It was just like the old days, but this was more lucrative, fun almost. The money had already been credited to an online account. The caller, although evidently in charge, was also fearful of betrayal. It was far easier to just pay the man.

Keep your friends close, and your enemies closer still.

It was an old adage, but one never truer than when associated with a Soviet-trained, goal-driven and quietly furious individual.

Cade woke with a start. Climbed out of bed, got his bearings and stood, listening. The wind had picked up during the evening and was now playing games with his sub-conscious. A metal dustbin lid had become dislodged somewhere, blowing against a gate and spinning to a stop. It was enough to wake the dead, let alone an already-exhausted Cade.

Satisfied he was not just hearing things and content that the most menacing threat was after all only an inanimate object he relaxed, visited the en suite bathroom, urinated carefully, mindful of leaving any evidence for the female of the house to find the following morning, rinsed his hands and returned to bed.

O'Shea failed to move, deep asleep and lost in an agreeable reverie from which she had no wish to be disturbed.

Cade was asleep in seconds.

Timing his movements with those created by the agreeable weather conditions, Iliescu was able to climb the stairs to the apartment, quickly and unheard. His night vision was excellent, and he was able to walk around the lounge almost nonchalantly.

He took a moment to admire some landscape photography, brilliantly observed and one, a monochrome seascape appealed to his artistic mind, if he were a burglar he would have taken it, if he were a friend he would have subtly asked for a copy. But he was neither. A pity, he particularly admired how the person behind the lens had captured the golden hour, had observed the shadows and had cropped the image to focus the mind. It would have easily graced the walls of his home.

He carefully picked up another photograph, a simple portrait in a sun-bleached birch frame. It was her. He studied her in the ambient light, long enough to confirm the target.

The caller's words were deliberate yet ambiguous.

'Cut a piece from her and remove it – send it to her lover at his work the following day. Let them realise we can strike at their heart, at any time.'

Iliescu found the whole task bothersome. He would much rather be entering the bedroom of a government minion in the country that had created the monster – a senior official from the National Library, perhaps? Yes, that would indeed do.

He would sedate the official's wife, quietly going about his task and with the clinical efficiency of an anaesthetist.

Propofol would swiftly enter the victim, sedating her in moments. As a fast and short-acting narcotic, it was ideal for his task. Her husband would be next, but his dose would be lethal.

With a cursory and complete check for the presence of obvious forensic evidence, *Copil de umbra* could leave the building and blend back into the place from which he gained his name.

But no, this client was different. This client did not want him to murder someone. Why make a difficult job harder comrade? He made a mental note to track down the individual, and when the time was right, he'd be sure to educate him on the finer things in life, taking a particularly pleasant moment to consume the bastards exquisite French brandy in front of him as he watched him beg for forgiveness, cable-tied to a chair, the hypodermic needle delivering its consignment, widening his eyes and flooding him with the realisation that this was to be the end.

He often despised his clients more than the target.

It was becoming a regular thing too. Haunted by the demons of his past, of the government that betrayed him, but equally, driven to do the right thing. He wanted to earn well, to exploit his skills, but at the end of a task he also wanted to retain the moral high ground.

Enough. He must not let his desire for revenge cloud his judgement. His need for secrecy meant he had to be lucky all of the time, but his client only once.

He approached the bedroom door, took hold of it firmly and confidently moved it an inch forwards and backwards. Good. The owner of this home was as fastidious as he was. There was simply nothing more inconvenient than a creaking hinge to upset the evening.

Some said he was obsessive, compulsive even, but he had washed his hands of them, five times.

He entered, confidently placing one foot in front of the other, just like God had intended. He was at a heightened state of alert, the hundreds of microscopic hairs on the back of his neck standing in line, always an indicator of an imminent threat.

He'd done this a thousand times, both in practice and in reality. There was one time in Prague where he'd brushed the back of his hand across the naked breast of a diplomat's wife. It was wrong, and he told himself he must never do it again. He was a professional intelligence operative, not a damned pervert. But she was rather beautiful.

When challenged, he explained to his supervisor that he needed to learn which parts of the human body responded to the lightest of touches. It was all part of the training programme and the diplomat's wife had undoubtedly responded.

The present difference with these two individuals who slept, blissfully unaware of his presence, was that they worked for a government with whom he had no experience, and in truth that concerned him.

His intelligence brief was simple, almost too rudimentary. What it failed to do was to outline the risks posed by his target. The female was a civilian, ex-police officer and now an analyst. She wouldn't pose a problem, surely?

The male was another case altogether. The document he had read and destroyed stated that he was a successful officer, with experience in a number of United Kingdom forces, that he had orchestrated a counter-strike against the client's own men. He was close-quarter battle trained and could use a handgun and as such should be considered a threat.

He looked anything but a threat as he slept like a baby next to his lover. He looked at them both, wondering whether they had recently made love or whether they lived a mundane lifestyle like so many couples. He chose the former, if nothing else it allowed his mind to wonder away from the danger of being caught. It was how he worked best: relaxed.

He carried out a risk assessment on the male. He was on

the other side of the bed and that provided Iliescu with valuable seconds should he need to exit rapidly. He looked physically in good shape, but the Romanian had the element of surprise. One good blow to the solar plexus would render the male ineffective long enough for him to leave the building and disappear.

Whilst the male slept in his newfound home, his uninvited guest continued with his task, allowing him the slumber he clearly needed. And besides, despite what the client had ordered, these two people had never harmed him and in a bizarre way they were connected – law enforcement brothers in arms, Intelligence Officers and all that.

He methodically swept the room, looking from left to right, taking a moment to close his eyes and just listen. Nothing, not even the sweep of a second hand on a clock.

He removed a scalpel from his sleeve pocket, it provided a hint of light, its tempered, sterile blade sitting at the end of a modest black plastic handle. Costing only a fraction of most surgical items, it was the essential catalyst for any surgery, so exquisitely sharp and yet so brilliantly simple.

She slept on her left side; her face looking straight at him. He lowered himself onto one knee and leant across her body. He could hear and feel her breath. She was naked, but it failed to distract him. Using the blade, he sliced a locket of hair and placed it into a plastic zip-lock bag. It would later be dropped into a pre-addressed envelope.

Content that he had got what he considered to be a piece of her, and contrary to the more sinister desire of his customer he began to stand up. His task was complete. If the customer wasn't happy then fine, he could come and have a face-to-face discussion about a refund.

As he turned to leave, he realised that in only carrying out the modest act of removing her hair he was in danger of damaging his reputation. After all, a skilled practitioner could remove the hair in a train carriage without alerting the donor. The client needed to know that their message had been delivered.

He exhaled silently. The couple were oblivious, sleeping soundly.

Iliescu stood still and thought deeply, rubbing his chin, backwards and forwards with his left hand whilst the right held the scalpel with the deftness of a surgeon.

He slowly let the air part from his lungs, and then gently inhaling once more. It was all he could hear.

'Damn you people. Why can't you just let me kill them and move on? Why does the job have to be so fucking difficult?'

He knelt down again, watching the male who had moved from his right to his left, placing his left arm up under the pillow and settling again. Now both people were facing him.

He placed the tip of the scalpel onto her neck, adding enough pressure to rouse her. She didn't move. He had carried out this act before and he knew that the neck, contrary to popular belief, was not as sensitive as the back of the hand, the forearm or cheek.

As long as the action was deliberate, decisive and swift he would be fine.

He started the cut just in front of her ear, under the jawline. Following the line of her sternocleidomastoid muscle, which acted as a guide, he drew the blade down her neck, stopping at the collarbone. The cut was made with the precision of a physician, only a millimetre deep but enough to allow it to bleed. It would heal in days, no worse than a shaving cut for a male.

But the point had been made. The message delivered.

He waited for a reaction. Nothing. As he expected. He was a professional, after all.

He placed the blade back into the pocket where he had located it and retraced his steps, gently closing the door as he left. He walked back down the left-hand side of the stair-case, through the lounge and out through the main door, closing it quietly behind him and removing a piece of cloth from the Yale latch, allowing it to slip quietly back into place.

A masterclass in burglary had just taken place in central London, and a young woman would only know how close she had come to death when she woke to find the blood on her pillow.

He got to the ground floor, waited and hearing no sounds other than the cry of the wind he removed the latex gloves that had protected them both and exited the main door, turned left and walked off into the night. He would dispose of the surgical items the next day, dropping them overboard from the passenger deck of the cross-channel ferry that took him from Dover to Calais.

Once back in France he could recover, relax and enjoy the benefits of a lifestyle paid for by people richer than him. Living, for now, in a rented farmhouse in the Bordeaux region he looked forward to a glass of Aloxe Corton, the famed red wine from Burgundy.

He needed to support the local industry and besides he enjoyed the taste of his local wine, which, as luck would have it was one of the finest Pinot Noirs in the world.

He allowed the liquid to empty into his favourite glass before he swirled it around and around, allowing the fullness of its flavours to collide with his senses. It was only two years old, not yet mature but ready to drink. The heady mixture of preserved fruit and blackcurrant delighted his taste buds and the colour, the colour was garnet, crimson and red. A deep and satisfying red not unlike the blood that had gently seeped from that poor girl's neck.

He leant back in his aged leather armchair and exhaled, forcing the stress of many years from his lungs.

For now, his work was done.

CHAPTER SEVEN

Early the following morning the weather had altered for the worst.

O'Shea fumbled for her alarm and placed one foot out of bed, took a moment to settle her equilibrium and then walked quietly towards the bathroom.

She switched the light on but kept her eyes closed. It was part of her daily routine. She ran the hot tap until it got up to temperature and then began to splash the refreshing water onto her face. Her eyes opened, the remnants of the night slowly allowing her lashes to prise apart.

She was joined by an equally half-asleep Cade who carried out almost the same regime, stood behind her, his arms casually draped over her shoulders, hands heading south towards her cleavage, but his eyes opened instantly when he saw his girlfriend's neck and shoulder.

"Carrie, when did you start shaving? Is there something we need to discuss?"

"What the hell are you on about?" O'Shea asked. She

wasn't at her best in the morning and she was fighting a losing battle with her lashes.

Cade stepped forward, took a flannel from a nearby radiator and gently wiped the encrusted dark blood from her upper body. It was then that he noticed the cut.

"Carrie, what have you done to yourself girl? Look."

She was now fully awake and staring back at her reflection. Her hand favoured the wound, pressing on it for a few seconds before she released it and stared at herself in the mirror.

"I have no idea."

She turned to look back at her bed, the pure white cotton bedsheets and pillow cases were stained with her blood.

The rational part of her brain tried to formulate an explanation. Life was strange and had a habit of presenting stranger scenarios but this one had no obvious explanation. She had no recollection of injuring herself, and she was absolutely certain that her newfound lover had not tried to kill her during the night.

Cade felt unsettled at what he saw, but forced himself to play it down. Somehow she had cut her neck, and, girl it was already healing. Best leave it at that.

O'Shea had the same unnerving feeling, but did exactly the same as her man. She lived a professional life that existed around the need to collect data, to provide intelligence and support investigations. As things stood she had some primary information; pure, analysed intelligence couldn't follow as she had no idea how it had happened and therefore an investigation was considered unlikely.

It was a freak event without explanation.

"Time for breakfast?" asked a reassuring Cade.

· · ·

Seven miles away rain was pounding off the pavements of Braybrook Street, London and creating hard work for the perished wipers on Gabor's newly acquired Peugeot 306.

The bland silver car sat in the side street adjacent to Wormwood Scrubs Park and in view of the iconic British prison of the same name.

Gabor was sat in his own car. At least that is how he viewed it for now, his, until taken away from him. He was in the driving seat, but not in control. Behind him was a thin but wiry individual who was by far the most paranoid person he had ever met. Most likely a heroin addict. He was constantly shifting about in his seat, looking left and right and up and down the street, as if the might of the United Kingdom police force was bearing down upon him.

Had the male have looked through his steamed up passenger window, or taken a moment to wipe the vapour away with his hand, he would observe that Gabor had parked immediately alongside a small memorial.

The memorial, brown marble with gold lettering and detail sat among the grassy verge of the famous common land and acted as a reminder of a summer day in 1966 when three plain clothes Metropolitan Police officers were shot and killed after they stopped to question three men in a car, a car that in its day most likely aroused as much suspicion as the silver Peugeot and its occupants would in the present time.

The offenders, almost certainly afraid of being found with a firearm in their car, were later convicted of killing all three officers, two of whom were detectives the third, their uniform branch advanced driver.

The irony was that the Metropolitan Police decided to create a specialist firearms branch – CO19 – as a result of the incident. A manhunt took place, two of the criminals were apprehended swiftly, however the third male, Harry Roberts, managed to evade capture using previously acquired military and jungle training. He was a career criminal who would eventually serve forty-eight years in a number of British prisons – one of the longest sentences in British history.

His accomplices were not so fortunate. The first, John Duddy, died in prison. The second, John Whitney was released early on parole, causing huge unrest among the judiciary and renewed heartache for his victims' families. Whilst hardly a consolation for the family, Whitney's life ended violently in 1999 when he was beaten to death by a heroin-fuelled flatmate.

The proximity of the Peugeot to the scene of the massacre was uncanny. When the male did eventually wipe the glass clear with his hand he noticed the memorial, its words and the police crest. He had no idea what the location was famed for, but shuddered involuntarily.

He had no need to worry. He was just another shifty-looking male sitting within striking range of a high security prison. The place was full of and surrounded by them.

Gone were the days that the nearby officers' quarters would have acted as a deterrent, now mainly in the hands of private owners: they were just houses that happened to adjoin the Victorian monolith.

Curtains occasionally twitched, but the inhabitants were too busy watching daytime television to care about the outside world.

Sat in the passenger seat and all together calmer was an older male. Gabor knew he was also Romanian and from his demeanour he knew he was in charge. His voice was familiar and he made no effort to remind those present who was actually in control. Calm, measured, but menacing.

The rear seat passenger was just along for the ride – and to slice open the driver's throat should the need arise.

The front seat passenger exhaled a dense cloud of cigarette smoke which mixed with the dank vapour already present in the Peugeot and forced the driver to lower his window slightly. The older male turned towards Gabor and spoke. It was at that point that the younger man focused upon the hideous, recent scarring to his face.

Feeling it was the right thing to do and a compassionate act, Gabor asked him the obvious question.

"What happened to your face?"

The male shook his head and blew another veil of smoke up towards the already tarnished roof lining.

"Let us say I had a disagreement with a whore."

Gabor laughed uncomfortably.

"My young friend, there are times when to laugh."

Gabor nodded eagerly.

"But this is not one of them. Laugh at my misfortune again, and you will look a hundred times worse than this. We will send a piece of you home to your beautiful mother every week until you are finally able to be laid to rest."

"I'm sorry. Sorry..." He held up his palm in a consolatory gesture.

"Another sign of weakness. Never apologise. See? You simply cannot win can you?" Now he laughed. "Relax. You have done well for us, the boss is very pleased. Now you must go to the next level. There is only one answer, and that is yes. We will meet near this location tomorrow night and we will hand over the equipment that you need. We will send a text providing the exact location. Until then, you do not contact any of us. And keep off the streets. Your days of making small money are gone. Do this last act and you can go home a rich man. Do I make myself clear, Dorin?"

"Yes, sir."

"Good. Very good. You will receive your rewards in heaven, or sooner, depending upon what your currency is. Mine, should you be interested, is US Dollars."

The insipid male in the rear seat laughed, revealing a mouth full of damaged, bloodied and blackened teeth, a pitiful legacy of his decade of drug abuse. His eyes were not windows to his soul but dark portholes that led to a cavern of self-loathing and paranoia. It was the first time he had been in a position to make some money since being released from the prison an hour or so earlier. He needed to buy drugs again and without exception would do anything to get them.

Artur Gheorghiu turned to look at him and placed a hand on his knee, slowly adding more pressure until he had found a trigger point.

"And you can keep quiet too, you fool. Go and open the door to the car. I do not wish to get wet."

The male hated him, but at the same time needed him. His past was so full of promise. Once the best at his trade in Eastern Europe, he had a reputation, but now, he just had a past. His future looked dismal, and he could see how awful it looked every day.

As he shuffled to leave the Peugeot Gheorghiu smiled at Gabor, he winked too but it was indiscernible, his eyelid being so badly damaged it gave the perception of a permanent stare, and that, among other things, unsettled the young Romanian.

"Smile. You are among friends. Now, drive away and don't look back. Until tomorrow."

He nodded. "Until tomorrow."

O'Shea walked into the office a few seconds ahead of Cade and was greeted by an ebullient Roberts.

"Alright treacle? How are you this morning?"

"Fine boss, you? Oh, and boss?"

"Carrie?"

"Please don't call me treacle."

"Indeed. Ah, Jack, my good man, and how are you? Did I ever tell you my dear old Auntie Dot who lived in Lewisham had a pair of lovebirds?"

Cade, still unsettled by the earlier incident, was in no mood for games.

"No, you didn't Jason. Did I ever tell you I set fire to my former inspector's home whilst he slept soundly inside?"

Roberts noticed a shift in his colleague's demeanour and asked him to join him in a side room.

"You OK, bud?"

"Honestly, Jas? No."

He explained about what he had observed at O'Shea's flat earlier.

"Weird. Any thoughts on how it happened?"

He hadn't, and that made it twice as bad.

They read the overnight occurrences and discussed the plans for the next few days over a cup of English breakfast tea. They were joined by an unshaven Del Murphy.

"I'll have one if there's one going boss!"

"Jesus Derrick, look at you man, you look like you've been up half the night. What's her name Del? Or, in these days of enlightenment, what's his name?"

The now-gathered team laughed at Murphy's expense, but he was in no mood to be the butt of their misplaced humour.

"Actually boss, I've been working with a source, not quite A1 but heading that way. She's given me some good intel up till now, but the latest looks right on the money. Some chatter about our Eastern European friends."

Roberts was intrigued, and Cade's ears had tuned in to the conversation. He slid his office chair in their direction and sat among the growing group.

"Pray, do tell my good man." Asked Roberts in a Shakespearian style.

"Well skipper, this bird I've been seeing 'as given me a few bits of decent source info, mainly about the Albanians in town. Some of it has been actionable, some not. But last night she wanted to meet up about a bloke she knew from the past, Romanian geezer who she knocked about with in the old days. Got a ten stretch at Scrubs for a failed bank job where he tried to blast the safe to bits – he's just come out."

"And...?"

"And 'es been back in touch with 'er already, wanting a bit of the other."

"Sorry Del, I'm not with you. How is this relevant, other than him being Eastern European. Expand before you lose your audience."

"She's a tom boss."

"This city is full of them Derrick and I'll remind you to be careful handling a prostitute as a source on your own, it's fraught with danger."

"No boss, not this one. We went to school together. She's different now to how I remember back in the fifth form. Very high class."

"Is she now?"

"She is way out of our league boss, and importantly out of reach of the lad who's just been released from the big house. Turns out in his day he was quite something, he was nicknamed The Chemist or some such shit; into mixing stuff up and blowing shit up, but the passing years have not been kind to him at all, that and a hundred quid a day drug habit."

"Go on."

"Well, it transpires that my source has seen this geezer with a right old stash of notes. He's only been outside for a day or so, so where's he getting 'is cash from? According to Lucy..."

"Lucy?" asked a now very interested Cade.

"Sorry guv, Lucy Thomas, the call girl I was telling you about. Bit of a cracker, actually. As I say back in the day, she was different. She's grown up a lot since then, got a collection of toys that would make Hamley's blush."

"Indeed."

"So what is this Lucy doing with an Eastern European criminal with a heroin addiction when she could pick from Arab sheiks or rich American businessmen?"

"Fair point, guv. It's not just the money. It's how he's talking to her. Talk of a big job, of explosives, that sort of thing. Her old man was in the British Army, did a couple of tours in Ireland. She likes this bloke guv, but hates terrorists. Hence the chat with me. Shall I hook up a meet with her? Perhaps you can ask her those questions yourself?"

"Do just that Derrick, my son. Jack will come with us to chaperone us in case we end up in some bizarre threesome. Carrie, before you start the overnight scan can you get a message to the boss to let him know we won't be at the morning briefing – we've got a date with a gorgeous and exotic lady of the night."

Roberts was drawing an outline of a girl with an hourglass figure as he looked back at Del Murphy.

Cade looked at O'Shea and smiled. He winked and mouthed the words 'miss you'.

She set about deliberately sharpening her favourite pencil as she mouthed back, 'Good. Make sure you behave yourself.'

Given the extent of the morning traffic, it was a wonder that they reached the apartment quite as quickly as they did. It was less than a mile as the crow would fly, but still took them twenty minutes of stop-start commuting.

Roberts had allowed his subordinate to drive. He was starting to feel the pressure of the last few weeks and needed a chance to close his eyes. Somehow he managed to drift off but sustain a complete conversation with both the driver and Cade who was ensconced in the back passenger seat also trying to grab a moment.

"Now listen Del, let me do the talking, I spent some time on Vice and I know how these girls work, they can be quite manipulative when the need arises. I got taken bloody hostage by one once, tied me up and whipped me and everything."

Cade was quick to join the tale, "So did you charge her Jason?"

"I did, Jack. Fifty quid and I got a twenty percent discount off my next visit!"

It flew straight over the head of Detective Del Murphy.

"We're here, boss. You sure you don't want me to come up with you and Inspector Cade?"

"No Derrick, we will be absolutely fine, thank you. You park the motor and I'll text you when we are done."

Murphy was old school so he did what he was told but felt he needed to add just a dash more sauce to the recipe.

"Skipper, there's something you need to know..." His words were lost in the maelstrom of morning rush-hour traffic so he put the window back up, dropped his seat back slightly and listened to Radio 2 until he drifted into a neck-snapping slumber.

Cade and Roberts reached Lucy Thomas' door after a rapid ride to the fourteenth floor. Cade was whistling the first few bars to *The Police* song about a prostitute as Roberts tried to suppress a naughty schoolboy giggle.

"Jack, stop it, man! We need to act like a couple of pros..."

They paused, looked at each other and started laughing at the most inopportune moment, and as luck would have it as the non-descript door to 1412 opened.

Standing in the doorway and at least six foot in her stockinged feet was the rather lovely Lucy Thomas, immaculately made up, her post office red lips were pursed, ready for action. Her hair, flaxen with a hint of strawberry, was tied into a hastily created pony tail. She was slim but not overly so, and her hips were emphasised by the way she stood, leaning casually against the door frame. She wore a rather red and very clichéd silk wrap, which was embroidered with the familiar emblem of the Mandarin Oriental Hotel Group in some far-flung corner of south east Asia. A dishonest acquisition or a gift from a lover?

"You two boys going to just stand there wetting yourselves or are you going to come in, I'm a busy person, time is money and all that. Delboy tells me you want to speak to me?"

Her voice was unusual, distinctive; rasping but alluring. Each word was measured, assured and brimming with experience. She looked up and down the hallway as she ushered them into her spacious and well-appointed home.

Roberts coughed nervously, still trying to hold back the urge to giggle. His collegial relationship had strengthened with Cade to the point where he had quickly considered him a friend and one with whom he could now have some fun – among the chaos that had recently consumed them both this was a good thing.

"Very nice pad, Miss Thomas. Delboy, sorry Detective Murphy said you could help us with some information about our current investigation. Is this true?"

Thomas walked to the kitchen, "Fancy a coffee? I'm parched, I spent four hours getting rather acquainted with a Jordanian businessman last night. The way he was going at it I think he was drilling for oil the dirty little bugger."

She laughed a laugh that was not in keeping with the image that Murphy had portrayed. It was a deep-seated roar, the kind that could easily have been equated with a dock worker or bricklayer, the antithesis of the inhabitant of upper-echelon male sexual fantasies. All that said, neither man had ever seen such an attractive tradesman.

In spite of the image and the developing rapport, Cade couldn't help feeling that there was something more to Thomas.

With perfect timing she looked at him and smiled emphasising her impressive cheekbones and aquamarine eyes.

"Sugar? Or, as I suspect with those ocean-blue eyes, are you sweet enough already darling?"

Cade laughed politely, if not a little awkwardly, and replied, "It has been said Lucy. Now, tell me what you know about a recently released Romanian."

"Dear God, no foreplay? Come on gents, Delboy and I spend at least an hour flirting before we get down to it. You can do better than that...surely?"

Cade looked at Roberts, who had withdrawn slightly and

was now sipping on his overly strong coffee and physically indicating to Cade to take the lead.

"Lucy, I'm all for foreplay but this is important, can we just go straight to full sex, you know, leave out the part where I tell you I love you?"

"Toys?" Thomas was almost insistent.

"No!"

"What about a bit of bondage? I could strap you to my headboard with your Marks & Spencer's tie and we could talk about the first thing that comes up..."

"No, no, no. How many times Lucy?"

"Me? I can go all night, Inspector Cade, I'm not sure about you." She turned to Roberts, "And what about you, sir? What's your pleasure? Let me guess...your friend here doesn't like my idea of M&S action, so what say we indulge in a little S&M instead?"

Roberts was quick to cut her off in her prime "No, seriously, that will not be necessary. The three of us need to get down to business before one of us ends up getting hurt."

Thomas placed her coffee on the black marble kitchen worktop, walked over to Roberts and inclined towards him.

"So sugar, now we are getting there, you want a threesome? Well, honey, why didn't you say, I'm game if you are, as long as old blue eyes over there gets to finish me off."

Roberts stood and tried to regain control. He gently pushed Thomas back with his left outstretched palm but the six foot tall Amazon resisted, now playing games with him and enjoying the audience.

She leant in further now, dominating him. Cade watched with veiled amusement, observing his partner losing the battle but prepared to step in should the need arise. He knew that escorts could fight their way out of most corners.

And the one first-hand experience he'd had taught him that they didn't play by the Queensberry Rules.

"Listen, love, we just need to talk. I'll pay you for your time but neither me nor Inspector Cade want to be tied to your furniture, spanked, licked, spat on, shat on, smothered in apricot yogurt or have anything cold, metal and shiny shoved up our collective arses. OK?"

Roberts had felt so intimidated that he knew had to push on whilst he had the upper hand.

"And another thing...I do genuinely only want you for your brain, not your body."

It was then that the slap landed on Roberts' face, and it was a ferocious slap too, probably heard by Murphy fourteen floors below.

"Bitch! I'll have you know my body is prized by men all over this city – no, make that all over the world!" The altogether darker Lucy Thomas was now enraged and strutted back towards the retreating Roberts, her hips sashaying from side to side.

Roberts reacted a little too hastily and pushed Thomas backwards. She staggered slightly and fell unceremoniously onto Cade. Now the fight had really started.

Cade pushed upwards, trying to rid himself of the blonde bombshell as Roberts moved in to drag her off him. Recognising the fun had only just started, Thomas lashed out with a foot and caught Roberts squarely in his testicles. He dropped onto her whilst clutching them and gasping for air. Nausea rose up and he took a moment to acknowledge that this was possibly the least erotic thing he had ever done.

Cade, sensing that things could take a turn for the worst, grabbed hold of Thomas' arm but connected with the silk robe instead. He was somewhat surprised to feel her strength as he struggled to hold on to her.

The three of them fought against each other before landing unceremoniously onto the expensive and no doubt authentic dark blue Persian rug.

Lucy Thomas had got the threesome she had desired. Her language now resembled the aforementioned dock-worker and her actions befitted a scorned fish wife. This was not in any way, shape or form turning out to be ideal for the two investigators.

Whilst Cade and Roberts battled to rid themselves of the happy hooker she hung on for grim death, not unlike a carnal rodeo rider, aroused at the physical interaction.

As the skirmish continued all three began to tire. Cade thought for a moment about ringing Murphy but he knew it was futile. For now, he needed to protect his own assets.

He found himself on top of Thomas and tried to restrain her, conscious of harming her but also aware that his colleague was underneath, shouting and pleading for mercy.

Cade looked across the room and saw a reflection in a glass display cabinet, it was a sight he wished never to see again. The three people thrashed around like competitors in a deranged game of Twister, which had transformed into something befitting a well-thumbed and slightly adhesive page from the Kama Sutra.

Knowing he had to resolve the matter – and wondering how the hell it had got to this – he grabbed her ponytail and yanked it forcibly. On the second heave the pigtail extension moved towards Cade, causing him to fall backwards, pushing Thomas' lithe and much-used hips into Roberts' face.

All that the detective sergeant could think about was his dear wife – what would Cathy she say if she could see him now?

Mother Nature, herself a playful thing, chose this very moment to reveal some extra facts about Lucy.

Her exquisite honeyed hair was far from natural. Her wig had masked what was actually a reasonable amount of mousey brown hair that could, and probably did, find itself transformed into differing styles. Mrs. Nature, not content with giving up without a fight, also chose to inject some previously secure information – and the evidence hit Roberts squarely in the face.

Thomas' equally silky underwear had shifted during the melee to reveal a rather healthy, previously restrained and altogether impressive phallus – and Roberts was within seven inches of it.

His arms were pinned to the rug by Thomas' legs, and Cade's own weight ensured that neither could move.

Cade was still astride her, now holding the once-glorious flaxen crown, and could hear his colleague begging for help. Whilst he was now fully aware that Lucy was not a natural blonde, he had no idea whatsoever that the girl called Lucy was in fact a man. A man called Thomas.

A six foot tall, well-hung, wig-wearing bi-curious call girl who was about to ruin Detective Sergeant Roberts' day, week, month and year.

"Any joy, Carrie? They've been a while." It was Daniel, wondering where his second in command was.

"Sorry boss, clearly something has come up with the hooker they've gone to pump for info."

"Right, well get on the blower and let Jason know he's going to get a right mouthful from me when he gets back. Our meeting has been in his diary for at least a week."

Daniel returned to his office, unusually angry. He was normally the brightest part of each morning, O'Shea knew, even after the relatively short time she had worked for him that something was wrong.

Roberts pushed with all his might against a pair of hairless thighs that now bristled with muscle, tendons and ligaments; that no longer appeared sexy, now they were more athletic and glistening.

The overly large testes, however, were a different proposition altogether. They sank onto his cheek, hairless and sweat-laden, causing the sexually bashful Roberts to wretch. It was one thing to sleep with his wife and to do the things that they did, behind closed doors and occasionally with the light on, but this? This was wrong on so many levels.

Cade had now got Thomas by the neck and was starting to increase the pressure on her carotid when he looked down and saw the offending member. Rather than restrain 'her' it was all Cade could do not to burst into uncontrolled laughter.

Thomas had also realised that the game was up, the fight over, and began to plead for mercy.

"OK, OK fellas, enough is enough. You win. I have my looks to consider. I promise I won't kick off again. Girl Guides honour."

"Bloody Boy Scouts more like!" replied a genuinely horrified Roberts. "You had your fucking balls in my mouth at one point. For the love of all things holy, when were you going to tell us?"

Thomas looked genuinely upset. "But I wasn't boys. That's just it. I'm Lucy, not Len. I'm a girl, I'm a woman, just accept me for what I am?"

Roberts was still incensed.

"I swear if you start singing '*I will survive*' I'll knock your bloody teeth out."

Cade, sensing that things were far from calm, offered to put the kettle back on.

"Guys, I think we can all put this behind us. Tom, Lucy, whatever your name is I think you need to start talking, and fast or I'll happily put you in restraints that you won't enjoy. Deal?"

Lucy Thomas wiped the smudged lipstick from her face, rubbing a solitary piece from her front tooth and apologised, first and foremost to Roberts.

"I'm really sorry. I don't know what was about to come over me."

She looked at Roberts who shook his head and replied, "I can assure you it wasn't going to be me love. I mean, really? Do you actually think I would go anywhere near a cross-dressing prossie? I'm a married man!"

"Excuse me, mister, married men make up many of my best customers. And for the record, I'm trans and proud." Thomas' anger was starting to boil again. Cade stepped in.

"Lucy, I can call you Lucy, can't I?"

"You can blue eyes, but he can't," replied Thomas with a theatrical palm wave towards Roberts who was still nursing a pair of frantically pulsing orbs.

"Good, then start talking. I want to know when you met this individual, actually, I want to know his name, who he associates with, where he lives, where he gets his money from, when you plan to see him again..."

Thomas cut Cade off mid-sentence, "I can tell you all of this honey, I can even tell you his favourite bedroom pastime – he likes to do it 'prison style'..."

"Lovely, do not tell me another thing about his needs, just the facts. Just the facts."

. . .

Cade spent another hour talking to their newly hired source. He even managed to convince Roberts to join in and before long it was Roberts who was obtaining the most information. Unbeknown to them both it would be the start of a longstanding and closely guarded intelligence relationship that would see the two become as close to friends as a Metropolitan Police detective sergeant and a bi-curious, bisexual working 'girl' could be.

The Romanian customer had indeed seen better days. Thomas explained that they had first met in the mid to late nineties when he was running stolen goods out of central Europe into London.

Constantin Nicolescu – son of Nicolae, or Constantin as she had only ever known him – made out he was shocked when he first saw Thomas naked in a spa bath, but the reality was he knew exactly what he was getting involved in – and was hardly in a hurry to leave. He visited once a week whilst in town and then whenever he returned to the area.

She had no idea where he lived. His only obvious associates were also similar looking, so she assumed correctly that they were from the same region.

The only thing he had told her was that he was now in possession of more cash than he had seen for years and that he had worked out a way of getting more. He laughed when he told her that he intended to explode onto the London criminal scene.

She didn't take him literally, and anyway it wasn't her business. He was a customer after all, and rules were rules. But terrorists were terrorists – it simply didn't matter how you dressed them up.

The only rules that existed since his release from Wormwood Scrubs were that he could not involve his friends and there was to be no kissing – not with that mouth – it repulsed her – but the money was good and in a bizarre way he was kind to her, unlike the Middle Eastern nobility who thought nothing of beating her and sharing her around. Of all her customers, they were easily the cruellest.

The two officers made a point of a professional goodbye in the hallway of Thomas' apartment building. She knew that in order to avoid a clutch of actual bodily harm charges she had to provide timely information, and often. She assured them she would, but insisted on a code name for when she rang in to speak to them.

All of the obvious names were gone: Vixen, Foxy, Kitten and Tiger.

Cade thought that the name Lucy Thomas sounded vaguely, phonetically, at a push, and without any other possible names, a little like 'illustrious' and his old school friend had served on the Royal Navy aircraft carrier *HMS Illustrious* – he repaired Sea Harriers – or jump jets as they were colloquially known.

Jump Jet seemed appropriate but too downmarket for the undoubtedly upmarket Thomas – but Harrier, at a stretch, sounded just right. And so she became Harrier. As with most covert human intelligence sources, her name was as much a mystery as the intelligence she provided.

A few hours after they had arrived at the apartment, they were travelling back to the Yard. Neither Cade nor Roberts said a word to Murphy en route, but as they pulled into the car park he got out of the car and spoke.

"Boss, I was trying to tell you something about Lucy that I felt you needed to know, but you couldn't hear me above the traffic."

Roberts did his utmost to hide his eternal shame.

"Oh yes, Del and what would that have been?"

"Well, boss, Lucy is not all she seems, she's erm a little..."

Roberts held up his hand, whilst the other sat in his trouser pocket nursing a still stinging testicle. "Derrick, there is nothing you can tell me about that lady that will upset me. Lucy, Jack and I got along just fine. We managed to obtain a lot of quality information and we will meet again whenever she has more to tell us. Cracking girl, very courageous wouldn't you say Jack?"

"Oh indeed, the girl has got some balls that's for sure Sergeant."

Murphy went back to his desk, looking a little bemused as Roberts ushered Cade into a side office.

"Jack, what we saw, felt, touched, tasted, smelled, did... back there....it must never be discussed again. Ever. Never."

He shuddered involuntarily. "I need to gargle with bleach."

"Gentleman's honour Jason." He put his hand out, allowing his colleague to shake it vigorously. Roberts was walking away when Cade called out to him, pointing to below his nose.

"Jas, you've got a stray hair on your lip."

He left Roberts in the office manically brushing his face with his spare hand as he gravitated with a wicked grin back towards an industrious O'Shea.

"Well hello, Inspector, the DCIs looking for you two. Hope she was worth it?"

"Carrie, you simply have no idea. None whatsoever." He

shuddered and walked along the corridor to the nearby office.

Roberts and Cade spent another half an hour briefing the detective chief inspector, strategically leaving out the finer details of their meeting.

"We learned a lot about an individual of interest but the only problem is sir, we don't know where the next job will be. I recommend that Jason keeps his hand in with the informant. I think she can come up with the goods."

"Whilst you have been out and about painting the town red, Carrie and her colleagues have been running the numbers again. It transpires that the ATM jobs are reducing. A few here, a couple there. The bottom line is unless anything significant occurs the commander will pull the pin on Op Breaker."

Cade went first.

"Boss, this is crazy we are *this* close!" Thumb and forefinger were used to support his words.

"He's right, sir. Just another few weeks."

"I hear you both, but with knife-point robberies escalating, the commissioner is losing interest. Get out there and start rattling some cages, but gents, no overtime."

All three men sighed. Despite the message that Daniel had delivered, he, too, felt that they were as close as Cade had indicated to locking up some seriously motivated offenders.

Daniel cleared his mind and spoke.

"Gents, I've only been on board for a short time, but I give you my word that I will back the team to the hilt. But please realise as much as I think you are all great, doing a great job...there is only so much I can do when it comes to three rounds of scissor, paper, rank."

Cade nodded. "At risk of being rude I doubt any of us are going to get promoted any day soon so we need a sharper pair of scissors."

CHAPTER EIGHT

THE FOLLOWING NIGHT, DORIN GABOR LEFT HIS BEDSIT room and walked quickly to his car. He had met Constantin earlier in the evening and the package had been exchanged. A simple, non-evidential trail; no chance of betrayal.

Whilst he didn't trust the other male Dorin could see some light at the end of the tunnel. He finally had a chance to become someone in his home town, a man of means who others would respect. All he needed to do was to assemble the devices, attach them as he had been shown and then make the hour-long journey to the channel port of Dover, drive his car onto the ferry and head across Europe for home, raising neither interest nor suspicion – in a now practically borderless Europe it has never been easier.

Artur Gheorghiu had promised him a brighter future. So far he had paid him well and treated him like a son. So why did Gabor feel such an overwhelming desire to get the job done and leave?

The older mentor was at the forefront of Gabor's mind as he approached the first ATM. He'd already done this a hundred times. But he felt a nervousness that he couldn't explain. The device was almost identical to the equipment he had become familiar with, with a subtle addition – but the new equipment in the boot of his car was far from it. He had never seen such things before. He could guess what they did, but would he be right?

As he attached the plastic surround onto the first ATM he could think of nothing but the other items. Successfully in place he checked his environs and left on foot getting back into his vehicle a few hundred metres away. It was almost muscle memory in action.

At the second machine he repeated the act. And then drove onwards a short distance where a pre-selected machine from the same bank group was to become the host for another device.

Sat in his car in a darkened corner of a side street, he sent a text message to Gheorghiu.

'It is done.'

Gheorghiu deleted the message and deliberately failed to reply. When the day was over he would destroy the SIM card. He was a professional. Why leave those bastards any clues?

In the next Borough Constantin sat in his poorly lit flat counting his money, again. He was restless. He needed to see the girl again. Perhaps tomorrow night when his job had been completed?

He picked up a backpack, left the flat and walked a short distance before head-down boarding a bus which carried him for three stops before he stepped softly onto the pavement, matching the speed of the approaching walkway expertly.

Gabor saw him approaching. He illuminated the side-lights on his car earning a solid rebuke from the older male when he entered the car.

"This is not spy film, idiot. From now onwards just do as you are told. Nothing more. Understand?"

He did. He swallowed audibly, causing Constantin to smile a ruined smile.

He placed his hand upon his shoulder. "Right Dorin my boy, let us go and earn some *real* money."

Across the city another duo were attaching identical devices to cash machines at branches of another of the 'big four' banks: Arrive, sweep the area for witnesses, ensure your identity is obscured, attach device, leave. The instructions were simplicity itself.

Jackdaw had asked his brother to turn up the heat. He gave him no particular instruction, but he did say he was no longer motivated by money. What he craved was a reputation.

Stefan recalled his words, 'Bring some distractions to the pathetic capital of England.'

"As you wish big brother, with your fancy name, and your illicit lifestyle, I will do just as you ask."

In the south of the extensive capital city, a third team mirrored their colleagues' activities. None had ever met, but all were trained via stammering, poor quality video recordings. A fourth team were a few minutes behind them working feverishly to make up lost time in the south west.

. . .

"OK Dorin, now we carry out stage two." He playfully rubbed Gabor's hair, causing the younger male to pull away. It was obvious that Constantin found him attractive, but Gabor did not reciprocate. He would take his time with the young man. The rewards were beyond exhilarating. He began to weave his trap – he was the funnel web and the good-looking boy, the fly.

"Get the equipment like you have been shown. I will check the street is clear. I have dealt with the cameras." He raised his eyebrows, adding what he thought of as a hint of chemistry to their relationship. "I am good, yes?"

Gabor could sense that things had changed. Now he was unsure who to trust the least. The boss who would probably slash his throat given the opportunity or this toothless predator who was clearly flirting with him? He felt sick. He decided that a penniless escape was better than any financial security.

He would do this job and then escape, head home to his mother. If he had to he would try to kill his teacher.

Constantin almost hissed at Gabor. "Come on boy, bring the final parts and hurry – we have one chance to do this. Time is against us. We must not get caught!"

Gabor looked down at his left wrist. His recently acquired watch had not missed a beat. It meant more to him than his car. He had no idea at all that he was its second owner.

CHAPTER NINE

ONE HOUR LATER, THE FIRST DEVICE IGNITED. IT HAD technically failed, but it caused some damage. Hardly a worthy distraction, it left the ATM housing partly molten and the cash machine rendered useless for a day. Constantin would not take the blame for this and unless the boy was willing to entertain him it would be reported as Gabor's fault entirely.

The normal method of operations required the team to place within the moulding a cell phone, a false aperture, and a data recorder. It was all they needed to obtain the bank information and PIN number, which would be cloned later. Childs play. But this device was unique in that it contained a very small amount of explosive – far from enough to kill anyone, but sufficient to create the distraction the Boss had requested.

Each cell phone had a timer, the timer had been set for an hour and countdown had begun when the teams had pushed the housing against its host. The phone created a small electrical charge, which in turn caused the solid pack electric blasting cap to initiate a secondary explosion in a minute amount of explosive.

The intention was to cause a commotion – the loss of human life was far from the minds of those responsible – and this would be critical should they be apprehended and held under the robust anti-terrorism laws that were sweeping across the country.

The plan, like all best laid plans, was for all of the devices to activate at the same time.

The first had failed.

Constantin was furious with himself. He had been employed as a civil demolition technician in the late eighties. Young, poorly paid and poorly trained, he had taught himself most of what he knew. He read books, he carefully sought information, and he experimented.

Constantly struggling to find a way to feed himself, let alone his extended family he began to hone his skills and as the months dragged on towards December 1989, he realised an ambition above anything financial – to strike back at the hated Romanian leader Nicoli Ceaucescu and all that he stood for.

He despised the dictator for what he had done to his people, living a life of obscene luxury whilst his subordinates lived in fear, misery and abject poverty.

He felt he could help support the anti-government uprising in his homeland but was held in custody after being arrested at a protest, long before his skills were ever able to be used. He was frustrated beyond belief. The fact that over a thousand people died as a result of the revolution angered him even more so. He became bitter and spent hour after hour fighting with internal dialogues that urged him to seek revenge.

It was whilst he was in prison he trained his thoughts

away from retribution and back towards financial rewards – if he couldn't earn a wage legitimately then why not use his skills to his benefit?

He began slowly, cutting holes in bank roofs and abseiling into the buildings using rudimentary equipment. His first job, alone, always alone, made him a week's salary. Hardly worth the risk. But as time moved on he became more adept, better prepared and able to identify his targets. Soon however he had to leave the country he called home for fear of capture. He moved north, stopping in places that had appealed to him as a child, at each stop he earned enough to live on. His progress was slow, but he was for the first time in years a contented man. He had never found the love of his life, over time his work became his mistress.

It was in Cologne, Germany, that he first met his nemesis. Flush with money from the recent burglary of a savings bank, he was unwisely seen in a bar with a significant amount of cash. A pretty off-duty bar maid convinced him to buy her a meal after work. Like Constantin, she was able to converse in Russian, and they got along very well. The couple ended up at a five-star hotel for the night, which he insisted upon paying for.

Sex occurred, but it was clear he hadn't enjoyed it. She had been satisfied and for her that was all that mattered. Whilst he slept she had the opportunity to steal his possessions and leave the hotel, blending back into the city and immune from capture. However, rather than steal from him she had seen a different financial opportunity and so introduced him to the noxious drug heroin. Why should she be its only slave?

Constantin had never experienced such feelings – the initial rush created by the drug took him by surprise, the girl brought out the best in him, just touching him was enough, the sensation was intense, beyond anything he had ever experienced, hour after hour she played with him until he became so drowsy he was unable to remember his own name. Soon afterwards he despised her and was so emotionally disinterested in her it would have shocked him, had he have been capable of connecting two thoughts together.

He had heard many people talking about the first rush that heroin provides, but always thought of them as weak. Until now. Now he just needed to visit the cruel mistress, just one more time. Just once.

He stayed with the girl for a month – he called her the girl because he simply could not remember her name. By then he was dependent and penniless. What she hadn't taken, her friends and dealer had.

He tried to self-treat – trying his best to withdraw but the constant itchy skin, restlessness and vomiting, diarrhoea and cold flashes made him miserable. There was only one way to counter the dreaded symptoms. He had to get away from the girl, the city and the endlessly available supply of drugs.

In a rare moment of sobriety, he left mainland Europe and arrived in London. Days later he had entered the previously considered fortress-like building of a provincial bank and had blown the front of their safe off. The explosion had taken him by surprise, but it was his new drug. The thrill was incredible. And the rewards far outweighed the risks.

What satisfied him more than anything else was the ability to choose when he wanted to experience an entirely different high. For now, it seemed that he had finally found a replacement for the dreaded drug that had entered his life and stripped him bare of everything he had ever worked for.

Staying at opulent hotels, he was soon exposed to the hedonistic world of pleasure that only cold, hard cash can provide. Drink, a new drug had laid bare his deep-seated addiction and soon he was seeking out a new dealer.

It was around this time that he first met the girl called Lucy. Against her judgement, but in return for a healthy reward, she introduced him to the local heroin trader. It wasn't a moral issue – she just despised the drug and how it had led to her younger brother's death.

From the moment that Constantin met her, his entire life was a fabrication. A drug-fuelled fantasy that enabled him to take greater risks and each time he entered a financial building, intent on removing some or all of their profits, he increased the amount of explosive that he used.

Constantin and Lucy continued to see one another for a few months – he even accepted the fact that she was a professional escort and insisted upon her taking precautions. The truth was, he had fallen in love with her – bizarrely, given that he knew that she was also living a momentous and almost paraphilic lie. Drugs had not removed his ability to judge a situation. It was his repressed sexuality that confused his state of mind, but if Lucy was happy, then so was he.

His opiate-based legacy had soon led him to accepting more demeaning roles, anything to be able to live. Quickly desperate for money, he had met another male in a pub on a quiet and miserable Thursday afternoon. The male was drinking vodka and offered to buy the second round. A simple act of kindness was all it had taken – that and a comforting conversation in his mother tongue.

The male spent the next few hours convincing him to

join his team. They talked about the revolution and toasted the future of a new Romania. The male liked what he heard and had a role that would reward his skills. No, the job would not be as satisfying, but his expertise would be utilised and he would be rewarded well. It seemed to be an ideal situation for a man who had little else to offer.

Constantin was not attracted to the male – more to his proposals.

Best laid plans: He was caught exiting a bank on only his second attempt and sent to prison by a judge who sought to make an example of him, later describing Constantin's offending as a 'Gaussian bell curve of gluttony'.

Locked down, hour after solitary hour in Her Majesty's Prison Wormwood Scrubs, he learned a lot about people, and importantly a lot more about his field craft. He read book after book about chemistry to the point where he convinced himself that he could easily initiate a device that would blow a hole in the extensive walls of a prison whose first construction began in 1874.

He was also, rather forlornly, able to obtain the drug of his choice and so his addiction flourished behind the Victorian façade of one of Britain's most notorious prisons from which he never escaped, nor truth be told did he eventually ever want to.

Whilst they housed him, cared for him and fed him, he could live a life without care. His body slowly began to rot, his mind quickly evaporating. The only thing he could remember was how to destroy things.

And her, yes, even in his darkest hours, he always remembered her.

• • •

What his sentence did do was focus his thoughts on how he could exploit his knowledge on the outside. He agreed with himself, for it was easier that way. He made a personal pact that the moment he got out of that miserable place three things would happen.

One, he would find that bastard Gheorghiu who he had met in that miserable English pub that served warm, inferior vodka and remind him what loyalty really meant.

Two, he would carry out the most spectacular bank raid yet and three, most importantly he would spend his ill-gotten gains on one more night with Lucy.

Oh, and four, he would place his addiction into an envelope, carefully seal it and send it, somewhere, anywhere, he didn't care, as long as it was as far from him and his inherent weaknesses as possible.

That was then. His past had a habit of visiting him whenever he allowed it a split second to invade his consciousness.

'Focus, Constantin. Please.'

Whilst Constantin did not witness it the second device was far more impressive. The blast tore a hole in the facia of the cash machine, sending its component parts across the street.

Small, effective and demanding attention. Stefan would be pleased. Jackdaw would be delighted.

The subsequent explosions, although small, were loud enough to be heard across various parts of London and in a city not immune to terrorist activity and occasional gunfire it was enough to cause some nearby residents to call the police.

One resident described the explosion as 'annoying' – it had interrupted her television viewing. Another was more descriptive, if not guilty of a little embellishment, explaining to the call taker that it sounded like 'the gates of Hell had opened!'

A third was perhaps the most informative. Pete Deighton was a thirty-year veteran of both the British Army and latterly, a police officer, now retired. He'd cut his teeth as a royal engineer, in particular as an explosive ordnance disposal technician.

He described the explosion as being exactly the same as the noise a detonator or blasting cap would make. He was spot on. Pete Deighton always was, he was a true gentleman and as his oft-used own pun went, a mine of information.

The first officer to arrive at the scene of the ATM blast updated his supervisor, who in turn told the CAD inspector that what they were looking at was an explosive device – not a cashpoint attack. This was enough to raise a few eyebrows and when the third one had been reported the CAD inspector hovered his index finger over his speed dial for a second. Should he call out the Met's own Bomb Squad or refer this to the local Royal Engineers?

He pressed the number 3 digit on the phone and began briefing the call taker.

Three minutes later the Metropolitan Police Ford Transit van exited its home and travelled swiftly across the city, crew on board, suited and ready.

Satisfied that the appropriate call had been made, Inspector John Ballard paused and then made another call to an old contact in Rochester, Kent, the home of the nearest available military EOD team.

"Geoff? John Ballard. Yes, very well mate. Listen, I've got a series of events happening up here and think you should be aware – our own squad are en route – and it may be nothing – but I want to inform you now in case this develops."

He began to outline what he knew to date and was careful to differentiate between fact and opinion.

"On one hand, we have a series of attacks on bank cash points and on the other we now have explosions at cash points. I'm sure they are connected, but I've seen my share of mayhem over the last twenty years."

"So, what's the real connection? Surely you don't get interested in these sorts of events?"

"You are right, Geoff, I don't. But these attacks have a link to a small group of Eastern Europeans who we think have begun to perfect this m.o. It's pretty lucrative stuff, but now the risks are increasing with these bloody explosions. Call me paranoid."

"You're paranoid, mate," replied a broad Birmingham accent, "But I'll consider myself informed. Keep me posted John."

In the preceding hour, Gabor and his unwelcomed mentor had worked with their own mix of diligence and paranoia to complete their task. Both men pulled their hoods around their faces, scarves already in place to cover their mouths.

Constantin gave the instruction to Gabor to start to prize open the cash slot with a crowbar whilst he ran to the car, grabbing two hoses, a sledgehammer and a length of wire.

He got back to his accomplice.

"Good, now go and get the cylinders. Quick!"

Gabor was back in seconds. He fed the two hoses into

the gaping mouth of the machine, stopping when he was physically unable to push any further. The wire followed.

Each hose was in turn attached to a cylinder. One contained acetylene, the other oxygen. If they had been able to park Gabor's car nearer to the scene they would have done, but for this event they would have to compromise.

The older male took control now – this was the critical part of the operation, far beyond the scope of a mere, albeit attractive boy. He skilfully allowed the gases to decant into the bowels of the machine, leaving them for two perilous minutes until he was ready to introduce a spark.

He'd seen it done many times in Eastern Europe and he had heard similar tales from South Africa – admittedly he'd only seen it on CCTV footage but he had practised it in his head many more times. The trend had only started that year, but was spreading with such intensity that the major banks had no response. The damage caused to their branches was almost as financially harmful as the actual loss of cash.

He had been allowed one trial run the day before at an old quarry in the nearby county of Essex. The explosion, given its simplicity, was gloriously spectacular.

"Come, Dorin. Hide with me behind this wall Come, now!"

Gabor was unsure, cautious almost, but Constantin's next words re-emphasised what they were dealing with. There was a sense of urgency, of excitement.

Quietly, he had hoped that this dark and deviant character would stand just a little too close to the bank. His thoughts were interrupted by his overly-eager abettor.

"Any moment now that cash machine will explode. Just like Gheorghiu and I explained. Remember? The front hole lets air in and the door on the back of the machine. It lets it out again! Simple. The gases mix and when we add a little spark...it goes boom! Then all we do is smash the wall down with the crowbar and hammer, and we take the stack of money and run. Ready?"

"It is like my chemistry class – chemistry meeting with physics, no?"

Constantin was too excitable to have the slightest interest in what the boy had just said. He considered his work an art form, alchemy, without the gold. He would turn a simple exchange of gases into a masterpiece, one which he considered, morosely, to be a waste of talent for many of his customers – and victims.

He was particularly focused, but managed what he considered to be a sincere smile before asking again.

"Are you ready?"

He was far from ready. What would his mother think of him? He had had such a bright future ahead of him.

"Ready."

Gabor stepped out from behind the wall but felt an instant grip on his arm.

It was his partner. His strength belied his physically poor condition.

"Get down you fool."

The explosion that followed was quite the most spectacular thing that Dorin Gabor had ever witnessed, heard or felt. In fact, he felt it before any other sense had been aroused.

There was no blinding flash of magnesium-white light, no obvious flames. If he was honest he daren't look, albeit if he had of looked he would have witnessed an impressive orange fireball. The surrounding air appeared to vanish, for a second he felt he couldn't breathe. The noise was intense, almost catastrophic given their proximity to the device. But what he did realise was that this was by far the most stupid, dangerous and undeniably amazing thing he had ever done. He found himself hugging his partner in crime, who just smiled an equally wide but broken smile.

"Come, brother, now we must hurry, this is where we make some *money*!"

Gabor ran with him, involuntarily rubbing his hands together.

They smashed down what remained of the machine surround and gained access to the rear, stepping over broken office furniture, walls and glass that had become victims of the attack. Gabor was amazed at the extent of the damage and more so that the police were not there yet. He recalled a feeling of suspended animation, as if he were able to operate in complete isolation with absolutely no fear of being apprehended.

He started laughing as he grabbed box after box of cash and stuffed it into one of a number of large canvass bags.

"Have you ever seen so much money, Constantin?" He asked, a huge smile emerging across his face.

His mentor had of course seen much more, but the taste of victory was sweet, sweet enough to overpower the acrid stench of garlic that surrounded them – a by-product of the toxic mixture of phosphine and arsine compounds released during the explosion.

They hastily rammed cash into the bags, climbed back through the void in the bank wall and ran as fast as they could, adrenaline coursing through their veins, back to Gabor's car.

All that was left was a vast hole, a debris field, a few hundred pounds in abandoned notes, and another statistic on a growing list of victimless crimes. And not one siren. Anywhere.

If the Jackdaw wanted notoriety, he had just found it.

His rapidly growing team had just carried out the first successful ATM gas attack on British mainland. At least the first that the banking industry would have to admit to, but it would not be the last and they would, for a few years at least be two steps behind.

Cade and O'Shea had foregone breakfast and had walked into work with four of the team, with a breathless Roberts two steps behind them.

"You've heard the news then Jack?"

"I have Jason, yes. What do you think? It's them, isn't it? It has to be."

"I'm a hopeless gambler Jack, so I'm putting it all on red."

"What exactly does that mean?"

"I have no idea."

The two were laughing about their conversation when they were joined by Daniel.

"Well, well, well, what do we have here then gents? A cynic might suggest that you and Jack have been running around town setting off a few firecrackers to court the attention of the media..."

Roberts was quick to retort, "With all due respect sir..."

"Which we both know means with absolutely none at all Jason..."

"We do boss, and normally I'd agree, but I mean it, respectfully, if you think this is really some half-cocked scheme..."

Cade intervened, "I'm pretty sure the boss didn't think that for a second Jason, and anyway, where can you buy fireworks at this time of the year?"

"Indeed – bloody big firework, Jack. Right Jason round

up that motley crew you call a team and let's get the white-board fired up. I want every fact on a timeline by nine-thirty latest. Give me a cast iron reason for me to go back to Frank Waterman so I leave his office with my reputation intact and not my balls in a bun!"

"You'll have everything you need, sir."

Roberts took the lead with his team, "Right folks, you heard the governor. If Breaker is to continue we need some real hard facts, I want these muppets locked up by the end of the week. They must be leaving more DNA evidence around the city than a teenage stag party. Let's get some enthusiasm going guys. Ask yourself what Woodie would have done!"

With the team fired up, Roberts ordered tea and coffee and a handful of what he liked to call 'celebrity biscuits' and then joining Cade and O'Shea adjourned to the briefing room, grabbed a pile of whiteboard markers and started drawing up the latest timeline. What startled them all was just how little 'time' had actually elapsed on the timeline.

"Morning Guv, Skipper, Carrie." It was Terry Campbell.

"Morning Tel, right, grab a brew and let us know any thoughts you have on this. Things have gone up a few notches overnight."

"They sure have boss. Like my dear old mum used to say, 'Life is like a box of chocolates, you never quite know whether to take the low road or the high road." He walked over to the whiteboard to act as the scribe.

Cade whispered to O'Shea, "Did he just misquote the great Forrest Gump or are my ears deceiving me?"

O'Shea beamed – it was the most amusing thing she'd heard for twenty-four hours. She hated what was happening in and around her beloved city.

Campbell was busy inscribing events onto the much-used whiteboard when a front counter employee walked in to the room.

"Sergeant Cade?" asked the employee.

Roberts was the first to respond. "It's Inspector, actually, Alice, but I'm sure he will forgive you. What have you got there, bit early for Christmas?"

"Motorcycle courier just delivered it Jason, very light, so it's not a gold bar!" She chuckled as she walked off, "I'll leave it with you darlin'."

Roberts slid the brown bubble wrap envelope across the desk.

"Special delivery for Mr Cade..." He playfully tapped the side of his nose.

Cade stopped the package with his palm and looked at the writing. It was a computer typed label with no return address.

He looked at O'Shea, "Too thin for a bomb so I guess it's an invite to the Queen's next garden party..." he tore open the envelope and instinctively looked inside to see a clear snap lock bag.

Roberts saw immediately that Cade's expression changed.

"What is it, mate?"

"I'm not sure, there's a small note in here too...stand by one..."

O'Shea continued to help Campbell populate the board with events, but became aware of Cade's silence.

"Jack?"

"It's nothing, Carrie, just something from my old force. Right, a cup of tea is in order, let's get our collective thinking caps on. Hopefully, we'll get the footage from the overnight job and we can start to put a few of the pieces back into the jigsaw."

"Absolutely old boy. The shame is that half the Met's finest now want a piece after that bloody explosion last night. Have you seen the headlines?"

"No. Show me."

Roberts took the signal, and both men left the room with Cade quickly walking into Daniel's office unannounced.

"Don't bother knocking, gents."

"I didn't sir. Put some gloves on and look at this."

Cade slid the envelope towards Daniel, who had removed a pair of latex gloves from his desk drawer. Roberts was equally intrigued.

Daniel squeezed open the aperture and looked inside. He saw it for the first time too.

"What is it, Jack?"

"Let it fall out, it's pretty clear."

The clear bag dropped onto Daniel's desk. The bag, not dissimilar to a container used by a drug supplier, was new and had a small label attached, upon which was written the date and the name: Carrie O'Shea.

"OK Jack, so it's a piece of Carrie's hair, other than it being weird what exactly does this mean?"

"Boss, I don't know, but I don't like this one little bit. I'm trying to think when someone has been able to get that close and importantly why would they take the trouble to send it to me?"

Daniel took a moment to sum up his thoughts, conscious that whatever he said would be taken as gospel.

"Jack, the cut on Carrie's neck?"

Cade was a step ahead of him, but didn't want to acknowledge the reality that was crashing into him like a charging All Blacks front row veteran. This was really going to hurt.

"No, sorry, boss. The two can't be connected. Can they?"

"Yes, Jack, I think they can. But I say again, what does this mean? Keep a close eye on that girl of yours, Jack. Given what happened with Nikolina, I do not want another one of our team going missing. Understood?"

"One hundred percent."

For once Roberts was not quick to add a lurid and mocking line.

The footage arrived into the office, the compact disc was removed from the container and the entire team gathered around to watch it. They were joined by a member of the Flying Squad, a specialist unit that was now paying the matter some attention.

Gary Preston, a ten-year member of the squad, had been there and got the T-shirt and he'd pretty much seen it all. But this latest series of attacks interested him greatly.

"So The Sweeney is on board at last, Gary my son? About frigging time. We've been asking for help for weeks and now we get a bloody explosion you are interested?"

Preston's reply was cool and calculated. "Yes, Jason I am."

"Well, with all due respect you can fuck off if you think you are taking this off us."

Preston smiled "Charmed I'm sure. I'm actually here to help as I have a background in explosive methods of entry. Can we agree to some entente cordiale rather than jumping down each other's throats?"

Cade leaned across the desk. "Jack Cade. Pleasure to have you on board Gary. Happy to learn from you."

Preston returned the olive branch, "Thanks guv, I've heard only positive things about you since the job with the bus. Terrible business. How's the backside?"

"News travels fast!"

"Not as quick as your arse, Jack!" Roberts was back on form.

Preston looked back at Roberts, "Look if it helps Jason, I've spent the last month in South Africa. The local police there have seen around a hundred of these jobs and they reckon it's the tip of the iceberg."

"So do you think this is the work of South Africans?" It was Daniel.

"No boss, far from it. I think your team is on the money. The recent ATM activity is classic Eastern Euro, they are the acknowledged experts but they are also adaptable. Why spend a day getting three or four hundred quid when you can hit one machine and take the entire contents?"

"But the risks are higher Gary."

"They are boss, it's the old risk versus consequences game. Some of their lower-level offenders are expendable."

"You speak as if you know a little more about this than I would have thought healthy for the squad. It's not exactly your remit this is it?"

"We've been watching them for a while, sir, if I'm honest. But you are light years ahead. If or when they move into using shooters, then we'll look to take over. Until then, it's your show."

The footage started. It revealed two subjects, all agreed they were most definitely male. They wore tracksuit bottoms and training shoes with hooded tops. All very stereotypical. However, unlike their streetwise local cousins, these boys were elevating the ante.

Daniel nodded to Preston, who took his lead.

"Right folks, see how these two are heading back and forth to the ATM. It tells me they have a car nearby, so that's a start point. Jason, perhaps one of your guys can draw a perimeter around the bank and check all CCTV locations?"

Roberts nodded.

Preston continued, "OK, now it's getting interesting. The guy on the left is collecting cylinders, one has oxygen, the other acetylene, and the wire enables a charge. Simple science really, but it takes some balls as I saw a good number of dead people in Johannesburg who failed to get the recipe right. This kit goes with one hell of a bang, trust me, I've heard it."

He talked the team through the process and then got one of Roberts' squad to slow down the imagery.

"Any second now...BOOM!"

The team was impressed.

"Shit on a stick would you look at that?" This from a very impressed Roberts.

"Amazing, isn't it? I've seen ATM imagery from Brazil that shows half the bank frontage blown away, it's a very fine art."

There was a light knock on the door. It was Cynthia Bell.

"Yes, Cynthia."

"Just had a phone call from the bank manager boss. He said that if it had been just before a long weekend, it would have been a whole lot more. But for now without a final tally, he reckons fifty thousand." She let the figure hang in the air before she walked back to her desk.

The team looked at each other before Cade spoke.

"Guys, girls, I think it's fair to say the ante has just been raised."

Roberts replied, "Agreed Jack, the problem was we thought we held all the aces but these bastards have a royal flush."

They rewound the imagery and ran it again. Cade spotted it at exactly the same time as O'Shea.

"Boss, the older guy...he thinks he's disabled all of the CCTV, but he failed to knock out the one at the pet shop next door. As a result, we can see him. I think the blast has blown his scarf away from his face."

Cade continued, "Just zoom in onto his face if you can, it's about 00:45:00....yes there! And pause. Right, get that image out to the masses. I want that toothless bastard in custody."

As soon as he had finished the sentence he looked at Roberts. It was a case of great minds.

"We need to speak to Harrier."

CHAPTER TEN

"Lucy, it's Jason. Talk to me."

"I'll talk to you if you use the right bloody name!"

Roberts looked around the office, noting that he was alone.

"OK, Harrier, talk to me."

"That's better. You need to get a grip on yourself, young man."

Jesus, he'd been on the phone less than thirty seconds and already she was flirting.

"Yes, yes, Harrier, enough. I need to know if you know anything about the explosion at the bank last night. Have you seen your man again?"

"No, and no. Next question."

"Do you have any way of contacting him?"

"I do."

"This is painful, Lu...Harrier. Can you let me have the number?"

"I can."

"Now!"

"Ooh, I love a man who dominates me. Such a refreshing change. It's..."

Roberts transcribed the number into his pocketbook and thanked Thomas for his time.

"Thanks for your time, Lucy."

"Excuse me?"

"For crying out loud. OK, I get it, it's fucking Harrier!"

"Ooh, now there's a nice thought Sergeant. TTFN." She blew a theatrical kiss down the phone, hung up and returned to applying his foundation. She had a busy day ahead 'and time, darling, well time is money'.

Cade and Daniel were discussing the bank raid when Waterman entered the office unannounced.

Cade motioned to stand but was ushered back to his seat.

"Gents. I see we have some new evidence to play with. The commissioner has given you another fortnight. So, two things. One, make this count and two, do not, I repeat, do not let them blow up my bloody branch. Waterman then proceeded to tell the credit card joke about his wife and the thief. Daniel and Cade feigned interest and laughed at the right moment before Waterman made his excuses and left.

"Two weeks, Jack. Enough?"

"Enough for what, boss? We still have no real clue what or who is hitting us. SOCO reckon there's bugger all from the bank, any evidence was destroyed along with the bank. Made one hell of a mess by all accounts."

"Brilliant, so we have a group of merry men robbing from the averagely well-off to feed the poor and no one has a blind bloody clue who it is?"

"Sorry sir, no, not yet. But we will. We just need a break."

"Don't we all, Jack. The sooner Mrs D and I bugger off to New Zealand, the better!"

"Boss, some bird called Fleming is on the blower. Wants an urgent chat with one of you."

Roberts stared at the ceiling. "Brilliant, all I need." He unnecessarily re-knotted his bright orange tie and got up from the desk.

Cade, ever the white knight said, "I'll deal with Fleming, you get some more work done on the research. I need to know if we have any way of plotting where this is likely to happen next."

As Cade walked off to answer the phone he heard Roberts say, "The impossible I can achieve Jack...miracles? They take a little longer!"

Cade picked up the phone.

"Jack Cade."

"Ah Detective Chief Inspector Cade, good to speak to you. Julia Fleming from the BBC. How are you?"

"I'm fine, Julia, tired but fine. It's Inspector, by the way, I haven't quite reached the heady heights of DCI yet. How can I help you?"

"Thank you, Inspector. Apologies for the promotion. I'm sure if you crack this case of terrorism, you'll soon get that third pip. Now, I've been talking to..."

Cade cut her off.

"Julia, which case of terrorism? Where? When?"

"Well, last night of course at the Barclays Bank branch."

"Julia, I need to meet with you, but what we discuss stays between you and me, for now at least. If you release any of it I will personally hold you responsible. I will charge you with obstruction and never, ever watch *Panorama* again. Do we have a deal?"

She paused, slightly bristling as a result of his brusque approach, but somehow she liked what she heard. He set standards, and she liked that in a man. Besides, he looked a bit of a dish from the recent press image, so yes, coffee would be nice.

Thirty minutes later, Cade was interrupted by one of the team.

"Boss, phone call again. Male this time, sounds foreign, sounds really pissed off too. Probably Romanian TV!"

"I'll be there in two."

He looked across at O'Shea who was staring into space.

"You OK?"

"Sorry?"

"You OK, you looked miles away?"

"Oh yes, just thinking."

"Anything in particular?"

"All sorts, Inspector. All sorts. Nothing to worry about."

"Dinner tonight, on me? We need to spend some time together."

"It's a date. I'll wear a red rose."

As Cade walked to the main office to answer the call he sensed all was not right with his girlfriend. He'd go back after the call and resolve whatever issue was eating away at her.

He picked up the phone smartly and said, "Jack Cade."

There was a moment of silence.

"Mr Cade. We speak at last. It has been a long time."

The voice was heavily accented, Russian? Possibly

Czech? It was almost that of an English person putting on a clichéd spy movie voice.

"I'm sorry, have we spoken before, Mr?"

"My name is far from important, Inspector Cade. But no, as you ask the question, we have not spoken before."

"But you said it has been a long time?"

"I did, yes. What I mean by this is that I have waited a long time to speak to you, we have so much in common – do we not, Jack?"

Cade paused, waving to a colleague and writing down hasty notes on a desk blotter.

'GET THIS TRACED!'

The officer ran off to find Roberts, unsure just how he was going to carry out Cade's request.

"I'm not sure just what we have in common, sir, but please go on, tell me how I can help you?"

"Ah, the ever well-mannered English man. How charming you are. I'm sure women flock towards you with your impeccable etiquette and boyish good looks. Women like Miss Carrie. Such a lovely girl, not pretty in the conventional sense, but lovely nonetheless."

Cade was now very interested in the conversation. He looked around to see if anyone else was as attuned as him. Roberts appeared and held up a piece of paper.

'No idea, Jack. We are running it through the telephonist.'

Cade shook his head. There must be some way to trace the bloody thing.

The voice spoke again.

"Mr Cade. I can help you. Write down this number. It is the number you are frantically trying to trace. Why make your life so...difficult. We can work together."

The voice laughed. It was a distinctive laugh, animal-esque, haunting.

Cade took the number and handed it to one of his team. He shrugged his shoulders, aware that it was futile. The voice wouldn't deliberately give his location away, and Cade knew the voice belonged to someone sinister. This was not a routine welfare call.

"Thank you. I am obliged to you. So, again, how can I help you, Mr...?"

"Jack, Jack, Jack..." He said it quickly, in succession, his tone slightly raised. Again, there was that visceral tone to his voice.

"It is about how I can help you, my dear. Like I say, we have so much in common. You are a leader. I am a leader. You are a good-looking man, I am a very good-looking man. I have wealth, you on the other hand don't, but you have your principles and they are like jewels to you. Why, Jack, we even share a name."

Cade listened intently, trying to decipher the meaning of the call. The voice continued.

"You like women, I like women. In fact, it appears that we liked the same woman. That was such a terrible shame, Jack. You see, a girl like that cannot be shared among two men – for fun yes, but not for love. Never for love. And I loved her, and I love her daughter and you made me punish her dear mother, Mr Jack Cade. You. Not me. No, it was you."

The faceless voice took a moment, then continued.

"You see, her death is your fault. You killed her. I'm sure she thought of you last as the water seeped painfully down her throat. Glug, glug, glug..."

"Who the hell are you?" asked a now angered Cade.

"Aha, now we are interested. Me? I am no-one, a black

shape that swoops in to watch a funeral, a mischievous being that steals jewellery, a bird that pecks the eyes of the dead from their lifeless bodies, Inspector. Peck, peck...peck. ”

Cade could visualise it now.

"Look, what exactly is your point? You said you could help me. I'm intrigued." He was trying his best to remain calm, in control, with the upper hand.

"But I can. Here is what you must do. That pen in your right hand. Start writing."

Cade pressed the pen into the surface of the paper, wishing it was the male's carotid artery. The pressure was building when the voice started to outline his needs.

"Number One, Jack – you need to relax. You must stop the rather attractive Miss Fleming from writing a story about my people being terrorists. This is an outrage. We are connoisseurs of crime, not terrorists! Even criminals despise terrorists." He laughed his trademark laugh.

"Are we at least in agreeance here, Jack?"

"OK. You are just simple thieves? Agreed?"

The voice laughed again.

"I see what you did there. Number Two. Go and investigate someone else, Mr Jack. There are plenty of Albanians and Russians in your city, West African money men, Jamaican Yardies. Go and trouble them instead. Leave me and my people to earn some money to feed our starving children."

"And three?"

"Oh yes, of course, Number Three, my favourite thing of all. Keep a watchful eye on your girl, Inspector, she may not be as pretty as my poor, wretched Nikolina – and nowhere near as pretty as my beautiful daughter, but to be fair to your girl, she has something interesting about her." He was quiet for a moment, but then continued slowly.

"I can see that. I see why you protect her. Yes, man to man, I understand why. Is she fun in bed? I imagine she is. The quiet ones often are in my experience. So quiet, so shy, until the door closes. But please understand also that I can cut her out of your life in a heartbeat. Tick, tick, tick..."

He left the last word to hang until Cade broke the silence.

"OK, I've listened to you. I will do my best to work with you, but you have to..."

"Jack, please. Do not start with your negotiation techniques. Seriously, do not insult me." His voice was now raised, angry. "Just do as you are told or next time...next time the scalpel will go just a little deeper, sliding beautifully into the carotid, so much pressure..."

Cade held the phone to his chest for a second, trying to think of something rational and nonchalant in response. His silence was all he had to offer.

The call continued for another eighteen seconds.

Alex knew he was listening and enjoyed watching the fine silver second hand on his exquisite mantel piece clock slicing across its pure white face, just like Copil had done with the girl.

Sweeping, deliberate, necessary. Deadly.

"Bye bye Jack."

Cade gathered the team quickly, almost shouting.

"Right, I've been told not to tell anyone this, but here goes."

He outlined the conversation he had just had with the male. What he deliberately failed to do was repeat what the voice has said about O'Shea.

'When the time was right, Jack, when it was right; not before.'

"I'm told we couldn't trace the call, but if I was a gambling man, and trust me I've never won a bloody thing on the horses then I would slap a grand on this caller being connected to Nikolina, the bank attacks and the pursuit involving the bus. I believe I have just had my first conversation with the man who refers to himself as the Jackdaw."

"We need to lure this bastard and his team into the open. They are greedy. It's just a matter of time. Any thoughts?" He scanned the room. It was Campbell who responded first.

The team braced for the mixed metaphors that were sure to follow – but they were all slightly disappointed.

"Bird in the hand boss, is worth two in Shepherd's Bush."

It was a direct homage to the area that the team were working in, albeit it was another jumbled up metaphor.

Roberts responded first.

"Terry my son, just what the sweet fackin' child of mine are you on about?"

"Easy skipper, we catch the guy with the missing teeth by using Miss Lucy to lure him out into the open. Nice and easy, lemon squeezy."

Roberts looked at Cade who was still trying to process the earlier call.

"I think our Tel is onto something, Jack. Agreed?"

Cade had little energy left to disagree, and besides, he thought it was the most sensible idea yet.

"Agreed. Right, get on with it, I'm off to meet Julia Fleming. Carrie, grab something to write with and a voice recorder. I want to make sure I stay on top."

He looked back at Roberts, who was busy poking his

index finger into a hole made with his other thumb and forefinger.

O'Shea walked past him and slapped him across the back of the head.

"Sorry, guv, must have slipped."

Cade walked into *Shot,* a new café not quite half a mile from Scotland Yard. He closed the door behind him.

An attractive woman, in her thirties with a short and well-cut head of hair that one moment shone chocolate brown, the other it was flecked with hints of deep vibrant red. She stood and motioned towards him. She was visibly put out to see O'Shea was with him.

"Julia?"

"Yes, you must be Inspector Cade? And this is?"

Cade disliked her dismissal of his colleague – more so he disliked it because he considered her to be his lover too.

"And this Miss Fleming is Carrie O'Shea – in my opinion, the finest criminal analyst on both sides of the Thames. She's my go-to person for crime science matters, knows just what to do with a hypothesis, and is truly wicked with a freshly sharpened pencil. She's also a great friend and is more often than not one step ahead of me."

Fleming appeared defeated.

"I bet. Anyway, we need to talk. Carrie, can you get us some coffee, I'll pay."

O'Shea was quietly furious, but agreed nonetheless. She deliberately scraped her chair on the stone floor and walked up to the counter, ordered three coffees and three scones, hers with apricot preserve, Flemings was chosen with raspberry jam. O'Shea hoped the pips would be stuck in the bitch's teeth for days.

The waitress brought the coffee to the table five minutes later. Fleming and Cade were deep in conversation with O'Shea making notes and interjecting at appropriate times. Fleming found herself warming to the pair and ventured to ask a question.

"Jack, are you two a couple?"

"Why do you ask Julia?"

"Oh, I was just wondering, you seem so close, if you aren't perhaps you should be, after all you seem to spend all day together."

Cade paused, sipped his coffee, smiled momentarily, almost imperceptibly, and continued.

"Julia, would it matter one iota if we spent all night together too? Would it change things in your eyes? Might it feature in your subsequent story? You know, a nice catchy headline. 'The long arm of the whore'..."

"Mr Cade, I work for the BBC. We are not the tabloid press, and as such are not known for our smutty one-liners."

He had the upper hand now. "I'm pleased to hear it, Miss Fleming – it's why I choose to watch your programme. Now that we've got the power-plays over, can we establish what you need from us?"

"Thank you, I'm sure you feel I deserved that. I want to be able to ride along with your team as they hunt down these...men. You say they are not terrorists, I agree to differ. But I will report on the facts. When can I start?"

"Ten minutes ago, Julia. You'll need this ID, and you are to report to Detective Terry Campbell. I want you to feature every word he says. You have my cell phone number, ring me if you need anything. Do not screen anything without me seeing it first. Miss O'Shea and I have some serious matters to attend to. Thank you for the coffee. Catch up soon."

He slid his chair back across the floor, again deliberately as he had seen how it set her teeth on edge the first time.

Ever the successful professional, Fleming felt she had retained the upper hand as she watched the two police staff walk out of the bustling café and back towards their headquarters.

The same waitress enquired if everything was to her satisfaction and handed her the bill. She looked at the total and called the waitress back to the table.

"Jamaican Blue Mountain coffee?"

"Yes madam, it's our finest. We think it's the finest money can buy, actually. Did you enjoy it?"

Fleming shook her head as she fumbled for her credit card. "Oh immensely. I'll need a receipt."

As the couple walked back to the iconic police headquarters Cade smiled and brushed O'Shea's arm.

"She was right, she did deserve that. If I'm not mistaken that was Jamaican Blue Mountain coffee, was it not Miss O'Shea?"

"I wouldn't know Inspector, I'm just a simple analyst."

"Glad you are back, boss." It was Murphy.

"You missed me, Del?"

"Always guv. Anyway, some geezer has been on the dog and bone asking for you. I told him to ring back."

Cade froze.

"Russian accent, Eastern European perhaps?"

"I've got no frigging idea, guv, 'e just wanted a natter with you. Sorry."

. . .

Just over an hour away in the historical Kent town of Rochester, Constantin sat naked in a pile of money. He threw another handful in the air and then another. It stank of financial and criminal drama.

In an adjoining room, Dorin Gabor sat penniless but assured of his rewards. He heard Constantin call his name. Cautiously, he approached his bedroom door and knocked.

"There is no need to knock, come in, boy. I have something for you."

Gabor eased slowly into the half-light. Sat on a dank, off-white mattress as stained and flaccid as the man himself, Constantin was hoping the sight of his naked body, the abundance of money and the sheer thrill of the last few hours would be enough to entice the boy into the heart of his temporary and squalid lifestyle.

He had even contemplated giving up the drug if this beautiful young man would relent – and give into his clear yearnings for the older, more experienced man.

He tapped the edge of the bed.

"Do not be afraid, Dorin. Come in, come and claim what is rightfully yours. Take a thousand, I'll help you count it. Have a drink with me, you have earned it. Then we must shower, to remove the evidence of what we have done."

He looked directly into the younger man's eyes before continuing.

"Perhaps, I should say, what we are about to do."

The tutor was becoming aroused, but his apprentice showed no interest, physically or otherwise.

"I am sorry, Constantin, I just need the money. Please understand. I do not mean to offend you. You are very kind to me but...I like women..."

His heart said 'grab the money and run', his head merely said 'run'.

Constantin sighed, looked up once more and spoke. He was still sat on the bed in the half-light. Growing less aroused by the second and beginning instead to feel uneasy, embarrassed and ashamed.

He asked a question.

"What has become of me, Dorin? Look at me. Help me and I will reward you with whatever you need to make a good life for yourself back in your home." He paused. "Please."

It might be a mistake, a ploy to lure him into a relationship he would never be willing to embrace, but he had saved him from injury and he had already rewarded him handsomely. He decided that he would help him. For now, this was all he had. A decaying counterpart, a deadly occupation and a fusty, unloved and deliberately anonymous home in a street, town and place he knew nothing about.

It was a rented end-terraced home on Pagitt Street. Long past its prime, the former home had become a shop in the 1930s and provided a much-needed service to the locals, who, back then, all knew one another.

Now it was an easy location from which to come and go, and no-one really cared whether they came or went. They were just two more men arriving and departing at odd hours, trying to appear guiltless as they went about their obviously nefarious acts and therefore were of no interest to the locals.

Except to Edward Francis.

Ted Francis was eighty-one. A true Kentish Man – depicted by the fact that he was born on the west side of the River Medway in the county that bordered the south eastern edges of London. He had made a career out of carpentry and was known as a quiet and unassuming soul who had an eye for detail a peregrine falcon would kill for.

He was one of a kind now. Born and bred in the same home, his home for over eighty years. His parents had died there, his younger sister had died there too, a victim of polio only a number of years before it had begun to decline. She had a son out of wedlock who was spirited away to live with extended family in Broadstairs, a lovely English town on the Kent coast. The boy would grow up to be strong and resilient, unlike his poor frail mother.

Ted had worked in the area, unable to go to war because of his flat-feet. He felt ashamed watching his boyhood friends departing to France, and the feelings never left him. Ironically, many of those young men never returned and Francis felt alone in so many ways.

In the post-war years he had helped many other tradesmen to rebuild the heavily bombed Medway towns. He worked tirelessly, his contribution to the memory of his pals who had failed to come home.

Having witnessed the rebirth of his home town he literally carved out a business repairing antique furniture, gaining a name as a true master carpenter. His attention to detail was exquisite.

His eyesight was phenomenal – for a man of his age. His hearing, too. It was just his hands that were ruined. A cruel legacy of a life of using manual woodworking tools.

He had painted the outside of his home seven times. Each time the front door would change colour, the rest of the woodwork remaining defiantly white.

"Not unlike the local population."

His current choice for front door colour was bottle green. He felt it symbolised a devout Englishman's home, and besides, he knew a Trades Officer who worked at the local prison and the only two colours George Miller could easily 'obtain' were Classic White, and 'Prison Green' as he liked to call it.

The entry point to this Englishman's castle had seen better days. The paint was peeling badly now, the bottom left corner starting to rot. It had been twenty-two years since he had made it the most resplendent home in the street. It seemed like yesterday.

"It seemed more like last week."

Off the street, inside the small hallway, he stood and watched. The singular spyhole had been a marvellous investment, fitted with care by the occupant just before he gave the door its new steam-train-green finish.

He'd added a doorbell too. Not one of those irritating, fancy, foreign battery gadgets, but a proper, wind-up doorbell that would last a month with three and a half turns.

It was last rung a year ago by kids playing trick or treat. It was neither.

"Bastards!"

If he could catch them he'd take them to the local Bobby, who'd give them a clip around the ear, and then he'd take them home to their father, who'd no doubt do the same.

"I should wind you up really, in case the milkman calls for his money," he said looking at the dome-shaped mechanism.

He was saying this to himself as he watched through the marble-sized glass viewing hole. He could see people approaching from the left.

"Indians probably, the street is full of them now".

He didn't dislike them, just their insular ways. He had heard that their food was an acquired taste.

"Why can't you buggers just get along with the rest of us?" he asked, to no one in particular.

The reality was, *he* was now the minority. An Englishman, in an Englishman's castle, in an Englishman's street. Living among a hundred other people, none of whom shared his ancestry.

"Don't get me wrong. I'm not a racist. No, not at all, I like these people. The women, yes, I like the women, rather exotic. The men, I can take or leave, they talk to themselves all the time. But the women I like. You'd like them too, Mother."

He continued to ramble on, stringing sentences together with ease for an audience of one. He was the epitome of loneliness in modern Britain: Born, bred, educated, employed, popular and hardworking, a man fashioned by his parents to inherit their modest home, among a real community where being inquisitive was a pre-requisite skill and giving a neighbour your last shilling was an act of simple kindness.

"They wouldn't give me the dew off their noses." He tutted, staring through the glass tube.

"Oh, here we go. The family at number seventeen are heading off to the mosque again, all dressed up. You have to give it to them, they are nothing if not keen. I've not been to church for months. I really should go. Father Gary would kill me if he knew I'd become so lapsed."

He hadn't been to Saint John Fisher in eighteen years. He really should go.

"I really should go. I have a few things I need to get off my chest."

And this is how he spent his days.

Sat in the kitchen, drinking tea, reading the coveted free newspaper, washing up his cup, wandering around the small but neat back yard, looking out into the scrub-land that was once the pride of the street and back to the front door.

What was left of the Axminster carpet was worn, his constant footfall leaving a trail from the rear of the property to the front door. Its trademark red and blue colouring was now all but gone, a few flecks of colour here and there were all that remained. Francis smiled when he reflected upon the time he had come home from school to find the carpet fitter finishing off the job.

He could hear his words as if he were stood in the doorway.

"Now then young man, what do you think about that? Your father has bought well there, this will last out his time…and yours, just remember to give it a good clean once a week and it will serve you well."

On special occasions he would go through the gate at the back of the property and walk through the vegetable garden. In its day it was the envy of the neighbourhood. He helped his dear Dad grow the finest produce there, most of which was sold for very little, or at best given away just to attract praise.

He couldn't recall the last time he'd walked through the larger garden, to the old shed, but he did remember that when he had, he couldn't find it.

"It was somewhere in the corner, just beyond the compost heap…"

He never used the best lounge. Mother wouldn't allow it. Such a shame, he would love to be able to go in and play the piano just one more time.

Sitting on the Kemble upright piano and as dusty as the instrument that it sat upon was a solitary black photo frame. The frame contained a simple, faded image of a smiling soldier, sitting post-passing out parade, tie slightly askew, surrounded by his mates.

The soldier wore a cap, upon which was fastened a gleaming badge. The Latin inscription read, *'Deus Vult'* – God Wills It. The call of the Crusades.

"I should ring Constable Brown about those two buggers across the road. Coming in at all hours with their bags. Full of money, if you ask me. Swarthy creatures, don't trust 'em. In my day I'd give 'em a bunch of fives."

He danced around the hallway, safe, practising his long-forgotten boxing skills, knocking down his opponent with a fierce single blow.

"They are in there now, no doubt plotting something else dark and devious. Right, time for a cuppa. Would you like one, Dad?"

Francis ambled back down the dimly lit, threadbare corridor towards the kitchen but was distracted by the letterbox slapping closed.

"Oh wonderful, someone has written to us. I wonder, is it the tax man? Or the dentist? Or...."

He looked out of his entrusted viewing device once more. Obsessive now, compulsive perhaps, he couldn't pass it. Resembling a bored businessman in a foreign hotel, staring out at the other dwellers and wondering who they were, where they were going, what they had been up to in the night?

He made a mental note to seek wise counsel for those thoughts before continuing his monologue.

"It's the Reader's Digest Mother, telling me I have won a million pounds. How truly delightful. I shall put it with the others."

He placed it on top of a neat pile of unopened mail.

His day unfolded. Hours blended into one another until the afternoon arrived.

Looking through the distorted tube, he saw the young male walking from the old shop towards his car. He was carrying the bag again. This time it was empty. Last night, when he arrived home, it was full.

"Lighter this time around old son. Much lighter. I could tell by the way you were struggling with it. Your friend too. His was just the same. I don't much care for the look of him, truth be told."

Ted had made a careful note in his kitchen, in his much-prized diary. He had come downstairs for a drink of water. Three minutes past one. a.m. Not four, or two. But three.

"And he had a friend too. They looked the same. The same origins anyway. One was older. You've had a much harder life, haven't you?"

He wrote down the description of the accomplice. Constable Brown would need that.

"Bloody Peugeot, French rubbish. You want to get yourself a Rover. Proper car that. Do you remember when you got ours, Dad? You said it was so fast you could catch pigeons in it! Pigeons! I ask you. Daft beggar. With respect. Tea time. Don't mind if I do."

The locals thought that Mr Francis was just an old fool who had lost his once pin-sharp mind, a nice old man who would have passed the time with anyone if they had only stopped to talk to him.

He only went out twice a week. Once to do his grocery shopping, the other to go to church. He always remembered the shopping, Mother had written down the exact route using the bus to town; he'd used the same list too, since 1982.

Those that knew him thought it was a miracle that he continued to survive. He confounded his critics and the welfare state, so independent was he that he had, for all intents, disappeared off the radar. A remarkable man indeed. But by Sunday had forgotten where the church was.

Constantin had first noticed the old man two days after he had arrived in the street. His hawk-like features immediately attracted his attention. The old fool considered the net curtains in his bedroom to be a shield from the outside world but Constantin was a hunter too – a heroin-paranoid, cynical, troubled man with few friends and, the old man had noted, none of them female.

'I can see you.'

The Romanian would engage in his own monologue, casting his watchful eyes up and down the street before entering his home. When he left, he scanned, left and right, right and left and for good measure he looked up to the rooftops. And, when his scan was complete, he would do it again. It was his obsessive behaviour that alerted him to the equally alert and elderly man across the street. The house with the now-faded green door.

"Yes, old man, I can see you. There you are again."

Constantin considered him a nuisance at first, but as the weeks passed by he became more wary.

"A man of your age should not be so interested in my activities. Go about your own business old fool. Leave me alone. Or I will upset your day. Trust me on this? I will upset your day."

The two carried out their singular conversations behind closed doors – a neighbourly joust with no victor.

Until now.

Now he had pushed the boundaries a little too far. Constantin knew that the slightest deviation in his behaviour would have the authorities looking for him once more. He simply could not go back into that place, that prison again. He would never see her if that happened and now, this new boy had come into his life. He would never see him either.

"Tell me Con-stan-tin, what is it to be?" he asked out aloud.

"Choices, choices." Either way, he could not afford to let the actions of a man twice his age ruin his already fragile life.

For Constantin – the criminal, there was only one answer.

The latest shot of heroin was taking effect, and with it his paranoia grew to a new level.

'Strike now. Deal with him. Go on, deal with him now. He has no one – and no one will miss him.'

He shook his head, blinked furiously, trying to counter the effects. His skin was flushing, itchy, his mouth drier by the second.

The biggest problem for Constantin – the addict was how short term the pleasure had become and how quickly the post-euphoria low reminded him why he should stop.

"Come, Dorin, we have to visit the old man across the street. He needs our help. I wish to give him a gift. He has deserved this."

Gabor was fascinated by the dichotomy that he was witnessing. One moment his teacher was conspiring to demolish bank vaults with explosives, the next, offering a charitable hand to an elderly and lonely man.

"Constantin, you are a nice man after all."

"Thank you, Dorin. Let us talk to our friend. You might learn something from our visit."

He pressed the doorbell. It was a pointless act. Francis had left the terraced home, catching the local bus to the supermarket where he would once more purchase the same groceries that he had purchased for as many years as he could remember. Many of his peers couldn't manage half of what he did. He only wished he could remember who they were.

Constantin shuffled from toe to toe. "No answer. A pity. The old man asked me to look at his oven. He told me a week ago that it did not work. We cannot have a neighbour without the means to cook his meal, can we Dorin?"

It was entirely rhetorical. He knew the answer before he had asked the question.

"Come on, we can get around the back. The old man told me it was OK."

They walked through an alleyway six doors away and disappeared into a different place, one full of conservatories and poorly landscaped gardens, of budget water features and wind chimes. Of overly large satellite dishes and a pungent mix of spices, bombarding the olfactory system with hints of turmeric, onions and chilli, and pepper and cardamom.

Gabor felt hungrier than he had done for weeks. They had existed on frozen microwaveable meals, barely enough to keep a flea alive. The notion of burgling one of these homes, in order to gain a decent meal suddenly seemed entirely appropriate.

Six houses along from the alleyway they found the old man's home. The grounds were larger than he anticipated however the once-immaculate vegetable garden was incredibly overgrown, nettles had overthrown runner beans and blackberry brambles fought for space alongside noxious weeds of at least a dozen varieties.

Unable to open the gate, they climbed over the wall, loosening the top and crumbling course of bricks before rolling clumsily into the undergrowth. They walked slowly, unsure of what lay under their feet. A garden fork stood defiantly in what was once a fruit garden. It had been there since the end of the Vietnam War. One delicate push and it would have snapped, its perished wooden handle exhausted from years of exposure to the elements, now almost dust, held together by time, goodwill and the ceaseless forces of nature.

A lot like Edward Francis.

Gabor tripped and fell, right arm outwards to break his fall. He clattered through what remained of a glass cloche – built by Francis many years before and designed to aid the growth of vegetables. Its glazed canopy simply gave way, the glass pane almost vapourising as it shattered beneath him. He survived the fall with only his pride injured, Constantin giggling at him as he tried to right himself.

He held out a hand, which the younger male took. As he stood up, they both began to laugh. It was the moment that the teacher had aspired to, but he knew he had to retain an air of superiority. The real opportunity would occur when the time was right.

"Come on! He could be home any moment!"

Gabor, brushing the debris from his forearm, turned back and asked, "Do you really think he would find us in here? We could be here until the war ends – like those Japanese soldiers!"

It took twenty minutes of skin-tearing activity to reach the kitchen door, also a faded Prison Green, it could tell a hundred stories, probably more.

It was the oft-used entry to the home, when it had been a gathering point for the local neighbourhood, keen to share in idle gossip over a cup of tea or to purchase some of the highly prized vegetables.

The two males had no interest in the history of the home, nor for that matter its occupant. Gabor was now along for the ride, unaware why he was here, navigating through dense undergrowth and slashing himself upon the wicked thorns.

Intent upon kicking the door inwards, the older male tried the door handle first. It was open.

He turned the resistant handle and pushed the door into the kitchen.

"Hello?"

He was out.

"Why are we here, Constantin?" Gabor felt uneasy, something deep in his psyche was sending signals that he didn't feel comfortable with. For some reason he was able to justify demolishing a bank building, but entering the home of an elderly male seemed morally wrong.

"To give the man what he deserves. He is alone. With no one to watch over him. Do you not think this is right that we should pay him this attention?"

Half an hour away, Ted Francis had missed his bus. Now, faced with the option of waiting among strangers in an exposed bus shelter or walking home, he chose the latter.

"Be good for the legs. Won't it?"

He began the walk which took forty-five minutes, fifteen longer than it did the last time it had happened.

"I'll put it in the diary. Mum will be most amused. Bloody buses. They should bring back the trams."

. . .

Constantin told his student to search the house to make sure the old man had not fallen and hurt himself.

"Go upstairs. Check the front bedroom. It is where he sleeps."

"You are a kind person. Different to how I thought," Gabor commented as he walked along the hallway towards the front door.

The older male said nothing as he quietly searched the kitchen. He observed that the old fool spent most of his time here, even sleeping in a large, old, wing-backed chair. He doubted much of the upstairs was used these days, only that front bedroom, the one that he looked out from behind those grey net curtains.

Looking around the room, it was much like a museum, a time capsule of a working class family. Such a shame. He had always despised his history teacher, an insipid little man with no interest in his pupils. And as he despised his teacher, he also loathed his subject. What was in the past should remain there.

He saw a large box of cook's matches on the faded table cloth. On a shelf he noticed a candle, half burned but just enough life for another winter's evening. He picked the candle from the shelf and placed it next to the matches, then continued his search until he located the electrical fuse box.

With a simple flick of the main switch, the old system was rendered almost useless. He doubted that the interfering inhabitant would remember where the box was, let alone remember how to use it, but as a precaution he removed a couple of fuses and placed them into his pocket.

He heard Gabor walking back down the staircase and joined him in the hall.

"Anything?"

"No, it is strange. It looks as though no one has been in those rooms for a hundred years. The old man sleeps in the front, perhaps? There is a black wedding dress in one of the bedrooms, it is like a person, an old lady. It made me very scared!"

The dress was hanging on an aged wooden mannequin in the larger of the rear bedrooms and had been in situ for decades. It was crafted from lace and dated from the early 1900s, its sombre colour an indication that Francis' mother had married a widower. To wear white was practically forbidden by the society of the era.

Although they had shown great resilience in the Francis family, death had often been a feature of the household.

The dress had unsettled the younger male. He had closed the door on it as quickly as he could, a shudder running involuntarily through his body. It was as if the bride had returned to the room and was watching him, challenging him.

"What are you doing in my home, young man? Come on, speak. Answer me!" She fixed her intense eyes upon him.

He ran down the stairs, not daring to look behind him.

Gabor shook as he spoke to his partner.

"It was horrible. A ghost. Yes, an old woman ghost. I want to go."

"What are you talking about? Ghosts. Stupid boy. Come on, control yourself. We go when I have fixed this cooker. Not before."

"Good. I am frightened. Please. Let us go soon."

Constantin looked through the spyhole. Nothing.

"Wait!" He was looking again. There was the old man. He could see him in the reflection of a house window, leaning against a wall. Tired but near enough to home that he would soon become a problem.

"Come. We must go now."

Gabor went first, eager to rid himself of the disquieting feeling. He almost ran from the property and into the overgrown garden. He knew Constantin was two paces behind him.

Had Gabor looked back, he would have seen his partner in the kitchen, deliberately placing the matches and candle within the half-light of the sash window. The last thing he did was to open the oven door and turn the dial on the time-worn appliance as far as it would go.

He followed Gabor through the scrub, over the wall and into the alleyway.

They exited separately and walked down the street away from their own flat and Francis' home.

'Goodbye old fool, so nice to have met you.'

Constantin shuddered; not the actions of guilt, but the response to his body countering the impact of a Class A drug that controlled and consumed him completely.

A hundred steps from home Edward Francis paused in the street, looked around and sighed. He leaned on a wall. He hadn't felt this tired in a long time. It was now that he wished he had children to care for him. His sister's lad would be a fine strapping young man by now.

His thoughts meandered as he leaned against a faceless property. He began to revert back to his own halcyon days, memories of his sweetheart flooding back to him.

"Such a pity, she was a lovely girl. Should have married her then you fool. Yes, quite right, I should. I wonder if she's still around. Next time I'm at the coast, I will track her down. Yes, I shall do just that."

He had been there for at least half an hour when he picked up the shopping bags, wincing as the weight cut into his almost transparent flesh and shuffled the last twenty steps, placed his key in the mortice lock and turned it. The lock was sixty years old and still reacted as if it were brand new.

"Thing of beauty that lock," he said to no one but himself.

He looked up the street and then back down before entering and quickly closing the door behind him.

He wound the bell for old times' sake.

'Three full turns – and a half. No more and absolutely no less.'

He walked slowly along the hallway and into the kitchen. Out of routine, he awkwardly turned his left arm to turn on the light switch.

"Nothing. Come along. Let's be having you. Father, that bloomin' fuse box is playing up again."

The ambient light had faded quickly, leaving Francis to squint as he looked around the kitchen. He knew the fuse box was there somewhere.

"Where are you?" He scratched his head vigorously. "Where...*are*...you?"

He pointlessly opened cupboards. The worn out box was in the void under the stairs and Francis would never find it.

"I smell gas. Silly old fool. I must have left it on when I went out. I don't know what has become of you, Edward?"

His eyesight, although brilliant for a man of his age, had begun to worsen in low-light conditions and soon he was using his hands as a guide. He saw the outline of the candle and the matches.

"Good man. Clever idea. Just in case."

He removed a single, slender wooden match, its bulbous, trademark red tip, waiting to carry out its singular duty.

"Soon have the place nice and bright."

The potassium chlorate in the match head was blended to react perfectly to the friction of the box's striking surface, itself containing a fine blend of chemicals and powdered glass. The action would cause the red phosphorous on the strip to ignite the white phosphorous and sulphur, allowing the match to burn.

A simple, everyday routine, like so many brilliant inventions, and often overlooked.

The process was always over in a heartbeat; the remnants tossed away, forgotten.

Francis looked through the kitchen doorframe, along the hallway towards the front door. His eyes focused upon the doorbell, then the letterbox, the frame and the door itself. In a millisecond he scanned, his brain absorbing countless pieces of information.

And then he saw her once again.

His mother, Sarah, was walking down the hallway. She was wearing her black wedding gown. Her face was white, but her eyes were as violet and radiant as ever. She was a strikingly pretty woman, so astute and ceaselessly considerate.

She raised her left hand as if to warn him of impending danger.

As Francis' gnarled fingers slid the stick along the box's

striking surface he smiled at her. It was good to see her again after so long. The match did not ignite.

"You look wonderful, Mother, so elegant..."

He stopped. Something had triggered a response in his mind. It wasn't, unusually, the sight of his mother but the recurring smell. What his aging olfactory system was detecting was the pungent aroma of Mercaptan, a chemical added to natural gas to act as a warning to humans that a leak was occurring; so incredibly powerful that it only required one part in a million for Francis to notice it.

Constantin had unwittingly allowed the gas to escape in an almost perfect quantity. A room containing around seventeen percent of gas would create a situation where, unexpectedly, an explosion would not occur – the mix of gas being too rich. At around four and half percent and below, the mixture would be too lean. It was a similar process to providing fuel to a car engine; just enough and it would start, too much and it would flood.

The gas in Edward Francis' kitchen was balanced, perfectly. It only needed a primitive ignition source.

As his ancient, veiny fingers slid the stick along the box's striking surface the source was provided.

And time, what was left of it for Edward Francis, stood momentarily still.

The ferocity of the explosion would not have surprised the grand old man. He was, in reality, dead before he had even processed the thought. The ground floor living space became an intense and ruthless fireball, sucking air from every corner and forcing the weakest points to give way first. In the case of his terraced family home it was the windows which offered the least resistance, shattering across the garden and street, sending glass in every direction, much of it ricocheting off the opposite buildings.

The noise was next. Inside the property it was unearthly. As much as two hundred feet away it was enough to make unwary pedestrians fall to the floor. Two males were affected but only marginally, fortunately they were heading away from the blast wave.

The younger looked back. 'What had they done? What had *he* done? Dear God, that poor man.'

Surrounding windows also imploded with the force. Car alarms sang out to no one in particular. Birds ceased their late afternoon chatter. The local community came to a standstill.

Two school children, walking home after an event-free day were only able to stand and scream. They had no idea what to do, where to run. One, a twelve year old girl, was sliced open by shards of glass as she instinctively shielded her younger brother.

Inside the kitchen, Francis' body had reacted to the devastating explosion as only a human body might. Although the incident was not comparable to a high explosive detonation, it had enough pressure to destroy his hearing in an instant. His eyes were next, also destroyed. As the pressure increased and the shock wave hit him, his lungs and major organs ruptured.

Any remaining air in his lungs was super-heated, searing his airways. The pressure increased again to the point that the speed of the overpressure easily exceeded that of a hurricane-force wind.

Edward was virtually torn in two. His injuries were so severe that he would not have survived. Indeed, he would not have wanted to. His last vision had been of his beloved mother. He could only hope he was now alongside her.

. . .

Despite withstanding the constant attention of the Luftwaffe in the latter part of the Second World War, the lasting legacy of the family home was now gone, shattered, and vapourised along with its contents and the history of a modest hard-working and popular family.

What countless German raids, hundreds of Magnesium incendiary bombs and the almost constant fear of attack had failed to achieve had been undone by two total strangers whose only apparent agenda was a preventative counter-attack on an old man who might have been a little too observant.

The Francis dynasty had been whittled away like a fine oak branch on a boy scouts camping holiday until it was left with only one surviving leaf.

CHAPTER ELEVEN

"John? Geoff Galvin from EOD? How's things?"

"Great Geoff thanks. Bit of luck you finding me on duty – what do you need?"

"It's not so much what I need but what I have."

"Go on."

"Look John, when we last spoke you were concerned about the rise in ATM attacks. I've kept a weather eye on things and to be fair there hasn't been that much activity, but last night..."

"Geoff, there have been no attacks in north Kent, I would know..."

"You would, but that's not why I'm ringing. Local Fire turned out with half of Rochester to a house explosion down here yesterday. Due to the blast radius we went to the job as well. Just a precaution really. There's a shed-load of old Second World War ordnance in that area. To be honest, it was good experience for my younger guys to see what a real blast wave can achieve. The bloody house was practically demolished."

He continued to explain in finer detail about how the hundred-and-ten-year-old property had all but collapsed, partially demolishing two adjoining properties.

"They found a single occupant in the ground floor – what was left of it, and what was left of him. Poor bugger, he didn't stand a bloody chance. Pretty certain at this stage it was natural gas. Always a highly entertaining bang. Bit of a loner apparently, but a nice man nonetheless. No obvious family."

Ballard had been listening patiently.

"I'm always glad to get calls from you Geoff but forgive me..."

Galvin cut him off.

"You want to know what this has to do with your operation don't you?"

Now the inspector was interested.

"Thought so. I'm not a copper. I leave that to you lot, I just save people from getting blown to bits. There were a couple of school kids injured in the blast. Both OK, cuts and bruises, local 'paper interest, that sort of thing. Anyway, they described seeing two males running from the property, and I don't mean for their lives. The little girl saw them coming out of a nearby alleyway that would have led to the target address."

Ballard interjected. "Let me guess at origin?"

"I don't think you need to John. Look, if you are interested the file is being handled by local plod and Fire investigators. But I reckon there's more to this."

"Not an accident?"

"Entirely possible. Until you discover that a car across the road from the address, well, what was left of it, had a couple of cylinders in the boot. A silver Peugeot. Oxygen and Acetylene..."

"Is that so? Geoff, thank you so much, I know a man who might just be travelling to Kent very soon. Look after yourself and again, thanks."

Ballard put down the phone and immediately re-dialled.

"Jason Roberts, good morning."

"Sergeant. Inspector John Ballard – CAD Room."

"Sir, how may I help you on this bright and breezy day?"

"Other way around Jason. I read somewhere that you are running a team looking at these ATM attacks. Correct?"

"It is indeed. Please continue to whet my appetite."

Ballard soon had Roberts salivating. He thanked him for the call, grabbed a black coffee from a passing detective's hand and ushered another away for biscuits.

"And get Cade. Now! Actually no, biscuits first and make sure..." His voice tailed off as he read a text message on his phone. "Make sure you get those nice ones with the chocolate bits."

His staff member had long gone as he knew what his boss wanted, he was nothing if not predicable.

Jack Cade had been at work early, using the ground floor gym to work a few things out, to cleanse his mind and hopefully maintain something of a physique. He'd left O'Shea in bed, having what he considered to be a much-needed lie-in. It was a risk, given the recent intrusion, but she was a big girl and he felt he needed to give her some 'space'.

Worse still he was having to contemplate the potential move to France to work with Interpol. This had become a 'head and heart' issue for the upwardly mobile officer.

Initially it was greeted with great excitement, but the more time he spent with O'Shea, the harder it had become.

He asked John Daniel the question that was circulating in his head, both during the day and in the quietest night-time hours.

"In the words of The Clash boss, should I stay, or should I go now?"

"Never heard of 'em Jack, I don't follow modern music, it's all garbage."

He paused, took a deep breath then continued, "Jack, what you do is down to you. If it was me with the decision to make, I would consider how much service I've got left and what I want to achieve. With three to five years in Lyon you could return as a superintendent. The problem I see before you is two-fold."

It was broadly rhetorical, but he admired Daniel immensely – and he valued his opinion. The two had only known each other for a relatively short time but the feeling was mutual. He had quickly come to realise that as mentors went Daniel was pretty perfect, offering a balanced and rational view on each and every subject.

"Do enlighten me boss. Worst case clear my head a little, it's been pretty full on lately."

He smiled "It has somewhat Jack. What with pursuits, gun shots, bus crashes, death, mayhem and bloody plague – and that was only your first forty-eight hours in London. And now the activity around Op Breaker."

"Absolutely boss. I reckon another few weeks and things will settle down and I can head back to Nottingham, hand back my Metropolitan Police pips and regain my old job back at the airport, put my feet up and relax into a future of profiling attractive and mysterious international travellers."

"Is that what you want? What you really, really want?" asked Daniel.

Cade was desperate to ask his manager if he was a Spice Girls fan but thought better of it given his comments about modern music.

"Not anymore. I want to spend more time with Carrie. I'm enjoying the job here in the city and if you'll allow it, I'd like to stay. Equally, France is beckoning. I'm torn."

"London's calling Jack."

"It is, boss. I know. Are you sure you've never heard of The Clash?"

Daniel shook his head dismissively. "Not a clue. It's getting busier with Breaker stuff, I think you need to spend at least another week on it. London is drowning Jack, and I live by the river."

Daniel tried his best poker face, but he failed. He'd been playing Cade like a sailfish.

"Sir, with respect..."

"I know, Jack, I know. I loved The Clash back in the day, but The Spice Girls, not so much."

Cade had walked out of the boss's office with a smile on his face. He was still undecided about the future. Truth be told he wanted his newfound, pencil-wielding, slightly obsessive, sexually charged girlfriend to travel to France with him, but when he had mooted the idea, she seemed a little cool. He would work on her next time she needed a shower.

Walking back to his desk he was interrupted by a colleague.

"Guv, phone for you. No idea. Sounds bleedin' foreign. Don't they all these days!"

Cade had been so unsettled by the call he had received from Jackdaw that he had installed a recording system on his phone. He left the handset in the cradle, pressed the button and started to talk.

"This is Inspector Cade, who am I speaking to please?"

There was a feint crackle on the line, a discreet echo. Long distance?

"Good morning Inspector." The voice was accented, but educated. Cade was beginning to be able to differentiate between the former Eastern Bloc countries now. This voice was most definitely a 'Romance' language, not Slavic which ruled out Bulgaria and Russia.

"Good morning. How can I help you?"

"My name is Valentin. Telling you this is not without risk, Inspector. My acquaintances call me Copil. You can call me Valentin."

Cade was writing down notes and passing them to Cynthia who had quickly steered her typist's chair alongside his. He had written 'IP database' in black and had underlined it twice.

Then he wrote Red, Blue, Green, Orange and Purple. The key notice colours adopted by Interpol covering the wanted notices, extradition cases, modus operandi, intelligence and risks posed by entities such as Valentin.

She knew what he wanted and raced over to a stand-alone computer where she accessed the Interpol database in Lyon, France.

She began to search for names, red or blue notices first, then the other flags, lastly for nicknames or a combination of all search fields. She even typed in Valentin.

And there he was: Valentin Niculcea. Wanted by the Romanian authorities for crimes against the state, cyber-crime, membership of an organised criminal group, crimes of violence and fraud. The list seemed to go on forever but Cynthia found herself questioning whether it was entirely accurate – found herself trusting the voice on the end of the phone.

Cade continued. "Hello Valentin. How are you?" The conversation had a déjà vu feeling to it.

"OK, first I must apologise. You are probably recording this conversation, yes?"

Cade had an uncertain feeling, but something propelled him towards the truth.

"Yes."

"Thank you for your honesty, Inspector. It helps me to assist you. I am running a binary encryption programme over the call, so please, do not waste your time trying to track me, or for that matter, record me. My people were working on cryptology before Scotland Yard had left kindergarten Jack. Sorry, do you mind?"

"No, call me Jack, Valentin." It was becoming like a game of ping pong and Cade felt as if he were twenty points down already.

"I have called you to discuss the matter of explosions in your city. The BBC reporter has called them acts of terrorism, would you agree?"

"No sir I would not. Would you?"

The male laughed. "Indeed, no. I have witnessed such acts, I have, possibly even carried out such acts – all in the name of the state you understand? It is a matter of great conjecture. But these men are just amateurs. You see Jack, I have been hired by them. They have paid me well. I was happy to work for them, even to carry out specific tasks, tasks which allow me to use my expertise. But now things... are changing."

"Do continue. I am very interested in what you have to tell me."

"I have no doubt. You see, I am a professional man Mr Cade, well trained by my country. Like you, I worked for the government at a time when we had the best intelligence services in the world."

"You are Russian?" Cade was looking for evidential support.

"Hardly Jack, no, I speak Russian of course, German too, and French, but no, I am Romanian. And we are proud people, not all thieves like the media portrays us. I fought against the government of my country because they took something precious from me and I will never forgive them. But I am still Romanian, my birth name was Iliescu, a proud name and I am honoured to be Romanian. But this group – the ones who call themselves *Primul Val...*"

Cade was writing furiously on the jotter pad and pointing at the keywords.

"...they are becoming more amateur by the day Jack. Richer? Of course, but they are getting, how would you say, sloppy?"

"Who are you talking about specifically?"

"The men who are blowing up your bank machines around London. Soon they will head to other cities and soon someone will be killed because of their foolishness. They are boys playing in a man's world."

"So what is your agenda Valentin? I wouldn't have thought a group of thieves would be of interest to a man with your experience?"

Cade knew, like all police officers, that all informants had agendas; some provided information for purely financial gain, others for a sense of social justice, but many did it for revenge.

"It is not for revenge Jack, if that is what you are think-ing? I want to provide you with information on this group of little children. They could harm me, if they could ever find me, which I doubt – and I am well trained, so when they choose to find me they will be harmed too. Jack, I do not wish to be labelled as a terrorist by any government. Please. This is all I ask. *This* is my agenda."

His words, his plea, sounded genuine.

"OK, but how do I know you are genuine?"

Cade had been joined by Cynthia. She had written a few lines on a virgin piece of A4.

'Negative database. Interpol spoken to. State that Valentin Niculcea is a.k.a. Valentin Iliescu. Nickname *Copil de umbra*.

Sought-after criminal. Former Romanian intelligence, now freelance following fall out with government many years ago. Possible home in Europe?

Never caught. Involved in 'collection activities' for crime syndicates.

Top class industrial espionage/burglar.

Message Ends.'

"How do you know I am genuine about what?"

"You say you want to help me. I need to know you are genuine and not working for the group you call *Primul Val*. By the way, what does that mean?"

"Oh, but I did work for them Jack. I just told you this. But that is in the past. Very much in the past. But now they are becoming – I do not know the word. In my language we say animal periculoase."

The dangerous animal.

"Why?"

"Good question. Because they are killing people Jack and they will kill more. They might even kill me. But I do not work for such people. I have a reputation. If you were to speak to your friends at Interpol they would tell you this."

He paused long enough to allow Cade to realise he was dealing with a genuine professional.

"So, how is that check going by the way, have you found out much about me? I am the best industrial burglar, et cetera et cetera, yes, yes I know. But now, I can perhaps work with you. No money. Just gratitude. We must never meet but it is time to repay my debts. I cannot do it for my own people so I may as well do it for yours. We are both Intelligence Officers and our profession is older than prostitution. Oh, and Jack..."

"Yes?"

"Two things. *Primul Val*, in my language, it means the first wave. But I hear Mr Stefanescu is rebranding. Secondly, whilst we are being so honest with one another. It was me. I ran a scalpel along the side of your girlfriend's neck...she was never in any danger. Tell her I am most sorry."

Cade was shocked to hear such a confession but needed corroboration.

"I...don't believe you. Anyone could have seen that scar the following day."

"Yes, Jack of course. You are right. But I am not anyone. And not everyone would have known about the piece of hair, would they?"

Cade paused, long enough to allow his new and unforeseen ally to breathe.

"OK, I choose to believe you."

"Jack, you choose what you like. But we need to trust

each other. I will ring you every other day. Every day if I need to."

"Trust? OK, this is your chance. Why do they call you Copil?"

"Very good Jack. Really, you should have worked with me back in the SRI. It is pronounced *Copil de umbra*." He emphasised the latter part, his mother tongue very evident.

"It means Child of the shadows, and it is where you will find me, if you care to look. Oh, and Mr Cade..."

"Go ahead."

"I have been...furnishing...the man they call the Jackdaw with information, for money. Yes, for money, I have no pension plan. Everyone has a price Jack, even you."

Cade missed a beat before asking the next question.

"What information?"

"They know where you have been sleeping these last few weeks."

Cade switched the hands free off and picked up the phone.

"Go on."

"They know where your girlfriend lives my friend. I am sorry. She is safe from me, but them, I don't know? Jackdaw has sent a message out to his teams."

"Saying?"

"Saying that he wants them to increase their attacks on the bank machines, to cause fear among the financial community and to cause you fear Jack, for forcing him to kill his girlfriend."

"There is a price on her head?"

"No! Not at all. That isn't how the Jackdaw works. He just wants her to suffer. There is a price on yours."

"How much?"

"One Euro."

Cade almost felt insulted.

"One bloody Euro?"

Valentin Niculcea, former Soviet espionage hero and one of the most experienced intelligence officers in Eastern Europe laughed, out loud.

"I like you Inspector Cade, I really do. You clearly think you are worth more. Jackdaw wants his men to harm and kill to show their loyalty. He has been betrayed so many times that he puts no price on loyalty. Watch over your girl my friend and I will watch over both of you. And Jack?"

"Yes."

"The bank operation is a cover. They have somebody close to the government. Money talks, in any of our languages. They plan to make a statement, or rather Jackdaw wishes to leave his mark, to pay back those that harmed him."

"But the British have never harmed him. Have they?"

"Quite right, but why target your own country when it has little to offer. Go for the jugular Jack, hit the rich nations first. Britain first, then Germany, France, Switzerland, he could even switch his teams to America – the Land of the Free!"

"So, who do they have on the inside and what for?"

"Good question my friend. The problem is, I have no idea yet. But I will. One day."

"OK. Stay in touch. You know where to find me, that is very clear."

"Why of course. I can trace you twenty-four seven as you say in your country. But as for me, until I am ready to be found please don't look for me. Do this and I will reward you with my services."

"How much do you charge?"

He laughed again.

"How does one Euro sound?"

The line cleared. Cade placed the phone back it its cradle.

"Anything?"

"Long gone guv, if he was ever there?"

"Well?" It was Daniel.

Cade blew air across his lips making them tremble. "Well, indeed. Not a bloody clue John. I seem to be getting half of bloody Eastern Europe either wanting to kiss me or kill me, this one wanted to help, some conversation about responsibility, about morals. Christ, I'm confused."

He explained the extent of the call.

"So what next?"

"He said he would contact me. I suspect from listening to him and from what Cynthia dragged out of the Interpol guys that we are best to leave him to run his side of the house. I certainly need an ally in the camp and he may be it. The last thing I should do now is hunt him down."

"Do you trust him?"

"Yes. But then no, of course not, but what other avenue do I have? Seriously, things are starting to heat up and we need all the help we can get. If it means I have to turn the other cheek with Mr whatever-his-bloody-name is I will."

"Just be careful Jack, he could be playing you."

"He could John. There is something about him though, the way he works, it tells me he's onside. If I'm wrong, then what is left of my tattered reputation can drift downstream to the land of the beheaded tall poppy. Right now we've got a group of God knows how many starting to impact on the financial quarter of one of the world's most influential cities and we know Jack Shit about them. Other than you and this fine body of people I need someone who *knows* what is going on. Not just someone who thinks they need to know."

"Well, I need you to know about some interesting developments in Kent if you are interested. House explosion down there yesterday, you might have seen it on the news?"

"The news? What's that boss? I haven't watched the news for a month. I haven't slept in longer. But do tell, explain why should I be interested?"

"Get Roberts, get a car and head down there."

"Is that an order?"

He smiled. "One hundred percent."

"OK, you are the boss, but you still haven't explained why."

"A silver Peugeot, containing two gas cylinders was found across the street. The car was almost destroyed along with the house opposite. The street looks like a war zone. Couple of young kiddies were hurt walking home from school."

Daniel knew, in fact he could see that Cade still wasn't engaged, but as he picked up the car keys and was joined by Roberts, Daniel delivered the game changer.

"Oh and Jack, the two men seen running away were described by a witness as being 'swarthy, one young, one slightly older, dark-haired. The older one had a pock-marked face and hardly any teeth.' The witness knows this because the older male smiled at her as he ran down the street, trying to stay on his feet as the blast wave sent everyone else onto their arses. Just thought you might be interested."

"Touché boss. On the way."

"Good, bugger off and get some fresh air and let Jason drive, you need some kip. The Kent ARV team are meeting up at Rochester to execute a warrant at the target address where they think the Peugeot was linked to. I'd get a move on."

He looked down at his notepad. "The officer in charge is one Sergeant Woods, call him up on their channel when you get nearer and bring me back a present."

Daniel walked purposefully through the corridor to brief a few of his senior colleagues.

Roberts made good time on the M2 motorway – the main traffic was heading north into London. At a steady one hundred miles an hour he was soon entering the town famous for Charles Dickens and his period works, many of which recounted the cruel and often hard times of Victorian life in the area.

Roberts was busy providing Cade with a running commentary of the region as he changed down to third to overtake a stream of vehicles, his discreet blue lights flickering in the grill of the Vauxhall Vectra SRI.

"My most favourite piece of useless trivia about the area is about James Bond. Did you know he drove along these very roads in *Goldfinger*, brilliant, eh?"

Roberts made a noise that he thought somehow sounded like a laser beam cutting through flesh... "No Mr Bond, I expect you to die!"

"I expect you to shut up Jason!" drooled a sleepy Cade, his head lolling back and forth on the headrest.

"Did you also know that Rochester has the biggest second-hand bookshop in Britain?"

"No. I did not."

"Or that in the early twelve hundreds it was..."

"Jason. Seriously, I will kill you, cut up your body and feed it to the pigs at the nearby prison farm."

"How do you know about them?"

"I just do!"

"Fair enough. Anyway, we are here now. Did you know that this station once..."

Roberts leapt out of the Vectra before Cade had the chance to throw something heavy at him. They were met by a uniformed officer who was in his early forties, greying at the temples, with shimmering blue eyes and an intriguing Robert De Niroesque arch to his left eyebrow.

The officer, a sergeant, was wearing the trademark black overalls of the Armed Response Unit and had a Glock pistol strapped to his right leg. He was diligently rolling a cigarette as his team busied themselves with equipment checks.

He walked over to the pair and put out his hand.

"Morning, Mac Woods, nice to meet you both. Time for a brew? Kettle's on."

The necessary introductions were made as Woods stowed the cigarette behind his left ear.

"Actually Mac that would be just superb," said an exhausted Cade.

"Oy Sharkey, get the kettle on you raving homosexual, can't you see we've got distinguished guests here from The Yard."

"Yes skipper, onto it now," replied a good-looking, thirty-something with a spring in his step.

"So, gents, what do you know?"

"Apart from the fact that James Bond drove through here one Thursday afternoon en route to a quite enormous book shop, not much Mac. We've been hit with a wave of criminals targeting our ATMs. It started at a lower level, then worsened, they are now using a mixture of gases to blow the machines to bits and steal the cash."

Woods was immediately interested and leaned against his Volvo T5, waiting to hear the rest of the story.

"Oh, nice. We've had a few of our travelling friend's rip the ATMs out of the wall with a digger and a long chain, all seems a bit much for a twenty-pound note which is what the last team succeeded in gaining, but so far, touch wood, no explosives. That sort of m.o. is a bit beyond them thankfully. That said, someone kindly blew some poor old geezer's house to bits yesterday of course."

"Any news on that Mac? Terrible job, poor old bugger."

"Indeed, it was Jason. At first the local Trumpton turned up with the entire entourage from Rochester Police Station. They soon realised there was no fire to put out, but they had to shore up what was left of the building, that's when they found dear old Mr Francis, lying in what was originally his kitchen."

Cade smiled at Woods' use of the generic term Trumpton, from the age-old British children's television series of the same name. Colloquially used by police across Britain to describe their fire brigade colleagues, it had remained in the vocabulary of generations of police officers.

"So why did your team become involved Mac? Seems as routine as a fatal house explosion can be? Or have I missed something?"

"Allow me to complete the picture, Inspector," said Woods as he lovingly crafted another cigarette between his fingers before running the tip of his tongue along the paper.

"A few months ago we had some uncorroborated intel about a group of Eastern European criminals operating on our patch. Source information indicated they were travelling across Europe to the ferry ports and using north Kent as a springboard to your patch."

Cade nodded encouragingly.

"The county has changed a lot over the last few years, people are really aware of Eastern Europeans now. It's a shame as there are some bloody good people among them, hard-working, trying to make a difference, etcetera, etcetera, but as with all walks of life, we only see the bad ones."

The tea arrived. All took a cup, and the conversation continued.

"So cultivating intelligence sources isn't difficult then Mac?"

"Far from it Jack, more a case of sorting the wheat from the chaff. But our latest stuff, well in my humble opinion, it's A1. We had an intelligence noting come through the system from Crimestoppers saying that two men were holed up in the very street in which Francis' house exploded. The source stated that the two men were not local and were up to no good. Most likely burglars."

"And?"

"And it went onto the pile with a lot of others. We are short of staff too Jack and we have to prioritise."

The two Metropolitan officers nodded sympathetically. The Crimestoppers charity phone line had seen some incredible successes, but like everything it needed resourcing.

"So why the change, why your team, why armed response?"

"Well, funny you should ask those three questions. The last piece of intel we received was so obviously from Mr Francis that we had to lock it down. It stated that he had seen two men carrying a lot of bags, and he swore he saw them handling large sums of cash, and the older male, who he described, was seen carrying a firearm. Given the explosion followed within a day of us receiving the info it seems apparent to me that they had somehow found out – either that or they had put two and two together and like Gary here had come up with eight. Clearly it was the beginning of the end for dear old Ted."

He looked straight at Cade. "We should have gone in yesterday."

Woods shook his head as he took a long swig of his tea and began to arch his eyebrow.

"Sharkey! Good job you can bloody shoot, this tea tastes like yak's piss! And I've drank yak's piss!"

"So do you expect to find the men in the flat?" asked Cade who was equally visibly critical about the beverage he had been served.

"Gents, I have no idea, but it would be nice to drill a round through the bastard. I used to foot patrol that street when I first joined and I can remember Ted Francis as a proud and lovely man. I often dropped in for a cup of tea." He yelled at his constable again, "Better than this insipid brown urine!"

Woods threw the remaining third of his tea to one side and theatrically licked his lips before continuing.

"He gave me no end of intelligence on local thieves. He had a nephew in the army as I recall, never stopped talking about him. He ended up heading to Northern Ireland and got involved in some covert shit. Moved up north last I heard. God help those two if he gets hold of them."

Cade shook his head. He had countless thoughts racing around it. Something that Woods had said struck a chord but he couldn't place why. Tiredness did that to a normally lucid mind.

The team were ready to go. Cade and Roberts offered to transport Woods in their car, he accepted, it was a good chance to complete the briefing and get to know him. He went to place the newly created cigarette behind his ear only to locate the one he had lodged there earlier. He stared at it for a while, shoved it into his overall pocket and muttered about needing to give it up.

With the briefing over and no further questions, the Kent Armed Response Unit pulled out of Rochester Police Station on Cazeneuve Street and headed towards their target.

CHAPTER TWELVE

As they pulled out of the rear yard Cade could hear Roberts whistling The Weather Girls' song *Raining Men*.

"Mac, you'll have to forgive my colleague's taste in music, either that or he has become bi-curious since a recent and somewhat frantic wrestling match with a transvestite informant of his."

"Each unto his own gentlemen, I'm more of a Showaddywaddy man myself."

"Sho?"

"Waddywaddy."

"Indeed. So tell me more about this warrant. What are the team hoping to find Mac?"

"Honestly? Two swarthy blokes, one who needs an urgent oral makeover and the other hot-footing it away from the locale with a rather large bag of readies. That and a pistol – and possibly some bomb-making kit."

"Explosives?"

"You never know boss, we have to plan for all such occasions. We've got EOD meeting us there too in case the place appears to be rigged up."

"Worst case?" asked a curious Cade.

"Worst case they have barricaded themselves in, then we'll have to produce Constable 'Sharkey' Green. He can send in a few cups of his noxious brew and hopefully flush them out. Either that or your colleague here can bore them to death with his local Kent-based trivia."

They all laughed, including Roberts who was fast becoming the self-effacing member of the team.

He asked another question as the laughter subsided.

"Mac, what if they have gone?"

"Fair point guv, it happens. Then it will be a good training run for the boys – we achieve on average nine out of ten failures. We pride ourselves on them. My commander reckons we are the worst-performing squad in the region!"

Six minutes later the team pulled up alongside each other in a side street. Woods directed the team forward, got out of Roberts' car and walked towards a white Leyland van which contained the regional Explosive Ordnance team.

"Alright Geoff, how's tricks?" Woods was vigorously shaking hands with and was obviously on first-name terms with the Chief Petty Officer.

"Bostin mate!" replied an ebullient Geoff Galvin, his broad West Midlands accent ringing out a phrase which meant he was feeling great.

"Good man, this is Inspector Jack Cade and his colleague Detective Sergeant Jason Roberts from Scotland Yard. They are investigating a series of bank machine explosions in the city and have an interest in the explosion that occurred yesterday. They will help search the target address once we have secured it. Any issues with that?"

"None at all. Just make sure no one breaks the rules, eh, Mac? You know the score, the second your boys reckon there's something afoot, they withdraw."

Woods nodded. There was no margin for error. None at all.

Galvin continued, "Tell me, Inspector. These the attacks, are they the same ones that John Ballard and I have been talking about lately? He's an inspector from your CAD room, gave me the heads up on this group a while ago. You really think they are trouble?"

Cade was shaking the soldier's hand briskly.

"Yes, they are one and the same. And I do Geoff, yes. Something in my water tells me we haven't seen the worst of this yet. Since I joined the Met team, we've had bus pursuits, shootings, bloody explosions, kidnapping and murder..." His voice tailed off as it dawned upon him just how busy the Breaker team had been.

"If you ask me, you'd be better off applying for a transfer then Jack!"

Cade responded with a laboured nod. It was all he could manage.

"Right, let's get this circus on the move, people." Woods took control and got his team into position. He carried out a tactical briefing, checked his own weapon, conducted a signal check with each of the team and nodded to the EOD team before pulling on his Kevlar helmet and winking at Cade.

"See you on the other side, boss. You know the drill?"

Actually, he didn't. In his relatively short service, Cade had only recently qualified to carry a weapon and handled a firearm tactically on less than three occasions and had never led a firearms team on a warrant.

Twenty-four hours prior and in the obscenely early hour's two Armed Response vehicles approached the road and lights-off quietly closed either end of the street.

One of Woods' men went forward, initially running along the line of the terraced properties, slowing to a tactical walk until he reached the front door. He stepped quickly but deliberately, up on his toes, checking in front and above. He knew his back was covered.

Plain clothed, he looked to the casual onlooker like a burglar – so he would be relatively safe, little chance of detection.

He silently put a small telescopic-handled mirror through the letterbox and had a quick look at the inside hallway. It was empty but for a growing pile of never-to-be-read mail on the floor. He noted there was little in the way to obstruct them.

The two-man team at the rear of the property were unable to see inside, but what they did do, under the cover of a teammate with a Heckler & Koch G36, was slowly and gently check the door, to see where the resistance was. With the site survey complete, they retraced their steps and returned to base.

Woods was now watching the whole event unravel from a small screen which was receiving signals relayed from the Kent Air Support helicopter. Hovering at a discreet distance so as not to give away their intention, the aircraft was a regular sight over the area, all the better to maintain an air of anonymity.

Three more staff were ready at the rear. Another had joined the officer at the front. Two local traffic cars continued to close the road off top and bottom and would add firepower should the need arise.

Constable Green leant against the white rendered wall of the adjoining address and waited. He'd done this a hundred times. He found himself looking across the street to what was left of the Francis' home. He signalled to the property with his eyes.

"Bloody mess!"

His colleague didn't have a chance to reply as they heard the familiar signal over their earpieces.

"*Stand by, stand by.*"

At the rear of the premises an officer was waiting for the signal to take down the door, it would be an easier task now that the pressure had been lessened by a small hydraulic jack.

The ever-vigilant Romanian had heard them coming. Quiet as they were his abject paranoia gave him the advantage. He could almost sense their arrival, could smell them. He looked across at Dorin Gabor, a young man with whom he had yet to become fully acquainted.

"We must go now. You come with me or you stay, either way you might die. Is it better to be running away to live like a coward than be a brave antelope, caught and eaten by a lion?"

Gabor was part-confused, part-terrified. He had seen his life unravel and wanted only to return to his homeland and live a normal life. But this man, this strange man, had a hold over him which he could not explain to anyone, least of all himself.

"Yes, I will come with you. But when we have got to a safe place, you need to explain what happened with the old man's house. Please."

"The old man was in our way, he would have sent me to prison, and you too Dorin Gabor, and do you think you would be safe? Fool. You would go to prison too. I would survive there, you would become a toy, a plaything for the older men. Better dead my friend than to be a slave to that place – to them. Trust me..."

"OK, I come with you. I won't tell anyone anything."

"What do you mean? Have you been thinking of doing this, Gabor? Of betraying me? After all, I have taught you. You would betray me?" The words were hissed from his fractured sneer.

The younger male noted the aggressive tone.

Constantin found himself trying to suppress panic. Only the drugs helped, and he was as far from the poppy field as he had ever been.

He had killed before. The old man was not the first, and he would do it again, but he could not harm this fine young man. He had so many plans for him. So, many, plans.

He pushed his hand into a small holdall and withdrew an ancient-looking revolver.

Gabor stepped back instinctively.

"Please, I promise I will not tell."

He looked exasperated. "Dorin this gun is for you, if they come through that door, shoot at them, before they shoot you. Understand?"

He did. He took the weapon and ran the fingers of his right hand over it. Did what many men did when confronted with a firearm and placed it up to his nostrils and inhaled the stench of black powder and machine oil.

"Is it loaded? How do I fire it?"

Sensible questions.

"Of course you stupid boy. The cylinder holds six bullets, squeeze the trigger, and it will fire. Simple! But Dorin, do not close your eyes, you need to see the bullets hit your target. I will be working on our escape. When we get to the street we will run, faster than we have ever run. There is a red Vauxhall car two hundred metres away, it is open. I have prepared it for our journey to Dover. We are going home, my friend. You and I are heading home."

He held him firmly on the left shoulder and attempted to smile. It became a leer, but the younger male took comfort from it.

"But what if...?"

"We do not go through our lives asking this question. We belong to *Primul Val*. What if? Can you imagine the Jackdaw asking this question? No, so neither must we."

The boy nodded.

"We will head to France and then Spain and meet up with him and he will make us very rich."

Gabor smiled a nauseous smile before reiterating.

"Rich?"

"Mai mult decat cele mai indraznete vise." *More than your wildest dreams.*

"Almost ready, folks. Once the boys have gone in and made everything safe, we can get you in there and you can do all your spy stuff."

"Understood Mac, just give us the nod and we'll be ready."

The Kent Air Support Unit relayed the imagery from the target address directly to Woods' Mobile Command Post and ran a secondary link to the nearby headquarters at Maidstone.

"Looks like everything's in place. No movement from the house. I prefer to go in at night to be honest Jack, but time is as they say, of the essence. Watch and learn, my friend. This will be a dynamic entry."

Cade nodded – part of him understood, but another part wanted to ask more questions. The simple fact was that a dynamic entry was the chosen method for such operations. This was a search warrant – but a methodical search would have to wait. Police officers the world over had learned, often with their lives, the difference between a rapid, safety-first entry and a slow, deliberate search.

Cade had been impressed with Woods' briefing. He clearly knew the capabilities of all of his men, but he repeated his well-worn phrases, regardless.

He hammered home the mission; dwelling on the difference between rapidity and careless use of speed when clearing the building. He necessarily laboured the need to be safe.

From their Intelligence colleagues they knew the approximate layout of the building, but each dwelling could be different, and importantly they didn't know where, and how numerous their enemy might be. Bursting through the door and into the 'Fatal Funnel' would leave them brutally exposed, their very bodies providing a perfectly back-lit target for any would-be offender.

"Remember boys, speed is of the essence. Dominate. Take control. But above all, let's get home for tea and medals. Just not Sharkey's tea, eh?"

Woods had committed a two-man team at the front and

rear of the building. The rapid entry team would go in via the back door whilst the unit at the front would remain ready to enter in the event of an unforeseen incident. In waiting and only metres away would be the remainder of the team, ready to secure the building and lock down evidence.

It all made sense. Putting more than two bulky, weapon-carrying staff into a room potentially filled with furniture was likely to exacerbate things. Adding a goal-driven offender who might not even speak the same language – was compounding things further.

For this job the team would enter, 'slice the pie' and split up quickly, reducing the opportunity to be killed with the same round. Once through the door, one officer would clear the left of the room, the other, the right. A third colleague would be ready to enter and support. Different forces did things in different ways. This was how Woods' team did things.

With a small kitchen, a lounge and a hallway on the ground floor, the whole initial phase would be over in minutes. With the area secured, the team would move upstairs, placing themselves in a far more vulnerable position.

What they did not realise was that this particular property had a cellar.

"Stay here Dorin, I will be back in a few moments. You trust me, yes?"

He didn't. But agreed.

Constantin made the call, tapping swiftly on his Motorola keypad until he saw that the call was connecting.

"It is me, George. I am ready. See you at the new house in fifteen minutes. I will not let you down."

"Make sure you don't. What about your boyfriend?"

The final word stuck firmly in Constantin's throat. So this was what they thought of him. 'Without me, you are nothing.'

But his mind was made up.

He removed the SIM card, carefully double-wrapped it and flushed it down the toilet. He waited long enough to ensure its complete disappearance.

He then walked onto the first floor landing and climbed up the pre-prepared step ladder, opened the heavy loft hatch and felt around for the torch. There, just by the wiring. Good.

He climbed down quickly and walked quietly down the stairs, keeping to the left to avoid the creaking wooden steps, Glock pistol glued to his right hand, ready.

He found the boy watching the back door intently. He admired his fine physique, the sculpted muscles in his back, his broadening shoulders and square-jawed persona. What he liked best was his innocence.

Such a pity.

"Dorin", he hissed, "Come quickly. The shadow outside that door is a police officer – he is here to kill you."

Gabor was ready to leave, he had complied with all of the instructions the night before. His clothes and modest possessions were in the luggage area of the Vauxhall. He carried no identifying documents, only an old service revolver.

"We go now, my friend, soon they will arrive and we must be one step ahead. Always."

He kissed him on both cheeks. An unusual act in his country.

. . .

"All quiet here, boss." It was Green, now in full tactical mode, the light-hearted banter parked up for another time.

"Yes, yes. Stand by, Hotel Nine Nine has a temporary download issue. All units stand by!"

The Eurocopter remained at hover, burning fuel, its observer calling up to the local air traffic control with their location and call sign – Police Thirteen.

Concise and clear messages bounced back and forth – given the motorway-like air traffic that passed through the area to the key London airports, it was essential.

On the ground the team was on edge, waiting. Green's feet itched; they always did at incidents like this – he considered the feeling an indicator that he was still alive.

"No sound from inside the property skipper. Quieter than a Charlie Chaplin film. Over."

The two Romanian men walked deftly up the stairs. Reaching the next-to-last step, Constantin stopped. Held his hand up and gestured for his partner to wait.

Gabor turned to look back down the stairs. It was the moment that Constantin Nicolescu – son of Nicolae had prayed for. He could not look into the boy's eyes.

He brought up the Glock, stared across the open sight and gently, deliberately, expertly pulled on the trigger.

He could feel the tension subtly change. Any moment now.

He was taught not to anticipate the shot, to do so often meant missing the target and he could not leave behind a wounded man. If he could not have him, then no one could.

"Farewell my friend."

Gabor, caught between foe and adversary, looked back up the staircase as the first round left the barrel of the

Austrian-made weapon. Being sub-sonic, he actually saw it in flight, for a second at least.

The Speer Gold Dot hollow point round was travelling at over a thousand feet per second, weighing one hundred and fifteen grains, or about seven and a half grams, it struck the young male in the sternum, shattering the round and the bony structure beneath his young skin.

Nicolescu felt the iconic trigger-reset and continued to pull the trigger. Another round left the weapon and hit Gabor in almost the same location. This time burrowing through his chest and causing chaos to his internal organs as the round fractured, each piece causing permanent damage.

Gabor stared intently at his master.

'Why?'

He tried to grip onto the stair-rail but his strength was evaporating rapidly. He dropped to his knees, trying to talk, trying to question why the man, who days before had tried to seduce him had now probably ended his life.

"Why?" Again. His voice was hoarse as he fought to swallow bitter, oxygenated blood.

It would be his last word.

The third round exited the pistol and struck him just above the left eye. He fell backwards onto the staircase and remained in an unceremonious position, spread-eagled on the steps.

Constantin's inner-dialogue was manic. 'Perfect – two to the body, one to the head'. He sprinted up the remaining step and onto the ladder. And found himself in the loft in seconds, pulling up the aluminium ladder behind him and discarding it into the void.

. . .

"Shots fired!" announced Gary Green rapidly but without a hint of panic.

"Shots fired!" The call was repeated over the radio.

Woods hadn't heard the discharge but knew from the tone of his senior man's voice that it was genuine. He now had a decision to make and one which would either maintain his career or end it. Either way, Cade was somewhat pleased he wasn't in Woods' boots.

"We going in Mac?" asked an excited Roberts.

"No, not yet."

Woods was speed-dialling his commander, whilst asking for a sit-rep from the ground and in the air.

Normally, as bronze commander on the ground, he would make the call to enter, but the intelligence had indicated the possible presence of improvised explosives. He was damned if he did...

"Guv, shots fired at the address, no new intel to support or negate the explosives. Can I go in?

His boss, a man with far less service, and a greater lack of humour paused and fumbled around behind his secure and well-ordered desk, clearly unable to make a decision. He was one of those that had been dressed for export – and subsequently ended up being Woods' boss.

"Leave it a minute then gas them Mac. Get back to me, I'll flag this with the Chief."

"Yes, yes, will do," was all Woods could offer as he disconnected.

"Skipper?"

"Go ahead Gary."

"We need to get in there now."

Woods knew this, but his hands were tied.

A minute passed. Woods could hear the second hand transitioning on his Casio G-Shock.

"Skipper?"

"Fuck's sake Gary – you'll be the death of me."

Woods threw his treasured cigarette to one side before keying the microphone.

"All units: strike, strike, strike!"

Constantin checked the simple timer that was strapped to the loft door. Thirty minutes should do. It was a basic device and one which he was not particularly proud of, but it would do. If nothing else, it would slow those pigs down.

He took one last look at the boy, then closed the hatch behind him and scurried along the roof void as fast as the structure would allow.

A peculiarity of some less-than-cared-for terraced homes in Britain was that the roof space was still shared, a cost-saving measure when neighbours were more trustworthy.

A row of the properties had been left with only partially bricked up gables and once he had discovered them he knew they would enable him to move quickly through the roof, traversing from house to house, undetected.

He paused, surprised at the heat that had been retained in the sagging roof, mopped his brow, thought of Gabor's expression, pitied him, then moved on.

There was no time to dwell on the past.

He was now eight houses away from the target address. His luck had perhaps run out? He opened a loft hatch and dropped precariously onto the landing. The occupants were not upstairs.

He could instantly smell a pungent aroma of ethnic food and felt intensely hungry.

'Push on Constantin, you must push on. You can eat if you live.'

He ran down the stairs to see a middle-aged Indian female, dressed in the black costume of her Muslim faith. She was as shocked as the male.

She saw the pistol in his right hand and began to sob, saying something repeatedly that he did not understand. But this was England, so she must understand the mother language, surely?

"Stop your crying woman," he said in accented English. "I am not here to kill you. Get out of my way."

The female was fearful of becoming another victim. Her local newspaper had talked about burglars targeting Indian homes for their jewellery.

To pre-empt his attack upon her, she removed her bracelet and offered it to him, pleading for her life.

"Woman, get out of my way, I am not a burglar." He threw the bracelet back at her with a sense of honourable pride and pushed by en route to the kitchen door.

He stopped, seeing the helicopter, still hovering, the predator of the sky, its electronic eyes constantly scanning the ground; today there was only one target.

'Me. They are here for me.'

He had to think quickly. 'What can I do to throw these dogs off my scent? They will be in the house soon...think.'

He looked back at the female who was still quivering, distressed and anticipating his next move.

He beckoned for her to remove her clothing.

She refused.

The words of the Qur'an were repeating in her head as she stood, steadfastly refusing to obey him.

...Not to display their beauty except to their husbands, or their fathers, or their husband's fathers, or their sons...

He spoke to her in English again – he could not speak her language and clearly she could not understand his dialect.

"Woman, take off your clothes or I will kill you – just the top and...the scarf. Now!"

She wanted to scream, to attract attention, futile given the lack of neighbourly kindness and empathy.

He pointed the weapon at her, causing her to sob uncontrollably and forcing her to comply. Her chestnut pupils were enhanced by the rapid reddening of her eyes.

She pulled the immaculate niqab headscarf away, fully revealing her face, which was framed by a thick head of shimmering coal-black hair which was offset with a solitary strand of grey.

He nodded to the burqa.

She grabbed hold of him, still pleading for clemency.

He swung his arm around and struck her on the forehead, causing an instantaneous gash to appear.

"Why can't you people just leave me alone?"

Once again he levelled the handgun at her. This was taking far too long.

"Take it off! Now!" He pushed at the clothing with the barrel of the gun.

Sensing it was her only option, she slipped the outer garment from her body revealing what he saw to be Western clothing. She was probably an attractive woman – to a man who found such things pleasurable.

She had just provided an opportunity to escape unhindered, albeit an entirely surreal one, but he had learned to ride his luck.

Fearing he would ask her to remove all of her clothing, she grabbed hold of him again, pleading in fractured English.

He struck her once more, intending to hit her with the back of his right hand, but instead he struck her above the left cheekbone, the hardened plastic stock of his Glock driving the bone backwards and causing immediate, intense pain.

She fell to the ground; playing dead, praying for leniency. At least she was alive.

All he needed to do was escape – he had no time for another brutal killing. He hurriedly placed the garment over his own clothes and slipped the headdress in place. He knew he looked preposterous; better foolish than in their custody – or dead.

He stopped for a second, dipped his finger into the blackened saucepan and let the spices burst onto his tongue. It tasted sublime.

'Move on fool!'

He opened the part-glazed door and looked right, along the row of houses and into the distance where the helicopter remained, indifferent, a hawk watching for its prey.

He hid his modest backpack beneath the flowing robe and exited, trying to a great extent to appear innocent.

The fusion of cultural clothing with Western garments was almost the local norm, it helped him to blend in and as quickly as his legs would allow he moved out of the small rear garden, into an alleyway and away to the south, and the car, his chance for freedom.

He left behind a quietly terrified female who had curled into a foetal position awaiting her salvation.

Nine Nine's observer scanned the ground with his powerful camera, paying particular attention to the old shop. He relayed his observations back to the Force Control Room and to Woods.

"Nine Nine, no movement on the ground over. The

street is, er....clear. No movement from the upstairs windows. At this time we will assume that both targets are still within the property. Nine Nine over."

Constantin could hear his own heart. It was pounding, desperate to escape his chest cavity. He daren't look back, but he also knew he needed to appear as normal as a wanted man in a hand-me-down burqa could.

Anyone in such a position would surely admit that they felt that the entire world was watching them, judging them, setting them up to fail?

But he kept walking; fifty metres, forty metres, thirty until he was there, alongside an anonymous rotting automotive relic of the nineties, no doubt the once-proud steed of a Regional Sales Manager, the only worn, sagging seat being directly behind the steering wheel – the rest resembling those of a freshly valeted showroom model, eagerly waiting for its highly excited customer.

Now it sat, anonymously on a side street, its flaccid suspension defiantly defying gravity, its damp carpets having long ago lost the battle with mould.

As he opened the creaking driver's door and threw the pack onto the passenger seat, he allowed his eyes to sweep up and down the street. Despite the fact that only a short distance away the police were conducting a raid that would fuel local conversations for days, he felt remarkably confident.

He climbed in, his olfactory system immediately reacting to the fetid air within. He wiped the driver's window and then involuntarily licked his fingers clean, leaving an acrid taste on the surface of his lips.

He placed the worn plastic-fobbed key into the ignition

and felt the much-abused engine labour into life. Without indicating, he pulled off from the kerb and headed for the safety of an anonymous, pre-arranged location, leaving an indiscreet cloud of blue smoke in his wake as he changed from first to second.

The heavily suited Explosive Ordnance team member who had approached the property under the cover of a police marksman, utilised his HAL Building Access Kit, which quietly and efficiently encouraged the door to open. He slid a CCTV probe into the room and declared the doorway clear.

He was superbly equipped for all threats but never had to resort to using any of his Access, Investigation or Render Safe methodology. Truth be told, he was somewhat disappointed, but reminded himself not to be complacent – that going home was always more beneficial than not.

"If this place is wired for sound, then I'm not a Cliff Richard fan boss." The time-served army engineer said as he fed back his on-site intelligence to the boss. "Very low key. There is a battery pack on the kitchen worktop and an egg timer. Amateurish at the very best"

"Received, do we give the green light to the police, over?"

"Yes, yes."

According to the police staff who had carried out the earlier site inspection, the aging, simple wooden door was supposed to provide a semi-belligerent resistance to the Method of Entry team – who had forgotten more than most conventional police staff would ever know about such things.

The 'doorman' was ready as always to strike the basic structure with such force that it would splinter or collapse.

However, if it was anything like the last one he struck a week before it would need another three well-aimed hits to convince it to release its grip. On that occasion when it finally relented it flew across the kitchen colliding with the owner and then her newly installed stainless steel oven.

The fact that it was entirely the wrong address simply exacerbated things and added to the poor sergeant's already-horrendous paperwork.

But this was altogether easier. The EOD staff had found the door to be almost insecure; less problematic, and therefore, to the cynical team waiting to enter, suspicious.

The first officer was in, his polished leather and denier nylon magnum boots trampling over a pile of part-filled black rubbish bags.

Swinging his weapon in a well-practised arc Pete O'Neil, nickname 'P-O' cleared the right side of the room, taking a split second to look up to the ceiling and then over the sights of his MP5 machine pistol down to the ground, checking for any sign of a trap. He knew that his partner in crime and a survivor of many off-duty 'epic events' was only feet away from him. Sharkey Green was nothing if not dependable.

Green had almost exactly mirrored P-O's actions; swift, deliberate and methodical. Neither had to shout 'clear' – they knew it was, and those waiting just outside the building also knew when things were going well. Call it intuition. But they did anyway – muscle memory.

"CLEAR!"

CHAPTER THIRTEEN

Green got to the next door, tucked himself up against the wall, lowered his stance and remembered to breathe. There could of course be a whole host of hidden atrocities waiting to ensnare them, but fortune, apparently, favoured the brave.

He nodded to P-O who gently pushed down the door handle and then eased the door inwards, allowing Green to see into the next room with an extendable mirror. Time in these circumstances did not equate to money, but rather whether one lived or not.

Again, he checked up, down and sideways. Nothing.

It was a lounge – of sorts. Sparsely furnished and reeking of damp; carpets, curtains and walls. Heavily faded wallpaper peeled back from the crumbling plaster to reveal brown watermarks and layers of previously fashionable coverings.

Remnants of past decades, in the form of a sagging corduroy brown sofa and an orange plastic footstool worked in tandem with an open fire, fringed in a seventies' surround that had not seen a naked flame in years. Together they did their combined but futile best to make the place appear homely.

The carpets were sticky. The team would remember to wipe their feet on the way out.

Green's frontal lobe had allowed him to process the whole room in a second. Everything, even the pile of unsolicited junk mail that had amassed upon the hessian doormat, adding its own distinctive aroma.

His Medulla, sitting innocuously within his brain stem, was carrying out the involuntary tasks such as breathing, which was quickened by the second.

Green had 'that feeling' – it had happened during a drug warrant a few years before, during which one of his team had been badly injured.

Instinct versus stupidity. Move on.

Being so sparsely furnished meant that Green could move forwards quickly, he broke to the left whilst P-O stepped deftly on his toes and to the right. They knew that two more members of the team had entered the kitchen and that three more were waiting on the other side of the main front door.

As they moved on, Green spotted the key to his suspicions. A door. Hidden behind a wall-hung rug – arguably the most valuable item in the entire building.

Green nodded to his colleague and reported in to his commander.

"Boss, sorry. Looks like we have a cellar to clear. May need more staff."

"Yes, yes. Stand by one."

Woods put his tactical thinking cap on once more.

"Is it locked?"

P-O checked and soon learned that it was.

"It is boss, how did you know?"

"I didn't, but my dear old granny always locked hers in case someone tried to break in via the coal hole. Leave it to the back-up team and move on."

Five minutes had elapsed.

P-O shifted his body position, swivelling his short weapon up into the stair void as Green waited for the signal to move from the left and to the bottom of the open-plan staircase.

As P-O lowered his gaze from the roof space onto the stairs he came face to face with the vacant gaze of a young male. As fearless and experienced as Peter O'Neill was, the image startled him. His finger flirted with the trigger for a nanosecond.

The man's eyes had long since lost the desire to focus on the world around him. His facial expression was indifferent; cold and pale. A solitary, blackened red hole was evident above his left eye.

P-O had only previously seen one such injury, the owner of which had survived, but when he observed the two well-placed entry points in his chest he was in no doubt that the man was beyond any help.

Despite his primary diagnosis, he placed his index and middle finger onto the male's hand and skilfully felt for a radial pulse. He shook his head at his team mate before speaking quietly into his tactical radio.

"Skipper, we've got one male, one oblique one. He's on the stairs. We need to move him to get up to the next level. Your call, please."

Out on the street, Woods processed the message. The coded conversation confirmed that one occupant was dead. He knew that this would necessitate a Scenes of Crime examination and a murder team – both of whom would want to crawl fastidiously across the site – and importantly, ensure that Woods' team had not been responsible for the shooting.

Every cartridge case would need to be located, photographed, bagged and exhibited.

Woods exhaled, craving the discarded cigarette.

Cade caught his eye.

"Penny for them, Sergeant?"

"Nice, cheers, boss. I've got a dilemma. As always, Uncle Woodsie is damned if he does and fucked up the jacksie if he doesn't. My boys have a body on the stairs and need to get up them to continue the search – with one more potentially hostile offender at the top of the bloody things."

Cade sympathised but was out of his depth. "I'll leave the tactics up to you Mac, but I think we both agree the body has to remain in situ."

Roberts nodded before adding, "Can you photograph it first, then move it?"

"I can Jason but I've got a funny bloody feeling about this job and time is not on my side, all I need now is that limp-wristed commander of mine to ring and engage me in some well-meaning conversation about Standard Operating Procedures etcetera, et-bloody-cetera..."

Woods' cell phone began to vibrate energetically. He smiled and shrugged his shoulders.

"See what I mean. I live in a world full of conspiracies – I swear it's like the bloody *Truman Show* here sometimes!"

He exhaled once more, deeply, deliberately, before keying the green button on his phone and allowing himself to smile radiantly.

He spoke with an emphasised smile. "Boss. How's it going?"

"Good Mac. You have my permission to go in. But Mac..."

"Boss?"

"No bloody heroics or my arse is on the line."

"Good call, Sir. You have my word."

He disconnected and called up P-O.

"Climb over him and deal with the matter in hand. And boys..."

"Skip?"

"Flash bang – no gas. My distinguished guests from Londinium would like to have a little walk, though as soon as you have made it safe and I don't think a mask would do much for Detective Sergeant Roberts' hair."

"Roger."

Another five minutes had passed.

Constantin was now nearly two miles away from the target address, driving as slow as he dared, trying to adapt to his new attire, all the while desperate to avoid detection. Where were the roadblocks? The armed police? Who were these amateurs?

Green and P-O waited for the stun grenade canister to clatter into the room. Another joined it a second later. O'Neill had learned that simply tossing them into the target area allowed an offender to kick them out of harm's way. Fire was always a secondary risk, but they would cross that bridge if they had to.

Both grenades detonated twice, the two-ounce charge in

each taking only a second to initiate. The bedroom was filled with a blisteringly white, three hundred thousand candlepower light. Anyone present would have been concussed, confused and utterly disorientated by the one hundred and sixty decibel explosion.

The two-man team were equipped to deal with both aspects of the grenade – wearing active microphones and ear defenders they would only hear muted reports, but were easily able to communicate with each other and their bronze commander.

Green felt the reassuring squeeze on his right shoulder, three times, the unambiguous signal to go. As they moved up the uncarpeted staircase, the smoke had begun to clear, enough to provide a view into an empty room through the lenses of their SF-100 respirators.

No furniture.

No-one.

Despite their masks, both men could sense the familiar stench of chemicals from the canisters.

The second bedroom was pronounced clear, then the bathroom.

"Boss, the upstairs is clear. No sign of a second offender. Only the loft and cellar to clear."

"Received. The other boys are seconds behind you. Just wait one."

Cade's phone vibrated discreetly in his trouser pocket. He removed the phone and lit up the screen. It was a text from O'Shea.

Heading out to buy lunch. How's it going? X.

He thought about not replying but sent a simple message in return.

Interesting x.

Roberts was trying to be discreet but failing dismally.

"Jas, if you want to read the bloody thing just ask!"

"Sorry mate – you and her are actually, you know, really something..."

Cade wasn't sure whether this was a statement or a question but replied equally ambiguously "Aren't we?"

Green and P-O had been joined at the top of the narrow staircase. The third officer had a pole camera – a relatively new and simple idea, but one which had already saved lives.

The officer, Steve '57' Heinz was the most recently qualified to use the kit and slid it systematically into place, teasing open the loft hatch, whilst P-O, who had stowed his MP5 and replaced it with his Glock, provided cover from within a bedroom doorway.

"Hello ladies, the B Team are just clearing the cellar. All quiet on the western front."

The fourth member of the team had joined them on the staircase with a tactical ladder. Green was the most experienced with this type of risk-laden search, and so had volunteered to go up and into the void.

Downstairs, a second unit had indeed cleared the basement.

"Boss, cellar is clear."

"Roger."

Green took over the comms again. "Boss, entering the loft. Stand by."

Woods did as he was asked.

Heinz flipped the loft hatch, pushing it up and into the empty space in one fluid movement.

He nodded to Green and corroborated with a clear and definite thumbs up.

Green rapidly climbed up the FDS lightweight ladder, its nylon slides making it all but silent. He had purposefully checked the safety catch on his MP5 – no point in having an actioned weapon if he couldn't use it. The weapon was longer than he would have liked, but it provided greater safety in the form of its attached Maglite torch.

The pinpointed beam of the torch illuminated the hidden recesses of the loft area. These areas normally provided problems to the search teams as they were a veritable dumping ground of much-loved treasures; Christmas decorations, books and dust-laden suitcases. This one, bar a galvanised water tank was completely empty.

Green poked his light into the types of places he would hide and where history had shown that desperate people would also seek sanctuary. Nothing.

And then he saw the void in the adjoining wall.

"Shit."

"You OK, Gaz?" asked Heinz.

"I am, but the skipper is going to be livid. There's a friggin' hole up here big enough to squeeze an elephant through. I'm going up. Get someone round to the next door property! Stand by on that."

He shone his light into the hole.

"The hole continues through to the next few properties. Looks like it's been like this since the Queen was a girl."

O'Neill transmitted the good news to his boss and prepared to follow his colleague up the ladder.

Green stopped. The smallest hairs on the back of his neck bristled. He shuddered involuntarily. Less than a foot from his head, and behind him, strapped to one of the joists, was the improvised device. A gift from Constantin Nicolescu. It required no glittery red bow but was delivered with genuine love.

As Green conducted a secondary sweep, the basic analogue counter diligently subtracted precious seconds from the time that Constantin had dialled in.

"Hang on, Pete. Something's not right. See if we can get the boys to do a recce on the other properties in this block. He's got to be in one of them."

He thought quietly to himself, 'this is all we bloody need.'

He kept one eye on the hole and scanned the roof space with the other. He paused, leaned further into the darkness, holding his weapon in his right hand as he gently brushed the decaying loft insulation to one side. There was something there, it was new, out of place. Foreign.

"Jesus H Christ on a bike!"

O'Neill had started to climb up the ladder but retraced his steps rapidly when Green began to exit the loft, almost landing boot-first onto his fingertips.

"Go, go, go! Bomb!"

O'Neill didn't need any more encouragement and slid the rest of the way down the ladder in one balletic movement. The other team members mirrored his actions, double-backing down the main staircase.

Three.

Two.

Green was almost out of the hatch, one hand on the wooden frame when the device detonated. The timer had reached its mark.

One.

Constantin was far from a master bomb maker but he knew more than enough to cause chaos – and the more he experimented, the more he fell under the spell of his new mistress. He loved how she captivated him, drank the air out of the environs with ease and dusted physical things to one side, slapping them away as a horse's tail might swat a fly. But most of all, he adored her authority, and her best was yet to come.

All he needed to do with the simple device was shape a small amount of plastic explosive – his homeland was awash with it – locate it in a place that would cause the desired demolition effect and consider the size, shape and configuration of his intended target.

His intentions were even simpler: create space, create time.

Any injuries to his pursuers were a consolation prize.

Green would later state that he saw the flash before the bang. He could taste the chemicals in the air and smell the metallic signature of his own blood. The detonation was flawed, its maker had hoped for more, but all it achieved was a dramatic splintering of the wooden roof joists where it had been located. And dust. An inordinate amount of dust.

The abrupt explosion had caused an immediate and intense flame which vanished in a micro-second. It had the

dual function of ripping the end of Green's finger clean off –
for the record, his right index finger – his favoured and infamous trigger finger. The most-feared in all of southern
England. Apparently.

The secondary function of the high-intensity heat was
that the flash cauterised the wound, searing it and sealing it,
like a tender eye fillet steak, served blue and dropped onto a
ravenous diner's plate.

Not normally one afraid of using profanities Green was
unable to utter a word for a few minutes. He lay on his back
looking up at the partially demolished loft entrance.
Processing his surroundings. The high-pitched whistling in
his ears was a temporary distraction from the overly present
and invasive sound of his heartbeat.

His specialist headgear had partly dislodged, enabling
him to be a part of the conversations that had commenced
around him. His team had recovered from their own awe,
stunned by the explosion and now operating in a fight versus
flight manner. One member had already rammed the ladder
back through the void – completely against his professional
instinct which told him, yelled at him, that there could be a
secondary device.

But he wanted that bastard.

The other team members were summoning further
medical help and securing their colleague, ensuring his long-
term recovery. None commented on Green's injury, which
looked significantly worse than it was.

The fall from the hatch had driven the air out of his
lungs and for a while he lay, gently moving his toes, then his
lower legs, moving upwards, each inch revealing hope as he
proceeded towards his back and neck and eventually down
his arms where he was able to wiggle his fingertips.

He chinked his wedding ring against the breach of his rifle and thought of his wife of ten years.

It was then he felt the intense pain in his other hand. Actually, it wasn't his hand; it was his finger, his right index finger to be precise. It was at this point that every other ache, pain and contusion he had suffered diminished rapidly. He felt as if his entire body was experiencing the agony of a hundred lifetimes through the microscopic median nerve that ran along the outer edge of his finger; that is, what was left of it.

Now, as he lay on his back on the threadbare carpet, his A-beta nerve fibre was carrying messages at an alarming rate up his arm, via the spinal column to his brain.

The A-delta nerve fibres were what made him suffer the exquisite pain.

Woods' radio hissed into life, announcing an incoming message.

"Skip, Sharkey's been blown up!"

The vastly experienced sergeant looked to Cade, then Roberts, then the sky before saying "Oh for...Great, just super."

He then keyed the microphone and replied.

"Received. Status please – I need more than blown up..." His broad Kentish accent appeared almost sarcastic and vaguely disappointed.

"He's lost his right-hand boss, some bruising too, and he's struggling to sit up properly...and his clothes are a bit torn..."

Woods thought the latter comment was unusual and could hear some commotion in the background. It was his senior man.

"...struggling to fuckin' breathe? Bruised? I'll have you know I've just been blown to bits by Al-bloody-Qaeda and all you can say is I've got a wardrobe malfunction. It's a wonder I can stand up…I despair I really do…If I'd still got my trigger finger I'd bloody shoot you."

He paused again, clearly suffering from shock. Then questioned his team.

"Well, go on, who has got it then?"

The team members took turns to shrug, shake their heads and deny ownership until Steve Heinz tapped the outer pocket on his one-piece overalls.

"All safe, Sharkey. I've wrapped it in plastic just like they taught us on the first aid course. Best we get you and it re-united at hospital."

Woods sensed great relief. He knew that Green would be able to survive this but was unable to cut back into the conversation, which continued for all to hear.

His team mate 'P-O', who was skilfully steering him away from the subject matter continued,

"Yeah, well you haven't stood up yet 'ave you Sharkey. I mean, you only got blown up a minute ago. And another thing, the least you can do is stay lying down until the ambulance guys get here. He was scanning the roof void and watching his partner for any change in his vital signs, knowing that all black humour aside from shock could kill in an instant.

"I probably saved your life, you ungrateful bastard – and – more importantly if I don't look after you, your Charmaine will have my bleedin' guts for garters. I mean look at the state of your trousers…"

Green lifted his head slightly and noticed that somehow the crutch of his one-piece overalls had been completely torn out during the blast, revealing what he artfully called "The Right Honourable Member for Kent."

It was lying to one side, slightly grazed, bemused almost.

However, having carried out its own post-blast assessment, it had declared itself fit for future purpose.

Green started to laugh. His body also began to shake as his system pumped Epinephrine around his veins. Heinz also started to laugh, as did O'Neill who pointed to Green's hand.

"You'll have to get someone else to pick your nose, kid. Come on, let's get you sorted, I reckon our man has long gone."

"Oh, you reckon do you? Let me at him, I can shoot with any of my other fingers you know...seriously, get me up that ladder..."

It was all he could manage before laying his back onto the frayed carpet and closing his eyes.

Woods was finally able to get back onto the conversation thread, ensuring that the team were able to function and advising that a paramedic was on the way as part of Galvin's team, being better trained for such incidents than most conventional medical staff.

He knew that his own team would strap up Green's arm until higher-level support arrived. His radio hissed a message again.

"Boss, we've found a female at number 28, Indian lady. In a bit of a state but she reckons our man ripped her clothes off her and escaped wearing them. Sometime before she heard the explosion. Might be worth getting our eye in the sky to check back over their footage for him. Other than that, all I can say is he's carrying a pistol, looks like an Indian bird and likes curry. Over."

Woods leant back against a garden wall and vigorously rubbed his scalp with his fingertips. He clicked the radio key twice indicating he had understood.

"Gentlemen, feel free to go to the house. I'm just going

to have a little cry then I've got a phone call to make and I suspect there will be a smorgasbord of Anglo-Saxon language present when I've explained that we've got a multi-cultural, cross-dressing terrorist and food critic at large in our county. I'll catch up in five."

Cade nodded to Roberts.

"Come on Jas, let's go and see what we are dealing with, I think Mac's got enough to do."

Roberts followed and added, "Jack, just what the hell *are* we dealing with here?"

Cade smiled without turning, "I honestly don't know Jason. But I think the next twenty-four, hours might be quite long and arduous, and you and I need to talk to our own cross-dressing source of information. Today. Ring Harrier."

CHAPTER FOURTEEN

Roberts had tried to contact Harrier – he reached the answerphone message and left a plea for an urgent response.

With Green en route to hospital and the scene locked down, Roberts walked quickly to the back door of the target address.

He joined Cade, looking around the terraced home. Their senses were filled with a blend of filth, blood and black powder. Knowing that a joint SOCO/CID team were en route they made the most of the chance to look around.

"His pockets are empty, Jack" said a latex-gloved Roberts.

"And the rooms are almost void of life, there's odd signs of occupancy but sod all in the way of evidence. At least we know what our man is capable of. What do you think about the explosion?"

"I'm not much of an IED expert mate, but this smacks of a diversion. If he'd wanted to he could have killed them all. Look what happened to the poor old bastard across the road...Jack?"

"Sorry?"

"You looked occupied, mate. What are you thinking?"

"Jason. Since I arrived on the scene I've been surrounded by war, famine and bloody pestilence. I'm beginning to take this personally. Not that long ago I was coming to terms with the fact that my dearly beloved was an eager member of the swinging scene, and more than happy to entertain members of my own force, then, within weeks I take up the chance to work at an international airport and I meet..."

"Petrov."

"Indeed. We get along like the proverbial burning dwelling, and she fills my head with a little too much information. I quickly heard the 'tick, tick, tick' of the roller coaster, dragging me up to the top of the first drop and honestly, I couldn't get off. I didn't want to. It was the diversion from reality I needed."

"Some would envy you, Jack. Pretty girls, car chases, mysterious Eastern European master criminals – all very Double O."

Cade snorted a small laugh. "Yeah, maybe, but this is not Hollywood and people are getting hurt, dying and suffering and I'm quickly becoming the catalyst. This is no longer about money – this is about revenge. And frankly, I'm worried who the next target might be."

Time had elapsed all too quickly. The pair continued their fruitless search for evidence, took a few photographs and headed back to an awaiting vehicle, shook hands with Woods, promised to stay in touch, asked him to pass on their best wishes to his team and left. They had made the prompt decision to return to London.

The drive back up the M2 was quiet, pensive, and about to be shattered when Roberts dialled a number on his phone.

"Well, butter my muffin top and soak it with strawberry jam, if it's not my fave detective sergeant and his dishy boss!"

Roberts had the phone system on hands free. As Cade accelerated past traffic on the expansive Medway Bridge, the conversation started in earnest.

"Harrier, listen to me. We have a serious situation that requires your help..."

"Oh, then if that's the case sugar hips I'm just the woman to climb on board the Investigation Express..."

"Harrier!"

"What?"

"Shut – the – fuck – up!"

No one had ever spoken to her in that way – and meant it. And she knew that Roberts was being serious, so, for once in her somewhat bizarre and controlling life she listened.

"Go on."

"Thank you. We are hunting for Constantin. We *have* to find him."

"What has he done this time? Another bank job?"

"No, if only it were that simple. He's moved on from blowing up ATMs – he's left that to the other syndicates."

"Yes, I saw there was another one overnight in Essex. They seem to be moving away from the city. Must be your lot putting pressure on them. So go on, enlighten me Jason."

"We believe he has killed an old man, completely innocent, and today a younger male."

"How?"

"That isn't important, Harrier."

"I need to know."

Roberts looked at Cade, who nodded.

"The old man died in an explosion. A gas accident, to be precise. But the Fire Brigade investigators are one hundred percent convinced it was designed to look that way."

"But you think it was deliberate?"

"Yes, sadly."

"My guess is, if he was even close by, then your old man had got in his way somehow. Constantin was a genius with all things chemical you know."

"I didn't. How do you know this?"

"Darling. Men talk when you have reduced their inhibitions. He could have been a chemist. He studied it when he was inside – prison that is. Read every book they had and then some. Reckoned there wasn't a thing he couldn't destroy given the opportunity. He told me once how his favourite things in the world were gasses, poisons and yours truly!"

"Charmed, I'm sure."

"And the male – how young?"

"In his twenties."

"Origins?"

"Eastern European."

"Gay?"

"I have no idea Harrier I never slept with him."

"Now who's being flippant, Detective Sergeant?"

Cade raised his eyebrows and continued north at speeds approaching ninety miles an hour. Any motorist who got in his way was reminded of his presence with a discreet flash of blue from behind the grill.

"Sorry, not called for. To answer your question H, I have no idea, but yes, possibly."

"Thank you. Where did he die?"

"He was shot. Twice in the chest, once in the forehead. Small calibre…"

"Jason, my dear, you are not listening. I asked where. Be precise."

"Rochester."

"For God's sake, be more specific."

The two police colleagues exchanged glances, shrugged shoulders and continued.

"On the staircase of a terraced house. To be precise."

"Up or down?"

"Not sure. Most likely up. He had fallen onto his back and the rounds hit him in the front, so yes. Up."

"And Constantin has escaped."

"Yes. How did you know, just a guess?"

"No. He called me from a payphone earlier. Last night too. He sounded paranoid. Said he wanted to see me, one last time."

Cade, sensing an opportunity, nodded encouragement to his partner.

"And? Did you say you would meet?"

"Of course. He pays well, and he'll be done in a few minutes. I know the tricks of the trade. He never hangs around afterwards. One last time might have some added bonuses."

"What time? Where?"

"Tomorrow. Seven o'clock. He said he had things to do tonight and tomorrow."

"1900 hours?"

"If you say so, sweetie."

"In the evening? It's important H."

"Yes. In the evening. Can I call you J?"

"You can call me whenever and whatever you like. But H..."

"Yes, J?"

"Do not let him into your apartment."

In a layby south of the River Thames, just off the M2 motorway, the red Vauxhall sat, engine running, windscreen steamed up; a solitary occupant hidden from view.

Minutes away, Bluewater, one of Britain's largest shopping complexes pulsated with people indulging in varied forms of retail therapy, all blissfully unware and frankly disinterested in the occupant of the car, who was eagerly consuming the heroin smoke that drifted upwards from its grubby tinfoil substrate. It found its way into a makeshift tube and into his body – its narcotic effect immediate upon his neural pathways.

The initial rush succeeded in calming him, allowing him to think.

He slumped into the worn seat and slept soundly for a few hours – as the world passed him by, oblivious to him and he, in turn, to it.

But his thoughts were forming now, more defined than ever.

First it would be Artur Gheorghiu. He must pay. Why did he ever accept his offer of work? He had enough knowledge to forge a new life without him and his people. And, if he had not met him, he would have not met dear Dorin Gabor. Such a sweet boy. They could have been lovers, in the end. It would have taken time, but he saw the look; that state of raw inquisitiveness that he had once shown, back in the motherland, in a beautiful government apartment where he too had learned to love and be loved by his fellow man.

"No! You *need* Gheorghiu. What are you thinking? Leave him. Get close. Leave him. Deal with him in the future. When the time is right. What *are* you thinking?"

He drifted again. The desire to sleep had become burdensome. He would have remained in a deep slumber if a heavy goods vehicle had not started up and pulled away from the layby. It felt like he had been asleep for seconds, but an hour had passed. The sun was starting to set, to drop below the industrial horizon, and yet people, western capitalists, continued to head for their Mecca.

"Don't these fools ever sleep? Bastards."

He ran the back of his hand across the windscreen, creating a small aperture in the condensed glass.

"And you, Mr Policeman. You are next. And trust me, you will be sleeping for a very long time."

He began to answer his own questions, his mind awash with thoughts. And now he was hungrier than he could ever recall. He looked down at his fingers and saw the turmeric stains, considered the passenger seat and noted the presence of the discarded burqa. He wiped his eyes. It had been a long day. A long week. A longer life.

'How have you ended up here?'

He shook his head, clearing his senses, and then asked himself another question.

"Why kill him? His suffering will be over too soon. To harm his woman is to harm him. Why should he have a person to love when mine has been taken away from me? Cause her pain. A slow, agonizing death. Then perhaps you will respect me. All of you."

. . .

O'Shea had sent another simple text:

Heading home, been a long day. Going to try some old-fashioned photography stuff. Come to bed and be very bad with me x

Cade opened the message an hour or so later. He remembered how Carrie had told him about her love of photography. He'd congratulated her on one of her landscape shots. He'd used complimentary words and hoped he had got it right. She seemed happy. He told her that one day he would hang a framed copy in his home and that perhaps, just perhaps, it would be a place that they could share.

The day had given way to the evening, but Cade and Roberts were still at work, having dutifully stood the rest of the team down. Now they were frantically trying to transpose the events of the day onto their system. Exhausted as they were, it needed to be done. He rang Daniel and appraised him of the situation.

"Jack, you've all done well. But we've got twenty-four hours. Sorry. I can't get a minute more. The deputy commissioner wants us to re-deploy to these street robberies. Without evidence – evidence of wrong-doing on our patch, I've got nothing to go back at him with."

Cade considered the words for a moment. He understood the quandary, but knew that the individuals they had been hunting and the group that funded them were capable of more, and he suspected that the lack of commitment from his bosses was the green light they were looking for.

"Sir. If we pull away now...well, you know my position on this. Remind the bloody D/C that we've had high-speed pursuits, murder, attempted murder of your staff, kidnapping. I mean really JD, how much more bloody evidence do you want? I'm sick of the up and down decision making here. I can't will these bastards to step onto the streets of London and start a battle with us. They are smarter than that. Shall I put a full-page ad in the *Daily Express*? They've stolen tens of thousands of pounds from ATMs and destroyed buildings in the process. The average street robbery results in twenty quid and a phone."

He took a breath.

"They've shot at police staff and endangered the public. Do you want me to go out and drum up some more business? It seems like I'm the Pied Piper of Bloody Hamelin when it comes to attracting the rats around here."

"Actually, Jack, I want you to go home. Rest. Catch up with that woman of yours. She looked tired too. We all are. We'll hit the ground running tomorrow and re-group. I'll give it one last go, but if I were a betting man, I'd say put it on *Street Robbery* by a nose."

"I've never wasted a penny on the nags boss, and I'm not about to start. Mug's game. I'll give it another hour then head around to see 'that woman' of mine and hopefully I'll be somewhat exhausted in the morning. Night."

He pressed the red button on his phone and walked to the kitchen, shouting 'Roberts' as he did so.

"Coffee, you old queen?"

"Queen? How very dare you? The most homoerotic thing I've ever been accused of was falling in love with two school bags."

Roberts didn't have a clue. "Go on..."

"My teacher said I was bi-satchel."

Roberts laughed. He was too tired not to.

"When you put it in such a politically correct manner boss, yes, I'd love a coffee."

• • •

fashioned English pub did; talk about the weather, about politics and most of all about football.

Fox bought the drinks, adjourned to a corner table and began the conversation.

"So Miss Caroline, how's life treating you? I hear the team has been busy lately. From all accounts, it's like the bloody Wild West out there!"

O'Shea smiled, "Crikey, it's a long time since anyone has called me by my full name!" She recounted some of the jobs that she'd either heard about or been present at and went into fine detail about the bus incident.

"Christ, girl, you were lucky. That said, I'm not sure this new man of yours is a lucky charm, you know. If you get bored, you know where to find me." He winked and sipped the top of his pint, gazing back at her inquisitive gaze.

"How do you know about Jack?"

"Word travels fast among retired coppers love. Besides, what else have we got to do but watch *Countdown* and gossip with other like-minded manic depressives on Facebook?"

"You need a hobby."

"Do I now? So what's yours?"

"Well, I'm a long way from retirement Foxy, but mine is photography. I've even started developing my own images. Jack says my spare bedroom smells like the ICI factory sometimes!"

"Tres romantique mon cheri!"

They laughed and O'Shea found herself relaxing whilst keeping a discreet eye on the time. Her drinking partner kept an eye on the door. Old habits died the hardest. Years as a Special Branch officer and close connections to Northern Ireland did that to a man.

"No really, it is an art form, it goes back many years. Jack thinks I'm mad. Blames my occasional 'absences' on chemical inhalation. I'm currently working on a technique known as the wet plate collodion process. I've bought a large format camera, which means I get to develop some amazing mono-chrome, that's black and white images..."

Fox was listening, but distracted.

"I'm boring you, aren't I Foxy?"

He smiled before adding, "No, absolutely not, I'm just trying to get my head around just what it is you are on about lady!"

She took a long sip of her drink and continued, buoyed by his interest.

"I use potassium cyanide as a fixing agent...it's pretty sexy stuff..."

"For Christ's sake Carrie, isn't that also pretty stuff lethal?"

"No, not at all. Well yes, very, but it's how you mix it, and where and with what."

"You've studied this and that worries me, I certainly don't want to make an enemy of you. Thank God you didn't know about this shit when I tried it on with you or I'd be in Highgate Cemetery!"

"You would you dirty old man, and rightly so. No, seri-ously, it's a safe process. As with all chemicals they are often stable in isolation, it's when they mix that things can... develop. See what I did there?"

He did. He still found her very attractive and that inquisitive nature and those come to bed eyes did nothing to diminish the sensation. But he'd had his chance and now his feelings were more paternal. He certainly felt old enough. He gazed at her for a while as she swept the room for risks.

The edgy, pockmarked male who had been leaning against the bar did the same, then looked away when Derek Fox caught his eye. He unhurriedly slid his empty glass back towards the barmaid, nodded, smiled a vacant smile and exited, turned right, then left and walked at a pace that showed purpose. Within minutes he was just another inhabitant of one of the world's busiest cities.

Fox took a brief moment to process what he had seen, considered the male to be a pickpocket, and placed the matter in File 13. If he tried anything on either of them out on the street, he would swiftly find himself en route to the local hospital. At fifty-four Fox was a young retiree and still very capable or inflicting pain; unless, of course, the recipient no longer felt it.

Roberts held The Sanctuary door for Cade who walked in, said good evening to Roger the landlord and found himself a chair in the private room that was almost always on standby for the various units that had adopted it as their own.

"Guten tag mon ami," said an upbeat Roberts before adding "Two of your finest foaming pints of brown dishwater and a couple of chipped bowls of what you fraudulently market as beef curry, if you please landlord."

"Jason, you can fuck off to the Jewel of Bengal if you want the real thing you know!"

"Please, Roger, I never knew you were so passionate about your culinary expertise. Slip a large sherry into a glass and come and join us, you sexy beast."

"Thanks, but no thanks I'd rather dip my balls in hot custard. Oh, and Sergeant..."

"Yes, barman?"

"As a special deal for you and your boyfriend, that'll be fifteen quid."

Roberts slipped the cash across the bar, ensuring it

absorbed some of the previously spilled drink that floated on top of the aged wooden surface.

"GFY Roger, GFY."

"Do what?"

"It's code. You wouldn't understand, you were only ever a traffic warden."

With drinks in hand and feeling smug Roberts joined a man he considered to be his friend and lately his boss and they did what most good police officers did after a stressful period – they laughed at the most inappropriate things and let what was left of their hair down, whilst Roberts extolled the virtues of heating a saucepan of custard to boiling point.

Half a mile away the same pockmarked male eased himself into O'Shea's flat, closed the door behind him and swept the rooms for inhabitants. It had been easy to find. The information Valentin had provided was extremely accurate.

Constantin was coming down from his latest heroin-fuelled nightmare and was now surprisingly fully in control of his faculties. His mouth was dry, sticky almost, but he had become so used to the feeling that it had become the norm.

Unable to produce endorphins naturally, he needed more excitement, more risk, greater danger and this was driving him towards his goal. Just as heroin was driving him uncontrollably towards an almost inevitable and somewhat painful death.

He was talking to himself, happy in the fact that he was alone in her home. He cared not that she might come home. She had entered the pub with that man, and it wasn't her lover. Clearly she was a whore and deserved punishing. He would like to punish her.

He opened her wardrobe, ran his hands along her

clothes, stopped, rubbed the silk lining on a charcoal grey skirt between his thumb and forefinger, then closed the door.

He stepped towards her bedside drawers and opened the top one. As he expected, it was full of personal 'things' – things he neither had the time nor the inclination to look at.

The second drawer, equally predictably, contained underwear. He carefully folded a few items over until he reached the bottom of the pile. His fingers adapted to the change in material. Cotton gave way to silk. He again rubbed his thumb and forefinger together, creating an exquisite feeling. He lifted the item out, held it up, admired it and then placed it reverently against his cheek.

He held it there for a while, content in the fact that he had truly invaded her privacy. But she was a woman, and that fact alone was reason to place the item back where he found it. His presence aroused him enough – she didn't.

He knew someone who would look extraordinary in the camisole. Even for Constantin this was on the wrong side of the moral compass, but still he rolled the sheer black underwear up, folded it again and placed it into his pocket.

He walked carefully around the flat until he located her photography equipment in a walk-in wardrobe that she had lovingly and rather cleverly converted. Her images were fine. He actually liked them. She had an eye for light. In another life he might even deign to hang one on his wall – if he had a wall, let alone a home. He admired talent, and the girl had it in bucket loads.

Pity.

"You pretty young thing. You have a lot of equipment here. Far too many chemicals for such a small space. Oh well, you live and you learn."

He located the exhaust fan, turned it on and laughed as

he started to open up the containers, gently distributing liquids and powders in the various trays that existed for such purposes. She had sagaciously installed the exhaust fan to extract the gases that would be emitted during the process. He would be deliberately less prudent, ensuring the wiring to the master switch was partially disconnected, appearing to the trained eye as if it had worked itself loose over time.

He should wear a mask and safety goggles, probably. He had spent so long working with and absorbing the impacts of commonly acquired chemicals that he appeared immune to their effects.

He wore gloves. He was reckless, but not stupid. Why leave obvious clues for her irritating boyfriend and his band of brothers?

He opened the bottle of hydrochloric acid and allowed it to vent.

Hydrochloric acid and potassium cyanide. Simple chemicals with potentially catastrophic side effects, and here they were in her own home. He didn't even need to bring the evidence to the scene of the crime. How perfectly fortuitous.

Once the two started to mix, to co-exist, to evolve, his work was done.

He carefully disconnected the wire on the fan. Turned off the light, eased the door shut behind him and left the room.

As he walked back along the street, away from the apartment building and further away from The Sanctuary he placed his hand into his pocket to avoid the cold night air. His hand stopped against the silk and he involuntarily rubbed it between his fingers once more.

He also carried out pointless but entertaining calculations in his head. It was how he had occupied his mind in prison when things had got so bad that he had contemplated suicide, not once, or twice, but daily.

If she weighed, for argument's sake about sixty kilogrammes she only need ingest half a gram of potassium cyanide to ensure her painful and untimely death, and, if Lady Luck were on his side, it would happen within two to three days.

Yes, the authorities would probably locate it as a cause of death, but they would attribute it to her carelessness, or better still, the hurried work of an inferior tradesman who never bothered to double-check his wiring.

He knew that around ninety percent of healthy people who weighed a little more than she did would die as a result of consuming a single teaspoon of the chemical. Furthermore, he knew that in many cases death occurred within hours.

That amount of the crystalline powder – a little more than most people would sprinkle on their breakfast cereals – was enough to ruin anyone's day. Both were readily absorbed into hot drinks, making it a perfect ally to the serial killer and willing accomplice to the suicidal.

He also knew that she would ingest the toxin even more effectively via the gas that was rapidly forming, and it would be this method that he chose rather than placing it into her drink in the bar.

The latter was far too risky in a building so clearly full of curious witnesses, of police officers, and, importantly, he knew that even the Russians had failed to kill the legendary Rasputin by placing cyanide into his wine.

Put simply, the alcohol and sugar in her drink would mix with the cyanide to form a less stable compound known as

Amygdalin. And this alone would be unlikely to kill her. However, the hydrochloric acid, quietly mixing with the cyanide in the darkroom of her London flat would.

Her home was insidiously filling with the gases present in hydrocyanic acid; a ruthless cocktail that had claimed so many lives in as many varied and tragic ways as one could imagine.

O'Shea looked at her watch, on this occasion, not discreetly as she had done a dozen times during the last half an hour.

Fox spotted the last three veiled attempts and relented.

"It's OK, I know you need to head home. You said an hour and I've had twenty-eight more minutes than I deserved. Carrie, it's been wonderful catching up. Can we stay in touch, if only so I can say I know a younger woman?"

She nodded, finishing her drink and walking up the bar to hand the glass over the counter.

"Goodnight all."

The darts contest had stepped up a gear, and the debate about Arsenal's chances against Chelsea had entered its next phase. It had been a somewhat unexpectedly pleasant evening.

Fox helped O'Shea on with her navy blue jacket, adjusted his own and held the door open.

They walked outside, O'Shea gathered her jacket together at the seams for there was a subtle chill to the air, as she was zipping it up Fox spoke.

"Allow me to walk you home, Carrie?"

"No, Derek, I'm fine, honestly. It's a few hundred metres, half a mile at best."

"I know, that's why I want to escort you home. This city is full of nutters...say nothing, Carrie!"

"Fine! But if you try anything, I'll stab you with a writing instrument."

"Ah, the famous, or should that be infamous pencil! Of course you have my permission to drive it into my carotid if I should so much as ask the fair lady for a kiss. Seriously, there was a guy in the pub I didn't like the look of. I think he was a pickpocket who chose the wrong watering hole, but you never know. To the door and then we part until we meet again. Deal?"

He held out his hand. She took hold of it and squeezed as hard as she could.

"Deal."

Cade and Roberts were on their second drink, having been convinced to play a game of pool with a couple of Roberts' old colleagues. Although only a room away, they had been oblivious to O'Shea's presence.

"Ten more minutes Jason and I need to get back. It's been a ferociously long day, and I promised Carrie we'd spent at least an hour together."

"Lightweight! Actually looking at the time I'd better make tracks or my Cathy will string me up." He looked at his old teammate from his uniform days and smiled, "Black ball, middle pocket."

He struck the blue powdered cue tip against the white ball, causing it to fly across the baize. It clipped the edge of the black, kissing it softly into the intended target.

"That, my dear boys, is how you play the noble game of pocket billiards. Thank you and goodnight!" He downed the remainder of his pint and grabbed his jacket.

"Come on, you old dog, I'll drop you off. Carrie will be

slipping into something silky as we speak, and the night is still young."

They got to the door when the barman called out.

"Night boys, have fun together!"

It was Cade who responded first, knowing the banter was just that, harmless fun between males.

"Roger, you have no idea what I am going to do with this fine specimen of a man when I get him home, no idea at all." He playfully tapped him on the backside to enforce the point.

"Good job you've got him to fall back on Jack, what with your missus seeing another bloke!"

The banter stopped. There. And then.

Cade was back in his old police force area, at a barbeque and staring straight into Grant Cooke's conceited little eyes. Life had just rewound to his earlier life, his old force and his old colleagues. The waves of deceit came crashing over him, and all he could see was the end of a futile marriage.

It seemed like only a few hours ago, but time had a way of compressing, and now it was unravelling once more.

He turned, like a self-assured western gunslinger in an arid street, and spoke quietly but loud enough to deliver his message.

"Say that again Roger, but be very careful how you phrase things, I've had a very long month and my temper is far shorter."

Roger Walsh paused, realising that he had unwittingly overstepped the mark and recognising that he was about to be outgunned he quickly apologised.

"Sorry, Jack. I thought you knew Carrie was in the other bar? She was here for about an hour, with a bloke. Tall, straight back, older than her, but they clearly knew each other. He looked like ex-job. I asked around. Someone said he was ex-SB, fella called Foxy."

"You say they left together?"

"They did mate yes, arm in arm, all cosy like. I just assumed..." He paused, "...sorry."

"No problem Rog, none at all. None at all."

Roberts looked at his boss and knew he needed to say something profound.

He placed his hand on his shoulder before continuing, "Jack, I know what happened up north. This is not the same. Carrie is not like that."

"Like what Jas?"

"You know, like you are imagining?"

"Mate, you have no idea what I am imagining. When you've found your naked wife, who you adore, frolicking around in a swimming pool, her perfect breasts, that I paid for, bouncing around in the waves, with three or four of your closest colleagues leering over her, and all you can possibly do is walk away, leaving her to her own fate... Then, and only then can you offer advice."

"But..."

"No buts, Jason. Drop me off at work, will you? I've got some paperwork to do. Perhaps by the time I get to the flat they will have finished whatever it is they have planned and he will have gone."

"Say he's still there? Then what?"

"Then I don't care how tall he is or what his background is, he's going to need more than a few plasters for his dented pride. Come on, take me to the office."

The man they called The Child of the Shadows didn't like what he saw. He respected the English officer and had made a pact to support him. The last week had taught him that he had made a sound judgement.

Watching the wireless close circuit camera he had had installed in an adjacent building weeks before, he inhaled a measured breath.

The device had appeared overnight, piggy-backing onto an existing surveillance camera, making it appear legitimate. It was an early prototype that he had 'borrowed' from a government agency with the primary intention of perhaps, one day, returning.

Whilst the quality was far from world class it provided him with a tactical view of the street, of Cade and anyone else arriving or departing the Old Queen Street address.

He had seen the British officer and his girlfriend arriving at all hours and generally, as the creatures of habit that they were, he would watch them leaving at the same time most mornings. He had observed their frantic attempts to avoid detection as they fell into one another's arms, through the heavy door and beyond. They made a splendid couple.

Tonight was different. Tonight there was a genuine chill in the air. He could tell the lens was slightly fogged and the people, oblivious and yet acceptant of the Orwellian scrutiny that surrounded them, pulled up their jackets to shield themselves from the northerly wind that whispered along the streets and probed into darkened doorways.

He chastised himself for not borrowing a system with a better lens, but what he saw was clear enough. A male entered the building, without a key, that is, without a conventional key. He was very proficient and hyper-aware of his surroundings, paranoid, and at best, distrustful.

Valentin Iliescu stared into the all-too-small monitor, which was remotely stationed, but allowed a bird's-eye view of the target address. The Romanian former operative had a number of these systems placed around the city – those that he didn't own, he controlled, and it was actually very easy, for a man with his background and latter-day contacts.

Roberts and Daniel were not immune from his watchful eye, but their existence, and that of their wives, never offered anything worth recording.

His plan – his task – had been to enter their lives discreetly and ruin them in any way that he saw fit. The Jackdaw had given him carte blanche to do so, 'do what you like, I am bored with the whole thing, cause them misery, but leave Cade for me.'

Iliescu studied the footage once more, 'There is something about you, my dark friend, something familiar…'

And then, as the previously obscure male left the property, it became all too obvious.

'Constantin. What on God's earth are you doing there? This is not your job. Your job is to blow up bank machines with your ingenious system and to train the younger boys to follow your lead, if you can leave your hands off them for a moment. You are not supposed to be getting so close. Your goal was clear; steal from the capitalist's, rip their financial hearts out, a thousand at a time'

Copil de umbra found himself facing a new challenge and a test of his loyalty. He had to make a choice. The new-found brother within the intelligence community who might be able to offer some semblance of immunity, or, more money, more than he had, which for the record was quite enough to lead a healthy and comfortable lifestyle in his provincial French home, where no one cared who he was – and never asked.

As always, he made a decision based on gut instinct.

He picked up his phone and dialled Cade's number. No answer.

. . .

O'Shea reached her flat, swiped her entry card on the reader and stepped inside. She trembled, trying to rid herself of the cold night air, then turned and smiled at Fox.

"Derek, it has been genuinely wonderful to catch up. I am not going to invite you in for coffee, as that will only mean you won't sleep tonight. And besides, Jack will be home soon, and as much as he would like you he's been hurt in the past and I don't want to give him the wrong signals – nor you. But we can meet again for coffee. Thank you for escorting me home on these mean streets, my white knight, in shining armour."

She stepped forward and kissed him on the cheek.

From afar Valentin watched, intrigued, but what he saw was not the actions of a woman with her lover, but a woman saying goodbye to an old friend, and contrary to what was apparently happening, he wanted her to invite him in. Constantin had been in her flat for a reason, and it would not be a pleasant one.

He spoke to the camera, to an audience of one. "Get out. Wait for backup. Do not let this friend go."

He saw her kiss him on the cheek before turning away and closing the door. The male looked up and down the street before turning left onto Storey's Gate and flagging down a black cab.

He dialled Cade's number once more. This time it transferred to an answerphone with a simple, soulless message. He cleared the line. He had to speak to him.

CHAPTER FIFTEEN

Her mind was awash with images of the past. She found herself reminiscing about her days at Hendon, the Metropolitan Police training centre.

She was a young girl when she had left home, after yet another argument with her belligerent father. He had been a veteran of the same force but had steadfastly refused to endorse her application to be a police officer – worse still, a police *woman*.

Leaving her troubles behind she had arrived on a cool March morning, most of her worldly goods packed into two large holdalls. Sliding the bags under her rudimentary bed she ran her eyes around the basic accommodation, imagining the ghosts of those who had gone before her. Far from being intimidated she was ready for the challenge, more ready than most of her male colleagues and that would earn her a reputation as a valiant, strong-willed foot soldier who would quickly become as popular with her peers as she would her superiors.

She was second in her intake, destined for greatness

when her career was savagely cut short – the direct result of a stubborn, foolhardy and allegedly more experienced colleague. She had so much potential. The 'accident' had deprived her of her calling, of a future as a naturally gifted investigator and myriad other avenues, all closed and never to be re-opened.

Her training sergeant had made reference to her uncanny ability to join the dots, to observe a trend, and had already pencilled her in as a worthy contender for a highly fought-over place on a subsequent Criminal Investigation Department course.

'Constable O'Shea has an eye for detail that many of her more senior peers crave. Example: Show her an unrecognisable crime scene and she will study it intensely, overlay a map and within hours will have located the exact location. What her local knowledge and technical expertise can't achieve, her human source skills can. Hers is an uncanny talent and one which the police would do well to nurture.'

That would cause her dear father even more consternation – a female bloody detective. What next? Promotion? For Carrie it was all going so well.

The noise of her own footsteps on the staircase jolted her back into the current time and place. Something in her sub-conscious alerted her to the intense awareness that she appeared to have for her surroundings. She had taught herself to walk around it in the dark, using her fingertips to gauge where she was.

She could almost hear the soles of her feet brushing against the woollen carpet, the breath exiting her lungs and her heart, quietly beating.

As always, since the crash she was working at nine-tenths – if only that selfish bastard had slowed down on that ill-fated day she would be one of the force's best thief-takers, with an assured and perfect mind for criminal investigation. Now, instead, she was trapped behind a desk and striving to get to the start of the food chain.

What most mortals failed to acknowledge was that Carrie O'Shea's nine tenths was the equal of most people working way above their capacity. When it came to pure analysis, she had few equals.

She hated the arrogant male who had done this to her and she hated the organisation for the way they had covered things up.

She opened the door to her flat, paused, reached around and perfectly located the main light switch. The room was bathed in cool light, familiar territory. An exquisite flat in an exclusive location and one, thanks to her benefactor she could fortuitously call home.

She scanned the room as she always did – the by-product of living alone. This evening the microscopic fibres in her nose sensed something unusual, untoward and foreign. It had a familiar note but she couldn't place it.

She shrugged off the ill-feeling but her head began to hurt, a mild pain, her eyes burned a little, but again nothing a dash of chilled water wouldn't resolve. But she felt slightly light-headed too.

Food. Yes, she needed to eat. Her eyes were burning due to the intense computer work she had been conducting for the last few weeks – a visit to the optician was overdue and this explained the gentle headache. Once again, Carrie O'Shea; the Detective.

But the headache was worsening.

Cade looked at his phone, noted the five missed calls and slid it across the desk. He did not know who had called, the message simply said 'Private'. He carried on writing his report but was distant, removed from his role, thinking about her.

Constantin had slipped out of the flat, onto the pavement and quietly into the darker side of the discreet but very upmarket road. He was rapidly heading towards the nearby refuge of a grey stone historic building, where he would wait, as an arsonist waits for the firefighter, stimulated by the sight of his destructive pastime and if providence was on his side he could plan the next phase whilst he waited for the drama to unfold. It just didn't get any better.

He wrote off the feeling of being watched as simply the result of drug-fuelled paranoia. But he was being watched. He knew it.

His plans were simple. More money, more drugs, more, of whatever he wanted. Jackdaw and that rent boy of his who had got him drunk on cheap vodka in that dowdy English drinking establishment; they could all go to hell.

He was on his own now, unhinged, rogue and afraid of no one, and of course, relishing every moment.

For the first time in years, he regretted his weakest of moments; accepting a Class A drug from a stranger. His skin itched, and he involuntarily scratched, paying attention to the inside of his right wrist, and there it was, the blue mark, the wave, the ink that enslaved him. He scratched at it until it bled. He needed to cut it out, piece by piece.

O'Shea walked into her lounge, slipped off her jacket and immediately thought of Cade – 'Come home now, it's my turn, I want to take up some of your valuable time.' Her eyebrows raised at the thought of what she might do with him.

She stepped out of her shoes; the relief was instant; it had been another long day. She dropped her skirt to the ground and flicked it skilfully with her left foot onto the sofa. Her shirt followed, but she expertly draped that over a dining chair, taking a moment to align the seams purposefully with the back of the seat. No longer quite as obsessive, but always driven by the past, Carrie O'Shea was changing slowly.

Her sheer blue lace bra found a temporary but indicative home on the bedroom door handle, it was so good to get it off. She kicked off her matching knickers catching them in one seamless motion and laying them on the edge of the bed. Just so.

If that didn't encourage him into their favourite room of the house, then frankly nothing would. It had been days; it felt like weeks.

Free of the encumbrances of the day and freer of her clothing she brushed her teeth, layered a mist of Chanel No 5 onto her neck and shoulders and walked without restraint around her flat. She caught a glimpse of herself in the hall mirror. She stood, side on and ran her hand alongside her breast, across the flat of her stomach and paused before thinking about heading a little lower.

'Carrie, you are a very bad girl. That sort of behaviour will have to wait until Inspector Cade gets home. And when he does, you are going to be a complete and utter slut. Every one of your lurid dreams will come true this evening.'

She glanced backwards and spoke into the mirror, "It's been weeks Jack, we owe it to each other..."

Her eyebrows raised twice in succession. She playfully slapped her own wrist and walked towards the homebuilt darkroom – if she couldn't be playful she might as well be creative. And what better way to be creative than photography. As Jack once said as he dragged her towards the compact, naturally dark room, 'Come on you, let's get in here and see what develops.'

She grinned as she walked across the open-plan lounge-diner but then sensed it again.

She felt confused, as if her blood sugar levels had plummeted, now the nausea was increasing. Her arms felt heavy, and yet weak, she became unsteady, as if drunk.

Her mind was on fire. Had she been drugged? Had Fox done this to her? Was he waiting outside to capitalise upon her situation?

"No, no..." She could hear her own words clearly, almost with complete clarity, but her physical motor skills were failing more quickly than she was able to react.

The imperceptible veil of gas was consuming her, wrapping its arms around her and crushing the air from her lungs; ivy encasing its host, clambering, twisting, turning, relieving her of oxygen, smothering her soul, quietly wishing to swathe her in its life-depriving clutches.

"Air, get to clean air...get on the floor, crawl." Her voice was now detached but guiding her towards safety.

She was confused and now hyperventilating, her heart rate quickening, panic was setting in, completely unaware why this was happening to her. She leant forward and grabbed the darkroom door handle, trying in vain to stabilise herself. The door eased slightly allowing a more concentrated blanket of gas to escape, now it was present at every level and insidiously entering her.

There was no sense of the oft-discussed bitter almond smell in her home, perhaps if there had been she would be in a more enviable position than she was now. She detested almonds. Her mind was still trying to process what was happening, she knew she was being attacked, but her attacker was absent.

'It must be the chemicals. The chemicals. The chem...'

It must be her fault. Her eyes blinked repeatedly as she tried to focus on the row of brown bottles, lined up perfectly on the white shelf. Then, as she slipped to her knees, she saw the open tray, full of liquid. Her last thought would be that this was a deliberate act. The diminutive young policewoman who had impressed so many with her attention to detail, her immense spirit and sheer resolution had lost the battle without as much as a fight.

She was forlornly unaware that her pristine, naked body lay next to the room that had become her emotional escape. She was hopeless, helpless and dying.

Around two hundred parts per million of the deadly cocktail had combined in the air to deprive her of her life and her dignity. Just another seventy units would have killed her instantly. Time was her nemesis.

As grey as the shadows he hid among Constantin could feel himself becoming tired. He needed another meeting with his opiate mistress, but she was locked in his car, calling his name.

His alternative mistress was the obvious solution. He recalled now, among the fog of war that clouded his mind and judgement, that he had intended to see Lucy, it was to be, possibly his last night with her.

It was coming back to him now, flooding back and encouraging him to make contact. He slid his phone from his pocket and held down the number three.

· · ·

Oblivious to the chaos Lucy dried her freshly manicured hand and answered the phone.

"Connie my darling, I've been expecting you. Guess where I am?"

He was in no mood for games.

"Tell me."

"I'm in the bath. Come over, you know where I keep the key. I'll wait right here for you."

She turned on the tap with her equally immaculate toes and soon felt the temperature rise.

Nicolescu processed her words and visualised her in the ornate claw foot cast iron bath.

"There is something I have to do first, then I will come to you."

Lucy Thomas hated secrets, but she loved a satisfied client more.

"OK Connie, but is there something you should be telling your Lucy?" She paused, long enough to create an uncomfortable silence. "Don't burst my bubbles sweetie..."

"OK. OK! I tell you, but if you mention this...to anyone, I will come over there and... drown you. I mean it. Make me a promise."

"I cross my legs and hope to die."

'Open them, more like...'

And then he did what he always did with his transvestite lover – he told her where he had been, what he had done, about the last twenty-four hours. As he sheltered in the darkened stone-arched doorway and she slipped deeper into the steaming bath, he told her everything.

But he stopped short of informing her what he was yet to do.

. . .

Valentin was still watching, the Imperial Eagle to his former comrade, the startled Baby Rabbit. But what he saw suggested that the rabbit had claws.

'Why are you standing there Constantin Nicolescu? What exactly are you waiting for? And who are you talking to on your phone I wonder?'

The younger of the two Romanian males lifted a glass to his lips and savoured the Armagnac that left liquid honey-brown tracks on the inner surface of his favourite lead crystal glass.

This time he said it aloud.

"Come on, what are you doing, who are you waiting for?" He deliberately read his lips, trying to decipher the conversation.

He dialled Cade again.

"Jack Cade. This had better be important!"

"Jack, it is Valentin, I have been trying to ring you. Something is wrong at your girlfriend's house. You need to get there quickly."

"Thank you, my friend, but I no longer have a girlfriend since she chose to find another man. Goodbye..."

The caller was unaware of Cade's history, of the wretched end to his previous marriage, of betrayal and disappointment. Cade himself was torn between the past and the present. His head refused to trust her a moment longer, but his heart, his heart knew that something was not quite right. Such a shame his foolish male pride would not relinquish the vice-like grip on the situation.

"Cade stop! Your girl is not with another man. I watched them at the door of her flat. She kissed him on the cheek and waved goodbye. I think they are old friends, nothing more."

The words came from a man described as a prolific assassin and now rather strangely; he was an ally, and his words seemed to provide solace to Cade. He shook his head, both physically and mentally. It was what he wanted to hear and now was back in control of his dreaded emotions.

"OK, so will you answer me a question Valentin?"

"Jack, we have no time for questions, you need to get to the flat."

"Just one. How do you know all this?"

"I have a camera on your home Jack, it has been there for a while, your colleague's too. I observed Constantin Nicolescu entering your girlfriends home, he entered carrying a small bag and left with nothing."

"And?"

"Jack! Need I remind you? He is a murdering drug addict who wishes to kill you all for taking away what he valued."

"What?"

"The boy he was with at the house in Kent. He is dead yes?"

"If you mean the one he probably shot, then yes."

"He is no longer thinking...rationally. You have been hunting him, no?"

"Yes. He is wanted for many things including murder and attempted murder, other offences too..."

He cut him off as the sentence was looking likely to be long and drawn out.

"I think Constantin will be nearby, watching you. I lost him in the darkness. Go to the flat Cade. Now!"

"OK, I'm going." He started walking quickly, then spoke again.

"Valentin?"

"Yes, I am still here."

"Are you watching Roberts too?"

"Of course."

"Is he home yet?"

"No."

"Thank you – I owe you. Goodbye."

He dialled the Control room, intending to compress four paragraphs into two lines but was put on hold and forced to listen to crime prevention advice on a monotonous looping recording. He left a brief but informative message before hanging up and auto-dialling Roberts.

"Jason it's me, get to Carrie's place as fast as you can. I've got back-up on the way."

"What's happening Jack?"

"I have no idea but a call from our Romanian assassin friend tells me something is very wrong. I'll ring for an ambulance, see you there."

"Jack, cancel the ambulance, they are on strike, went out at six o'clock tonight, them and the underground staff. Industrial action over pay and conditions. I'm not that far away, I stopped to get some..."

Cade cleared the line, grabbed his phone and a set of car keys from a nearby wall hook. Bypassing the lift he ran down the stairs to the ground floor. Floor after floor, it seemed to take an eternity before he burst through the fire door and into the car park.

He looked around the parking area. No one left. He was on his own in one of the busiest police buildings in the country. He dialled the number for the police control room again.

"Inspector Jack Cade from the Operation Breaker team. I'm en route to an address in Old Queen Street, South West

One. Get me some backup and a medic." He cleared the line once more and accelerated out of the building.

The Vauxhall's engine was being caned, each gear propelling the car forwards and into the red line. He brought the car to a rapid halt at the junction of Tothill Street and Dartmouth Street. This was the way he walked her home, but it was one-way.

He shoved his left index finger onto a dashboard switch which illuminated a set of blue strobes, sat inconspicuously behind the grill and conventionally very discreet.

Adopting the old adage of it being better to ask for forgiveness than permission he drove across the main road and up the one-way street, mounting the kerb to his left to avoid parked vehicles.

At sixty miles an hour, he knew that if somebody pulled into his path, he was doomed.

They did.

The elderly male businessman, who had also had an incredibly long day, had indicated to his right, looked over his left shoulder and pulled away from the kerb. He had done everything by the book, just as he had over fifty blemish-free years of driving.

The Vauxhall struck the front right-hand wing with a jarring thud, sending glass and most of Cade's pride cascading across the narrow London highway.

He looked at the other male and could see immediately that he was uninjured but about to explain to Cade in words of limited syllables just what he thought of the police officer's driving.

But his opportunity was lost as Cade was out and running. He paused, shoved a business card into the pinstriped-driver's hand and ran north. As he ran, he reached into his pocket to answer his cell phone.

"Cade."

"It's Jason. I'm here, where are you?"

Roberts could hear that his colleague was running, but had no idea just how far away he was.

"Do I wait for you?"

"No. Yes. We go into together. I'm a minute away." He hung up.

CHAPTER SIXTEEN

Cade was running faster than he ever had. His chest was wracked with pain as he piled air into his lungs, his arms trying their best to propel him forward. He rounded the last corner, having left one highly overpriced street for another.

He reached Roberts and scanned his entry card onto the door reader.

He took a brief moment to look up and down the street, gulping in air, trying to stand up straight. As with his workplace, the streets were deserted. Had he somehow missed an apocalyptic episode?

"Go, get inside."

They crashed up the stairs, oblivious to the need to maintain a covert approach. The main door to the flat was locked. Cade stepped back and rammed his right foot against the lock. Nothing.

He tried again, and again. Already exhausted he could sense a battle lost.

Roberts stepped forward.

"Jack, no offence but move. This door is going in."

He took two steps back and propelled his foot straight through the door panel which gave way instantly. Cade was so fast to react that he pushed the door inwards with his partner's leg still hanging through the door panel. At any other time, it would have been hysterically funny.

Cade was moving quickly, but sensed a significant odour. It started to affect him almost immediately. He called out to Roberts.

"Jason, stay out, get out! Call the fire brigade – there's a chemical leak in here."

As he was shouting Cade could feel himself plummeting, his eyes burned intensely and nausea welled up from his stomach sending acid coursing through his system, scorching his oesophagus and making him retch.

He instinctively dropped to the floor and in doing so probably saved his own life. The room was clear of any obvious vapour cloud but he was fighting a forceful battle – to see and to move.

He looked across the lounge and saw her lying on the carpet, half of her naked body was inside the dark room, the other stretched into the lounge.

Without pausing to question why she was naked he crawled, infant-like across the room, took a huge breath and prayed for salvation. He could hardly see now but his hands still worked. Grasping hold of her feet he pulled her towards him. Instinctively he wanted to hold her to his chest, to console her, but he knew that whatever the chemical was it was killing her and time was her only ally.

"Jack! Meet me half way, wrap this around your face." It was Roberts, offering lucid instructions to his friend and colleague.

Cade grabbed hold of the item which he saw was

Roberts' jacket. He wrapped it around his face and with a boost of adrenaline shuffled backwards towards his loyal colleague.

Roberts, never the strongest officer on the force, took hold of Cade's legs and pulled with Herculean strength, bringing both him and O'Shea back into the doorway.

A neighbour appeared. "Can I help?"

"Get her into your flat and open up all the windows and call an ambulance."

Roberts looked at Cade and nodded.

"Well done, mate. Look we need to get her to hospital. The clock may be ticking and we don't have the first clue what is wrong with her. This is no accident Jack."

The neighbour did as instructed – he'd put two and two together and assumed the males were police officers. He knew what his neighbour did, but in three years had never questioned what exactly. In fact, he had hardly ever spoken to her.

"Look gent's bloody awful news but the ambulance service are on strike. They are sending an Advanced Paramedic but we may have to get her to hospital by other means."

Cade didn't have time to respond – he was planning priorities: transport, detection and revenge.

All had their place, but the first was getting his girlfriend to hospital – by any means.

"Jason, ring nine nine nine for Christ's sake. Then try the Yard. Stop a taxi if you have to. Do *something*."

Cade was between the proverbial rock and its harder cousin. Police officer? Or caring, loving partner? His primary coping mechanism was to be a law enforcement officer. He knew his selfish mix of paranoia and stupidity had allowed her to be alone and he now believed – rather he now knew, that either the man they had been hunting or an associate was responsible for the likely death of the single best thing to occur in his relatively disordered recent life.

"She's unresponsive Jack."

Cade was deep in thought.

"Jack!"

"For God's sake Jason, do you think I cannot see that?" He looked up at the neighbour who was dumbstruck, "Sir, do you have a towel or a dressing gown? Anything, just give her some of her dignity back would you?"

The neighbour scuttled away and returned with his wife's dressing gown. They eased her into it. Although she was lifeless at least she her self-esteem had been returned.

Cade held onto her, willing the intrusive noise of motor-cycle sirens to grow louder. His singular prayer was answered as the BMW machine negotiated traffic and pulled up outside the flat. Its green-suited rider grabbed a pannier from the bike and was met by Roberts on the stairs, who identified himself to the medic.

"Normally healthy female, found unresponsive on the floor of her flat. My colleague who rescued her said he could smell a chemical of some kind. He was almost passing out. We've closed the door and called the fire brigade. I've got a patrol car en route too as there are no bloody ambulances."

The medic pulled a half smile, half grimace. "I'm here now mate, let's see what we can do to help this lady shall we?"

Cade acknowledged the biker and stepped out of the way.

"She's a photographer."

It made no sense to the ambulance officer who was used to hearing normally balanced people offer a raft of poten-tially valuable and often conversely useless information. He looked at him momentarily and then continued checking O'Shea's vital signs.

"This lady is in a critical state gents. We need that patrol car." He paused, unable to do a great deal more. "Photography?"

"Yes, I think that might explain the chemical smell in the flat, it was intense, over-powering. She was on the ground when I got in there. She was naked too. We don't know why. I can't think of anything else that might help."

It was obvious to the trained paramedic that Cade was also suffering partial symptoms of poisoning.

He walked into the hallway. He needed more than fresh air.

"Jas, I'll be outside if you need me."

A mile away Lucy Thomas was preparing for the night of all nights with a man who paid well and, when the mood took him, performed even better. But he was yet to arrive – metaphorically speaking.

"Where are you, my naughty boy?" Thomas dialled Constantin's number.

Unexpectedly he answered immediately. Quietly spoken he responded to her first question.

"Where *are* you? I've been waiting..."

He almost hissed his response. "I told you, there was something I had to do."

"Good, well, have you done it yet? And, how long will you be? I've got a bottle of Moet with our name on it and I'm wearing your favourite outfit..."

Thomas could hear the ambient noise but the man she was bizarrely attracted to failed to reply for a few seconds. His mind was otherwise engaged.

"Connie...what have you done...remember earlier, you said you were angry with someone? Have you hurt them? Come on darling, tell Lucy..."

Constantin was now the empty shell of a human being, stood in the poorly lit corner of a beautiful listed building, a doorway to a thousand stories and now his temporary refuge. What *had* happened to him? Had drugs deprived him of a life? And, if so was it so wrong to steal somebody else's?

He exhaled and spoke.

"Lucy, I cannot come to see you. I will send money but I must leave. I have killed people and now the police will kill me too. I do not...want you...to be near me anymore. I am hideous in many ways."

A moment of salvation and charity was entwined in a shroud of desperation.

"I am sorry."

She could hear him sobbing.

The skilled performer that she was Thomas allowed him to cry before asking a few more pertinent questions.

"Talk to me my love. I know you said you had been bad. Tell me where these people are. Tell me what you did. I would love to know all about it you very brave man."

Thomas used every trick in her extensive repertoire to extract a prompt response.

Valentin drained the last of the brandy from his favoured glass and lowered it onto the green leather-bound desk.

"Come on, where are you? Show yourself."

He strained his eyes onto the screen. Adjusting the brightness, trying to force the picture to improve.

And then for a brief moment he saw him again. A moment of clarity allowed the hunter to stare into the quarry's eyes. They looked as shallow as ever but more vivid, even within the monochromatic view that Valentin held they looked miserable. He was crying. Something had disturbed him into a state of emotion that was no longer just drug-fuelled. He was preparing for his next act.

Cade's phone vibrated in his pocket. It was a distant sensation, almost imperceptible, but he managed to engage his brain for long enough to open it and look wearily at the screen. What he saw caused him to exhale and let out an audible moan. It was Thomas. Too tired not to answer he pressed the green button.

"Put me on hands free Jack." He did.

"Is Jason there?"

"Hang on I'll go upstairs. Look, Lucy, this is not a good time. There has been an incident and I'm erm..."

"Jack, shut up and listen. Is Jason there yet?"

"Yes, go ahead," replied Roberts, using a vague form of sign language towards Cade, trying to establish what his most unconventional informant wanted.

"It's Constantin. He's told me everything. I'm scared guys. I think he's coming for you and then me. He talked about a boy being taken from him – I knew nothing about that – anyway...it doesn't matter. He blames you both. Look, the point is he's in town and I think he's near to wherever you are. I know about your girlfriend Jack. I'm sorry."

Roberts hurried her along. "Yep, we hear you Lucy but listen love we are in a serious state here. Carrie is dying, and your bloody boyfriend..."

"Client love, client."

"Whatever! He is guilty of a whole bloody pile of trouble Lucy and you need to do whatever it takes to help. Do that and I'll personally ensure you get a Get Out Of Jail card. If you don't I'll have you locked up for something within the hour."

Thomas could feel the alter ego slipping and was reverting to his natural self. Thomas' voice deepened and became more direct.

"Listen sunshine, if it wasn't for me, you and the rest of fucking Billy Smart's Circus would still be running all over town. He's nearby. Very nearby from what he has described and I don't think he's in a hurry to leave. He's got a gun too. And nothing to live for. Your call."

Both men knew she, or rather he was right.

"OK, this is what I need you to do." Roberts continued talking to her whilst Cade stood, impotent and empty, watching his girlfriend's life ebb away.

He turned to the medic once more, "Is there nothing you can do?"

"There would be if I knew what those chemicals were. Sounds like Fire are here. Let's give them some room. You do something useful and brief them whilst I maintain her airway. I've got a colleague on the way to help – we've been at breaking point Mr Cade. I'm sorry."

The first of the firefighters joined Cade who had found a new lease of life – again reverting to professional mode. He explained what had happened, what he had observed, what he had experienced. Roberts continued to talk to Thomas, explaining that when they gave the signal, he was to call back his number one client.

Thomas suddenly stopped Roberts in mid-sentence.

"Rewind, *rewind*!"

"What?"

"I heard Jack say something about a chemical, something about photography. Jason put me back on hands free now!"

He shouted so that everyone could hear him. The consummate performer, performing.

"It's cyanide! Constantin talked about taking a chemical to the flat to mix with something that your girlfriend had there already. He's mixed cyanide with hydro...look, that doesn't matter. Tell the fire crew to vent the place and get the paramedic to treat her for cyanide poisoning."

The paramedic looked at Cade and nodded, picking up his cell phone. The fire crew were already in the flat, inhaling forced, clean air via their breathing apparatus and ventilating the rooms whilst attempting to preserve the crime scene.

Cade interrupted the medic. "John, it says that on your overalls, so I'm guessing it's your name. I cannot express just how much this girl's life depends on your hard work, my prayers and her incredible fighting spirit. Now, we have a great chance to sort this out thanks to that person on the other phone, so tell me, John, why do I sense a lack of urgency on your part?"

"Mr Cade, I don't carry hydroxocobalamin, OK? I just don't have the space on board the bike. Most of the basic road ambulances don't either, it's such a specialised piece of kit – normally, we can get one of the other advanced crews here but they are flat out. You'll be aware of the incident running further north? And, you know a lot of the crews are on strike?"

It was a rhetorical question, designed to give him some breathing space.

"I am doing all I can to save your girlfriend's life. For now, I can keep her in a state of unconsciousness until we can get her to a hospital. Trust me on this?"

Thomas called out over the phone. "If the medic can't get hold of Cyanokit, then you need to listen to me – and listen very carefully because what I am about to say will make no sense at first, but you have to trust me more than you do John, Jason and yourself. Agreed."

"OK, go. Whatever you need to do."

"I need you to get a police patrol to head to a club on South Lambeth Road. It's called The Rack. The local cops will know where it is. When they get there ask for Master Toby. I will ring ahead, it's only minutes in a patrol car. Toby will hand a package to the officer – no questions asked, then meet the girl and the medics on the way to the hospital, she won't make it if you wait until you get there. Do this as fast as you can and your girl will probably live."

The paramedic spoke first.

"What's in this package?"

"Amyl nitrite."

It was Roberts now. "Lucy how the hell do you know about all this stuff?"

She laughed – a strangely relaxed moment given the circumstances. For a second he was a full-blown male again, the voice deeper once more and supremely confident.

"Do you think I've always been an overpriced feisty hooker Jason darling?"

Roberts offered no response.

"No, I thought not. I was a successful medical technician in the late nineties and dragged myself into the early part of 2000 as a trainee chemist."

"What went wrong?"

"Nothing, nothing at all. In fact, everything was very quickly on the up the moment I quit my job and walked into The Rack for the first time. Right, clear the line in case Constantin rings me. Let me know about your girl as soon as possible. Or else."

· · ·

Two patrol vehicles arrived, the first took Roberts south across the river as instructed. He had abandoned his own private car in the street, quietly hoping the business card in the windscreen would mean it wouldn't be towed by the morning.

The second car, an aging Rover 800 was parked half on the pavement, its strobe lights still flickering off the surrounding buildings. Its double-crewed team helped Cade and the paramedic manhandle O'Shea down the staircase as O'Shea's neighbour held the doors and then opened the rear door to the police vehicle.

With the patient on board and strapped in as best they could, the newly created team sped off with the medic following closely behind and talking to his own control room.

With the advantage of lights and sirens, Roberts soon found himself outside a faceless railway arch that contained the target address supplied by Thomas. As they pulled to a halt the younger of the two constables turned to Roberts.

"Jesus Skipper, you really going in there *alone*?"

Roberts was unsure what he meant and pulled an encouraging face.

"Seriously boss, that's one weird place and us being in uniform, well, not being funny and all that but we ain't going anywhere near the place."

Roberts had limited time so discounted what they were saying. But his instinct wanted quick answers.

"What the hell are you two muppets on about?"

The older of the two, Constable Sean Doyle replied in a Northern Irish accent that was sharp enough to slice bread, "Don't get us wrong here governor, we're not afraid, so we're not, it's just..."

"Just fucking what boys, I'm in a hurry?"

"You'll see, so you will."

The detective sergeant left the car, now unsure what fate lay before him. More concerned about his colleague's life than his own he made a rapid mental note to regale his wife with his stories of bravery, when and if he ever made it home.

Cade held onto O'Shea, her skin was grey and lifeless. Her hands were cold, clammy almost.

Worst of all she was unresponsive. His thought processes were hurried but now more rational than they had been in the flat. He knew he also needed primary medical care, but he was recovering faster than the woman, who was very recently described as his girlfriend.

His thoughts turned to the females in his recent life. And it was recent too. In a matter of a few months he had left his wife, started a new role, moved again, been shot at, spat at, bitten and abused. He had also immersed himself in one of the world's most exciting cities and met some incredible people, some incredulous people and if that wasn't sufficient, some quite simply bizarre members of the human race.

But notwithstanding the drama and excitement, he had also met an incredible woman. The perfect stranger. Compulsive at times, charming, flirtatious and possibly positively lethal, she may not have been everyman's fantasy, but she was Jack's.

His thoughts were interrupted for a moment.

The driver turned to Cade.

"Governor, we need to take a detour, there's an RTA on Westminster Bridge. We'll head south and meet the other team. It will all work out."

He nodded. Of course there was a car crash, why would there bloody well not be? Why not shut the hospital down with a fucking anthrax threat too and halt all the power supplies and cancel Tuesday whilst you are at it?

He turned to look at O'Shea as the orangey shadows of illuminated images from regularly spaced street lamps cascaded off the vehicle windows. Brightly lit shop windows beckoned. He was unable to focus on any of them, upon no one other than the lifeless female.

He loved her from the moment he first heard her, it genuinely did not matter what she looked like. Her voice had captivated him. She was livid, yelling at a manager, technically her superior, but only in rank.

The fact that she was above-average to look at helped. Her ability to place the jigsaw pieces into the puzzle was a professional advantage. That she was a vixen behind closed doors was a glorious plus point.

And now she was slumped against him, en route to hospital and possible deliverance, or on a journey to a better place. He loathed not being able to control the situation. Unable to talk he pulled her closer still and for the first time since he had been a child he prayed.

"Not much further boss. Hang in there. She'll be fine." The detached words of his colleague in the front passenger seat swirled around the patrol car cabin remaining unprocessed.

Her dreams were rich and colourful; a pity they were so intensely upsetting. Her skin pellucid, her eyes motionless, black. Ceaseless, prevailing low-pitched noises haunted her every footstep, petrifying her as she walked through a derelict building; alone.

Opening a door with a translucent hand she saw a hospital bed and equipment, tarnished but arranged in such a way it appeared to be waiting for her. She allowed the door to swing back into place, her senses were so alive she could smell Ether, taste blood and hear moans and distant screams.

She tried to pick up a note, seemingly left on an adjacent medicine trolley, however the message passed physically through her skin, bypassing her ivory-coloured bones, crushing miniscule blood vessels and allowing them to bleed into the surrounding air.

The note fluttered to the floor, face down. She tried again and again to pick it up, conscious that it contained something of great importance. Hour after hour she stood there using every possible means to turn the page over.

Footsteps. Somebody was approaching.

A nurse, in her fifties, greying blond hair tied neatly into a bun and looking immaculate in a dark blue uniform strode down the corridor towards O'Shea who froze, desperate to avoid being seen. This was a dream, right?

The nurse walked slowly past her, looking straight into her face, her equally lifeless eyes staring back. Had she seen her? She could feel her breath on her face, it was cold and smelt of decay. She walked to the note, bent over, picked it up and looked at it. Then she smiled, folded the note precisely in half and placed it back on the trolley.

As she walked away, she created a cool draught. O'Shea shuddered and began to cry, her name was visible on the foot of the document. The date and time alongside the location and cause of death were now very evident, each letter shrinking on the page until they were gone.

In the patrol vehicle, Cade felt her body jolt. And again. She exhaled deeply. And then she was still.

CHAPTER SEVENTEEN

Cade knew they could not afford to detour towards Roberts – this was a case, if ever there was one – of now, or never.

"Boys do whatever you need to do, break the bloody law if you have to. You have my permission."

Roberts' police ID had stayed firmly in his pocket as he breached the doorway of the club. Feeling inappropriately dominant he almost brushed the leather-clad doorman to one side.

"Detective Sergeant Jason Roberts to see..." he paused awkwardly "...Master Toby."

It was a simple, swift instruction in a place that at any other time would be just too surreal. He couldn't do it any other way. He needed to be strong.

The doorman was immense but appeared to have a softer, submissive side – he stepped backwards and beckoned with his left hand to a side door.

"The Master awaits."

Roberts, despite his external body language was genuinely afraid he would never leave the building again. He felt young, inexperienced and yes, for the record, attractively vulnerable. He thanked a God somewhere that he wasn't in uniform.

Cade owed him a debt of gratitude. However, now was not the time to cash it in.

A white male in his fifties with suspiciously black hair stood up from behind a large white desk. Had he have been positioned anywhere in the business district of the City of London he would have been taken for a stockbroker, a merchant banker or a solicitor.

He wore Armani was well as any man; classic navy with a subtle pinstripe, white shirt, blue tie, white handkerchief, Cartier watch. His hands were immaculately groomed, nails trimmed to perfection.

Through nephrite-green eyes he considered the man before him.

Slim, attractive and self-assured. He cared not for his dress-sense but he admired his audacity – walking into his domain without a conventional reason – his introduction had been enough.

He held out a tanned hand, upon which jet-black hairs bristled, an indication of his hirsuteness.

His grip was intense and surprised Roberts.

"Jason Roberts. I'll cut to the chase sir, you have something for me which I need now."

"Charmed I'm sure. Mallory St John at your service. It is pronounced Sinjun. Your driving licence, please?" He held out an impeccably clipped hand.

"What?"

"I made myself quite clear, Sergeant." Dominant.

Roberts, sensing a battle lost, handed over his licence. Submissive.

"I'll be back for that."

"I'm counting on it my dear officer." His eyes shone as he revealed a perfectly white and straight set of teeth and as it ran over them he also saw a silver stud in his serpent-like tongue.

"Take this, send my love to Lucy and do let me know about that poor girl. Now go, hurry along and decamp, as you boys in blue often say."

He ushered him away with his exquisitely manicured hand.

Roberts took the package and turned upon his heels, not wishing to look back, but ever-mindful that he had just handed over a key item of identity to a man clearly more adept at being in control than he was. He waved his own goodbye, trying to be dismissive but only managing to look outrageously camp.

The irony that he had travelled to the venue from Old Queen Street was far from lost on him.

Mallory St John sat back down, leant back in his walnut-leather chair at precisely thirty-two degrees and placed his feet up on the table.

He took a moment to admire the monochrome, size ten high heels before rubbing his hands together in anticipation.

A male employee entered the office. He was white, slender and outwardly submissive. His almost hairless body was criss-crossed with leather straps and shiny steel buckles. Despite being an employee he actually paid a weekly sum for the privilege of working for St John. By day he conducted himself as a senior manager in a blue chip organisation, but as the sun dipped below the horizon, he became Mallory St John's personal plaything.

The Master selected a ball from the desk drawer and threw it across the office.

"Fetch."

The male did as he was told, allowing St John to contemplate the attractive young police officer once more. He smiled, gently picked a piece of food from his teeth, examined it and allowed it to drop to the floor.

"Oh yes. I'm absolutely counting on it officer."

Back in the Rover, Roberts was immediately onto his phone.

"Jack, it's me, I'll be with you..." he paused, working out approximately where their journeys would bisect, "...in three minutes. Are you aware there's a crash outside St Thomas' Hospital? Ambulance versus van. Chaos. The lads here say divert to Guys. We are coming up behind you now."

Roberts was using the classic international police timescale. 'Now' was often designed to make the officer requiring immediate back-up feel more secure, when, in actual fact 'now' meant at least three or four minutes.

Cade yelled at his driver. "You said the crash was on the bridge, it's outside the hospital. We need to divert to Guys. Get to Guys, but when you see the other unit, stop. Just do it, please."

As Cade had finished the sentence the driver looked in his rear-view mirror and saw his colleagues approaching at Warp Factor Five. He slowed and then having conversed on the force radio, pulled over in the middle of the road. They were joined by the paramedic.

Roberts leapt out of the car, handed the ampoule to the medic and opened the rear door of the patrol car containing the patient.

Cade nodded at his partner. He was unable to do more.

"Out of the way, please." It was the medic, hypodermic in hand. He pulled the dressing gown to one side, dabbed the skin with an antiseptic wipe and stopped.

"Sir, do I have your permission to do this? What I am about to do goes against everything I stand for and have trained to deal with. I do not actually know what is in this bottle. Therefore, we should wait."

It was the first time that the notion had entered Cade's head. Damned if he did.

"Do it."

The surgically sharp tip of the needle entered her cold skin and allowed the liquid to enter her body.

Cade now prayed out loud.

"Right, go, get her to Guys. I will go ahead and brief the Casualty Team." John Parker got back onto his BMW lowered his visor and accelerated north east. The convoy followed.

Roberts' phone rang.

"It's me. He's still near the girl's house. How is she? How was Toby? How are you?"

"Too many questions Lucy. Carrie is not good, not good at all. And by the way Toby is called Mallory and took my bloody driving licence off me in lieu of the drugs and I am royally pissed off, truth be told. But thank you. If she survives, which is touch and go, then I owe you."

"Call it honours even Jason, you know, for when we first met. Oh, and by the way."

"Go on."

"You didn't have to hand your licence over! You obviously wanted to go back you naughty man. He does it to everyone. That's why he is the Master and you..."

"Lucy, Dave or whatever your bloody name is, if you call me a slave, just once, I'll kick your back door in!"

"Ooh promises, promises you wicked man. Let me know how the girl is. Now go, be brave my liege. The city needs you."

Roberts offered an expletive but Thomas had already gone.

Cade walked with the medical team as they examined O'Shea en route from the patrol car.

"Mr Cade, you say you think this is cyanide? There are no obvious signs with such poisoning so we have to be careful. Has she had any other medication? Anything at all?"

Cade paused, looked at the paramedic and knew he had to fall upon his own sword.

"She's been injected with an ampoule of amil nitrite. In lieu of a Cyanokit. There was chaos with the crash at St Thomas' – it was the best we could do."

"Your idea? Did you administer it?" The voice of the Canadian doctor was neither accusatory nor supportive as his head turned from Cade to the Paramedic.

Cade did not hesitate. "My idea – yes, on both counts."

"Then you may have saved this ladi's life, Inspector. Well done. Inspired." He checked O'Shea's shallow heart rate and started to instruct his team.

He looked at his junior colleague.

"OK, shall we do this?"

It was a rhetorical question but one designed to set the medical wheels in motion.

Doctor Anthony Hay, a native of Vancouver and in London for 'the ride' started to orate as he worked. It was for everyone's benefit, including his own.

"OK people. In patients with acute poisoning from hydrogen cyanide gas the principle acute care concerns are what?"

A wide-eyed and enthusiastic Korean female answered immediately.

"Hemodynamic instability and cerebral edema?"

"Good. Very good."

Cade knew this was how senior doctors worked with house officers, but he wanted them to stop discussing her as if she were a lecture topic and concentrate on providing some positive news. He knew enough about medicine to second guess much of what they were discussing. It sounded far from positive.

Hay continued, "Now, this normally healthy lady is rather unwell, once we stabilise her and add to her existing drugs...she may improve; however team, a couple of key points please?"

He looked around the room, his facial expression soliciting an answer.

"Continuous cardiac monitoring?" offered a freckle-faced male.

"Excellent."

"Respiratory and cardiovascular support?" offered the Korean doctor.

"Spot on – and I want to see frequent neurological evaluations too." He then looked at the staff nurse.

"Let's keep oxygenation at optimum levels please and monitor her cardiac stats. I'm not one hundred percent happy with her oxygen levels so I may intubate her, get some more of that lovely stuff into her lungs, give her the fighting edge. For now, let's look at serum lactates, chemistry and arterial and venous gases please Vicky. Thank you."

He turned towards Cade.

"Your partner will stay with us until her signs improve and I can be assured that she is on the mend."

Hay was about to walk away when he stopped to talk to Cade. He beckoned for the group to continue onto the next patient.

"Tony Hay."

"Jack Cade. Carrie's...boss. Partner. Confidante. Jesus, what a week."

He took a moment.

"Hey Jack, good to meet you. You can call me Tony. I only reserve the Redeemer for when I perform true miracles. Look, I think I can be blunt with you? Miss O'Shea is critically ill. She may not survive. Does she have family? If so, you should start to notify them."

Cade took a moment and soon realised that he had never discussed family members with her. Not once. And vice versa. He would instruct Roberts to do this. It seemed appropriate.

"Jack, the problem with cyanogens is that poisoning symptoms sometimes don't manifest, or importantly, become truly life threatening for many hours after exposure. We will be watching her like a hawk. You are welcome to stay day and night, or I can ring you if anything transpires. If all goes to plan we will need to re-evaluate her for the next seven to ten days. This wasn't self-inflicted was it?"

Cade's look provided the answer that Hay needed.

"You might want to be here or you might want to use your obvious..." He hunted for a suitable word... "Passion, to go and hunt down the Neanderthal that did this. My carefully chosen personal words of course, not the opinion of the British National Health Service you understand?"

Cade nodded wearily and looked at O'Shea. He had seen her in various stages of vulnerability, both on and off duty, but he had never seen her like this. Alive, but somewhere approaching death. A number of machines continued to monitor her vital signs and Cade could do no more than gently hold her hand. He was torn. Stay, holding her hand, waiting for one of two things to occur or leave her and track down the bastard responsible.

"How long Tony?"

"In that state?"

"Yes."

"Unassisted? Twenty-four hours at best. Hooked up to that gear? Weeks. If she's going to survive we'll know within two days."

He subconsciously looked at his wristwatch, a battered and much-loved graphite Zietner Chronograph that once belonged to his father.

Cade was also a man working against the clock and shook Hay's hand, allowing him to leave without the need for another word. They were both men on a mission, albeit entirely different.

He nodded at the two uniformed staff who had arrived to provide an increased level of protection to O'Shea. Both were armed and planning to spend the night at the hospital.

Cade beckoned for their car keys as his cell chirped into life.

"Cade."

"Jack, John Daniel. I've been briefed. I've elevated this to the next level. We are getting some buy-in. Jason and the team are out and about looking for the offender and uniform and ARVs are swamping the area. CID are talking to their sources. We'll get him Jack. Jack?"

Cade had abrogated himself of responsibility, leaving her bedside and now walking at a fast pace, a man with a plan.

He got into the Ford Mondeo and turned the key hoping his mind could unravel exactly what the plan was.

"Sorry JD, I've left Carrie at Guys. I need to get back to the scene. I'm useless here."

"I disagree, you should stay. I'm heading in to work, let me know if I can do anything..."

Daniel was the iceberg; the tip, the middle and the bottom, the archetypal mentor. He knew what to say and when, but Cade had already hung up and was now accelerating towards O'Shea's flat.

Roberts was back in Old Queen Street area, with Dave Williams and Detective Constable Chris White the newly arrived replacement for Clive Wood. He was gathering evidence at a fast pace but knew that there was no way his team would or should deal with the file. As soon as the local staff arrived he would hand over, removing himself from the chain of evidence.

"Right boys, here's the plan. We throw a net over the local area. Jack reckons our man is still somewhere nearby although God only knows why he would be unless he's like one of those weird fire starters. We get uniform to patrol the wider area – where possible a few on foot would be good, then we hunt him down and nail the bastard to the cross. Any questions?"

Cade was inbound to Old Queen Street when his phone started to vibrate once again.

Private number.

"Cade."

"Valentin."

"Go ahead."

"You are hunting a wounded animal Jack. I don't think he will give up easily. I wish I could be more useful but for now I am tracking everywhere. Your own people need to search the camera systems, talk to their informants, think like hunters, there is no time for kindness. I believe he will kill again. He has crossed the final boundary. He has nothing to lose."

"Valentin, do me a huge favour?"

"Of course."

"When this is all over, reveal yourself, I will offer you as much protection from prosecution as I can, but worst case can we meet, anywhere in the world, somewhere you consider safe? I just want to shake your hand. I am in your debt, and that is not something they teach us to admit at training school."

"It is entirely possible that we will meet. One day Jack, one day, until then I will help how and where I can. For now you need to know that this team is bigger than Constantin. They are still operating all over the south of England and their numbers are growing and they are operating right under your feet – their plan is to head north soon. One unit has committed three hundred offences against one of the largest banks by aiming at their cash point machines. Three. Hundred. Where they are not gaining actual cash they are obtaining data, and in the right hands that is just as valuable. I will leave you to work out the numbers Jack but it is fair to say somebody, somewhere is smiling. And that person most likely calls himself Jackdaw."

In the preceding weeks Cade had heard that bastard's name on many occasions but had intentionally decided not to dwell on who or what he was. Once he worked out the where then he could seek some wider assistance from his international colleagues and perhaps his new-found and unanticipated friend.

"Thank you Valentin. For now, I have three priorities; Carrie, your friend Constantin and somehow I need to influence my leaders to put some greater emphasis on locking up these bank offenders. As you say at a hundred thousand pounds a team they are making somebody a very rich man. But he will wait for now, his day will come, and when it does, I want to be the one who wraps my hands around his throat like a Scotsman caresses a caber..."

"Positive words my friend but I suspect you will remain frustrated, he is evading bigger fish than you Jack. Right now he is laughing at the European authorities more than I am, and I have...as you would say, the sense of humour too."

Cade paused. "OK, Valentin I need your help and I will get you the rewards – I suspect that for you this does not mean financial. Help us find Constantin and then do your best to direct us towards the offending teams that are hitting the banks; I can get more staff directed at that operation. Then tomorrow, perhaps another time in the future we can both track and capture your Jackdaw."

"Of course, but for now I must continue to gain his trust. He is not an enemy of mine. Albeit I do not like him. I will ring him. Do not forget, Constantin, he is somewhere near you – he too hides in the shadows, he is your priority."

Cade looked at his phone and wondered out loud when the sun might add some light to these bloody shadows that everyone seemed to excel in hiding amongst.

The screen was empty, the caller's private number message now gone. He sighed, steepled his fingers to his lips and blew through them as he attempted to gather his thoughts.

He was back at Old Queen Street. The flat was taped off

with a local team on site, a Scenes of Crime Officer was examining every surface that might hold a fingerprint. A cheap-suited detective sergeant was pointing out evidence and directing junior staff. For all intents it resembled the hypothetical scene from a televised crime drama, just requiring a distant voice to shout 'cut!' and bring everyone back to a sense of normality.

Cade was met by Roberts.

"Jack, what the Jesus and Mary are you doing back here? What about Carrie? Jack?"

"I've had this from JD mate. Just realise I need to do something. I can't sit in there and stare at her lifeless body for another second. Her skin was grey. No amount of frenzied hand rubbing and compassionate words are going to bring her around Jason. We both know that. So let's focus on the here and now shall we?"

Roberts sensed the futility of arguing the point and suggested they double up to search for their target.

"Let's not forget this bastard might still be armed," Cade offered to anyone that might listen. "Any doubt. Any whatsoever and we wait for armed back up, do I make myself clear? We've done enough damage for one night. Right, pair up and let's throw that net over this noble city shall we?"

Cade's team were joined by a sergeant and four constables, a local dog unit and the promise of air support. More staff were on the way. Roberts' team of detectives were already mobilised, combining old-fashioned policing with its more modern brother – CCTV. It was everywhere, but you needed to know how to interrogate it and these officers were expert at it.

"You can drive Jason. Valentin stated that he believes our man is somewhere nearby so we work in eccentric circles. I suggest we let the uniform boys and girls patrol and we park up and watch and listen. Sooner or later he's got to break cover. And when he does the might of my adopted police force will pounce on the bastard. I so hope he puts up a fight."

Constantin had been still for an hour. He was in agony. His feet ached, his body throbbed, his headache was pulverising his ability to think. The heroin hit had long worn off. He needed more, but he knew that to break cover whilst the police activity was so dynamic was tantamount to surrender.

They were everywhere. Look at them, they hadn't got a clue, not even their dog could find him. And Cade and his sidekick boyfriend? They were pathetic. He could have outwitted them when he was just a boy back in Craiova, back in the motherland, back home.

"When I escape from you tonight, it will be the start of my retaliation. My chance to look you both in the eye and smile as I drive the knife through your heart. Your girlfriend is already dead, and that was all my pleasure. I will kill you both in a different way. Yes. Different. More violent." His conversations were becoming more animated by the second.

"The girl? I put her to sleep. You? I will make sure you never sleep again."

He became aware he was talking to himself once more. Scratching his itching limbs, his body involuntarily jolting.

"Go. No, stay." His senses were heightened allowing him to see and hear with greater clarity.

"Go."

Cade was sat with Roberts. They were sharing a bar of chocolate. The sugar hit was desperately needed by Cade who had realised he hadn't eaten – at all, since, actually he couldn't recall but it had been a lengthy amount of time.

"Jas we need to focus on this group. Constantin is one man, and he is manipulating our numbers, we have to remember that there is a bigger group out there, stripping ATMs bare as we speak. We need JD to push this issue up the food chain."

The issue of food was also making Roberts intensely hungry.

"McDonald's, Jack?"

"Seriously? You think I'm in the mood for a bloody Happy Meal, Jason?"

Roberts looked hurt.

"No, I just thought you might be hungry. Just a gesture of human kindness."

Cade realised his response was unfair, they were all tired.

"Is there one nearby?"

"There is."

"Then I'll pay. I hear that the toy is a Buzz Lightyear this week."

"Twat."

"You started it!"

For the first time in weeks they laughed, the adrenaline was abating and for a change serotonin flooded their inner selves. Roberts drove along Victoria Street and parked directly outside the iconic fast-food outlet. Anyone who had a problem with them doing so could take it up with the Commissioner.

Roberts clipped his personal radio to his belt, activated the vehicle remote and walked into the always-busy restaurant and straight to the front of the queue.

"Big Mac please my love. No, make that a McBean burger combo and my friend here would like the Buzz

Lightyear Happy Meal with extra large fries, a dozen chicken nuggets and a McDonald's cola. Thank you."

Cade was in no mood to argue.

"McBean?"

"Oh yes, I forgot to tell you, from this day I have become a vegetarian. No meat shall pass these lips ever again."

"Why?"

"Why not? Have you chewed any ears other than mine lately? No? Well I have and even the thought makes me heave"

Again, he did not have the energy to argue.

By the time they had discussed Roberts' new health regime their food was on the counter. Roberts attempted to pay for it but was recognised by the manager.

"This one's on me Jason, even the Buzz Lightyear – you boys looked absolutely knackered!"

They began to walk out of the store when Cade saw a young boy enter with his mother. His whiter-than-white eyes stood out from his conker-brown skin as he recognised the toy being offered to him.

"There you go young man. My friend here has Buzz already. He was hoping for a Woody tonight as he hasn't had one for a very long time." Cade patted him on the head and walked to the car sinking his teeth into the quintessential chicken.

"I hate you Jason."

Getting into the driver's seat Roberts laughed and offered him some of his vegetarian meal.

"I'd rather sleep with Lucy Thomas."

"Noted boss. I'll arrange it – she loves fresh meat."

· · ·

Constantin decided he could wait no longer. He had to leave the area. He could almost smell the dogs closing in. He knew if he climbed up the building he might evade them. But that took strength and it was something he was lacking. He exited as nonchalantly as he could from the gated area of the stone-balustrade walls and began to walk towards Great George Street.

He turned right, desperately trying not to look behind him, head down in a city of head-down people, not really knowing where to go. He had seen a tube station on his travels. He would go there. Safely on board he would allow the train to take him away from the hunters and then ring Gheorghiu. As much as he hated him, Artur Gheorghiu was the only ally he had in a city that was crawling with adversaries.

And once he got close to him, he could wipe the smile of his face too.

Cade was contemplating his nuggets when the radio announced its presence.

It was a breathless section constable trying his best to run and provide a commentary.

"Parliament Square Gardens towards the river..."

Cade threw the fast food out of the passenger window.

"Go Jason, go! It's got to be our man."

Roberts was already accelerating along Victoria Street whipping in and out of traffic, sirens on, strobe lights rebounding from vehicles and buildings alike.

The radio had come to life as it always did during a chase. Everyone, everywhere, wanted a piece of the action. The Comms operator struggled to maintain control as uniformed and non-uniformed staff jostled for airtime. The local dog handler was also trying to attain air supremacy. The problem for him being that with the amount of foot traffic still present on the streets he could never freely deploy his jet-black German Shepherd Zeus.

"Through the gardens, still towards Big Ben. Male...short hair, dark clothes...small backpack."

The officer was almost gasping. He was, always, at a disadvantage. The hunter tracking the hunted but carrying twice as much weight and up against a prey that was drowning in adrenaline.

"Over Parliament towards Westminster."

The Comms Operator repeated the directions for all to hear. Waving to the duty inspector with one hand and typing with another.

Staff were focusing upon the area, moving in from areas across the region. Two ARV teams were also en route.

Cade and Roberts were now on the hunt as well. Most of the pursuers wanted the arrest, the 'collar', for the two more senior men it was a very personal matter of putting the animal back into its cage.

"Stand by, into foot traffic, tour group, heading to the Houses of Parliament."

"Do not lose him!" It was Cade, talking to no one in particular but to everyone involved.

It was easy to forget that regardless of the time of day this was one of the busiest cities on the planet. There was always someone, going somewhere.

As Roberts pulled onto The Queen's Walk he could see the problem. People.

People going about their business, people going to and from their businesses, and tourists. Hundreds of tourists. Did they not have hotels to go to?

Constantin was exhausted, but he knew that to stop now

was to give in. He needed to walk, not run, to blend in. They wanted him for at least one murder, possibly two. And then there was the girl. And the banks. With a well-funded lawyer he might even be acquitted. His mind was trying to process too many things at once.

And the gun. There was the issue of the old handgun. He could feel it near to his ribs, tucked up inside his jacket pocket. The same one he had used to kill Gabor.

He chose to retain it. He knew he could not take on such a well-equipped enemy, even a cowardly one like the British with their rules. As soon as possible he should discard the weapon. But where? A bin?

There were no bins, a legacy of historical anti-terrorism measures which saw the streets of London largely stripped of such facilities. He had to remove himself from the chase and dispose of as much evidence as his fatigued mind would allow him to. As he half-ran, half-walked he saw the opportunity. There, opposite one of the city's most recognisable landmarks was his escape route. He could hear footsteps, running, at a faster pace than those of the tourists that provided him with basic cover. They were closing in now.

The wolf into the bear trap.

CHAPTER EIGHTEEN

His lungs hurt more than his head, his legs were leaden but still providing forward momentum. He needed to stop. He had to stop. Just give up.

He didn't have enough energy left to run another step but worse still he knew he couldn't afford to spend another day in prison. This time it would be the death of him.

He thought of firing the gun into the air. It would provide a distraction in a city already on edge. But he knew it would draw immediate attention to his presence and he would become a target.

He had seen how they had gunned down his innocent friends.

He carried on, shuffling through the crowd, but strangely, part of it. No one raised an eyebrow at the sight of the broken, manic individual that he had become. No one cared where he was heading, as long as he was heading the same way and didn't impede upon their own self-satisfied journeys he would be ignored.

Fifty metres ahead he saw a cleaner pushing a trolley

upon which was attached a large rubbish sack. As he approached, he withdrew the weapon.

Streets away a camera operator was watching the live feed from the Westminster underground station. An hour into his shift he was still vigilant. He had waited a year to be a part of something different to the day-to-day hustle and bustle of commuter-based chaos. Something other than lost children, pickpockets, prostitutes and passengers seeking to obtain another free ride.

And there it was.

"A man with a gun..."

No one heard him at first. He wasn't entirely sure if he had said it aloud but he said it again and this time he attracted attention.

"He's got a gun. The guy there, near to the barrier, to the left." He was pointing animatedly at the screen, his right index finger pushing into the soft coating and forcing the image to distort.

His duty manager appeared on a high-backed typist chair, rolling himself across the office floor at high speed.

"Move! And if this is another passenger with a cell phone I will personally march you out of the building and kick your arse with my size tens."

But he was right. Immediately in front of them, tangible, apparent and two-dimensional was a male who stood out from the crowd for one reason. In his left hand was a firearm, an older-looking pistol, but a firearm nonetheless.

Constantin had no real desire to shoot. He'd killed already. His exhausted mind concluded that a neutral onlooker might even forgive him for another one, or two deaths. Honestly, what difference would it really make? For a brief moment, he felt that he could genuinely be acquitted of the second murder, he might say it was a simple case of self-defence and that he somehow feared for his own life, at the hands of a person a good defence lawyer would later say was evil, goal-driven and the true architect of the operation.

'Do not be fooled by the young man. He was a brilliant tactician, wise beyond his years. Do you really think a washed-up heroin addict like my client could be so cunning – as to kill a harmless old man?'

He could hear his defence lawyer now, skilfully swaying the jury, convincing them that his client would have committed only a crime of self-defence, of *passion*. He would argue that he would have only ever killed for the chance to possess a sound mind.

'There were no witnesses to the passing of the old man. He lived alone, and he died alone. It was an accident. You must see that this could have happened to anyone, at any time...'

Internal monologues aside he knew that if he started shooting innocent members of the public in a crowded train station, he would be labelled a psychopath, a cold-hearted killer – a terrorist – in a fragile nation, perched precariously on the edge of its collective seat, poised at the highest security threat level in years.

His mind spun; between creating a loud and defiant distraction and disposing of the weapon, it spun and twisted and replayed over and over. The rational partition of his brain told him to drop the gun into the trolley, to ignore the looping footage in his mind.

Another robotic and spontaneous feature of his past saw his left hand slipping into the jacket pocket of the male immediately in front of him. It was the unemotional aspect of the transaction that made it imperceptible to the victim who was oblivious to his gossamer touch.

Caring but in an uncaring world the victim strode on

towards the turnstiles, desperate to get home. Resorting to muscle memory his right hand moved into the unzipped pocket where for a moment he swore his wallet had been. It had gone. But hang on, where? He had only used it minutes before. He searched once again tapping outer pockets, searching inside each, again, and again.

In a heartbeat it had vanished. In another he realised how.

He saw police officers, more than usual, but that was London for you. Picking one from the crowd he called out.

"Excuse me!"

It was the last thing the young officer needed. Couldn't this irritant see he was on the hunt?

Without being so unprofessional as to push the victim out of the way the constable suggested, rather forcibly, that the male should report the matter to his nearest station and that for now, 'sir, things were a little busy with something more important'.

If he had taken just a moment to talk to the victim, he may have learned something that later would save countless hours.

"But I have been robbed."

"It's not a robbery – just simple theft sir, probably kids. Seriously, report it to your home station and let the banks know, the thieves are probably in the process of handing out your bank cards as we speak…I had my credit card stolen last month. I didn't report it as the thief was spending less than my wife…"

The victim raised his hands in the air and shouted at the rapidly vanishing officer.

"You think that's funny? Really? I hope… I hope you get chlamydia!" Exasperated he pushed his way back through the crowds.

Two suited males came towards him at a pace. He sensed that they were also police officers but thought better of stopping the blue-eyed one. He looked as if he wanted to kill someone.

"Yeah, don't mind me. I'm just the bloody victim!" The male called out to Cade who brushed him aside but then stopped in his tracks.

He beckoned to the male.

"Come here – please."

"Oh, a member of the judiciary with some manners at last." Either that or he was about to cause him some immediate physical harm.

"Sir, I am beyond busy right at this moment. Do you want my help – or not?"

The male, sensing an opportunity to tell his tale of woe side-stepped the crowds and regaled Cade with his story.

Constantin examined the contents of the wallet on the move. His street craft had not eluded him, despite his shattered mental state. A rapid search of the contents revealed enough items to get him away from the area and, as he felt intensely hungry for the first time in days, if luck was on his side there may just be enough cash to buy a meal.

He swiped the Oyster card over the turnstile and was quickly heading deeper into the station, down the escalators and towards the trains. He could hear them approaching and felt the rush of air as they arrived and departed into the crowded platforms.

Above ground officers pushed their way into the station, trying their best to be as discreet as possible, aware that their own panic could instil a stampede of sorts. Uniformed police staff familiar with the building made their way to common areas, looking for a male roughly fitting the ambiguous description passed to them by their colleague.

The London Transport control room finally got the message across to their police peers who were having signal problems with their recently issued radios. It had been an ongoing problem with the various police forces based in the capital, who despite working incredibly close to one another could rarely communicate on a reliable network. Heading underground only exacerbated things.

"Yes, a male, by my guess European, in his forties, he had a handgun. In his left hand. My team member saw it clearly. We have back-tracked on the footage and we also think he took someone's wallet. He used the card to get through the turnstile."

The message was relayed to those staff present in the station. Some had remained on the street, hoping their target would exit, like a fox revealing his presence from a wooded copse, craftily evading the hounds.

Others continued to search toilets whilst a few more, their numbers now growing, moved down the escalators and onto the platforms.

A black-haired sergeant approached Roberts seeing his tell-tale radio in his left hand.

"Alright gents? No sign of the bastard. He's long gone."

"Yes, and with some poor bugger's wallet. Stand by a second."

Roberts held the radio to his face and broadcast some new information.

"All units Westminster Station. The suspect male is called Constantin. He is possibly in possession of a handgun and a wallet with contents in the name of John Kelly. All staff to avoid direct contact, sightings only, repeat sightings only."

On the street another ARV team arrived, checked their weapons and made their way through the crowds towards the platforms.

"Where are his team Jason? This bastard is not operating alone. It's not how they work."

"Offshore? Creaming the profits off the top whilst the minions take all the risks?"

"Possibly. Probably, but a city this size allows people to operate right under our bloody noses. Constantin's boss is in town. I've got one of my strange feelings."

He shuddered.

In a warm hospital bed a stone's throw away O'Shea's inert body also twitched involuntarily. Her cruel reveries had returned. Her mind was the only part of her that had remained active. The images that flashed into her dreams were coherent, filled with washed-out colours, and sounds. She could see herself, but she was unaware whether she was alive or dead. The images that surrounded her made her wish for the latter.

A mile away, sitting in a corner of the American Bar, an iconic part of the equally lavish and sought-after Stafford Hotel a muscular blond-haired male leant back in a red upholstered armchair, steepled his hands and spoke with a confidence born out of success.

"Go upstairs, or go out and buy something. You are annoying me. You know where the money is. I have business to discuss. Can you not see this? Go on, go before I have to consider something unpleasant to do to you."

He held her slender hips in both hands and pulled her towards him. She bent down and kissed him, leaving scarlet lipstick on his left and right cheeks.

As she made to stand up, he pulled her back down onto his knee, allowing her all-too-short skirt to ride up. He slipped his hand beneath her cream silk blouse, running his fingertips beneath the ivory-coloured bra and over her breast.

His male business partner feigned looking away.

"That feels nice?"

The girl giggled and pulled away but he was stronger.

"I asked you a question."

She cleared her throat and replied.

"Yes, it feel nice. I like it. Now, I go – and buy a new dress and underwear. For you. For you Stefan."

He smiled, it was the smile of a man surrounded by the trappings of his illicit gains. The stuffy, classically dressed, pinstriped males scattered around the bar despised his sort. New money. Russian, probably. Yes, Russian.

'Look at him with his beautiful girl and his endless supply of cash. His sort has no place here.'

But they came and their numbers were growing.

To make matters worse to the pinstriped voyeurs, the male appeared to be held in high regard by the staff – either that or they feared him. The stockbrokers could only assume.

Stefan Stefanescu summoned the immaculate bar manager to his table.

The Frenchman had been a part of the fabric of The Stafford since the late nineties. He had replaced the much-loved Charles, an equally iconic part of the hotel's history who had served business people and celebrities alike for over forty years.

The Frenchman longed to continue the work of his adored predecessor and also hoped to stay, at least for a while. Always elegantly attired, he wore a blue suit, white shirt, a waistcoat and navy blue tie, matched with a handkerchief, folded, just so.

He too loathed the blond, but he knew that his money was as good, if not more plentiful than anyone else's. He noted that his money was tangible, unlike many of the bankers who became richer each day but never appeared to have cold, dirty cash in their possession. Nevertheless, he always turned down their tips, generous and tax-evading though they were.

"Bonjour Monsieur Stefanescu. How nice of you to join us." Measured, professional but tainted with an underlying distaste.

"Yes. Isn't it?" He laughed, causing the male to his right to join him. It was false and everyone present in the exclusive bar could see how he had forced the response. He was either very shallow, astute or lived in fear.

"I trust you are well my friend?"

"I am, sir. Very. Thank you. Now, how may I help you today?" replied the Frenchman.

He was engaged in a conversation that to a casual onlooker might indicate that the two males knew one another. Nothing could be further from the truth, for neither had ever met. But the man, originally from Lyon had carried out some basic research and as with all of his more interesting patrons he knew enough to avoid conflict.

"Well, I am delighted to hear that. And you will be delighted to learn that business is good my friend, very good actually, I have an obscene amount of money burning a hole in my wallet. So I require you to make a recommendation between..." He glanced at the wine list before tapping onto a particular line and then another, "...this one, or this one."

The Frenchman knew that the Romanian gentleman was far from well-bred, but he was not ill-educated and above all, in his defence he appeared to have taste, and was clearly able to make a discerning choice himself without any guidance. But, it was a game of cat and mouse designed to impress those that observed him. Stefanescu knew that the cellars beneath the hotel were built in the 12th Century, their walls had eavesdropped upon many tales and held within their white-painted brick walls the confidences of Lords, and Ladies and the desperate and vital secrets of Kings and Queens.

So stout were the cellars that they had withstood not just the test of time but also the onslaught of the Luftwaffe during the Second World War, who despite their targeted and persistent bombing had been unable to destroy the collection of around eight thousand bottles of the finest wine.

The Frenchman cherished the chilled rooms and their climatically controlled contents, but loathed equally the fact that this bleached, muscular male before him would dare to even ask for his advice, let alone be in a position to afford to have a choice.

Nevertheless, he smiled and nodded downwards and to his left and quietly pressed his hands together before continuing.

"Very wise and considered choices, sir. Of the two, as you are not dining and simply want to enjoy the flavour then of course I must recommend the Bordeaux. The Chateau Petrus 1994 comes from a very fine vineyard Mr Stefanescu. Even during the rainy periods between ninety-two and ninety-three they managed to produce some rather splendid wines. However the Ninety Four is my choice. You have selected very well. May I return shortly with a bottle?"

Stefanescu nodded condescendingly.

The Frenchman returned briskly, he would never run in front of a customer, regardless of their wealth and power. He expertly slid the cork from the neck and decanted some of the contents into an overly large red wine glass.

"As you will see it is brilliantly opaque, a dark purple, perhaps almost black in colour. You will immediately taste vanilla, and cherry. If you dwell a little longer, you will detect a hint of cassis as layer after layer reveals itself. This has been cellared for ten years now sir and in my opinion is as close to perfect as..."

The blond held up his hand, and allowed each finger to drop back into his palm before he formed a fist, then slowly opened the fingers again, back into a palm. It achieved nothing but reminded the waiter, for that is all he considered him to be, exactly who was in control.

"You have stopped talking? Good. Then pour two glasses and leave the bottle."

"Of course sir. It would be my pleasure. Should I add it to your account?"

It was a purposefully rude question.

"It would be rude not to. Do you take me for a thief?"

The Frenchman knew that his true answer would encourage a swift response, albeit probably a violent one.

"But of course not sir!" He laughed, uncomfortably.

He expertly poured a measured amount of wine into Stefanescu's glass then turned to his guest.

"Sir? Are you happy with the same?"

The voice was unexpectedly English. Controlled, considered.

"Absolutely. Thank you."

The male who was wearing a lighter blue suit, pale blue shirt, brown shoes and a sapphire-coloured tie nodded to his host, raised his glass, swirled its contents gently, inhaled its aromatic fragrances and took a healthy sip.

He acknowledged the quality of the wine and gently clashed his glass against the Romanian's.

"Salut."

Stefanescu smiled before offering a mocking and accented English "Cheers!"

The Frenchman accepted his presence was no longer appreciated and once again nodded his head indiscernibly and discreetly blended back into the environs, slipping his prized corkscrew into the pocket of his waistcoat – in truth he wanted to drill it into the patronising bastard's eyes and pluck them, as one would *escargot*, neatly from their shells.

As the Romanian took another sip of the rich red liquid, his phone began to ring.

"Yes?"

He raised his eyebrows to his invitee.

"What now? I have just opened a three hundred pound bottle of wine. I have our guest with me. Can it not wait?"

It couldn't. He closed his phone and placed it into his pocket.

He beckoned the Frenchman back to his table.

"I have to leave. But I will be back. This wine will not keep. Give it to my admirers at the next table. They appear to be most interested in me. Now, if you would, my car, please."

He ushered him away with a firm push in the small of his back.

He turned to his guest. "I am so sorry my friend. As you can see I have to go, such poor timing. One of my...staff...is in need of some...advice. I will ring you so that we might continue our little conversation. I feel you and I have plenty more to talk about – we have the same business ideas, do we not?"

He shook hands firmly, a test of strength which the guest was equal to.

"It would appear so. Do not leave it too long."

Hewett drew him closer and whispered into his ear.

Stefanescu replied, then spoke louder, "I will ring you as soon as I can. Maybe tomorrow?"

He smiled at the table of businessmen and waved indifferently before feeling in his jacket pocket for his phone, mouthing the word 'enjoy' as he walked past the group. He squeezed one purposefully on the shoulder before lowering the half empty bottle onto their table.

"Ciao."

He dialled. The call transferred to an answerphone service. It was a default message offering a random caller no clue to the owner's identity.

"Brother. I am sorry to drag you away from whatever you were doing. Another attractive whore perhaps? Things are becoming interesting here. I feel I may need to leave soon. I will get my best people to leave also. The rest can make their own way. One in particular, well, he is not likely to make it, the authorities are closing in on him as we speak. He should be shown some loyalty but since when did our family ever show anyone loyalty? Pick up the phone..."

He was aware that he was no longer offering relevant information and if his brother was even listening, he enjoyed being in control, he always had, so he pressed the red button on his Motorola and ended the call.

• • •

The Englishman stood, slipped his chair quietly back into its place, emptied his wine glass, placed it quietly onto a leather coaster, straightened his single-knotted tie and walked out of the bar. Within a minute, he too was in his car and dialling a number on his phone.

The phone rang for a while, so he leaned back in the leather seat, bracing his left foot on the rest and propping his right elbow onto the door trim of the Nordlichtblau Audi S6.

Clouds were starting to appear on the horizon. A few isolated specks of rain landed on the green-tinted wind-screen initiating the auto-wipers which arced across the glass, clearing it temporarily.

The Audi engine started without drama, its driver selected first and accelerated into the traffic. He stopped at the first set of lights. The rain was more persistent, larger drops struck the screen, causing the driver to increase the speed of the intermittent wiper system.

Pedestrians walked, strutted and shuffled past him, oblivious to his presence. Some raised umbrellas whilst others pulled their collars up against the mounting squall.

There was a storm developing somewhere.

As Stefanescu walked through the lobby, he received another call. It was a very familiar voice.

"Do what you need to do, remove the fool from the operation, I want him back here where he can do no more harm."

"Why not let the British authorities kill him? It would save a lot of time and trouble."

"It would brother, but he has been a good foot soldier for us, he has made us an obscene amount of money for doing...nothing. I think we owe it to him to get him home. Don't you?"

So he did reward loyalty after all.

Gheorghiu had also disconnected his phone and quickly walked out of the familiar fast-food restaurant and onto the street. He had promised Stefan that he would support Constantin. Everyone agreed that he was becoming a liability but his skills were reaping rewards, day in, day out. He had other skills too and for those he was both famed and feared.

He had trained the disparate team of young men and hired the one or two willing women that entertained them at night. To date, they had so far targeted nearly four hundred bank and retail point-of-sale machines.

The numbers, per capita, were staggering. Constantin was paid reasonably well. Gheorghiu better. Who actually knew how much the Stefanescu's were earning?

With at least two-thirds of the intended victims unaware that their accounts had been compromised for around a week it was as close to the perfect, victimless crime as they could commit. Their boss was right. Why risk interaction with a victim when this type of offence could be committed, over and over, and when you thought you had enough, over again?

Resembling a plague of locusts they would strip London of all of its natural wealth, victim by victim. Then, when the risks outweighed the consequences they would move on, probably to another British city, possibly a European one. A number of factors would influence this decision. Their appearance in the local and national media as a result of continued pathetic and xenophobic police warnings, their own confidence and their nerve, all would act as a guide to where and critically, when.

Gheorghiu dialled a new number. It was eventually answered by a breathless, almost panicked male.

"Yes? What? Is that you...?"

Gheorghiu cut him off.

"Do not use my name, get onto the next train. You need to be on the Circle Line. Are you listening?"

There was a pause. Gheorghiu could hear the varied sounds of the underground. The public address announcements, the noise of the trains and the constant pulse of commuters. It was the white noise of a major city, broken down into its key components it would provide a fascinating insight into modern-day London but to the Romanian it was just noise.

"Well?"

Constantin responded.

"Yes. Yes, I am listening. I am heading deeper underground. Which train?"

It was clear he was not listening so Gheorghiu yelled down the phone.

"Circle! It is the yellow line on the map. Get on as soon as you can. They will be following you."

This didn't help.

"Then I will shoot them."

"No, brother, you will not shoot them. You will NOT shoot anyone or our boss will feed you to the pigs. Get on the train as I have instructed you to do, keep your head down and get off at Blackfriars. I repeat, Black-friars. It is the third stop. You will be on board for five minutes. No longer. Tell me you understand?"

"I understand."

"You have money?"

"Yes. I do now."

Constantin was walking faster now, down stairs, onto escalators, a frightened hare desperate not to get caught in the headlights. His breathing was laboured. He needed to eat; he needed another shot of heroin. He needed to be home. Away from all of this. Away. From everything.

The underground system was incredible, a feat of engineering as impressive as any other, anywhere, but he had no time to admire the shining steel and concrete architecture. He rubbed his eyes then wrung his hands together, shielding his nervous demeanour, but to the trained eye failing badly.

He could hear shouting behind him. Resisting the urge to turn he carried on, faster now.

The voices weren't gaining, but he knew instinctively they were calling to him.

He began to panic, pushing past other travellers, those that resisted were encouraged to move. He had made the decision, contrary to Gheorghiu's instructions, that if anyone got hold of him he would fire his weapon. He now had nothing left to lose. The syndicate that he was indebted to would not support him anymore.

He could see the train ahead. He started to run.

Roberts had temporarily lost Cade in the crowd. He had pushed on with a few staff at his side and assumed that his partner was alongside him.

About a hundred metres ahead he spotted the target,

running, pushing his way through the throngs. He looked again, and he had vanished.

Constantin had dumped his jacket, dropping it on the floor, allowing it disappear beneath the orderly pedestrian stampede. A few kicked it to one side and in seconds it was laying against a wall and out of sight.

It gave him long enough to gain an advantage.

Roberts turned and saw for the first time that he was alone among hundreds. But he had a goal now, and he wanted that bastard as much as the next man. The dreaded 'Red Mist' was enveloping him, altering his natural sense of self-protection, urging him onwards and into harm's way.

He stepped onto the downwards escalator and caught a glimpse of his quarry once again. Grabbing his radio he raised it to his mouth and pressed the talk bar.

"DS Roberts to all staff Westminster, target sighted, heading towards..."

But his words were lost. All his control room staff heard was a garbled message, encrypted and impossible to decipher.

Falsely assuming his colleagues had heard his update he started to run. Constantin sensed Roberts gaining on him. He could hear his own breathing, the increasingly loud beats of his heart were fighting for attention and adding to his general sense of panic.

Roberts was running faster now. Faster than his target. He offered another rapid update into his radio but it was another message sent but never received. Knowing that his colleagues were a step behind gave him the momentum to pursue the male.

. . .

The train was in front of Constantin now. He just had to get on and pray the door closed in time.

The red and white train, number 5540 was long past its prime but it carried out its duties valiantly, around and around on the circuitous journey that gave the service its name. It was a relatively shallow underground line, but he felt as if he was compressed beneath the earth, trapped in a tube and feeling ever more claustrophobic.

The doors were open and as he stepped quickly into the body of the train; he turned right, allowing himself to make the most of the entire length of the series of carriages. The familiar voice message warned people of the need to take care as the doors were closing.

Cade was gaining on Roberts who in turn was approaching the train at speed. As he reached the door it began to close, he threw himself into the gap and collided with a passenger who immediately did what most metropolitan commuters did and ignored him.

He was aboard. With a hungry, goal-driven, heroin-addicted, gun-carrying murderer. And, as the train moved off he realised that he was quite spectacularly alone. A solitary police officer whose actions were likely to be either gallant and recognised or foolhardy and soon forgotten.

Surely the public would come to his aid?

As he looked briefly back onto the platform he saw Cade and two other uniformed officers.

His lip reading skills were advanced enough to work out what Cade was saying, and it was far from pleasant.

He stood for a while, looking down the train, trying to pick him out. There was no obvious sense of panic anywhere so his gun must have been disposed of or be hidden out of sight.

Roberts felt that he stood out, a beacon that shouted 'Look at me!'

But for all his fears, he was, to the masses, just another passenger.

He started to walk now, checking as discreetly as he could for his target whilst attempting, probably unsuccessfully, to look similar to any other miserable commuter whose only barrier to civility was a vacant stare or a deliberate air of indifference. His only weapon was a baton and a warrant card, that and his uncanny ability to think on his feet.

Actually, what *was* he thinking?

Cade had updated the control room and re-assigned staff to meet the train at the next stop, called Embankment. He turned around and made the slow journey back up through the station until he got stepped out into the light and onto the street.

The black-haired sergeant appeared again.

"We've searched everywhere boss. Not a trace. I think your boy is long gone. It's been a long day. We are heading back to base unless you object?"

"I do mate as it happens, sorry. My man is on that bloody train that just left platform two. I need you to get me to the next stop on the Circle Line. Sharpish."

"Roger." He whistled to a member of his team. "Get the boss to Embankment underground and stay with him. We'll be two seconds behind you."

Cade liked how his instructions were followed to the letter and without question. He got into the back of the patrol car as its driver and co-driver jumped in, adjusted their body armour and weapons and headed south before turning immediately left onto Victoria Embankment and accelerating for a hundred or so metres before coming to a halt.

Regardless of the fact that their vehicle was highly visible and festooned with strobes and creating enough noise to wake the grandparents of the dead they were stuck fast.

"Jesus when will this traffic ever improve boss?" Asked one of the authorised firearms officers.

"Your guess is as good if not better than mine. How long?"

"Ten minutes tops boss," said the young AFO.

He knew that on average the underground service would make twice the ground that they would, trying to fight through traffic and an endless sea of pedestrians.

They got as far as the approach to the Hungerford Bridge when Cade realised they were destined to miss the damned thing. What *was* Roberts thinking?

"Can we get some more units to head straight to the Embankment station? This bloody pain in the arse is running us ragged here and I'm getting just a little tired of him and his friends."

"Leave it with us governor." The co-driver called up the control room and relayed the message.

An anonymous and overworked voice replied. "Will do. We've got a unit nearby but they are en route to a reported stabbing. I will re-route them as soon as I can."

"Tell them we've got a matter of minutes. Try BTP. Tell them we need armed staff."

The latter suggestion had escaped his mind until now.

British Transport Police were a standalone force, created to manage the vast transport networks across the British Isles, just like their Metropolitan counterparts they had staff in many departments including AFOs.

On any other day Cade might have found himself admiring the bridge, the work of the industrious British engineer Brunel. Diagonally opposite was another feat of engineering that the great Briton would have found equally alluring, a giant Ferris wheel known by most as the London Eye. Cade looked at that instead and wished he was stood in one of its many ovoidal capsules, looking down from its four hundred feet vantage point at the ants below.

And he was in just the mood to stamp on one.

The Circle Line train made impressive progress, its carriages creating a draught and a growing back pressure as it approached the Embankment station.

Roberts was stood by a doorway now. His heart was beating a little faster too. Where was he? He saw him board, so he had to be there somewhere.

Artur Gheorghiu was ever-reliable. He resisted the light breeze that rushed from the tunnel, partially closed his eyes to avoid the dust and waited for the train to stop before stepping from the platform into the brightly lit third carriage.

Roberts was hedging his bets. Half in and half out of the door he watched as best he could. He grappled for his phone, withdrew it from a pocket and checked the display. His battery was flat.

'Bloody marvellous.'

He could try the radio again, try to attract attention, but his aim was to surveil not to attract attention. The minute Constantin saw him one of two things could happen. He could run or he could fight. If he chose the latter, cornered and vulnerable it could easily be Roberts who would come off second best.

It was Gheorghiu who had now become the hunter. 'Where are you?'

The doors were about to close. Roberts chose to stay on board. To ride his luck, at least to the next station where with fortune on his side Colonel Cade and the 1st Cavalry might arrive.

Gheorghiu was scanning as only a first-class operator would. Although the carriages were packed he was soon able to distinguish who might not be and importantly who might be a cop. He had a sixth sense when it came to picking them out.

And there he was. The man in the next carriage, trying his best not to draw attention to himself.

The carriages were busy but not packed to capacity as they always were in the early and evening rush hours. Gheorghiu walked surreptitiously through the carriage and sat diagonally opposite his team mate.

He nodded. It was a nod that spoke volumes. 'Do not look at me more than you have to, do not speak to me and above all do not give anyone a clue that we are associated.'

Constantin was wise enough to obey the rules. He was feeling awful. His head was in a vice-like grip, his eyes burned, he was nauseous beyond belief and on edge. But he obeyed the rules.

His partner indicated right with his eyes. Again, it spoke many words in one simple almost undetectable action.

'We have company my friend. Stay calm. We can do this you and I. Hate me tomorrow by all means, but for today we are brothers.'

Constantin replied with a barely visible nod as around him other commuters ignored one another, staring everywhere but into the eyes of their fellow man.

The train was picking up speed. Roberts discreetly

turned down the volume on his radio and edged forwards. His target hadn't spotted him. He had the advantage. A few minutes and they would be at the next stop.

'Why wait?'

He started to walk through the carriage, opened the door that joined the two units together and edged past an anonymous traveller who was trying to balance whilst reading his half-folded newspaper.

Cade could wait no longer. He opened the back door of the BMW 5 series and started to run.

"You'd better go with him. I'll find somewhere to abandon this."

It looked closer from the back seat. After the first hundred metres, he was regretting it but kept running. The younger officer was catching him, despite the additional weight of his equipment and firearm.

Visitors from far and wide, previously marvelling at the sights and sounds of the city were now either sheltering, shielding their loved ones or considering running for cover – in doing so misjudging the situation entirely, but they had watched enough news bulletins recently to know that the heartbeat of a major city could stop at any moment.

Cade reached the Embankment underground station and entered, running towards the aging turnstiles. A few attentive staff members made to stop Cade who produced his warrant card and indicated his intention not to stop. The sight of the pursuing black-clad officer added an assurance that their fate was in good hands.

The officer yelled "I'm with him, open the gate!"

The pair were soon approaching the platform with the third officer a few minutes away. BTP staff were en route from nearby Temple underground and racing towards them. No one had considered stopping the train. It was that easy.

With a hundred people on board, the doors closed again and the train moved away from the platform and began to pick up speed towards its next stop only a few minutes away.

Cade and his temporary team saw the train depart.

He ran towards a guard waving his ID.

"Is there another train coming? I need to follow that one." It sounded nonsensical. It probably was, but he was getting a little desperate.

The sixty-year-old weathered face of the West Indian guard broke into a smile.

"Man, dis is not Hollywood. Ya can't go around chasing a train!" He laughed a normally infectious laugh before continuing.

"What ya gotta do is wait for the next train and that will come in..." He looked at his watch, gifted to him for forty years of continual service, "...in about ten minutes."

"A man might be *dead* in ten minutes!"

"Mister, we could *all* be dead in ten minutes, calm ya skin, let me think. I need to think. Now, there is a way..." He unfolded a much-loved timetable and mused at the options, oblivious to the fact that his customer had already walked away.

Cade saw Roberts but chose not to communicate obviously with him, however his Anglo Saxon lips moved at the same time as a string of profanities were emitted. Pausing no longer, Cade had already turned on his heels and was running back up towards the patrol car.

The AFOs shrugged their shoulders and joined him.

. . .

Valentin Iliescu dialled an international number and waited for it to be answered.

"Yes?"

"It is me."

"So I hear. What news from London?"

"He believes everything I tell him."

The voice laughed. "Good. So he trusts you. You have done well. My brother is there, but I am sure you know that, there is little you do not know. He tells me that a few of our people have caused him to get a little angry. I have told him to take the lead, after all I put him in control of the British operation as a test."

"Cade and his partner are being run into the ground by your team. You are always one step ahead. Very impressive – and the money must be equally so. As the American capitalists would say, 'it must be rolling in'."

"Oh trust me, it is."

"And all your teams have to do is steal from a few locations, cause a diversion and move on. They are creating a reputation in the heart of the wealthiest financial centre in the world, and the authorities are almost allowing them to continue. But the risks are increasing each day, they will leave London soon, no?"

"Yes, you are right, but in time, not just yet. I will tell you later. Mr Cade needs to think that we are heading into the lion's den and you will support this, tell him that we are stepping up our operation and will be targeting shopping centres, supermarkets, petrol stations, train stations anywhere with an electronic point-of-sale device."

"You want me to tell him what you intend to do? Where you intend to target?"

"Absolutely. Let him believe that we are falling into the lion's mouth."

"When in reality?"

"We are heading into his body and ripping out his throat."

Valentin took a moment before he continued the conversation.

"There is already a lot happening here. The police are hunting for your team but focusing on Constantin. He is your weakest link now. They have deployed a lot of their people, they are armed and he is dangerous. This will shine the light upon your team. He will talk. It is a poor combination likely to cause you…heartache, would you agree?"

"I would."

The Jackdaw crowed as he briefed the man they called The Child of the Shadows, outlining his plan for a lucrative, targeted operation centring upon one of the city of London's most iconic annual events.

"Your plan is indeed impressive, very. I thought you were only interested in bank machines? Do you have a Plan B?"

"Of course it is an impressive plan Copil. And yes, I have a Plan B, and that is even more audacious. When have I ever been anything but impressive?"

He didn't wait for an answer before continuing.

"My dear brother will deal with the situation you have outlined. My days of placing myself in the way of harm are gone for now. I have a little girl to think about and one day I shall reunite with her and give her even finer things than she has now. Nevertheless, today and tomorrow and the next day I must empty the bank accounts of the foolish English and whilst they concentrate on that I can begin to turn off their life support. I have them right here." His grip whitened his knuckles. "And for that I need my dear little brother's help. He wants to be a great and important piece on the chessboard, he wants to be the

King, but I am the King. This is his chance. What do you think?"

"You are indeed the King. Stefan tried so very hard, but sadly is only the Bishop, just the Bishop. Moving around the board in simple diagonal lines. He is a valuable piece at times, but limited in his strategy."

"And Cade?" He put emphasis on the name, almost spitting the word down the phone.

"Cade is half Knight, half Rook, more flexible than you give him credit for. Be wary."

"He does not worry me. His other team members? What of them?"

"Pawns. Nothing more."

The voice sighed, almost knowing what was coming.

"And you, Valentin, tell me, what are you?"

He paused, took a sip of warming Calvados and before finishing the call said, "I am the Queen of course, I move where I want, in any direction."

CHAPTER NINETEEN

THE TELL-TALE SIGNAL WAS ALL ROBERTS NEEDED TO observe. He had been in the job long enough to recognise an NVC – a non-verbal communication.

The male in the next carriage had looked at him, for a split second, but his reaction was enough. It was the involuntary wipe, his left hand across his mouth, and it was all Roberts needed to observe. He'd been taught well many years before. His police tutor, Rob Wilsea, a career-constable and thief-catcher extraordinaire had handed down the sixth sense and field craft of twenty years and a young, fresh-faced Constable Jason Roberts had absorbed everything, chamois-like, desperate to ingest, to learn as fast as he possibly could. His thirst wasn't insatiable, it was gluttonous. Where knowledge was concerned he could drink from a firehose.

"When you see that bloody face wipe – pounce. You mark my words kid. He's guilty, every ruddy time!" Wilsea's words were now echoing around the stark metallic envelope of the train carriage.

The male was staring down at the grubby, well-worn flooring. Overly conscious of his actions, desperately waiting for the next stop and a chance of escape.

Roberts leant back, just out of view and keyed the microphone on his radio, whispering almost, hoping that his words would be heard.

"Alpha Five-Five MP – I need urgent assistance. I'm about to arrest a target offender. I'm on the underground heading towards..."

Christ! Where was he heading? He looked up at the map, scanning the vivid arteries and veins that criss-crossed London. Colours of the rainbow and iconic station names filled his view, 'Come on! Get a grip, man!'

It took two long seconds, but he blurted it into the microphone. "Towards Blackfriars."

No one heard him but the back-up he craved was already on the way, racing from different directions, converging on the station, a plan in place to capture a murderer and common thief. There would be no negotiation, little fuss and it would all be done just so; thoroughly British and all better for it.

As the train began to decelerate Roberts made his move. The carriages bucked and shook from side to side as they moved around on the aging rail system. He lost his grip for a second, but managed to grab hold of an overhead strap. He moved again, his quads bracing against the rodeo-like energy of the train.

Trying as hard as he possibly could to avoid detection his hand had been played, Constantin started to edge forward clutching more picture cards than his adversary.

Gheorghiu looked at him and discreetly shook his head.

'Not now. Wait.'

Paranoia was already weaving its spell and convincing Constantin that his days as a free man were limited, he'd soon be staring at a blank ceiling again, a faceless cell with bland whitewashed walls and the only decoration being a faded and lurid inscription from a former inhabitant. There was no way he was going back inside that bloody place. He'd made the decision to escape at any cost.

He stood up and paced left and right, then towards the door. He looked at the emergency stop system and knew that the train would halt in seconds if he pulled it. But could he get off? Where would he run to? This wasn't an action film – he couldn't run along the tunnel, find a hitherto unseen and convenient doorway and make good his escape up onto the brightly lit streets quickly blending into the urban chaos that enveloped him, providing him with a cloak of anonymity.

He had to fight for his freedom. Once more, he had to fight for it.

He turned towards Roberts who was now in the middle of the carriage with a raised hand which held a leather-clad warrant card.

"Stop right there. Police!"

Constantin looked around, contemplated grabbing hold of the young girl to his left, considering the value that a hostage would bring, but instead drew the aging revolver from his jacket and brought it up into the aim, staring intently at the foresight. He could almost smell the metalwork, taste the black powder.

All he could see among an ocean of faces was Roberts. Looking back at him. He looked scared, as if this was to be the last event of his life.

As he glared at Roberts, his mind returned to the gaudy,

damp stairwell of the two-up, two-down rental property in Kent; it struck him that it was the last time he was able to recall a brief and miserable home. It was also the place where he had watched a solitary bullet exit the barrel and drill into that young boy's forehead. He could hear the round now, slicing through his skull like over-ripe fruit being dropped onto a cold concrete floor.

He shook himself visibly and regained control of his senses. The nearby screams of passengers had brought him back to the here and now.

Those that could run towards the opposite end of the carriage did so, others cowered in their seats. Men who had previously failed to so much as give up a seat to a female now shielded them, some using their briefcases as a hopeless barrier.

"All of you go away!" yelled the Romanian addict, physically shaking and filling with adrenaline.

"I do not want to kill you. Just get...away from me! And you..."

He looked into Roberts' eyes. "Stay there or I will shoot you. I do not care anymore. Please."

It was the civil, almost courteous gesture at the end of the sentence that threw the experienced detective, long enough to unsettle him. He knew he had to recover rapidly and negotiate his way back out of the pit that he found himself sinking in.

"OK mate, I have no idea what you have done." It was a lie. He spoke slowly, trying not to be too patronising. He held both of hands out, open, offering a transparent and non-threatening gesture. It was textbook stuff.

"You are lying!"

"No, trust me. I am just here to help. To prevent you from hurting yourself. Give me the gun and you will not be harmed. Then you and I can both go home tonight." He smiled at him but it looked awful, in truth if he could see his own reflection it would have manifested as an indignant, worried sneer.

The train continued onward, all the while approaching the station, its driver oblivious, moving forward through the claustrophobia of a subterranean capital.

"Listen to me my friend. Hear what I am saying." He was now more deliberate. "Lower the gun. Please. You *don't* want to shoot me, it would be the worst thing you could do. If you do as I say you will be given a warning."

"I have killed people! How can you warn me? Do not lie to me. I am in control. Not you. Get on your knees!"

Roberts, trained, but unused to ever carrying a firearm on a regular basis found himself wishing he had one secreted about his person, one that he could draw and fire two rounds into his chest and one to his head.

Bang, reset. Bang, reset...Bang.

'Cover down, Scan, Re-assess'.

He could hear the range officer's words, muffled but concise. He was back there now, so much so that he too took his eye off the ball for a split-second.

Constantin's right index finger reduced the miniscule remaining slack on the trigger and squeezed. He had crossed the line now. The chamber revolved and the awaiting cartridge casing prepared for the inevitable firing pin to strike home, setting off the charge and propelling the heavy round along the barrel and toward its target.

Roberts' senses had stepped into hyper-drive. He could hear very clearly, intently, but strangely he was also able to taste the air that surrounded him, almost sense the bullet heading towards him, it was just a moment in time and for him, the end. He heard his kids, his wife, his father, and strangely, almost surreally the clipped tones of his elderly English teacher.

'You will come to nothing in life if you fail to work hard Jason...'

The train continued regardless. It was heading one way, at speed, the bullet in the opposite direction, but much faster.

A tightly compressed spring propelled the hammer forward forcing the firing pin to strike the round, pressing deep into the brass primer plate and releasing its explosive power. The gas pressure completed the process, allowing the bullet to escape.

Roberts was only five metres away. He watched the round leave the barrel. Actually *watched* it. He could see it turning in its flight, he swore he could hear it cutting through the air too, but in reality he could hear nothing. The noise of the revolver activating had almost deafened him and everyone else within close proximity, including Constantin.

The bullet seared past its target striking the aluminium carriage wall and ricocheted to a stop, lodging into the top of a worn velvety seat cushion.

Roberts tried to close his eyes; transfixed to the spot, he was unable to think.

Constantin pulled the trigger again, the cylinder repeated its earlier action. Weapons such as his, even ancient ones were relatively reliable, with fewer moving parts they were de rigueur for many criminals.

The hammer forced the pin forward again but this time the round failed to fire despite Constantin convincing himself that he had shot at the officer for a second time. Seeing no bullet in the air and noting Roberts' now rejuvenated and quickening approach, he fired again. Nothing.

He held the gun towards his face, precariously; it was a worryingly common action of even trained firearms officers when a weapon failed to fire in anger. He looked at the barrel, then at Roberts.

The police officer had made his move. Saying a symbolic goodbye to his loved ones he lunged at his target and caught him in the diaphragm causing a sizeable gust of air to escape. It rushed into Roberts' face, causing him to inhale the manic offender's week-old mortuary breath. Despite the stench he kept his own head as close to Constantin's as possible and hung onto him, grasping at anything and everything.

Surely someone would come to his aid – the train was nearly bloody full. Surely?

The revolver had clattered to the floor arriving at the feet of a young office worker who in a moment of oblique terror had kicked it further up the carriage and for now out of harm's way.

Roberts was fighting for his life, hanging onto Constantin, grabbing anything that he could, trying to inflict pain, attempting to immobilise him. He struck him in the pelvis with his knee again and again, driving the bony protrusion into the softer more vulnerable target area but the determined bastard kept fighting.

Constantin swung wildly with his fists, catching Roberts on the temple and the left ear. The high-pitched ringing providing an unsubtle reminder that his hearing had returned to normal levels.

Like many police staff Roberts had been taught what were known as 'Home Office Approved Techniques' – methods of self-defence that were reliable in a classroom situation but practically useless in a feral street fight where the offender had ten times more to lose, and a barrel-full of adrenaline on tap.

He was sensing very quickly that his energy levels were sapping and realised his gentlemanly fighting techniques needed changing. He ran his fingers up and over Constantin's eyes and clawed at them, feeling the skin ripping under his immaculately short fingernails.

Constantin screamed in pain but fought back.

Passengers were now frantically dialling on their phones, some to their loved ones; some to the police. For them this was their Ground Zero. They had left home as a commuter but now found themselves a part of what the media would refer to generically as a developing situation. They were the news in the breaking news item.

They could see that Roberts was getting the upper hand. He was punching now, striking the opponent's face with his clenched fist, propelling his palms up and into his rival's septum, trying deliberately to break his nose. He was equally feral now; he wanted to force that bone up and into his skull. He wanted to go home to his family.

He struck again, this time feeling cartilaginous matter shifting under his palm with a resounding crack.

Roberts' senses were now reduced to sight. He couldn't hear and even his sense of touch appeared to have departed. He knew he needed to stay on his feet, once he was down, he was out.

He caught a glimpse of movement to his right, a male, non-descript, but a potential saviour. At last. He softened his grip, knowing he was rapidly running out of strength and waited for the male to come to his aid.

The moment he felt the male grabbing for his handcuffs he knew he had an ally. The pouch, attached to his trouser belt popped open allowing the highly polished Smith &

Wesson 'cuffs to slip out. He had set them, as any good officer would, with the ratchet primed on its last tooth, allowing for rapid deployment.

He saw a hand enter the maelstrom and shouted out, as loud as he possibly could.

"Get them on! Now!"

The male rammed the first cuff onto a slim wrist which did little to resist. The mechanism worked perfectly, encapsulating its target, shutting with a deliberate, high-speed set of clicks.

Roberts was incredulous. They were on the wrong wrist. His.

"For fuck's sake. What are you doing?"

The male rammed his fist into Roberts' ribs, cracking one and splaying another, tearing the intercostal muscle that separated the ivory cage. He struck again, and again, once more cracking another of the fine bones.

With Roberts dropping to his knees in agony Artur Gheorghiu knew he had control. He pulled on the empty handcuff link and dragged a subdued Roberts for a metre, slamming the cuff against an upright, brightly painted pole and incarcerating him onto the pole and within the train which continued, regardless.

People stopped speaking. Their phones idle. Their loved ones forced to listen to the dull groans of one of London's finest.

Constantin had recovered the handgun and swung it around wildly, pointing it at anyone who looked remotely capable of intervening. The only noises that could be heard were distant whimpers, the train carriages creaking and moaning and then silence.

It was the type of silence that people later recall – when

in fact their brains are scrambling to understand what is occurring.

Roberts lay on the grubby floor, his fight over. His arm was bent at a perverse angle from where he had fallen. He looked up at the two males.

"Why?" It was all he could say, his breathing laboured, each word a struggle.

Constantin knelt down and with his grubby fingers forming a lever under his chin, lifted his face, stared at him and said "Because you would not just let me leave. All I wanted was to have enough money to live a good life. Is that so much to ask?"

He moved his hand and took hold of Roberts' face. His grip was vicious and determined, as if he were exacting the revenge of years of hardship on Roberts and no one else. The pressure was intense, as if he was trying to crush his molars into a fine calcified powder.

"I do not kill people for the..." He searched his mind for the right word, "...fun. For the hell of it. But people like you, in authority, people who stop me from being *me*, then yes, those people I will happily kill." He looked around the carriage, expecting to see somebody prepared to take a risk, but no one moved. Most didn't dare breathe.

"The government that oppressed me and its servants, yes those too. I am Roma and proud. We are a proud people, Sergeant Roberts and men like you hunt us like rats. But even rats have pride. We have lived with a reputation for centuries. But we are good people. That is why I kill. Pride. I kill in the name of..."

Roberts found his second wind. Realising that his life, ironically given his location, was very much on the line, he spoke, quietly as first, then more determined, more resilient, belligerent almost, and with a heaped tablespoon of reck-lessness.

"You are as bad as the rest of them then? My colleagues will hunt you down, rat or otherwise and you will end up in prison once more. And another thing...and when you talk to me mate...it is Detective Sergeant and nothing less..."

His head dropped to the floor. At this level he could smell the rubber and leather and the long-departed contents of a hundred thousand different soles; he could taste the bitterness, the detritus and daily flotsam and jetsam of a city that moved its people around on foot, underground. He was one of them, normally, a quiet soul watching life pass by, through the window, the blurred images of a commercial world whipping past as the train progressed at speed from tunnel to platform.

Using the reflection to keep a weather eye on the people around him Roberts was on one hand a commuter and on the other, a guardian. The job did that to you. You never quite switched off. But now, lying face down on the indus-trial surface of what for many was a necessary and conve-nient way to get from A to B, he was done. His hearing remained but his other senses had almost admitted defeat.

Constantin stood, lifted Roberts' face with the tip of his foot as if he were examining something putrid and then smiled a vacuous smile.

"There is nothing left of me to imprison Mr Roberts. We will be gone soon. Then, you will never..."

Gheorghiu looked at his colleague and shook his head once more.

"Enough, we need to go. We must always be one step ahead. Tell him nothing."

Constantin lowered himself in what appeared to be an act of conciliation. His hand was close to Roberts' face, his tawny-stained fingers tapping him and stroking his cheek. Roberts retched at the stench of month-old nicotine.

"Goodbye. Tell your friends not to follow us."

Roberts struggled to focus but he could clearly define the image that adorned his attacker's wrist. A simple design, overlaid across the arteries, bright blue and in the shape of a wave.

He could hear his own laboured breathing and shifted awkwardly, trying to find a comfortable position. The train was slowing and would soon be at its destination. Cade would be there along with the might of the Metropolitan Police, waiting and ready to lock these bastards up.

He exhaled. The pain is his chest was awful. He swore he could taste blood, oxygenated and bitter.

As he opened his eyes, he saw the booted foot heading towards him. It was aimed squarely at his handcuffed arm. It was more a stamp than a kick. The blow was nauseating as it punched through both the radius and ulna, breaking both instantly and causing part of the radius to erupt through the skin of his forearm.

The skin around the injured site blackened immediately then bled.

The second blow hit him in the chest, targeting the already broken ribs. The offender held the boot against the bones for a fraction longer than necessary, twisting it slightly as if extinguishing yet another cigarette.

Roberts waited but the third wave never came.

They left him chained to the pole, a twisted and broken man with an audience too afraid to even move.

Cade and the two AFO's were making progress but struggling to keep up with the pace of the underground. BTP officers called up on channel two, stating that they were seconds away. Another three units, including one from south of the river were also en route. A colleague in trouble meant that staff from every facet of the force had dropped everything to get to his side. It was a universal response.

Cade leant forward. "You carry spare weapons?"

"We do sir but..."

"It's an order, son. I do not have time for buts right now. Stick it in your statement. Hand me the Glock and a magazine. I don't intend to carry a warrant card to a gunfight. I'm sure you would agree. Agreed?"

The younger officer looked quickly at his senior colleague who nodded and carried on driving.

"Absolutely guv. You're the boss." He withdrew the Austrian pistol from the gun safe and handed it over his shoulder, quickly followed by the magazine.

"Weapon is safe."

"Thank you."

Regardless of the safety briefing Cade withdrew the chamber flag and pulled the ribbed slide back quarter of the way, checking for a round. Seeing it empty he slammed the seventeen round magazine into the stock and racked the weapon. His left hand moving rapidly and efficiently, backwards over his right shoulder.

"Sorry boss, haven't got a holster. You be OK?"

"It won't be in the holster mate. How long?"

"Two, maybe three."

The train reached the station; the doors opened and its passengers disgorged, some were walking at a pace, oblivious to the chaos, others ran; some were powerless, unable to put one foot in front of the other. Men and women wore panicked expressions, panicked but relieved. In such tight confines the business-as-usual pedestrian carnage aided the two comrades who were able to move quickly through the station.

A lone female, a lifelong officer in the Royal Air Force had seen enough, now mobile she had made the decision to follow the pair, and if they separated she'd follow the one who looked ravaged by heroin.

"Yes, you bastard, I'm following you."

Having seen the way they had attacked the officer she knew it was her duty to track them – it wasn't without risk, Air Force or not she was only an Education Officer, hardly a combat pilot, but she knew right from wrong and this was wrong on every possible count.

She dialled 999 and spoke as she walked.

She was physically and mentally fit, and typical of Her Majesty's Forces as she had displayed an early and uncanny tendency to win on the athletics field, she soon found herself spending as long training for an event as she did teaching junior staff. Her bosses had been quite candid.

'Why let work get in the way of beating the army?'

And she could keep up with these two all day long.

On a rare day off from nearby RAF Northolt, Flight Lieutenant Mary-Jane Shipley was the epitome of the girl-next-door.

She favoured plain hair, plain make-up and had a willowy frame, the result of years of what she considered to be 'competitive ballet'. Plain she might be but in many aspects she was the envy of many of her more 'rotund' and more colourful friends.

She was attractive in a very addictive way. Men wanted to be with her, they adored the way her nose crinkled when she giggled and how she laughed openly at their appalling attempts at humour – and yet none had ever conquered the fear, simply to ask her out. Perhaps it was the fear of being beaten to a pulp if they went too far?

And so she became their friend rather than their lover. Which was rather a pity as deep down she had an appetite as large as her lust for life.

She'd joined 32 Squadron Royal Air Force and revelled in the opportunity to meet with VIPs and the British royal family. Her latter-day role was more liaison than anything else, but her core, the very heart of her was a fighter.

She could still beat her male colleagues hands down at arm wrestling and had a strength of mind to match. With a brown belt in Shotokan karate and another, more recently in Taekwondo she revelled in a good scrap. Where she lacked in physical strength she excelled in speed, often using her own attacker's energies against them.

She also had a spirit that contradicted her relatively tender and sheltered upbringing as the only daughter of strict Christian parents, both teachers from the west country county of Devon. The day she passed out at RAF Cranwell her father had wept. They were genuine tears of pride. All he needed to do now was protect her from the dangers of conflict.

"Pick your battles, my girl."

And so, to appease Mr Shipley, as his pupils called him, she moved into the education branch and in her father's defence had never looked back. She had found her vocation, life in the forces, teaching but ready to fight should the day ever arise.

She'd never had a boyfriend, not even close, but she had plenty of friends who were boys and she was immensely popular. Never the twain.

The night before, under floodlights, she had acted as a

pace runner to a male colleague, in training for a joint forces long distance event. She cruised along, engaging him in conversation, at one point even telling a joke. He loved and hated her at the same time.

In truth he loved her; she was just Flight Lieutenant "MJ" to her colleagues, but to him she was simply Mary and rather beautiful. He was desperate to tell her, even more so to marry her, just hadn't got the first clue how.

She had missed it entirely, the subtle nuances were simply that, too subtle.

Leaving him at the trackside she jogged away. It helped her to cool down on the way to the dojo where she would train for two more hours. Her aim, in her latterly discovered Korean martial art was the next phase, a belt, nothing more elaborate than that. And this one happened to be red.

Her teacher, a Californian with straw-coloured hair and a physique that belied his sixty years, was a man of few words. However, she could still recall them as he handed her belt over at a recent grading.

"Red. The next phase, and never forget, red is for danger. You are almost there. One more step."

She'd risen early as always, brushed her hair, tied it in a simple ponytail, flossed her teeth, rinsed, paid limited attention to her appearance and having donned a tracksuit and waterproof jacket had travelled across her favourite city.

She adored the underground, seeing it as a splendid way of navigating, avoiding the above-ground traffic chaos, in itself a positive thing as she had never learned to drive.

It was a great day. It was always was. She lived to be alive, despised cruelty to her fellow man and above all, hated bullies. And now she was behind two, keeping pace, easily.

'All day long!'

One was evidently struggling. That copper had landed a really good strike on his leg and he was paying the price. She decided that if she got the chance, she'd kick him too.

"Yes, I'm still in direct line of sight. They are making their way towards the exit. One is limping slightly, I'm going to stay with him. He has the gun." She was whispering, pointlessly as the ambient noise of the tube meant that her targets couldn't hear her if they wanted to.

The control room operator at the newly opened Bow Command Centre was frantically typing into the police system whilst a wave of the hand attracted her supervisor. She pointed to the screen. It took less than twenty seconds for the team leader to read, digest and disseminate the information.

The rapidly typed message read:

'2 x males – both IC1 – one wearing a blue jacket. Carrying a backpack.
**Older of two has a gun*. Revolver.*
He is limping. Has a fresh cut to his face, near his eye.
Speaks with an accent. Russian?'

The text was free hand, without analysis and beginning to fill with acronyms and codes which to the untrained eye were all but impossible to read: IC1 was standard police code for a white European.

"Are they both armed? How do you know it's a gun?"

"I can't answer the first question, sorry. One is though, definitely carrying a revolver and to answer the second question, I've fired enough to last a lifetime."

Shipley continued, it appeared that she did so without even taking a breath.

"The one who is limping shot at a police officer. He missed. The officer is still on the train, they handcuffed him. He needs help quickly – nasty injury to his arm."

She looked ahead, lifting her head to maintain the view in the growing crowd.

"What is your description please?"

Shipley described herself briefly and without question. Then she continued her commentary.

"OK, they are starting to get ahead of me, stand by a second I need to move faster."

The operator could only wait, her right headphone full of background noise. He wanted to warn her.

At the same time at least half a dozen other callers had rung the emergency services, many now from what they considered a safe place. Their first call had been to the police. One, in a panic, rang the Fire Brigade. Another pulled the emergency cord, rang her husband, then the police. Most had left, either continuing their commute or running anywhere they could to avoid conflict.

A suited female sat on the floor of the train as it waited at the platform, doors open, her hand rubbing the back of the complete stranger who was now almost unconscious, manacled to the bright yellow, cold metal pole.

"Stay with me, officer."

Roberts cracked open his left eye, swallowed deeply to avoid vomiting and uttered, "I'm hardly going anywhere, am I my love?"

"Guv, control room have a sighting of our targets. One wearing a blue jacket, carrying a backpack. Got a limp.

Being followed by a witness. Stand by…one male has a firearm, seen by the witness. She's RAF apparently, giving a commentary. On an escalator."

"All units Blackfriars. Two IC1 males responsible for a serious assault on a police officer. One is known to be armed with a revolver. One wearing a blue jacket. One is limping… he has the firearm. A witness has been following but has temporarily lost sight. Witness is a female, wearing a tracksuit, hair in a ponytail. Stand by for further. Now towards the bridge. Units attending please acknowledge call signs."

And so the flow of information slowly increased. Piece by piece it was processed until the dozen or so staff who were now on the ground and heading rapidly to the scene, knew roughly who and what they were looking for.

In the middle of a field in broad daylight their two wanted offenders would stand out like fresh red wine on a pristine wedding dress but here in the heart of a pulsing city it was easier than many realised simply to lose a target, especially if the target steadfastly refused to play by the rules.

"I need to stop. Just give me a moment. I can't breathe." It was Constantin.

"Brother, if we stop, we die. And I do not intend to die in England. Not today. Not ever. Now come on, keep moving, just another hundred metres and we will be free. Keep moving or I will shoot you myself."

Constantin looked behind him and saw an organised crowd; people to meet, places to go. To the left and walking quickly, talking on a cell phone was a thin girl, with what he considered a pale and uninteresting face and she was looking at him. She stopped, tried to blend back in, but he had isolated her now. He shuffled forwards trying to maintain Gheorghiu's pace. They were up now and out onto the street, walking quickly with the southbound foot traffic.

"This way, quickly, we must separate, head up the street, towards the old sandwich bar. Take the door on the left just before the red phone box. It is safe. I'll meet you in two minutes. Remember what I told you on the train. Now go."

Gheorghiu knew he could also be a target, but he realised that the police were after Constantin, first and foremost. He took a minute to watch, observe and sense what was happening. There were police converging on the street, cars came across the bridge, one from the north too, the cacophonous noise of sirens surrounded him. Before long they would be everywhere and the luck that had guided them so far would soon end.

A thin female stopped at the edge of the station exit and looked up the street and then to her left, across the bridge. She was not police, somehow he had a sixth sense about her, but she wasn't a conventional passenger either. She had purpose, a mission, although he wasn't sure what. He looked away, turned and carried on towards the same door that his partner had now reached.

She followed. Looking down at her phone she saw that she had been cut off, so pressed the green icon and re-dialled.

Constantin was beginning to panic. He could almost smell his pursuers; any second now he would hear them shout his name, feel their cold, bony hand on his shoulder; die at the hands of their firearms or slowly decay in one of their prisons.

He reached the door and walked straight through, nonchalantly, following instructions, pieces of simple data that had somehow managed to navigate through the nauseating haze of a still-recent drug intake.

Perhaps, he pondered, in a part of his brain that allowed another conversation to continue unabated, the drugs had kept him alive? Perhaps.

'I need more, that is true. But later. Now, I need to live.' He pressed on.

A prematurely balding and wiry-electrician walked straight into him, head down, busy trying to complete his work so he could get away, and where possible avoid the inevitable traffic chaos. He intended to spend at best an hour with his new and rather-flexible girlfriend before once more stepping back onto the hamster wheel of municipal life.

"Oy watch it pal, you wanna slow down there chief. 'Ere, you alright? You got yourself a nasty little cut on your eye. 'Ad a scrap wiv your missus?"

"My wife, she find out about other woman!" He emphasised his natural accent, in a successful attempt to avoid a full conversation. "I go to cellar, do plumbing."

"Fill your boots, chief. I haven't been paid this week, so I don't give a monkey's who goes in. Careful though, it's wet through down there."

The male was already walking away into the shadows, resolute, and for all the world just another illegal migrant tradesman living a downtrodden life.

"Women eh? Can't live wiv 'em, certainly can't live wivout 'em. See you later, lock the door on your way out, don't want any more bloody squatters in there do we?"

And with a whistle the youthful tradesman left the corridor, walked through the partially boarded-up entrance and headed for his van.

Gheorghiu watched him exit and made a similar

purposeful approach to the partly derelict building. Without looking behind him he walked in and slid a wooden hoarding into place, creating a temporary barrier. He stopped, listened for activity, other than the chaos outside, and smiled. He exhaled slowly, adapting to the reduced light. Almost there. He could be guaranteed safety if it wasn't for his boss's misplaced loyalty to that helpless drug addict. So what if he brought them more money than they had witnessed for many months? They could train new, younger, expendable boys to do the same role.

'Enough thinking. Get moving.'

Cade and a growing team were rapidly through Blackfriars station, searching as methodically as they could, all the while waiting for any updates.

"Anything from the control room teams? Or our friends at London Transport?"

"Not a thing, guv. It's called TFL now, by the way... Transport for London." He stopped.

"Hang on, look down there!" He was pointing with his non-master hand, the other staying firmly on his weapon.

The officer had been attracted by an underground worker, waving but not wanting to shout, for fear that the attackers might still be in the area.

As they ran towards the guard, weapons in the low ready position their radio hissed back into life.

"TFL have a sighting of our target. He's no longer alone. In company with a younger male. They were seen to exit Blackfriars and turn left. Time delay about three minutes."

Cade was becoming rapidly frustrated, angry at the level of their ill fortune.

"Exit? Jesus H Christ! Right, you two see what he wants. Guys, you two come with me."

He called up on the local channel.

"Cade, all teams at Blackfriars. Let's concentrate our search in the Blackfriars Bridge area please, get into offices, ask questions and remember one of these...people...is armed. Control, you received?"

His instructions were acknowledged and followed by another update.

"All units Blackfriars, DS Roberts is on an underground train with a member of the public, a number of calls coming in, he's alive but injured. The train has been stopped."

"Cade. We'll deal with that." He looked around for another staff member.

"You! I need to get to the train that has just arrived from Embankment."

The sixty-three-year-old female Dominican questioned him immediately.

"Seriously? You want me to go to the train when there are men, with guns? Are you crazy?"

Cade had begun to question over the last twenty-four hours whether he was indeed as unwise as the subterranean veteran was suggesting. He'd crammed more into a day than most would deal with in a lifetime.

"My love I don't know if you have noticed, but we all have guns?"

She hadn't.

"Good, so now you know. I would suggest you are a damned sight safer with us than you are stood here on your own with a bloody whistle. Your call."

She paused, sucked air in through her overly white teeth and started walking.

"This way, gentlemen, this way."

They reached Roberts in less than two minutes. Cade instructed the team members to ensure the train remained on site and also double-checked that they were happy that the platforms and surrounding areas were safe.

"And find out how long the ambulance staff will be. Get someone to fast track them down here!"

He stepped into the train and walked a few metres before kneeling down, smiling at the attending female and placing a hand on Roberts' shoulder.

"Don't tell me, you should see the other guy?"

Roberts could only laugh a shallow, controlled laugh.

"Fuck off, Inspector. This is Emily, by the way. She works for Deloittes. Lovely girl." He was grey with pain. "Have you caught the bastard yet? I want five minutes with him. He's smashed my bloody arm. Look at it. Actually, I can't. I feel sick. I'll never play the guitar again..."

Cade looked down at him, carefully undoing the offending handcuff but still causing his colleague to scream. He laid the damaged limb down at Roberts' side, deciding that any further manipulation would just be cruel.

"I didn't know you played the guitar?"

"I don't." They both laughed, causing Roberts to wince and cough up some more fresh, bright red blood. He spat it onto the train floor whilst trying to ease himself onto his good side. A trickle of red-tinted saliva clung to his chin. He wiped it off with his good hand.

"God's sake, Jack. What have we done?"

"I am not entirely sure, my friend. We've poked the hornet's nest, that's for sure. We'll get 'em. Mark my words. They won't just be able to disappear, big city or not, people talk, and when it comes to informants, I'm going to empty JD's CHIS budget overnight."

Cade knew, in reality, that a CHIS – or Covert Human

Intelligence Source was possibly the only way Cade and the Breaker team might find their targets now.

"Come on, pal. Let's get you comfortable. There's a shit-tonne of cops out there looking for them. Don't know about you, but I've had a guts full of action for one day. How does McDonalds sound? I hear they've got a new Happy Meal..."

"Nice. I fear it may be hospital food for a while." He exhaled, twisting, trying to find somewhere resembling comfortable before slumping back down onto the train floor and slipping back into a state of semi-consciousness.

Cade looked at the girl-next-door-pretty Emily who had given up adjusting her pencil skirt and now sat in a position that also offered basic support and comfort to both her and Roberts.

"Thank you, Emily. I'm sure this will be the start of a beautiful friendship."

She smiled and nodded. "It's OK, my pleasure, we should help you guys more often, but we don't always have the chance – or the courage. Sorry."

Cade was about to remonstrate. She had done really well to keep his colleague's spirits high. He looked through the doorway and saw that more staff were arriving, along with a motorcycle paramedic.

He looked familiar.

"Hello mate. We meet again. You seem to attract chaos. How's your female colleague, any news?"

Cade was horrified. For many hours he had been so pre-occupied he hadn't given O'Shea a second thought.

"I have no idea, mate, I'm ashamed to tell you. I'm sure she will be fine."

"I'm sure too." He wasn't. He looked down at Roberts. "Now then fellow, what's happened to you, some weird stuff at the club you went to or did you try to ride without a ticket?"

Shipley was thirty or so metres onto Blackfriars Bridge. She looked across its ornate span into the Borough of Newington. She saw nothing except a river of pedestrians that she had no interest in. She turned and jogged back, stopping alongside an iconic and latterly it seemed unused phone box.

An electrician was busy arguing with a Traffic Warden, the tradesman was getting visibly angry, telling the 'Officious Nazi' just where to place his ticket. Shipley intervened.

"Gents, sorry to burst into your debate, but have either of you seen two men in the last few minutes? One possibly carrying a backpack. Got a limp. Probably in a hurry?"

"Madam, I am trying to do a job here. I have seen hundreds of men, in the last hour. You expect me to note the descriptions of everyone I see?"

"No, I..."

The 'spark', as electricians were often known, now sensing a possible ally joined in.

"Oy Hitler, do us both a favour. Yes darling, it so 'appens I have. But I only saw one, he's a plumber, Polish I think. Had a cut on his eye. Said his missus walloped 'im for playing away. You Old Bill, are you? Thought so."

Convincing himself Shipley was a police officer he continued, "Went into that building there, just before Adolf 'ere started reading the Riot Act to me. I mean, seriously, 'ow's a bloke supposed to earn a bloody livin' around 'ere when you've got the Waffen SS strutting around like it's nineteen thirty bloody nine? Eh?"

He looked around, enjoying his new audience of one, only to find she had gone.

"What is it wiv this place? It's like everyone I talk to is part aborigine. There one minute – gone the next!"

Shipley had moved on, conscious of the need to remain at least in visual contact. She checked her phone and thought about dialling but knew she couldn't search and speak. If all hell broke loose, the electrician would come to her aid. She pressed on.

Stefanescu had abandoned his vehicle, on double yellow lines on a Thames-side street called Bermondsey Wall East. The car was void of any incriminating evidence and would be towed soon, and someone, at some point, would go and claim it from the compound. Or not. He had never registered it as his. As with all the vehicles he drove, it was a clone. High powered, high value but ultimately worthless. He'd just place an order to have a new one stolen.

He checked his phone for messages and increased the pace, walking past a bronze statue of an elderly male, sat on a bench staring across the walkway at two more statues, one of a little girl, the other, perched on the river wall, a cat. On any normal day, any normal individual would stop and admire the artwork, or possibly even have a photograph taken.

He shook his head, mocking the English before pacing towards a boardwalk and crossing over a small white footbridge that descended to a mooring. Without even looking for a custodian or an owner, he climbed aboard a small boat and checked for keys.

Finding nothing, he moved onto another. A male shouted from the footpath. He simply cupped his ear, shrugged, waved back and started the second boat.

Once he had left the small berthing area, used by a local

Thames river cruise company he moved upstream as quickly as he could. The tidal flow was impressive and enough to propel him along at just below the locally posted limited. He wanted to get somewhere quickly but not attract attention. He pushed on. The tide was in his favour and coming in rapidly.

Ahead and to his right lay the landmark sites of Tower Bridge and the Tower of London. He was disinterested at best, keeping any eye open for anyone in authority who might be watching for him specifically, or an over-eager official looking to make his quota. Either way he needed to remain anonymous. He kept left, under the bridge, and took a moment to look up, dwarfed by its impressive span and architecture.

The Tower was equally imposing. He looked at it and thought aloud that it would have made him a fine home.

He'd keep the jewels too, naturally.

With his phone in one hand and the other on the wheel, he was making progress, tucking in tightly alongside *HMS Belfast*, a floating leviathan of the last world war.

Although he was making excellent headway, he wanted to go faster, but whilst the tide was on his side, time wasn't. He had misjudged the duration of the journey, wishing now he had sought out a vessel closer to his pre-arranged meeting point. Damn the authorities, who were they to control him? Or, was he in fact just like them?

Cutting under the Millennium Bridge, he was at last in reach of his end destination, Blackfriars.

Looking over his shoulder he began to time his change of course, looking left, right and ahead, an eagle scanning its environs. There were people everywhere; on the river, on the bridges and on land. But in a throbbing metropolis was anyone really interested in his activities?

Two minutes.

"I hope you have followed the instructions?" He asked aloud, more than anything to himself, for no one else was close enough to hear.

Shipley moved quietly through the ground floor of the former café, checking rooms as she went, placing her phone onto silent. Quite what she was going to do when she caught up with them was something, unusually for one so highly organised, that she had not yet considered.

Much of the ground floor was a building site. Why would they hide here? Knocking over a half-empty bottle, she ground to a halt, waited, her breathing overly loud. She measured it until she was able to calm down and move on. The next room was lighter, its old sash windows, jammed in place by years of over-painting allowed a stream of light into the space, creating pockets of chromatic bright light in a sea of dust. She brushed it away and realised that the particles had been caused by recent human disruption.

They were here.

CHAPTER TWENTY

John Daniel was about to leave Scotland Yard when he sensed a figure in the doorway to his office. He pulled his glasses down from the top of his forehead, slid them into place and looked up.

It was Frank Waterman.

"Frank, how are you, sir?"

"Better than you by the looks of it, JD. About time you took a break. How's it going? How's Lynne? I heard about Roberts."

"Thanks, yes, bloody awful actually. Lynne is great thank you for asking. Roberts? Lucky to be alive and pissed off. There you go, all three answered in one easy sentence."

The desk phone chirped a familiar classical melody.

"Daniel."

He listened briefly, then exhaled without any difficulty and looked up at his boss whilst shaking his head gently.

Waterman was right. Time to head home.

"Penny for 'em, John."

"It's O'Shea, she's taken a turn for the worst. Not

looking good, what with that and the RAF girl too. Cade's out on a manhunt for the bastard that got them. God help him if he finds them first."

"Remind him of the ancient laws of England and Wales, please John. As for O'Shea, does he know?"

"No."

"Then keep it that way, John."

"Will do, Frank. Oh, and Frank, did you want me for something?"

He had already started to leave Daniel's office but shouted back, "I want you to spend some time with Hewett. An opportunity might be coming up to work in France – but of a joint op with our boys and Interpol. He's the man to broker it, for you and Cade too if he can make his bloody mind up on his future. But for now, it'll wait."

Waterman had slipped Hewett's embossed business card onto the desk.

"Give him a bell, but do it tomorrow. He's a good man. Not to everyone's taste, bit too handsome for my bloody liking, but as an operator he's first class, and he seems loyal, and importantly, I trust him too. Go home, John. That's an order."

Daniel tapped the cell phone details into his phone, placed the business card into his desk and shut the drawer and locked it. He hit Control, Alt and Delete, locking his computer before pushing back the leather office chair and picking up his car keys.

In the lift on the way to the car park, he rang his wife.

"It's me." She knew what was coming. "Sorry. I'm likely to be late. I owe you one. Again. I'll grab some dinner on the way home."

.   .   .

Shipley was on her toes now, walking skilfully through the building and wishing she had a firearm, or better still a few of her colleagues by her side. She also thought about her running partner and for the first time she acknowledged that he kept interrupting her thoughts, entering her mind when her guard was down. She made a mental note to ring him, or better still, head to his room and show him, physically, how much she thought of him.

She paused, listened, and moved forward. The smallest hairs on the back of her neck stood up, she shuddered but wasn't cold. She swore she could hear someone breathing just around the corner. She exhaled, tensing up her diaphragm just as she had been taught.

She knew that in order to continue the hunt she had to take two, possibly three steps into the half-light. Discarding the opportunity to find a weapon of opportunity, she would rely on her hands and feet. She stepped down, one step, and then another into the cellar. The electrician was right; it was wet through, a trace of mildew and aging paint clung in the air. If she had stood still long enough, she could have heard the flaking cream-coloured emulsion fluttering from the walls and onto the surface of the dank water below.

She waited a moment, blinking, allowing her eyes to acclimatise, and then gently stepped into the pool. A pump lay in it, discarded and clearly ineffective. The water was about six inches deep and still. If she could see clearly, it would have been green and opaque. She could hear water running nearby and decided to follow the sound to its source. She closed her eyes, allowing her hearing to take primacy.

Bottom left. She moved towards the sound. She could feel her phone vibrating furiously in her pocket. There was no time to answer it.

. . .

"No answer from the informant boss. Control room staff are trying to track her on available CCTV as we speak."

"Thanks, keep me informed and let the control room know everything – if we have new information, they get it in the very next call. Everything, alright?" He patted Roberts on the back, gently but with enough strength to make him realise he was going.

"Got to go Jase, I, or rather we, need to find these scum and get them locked up. I'll come and find you as soon as I can and I promise, when this is over, I'll treat you to guitar lessons. Right, I'm out of here."

For the second time that day, Cade handed someone he cared a great deal about into the care of a sole paramedic. He didn't have to say another word.

Cade and three staff left the claustrophobia of the platforms and made their way back up towards daylight, passing two more ambulance staff heading in the opposite direction. The police team were soon joining the hubbub of daily activities and the tumult of vehicular traffic that crisscrossed over the bridge, heading north to south and vice versa. Cade found himself wanting to be below ground again, it was quieter and allowed him space to think.

He stood for a while, getting his bearings, trying to listen above the din.

"Where to boss?" It was the youngest of the three staff, clearly keen to arrest or shoot someone. He was a follower and as with all followers, he needed a leader to galvanise him.

"Just give me a second boys. I can't explain why, but I've got a feeling she's close, and if she's nearby, then they are too. Call it intuition, call it balls-to-the-wall exhaustion, but bear with me?"

Who were they to argue?

. . .

Her shoes and socks were saturated, and she was now cold, but the red mist had lowered. There was no way she was turning back. The police needed to know where the two offenders had gone. Better still, if she could detain them they could arrest them and allow the officer on the train to have some justice, preferably summary and out of the way of prying eyes. Down here, off the beaten track, would be just perfect.

She came to a door, half open, stuck fast in deeper water. She squeezed into the gap, struggling, even with her slight frame. As she emerged into another corridor, the first of two rapid blows hit her. One to the face, the other to her left arm.

She was stunned by the impact but switched into fight mode. She moved backwards quickly, re-adjusted her footing and focused on her target. It wasn't the drug addict but a slightly younger, stockier male. He was holding a length of wood in his right hand. She'd strike that first – if only she had the space, if only this bastard was on a mat, in a brightly lit gym. She would literally kick the shit out of him.

She tried to kick out, but the water reduced the power and direction of her primary weapon. The male moved back, countering a possible blow and struck back, hitting her again on the upper left arm. She had to isolate that weapon.

She punched out, exhaling, driving the air up through her lungs and let out a considerable yell. Her fist, expertly positioned, struck his right bicep, sending a shock wave through the muscle and nerves. His reaction was instantaneous, he dropped the wood into the water and almost involuntarily lowered his upper body to retrieve it.

He'd planned to show her how to have some respect. It

was a naïve mistake.

She drove her knee into his chin, knocking him backwards into the water. It felt good. She was in a cat stance, ready for the next counter. She was bouncing from left to right; even the water couldn't stop her now.

"Come on. Try again." She was actually enjoying the fight and resisting the urge to react to the pain that coursed through her recent injuries.

She looked beyond her opponent, who was recovering from the surprise strength of his sparring partner. There was the addict again and now he was moving through the water rapidly, causing small waves to lap against the decaying walls. She could see he was holding a hammer.

She was ready for him. His colleague had made a mistake, and she hoped he'd do the same. She'd immobilise his fighting arm in two seconds, then drive her palm up and into his nose.

Her teacher had always told her, "Leave this as your last resort, MJ. If you get it right, it will be very wrong for your opponent. Very wrong indeed."

The younger male was trying to get up. She slammed her right fist into the top of his head and then another onto the collar bone, rendering him, for the short time, ineffective.

The room was noisy now, sounds of water sloshing back and forth, of pain and energy being consumed. It was confined chaos.

She couldn't reach the older male, but if she could she would have hit him so very hard, the vile little weasel. Look at him, with his hideous face and loathsome smile.

She made her first mistake at that very moment. In the worsening light, she failed to see him throw the hammer. It left his hand, rotated twice and hit her, shaft first between her eyes. At first the noise was worse than the pain, but then the headache started. Her vision was blurring and pain encompassed her. Her natural human reaction was to place her hands up to her face, and in doing so she lowered her guard.

She felt hands on her lower legs, dragging her down. She fell backwards, striking her shoulder blade on a submersed hazard.

The hands dragged her by her feet, through the water and quickly submerging her face. She knew not to scream, instead keeping her lips tightly sealed.

Gheorghiu had the strength of an ox. He was up now and standing, and pulling her unceremoniously through the building, away from the street and possible rescue. Constantin was forging ahead, just as he was told. He moved down another level, lifted a hatch in the floor and exposed a tunnel. His partner was alongside him now, still clinging to the girl who was recovering and starting to resist.

As they picked her up she lashed out, striking Constantin under the nose. He heard the cartilage break, a deep-seated cracking sound reverberated inside his head – the noise was awful, like a stubborn tooth being extracted.

He punched her squarely in the face.

Gheorghiu held her now, his strong hands under her armpits.

"Go down. Now!" he yelled at Constantin.

His instructions were obeyed. As the bloodied and more senior male disappeared down into the void, Gheorghiu waited a second and then pulled her to the edge.

She struck him twice in quick succession with her right elbow. He blocked the first, but the second landed on his left eye socket.

"Stupid bitch. I am going to kill you as soon as I get chance." He tensed his muscles, sucking the life out of her;

she was partly through the hatch now, her legs were twice as heavy as normal and now useless as weapons, worse still her arms were trapped, entwined in his.

She looked into the space below, which was a little brighter; she was aware of a source of stronger light coming from her right. There was water again, deeper and stronger smelling: mud, dirt, pollutants, life, death – the many odours of an historic waterway were assaulting her olfactory system and playing havoc with her mind. The close confines of the tunnel seemed to exacerbate the smell making her to want to vomit.

She could feel herself passing out and knew that she needed to conserve energy. Whatever was coming next, whatever plans, albeit spontaneous ones, were hardly likely to be pleasant.

Gheorghiu looked down. Below him was a perfectly round, Victorian, brick-built tunnel. Like so many similar structures it was built in the late eighteen hundreds, its purpose was simple but beautifully executed, to allow waste water into the Thames.

Without compassion, he dropped Shipley feet first. She landed with a watery thud, knocking what air she had left in her lungs rapidly out of her, the fall tearing the ligaments in her left ankle. Gheorghiu lowered himself down and landed, trying his best not to roll his own ankles on the awkwardly curved brickwork.

Shipley's now semi-conscious body had hit the water below and immediately started to drift away from the large iron grid that separated them from the tunnel and the River Thames.

The two Romanian men were now in the ancient sewage system, trying to formulate a plan. They needed to escape but also prevent the irritating girl from either following them, or worse, giving evidence against them. They needed to kill her. There were no longer other options. However, there were no weapons available either. The older man started to look around the tunnel. There had to be something they could use, other than their bare hands.

He wasn't averse to killing, but he feared the physical contact that was required, making him, rather idealistically, a resourceful killer, one who normally thought of his work as an art form. The inquisitive and foolish old man, for example, had died a remote death with no tangible connection to Constantin. The girl too, overcome by a simple chemical reaction. It really was all too easy.

But not the boy. He was somehow different. Both he and his executioner had watched the bullet that struck him in the forehead; its rapid, yet conversely slow flight had ended his all too brief life. It would be one of Constantin's few regrets.

He searched further. The incredible brickwork that surrounded them was worn smooth from a century of activity, but testament to the sheer skill of the men that had laid each one a hundred and fifty years before their arrival, not one single brick was loose.

Constantin scrambled beneath the water, noting that it was starting to rise.

His fingers grasped an object, and he immediately started to pull it from beneath the surface. It was a chain which was attached to the grid in front of them. A length of rope, slippery and stained but still intact, was tied to the end of the chain. It once had a purpose, he was sure, and now he had found another.

What they were standing in was part of an old sewerage system but also an outlet for another of London's great river systems, the River Fleet. The same river that gave birth to Fleet Street and its world-famous newspaper industry.

Now practically invisible to commuters and tourists, the Fleet made its way across north London, now almost entirely underground, running for four miles from one of its sources on Hampstead Heath. Since Roman times the river had provided transport, trade and even, during the river's purer days, a source of health.

That the tunnel system still remained so intact was credit to its engineers and builders who had constructed it some forty feet into the ground and allowed it to wash the waste of thousands into the serpentine waterway that endlessly flowed out to the east and eventually into the North Sea.

Constantin could sense the arrival of the incoming tide. What he didn't know was that the tunnel they were in, could flood to its ceiling in half an hour. It was a salient fact left out of the conversation he had held with his boss when the rapid plans had been made with the owner of the dilapidated café, a fellow countryman who was happy to accept a few hundred pounds to turn a blind eye.

Gheorghiu called over to his partner, raising his voice against the growing noise of the incoming waters. "Grab her, get her hands and tie the rope to them."

He tried, but the rope would not hold.

"Around her waist. I'll deal with her wrists."

He tore a sleeve from his shirt and bound it around her slender wrists. She started to struggle once more, using the last of her strength against her attackers. She kicked out wildly but missed with each attempt.

The realisation of what was about to happen began to overwhelm her.

The rope sealed against itself, sitting on her hips, tied

behind her back. The second sleeve had now been formed into a gag and wrapped tightly around her mouth.

Constantin approached the large ironwork gateway and looked out into the Thames, which was rising with alarming speed. He turned and started to wade through the water, back towards Gheorghiu and passing the girl who was trying to maintain her balance in the deepening current. She looked pathetic, worse still she felt pathetic.

As Constantin struggled past her, he stopped and took hold of her shoulders. He lifted her hair in his hands, feeling its weight. It was wet and burnished, almost raisin-coloured in the available light, he hadn't noticed its beauty before now but it reminded him of the colours of a bird he had nurtured when just a small boy, for days he had fed it by hand before placing it back into its nest. For a short time, he reflected upon his childhood; what had become of the kind, compassionate boy? What had led to him becoming such a sadistic and uncaring creature?

Born to a young and single mother who could barely look after herself let alone a new-born son, she had been threatened with imprisonment for twice trying to drown him during her repeated heroin-fuelled escapes from reality, unable to cope with his torrid home life he ran away from his village and home at the age of thirteen.

It was the start of everything.

His infatuation with drowning – with death – and how to convey it.

He looked into the British girl's eyes. They displayed a mixture of defiance and fear.

Was this the opportunity she needed? To appeal to his better side? To possibly reduce the odds?

Constantin shook himself back into the present – he would offer no such chance. His own eyes were as cold as the incoming tide. He smiled, reached around her neck and tightened the gag and then stepped to her side, knocking the back of her knee with his foot. She buckled and fell into the water and was partly submerged once more as she fought to remain above its surface.

Neither man looked at her as she flailed around in the tunnel. They had their own lives to save. If she had not been so foolish, so belligerent and so bloody brave, then perhaps things would have turned out better for her.

The water level rose around her, she was floating now, all but gone.

"Leave her, she can do nothing to us now, brother. We need to get to the next tunnel. Stefan will meet us. Come on...we must go. We have only fifteen minutes."

"Boss, one of the control room operators has managed to triangulate the girl's signal. We are apparently right on top of her last transmission. You're right, she's here, somewhere."

Cade was pacing now, not too dissimilar to an expectant father. He knew it was pointless carrying out a random search, they rarely achieved a result. Whether it was a missing child or a criminal on the run, it took method, structure and discipline to find them.

Cade began to do what he did best in these situations, scratch his head. He walked towards the bridge as his emergent team followed two steps behind.

He knew he had to re-engage but was seriously wondering why he appeared to be the only bloody supervisor for miles around. It was a force of some thirty thousand staff. Where the hell were they all?

"OK, two of you get over the road and start asking questions in those buildings. Ask about CCTV, get names and get phone numbers, this is rapidly becoming another bloody murder investigation. You know what to do, be police officers for Christ's sake!"

Two staff did exactly what they were told and ran, dodging traffic, and soon disappeared into a large commercial building. Given their para-military appearance, Cade was sure they would get the answers they craved.

"You, get back to the underground station and watch for signs of life – please."

"Will do, guv."

He was back in control.

"And you two come with me. Let's see if my gut feeling is right."

They walked towards the old sandwich bar but were flagged down by an exasperated parking warden.

"At last, I asked for back up ages ago. He could have killed me by now!"

Cade was far from in the mood for such an intervention, but swiftly reverted to street cop mode.

"I'm in a hell of a hurry. Are you injured? Is this man an immediate threat? Can it wait?"

Unusually, the electrician answered first.

"No, he's not, neither of us are. Am I a threat, 'ardly but to be fair if he'd ticketed your motor you'd be pissed off too? I'm trying to earn a living here boss, please see reason. Can it wait? As it 'appens not really, I've got a date with a very innovative gymnast."

It was the most amusing response Cade had heard for days.

"Strikes me a warning would suffice." He looked straight at the warden. "Now, if you don't mind, I've got armed criminals to bloody well catch."

He went to walk away when the electrician grabbed his arm.

"Chief. Thanks, I'm just an honest man trying to earn a living. You looking for the skinny bird in the tracksuit? She's one of yours, isn't she? I knew it."

"What?"

"One of your lot. She was chasing two right dodgy looking blokes. One of 'em is Eastern European, a plumber, he said he was Polish, but I know pony when I hear it."

Cade stared at him, quizzically.

"Pony? Pony and trap. It's rhyming slang for..."

"Yes, yes, I get it. I just want you to finish your bloody story!"

"Well, I didn't believe him to be honest, but I'm knackered and just want to get home to Nadia."

Cade was getting more tired by the second. His colleagues were fanning out now and scanning the streets for any sign of a clue. Another patrol van stopped outside the underground. Four staff, three constables and a sergeant got out, adjusted their yellow coats and set about showing a presence in the area.

Cade had the firearm in his right hand now and was commanding the attention of those around him.

"Sorry? From the top. Nadia? Who the bloody hell is Nadia?"

Staring at the Glock, the electrician continued. "Jesus, don't you listen? She's the gymnast, named after Comaneci, the Romanian girl, the Perfect Ten. I always fancied her. It was her accent see, I can spot a Romanian voice from as far away as Bucharest, further if she is attractive!"

Cade looked straight at the male, "What is your name?"

"Kevin. Kevin Brock. KB Electrical." He produced a grubby business card from his overalls.

"Kevin, I have been awake for days. I have no need of a rewire or even an additional and all together convenient extra socket. I am actively pursuing armed offenders and am at great risk of losing someone I...love...most dearly."

Brock nodded encouragingly.

"Given the cocktail of exhaustion, frustration and absolute desire to be somewhere else other than talking to you two, please do understand if without so much as a warning I should suddenly shoot you in the spleen."

He understood. The warden was smiling smugly now.

"And you, you overly vindictive fascist, would be a close second, ideally with the same bullet. I'm conscious of saving money, given the state of our budget. Tear his ticket up and go and annoy someone else."

"Nice one, guv'nor." The electrician was the one smiling now.

"Seriously, I will shoot you, Kevin. Now if you don't mind?" He walked away, back towards the bridge, sliding the firearm awkwardly between his waist and his trouser belt. It felt ridiculous, so he carried it in his left hand, caring not what the public thought upon seeing a scarlet-eyed gunman walking towards them.

"Left!" It was Kevin Brock again.

Cade ran his palm over the stock of the Glock but thought better of it. Why destroy what was left of his already tattered career?

"Go on, you've got my attention. You said left?"

"I did, sir. She went in through that hording there by the phone box. She followed the two blokes. I've been trying to tell you but…you were somewhat focused on shooting me in an organ that I can live without."

With a half-smile Cade said, "I was, wasn't I? Apologies. Out of order. Thank you for your help, Kevin. Enjoy Nadia – give her one from me."

Cade whistled to the now under-employed staff member at the door of the underground. He ran to the doorway and joined Cade, who was already pulling the plywood panelling to one side.

"Another call from control boss. We are spot on. The signal is coming from this building."

Cade nodded back towards the young electrician and entered the doorway. He hoped he was in for a great night, the lucky bastard.

He looked back at the younger officer whose face was a picture – part fear, part excitement. He snorted as he recalled his own first day on the job, charging into a house in a leafy suburb of Nottingham to arrest a man who was pointing a shotgun at him and his wise old sergeant. Hindsight told him it was madness, but wild horses wouldn't have dragged him away from the opportunity.

"Turn your radio right down, we don't want anyone startled, do we?" Cade finished the sentence with a reassuring pat on his arm and a wink of his trademark blue eyes.

Raising his pistol into the low-ready position, he entered further into the building.

The Audi S6 pulled to the side of the road. Its wipers had now ceased their continuous arc. The car was tucked tightly into the kerb of Melbourne Place, just off the ever-busy Strand, and behind Australia House, a place where his car and face were familiar.

Exhaust gases emanated from the Audi's twin chromed pipes as its driver waited patiently. He would wait here, regardless of the improbable risk of being asked to move on.

He looked into the rear-view mirror again and smiled, his eyes narrowing, revealing the beginnings of subtle crow's feet. They were the legacy of years of long, painful hours; endless government meetings, countless false smiles and promises, most of which were broken as soon as they were uttered.

He acknowledged the hint of grey appearing on his suntanned temples; there was nothing to fear. Apparently the ladies liked it, some even loved it, for them grey was the new black.

He leant forward and pressed the power button on his Hi-Fi. The Bose speakers announced his favourite fast-driving soundtrack. He turned it up, indicated right, glanced over his right shoulder and entered the line of traffic. He accelerated along Arundel Street before turning left and joining heavier traffic on Temple Place.

In a hundred metres he looked at his watch, his favoured Rolex Submariner, a recommended timepiece that he had rewarded himself with a few years before. He would often admire the movement, the dark, perfectly painted black face and complimentary bright white sweeping second hand, and the steel bracelet. He liked that especially, for again he was able to liken himself to its manufacturer's official description:

It maintains its beauty even in the harshest environments.

The whole package was, he thought, very much like himself. Beautifully presented, exquisitely constructed and evidently, perfectly designed and singularly reliable. When he first slipped it over his wrist in the discreet city jewellers he had stood and admired it, as the manager nodded an approving and somewhat sycophantic nod.

"Excellent choice, sir. And may I say one, which unlike people, will never let you down."

And that was Hewett's cathartic moment in life. A bloody watch. He'd broken a thousand hearts and brokered many more deals for the British. Despite his relatively young years he had been supremely successful as a negotiator among men – and a fair few women too, most of whom, with the notable and praiseworthy exception of the borderline nymphomaniac from Slovenia, had been taught the ways of the world in a single night, in a king-sized bed, and all at the expense of the host nation.

He was nothing if not a supremely capable operator.

But that was then. He was fed up to his immaculately white back teeth. Good old reliable Johnnie Bloody Hewett. Well, frankly, enough was enough. Why should he burn both ends of the candle, day after day, for a high-end five-figure annual salary when a few equally long days of using his supreme experience could net him more, a lot more?

He began to sing, comfortably aware that the heavily tinted green glass shielded him from embarrassment. Not that he really cared anymore, well, not that much anyway.

For Johnnie Hewett, the day was just getting better. His fingers mimicked a pair of Hickory sticks beating an imaginary drum as they bounced again and again onto the hand-stitched black leather steering wheel. Frankie sang about *Two Tribes*.

As he merged with more traffic on Victoria Embankment he slowed once again, admiring the view as he always did. He was devoutly British, through and through, the product of British parents, both of whom, having served overseas with the Foreign Office, were once also fiercely patriotic.

His eye caught one of the two silver dragons that sat either side of the road. Boundary markers for the City of London, they were just one of the hundreds of historical effigies that marked out London as a city of culture, statues, like so many, missed by the millions that walked and drove by them every day.

However, as much as he admired them, his gaze was drawn to the iconic London Eye, for him a symbol of success, of wealth, of 'look at me'. He clicked his thumb and forefinger together and pointed at it, "That's more you John-nie, my boy. Sleek but not too shiny!"

He dropped down below the skyline as the Audi cruised into the Blackfriars Underpass. He lowered the driver's window a touch so he could hear the Audi's engine note reverberate off the enclosed walls as Frankie and his band belted out the chorus.

John Daniel was also making progress through the relentless city traffic in his altogether more basic Ford.

He had made the decision to head towards Cade. Driving a desk was fine, but like most career cops Daniel missed the thrill of the chase, and since the new boy had arrived, it seemed as though the chase was not only on; it was permanent.

He was fit enough still, so why not? "Just don't tell the wife", he'd said to an audience of one as he skilfully whipped through the traffic, darting into gaps and grabbing opportunities as only an experienced London commuter could. Faint heart never won a fair lady, and timid driving didn't get you to the church, or anywhere else for that matter, on time. He changed up through the gearbox and got the hatchback up to sixty. Not once had he used the discreet lights or sirens.

He was on the Blackfriars Underpass now, also heading east. He came up behind an Audi and admired it.

"Nice car," he said out aloud, pulling alongside and performing a double-take as he recognised the driver as Hewett.

The traffic was slowing them both now as they progressed in a stop-start manner along the partly tunnelled route that snaked alongside the Thames.

Daniel fished around for his cell phone, opened it, typed an 'H' and found Hewett's number. It began to ring. He looked across and saw Hewett doing his utmost to ignore the call. After eight rings he answered.

"John Hewett."

"John, John Daniel. Frank Waterman asked me to ring for a chat. I'm on the way to support a colleague but seeing as though I'm actually alongside you I thought I would strike whilst the iron was hot. After all, neither of us are going far in this bloody traffic." He laughed, forcing a response from Hewett who looked genuinely startled.

"Indeed. Bloody traffic. John, would you mind, I'm waiting for a rather important call, from the um...Home Office. I'll promise to catch up soon. Coffee, at my place, how does that sound?"

Daniel knew how and when to recognise being fobbed off, but decided to play along.

"Sounds good. I'll crack on with rescuing Cade."

"Cade?" Hewett no longer seemed to be in such a hurry.

"Yes, one of my team, you've done a bit of work to support him already."

"Yes, I'm aware of that John, but what has he done now?"

"Oh, other than causing chaos across half of London chasing a bunch of bloody tearaway Eastern Europeans hell-bent on emptying our ATMs...not much, really."

"Sounds fun. So exactly where is he now?"

"Your guess, John. Your guess. Last update I had was that he was heading into a building to follow a girl – who might well have the answer to who tried to gun down one of my staff on a tube train a short while ago. It's a rather convoluted story, but needless to say Cade seems to be on their trail. I pity anyone who stands in his way."

"As I say, sounds fun. I miss the chase, John, more international stuff these days, dashing here, flying there, you know how it is I'm sure. Anyway, I've taken up enough of your precious time, look after that bounty hunter of yours, I hear he's been offered a chance in Lyon. My advice would be to take it and get out of town before he becomes a target."

Hewett cleared down, leaving Daniel to ponder what the last line of the conversation meant. He saw the Audi accelerate briskly and indicate left. It cut across the two lanes and disappeared up a side street.

He decided to make some progress himself, lifting the lid on the central armrest and initiating the sirens, the flickering strobes beneath the grill added to the effect and he was soon dominating his way through the underpass, enjoying the thrill of rapid response driving through almost stationary traffic. Who wouldn't, given the chance?

The two desperately wet and exhausted males clambered through the larger tunnel and into a smaller one, slightly higher, above the current high-water mark.

Gheorghiu looked back, seeing his colleague immediately behind him, he pressed on into the dark.

Ten minutes later, but only a hundred metres away, they turned left and headed back towards the light. The stench inside the tunnel made them both heave. Even Constantin, who, upon self-reflection had sunk as low as he could go, now considered this to be the lowest point in his life. He wished his bastard of a mother had drowned him when she had the chance.

Minutes later they had reached the metal grill, similar but less significant than the last they had looked out of, across the green and grey surface of the River Thames.

Dropping down the outlet, they collided with the aging metalwork and paused for breath, wiping their faces of filth.

"OK, Constantin, like I told you. Yes?"

The older male nodded and laid down in the rising water, his back to the tunnel and his feet up against the rusting grid. Gheorghiu joined him and they began to kick the framework of the Victorian ironwork. It resisted.

"Kick harder. This grid is all that lies between you, me and the outside world. If we are caught, especially you, then the game is over. The next bars we will see will not be so weak. Kick!"

Stefanescu had slowed the stolen boat to a crawl. He'd been travelling at twelve knots in the King's Reach, and at that speed was not likely to attract anyone – lawful or otherwise. But now he dropped the speed again, almost drifting at three to four knots. The on-board VHF radio hissed into life on channel 14. He expertly ignored it and whatever the bland male voice was saying.

The depth of the river allowed him to edge up to the Embankment. He cruised eastwards and came up alongside the First World War vessel, the *HMS President*, her black hull and white superstructure standing out against the green-stained river walls.

Almost anticipating a voice, or a shout of warning that never came, he was on edge, coiled and ready. Why did he always have to be the one to expose himself to such danger when his useless brother lived a risk-free life?

His mind wandered as the smaller boat reached the end of the *President*.

Trying to be discreet was becoming a nuisance. He accelerated slightly; the bow lifted, and he navigated down the river towards the Blackfriars Millennium Pier. A few minutes later and looking over his shoulder he was back alongside the impressive river walls once more. He could see the meeting point ahead.

Cade turned in the half-light and beckoned to the younger officer to join him.

"Any news on that radio of yours?"

The constable was wearing an earpiece now, a moment of inspiration following the instruction from Cade to turn the volume down.

"Nothing governor. Shouldn't we wait for backup?"

He was right.

"You're right, but we haven't got time. Go back if you need to. I won't hate you, but when they are dishing out tea and medals at the palace, don't come crying to me when your name isn't called out by HRH. Besides, they won't attack us, we're the coppers!"

It didn't help at all, but like so many junior police staff it was often easier to agree with a senior officer than it was to walk away and face the dreaded 'canteen culture' conversations that followed later. And this boss seemed like a good bloke. He paused for a moment to think of his family, then nodded and stepped into the shadows.

Cade held up a hand – military style.

'Stop. Wait.'

"Did you hear something?"

"No, sir."

She was holding her own, kicking against the tide and holding her face up to the grid, turning at every opportunity onto her back and trying to relax. If she could just stay afloat sooner or later, someone would come to her aid.

The gag did its job, tied tightly across her mouth, and reinforced with the pressure of the water prevented her from screaming, but more importantly it now caused her to panic. She knew she had to take control. How much longer could she sustain this? As fit as she was, she was beginning to lose the battle. She was drowning, second by second.

She began to think of her parents – the two people that meant the most to her, then remembered once more the day she passed out, resplendent in her number one uniform, and how her father had wept. They were genuine tears of pride. He smiled, but it was a forced smile.

"All I need to do now is protect you from the dangers of conflict. Please pick your battles, my girl."

Her mother stood behind him, trying to summon her own smile. What would they think right now, what would they think?

Her upper body dropped below the waterline and she began to sink to the brick-lined base of the tunnel.

Let go, Mary. It's OK.

· · ·

"It's giving way, brother! Kick harder! Once it is loosened we can make enough space."

The encouragement was all he needed. He leant into the grid and drove his right foot into it again and again. It started to move. The stone was strong, as robust as the day it was laid, but the union between the brickwork and the iron was weaker; age and a combined daily onslaught of water has loosened its grip.

"We only need enough room to slip through!"

Although Gheorghiu was shouting, no one other than his immediate companion could hear him. Not the river users, the oblivious pedestrians walking along the Embankment above them, not even Cade and John Nicol a constable barely out of his probationary period and now following an older, and he'd hoped far-wiser boss into yet another unfamiliar situation.

The bar lost its battle. They took it in turns to feel below the surface until Constantin managed to get a strong grip. He was beyond exhausted but the chance of salvation, monetary rewards and the first hot shower in a week provided all the encouragement he needed.

"Brother, I will hang onto the bar with all my strength. Get behind me and pull me backwards. We will do this. Stefan will be here soon. To save us."

Gheorghiu was now subservient and had wrapped his powerful arms around Nicolescu. The combined strength of both men moved the bar for the first time in over a hundred years.

Gheorghiu pointed below the water.

"We need to get down there and swim."

Constantin looked astonished.

"No. I cannot do this. I cannot explain. But you go. I will stay."

Gheorghiu wiped more water from his face and breathed in heavily through his nose, anger building.

"The reason I am here, up to my neck in human waste, is for you Nicolescu. I could be in a hotel bed with a whore now, but for you. The boss thinks you are worth saving – that you have skills that he needs – needs to reward! And this is how you reward me?" His face reddened. He leant forward and grabbed Constantin by the scruff of the neck.

"Whatever the reason, you are going. When I count to three, you go down and I will push you through. It is just a second underwater. When you get to the other side, hang onto the bars and stay quiet. Either that or you can go back in there and die with that stupid girl. You can drown too, for all I care. Go on, you selfish little man. Go back and die."

If only to spite his departed mother. He took a deep breath and closed his eyes. "OK."

Hewett pulled into Broken Wharf and slowed, easing the Audi into a business area surrounded by barriers and CCTV systems. It was a nightmare location, but one he felt confident he could talk his way out of. He would stay in the car, exiting only under extreme circumstances. If the police came, he would identify himself and forget about his plans, either for the very near future or, if the circumstances altered, forever.

They had absolutely nothing on him. Amateurs, at best.

He checked his watch. Reliable as ever. He looked at his phone. A full signal, but no missed calls. He could wait. No one would dare move him on.

· · ·

"It's there again. Did you not hear it that time? A dull knocking?"

"Yes, I heard it that time, boss."

"Come on mate, let's go and whilst we are up to our nuts in bad guys please call me Jack. OK?"

They moved more rapidly through the same hallways and down into the building until they came to the cellar.

"Looks like we get wet from here on in pal."

They moved quietly and in sync. Cade liked Nicol, he was young but mature and looked like he could handle himself in a fight.

They reached a semi-open, partly flooded doorway and squeezed through. Cade was waiting for the almost inevitable blow to the head – so always went first. He heard the sound again, closer this time, but it had changed, it was no longer industrial; it was animal. To be precise, human.

CHAPTER TWENTY-ONE

Daniel pulled his car onto the pavement behind an eponymously named Transit van.

He slipped his phone into his pocket, got out and locked the car. He was joined moments later by the shift inspector who had also just arrived on scene.

"John Daniel." A quick shake of hands took place.

"Andy Jennings. Marvellous weather. What do you need my team to do, boss?"

"Thanks Andy, shake the trees, lift the manhole covers, do whatever you can to find anyone connected to the attack on DS Roberts. Oh, and if possible locate my DI would you. He's a northerner, probably likes warm beer and rugby league, a little out of place in the big city. But for Christ's sake don't say I told you or he'll have my guts for proverbial sock stays."

Jennings, a young veteran, was already en route to his team of five when Daniel called him back.

"Sorry, Andy. Between you and me, if you see a rather

nice Audi pull up with a good-looking bastard behind the wheel, will you let me know? Immediately."

"Absolutely sir. One of ours?"

Daniel paused. "I thought so. But I'm not sure anymore, I'm not sure."

Hewett tried his best to relax. He ran his hand over his cell phone, saw Daniel's number on his list of recent callers and gently pressed his index finger against the call button, causing the crystal display to distort but not enough to initiate the call.

He knew he was about to make the biggest decision of his adult life, a chance for a truly hedonistic lifestyle, and all he had to do was betray everything he had publicly stood for. And he had stood for it for rather a long time; for how long, he couldn't recall, but it had been a while.

He had said and done the right thing over and over again, he was what the Foreign Office chiefs described as 'highly thought of' and in order to get to where he was now he had had to bend the rules occasionally – they all had, they all did. But a debt was a debt, and one he knew he had to honour. Why he had ever allowed himself to become embroiled with them, he would never know. Was it the cars? The girls? Or the bizarre antithesis of loyalty that attracted him?

He was on the first phase of the roller coaster; tick-tick-tick, and heading to the top. When his solitary car reached the summit he had a choice, get off or stay on board. Was it the thrill of the ride that drew him in?

Or was it the chance to be truly debt-free?

His windscreen was starting to fog, so he turned the ignition back on. Better to give the impression that he was only a temporary visitor to the myriad sets of prying electronic eyes. He watched as the mist danced away from the green glass and then gazed across the river, to the south.

His phone throbbed against his left thigh and brought him promptly back to life.

He looked at the screen. Private number.

"Hewett."

"Oh dear Mr Hewett, why so formal? I would have thought with everything that my dear brother had told me that we would now be classed as friends."

The voice was familiar, accented, but not Stefan's. It began to laugh, sending a chill across Hewett's neck and shoulders.

"Jackdaw?"

"Please. That name is reserved only for people who fear me, Johnathan. You surely do not fear the man who saved you from financial ruin, do you? Who bailed out your parents' considerable socialite debts? Well, do you?" He paused for effect.

"Who provided you with the means to buy that car that you now comfortably sit in? Turn on the heated seats Johnathan you sound like you have a chill, my friend."

Hewett shivered again. He had to stop this, redeem himself before his own people even began to learn of his treachery. They would support him, he was sure. But in truth, he was far from sure. In fact, he was sure of only one thing. They would hang him out to dry.

Jackdaw was still waiting for a response. "Are you there, Johnathan? Speak to me. Tell me you are still with me, with us...come on, you just have to say the words."

"I could hang for this, you know."

"Who was it said 'We must all hang together or assuredly we will all hang separately?'"

"Benjamin Franklin."

"Thank you. I do so like to be educated. And you Johnathan are a very educated man, a company man, a government success, in the ascendency too from what I have been told, you have lived a perceived wealthy lifestyle, but we both know you will never be rich. There is a difference. I am that point of difference. You know what you need to do. Now do it."

The tone changed – more menacing, accentuating the last two words.

Hewett altered his own voice, mindful of the fact that he needed to shield any outward sign of fear, but his caller had already disconnected, parting with the advantage.

He sat alone, his mind was in tumult – damned if he did. His parents' lavish lifestyle had come with a price and their precious son had followed in their footsteps, except his debts had been less naïve, more illegal. Underground and reckless, but oh so exhilarating. He had become just another gambler with breeding, a class act with an exponential obligation to a man he had never met and who offered him a lifeline via one of his more adventurous and alluring employees.

Hewett claimed diplomatic immunity, but it meant nothing to a borderless group whose reputation and tactics alarmed even their most avid enemies.

He stared into his rear-view mirror. His normally smooth chin was covered in a light stubble, his eyes red and his skin pale. He hadn't slept for days and when he ate he soon expelled any of the valuable nutrients from his body.

'Just this once' he had said as he signed over the four hundred thousand pound debt to Alexandru Stefanescu.

He shook his head.

"Bastard."

. . .

The Jackdaw grinned as he placed the classic-looking Bake-lite phone handset into its receiver.

"I *am* such a bastard. But I am *your* bastard, Mr Hewett."

"No sign of 'em boss. It's as if they've vanished. We'll keep searching, they must be nearby."

"Thanks Andy." Daniel involuntarily turned three hundred and sixty degrees and came back to the same start point. Nothing had changed.

Roberts had arrived at St Thomas' Hospital and breaking all the rules had been allowed to leap-frog the queue. His injury had been triaged, he'd been made as comfortable as possible and was now on his phone, trying to ring his wife. He looked up at the two uniformed staff who were stood at the door to his side room.

It was a look that said 'I appreciate you being here boys, but really, right now I just want some space.'

The phone was answered after four rings.

"Hi. It's me." He took a quick breath; time to compose the lie.

"I've had a bit of an accident."

He'd decided that tactically speaking it was a good idea to massage the truth slightly. The fact that his radius was in two pieces was one thing for his wife to contend with. The fact that he had avoided the impact of a nine millimetre round, not once, but twice was something altogether different. Hopefully, it would remain his secret.

He outlined a version of the truth and said that yes, in the scheme of things, he would appreciate her coming to the hospital at some point soon – but sort the kids out first.

"No, honestly, nothing else. It's just been a busy few hours."

It was a horrendous lie; it had been a chaotic few weeks and despite the pain he was glad of the rest.

"Anyone else hurt babe?"

"No. Just me. Look hun, I've got to go. I'll ring you when I can."

Another lie.

He pressed the red button and ended the call, leaned back into the pile of cushions, none of which offered anything like comfort, and allowed his head to sink into the one that stood out as the most pleasing.

As soon as he had relaxed, the pain started. The throbbing pulse of agony got worse by the second. The temporary cushioning effect of the soft splint only suppressed the pain for so long. But it did allow him to think.

It was only then that he realised that O'Shea was technically in the same hospital. St Thomas' was part of the amalgamated Guy's and St Thomas' hospitals. He was in the A&E Department and she was in the nearby Urgent Care. But they were, for all intents, miles apart.

He stared at his own reflection through dilated pupils. "Christ, how could I forget?"

He looked outside, called out and got the attention he craved. One of the two uniformed staff walked in.

"Yes skipper, what do you need?"

He took a moment to contain any thought of being wheeled to her by two armed guards.

"Get someone to find out how Carrie is, please. Now."

"Carrie boss?"

"O'Shea. She's one of my team. Best analyst in the force. We, I, allowed her to become a target. I need to know how she is. Fast as you can. She's somewhere in Guy's."

In the Victorian sewer, Constantin ducked under the greasy surface but immediately panicked and started to inhale water. He shot back to the surface.

"I can't do this."

"Then get out of my way and let me live. Go on, move out of the way. I am far too young to end my life in an English sewer...with a rat."

"OK. OK. I will do it." He was fooling no one.

He nodded repeatedly, convincing himself to go, looking through the bars, focusing on one in particular, then past it and out into the river. He lowered his face to the water once again.

No longer sympathetic, Gheorghiu slammed his palm onto the back of his partner's head and pushed as hard as he could, driving the older man down into the water, and then using his thigh he propelled him deeper into the river.

Half way through, Constantin opened his eyes. He didn't see the outline of his mother, or ethereal beings, or for that matter anything other than opaque and cloudy water, a series of metal bars and then in the distance, dark, cold, deeper water.

Gheorghiu was kicking him now, using his feet to get him to the other side. He waited a moment, cognisant of the fact that he couldn't go until the channel they had hurriedly created was clear.

'Where the hell was he?'

He was back. There. An infant at his dear Mother's hands. He looked up but all he saw was the impassive face of a broken woman pushing him down into the water, tears in her cold, detached eyes.

"Merge. Lasă-mă în fiul meu."

"Go. Leave me, my son."

He wanted to speak to her. To ask her for forgiveness, quite what for he did not know. But soon her face became a façade, a featureless embodiment of a once-proud woman.

Just as everything he saw indicated that Constantin was about to give up, Gheorghiu watched him emerge on the other side in a panic, exiting from beneath the water as if he had seen a ghost. He was ten to twelve feet away from the entry point, having quickly drifted with the tidal flow. He was now clinging onto the railings, skin white as freshly blanketed snow. Silent.

Gheorghiu dropped below the surface and using the railing pulled himself along, swiftly, bursting into the main stream and joining the still silent Constantin.

"It is OK. You did well. Look, Stefan is coming." He smiled, but received nothing in return.

The boat was drifting now, Stefanescu coaxed it towards the wall, caring not whether he damaged it, but cautious not to deprive himself of a means of escape. His two colleagues had one chance only.

He held the boat against the wall, staring ahead to locate the two members of his team. The sheer scale of the river and its surrounding architecture made it difficult to spot them. And then, only a short distance away, he saw Constantin, then Gheorghiu, vermin, clinging to the bars. Filthy, cold and apparently afraid.

Gheorghiu was the first to pull himself up onto the stern of the boat as Stefan held it in position. Once safely on board he put a hand into the water and grabbed Constantin.

"Come brother, we have to go. Now!"

Stefanescu could see that both men were as good as in the boat so accelerated, away from the wall and away from danger. Gheorghiu was still holding onto the hapless older man who was exhausted from days of abuse, adrenaline over-dose and complete tiredness.

Constantin could feel the cool water pulsing around his body and found the temptation to let go almost unbearable. But something drove him up and into the hull.

Cade and Nicol had found the entry way to the main tunnel.

"Jesus, I doubt anyone's been down here since the war Jack."

"Don't be too hasty, mate – look around you. There are marks on surfaces everywhere. There's been a struggle here, and recently, and I don't mean during the Blitz."

"You are right, boss. Over here. I didn't spot it at first, but there's a hatch."

Cade lowered himself to his knee to get a better look, then lower again. Beneath him, he could see the same perfectly constructed brick tunnel.

"It's part of the old sewerage system. Work of art, shame, it stinks to high heaven. I'm guessing they've gone this way. They were lucky, or they knew this was here. Either way, we need to go down too."

He cautiously looked left and right, sweeping his pistol in a deliberate arc.

"I can see more light to the right, it must be an outlet."

Contrary to the fabled imagery of a waterborne death, Mary-Jane Shipley wasn't having life-centric and dreamlike footage flashing before her. She had given up. Another victim of the ancient waterway and the second in a desper-ately short space of time at the hands of European criminals, all of whom exhibited the same simple blue mark on their right wrist.

How she died did not concern them, that she did was all that mattered.

But as fast as she had willingly turned her back on life, something concealed deep within her, physically, or residing in the darkest corner of her mind had shunted her brutally back into life.

She jolted, gagged repeatedly as she tried to expel the water and then began to thrash about, forcing herself onto her back. She was a Shipley. And despite her parents' detestation of Anglo-Saxon language, she found herself thinking 'Fuck this, and you, and everyone else. I am *not* ready to die.'

With a final push she elevated her body out of the water – it was a display of defiance if nothing else, but it was likely to be her last.

"Boss, in the water!"

It was Nicol that spotted her first. Her dark clothing had disguised her presence in the tunnel superbly, but now she was very evident; face down, suspended below the waterline and lifeless.

"Wait!" hissed Cade, causing his younger colleague to throw him a questioning look.

"Boss, we need to go. We need to get down there."

He was right of course, but Cade was doing what he was trained to do.

'Stop. Think. Plan.'

The next few seconds would make no real difference, but may save three lives.

Who was the person in the water? Was it the female? Was it safe to go down? Was it a trap?

He looked at Nicol, who was already preparing to drop down.

Cade held up a palm. "John, try the radio again. Somebody may be listening to the bloody thing."

"MP from Whiskey One Three." He repeated it twice.

Almost directly above them Jennings, in the comparative calm of the chaotic high street, heard it at the same time as the control operator.

They had received Nicol's last transmission.

"Go ahead."

Nicol outlined his situation and location and said he was going off the air – but they needed help. The two targets were no longer in sight, but it was assumed they were somewhere in the labyrinth of tunnels that intersected beneath the city.

Jennings cupped his hands and yelled across the road.

"John, did you hear that?"

Daniel, sensing a turn in events, was running towards him now and replying at the same time.

"No. What've you got Andy?"

"They are somewhere below us. In a tunnel. A sewer."

"Typical of Cade to be in the shit." It wasn't meant to be funny.

Cade looked at Nicol. He trusted him, and the situation needed the trust to be mutual. They both nodded.

"Let's go."

He rammed the pistol into his trousers and hoped for the best as he lowered himself through the hatch, dangling as far down as he could to lessen the impact of the landing.

He dropped into the water and tumbled, but survived the descent without injury. He stood and guided Nicol, catching him and reducing the impact of his own entrance into the tunnel system.

They were both wading towards the grate, as fast as they could, now practically abandoning any sense of risk assessment.

Cade took hold of the lifeless body, trying desperately to raise it above the water. Nicol joined him and clawed at the gag. Between them they managed to keep her mouth clear of the river, but it appeared to be a losing battle.

"We need to get underneath her John."

It wasn't an order. It wasn't the time for such things. Moreover, it was a commentary of humanitarian need. Nicol's face told Cade he needed to go first.

"I'm sorry, boss, I've got a real issue with water."

"OK, mate, I'll go first. Have you got a knife?"

Nicol fished around under the surface until he located one of two pouches on his belt. One contained handcuffs, the other his faithful Gerber multi-tool. He presented it to Cade, who gripped onto it and started to lower himself under the girl. As his face connected once more with the frigid water and his eyes were about to close he heard a sound.

A boat? The Police launch, perhaps? Lord knows they could do with the help.

He looked through the water to his right and saw a boat appearing in the aperture of the tunnel. A well-dressed male was at the wheel. Behind him two dishevelled men were pressed up against the hull, cold and clearly wet through.

Cade turned to Nicol. "It's them!" Does that radio still work?"

Nicol pressed the microphone, but the set had died.

Cade fumbled for the Glock.

"Can you shoot?"

"I can boss but...we don't have a reason..."

"No time for buts John. I need to get this girl back into the world of the living. Shoot the bastards. And that *is* an order."

Like many British constables, John Nicol hadn't actually ever fired a pistol, in anger or any other way. He looked over the top of the sight and squeezed the trigger, not quite believing he was doing it.

He anticipated the first shot which ricocheted off the bar immediately in front of him, passing harmlessly back into the tunnel. The brass cartridge case dropped to his right and hissed into the water.

He fired again. The trigger reset, reacting like clockwork. And again. It was surreally addictive. He had given no consideration to what might happen if he was to actually hit someone.

The noise was deafening in the confines of the tunnel, even under water Cade could hear the resounding boom.

He pushed up into the girl's back, using the tunnel to brace his feet and keep her clear of the water. The idea, best laid was that Nicol would commence CPR until help arrived. But like most of Cade's recent strategies, it had not gone to plan.

Nicol fired again.

Jennings heard it and looked at Daniel and smiled.

"That'll be the Fat Lady singing boss. Let's go." He turned to his team, who had re-grouped upon hearing the gunshots. "You two get to the bridge, let's have some eyes on the situation."

Daniel was in full tactical mode now. "And we need to think about air support. Get them up Andy. Now."

• • •

Cade groped around in the semi-darkness, running his hands across her submerged body, frantically trying to locate the bindings that prevented her from surfacing. He opened his eyes but the cocktail of river water and waste stung, but he knew he needed to at least try to see. Like many people in the same situation, Cade resorted to touch.

His hands were moving rapidly around her, darting here and there until his fingertips brushed against a coarse surface that instinct told him wasn't clothing. Rope. Thick, industrial, saturated hemp.

He started to cut, at the same time telling himself not to breathe.

The Gerber sliced through the rope, strand by strand, but Cade needed air. He pushed back up to the surface and inhaled as fast as he could. He shook his head and cleared his eyes. Nicol was still firing.

Cade could see what the problem was. They were so low in the water that Nicol had lost all sense of perspective – he was firing over the top of the boat.

"Give me the gun!"

He grabbed the polycarbonate grip and settled his thumbs into a firing position, breathed and stared over the tritium front site. His target wasn't the driver, he wanted to get the remaining rounds into the hull. If he couldn't legally shoot them he was sure a magistrate, somewhere, would agree that in the circumstances sinking them was lawful under a long forgotten sub-section of the River Thames bylaws.

As he gazed up and over the site, both eyes open he found himself looking straight at the person behind the wheel, specifically, straight into his eyes. One was dark, chestnut brown almost, but the other was lighter, more distinctive, hazel.

Cade's vision was intensely accurate. He could see the difference in the colours, almost to the point where everything else didn't matter. The male was quite impressive, tanned but arrogant. It would be the word that Cade would use over and over again at later debriefs.

"He was arrogant."

"That's hardly a description, is it Jack?"

"You weren't there. He was cold. Cold and bloody arrogant and I will never forget that face."

He exhaled and pulled the trigger towards him. He had ten rounds left. The first drilled through the hull, the second, rushed, skipped across the surface of the water, which did its best to slow it down a little. The third was on target. And again. He was firing rhythmically now.

Nicol had overcome his fear and was doing his best to keep the girl alive. Praying in his own probable aquatic grave for an end to his insanely exciting tour of duty. He'd accept normality from this day forth.

The boat was moving out of range, the two males in the rear had dropped out of sight but the skipper was still in view. Cade had a choice to make; fire all three remaining rounds in a burst and hope for the best or fire two in succession into the hull and take his time with the last round.

Bang. Bang. The fifteenth and sixteenth rounds hit the boat, splintering fibreglass around the cockpit. A shard of the razor sharp material hit Gheorghiu in the thigh, causing him to yelp. It felt as if he had been stung by a wasp as the blood seeped from the incision into the damp material of his trousers.

Stefanescu ignored all maritime protocols now and rammed the throttle into its highest setting, causing the damaged boat to surf up on its keel, the bow lifting out of the water. He was now a target.

Cade settled himself against the railings, closed his left eye and released the air from his lungs. The round left the Glock without telegraphing its escape. On a range it was the perfect shot. Knee-deep in filthy water, cold and pumped full of adrenaline, it was a bloody miracle.

The bullet tracked across the Thames, chasing after the boat and its occupants as a peregrine falcon hunts its prey. Fast, targeted and ruthless.

Made of copper for maximum fragmentation, it entered the boat and struck Stefanescu in the left arm, blowing flesh away from bone and exiting up through the canopy, shattering the plexiglass windscreen and disappearing harmlessly down river.

To an untrained observer it sounded like a knife being pushed through soft fruit, to a surgeon it was the sound of internal chaos as blood vessels separated, discharging their precious fluid into the surrounding masses.

The slide flew back on Cade's pistol, announcing the empty state of the magazine. Even if he had a replacement, it would have been futile. They were gone now. Gone. But far from forgotten.

CHAPTER TWENTY-TWO

Stefanescu heard the round hitting his arm.

"Pwwwt!" It was a peculiar sound and one which didn't particularly herald the pain that followed. High pitched, a whistle almost, it announced itself above all other sounds and managed to make its presence known above the cacophony of the protesting outboard motor.

He knew he had to prioritise, but human need was rapidly overwhelming his thought processes.

'Once again brother you leave me to fight for myself. I despise you.'

He was distracted by the sight of blood which was quickly, but not rapidly staining his clothing. In order to prioritise, he focused on the pre-arranged landing area – a small beach that was only exposed at low to mid-tide and below the place where Hewett had said he would be waiting.

Stefanescu did not trust the Englishman. Not at any point in the past and certainly not now. He half expected him to fail in his initial mission. Why his brother had involved him he did not know, there were, as the English often said, plenty more fish in the sea.

He looked backwards into the main passenger area of the small but surprisingly capacious boat and began to weigh up the issues before him. He nodded to Gheorghiu.

"You OK brother?"

He nodded. "Cold, tired…"

"These are things that will pass. Temporary states of mind. I need you to be my strength in the next few hours. You are bleeding."

Gheorghiu looked once again at the small wound and wiped the blood away, then rubbed his hands together until the red liquid dried into a metallic-smelling paste.

"I will be OK. You?" He pointed needlessly at the more impressive wound on Stefanescu's arm.

"I've had worse playing with my big brother! But see if you can find a first aid kit, somewhere up front, I need to stop the bleeding soon."

Gheorghiu tapped Constantin on the face, stinging his already frigid skin.

"Wake up little one, we are almost there. Another twenty-four hours and we will be home."

He took a moment to sigh and consider the last few weeks. The promise of easy money and luxuries had been too much of a temptation to ignore, but as he shuddered against the breeze, he found himself longing for familiar surroundings and normality. Boredom seemed like a perfect option.

Constantin had dragged himself back into the here and now, away from the perpetual nightmare that haunted him and wondered whether the escape from the tunnel might have been the cathartic moment he needed to move on in his own life. If he could rid his body and mind of the constant craving for chemical stimuli all the better. He shuffled forwards and told Gheorghiu to take the helm.

Gheorghiu had a twenty-second briefing and took over the wheel from his injured boss.

Constantin spoke to Stefanescu, as loud as he could, without obviously shouting, paranoia once more convincing him that everyone in London was watching or listening to him.

"Let me deal with the wound."

"What do you know about medicine you fool? I don't see what my big brother sees in you. You are a burden to us all. If we are caught..."

Constantin stepped up a gear, raised his right hand and placed his index finger on his boss's lips.

"You need to conserve energy my dear friend. The bullet caught your cephalic vein...it will continue to bleed quite badly but you will not die if we apply pressure. Here, push this into the hole until I can find a clean bandage."

Stefanescu did as he was told. As he leaned back against the hull to steady himself he looked straight at Constantin.

"So where does a failure like you, a washed-up drug addict...learn such skills? Military?"

He smiled a sarcastic smile. "You see me as the broken bottle in the children's playground don't you? Actually, no, I am self-taught and then when I learned how to blow things up they taught me how to repair any innocent victims who got in my way. Not once did that happen. I was an expert. There are not many basic injuries I cannot deal with. I learned on pigs, but I often find they have more manners than some of my patients. I may be... washed-up, but I have just stopped you slowly bleeding to death."

He emphasised the last point with a tightening of the

dressing, announcing he had completed his job in rapid time.

Stefanescu nodded. "Thank you."

"It needs more work, but we will do that later."

They were both reminded of the present when Gheorghiu shouted back to them.

"One minute!"

Nicol surfaced with an immense gasp. He'd cut more of the fibres away but it needed one more attempt.

Cade tossed the empty pistol towards the secondary tunnel, partly hoping it would remain dry, then focused on the girl. She was not the main concern.

"Well done John. I'm going back down. Just try to keep her above water, we don't have long – talk to her – and listen out for the troops. There's no way they couldn't have heard that bloody racket."

"Will do, boss. Did you get them?"

"I have no idea." He ducked under the water, knife in hand, re-traced his steps and started cutting. Part of his psyche told him to stop, to give up, but the balance, the desire for the far-greater good urged him onwards. After all, he had bugger all else to do.

He opened his eyes again, allowed them to focus and started slashing at the hemp fibres until they gave way. Almost one by one they ruptured, letting go of their captive, swirling around in front of his eyes before being spirited away on the tide. It took a minute – a lifetime, but she was free.

Cade surfaced with a clear idea of what to do next. If it worked, it would be more extraordinary than anything else he had ever done, and in a few frenzied weeks he felt he'd done enough to write an entire book, a sequel. A bloody trilogy in fact.

Hewett was tapping the black leather steering wheel, drumming his fingernails onto the four silver rings that adorned the centre boss.

There was no music this time, no confident arrogance. He was at the point of no return, in his head he had already turned left and accelerated towards an uncertain future. But his heart was saying 'Stop! Turn back you fool, save your soul and your reputation while you still can. No one will know.'

Jennings, Daniel and a growing number of troops were pushing their way through the watery debris of the old café, fighting to get to the source of the commotion below them.

"Are we safe doing this boss?" It was Jennings this time, questioning the mentality of taking a stick to a gunfight.

"Stay or go Andy, either way I'm going. I've lost too many of my bloody team not to."

He clambered over discarded building materials and indescribable rubbish, through the half-light and down into the building, following the two previous groups that had made the same journey.

Within five minutes they found their way to the hatch. They needed no further encouragement – Daniel held up a hand for silence. Below them was not the sound of a struggle, but a fight for life.

"One and two and three and four..."

He lowered himself to his knees and leant through the hole, initially retching at the stench of the old tunnel. He looked down onto a surreal sight. A uniformed constable was leaning into the curved brick wall, waist-deep in water with the saturated body of a female laid across his lap. He was pushing rhythmically onto her chest which explained the counting.

At his right and cradling her head was Cade, providing life-giving oxygen, his lips sealed over hers, no longer concerned about water-borne hazards.

A solitary rat lowered itself out of the nearby secondary tunnel, slipped down the polished brickwork and nonchalantly swam past the group, its head only just above the waterline. Seconds later it had vanished, swimming through the grate and out into the main river.

Cade, who despised the creatures, hadn't even paused from his duties. At any other time he would have happily clubbed it to death. He had his reasons, disease-carrying bastards.

Daniel was unsure whether to break the momentum but knew that Cade needed help. He called out.

"Jack, it's me. I'm ruining a perfectly good Aquascutum suit here. Anything I can do old chap?"

It was the understated Englishness of the situation that finally made Cade laugh after so many days of turmoil.

"Do you know what? A cup of Earl Grey would be delightful."

"On its way, sir. As it comes, no milk. Now seriously, what do you need Jack?"

"Get a few of the lads down here, not too many, it's not good underfoot, we just need a break. Tell them to leave their dignity up there, it's festering down here. And get us an ambulance team ASAP. I have no idea if this girl is going to survive boss but I'll be damned if I'm going to allow her to end her days in this shit hole."

"All points noted old son. Ambulance will be here soon,

ETA about five. What was all that bloody racket earlier? Did you see them?"

Cade exhaled into Shipley's water-filled lungs, knowing he was probably doing more harm than good. He handed over to Nicol and continued talking.

"John here got off a few shots. For the record he's not a qualified AFO – but authorised or not he did a fine job with the pistol so let's just forget that little matter shall we and blame me if he hit anything? He was under orders after all. Wait one..."

He returned to propelling deep lungfuls of air into the prone, lifeless girl.

"...OK, I got off half a magazine, I'm certain I hit one of them, probably wrecked the bloody boat, but you'll have to deal with that out of Westminster's budget. They went that way, small cream coloured day cruiser, blue canopy. Took off like a scalded cat."

Another lungful of air was dispensed as Cade allowed a fresh-faced, blond-haired constable to lower himself into the void and take over. He wiped his own mouth before commencing – as if he was afraid that his benevolent gesture was going to infect her somehow.

"She's past caring kid, just crack on, ambulance will be here soon." Cade stepped away, his legs started to shake as he leant against the slippery surface of the tunnel wall, trying to steady himself. A combination of exhaustion and location was conspiring to frustrate him beyond belief. He felt like he hadn't eaten in days and probably hadn't.

He continued to talk to Daniel without looking at him. "We need a ladder boss. Sharpish. I have to get out of here before I dissolve and the medics are going to need some method of extracting her, regardless."

Daniel realised that despite Cade's efforts he had no obvious idea whether she was alive.

"Roger that Jack." He passed back the messages via Andy Jennings who was happy to remain out of the tunnel and save the Met Police a further dry cleaning bill.

"If we pass down a belt could you allow yourself to be pulled up?"

"I don't think I've got the strength John. I'll stay here until you can provide another fresh set of hands. Young John here looks like he could do with one any minute now."

He walked through the water and motioned to Nicol to stop the compressions, allowing him vital rest. All he had to do now was concentrate on the intense cramp in his legs.

"Paramedic is here Jack. Fire Brigade a minute away with a ladder. We'll have you all out before you can say..."

"Moist?"

As he said it he knew it rang a bell. O'Shea hated the word.

Gheorghiu swung the boat to the left, let go of the throttle and prayed that they would beach in one piece.

"Hold on!"

With the engine cut, the boat's only noise was when its keel started to run along the submerged debris field that littered the river. The noise increased to the point where it started to attract attention, not ideal, but they had now gone beyond the tipping point.

Two people, foraging with metal detectors on the developing shoreline heard the boat before they saw it, one began to try to outrun it, his boots sinking into the mud and shale.

It narrowly missed him and continued along its trajectory until slithering up the beach and stopping about twenty feet short of a dilapidated iron ladder that clung belliger-ently to the river defences.

Constantin was out of the boat in seconds. He had been told what to do and who to look for. He forged through the mud, not wishing to spend another second near it and was clambering up the ten rungs, reaching the top of wall and rolling over the top before stopping to get his bearings.

'You will see an Audi.'

Gheorghiu guided his boss out of the boat and they started to trudge up the beach towards the ladder, caring more for their escape plans than the welfare of any passers-by.

Gheorghiu got to the top and leaned back down to help Stefanescu up the ladder.

Constantin ran left, it was his only option, a sturdy set of gates were stopping him from running into the nearby upmarket apartments.

Twenty seconds later having turned right and away from the river he saw the car.

Abandoning all counter-surveillance protocols he waved frantically.

Hewett looked up from his thoughts and saw a male waving, he was covered in mud, wet through and had an almost manic appearance. He did his best to ignore him initially but noticed he was getting closer.

He instinctively pressed the central locking master button with his elbow without taking his eyes off the male.

'Start the car John, start, and drive away.'

The male was now banging on the driver's window, forcibly enough to break the glass.

Hewett had seen and heard enough. He lowered the glass a fraction and yelled.

"Get off my bloody car before I come out there and teach you a lesson. Go on, piss right off. Go!"

As he finished the sentence, he looked forward again. Two more males were travelling faster than walking pace, unable to run for reasons not immediately apparent. But he noticed the older of the two was also wet through, muddy and in a hurry. He was partly guiding the younger male, a blond-haired individual who had a bloodied-bandaged wrapped around his arm. He was comparatively dry but his feet gave the impression of someone who had just run an assault course.

"Jesus Christ it's him. Look at the state of him."

Stefanescu reached Hewett's car, leaned on the bonnet and demanded he let them in.

He lowered the window further. "But you are shat up to the eyeballs man. I'm not letting you anywhere near my car. Seriously, bugger off." He pointed disparagingly towards Stefanescu's dishevelled team. "And I don't want another thing to do with this, or you or them."

Stefanescu stepped forward, leaned through the window with his right hand and gripped hold of Hewett's collar. He stared into his face, noting the blood vessels around his blue eyes. Stefanescu's own complex eyes were glaring back, his lips had tightened across his teeth and his nostrils had flared slightly. Classic signs of preparation for attack.

He rolled his fist up under Hewett's chin and pressed into his larynx.

"Ring my brother Mr Hewett. He has something to discuss with you – it relates to your parents and their ongoing welfare. I hear they are enjoying retirement in France." Stefanescu was smiling. There was no warmth though.

Hewett knew he was cornered.

"I don't need to ring. Get in. But be careful with the seats."

The Romanian turned to his partners in crime. "Get in, we need to move before we attract any more damned attention."

As Stefanescu sank into the black leather seat, the Audi engine started. Hewett put it into reverse and started to swing around into an opening. He turned the car around and began to drive back towards the main road.

"There, my good friend. Isn't that better? Do you know where to go?" He raised his eyebrows quizzically before wiping mud from his legs deliberately onto the seat covering.

Hewett was visibly furious but knew he had to pick his battles.

"You stink. And those two in the back smell like a cesspit." He lowered the rear windows, enough to let air in but not so low as to allow people to look in.

"Better to smell of a sewer than of fear itself Mr Hewett. Turn left here, get over the Thames and head south on the A2. As fast as you can. We have another watery tunnel to get through."

"How are you going to do that without a vehicle?" Hewett asked incredulously.

Stefan's wounded and exhausted answer was tinged with a gentle amount of laughter as he leaned forward slightly and pressed the heated seat button, needing its warmth to sooth his shattered body. He grinned, gripped Hewett's chin with his good hand and said "It's simple. You are coming with us Johnnie. You, are coming with us."

. . .

The London Fire Brigade had arrived with a portable light-weight ladder and were busy assisting with the extraction of Cade and Nicol. Two recently arrived police staff had stayed below to provide support to the paramedics who had earlier been lowered, with life-saving equipment into the brick-lined tunnel.

Cade had wanted to stay in situ but knew he was in the way, and Nicol had tried his best to remain but in truth couldn't wait to leave.

They talked a few things through, a classic tactical debrief between a great leader and a willing follower. Nicol was sent up to the street to get cleaned up and allow himself, upon orders, to get a rapid check-up from another ambulance crew.

Cade was on hand to help pull the rescue stretcher up and out of the dank water below. It was more a demonstration of his commitment to her than a show of strength. He was beyond fatigued – more than at any other time in his life.

"Let her go now Jack. Incredible job. It's down to her resolve and the skill of the medics."

Cade stopped the stretcher crew for a valuable few seconds and knelt down beside the lifeless body before whispering into her chilled and clammy ear.

"Who are you? Eh? Why did you go down there? Whoever you are, thank you. I'm sure your parents are intensely proud of you. I know I am. You'd make a great member of my team..."

He held her equally icy hand.

He looked up at the senior paramedic. "Well?"

He shook his head subtly. "I don't think so, mate."

. . .

Jackdaw's phone trembled in his hand. He was waiting for the call. He pressed the green button, breathed in slowly and spoke.

"Yes. Speak to me brother, tell me only good news."

"I spent far too much of our money on a bottle of wine that I never finished. I stole a boat, caused chaos on the River Thames and rescued your two men before being shot in the arm. Then survived a boat crash and found myself being refused entry to Mr Hewett's very nice Audi motor car. Which I believe we paid for. Then I spent a while convincing our friend Johnnie that he would take us all for a ride to Chatham and from there, home."

"It sounds boring brother. You are weary. You really shouldn't be quite so specific."

It was a gentle warning to a clearly tired brother who had not considered that he might be the subject of audio surveillance.

"Tell me, what else did you do whilst you were in London? Did you see the Queen?"

It was code and one which only the two brothers knew.

Stefanescu admonished himself.

"Of course. She sends her very best wishes. Her servants have followed their orders to the letter. They are out in the kingdom now, making the most of the weather. The princes and princesses, butlers, horsemen, waiters, and court jesters, all of them, doing what they do best. Doing it all for their country."

"That is indeed excellent news. Soon we shall also feast like royalty. Your carriage awaits, you leave at four o'clock. Don't be late brother. Oh, and give my regards to the driver."

. . .

Daniel's phone battery was hot. He had made and taken countless calls in the last hour and expected it to go flat any moment. A quick text was fired off to his beloved – the key to any good police relationship always followed the mantra: 'Happy wife – Happy life' – and don't forget the flowers.

If all else failed, blame someone else.

Hi. I'm running late. Blame Jack.

"Right mate, we need to get somewhere we can hose you down because with all due respect...you stink. That'll do nicely." He pointed over to the Fire Brigade who had set up a Hazchem shower to rid their own staff of the stench of the tunnel system.

"Mind if we borrow this for a second boys?"

"Make yourself at home chief. Don't drop the soap though!"

Cade stepped under the water which by comparison to what he'd been submerged in was warm and luxurious.

He exited, rubbing the excess from his face and gratefully accepting a towel.

"They are still working on your girl Jack."

"Which one?"

"Sorry. The girl in the ambulance, God only knows who she is and why..."

"I asked her the same question John. Do we know anything about her?"

"Not a clue. She's got three pennies in her pocket and a season ticket to the underground. She got off the train here for a reason but we may never know why. It could have been her intended stop. She's got some guts I'll give her that. There's no way she went down there by accident. She's followed them deliberately."

"Agreed. Just need to find out why." He finished drying himself as best he could before tossing the towel into a black bag. Blinking out the last of the water he focused on his boss.

"Christ, John what is going on?"

It was a fair question.

"Well, I can tell you that my division has never been so bloody busy Jack. I'm beginning to wonder what it is about your blanket that attracts quite so much shit. I know we've done this before but we need to whiteboard this and start at the beginning. What we know is we have a team, or teams that have worked out how to exploit our financial systems, but importantly, somewhere in amongst that nest of vipers is a leader and a hierarchy – and a traitor or two."

"Two?"

"Yep. Call it gut instinct" said Daniel, doing his best to ignore the osmotic effect taking place in the hems of his much-loved suit trousers, whilst trying to find a clean corner on a borrowed towel and absentmindedly wipe something noxious off his shoe onto a nearby kerbstone.

"I'm not with you?"

"One of them is your man Copil. We still don't know why or even if he has turned, but if he has and if we act with caution, he could be our ace card. Or, he could lead us away from the action."

Cade nodded, starting to feel vaguely human again.

Daniel carried on. "Talking of which there have been four explosions in the last twenty-four hours around Greater London, all connected to banks, over a hundred ATM attacks and we've even had a report about a supermarket in Essex being the victim of a point-of-sale device being swapped. This is a clever team Jack but there's more to this."

"You can say that again. They've also got some nasty

bastards among the hierarchy you alluded to. I'll bet what's left of my reputation that they've chalked up a few murders in the south of England, shot at our staff and ripped thousands of innocent bank customers off via the ATM jobs. But all that aside I think this is a cover for something bigger. I have done for a while now and on that, I think you and I agree."

He knew he was tired and hoped he was making sense. "They know too much JD. Got any ideas?" He leaned back against the bright red fire tender and closed his eyes, willing them to stay closed.

Daniel continued the conversation.

"Jack. I think we are having the same thoughts. I've probably been around a while longer than I should have been, but my instinct never betrays me. I know that they've got someone close. I'm hearing some chatter on the human source channels suggesting the involvement of diplomats. But it doesn't compute. As it stands I haven't the slightest idea where they could fit in, and why. We'll figure that in time. But for now, one of our priorities is to identify our problem child. Assuming it's not you, which I think we can take for granted, and it's certainly not me, and it's none of the team."

Cade shook his head vigorously, guzzled a welcome and hot and sweet cup of tea as quickly as he could and said "Agreed, one hundred percent. It's none of our lot."

Daniel grabbed what was left of Cade's tea, almost emptying it in one swig then flicked the rest across the pavement.

"And finally, with those two poor buggers in hospital I'm happy it's not Jason that's our Judas, and something deep down in here says it ain't poor old Carrie."

Cade's eyes opened immediately.

"Bloody hell John. I need to go and see her. I'm a V12 engine running on four cylinders and someone has filled my tanks with diesel." It wasn't funny, but he giggled inappropriately, his blood sugar levels had plummeted and he was on the verge of collapse.

"Let's get you cleaned up first Jack, and get some food into you, then we'll go. I'm sure she'll be fine."

"I somehow doubt that, Chief Inspector. Every other female I seem to come into contact with leaves me alive and miserable, or happy but dead."

The door of the ambulance burst open causing Cade to rock back into life.

"We've got a pulse. Heading to St. Thomas'. Well done. Seriously." The paramedic's animated thumbs up was a massive boost. The brightly marked rear door of the ambulance was closing as it edged into traffic and lit up, announcing its presence to all and sundry. 'Please move out of my way – this might be you one day.'

Daniel slapped Cade on his shoulder a few times. "Well, perhaps that young lass is about to change your success rate."

Cade looked up at a brightening sky and put his head against Daniel's shoulder.

"Perhaps there is a God after all John? Let's get cleaned up and get to hospital, we can kill three birds with one stone, seeing as my presence in your fair city put them all there."

"Sounds like a plan. I need to talk to you en route. I'll drive, you can close your eyes and listen."

He turned to Jennings. "Andy, mate, thank you. When this has calmed down I'll come and see your team with a cake or two. Top work all round. Can I leave it with you?"

It was an iconic phrase among police specialist units –

the subtle handover from a suit to a uniform that was always rhetorical. This was a great manager, Jennings could tell and for once, having it left with him was actually flattering.

They returned to Daniel's vehicle got in and set off for the hospital. Daniel turned the heating on full and drove through traffic until he got to a petrol station.

"You stay in the car, you stink! I'll get some food and a couple of fresh coffees. Stay warm."

Cade put the passenger seat back a few notches and closed his eyes. He was quickly drifting off into a head-snapping sleep, his neck jolting him back into an awakened state at least three times as he fought to keep his eyes open. He stared at Daniel, queuing up for refreshments and realised he was looking at a naturally gifted leader. As he stared through the windscreen, he remembered that he had wanted to speak to him about something but at the time had declared it as unimportant.

"Ever the diplomat John."

His stomach rolled, and he felt nauseous but sleep beckoned once more, washing over him, drawing him in, until his eyes gently closed and this time his head dropped against the passenger window. He was gone.

His eyelids were fluttering, already in a deep sleep, his dreams surfaced once more. Under water, reaching out, clutching, grabbing hold but not quite accomplishing his goal. Surrounded by obscure shapes, some almost human, others fishlike, swimming just within reach and then gone, scurrying like alarmed small fry into the dark green weeds and out of harm's way.

He turned around in the water, trying to find a more advantageous way to see them, to see their faces but it never got beyond this point, as the scene replayed over and over again until the sense of frustration was palpable.

He could hear Daniel talking – distantly, but he knew, even in the depth of his dream that it was Daniel.

"They know too much Jack." It was his own words but spoken by his boss.

The current began to quicken, carrying Cade deeper, down towards the river bed where myriad obscure shapes lay. He felt that he wasn't alone, that eyes were watching him, even in such a cold and miserable place. The deeper he went, the darker it became until all available light had vanished and he was alone.

He was struggling against the tide, forcing himself to turn, fearing something, but desperately unaware what. He began to cry, his tears coloured the black water and then dispersed into the aquatic mire. Voices, from somewhere, began to shout his name, almost rhythmically, but it was a slow fractured chant, not with any discernible beat, just over and over again.

He looked up to where he thought the surface was and began to push up and away from the bottom of the river, for every stroke up he was dragged two back down again. His chest began to pound as he forced himself to conserve the last of his remaining air.

It was becoming easier to just inhale.

A shape appeared alongside him. Its body was human without any doubt, but its face was non-descript, androgynous, a void. It held out its hand. Cade could see through it, through every limb, the skin began to peel away, rotting before his eyes. It was hideous. But as he swam upwards towards the surface, the body began to take on a new form. Its skin appeared to heal, its hand grew stronger and more opaque and now it led him towards a strengthening light source, pushing through the plants, shoals of inquisitive fish flashed here and there and he knew that he needed to continue. This was far from a simple nightmare. It was tangible.

Within feet of the surface, Cade turned and looked at the figure. Its face had transformed and no longer alarmed him. It was someone he knew and in his presence he had always felt safe. The figure was now much stronger, definable and physically too, it propelled Cade up towards the sun. He turned to look back, but the figure was drifting downwards once more. Its face was now unblemished, handsome in an old-fashioned way and recognising its task was complete it simply smiled and nodded, gently holding up its right hand as it blended back in with its surroundings and as quickly as it had appeared had departed.

Cade reached the surface which was shrouded in a still-dark veil, it almost ensnared him, unwilling to let him make the last part of his journey, but he was damned if he was going to give in now. With a final push, he broke the surface and hauled air into his lungs.

He shuddered violently and was awake.

His heart was beating rapidly as he took a moment to look around and saw Daniel sat in the driver's seat, quietly sipping on his coffee.

"You OK there old son?"

Cade exhaled. "Yep. Just fine." He wiped a tear from the edge of his eye.

"Strikes me you were having one hell of a dream Jack."

"I was, I have it a lot lately."

"Anything you want to discuss?"

Cade thought for a second before speaking, "No John. Thank you. I'm fine. I think I just need a holiday but we both know that won't happen for a while."

He picked up his coffee and began to slurp its scalding hot contents through the aperture in the lid. Daniel started the car, looked over his shoulder, indicated and merged with the traffic.

He motioned towards a hot sausage roll. "I've eaten one whilst you've been asleep, I thought I'd save that one for you."

Cade managed to raise a smile. "Thanks. I think."

He stared out of the window as they whipped through the comparatively light traffic that was beginning to build, taking the commuters south and home once more. He was lost in the middle of it all, trying to focus but fixating on a familiar tail badge of the car in front – for a moment he could have easily fallen asleep again but quietly pinched the skin on his thighs in order to stay awake.

As he took another sip of the liquid, he realised who the dream figure was.

Exhausted, his mind wandered again and his eyes were soon glazing over as he fought to focus on the depth of the London skyline. He knew he had to be buoyant when he visited his team in hospital, however despite willing himself to concentrate he was drifting again. He jolted as he spilled some of the coffee onto his leg.

"Bastard!"

"Thanks, you can buy your own in future you miserable northern twat!"

"Bollocks to you, Chief Inspector."

"And bollocks to you too, *former* Inspector!"

"Touché!"

"You deserved it. You know I only ever look out for your best interests Jack. And besides I bought you a sausage roll too..." He pointed towards the microwaved offering as if it were made of gold.

"You call that food?" He held the oil-stained paper bag aloft.

"Oh, trust me I've eaten worse."

"Oh trust *me*, so have I. I once ate a live sea slug for a bet and it probably tasted better than that bloody thing!"

Daniel winced, raised his index finger and continued.

"Ah. But when you are married to one as adorable as me, who is an absolute whizz in the bedroom and even better in the kitchen then you learn to appreciate the finer things in life kid. I learned to tread very carefully when it comes to complimenting Mrs Daniel and her catering. She has a dream of opening a nice little restaurant one day. In some far-flung land."

"And I suppose you pamper to her every desire boss?"

"Au naturel Jack, au naturel."

"Ever the diplomat John…"

He took a bite of the food and confessed that it actually tasted superb. As he savoured its flavour he stopped, hastily swallowed and turned to Daniel and began to quote verbatim from his meeting with Nikolina Petrov at East Midlands Airport.

"You see Jack, what Alex learned – he's a fast learner – was that if he found the right people, he could get more passports, and more passports means more fake diplomats and more diplomats…" He finished swallowing the last of the food. "Means…more money."

"Jack I have no bloody idea what you are rambling on about!"

"Of course!" He clicked his finger and thumb together loudly.

"OK. Are you going to let me in on this or do I have to tell everyone that you cry when you dream?"

Cade looked at Daniel, a man who he trusted implicitly.

"You've just crossed the line John."

The look that accompanied the sentence spoke volumes and Daniel knew he'd overstepped the mark.

"Fair play. I apologise unreservedly."

"It's not a dream John. It's a bloody recurring horror movie. I can't take control, I'm adrift in deep, dark water. Black water. I can see a way out but I can't ever get there. There's always a figure waiting in the half-light..."

"OK, doesn't sound good. Perhaps something we can help with when this has settled down a bit? I could talk to our Doc?"

"Thanks. I doubt it would do any good."

Unannounced Daniel pulled into a bus stop and applied the handbrake.

"Do the tears flow every time?"

"No. Just this time."

"Any reason?"

"I saw the face for the first time John."

"And that was a good thing?"

"It was. Normally the figure is impersonal, faceless."

"And today?"

Cade recounted a story as they sat at the side of the road. Daniel knew they needed to move on with their enquiry, but felt that what Cade was about to say was more important, if nothing else for his own welfare, and a truly brilliant manager would always adopt the 'two ears, one mouth' principle. So he sat and listened.

"In a nutshell that's it. I never got to attend his funeral. To say what I needed to say. To put my own house in order and to let people know that I loved him. It broke my heart. And it still hurts me John, every single bloody day. Do you have any idea what it is like to be the eldest son and have your eulogy read out by someone else?"

"No, I cannot begin to imagine my friend."

"Well. Today the dream came back. I saw the face of my father and he smiled. All was well John. We made our peace, and he guided me, up and away from whatever it is that haunts me, towards my own salvation, away from the nightmare that invades my every waking thought."

"I'm pleased for you Jack. I really am. Can't have been easy. But you might have some clarity now."

He turned the key and re-joined the traffic.

"We'll never discuss this again Jack. You have my word."

"Thanks boss. Oh, and there's something else he taught me."

"Go on."

"To listen to the voices in your head. Sometimes tell them to piss off and go and annoy someone else, but when they keep repeating themselves, there's a reason to listen."

"I'm all ears," said Daniel as he entered the police parking bay outside St. Thomas' Hospital.

"*If he found the right people.*"

"Jesus Jack I know you are tired but this is exhausting me!"

"Call yourself a detective? The Right People. Alex Stefanescu needed to find the right person. A person connected to the diplomatic trade. You are hearing chatter about it from your Human Source staff. We know that this group, the Seventh Wave are ripping us off for thousands but we also know, or suspect, there's something else, and just lately you've had your doubts about one person who is connected to every possible link in the chain."

"I need to demote myself Jack. Put me out of my misery." He was toying with the idea himself now but it was clearly too obvious.

"Name me the one person who has been involved in

getting me up close and personal with the players in this group? The person who managed to get Petrov out of the detention centre, the one who everyone admires? The one person that the government appears to place on a pedestal? Sophisticated, smooth, well-connected...and yet the one person that no-one actually knows a damn thing about."

Daniel was staring at Cade, impassive, and finally aware.

"Boss, you've had your doubts too. Tell me you haven't?"

Daniel didn't say a word for almost a minute which spoke volumes, but when he did finally utter them his words were brief and emotionless.

"Do you really think so? I hate to admit it but I'm one step ahead of you. I've felt it for days now. People do strange things when you least expect them to. In his case he has so much to lose. He's well off, well connected and successful."

"He's all of those things and more JD. But the answer lies beyond money. He's either being blackmailed, is involved in such a thing and or is the architect of some wonderfully planned attack on the state." Cade finished and looked at Daniel.

"How could he Jack?"

CHAPTER TWENTY-THREE

CADE AND DANIEL APPROACHED THE NURSING STATION, identified themselves and asked where both of their staff were located.

"Not ideal that they are in separate areas Staff," said Daniel talking to the senior nurse on duty, pretty in an unconventional way, she had a gently slanted but captivating smile and cocoa-coloured hair tied into a perfect bun.

"Makes my job a lot harder. Any chance we could move them closer together? I have a risk assessment to conduct as they are both potentially still in harm's way. In doing this I'm also protecting your staff too..."

He let the last words hang in the air whilst fixing her gaze with his and using all of his well-established charms on a nurse clearly well-versed in such offensives.

"And if I do that for you, Chief Inspector, I have to do it for everyone."

"Of course..." He looked discreetly at her name badge. "Of course...Kellie. I completely agree and understand entirely, but not everyone has been poisoned or shot at. I really need you to pull the rabbit out of the hat for me."

He leaned forward and brushed her hand with his.

"Please."

Kellie put both of her hands to her side palms facing Daniel as if pointing at something and almost sang the words "Da-dah!"

Daniel looked at her blankly.

"Call yourself a cop? I'm being your magician's assistant. Leave it with me. For now Mr Roberts is on the Acute Admissions Ward and...Miss O'Shea is in Intensive Care. By the way I get off at 22:00..."

Cade smiled and interjected as he dragged Daniel along the corridor.

"Come on boss, we've got a risk assessment to write. Thanks Staff Nurse. Much appreciated."

They got around the corner and headed to a lift. The doors opened and Cade entered first, pressing a button illuminated in blue. It read L1.

As the doors slithered to a close, he spoke.

"You dirty old dog! I never knew you had it in you."

"Hey less of the old Cade. Anyway, it's all a game isn't it? They love it those nurses."

The lift announced its arrival, its stainless steel doors opening as a detached and subtle female voice purred. "Level One."

They walked out onto the new floor and looked around for signs.

"Does Mrs Daniel dress up as one occasionally?"

"Now who's crossed the line? This way by the looks of it."

They arrived at ICU first. Two armed staff spotted the IDs and moved to one side with a nod and some small talk.

Daniel stepped back and allowed Cade to enter the side room. Seeing O'Shea lying in the bed, motionless but evidently alive he made the decision to leave Cade alone.

"I'll go and find the other patient mate. Take your time yeah? Looks as though she's out of it, but don't forget, they say they can hear your every word. Ring me when you are done."

Daniel was about to walk away when he turned and added another few words.

"Oh, and Jack...don't forget."

Cade looked at his boss curiously.

"Tell her. While you still can."

"Tell her what?"

Daniel smiled and walked away along the sterile corridor towards the Acute Admissions Ward, passing temporarily displayed works of art by local schoolchildren, each depicting colourful scenes and stories much-loved and only understood by their adoring parents.

He reached the ward and was directed to Roberts where he found his colleague dozing in a stereotypical hospital bed.

"No need to salute Sergeant, stay where you are!"

"Jesus boss you startled me. I thought you were another doctor, come to brutalise me."

"Best I don't ask. Silly question..."

"Awful it was. I doubt I'll ever play the piano again, sir."

"It was a guitar earlier."

Roberts laughed, "Yeah it was wasn't it." He winced as he moved, the deep bruising on his lower body was starting to impact. "Is someone covering for me?"

Daniel took his cell phone out of his jacket pocket, looked at the screen, decided to answer it later and carried on with the conversation.

"Yes, Paul Clarke is now officially you." He let that information sink in before continuing. "They got away Jason."

Roberts slumped back into the multiple pillows that jostled for superiority and exhaled slowly.

"I'm really beginning to hate those bastards boss. How is it they are so lucky all the bloody time?"

"No easy way to break this to you Jason, but they have a first-hand line of information."

Roberts, nursing the mother of all headaches looked straight at his chief inspector and shaking his head said, "It's not one of my team guv'nor, and it's not Jack. No way. He's invested every waking hour into finding this lot – he's got a few debts to repay but he would never do anything underhand. Never."

"Are you expecting me to disagree?"

"No, just hoping you don't. I can't deal with much more. I've lost one, nearly another, seen a key witness brutally killed and taken a beating myself." He adjusted himself in the bed, desperate to get comfortable, before continuing – his speech deliberate as if he was searching for every word. "If a few months ago someone told me a team like that would resort to this level of violence just to steal cash from bloody bank machines I'd have laughed in their faces."

"But now?"

"This morning, when I left for work, I was beginning to think they were just well-organised with a violent element. But now, given what's happened in the last week, I'm not sure what we are dealing with. There's something missing in the intel picture."

"And that my friend is why you are a detective sergeant. The answer, the sixth degree of separation that everyone goes on about lies very near and is an anagram of Hewett and Complete Bastard."

"No?"

"Yes…Good old, kind old, everyone's best friend and the government's pin-up boy himself. And if I get my hands around his manicured bloody neck, I'll ring it like the last fucking turkey in a Dickensian Christmas novel."

Roberts lay with his eyes closed, almost unable to contemplate what he had heard, but burrowed deep for a morphine-laden reply.

"It was a goose," was the best he could offer before he succumbed and fell asleep.

Daniel stepped away and tapped a number into his cell phone and whispered, "No trust me, it was a turkey…"

"Towards the A2 Johnathan and as fast as you can without being stopped. Head to Chatham, it's about half an hour from here, if you stick to the speed limits."

"It's at least forty-five minutes and forgive me but I know where bloody Chatham is, what I don't know is why we are heading there."

Stefanescu shuffled to his right favouring the wounded arm.

"Because that is where we get rid of this car, it's far too obvious now, every officer in the south of England will be looking for it at some point, if not already. Stay on the motorway and keep just on the limit. Nothing out of the ordinary."

"And when we get to Chatham I take it you lot bugger off and I wait for the next set of instructions like some ever-willing lapdog?"

Stefanescu said something in his mother tongue which made the other two men laugh – they clearly laughed at everything he said as in translation it wasn't really that amusing.

"No, not at all. We have things to arrange, so we will be busy. And you appear to have forgotten that you are coming with us."

Hewett said nothing, sitting bolt upright he stared through the tinted glass, neither looking left or right and fixed his eyes on the road ahead as he tried somehow to contain his mind, which had become a cruel windmill of emotions.

Cade stopped at the door to the private room which was situated at the side of the Intensive Care Unit. He flashed his ID to the loitering and clearly-bored officers and asked for some privacy. They had been warned he was en route so did not challenge him – his look said he needed to be taken seriously.

He waited a moment, took a necessary breath and entered the room.

The almost blue-grey of the hospital lighting appeared to highlight the stark whiteness of the sheets that surrounded her, tucked in immaculately, as if she was on display to a mourning public. It was this fact that caught him off-guard – not the constant thrum of machinery or the rhythmic blinking of the blue and green neon lighting. To the average passing member of the public it would have been easy to think she was laid to rest, awaiting her loved ones, intact, whole, but no longer alive.

Her skin was pallid, but not grey as he had expected and as the doctor had warned him – she had some fight left in her and it lifted his spirits. This girl could survive whatever Mother Nature or Any Other Bastard threw at her. She was breathing, but in a gentle, shallow state. The doctors had previously intubated her and were now trying to allow her to breathe by herself – but it was evident that she was in a comatose condition; alive but absent.

Cade could feel the emotions, physically, wrapping themselves around his stomach, like a knotted rope, twisting and pulling the life from him. His heart ached so much he felt nauseous, and he was aware of becoming breathless. He tried to compensate by breathing faster but this only succeeded in making him more light-headed. He grabbed hold of the bed and forced himself to exhale. And again, until it passed.

She hadn't moved.

He wiped a sizeable tear from his eye, which had been sitting, waiting for the eyelashes to release their relentless hold.

He edged up alongside the bed until he was level with her face. The pure-starched sheets were folded perfectly below her chest revealing a hospital-issued and unflattering nightie which gaped awkwardly and revealed a cleavage that had first caught his eye many weeks before.

He ran his eyes over the clothing and felt for a moment that what he was doing was morally wrong, but he couldn't stop.

Did not want to stop.

He felt that somewhere deep in her current state she would approve. It caused a much-needed moment of levity.

Her breasts were an agreeable surprise when she had first leaned forward in the office that day; exquisitely shaped, larger than he was ever allowed to imagine them, bridled under their staid, business-like blouse. But the pretty white flower detail on the front clasp told its own tale. Here was a girl that relished dressing up, and, he considered, or rather hoped also enjoyed the thrill of lovemaking.

He needed no more convincing that she was able to equally make love with her body and her mind – but it was her eyes that actually, really attracted him. They spoke to him, shouted at times, swore too, but always drew him, a Siren to the rocks.

She was able to hold an entire conversation, by using them without a word being uttered. It was said that they were the window to the soul, and he once found himself daydreaming about their delicate colours and what they concealed in their brief but powerful gazes across the office.

He formed the opinion that there were two sides to this girl – possibly more.

One, a strict, almost business-as-usual, industrious and fastidious employee who would appear to the onlooker to have an iceberg exterior, an exterior with only ten percent visible above the waterline that no man had ever been able to conquer, although many had tried.

When she let her professional guard slip a little, she might – with the right sparring partner – allow a brief moment, an interlude of mild flirtation. But only ever ten percent, not a decimal point more.

It was the remaining ninety percent that intrigued Cade. He had quickly convinced himself, in his many internal dialogues, that her coolly proficient exterior concealed a submerged, simmering, torrid underside. He didn't require any convincing that away from work she was likely to be different; in her apartment, the lounge, more relaxed, the bathroom, warmer, revealing, playful, gently adding pressure to a saturated sponge and letting its warm water trickle along her body, she would control its path, so that she, and she alone would benefit.

In the kitchen, laying bare her deepest feelings, revealing herself; calm, serene and yet shy, hesitant and almost a little nervous, undeniably mesmerising. She enjoyed it here very much. A step or two onto a balcony to reveal her nakedness to an awaiting world, feeling the cold air snapping at her skin, flushing her body with blood, racing to her extremities. During the day, this was a treat, a not-so-subtle naughtiness that excited her – but at night, under the stars she would step out a little further, revealing more of herself, quietly, daringly hoping someone would be looking at her. Somewhere.

In the bedroom he was utterly convinced that she would only ever be a completely devoted mistress, in every possible way, perspiring, physical, vocally giving herself up to him at levels she had previously never considered possible let alone likely. She wanted to become enslaved within and by his mind, soul and body.

Since the early days of teenage development she had stood out from her peers – a shock of dark, curly blonde hair that had slowly darkened and grown to cover her shoulders. She had a misplaced confidence with older men and some would quietly muse at the idea of taking advantage of her. Her looks and physical presence were a heady cocktail to both men and women that she had worked with, and for.

She was flirtatious – oh without a shadow of a doubt, but this was often mistakenly read, especially by the officers' wives as a predatory habit. Nothing could have been further from the truth. There were one or two of the compassionate officers that she found attractive, but in a way that was more fraternal than flirtatious. And she knew how to flirt. She knew how to dress – both on and off duty.

She favoured darker colours but could look good in anything; white was conventionally pretty, virginal with a hint of confidence, but it had to be pure, not off-white. Blue, slightly racier; shades of red lay in her second drawer down, unused, folded, just so. Various other colours competed for attention, grey, purple, cream and even something bought on a complete whim from an anonymous site, shiny, almost cheap. It had forever remained in its wrapping. Cheap and cheerful, and that was not Carrie O'Shea.

Black. Black was the one true colour that brought out her inner self, allowed her to edge away from the wary, to the potentially teasing, lead-you-by-the-hand lover. Her favourite matching set of bra and knickers was elegant, with a white ribbon detail at the front and a strong underwire on the bra to enhance her natural shape. She loved it, adored catching a glimpse of herself in one of her many mirrors and more than anything else wanted to be seen wearing it. But not by just anyone. Just someone. Someone who wouldn't take advantage of her, as they had done when she was younger; those that had exploited her brittleness and told her to remain subdued, quiet – responsible for nothing, but guilty of everything.

How she functioned sometimes, remained upbeat, coped – that was something that only she could control – and control it she did. There were no alternatives. Years later she had emerged from a physical state of anxiety, the partially coloured butterfly through a sea-mist of mental anguish, out into a brighter world, notwithstanding she would always carry an heirloom of culpability.

For those that were fortunate enough to really get to know her, it was parent that the legacy ruled her head and heart, when and wherever she allowed it to.

It was the need to place two defiant fingers up at men and a society that judged without pausing that led her to finally put herself first. It wasn't a textbook, social media cathartic moment that led to this, more a situation where she had emptied the bottle – or bottles and had sat on the level crossing, silently waiting for a train that never bloody arrived, and ever since that lurid moment, her favourite time of the day had been waking – she considered every such occurrence a bonus.

She would slip out of bed and luxuriate in the shower, applying oils and an expensive shampoo, then, after slowly and rather deliberately drying herself select the chosen underwear for the day ahead – underwear that had earlier been laid out on an ottoman, alongside a dark, black, silk kimono, folded perfectly.

Of all the clothing items she owned, this was her favourite. Its feel, soft, sensual and cool was always perfect, better still when it had nothing to resist its removal, its journey from on to off which she had practiced over and over again in front of the full length vintage bedroom mirror, allowing it to slip from her shoulders and quietly onto the carpeted floor, imagining the hidden male stood behind her, naked in the shadows, controlling its demise.

She was a rare one indeed, able to stand her ground when the need arose but equally able to lay back, close her eyes and think of England's green and pleasant land. To enjoy and conversely to be enjoyed.

Cade recalled in the early hours and days following their first meeting how he had tried his best to avoid eye contact with her, allowing them to dart back and forth in time with her own sideways glances, but each time he looked, he picked out the delicate black lace that wrapped itself around her and accentuated the outline of her body.

It was only later when she had laid herself bare, allowing

him to admire her without any obstructions, either physical or professional that he had realised just how much he was attracted to her. He felt it physically too. The mere thought of her was enough to create a tension of physicality and need. He could close his eyes at any time and see her, standing, naked from the waist up, revealing herself to him for the first time.

He was doing it now.

Her skin was slightly tanned, almost olive in normal light and her arms and shoulders bore a sense of physical exercise, not slender but beautifully formed and he liked it.

For the record, she abhorred them, covering them at every opportunity. Cade considered it a terrible shame and tried his best, without appearing over-eager, to encourage her to reveal more of herself.

He placed his hand on her chest, clutched at her left breast and then held onto her as tight as he could without causing her pain, before running his hand quietly and slowly down and over her stomach, stopping, placing his fingers between the buttoned down gown, hesitating – again, to an onlooker it had all the hallmarks of being so very wrong. But he didn't care. He whispered something incomprehensible – aware of Daniel's last words.

He moved his hand back up to her collarbones and stroked them with a feather-light touch before running the tips of his fingers around her neck, pausing on her throat and then turning his hand over, used the back of his fingers to caress her cheek. He held them there a while before moving his ring and index finger onto her lips, allowing them to part softly. They were dry, but he recalled how simply striking they were, crafted in subtle colours, their shape outlined in a darker shade and emphasised when she smiled.

It wasn't a beaming look at me smile, but it had an impact on him every time it happened. It spoke volumes, and offered, to the educated, an idea that she was thinking about something deep, possibly meaningful, and occasionally, when she allowed, a little too naughty for public discussion.

Her vocabulary was extensive and at times Anglo-Saxon – but she saved the best for one place only.

Her mouth was small, concealing a delicate tongue, pointed, perfectly suited to seeking out the most intimate of places, she would occasionally mirror Cade, who licked his lips when deep in thought, often appearing flirtatious – without the slightest intent. But it drove her wild.

He stood and stared at her, taking in her perfect imperfections, trying to swallow, his throat felt as it were lined with razor wire. He wanted to sob but something held him back, perhaps with the fear that if he started he might never stop.

He leaned down and murmured into her ear – 'Carrie, it's me, Jack. I'm here now. I won't go until I know you are safe...I...there's something...'

He'd made a career out of saving people, both good and bad but knew that Mother Nature, at her worst would always have the upper hand – and here she was, clasping onto his girl.

'Let her go...please.'

His own feelings of emotion were driving up through his body, volcanic, earthy and tectonic, out of control. He started to shudder, his chest heaving, he breathed again.

'Control yourself, man. This is neither the time, nor the place.'

Balanced once more he continued to stroke her face, reminding himself of the first time he met her and how he adored her feistiness, her very direct approach, but also her deeply hidden self – the one that was evidently only ever saved for one man. He envied him greatly.

He moved his head slightly, lowered himself down towards the bed and held onto her. He breathed in her scent, evoking memories of the hallway and stairs that led to her apartment and the mystique of her bedroom. At the time he was dragging himself out of a pit, unsure in which direction to head. Now he was alive – but praying for her to re-join the world of the living. The still fragrant nature of her matted hair seeped into his sensory system, it was fresh, slightly citrusy, lime, or was it lemon? Whatever its origins it was never overpowering. She rarely wore perfume, she didn't need to.

He knew that a staff member or colleague could walk into the room at any moment, but he no longer cared. He rested his cheek upon hers and imagined her reciprocating, pushing against him, exhaling as she whispered into his ear, again, broken indecipherable words but with an undercurrent of passion, of loyalty and inquisitiveness. 'If I kiss you Jack Cade will you reward me?'

His lips kissed her cheek, moved up slowly onto her motionless eyes, hovering, feeling her lashes brush against him before running his own kiss back along her face and onto her lips. He hesitated. This was wrong. He continued, even in her current state there was a sense of reaction from her, the forbidden fruit wanting to be consumed, piece by perfect piece.

He lowered his lips back onto hers and tasted her briefly; they were as dry as he imagined – again, he cared not. He kissed her again, deeper this time. Short, perfect kisses – as if something was telling him not to proceed, but she tasted so incredible, he wanted to remain there forever, skin on skin, breath on breath, before picking her up, carefully, respectfully and bringing her to his chest.

If she was awake now he knew, there and then that he wanted her more than he had ever realised. The office play, the sideways looks, the less-than-subtle flirtation now all a thing of the past. She may never survive and he had wasted the opportunity to tell her exactly how he felt – he had so many opportunities, so many chances to set the record straight and ironically, despite his inbuilt fear, to tell her exactly what she wanted to hear.

'Tell her Jack.'

The times that they had walked along the nearby streets, business-first, passion later, a careless stray hand brushing against the other, interplay at its finest. And now, he may never see her again. And it hurt. He felt as if he had been struck by a freight train, its carriages heavily-laden and stopping for no man, least of all him.

'Fuck you, Jack Cade will you just explain how you *feel?* I don't care whether anyone else but us knows. It will always be ours; coveted, sheltered and beyond surreal. Ours, bound in trust. Alone...'

A tear broke the seal, flooded over his eyelid and dropped onto her face. He went to wipe it away, but it had run down her soft cool skin, onto her neck and had been absorbed by the sanitised cotton linen beneath her.

He was in danger of unravelling, of finally letting go of years of denial – he'd been hurt beyond belief by another and here he was, exploiting the most resilient girl he had ever met. The one who told him how it was, in every situation, but always found a place for humour, guidance and angel-like compassion. She was not what people saw on the surface – she was a still water but her truest character was only ever revealed to those she trusted. And she trusted Cade with her life, her heart and her soul.

He kissed her once more and quietly spoke into her small and delicate ears.

"I love you Carrie. I suspect I always have done. I wish we had met long ago. Stay with me, but know, if I should lose you then I will be waiting..."

He perched on the edge of the bed and watched her breathe, staring for so long that he was unable to focus. It took a fraction of a second to drift into a place where he could finally lay next to her, naked under a simple, single cover, feel her push back against him, his arms wrapped around her, one across her stomach, the other her chest, his face buried in her immaculately crafted hair as they made love for hours – this was not the frantic, athletic sex that he was occasionally used to, this was the beginning of a new journey with another person; gentle, exploring, passionate, seeking, crying, smiling, exhaling.

He reached out and brushed her hair, so gently that in a waking state she wouldn't feel his touch. He held his breath so as not to disturb her. He felt the texture of her hair, silk and satin and natural oils which accentuated its colour. He wanted to carefully cut a small lock from her head and store it in a corner of his life where he could revisit her in his own time, raising it to his face and allowing its scent to wash over him like a wave. Someone else had already carried out that act, it seemed wrong to now replicate it for his own needs.

This collection of feelings was nothing like his former life with 'her' – Penny, his outrageously playful and now estranged wife – but so far, it was only a dream, the almost-mistress, the cliff-edge lover that he craved with so much passion that it was physically painful. And, if fate played its hand, if he never saw her again, never able to reach out and embrace her, draw her towards him, holding her as close as he actually, physically could, inhaling her every scent, then life was probably not that special after all.Something told him that despite the intensity of his feelings, he would never fully experience her and that, was too much.

Let her go.

Carrie, in her comatose state could hear Jack and physically feel the intensity of his presence. His hand on her breast, caressing, loving, desperate.

She pushed into him, meeting his hold on her but he appeared unaware of her emergence from her intense slumber.

She was stirring, shifting in the bed, allowing the gown to gape, to reveal herself to him. Her lips were dry, and that was very intentional.

'Kiss me, gentle kisses, pause, hold me, accept me and let me invade your head and heart and let me be present in your every waking moment...'

She could hear her own voice, her thoughts and his. They were at her place; she knew because she had seen the large black door, standing, open allowing access from her street and straight into her bedroom. But things were somehow different. She was struggling with an unseen energy that prevented her from moving forwards. Over and over in her dream-laden condition she fought the glass ceiling that prevented their union.

His tone was fractured, distant almost as if he were frightened. But she was alive, so why was he afraid?

There was no music, no other sounds, even passing people, vehicles and the humdrum of a frantic lifestyle was missing.

She caught a glimpse of herself in the glass walls that now surrounded her. She was wearing her favourite underwear, bought, very recently, for him. And she felt exquisitely at peace as she stood before him. She reached forward and took his hand, feeling its strength, looking at his forearms, the gentle rippling of tendons and the tanned skin all appeared before her in intricate detail. She could hear the second hand of his watch ticking.

She was awake. She was alive.

If she died now, she would die knowing what love really was...finally. Heaven sent, without a doubt.

Better to have loved and lost, than never to have loved at all...

For Cade it was too much; to contend with, or even think of. He had to compartmentalise the thoughts or he would slowly drift into a deep valley of blind frustration and discontent.

He had her in his heart, and that counted for something. His thoughts were his alone. He could close his eyes at any given time and see her, not in a blurred, dreamlike state but in total clarity – she was tangible. He didn't always need to be standing next to her, holding her to his chest, breathing in her spirit and deepest, intimate thoughts.

But he questioned when that would happen again – and it couldn't, soon enough.

His priorities had changed. She was alone but in the hands of professional people who knew that only time would either heal her or take her away from him. He knew he had to allow them to do their jobs and he, his.

He now had to find the bastard or bastards responsible for stealing her from him and that was a dish better left to go cold.

He pulled away, held her hand, and squeezed it as hard as he dare – he never wanted to hurt her again – he straightened, composed himself and walked quickly out of the room. Let her go. Let every part of her go or watch from a frantic corner as everything connected to him impacted upon her. Decision made. Adore her though he might, it was time to move on. She might forgive him, one day.

The constable immediately outside the room saw Cade's face and unsure of what to say decided on brevity.

"You OK boss?"

Cade smiled a forced and pained smile. "I am now mate. I am now."

As he walked back along the same corridor towards where he had left Daniel he stopped, turned around, stared at the walls, then the ceiling and then walked again.

Should he stay, or should he go?

"You have made your decision. Leave it now. Do not go back." He didn't quite believe himself but of the two options it was the only one that was viable – to maintain the doting pseudo-lover was only going to end in tears. Release her spirit and walk away. If she was still there when he returned, if all of the other eight, or nine or ten planets were still aligned, then fine, pick up the pieces.

For now, it was nothing to do with revenge – this was good old, plain old policing, concentrating on the things he could change and leaving everything else to Lady Luck. And if you believed that Jack Cade then...

He continued towards Roberts' ward dragging a sense of composure from deep within his own wounded soul. As he left the corridor and saw his two colleagues sat in the ward chatting about something inane, O'Shea's right hand moved, subtly, but in her subconscious mind she was reaching out for him, clasping for another hand to hold. He was there, somewhere.

O'Shea could sense him nearby but the glass walls and ceiling of her cell compressed her tightly, holding her in place.

"I need to get to him," she announced to a doctor, stood studiously at the side of her bed.

"I need to get to him now. To tell him."

She could sense her own frustrations buried deep within her dream.

"Tell him what Miss O'Shea?" asked the faceless health worker.

"That I love him. For fuck's sake, can it really be that hard? Just call him, he's only just down the corridor. Shout his name and he will come back…"

Her words cycled over and over again, she had no strength, and despite tugging at the doctor's arm it made no difference, made little impact. Her fever was encompassing her rapidly, her own mental vultures were circling above, waiting for the moment to swoop.

She screamed Cade's name repeatedly, but it felt as if she were powerless; dying, slipping into a deeper void, where no amount of physical or mental energy would make the slightest piece of difference.

She was. And it wouldn't.

Cade met Daniel at the door to the unit.

"Boss."

"Jack."

"How is he?"

"He's fine, you?"

"Fine."

"Liar."

"Granted."

"Jack, you know we need to leave these good people at the behest of the medics don't you? We could stay for hours, days probably, but it would not achieve a bloody thing. Jason will be discharged today, possibly tomorrow. He'll head home to recuperate."

"And Carrie?"

"Sometime."

Cade repeated the word. "Sometime this afternoon? Sometime this evening? Sometime bloody never John? I need to know when she will wake up."

A junior house doctor popped his head around the curtain and spoke, as they all do, in a staccato medical tone fashioned from only six years working in the trauma industry.

"Sorry to eavesdrop gentlemen but with her diagnosis the best-case answer is c) – sometime..."

He paused, allowing the news to circulate. Sensing a line crossed, he attempted a smoothing of the waters.

"By that I do of course mean she could also make a full recovery, physically at least. We have no idea, no glistening ball of crystal on where the next few days will take her. Trust me, I'm a doctor."

He was Polish or German, or Welsh; normally this level of information was critical to the natural investigator but after the month he had experienced Cade couldn't care less where he was from and who he was, as long as he prolonged her life.

He found himself thinking that actually it was a good thing that he was away from her or her invasion of his mind and body would be complete and he'd never achieve anything. She had such a profound effect upon him – even in her half-departed state.

What he feared was loving again. It wasn't commitment per se, more a case of anxiety ruling his head.

He nodded at the doctor; it was in preference to causing him so much harm for his overly honest opinion – the place was busy enough without another casualty.

He gently shook Roberts' hand.

"I need to go, mate. You realise? I...or rather we, what's left of us needs to hit the road and carry out some summary retribution, all under the auspices of the law you understand?"

Roberts, who was still pumped full of morphine started to laugh. He caught a sideways glance from Cade.

"Sorry Jack, I'm just having funny thoughts. I think it's the drugs. This is some powerful shit!" He pointed to the pump next to him, tapping the device lovingly and grinning inanely.

"OK mate, what's so funny?"

"I was going to start singing that song...*Hit the road Jack.*"

"And?"

"And I could see three black female backing singers walking in from around that curtain singing no more!"

He started giggling which was unexpectedly infectious. Daniel looked away, biting his bottom lip. A nurse excused herself leaving Cade to fathom out whether it was an absolute insult or indeed a moment of levity.

He began to walk out then spun around and burst into song.

"What did you say?"

Roberts was trying to respond with a line from *Hit the road Jack* but was unable to utter a coherent word due to his drug-fuelled haze.

Daniel started clicking his fingers in time as Cade finished with the line about not coming back.

The two able-bodied men pseudo high-kicked out of the room in time to the music, leaving their friend and colleague unable to talk for a fit of giggles.

Daniel stopped after a few metres.

"Come on, enough of this cabaret, we have to go. That's an order."

"Good. I need something else to focus on. After all, I've done sweet FA for the last few weeks."

They had reached the car park when Cade's phone chirped into life. He pulled the handset out of his trouser pocket to see a simple text message.

South East Coastal port. Tomorrow morning. Your man is with them. Copil.

Cade turned the screen towards Daniel.

"I'm thinking the White Cliffs of Dover?"

Daniel took a second the replied, "Just have to wait and see won't we?"

"How does he know this? And more importantly, do we trust him?"

"I have no idea. And, as for trust, no less than I trust Hewett, Jack. No less. So in my book that equates to not very much at all, but forgive the pun, any port in a storm."

He pointed through the windscreen where the clouds a few miles in front were changing colour dramatically, light grey to darker hues, almost green.

"Hardly a great night for fireworks is it?"

"I guess it depends upon which type John."

Stefanescu's cell phone also throbbed into life. He fumbled for the green button and jammed it between his shoulder and his left ear. The voice he heard was familiar if a little strained.

"Hello brother....how are? How are my team? How is Mr Hewett?"

"We are all OK. Mr Hewett is just fine. He is aware he is coming with us. As usual brother, I have done everything whilst you sip expensive brandy, smoke American cigarettes and play with your whore of the week. Where is she from today huh? Mexico? Brazil?"

Alex snorted a sarcastic laugh as he took a moment to ignore the comment.

"Stefan, if it wasn't for me you would still be a moderately successful gypsy. Do not ever forget this." He directed a stream of air over the last word whilst driving his fist into the black granite worktop of his jet black kitchen.

"And if it wasn't for me, brother, you would just be a gypsy with money..."

There was a pause, a brief moment for both to have the upper hand before Alex continued, business-like once more.

Smiling. "OK, you win this fight. Let me remind you that we both win if we stay strong and keep to the plan. You surely agree that the plan is good little brother?"

He hated how he called him by that name, had done ever since he was able to comprehend that his older brother had a sadistic streak.

Alex had recovered – for now. But his tinder-box temper was so close to the surface it would only take the merest hint of tension to drive him over the edge. He was pacing again, favouring the knuckles on his master hand, unsure why they were blue and painful.

A lack of a reply from his younger brother was taken as an affirmative. He agreed with the plan.

"Good. We need to start Phase Two – bring in the new

children...let them learn, give them a free reign to exploit the British mainland, let them take risks, the more the better, I always succeed when I cling to the cliff face, the chalk filling my nails as I slip towards the next life. It is the thrill of waiting to fall Stefan. Deciding upon your own destiny. They say don't look down. But you should, all the way to the bottom. Imagine falling and the feeling of hitting the ground. You really should try it sometime. "

His brother could hear in Alex's tone that he was slipping back into a state of agitated behaviour once more – and this was a warning sign. He had first displayed symptoms of subtle obsessions as a young child, enough to cause his devoted parents some concern – but in a post-war, late-Forties communist annexe of the Soviet Union to even think about asking for such help was a sign of weakness. His true psychoses hadn't manifested until much later, but in any event and shortly after he had suffered his first major lapse.

He had strapped his mother to a wooden kitchen chair and having stupefied and blindfolded her he slit her shins carefully before he had ripped the varicose veins from her legs, with his bare hands. He despised their imperfect appearance, a bulging, green anachronistic legacy of her apparent youthful beauty. He wouldn't know what she had looked like, for the state had burned every last picture of her as a younger woman. He told himself this – but he knew the truth. He took her love and crushed it. And yet he worshipped her. He told her this as he mopped up the congealing blood and rinsed the kitchen floor repeatedly.

It was the first episode and the trigger for what followed. He had started to have thoughts about experimenting on animals but abhorred this – it was so cruel. Arson had been a substitute, watching the firemen arrive with their rudimentary equipment had provided a suitable thrill. The doctors spoke to him for hours, about his thoughts and deeds. He had answered honestly, and they declared his condition to be a direct result of having come home from school one day to find his mother slumped into an old chair, dead.

He had killed his father with a hammer. Comparatively speaking it was an altogether easier scenario. There was no love there and to expend any more energy than was necessary seemed like a total waste of his talents. As he disposed of his body, he recalled one moment of clarity – the point where he stopped and questioned himself why he had just done what he had. He knew after a moment of brief self-flagellation that he would do it again if the inner demons commanded it.

There would be no mortification of the flesh for Alex Stefanescu.

His time in prison had all but destroyed him. How anyone could return from that was remarkable – but it also explained why everything he created was genetically strong. Alex's daughter, was a fiery thing – all the virtues of her mother; positive, passionate, perplexing, capable, curious, charming: dangerous.

"We can afford to lose a few. None of them will talk, they value their families far too much. Those that rise to the top will take part in our own superb plot and we need to make sure things go with a bang. Remember, remember as the British say..."

Stefanescu was about to add his own tactical thinking when he realised that once more his older sibling had regained the upper hand. A blank phone display indicated that he was no longer on the line, back with his left hand on the stem of a cut-crystal glass containing Hennessy cognac and his right firmly on the ludicrously attractive rear of a good-looking girl. It was how he liked to end every call.

He vigorously slapped her and downed the warm liquid before inverting the glass and watching the last few droplets cling to the side before landing on her skin and trickling across the back of her taut and tanned legs.

"Remind me girl, where *are* you from?"

CHAPTER TWENTY-FOUR

THE PHONE RANG IN DANIEL'S CAR. HE LOOKED AT CADE and mouthed 'Frank'.

"Yes boss. How's it going?"

"Enough of the small talk, John. Where are you?"

He thought about altering the truth to suit the situation but recalled the much-loved, much-used police phrase: 'never bullshit a bullshitter.'

"Heading south Frank."

"Would you like to narrow that down a little gentleman? Are we talking south London, southern England, Monte Carlo or the bloody pole with the same name?"

"The second one. We've got some A1 source intel that suggests our targets, including Hewett are heading for the Kent coast."

"Hewett?"

"Yes. Frank, it's a long story. More than a hunch. He's involved and I suspect he's already up to his nuts. We've all been blinded by his natural charisma. I'm prepared to give him the benefit of the doubt – perhaps that the group have something over him but my gut says otherwise."

"Hewett?" he asked again, still in disbelief. "John if this is even partly true the fall-out will be monstrous. You realise this don't you? It could end you too. I need more than just a copper's gut bloody feeling."

"And your point, sir?"

"Do I really need to outline this in words of one syllable JD?" He paused, less for effect than to provide some thinking space. "OK, what is your plan?"

"I want to bloody locate them. Actually, I want to find Hewett and ring his bloody neck."

"I assume Jack is with you? Leave it to the locals John, they're more than capable. We can put a call into the Frontier Ops team at the tunnel and also alert Dover Harbour Board Police. The only other option is one of the other ferry ports. My bet is Dover. It's where I would head. More traffic. Not that that's where you are probably heading right now?"

He found himself being drawn into the situation and smiled. He'd been there once. Still missed the thrill of the chase.

He continued. "Not that you are continuing at warp factor five down the M2 as we speak, eh?"

"Not at the moment, sir, no."

"I've got a call coming in from the boss JD. I suspect he is going to re-affirm a little chat we had yesterday. He wants your team off this wild goose chase and onto some operation called Blunt – knife crime. The current sexy thing in the Met, apparently. Like I say, if it were my operation I would be leaving it to the locals. More than capable and all that. But unless I give you the direct order to extract yourselves from this pile of bovine excrement, just steel yourself to reply that we've not had this chat – seriously John, if the deputy commissioner finds out he'll have my nuts on a cracker and knowing his little ways it will be smothered with bloody Marmite."

"Thank you, sir. We appreciate this. At risk of being boring..."

"You've got twenty-four hours. Not a minute more. Stay safe and do not submit any claims for lunch in France. Clear?"

"Waterford sir."

"It's Waterman."

"I meant the crystal..."

"I know."

Hewett's Audi maintained a steady seventy as it crossed into Kent and headed towards the Medway Bridge. His raw instinct told him to drive to the nearest police station and hand himself in – or better still hand them over and escape with his integrity intact.

However, it was his reputation he valued more than anything else and they held the ace cards resolutely to their chests; his financial transactions, imagery of the meetings, phone conversations. It was all so well done.

The latter were damning, but the video imagery was career ending – they were a beautiful, young and at times athletic couple. It was just fun at first, but then it became addictive. No names, no promises. He was trapped, and they had cornered him perfectly. It wasn't as if he had enough to worry about with his debt programme and constant fear of a public, painful and very familial shaming regime. He found himself dropping into a widening sinkhole with no idea when the ground would next meet him.

"Left at this exit. To Chatham. We meet with a friend. Change the car and then to Folkestone. Give me your phone."

"Why? I thought we trusted each other Stefan?"

"You do. But I don't." He lowered the tinted glass and nonchalantly tossed the phone over the bridge. They had travelled at least two hundred metres before it slipped below the surface of the river and lodged into its muddy base.

"Well that's just bloody marvellous. If I get the chance I'm going to do the same to you. I had everything on that damned thing." He sensed he was getting angrier by the second but judged his audience, a sociopath, a psychopath and an unknown quantity. Hardly a favourable hand.

Stefanescu shrugged his shoulders and grinned.

"All things of your past Johnnie. Chapters that are now gone, shredded like your debts. Cheer up, soon you will have new friends, new numbers. Maybe even new debts. Right here, then left at the roundabout."

Hewett smiled internally. "You are not that smart you piece of...worthless human waste." He mentally stroked the second phone in his jacket pocket.

Fifteen minutes later, through medium density traffic they arrived at a neutrally grey industrial estate and were ushered into a stereotypical, shuttered unit whose only iden-tifying feature was the number fourteen.

The shutter dropped behind them. Hewett switched the Audi off and stepped out of the car. The immediate stench of lacquer provided all he needed to know that this was a body shop, and he soon imagined his beloved car would be wheeled into the booth and reborn.

To enforce this a male in his twenties began to unscrew the number plates and toss them into a bin, already full of similar identifiers.

"When do I get the car back?"

"You don't. And anyway, where you are going you need left-hand drive. We will buy you a new one. Perhaps a real car, like an AMG Mercedes. Yes? You like this, I can tell. Anyway, I need fresh clothes and a strong cologne." He playfully slapped Hewett on the cheek before walking away to answer his phone.

Hewett breathed in, deliberately slow, coating his lungs with acetone. He was in so deep now he could taste the polluted water on the back of his throat. He looked around but everywhere there were dark eyes looking back, questioning why the boss had this pale-faced and English man with him.

Hewett's attention was suddenly diverted to the adjoining unit. He could see clearly through a door and watched Gheorghiu helping another male remove a large tarpaulin from a vehicle. It was white, with red and blue details, appeared to be newly painted and bore insignia along the panelled-sides and on the driver's door.

Hewett looked closer. He could see the multi-coloured sweeping coachwork on the Renault Traffic van but was unable to ascertain its exact identity or purpose. He was joined by Stefanescu.

"I see you are intrigued Johnnie. Please, take a look. After all, you are one of us now. Go on, sit in the front passenger seat. Go!"

Hewett did as instructed. As he walked towards the van, he saw the familiar logo on the bonnet. Police Nationale. He felt a tap on the shoulder; it was Constantin.

"Get undressed. Put this on." His English was considerably better than Hewett's Romanian.

Hewett looked around for somewhere to dress.

"Oh dear. Are we shy?" Stefanescu asked the former stellar member of the British government elite.

"You will need these too."

Hewett looked at his own image on an ID card. His name was Charles Durand, and he was now, at least according to the card, a Brigadier-chef in the Police Aux Frontières, the team formed to patrol and control French borders around the world.

"I have done my homework Mr Hewett. I know you speak fluent French, and besides, you look more like an officer than Constantin. Get used to your new name and role. We will pass into France as soon as possible, whether we do so without causing alarm is *entirely* down to you. And please, do remember, I also understand the language enough to know if you are still one of us."

Resigned to the fact Hewett pulled on the dark blue boiler suit, adjusted the fit with a belt and clipped the ID into place on the left breast pocket. He discreetly palmed the secreted phone into the left trouser pocket.

"Tres bon monsieur Hewett. Vous avez l'air d'un officier!"

He caused his small team to laugh, many of whom also had a fundamental grasp of the language.

"Hurry up everyone. We need to be ready. The other teams join us tonight. We head for France at two in the morning then our new lives can begin. I do not know about you but I have plans for the weekend!"

There was no celebration, just a repeated nodding of heads around the twin commercial units as people resumed their tasks. Hewett stepped in front of Stefanescu and gripped him by the arm.

"Is there something you need to tell me?"

"No, not at this time Brigadier-chef. Do not worry, in a few hours you will see for yourself. *Primul Val* is about to be become headline news. But only when we are far away from this cesspit. Now, please remove your hand before I break it with my remaining working one. Come on, we need to eat and I know how much you French love your coffee and your croissants."

Hewett suppressed a feeling of dread and nausea, caught a glimpse of himself in the van window and prayed for rain – torrential rain, enough to wash the paint off the bloody thing and reveal to anyone that gave a damn that something wasn't quite right.

Stefanescu was quickly back onto his phone. Holding down the number four.

"It is me. We are ready."

He repeated it with the following five numbers – all pre-loaded for speed dialling.

Behind him the Audi was already stripped off its glass and was being wheeled into an awaiting booth as a panel beater began to skilfully alter its identity, happy to be using his skills and earning a living once more.

Cade and Daniel were doing their level best not to adhere to the local speed limits – heavily enforced in the never-ending road works. The wipers on the Mondeo swept a light shower off the windscreen as the grill lights illuminated the myriad red and white road cones.

"Move over, that's the boy," said a steady-nerved Daniel as he made progress through the traffic – which in typically British style parted like the proverbial sea at the sight of flickering blue lights.

Cade's mind began to roam as they surged through the red and white alleyway, each cone acting as a mesmerising aid to his hypnosis. Behind him in the City of London lay a great friend and a potential lover who he accepted, quietly, he might never see again.

The skies were clearer, and he had a future. All he had to do was let go of one or two things from the past and he could be free to pursue a new life. The force appeared to have adopted him – quite how he was still unsure – and with the skeletal remains of his former life now buried in his old home town he could head wherever he wanted to. He had to smile, unlike many a British fictional police character Cade had neither the demon of drink or drugs in his closet. But like everyone, he had been let down, and that was often enough of a catalyst.

Whilst he considered his immediate future he couldn't help but think about what else was on the horizon.

The job in Lyon and working with Interpol had its own unique appeal. Staying in London, a place he had only previously considered as a tourist location, had its own charm, and he felt that somehow he could adapt. He wanted more than anything to adapt with O'Shea. But what if? He was changing his mind with the passing of every traffic cone, aware of more voices joining his own internal monologue.

"Jack. Am I having this discussion on my own?"

Cade came to his senses, deciding to leave any decision to a time when he was at least able to remember his own name.

"Sorry John, miles away. You were saying?"

"Indeed. You need a rest pal. I was asking, what is your call? Dover? Or the Tunnel?"

The port of Dover was a place very recently dear to Cade's heart. Situated on the south eastern corner of the

Garden of England it had a maritime history ten times older than Admiral Nelson and had broken countless passenger records over the years as its impressive fleet of ferries, hovercraft and gargantuan catamarans had plied their trade between the ports at its French equivalents in Calais and Boulogne.

It seemed like only a matter of hours before that he had picked up the diminutive but fiery Nikolina from the Immigration centre and whisked her northwards to London – where it had all unravelled, from where both of their lives had changed.

'My God what an amazing woman. If only...'

The second option was Folkestone, or rather slightly inland at Cheriton where the infamous tunnel started its anfractuous journey underground, deep under the bedrock of the English Channel, meeting its French counterpart at the midway point or Point Median.

Officially the longest undersea tunnel in the world it had its own claims to fame, and for Cade was the lesser of two evils. He considered it more secure than the surface option at Dover and outlined his reasons to Daniel.

"OK, Dover it is Jack."

Daniel stayed on the M2 motorway avoiding the chance to divert onto the parallel M20, both of which headed south and terminated at the two very different ports. A few miles away their targets sat in old car seats, propped themselves against walls and generally rested, eating cheap and generic take away meals and sleeping where possible. Constantin embraced caffeine in place of any more noxious commodities.

For the first time in weeks he felt alive. He must never allow himself another moment of weakness.

· · ·

North of the River Medway another two Renault vans joined the traffic and headed south. White, far from unique and ready for their new identity they merged with the growing numbers of vehicles travelling towards the southern ports. At Chatham they exited and headed for the same industrial complex.

Further north, a young Eastern European male, twenty-three at the most adjusted his collar against the wind and walked quickly from a clichéd silver vehicle towards a doorway. He knocked four times. Deliberate, twice, then again. The door opened a fraction before it was unlocked completely and the male was embraced by another of similar age. The street-front room contained eight men now, all of similar age and build and all wearing almost identical clothing. They were waiting for one more to join them.

In a thoroughly miserable bedsit flat a mile away, Alin Vasile a twenty-four-year-old from the small Romanian town of Bucovat was waiting patiently for a phone call that he was promised would eventuate. He would receive the call on the onetime cheap Nokia he had been given a week before.

He missed his home. The nearby city of Craiova had always captivated him, its beautiful buildings and churches, its people were special too and he always recalled with great fondness the fountains that he danced under when just a small boy. He adored them so much, skipping through them on the way to a warm summer day.

He stopped his thoughts. Was it only so very recently that he was that same child?

He took a long breath and exhaled, blowing out the inferior British tobacco smoke and marvelling at how it found a draught that had otherwise remained veiled.

He missed home indeed, but the opportunities were too few, and so very far between.

His older brother had introduced him to Gheorghiu – a strong man, a man of principles and a man he admired.

'Come with us Alin, we will make you wealthy and you can return with your head held high – and leave the place you grew up in...for Craiova or better still anywhere you want to be in Europe, or America. Imagine that? The choice is yours. Come. Come with us.' Hope had become a drug as addictive as any other.

It was so personal, so crafted to him alone.

Such a pity he had given the same crafted speech to his eight young companions.

The call came. He lifted the phone to his chiselled and slightly pock-marked jawline and listened. He formatted the phone and removed the SIM card, dropping it between the floorboards of the austere room before exiting the flat via the fire escape. He walked quickly, head down and also pulling the collar around his neck. He was used to cold weather but he felt chilled today. He separated the phone from the battery and dropped them into adjacent and over-flowing waste bins.

Cade looked out of the window, in the distance he could make out the magnificent Canterbury Cathedral, for eons a centre of Christianity and a place not visited by Cade since he was also a boy. The rain danced across the passenger window, droplets twisting and turning before relenting to the air pressure and departing.

Lost in their hypnotic actions he too began to consider

his past, and his future; his mortality too, probably for the first time in his life.

As his woodwork teacher always said, 'Carpe Diem Cade – Seize the Fish!'

He always laughed as he feared the ruddy-faced bully. Such a shame he hadn't got a clue what he meant. But he had always harboured a desire to take one of his prized rasps and run it across the back of his hand – bastard – he had picked on Cade when he was at his most vulnerable. It was a strange moment of mental purification for the young Jack who had sown a seed of policing or enforcement of some kind which wouldn't bear fruit for years. As with many who were bullied he vowed to fight them in later life.

'Ripping of your skin Mr Adams, slowly, revealing the inner workings of your hand. Not nice is it?'

Cade was always aware he didn't have it in his heart to harm someone for no reason. But he'd make a few exceptions.

His own rewarding personal thoughts jolted him back to reality. He looked at Daniel who was as visibly tired as he was.

"Want me to drive?"

"No you're fine Jack. At this rate we'll be there in fifteen minutes." It was typical of police understatement when it came to judging distance and time. At the speed Daniel was driving it was more like sixteen.

The car phone rang. It was Kent Police's control room at nearby Maidstone, offering their services and acknowledging Cade's earlier VHF radio announcement that they were on their area and travelling swiftly across the county.

"We have staff at all of our ports, including Ramsgate sir. My boss just wants to make sure you appreciate that we have jurisdiction over this – but is happy to work with you of course. All we ask is that you keep us informed via VHF. Our traffic units are in place on the M2, A2, A20 and M20 plus our local units are aware that you are in the area. Confirm we are looking for a blue Audi S6 with four males on board?"

"Yes, over."

"Confirm whether armed or currently unknown?"

"Armed."

"Roger. And that they are wanted for a number of offences including GBH, burglary and theft?"

"You can add attempted murder to that. In fact, let's just stop it and then we'll tot up what we have on them when they are safely locked up"

"Copy that sir. Our armed cars are using the call signs Trojan on VHF 46 Kilo Alpha. If you can use Zero Two Mike Papa and designation Golf Tango we will monitor you."

"Golf Tango. Received thank you."

He turned to Daniel and with a twisted smile said at exactly the same time, "We forgot about Ramsgate."

Alin Vasile reached the second house in time to watch the sun start to set in the winter skyline. He liked this new city, a city of hope but he knew that he could not remain. He tapped the door twice, then again and entered.

"Hello my friends. Are we all ready to earn our fortunes?"

Some smiled, others clapped their hands together. One

stayed resolute, staring back at him without comment. The last one visited the bathroom for the sixth time since he last checked his watch only a few minutes before.

"We all know what to do and where to go? Once we have enough, we get back here and split up with the goods. You all remember where your vehicles are parked and which way we head home? Good."

He looked around the room sensing a few gaps in the information.

"Have I made myself clear? Do not fail to ask me a question – better to do it now than look foolish later, or worse still in prison with a man who will make you his late night plaything. Any questions?" He expected none.

There was one.

"So, you are the boss man?" It was the unyielding male who had earlier locked eyes.

"I am. Do you have a problem with this?"

"No, boss, not at all. I just needed to know. Now if that little boy has finished with his nervous visits I need to take a piss too!"

Dragos Saban left the room, pulled the warped wooden door closed behind him, slid the aging brass bolt into place, noisily closed the toilet seat and began his business. It was a genuine need as he too was nervous, but he failed to display his fear. He also took the opportunity to remove his own phone and write a text.

"Robbery. Tonight. Time unknown. Hatton Garden. Jewellery Convention. Leader is Alin Vasile."

He typed in the familiar free number and within seconds a member of the Crimestoppers team had received the message and was processing it, triaging the information and firing it off to the Metropolitan Police control room team.

He quickly located a contact in his phone under the letter V, then deftly typed in another message.

"All done uncle. Wish me luck. I am doing this for the family and for you so that..."

Saban heard a tap on the door. He paused and called out that he was almost done, flushed the toilet, overly washed his hands and cleared his phone of evidence as he took one last look at himself in the decaying mirror.

"...so that we can finally get you home, to the family, and where you belong."

In France, Valentin Niculcea drained his glass. He needed to stop drinking so much if his plans to retire happily in Bordeaux were ever to eventuate. In truth he had given up all hope of ever returning to his homeland but agreed that the ability to at least visit was attractive.

He deleted the text message from his nephew, praying quietly that Dragos would get across the border and once in France make his way to his gîte, where if luck and other factors allowed he could keep his head down, lie low for a month or so and then blend back into his hometown – a folk hero who had navigated his way across France and southern Europe during his escape from the authorities.

Niculcea picked up a less-traceable Blackberry phone and dialled a number.

"Jack, it is me. Can you talk?"

"I can."

Cade was beginning to feel comfortable with the conversations he held with the faceless ally.

"I think you may be heading in the wrong direction. I have a very close-held source that has just provided some information to your authorities – there is going to be a raid on the jewellery convention in London tonight."

"But that has nothing to do with what we are working on Valentin. Our local staff can deal with that."

"Correct. Normally. But this is a distraction. You and your team head south whilst Stefanescu's boys carry out the robbery. They stand to make a lot of money. They will be armed and only one of them has morals. Once they have carried out the operation, they will also head towards a port – this has not been confirmed yet. Are you still listening?"

Cade was making frantic and basic notes on the back of a McDonald's serviette.

"I am. Just one thing. You told me earlier that the group were heading to a port. But now you are saying they are carrying out a major robbery in London before they go? Have they not made enough money? What am I supposed to believe?"

"Jack. This is no longer about money – for the young, impressionable boys, yes. But for Jackdaw and his brother and their lieutenants, then no, this is all just a training exercise for the future, when their group will spread like a virus across Europe. Mark my words, this will happen. If you decide to walk away, to listen to your bosses, then you must be like the ostrich and bury your collective heads in the corporate sand. But they will march across Europe just as the Nazi's did when they hunted down their grandfathers. These are survivors Jack. Please, do not ever forget that."

"OK. Point made. Actually, what *is* your point?"

"Tonight there will be a robbery in London. When it is done, and it will be successful, the group will split up, some will head north where they will board a ferry to Europe.

Worst case they will act as a draw, taking your colleagues north with them. The others will head south and join Stefanescu, their plan is to cross the border using Hewett. Stefan and Hewett could be in either group, you need to decide which one you want. My advice is focus on the southern group. But Jack, within the group is one I want you...rather, I need you to trust."

"Tell me more."

Valentin outlined his nephew's connections, his agenda and his strict moralistic upbringing.

"And yet he chooses to risk it all playing with this bunch of..."

"Yes Jack, he does. You have no idea how much importance his generation, and where they are from put on material things. He values me highly too and I know his mother wants me to return to our home. I believe he is doing this act to support me. Little does he realise I don't need his help. If I remove him from the group now, he will be at risk. But Jack, you must appreciate that for now this is all I know."

Cade was over-tired, and it began to show. "Valentin, forgive me. I am listening, and I am tired and above all I am wholly pissed off with these people. Tell me what I did wrong and perhaps I can examine things and make amends, but right now I have twenty-four hours to find the haystack. All I need you to do is provide me with enough evidence to convince my bosses that there is a needle in it."

"Mr Cade, Inspector. If you listened carefully, I gave you the needle, you just have to decide where in the haystack it sits – north or south. Just watch you do not prick your finger on it when you find it."

Valentin had already hung up – he vaguely understood what the Englishman was alluding to – he wanted to help him, for he knew that in doing so Cade might return the favour. His own life had been mapped and yet somehow at the point where he chose to head over the faraway hills and into the unknown somebody had kindly turned the map the right way up.

'That is the direction you want to go in my friend.'

He looked at the Armagnac but decided against it, for now and for the immediate future. One day soon he would remove the stopper from a bottle he had hidden for a special occasion and share it with someone he trusted. And there were very few people who managed to sit in that category.

He considered the Englishman to be one of them.

Daniel turned to Cade and said, "Care to elucidate old chap?"

Cade replied through tightening lips, "If I knew what it meant, then yes, absolutely. I think we have an ally there, but I'm not one hundred percent sure."

He looked at his watch, "Ten minutes now, the Frontier Ops guys are expecting us."

Daniel was back on his phone, the handset jammed between his cheek and left shoulder and briefing the duty inspector at Camden who was already reading the Crimestoppers information.

"Yep, all over it governor, like the proverbial weeping rash."

"Just be aware that we think this group are connected to the team we have been hunting for weeks now, the ones targeting the ATMs all over the city."

"A bit up market this job isn't it? You know, compared..."

"Absolutely. But our human source believes that the ATM stuff was actually just a training programme for what is to come."

"And that being?"

"And that being, I haven't got a bloody clue. Needless to say we are committed at the coast, it would appear that every man, including his dog is aware, briefed and ready to respond. But as yet we don't know what we need to respond to, where and when, and potentially by whom." He counted the interrogatives off on his hands and realised he'd forgotten one. "Oh, and how!"

"Permission to mock openly guv and say we know two fifths of fuck all then?"

"Granted, Inspector – and trust me, that is forty percent more than we knew this time yesterday."

"So, do we have a cunning plan?"

"We do. It's called sit back, wait, and respond, using the much-loved but recently berated old fashioned policing technique of chaos, foot chases and a right-royal punch up down a dark alleyway. I can only wish you a quiet night elsewhere so we can focus your fine men and women onto one spot."

"Splendid, that's cursed that then boss! I look forward to this night with glee."

The poorly veiled sarcasm didn't hide the real message, which more simply said, "Should we just go and get the bastards?"

The two gleaming white Renault vans entered the Clerkenwell area of London at 19:55 hours – exactly.

At 19:57 hours – or nearly eight o'clock in old money, the first pulled up in Leather Lane, a stone's throw from Hatton Garden, the iconic and heavily guarded, much-prized diamond trading centre of the City of London.

Its driver pulled off the road and watched and waited for

the second van to arrive, which duly parked alongside two heavily shuttered businesses, that prior planning had shown lacked any type of CCTV coverage. The small camera that was is in situ was as false as the lettering on the side of the French panel van, the eight occupants of which sat tight and avoided any form of eye contact with the few and far between pedestrians.

The Argosy Shop Fitting Company logos and phone numbers that had been freshly applied and which were entirely fabricated offered an early alibi. Maintenance teams often entered the city to carry out such work overnight, and to the only onlooker, a disinterested nightshift worker heading to Smithfield Market, where they were parked was 'bang on' as the building was in dire need of a makeover and besides they didn't 'look suspicious'.

The local security patrols had already carried out their rudimentary checks and had moved on. The few remaining people who were contemplating doing some work on a hole in the ground had decided to refrain and take shelter in their own works van, comforted from the cold by a thermos flask of tea.

The conditions were, so far, perfect.

A minute later the vans had stopped further down the street, again, away from the sweeping arc of government and commercial cameras. The front passenger of the first vehicle removed the two-by-two square to reveal an extremely familiar logo and naming convention.

At 19:59 hours a stereotypical silver saloon car passed them, travelled along the same road, past the skeletal remains of partially erected market stalls and turned left again onto Greville Street. It drove quietly beyond the Bleeding Heart public house and began to accelerate, turning left once more onto Hatton Garden itself.

Having entered the unexpectedly quiet street the driver identified the location, selected after many similar journeys and steadily began to pick up speed. In his mirror, the driver saw one of the two Renault vans following him.

A hundred metres short of the sombrely painted and understated shop frontage of Hodgkinson & White the first van drove by the silver car, rapidly decelerated and stopped, effectively blocking Clerkenwell Road to any vehicular traffic.

The second van careered across the narrow carriageway, spinning one hundred and eighty degrees before coming to a halt and closing Hatton Garden to traffic trying to enter or exit.

The silver vehicle was now travelling as fast as it possibly could in the short distance left. Its driver took a nanosecond to consider his future before jarring the steering wheel to the left and forcing the car through the shop frontage. The glass shattered with a stupendous thump, but the driver, restrained and grateful of the protective cover of the airbag was fine. In fact, he was already out of the car.

"Hello Operator, what is your emergency?"

"Yes hello police please, and fire there's been a crash on Hatton Garden."

"Thank you. Any obvious injuries at all? Are you a witness? Is the road open?"

All standard questions and easy to respond to.

"I can't see love to be honest. No, not really, I'm busy. Erm, sort of, there are two vans that have crashed too, one's sort of blocking the street. Look I have to go."

"Hello?"

Call ended. 20:03 hours.

. . .

The resultant positions of the vehicles did in fact give the impression, to anyone with more than a passing interest that they had probably collided. Someone should call the police, but this was Hatton Garden, the home of the United Kingdom diamond trade. There would be cameras everywhere, little point then in calling anyone, someone would be there sooner or later. No one looked injured, probably a hint of road rage. Best carry on.

No, on second thoughts, best make the call.

"Hello Operator, what is your emergency?"

"Oh yes hello, there has been a crash, it's a bad one, on Hatton Garden."

"Yes thank you sir, we are aware, help is on the way. Are you a witness?"

"No, sorry. I was looking for a ring, for my wife, we've been married you see, forty-two..."

"Thank you sir, if there isn't anything else we are extremely busy tonight."

"Yes actually, there is, the two vans are your lots..."

"Our lots?" The operator bristled at the caller's slothful use of the English language.

"Yes, as in police. They are police vans my friend. There are men coming out of them are in dark boiler suits."

The caller was becoming more excitable causing the operator to cut over him, stopping him in his tracks.

"They've got guns!"

"So you are saying we have staff there already?"

"Absolutely – and some! And whilst you are on...we heard a bang..."

"Sorry sir, we have more calls coming in about an incident elsewhere. It's probably a training exercise. I have to go."

She lifted one earpiece from her head and turned to her colleague. "Do we have something happening in Hatton Garden tonight?"

The two elderly pedestrians who had been browsing for a new ring were the first to hear the silver car colliding with the shop front. They were a little shocked, to say the least. They had tried to tell the Operator that the sound they had heard was a real and loud bang, and would later declare it to be just like an explosion.

"It sounded like a bloody great big firework or a cannon. A proper one. You know officer, like those they fire on the Queen's birthday?"

Typical witnesses, they had focused on the less than obvious and had missed the literal.

The first charge erupted with a resounding crack knocking the hinges off the secure door to the lower-level vault. Hatton Garden was a warren of subterranean passageways and vaults, some were interlinked, others guarded fiercely by their justifiably paranoid owners.

The second charge turned heads.

The side and rear doors opening on the white vans did little to dissuade people, now gathering in their numbers that this was not a conventional crash on one of London's streets. Some counted seven, others ten as the darkly clothed figures spread out, almost in military fashion.

Perhaps the Operator was right. It must be an exercise. It was very impressive.

One of the armed men guarded the vehicle and Clerkenwell Road, his opposite number watched Hatton Garden and the second Renault. The remaining balaclava-clad offenders burst through the demolished shop front and into the conventional jewellery store. One person remained, sweeping a tactical arc with a short-barrelled firearm, away from the door and back out into the street, whilst his colleagues cascaded down the stairs and into the vault and very much into the life of Barry Hackett.

Hackett, was a fifty-nine-year-old retired police constable and night-shift guard for one of the annual jewellery convention storage facilities – the big guns of the jewellery world were in town and storage was at a premium.

He initially tried to stand, but was greeted only by the sound of a deliberately racked weapon. He knew enough to say nothing and do less. Instead choosing to point towards the vault with a deliberately straightened index finger. His mind was a tornado. Speak and get shot, say nothing and probably get shot anyway.

"May I speak?"

The male stood in front of him was caressing his weapon. His night-black eyes, the only thing visible through the flame-resistant headgear never left their target. The head nodded once.

"Guys, the vault won't open until the morning unless you have the code and I haven't – so shoot me by all means."

It wasn't going well.

The dark eyes that stared back at him neither pitied him nor gave him an indication about which way his life might head.

"I'll keep quiet. Yep. Best I do. Right away." He cursed his every word. 'For Christ's sake Hackett shut the...'

It was his last thought that evening, the butt of a rifle striking him across the rear of his neck, not once but twice, as he had always been physically belligerent. Far from permanent it ensured he wouldn't wake for a while. His hands were cable-tied, and he was rolled to one side, ironically out of harm's way.

"Four minutes."

The team leader didn't reply but heard the two important words. He watched as one of his team dealt with the cameras. There was nothing technical about the way he did it; simple and destructive.

The leader then tapped in the memorised six digit code and waited as instructed.

Out on the street Hatton Garden was now becoming more animated. A distant wail heralded the approach of the local section vehicle, containing a single police officer, sent to deal with what appeared to be a non-injury crash. A fire brigade unit was following and would have to pick up the pieces as the local Ambulance staff were already overly committed.

The numeric code allowed the tumblers to slip and slide into place almost without an audible sound and this was a benefit as the operator could only hear his heartbeat and the familiar and distant wail of a siren.

The door opened and three pre-selected team members entered, filling black holdalls with diamonds – it was surprisingly simple – as one would if they entered a supermarket and picked up fruit or vegetables. As specifically instructed, they ignored other gems, gold and conventional jewellery which was conveniently but naively stacked, ready for display at the forthcoming convention.

Candy from a baby.

"Six minutes. Now get the black cases."

Alin Vasile moved quickly, ushering his team upstairs. The last to pass him was the similarly aged and identically militarily trained Dragos Saban. Both had carried out and completed their mandatory national service only months before, hardly experts and both from the infantry they had learned enough to handle weapons, how to dominate an enemy and above all, especially so, they had learned the art of discipline, and command and control.

"Go!"

They both heard the radio message clearly and now Saban knew what to do next. He pushed over shelf units and stands before emptying draws of necklaces and bracelets onto the floor. A ruby necklace caught his eye, it would have graced his mother's neckline so beautifully. He bent to pick it up then kicked it away, a hundred thousand pounds of exquisite jewels pushed under rubble and left behind. Follow the orders!

He released the pins from two smoke canisters, tossed one into the vault and held the other as he bounded up the stairs, entering the main shop and dropping the second in the main display area.

Two more had been thrown and having struck the floor with their trademark 'tink-tink-tink' had initiated outside in the street and were effectively driving back the crowds.

Saban stopped alongside the silver car and dropped a white phosphorous flare through the passenger window. In seconds, the cloth upholstery had ignited and less than a minute later the cockpit was ablaze.

A few minutes after eight o'clock the ever-beating heart of the financial district of Britain had a low-level crash to deal with. Now, ten, fifteen minutes later the City of

London had an incident of note and it had just torn a gaping hole in its aorta.

Before the first response vehicle arrived, and in a little over ten minutes, the team had entered the building, selected exactly what they needed, ignored much more and had left. The two Renault vans had departed, one heading north, at speed, headlights flashing rhythmically, the second south across Blackfriars Bridge and towards Chatham.

In a display of sheer audacity the passenger of the southbound vehicle even waved to a patrol vehicle en route to the scene.

Chaos. Arrogantly. Organised.

Approximately twenty minutes later, as units still descended upon the area another call was received into the control room.

"There's been an explosion, somewhere near Hatton Garden."

The shift inspector wheeled himself across the control room and came to a halt next to his favourite operator Jean Gibson.

"Talk to me Jean."

"Guv, seems that there's been a report of an explosion near Hatton Garden."

"Yes, but we know about this, don't we? Isn't this the crash near the junction of...?"

His junior colleague held up her hand.

"No sir. This is new. Somewhere near the Embankment. Described as a series of loud, dull thuds, some flashes too."

"Jean, it's November the bloody fifth. Are we going to respond to every one of these?"

"Point taken boss. But Guy Fawkes Night or not are you happy to sign off on this?"

"We are rushed off our feet. Even with all of our resources we are running out. Unless there's blood coming under the door, then yes."

He navigated his way back across the floor and plugged his headset back into the desk as he began to monitor another five similar calls across north and then south London.

Gibson shook her head as she stared at the screen in front of her. She had experienced busy shifts, but this one was becoming quite memorable.

Team Three were deliberately unconnected to the first, second and fourth teams. Team Four was operating south of the river and were now emptying the night safe of the second ATM that they had all but demolished with an oxygen cylinder attack.

In Alex Stefanescu's simplistic view these were the Second, Third and Fourth Waves. His original naming convention for a group of organised criminals had been *Primul Val* – the First Wave. He liked it and defied anyone to disagree. His aim had always been to call his group of Romanian brothers the Seventh Wave – the most powerful in myth and legend.

In reality he didn't really care what they were called as long as they were successful and gained a reputation under the flag of their blue wavelike tattoo. What the four teams had intended to do in the central business district of London was create a financial storm. Hitting the banks and finance houses from as many angles as they could.

Whilst the northern and southern groups were

achieving success two more were operating with equal success east and west. One team sustained a minor and calculated injury by over filling the device with the deadly mixture. Stefanescu, and his brother, without a doubt, would care not.

These were all just exercises anyway, designed to test the equipment and the personnel for a time when they would really exploit the 'great' British people, who meanwhile gazed up at the night sky, 'oohing' and 'aahing' as tens of thousands of pounds of black powder and chemicals lit up the black velvet backdrop.

There were so many deep, powerful and plentiful explosions that anything significant was greeted with a cheer. The louder, the better.

Within half an hour the Metropolitan Police had almost run out of resources and were calling, unusually, for mutual aid from Essex, Surrey and Kent.

A patrol van heading north, into Essex and en route to the port of Harwich didn't choose to ignore the desperate appeal for staff, it simply didn't hear them as its only connections to the largest police force in the country were false, magnetic and hanging onto the side of the vehicle. Its driver tried his best to hide a smile as wide as the ocean they were planning to cross.

As false as the uniformed staff it contained, it did its utmost to convince any uneducated onlookers that it was wholly original. Strips of magnets were in place and doing their level best to adhere the world-famous Met logo to the freshly painted metalwork.

The van and its passengers were already booked on the late night crossing to Rotterdam and before they reached the port, the signage had gone, along with the false UK plates. Their van was empty, apart from the much-loved tools that corroborated their reason for being in Britain – the building trade had been kind to them – or so their well-practised story went.

'Thank you, officer. Yes, we have had a very good time. We have earned money in your country, but now we can head home to our people. Take care – until we see you again.'

Their story was cast-iron. The only diamonds to be seen lined the tips of their drills and they were mostly worn and in need of replacement. They were tired and heading home for a much-needed spell of rest and recuperation. They worked long hours, but the money was good. It was almost believable, the dream that they had worked towards.

The jewels lay beneath the false floor away from prying eyes, bagged and ready to distribute. For Jackdaw these were the glistening icing on the cake, the annual bonus for all his hard work, and yet he was prepared to give them all away, throw them overboard if he had to. He'd had diamonds before, some legitimate, some with a tainted past, but they were just carbon at the end of the day, like him and every other being.

He'd once personally mounted one in the belly-button of an Australian girl who only ever provided him with afternoon entertainment whilst his other whores rested. Unlike the others he grew to like her and even gave her a pet name based upon the colour of her hair.

She did anything he asked and some things he didn't. Cocaine was her fuel and of that particular commodity he had a trans-national pipeline as long as the Alaskan and Russian ones combined.

A pretty girl, eighteen going on forty, a sun-bleached-blonde and stereotypical surf chick, she had tanned and honed legs and a raucous appetite for Class A. She was once a refined, public school success, popular, in a much-admired girl next door way – but although her body was still in remarkably good shape her mind was shattered, a legacy of her misspent and sybaritic time in Bali.

The jewel, a conflict diamond sourced out of Angola only added to her raw beauty. He endeavoured to provide them to the females in his life that he loved or on one precise occasion had worshiped – but that carefully selected jewel had been of a shade normally reserved for jealousy.

It would transpire that one of his junior workers also found the allure of the diamond hard to resist and over the course of a few weeks he had discreetly visited the surfer in her room, marvelling at how, even in the discreet light he could see his face in the myriad facets as he made his way across her stomach, licking the downy blonde hairs before navigating lower, between her legs.

Lust and the reckless effects of cocaine made her worth the risk.

Some say he wanted the diamond more than the girl.

'Trust no one. Not even me.' These were the limited words that formed Alex Stefanescu's initial briefing to any new member of his team.

'Let me down and I will personally cut off parts of your body and feed them to you. Piece by piece.'

It was a reputation that had served him well since his days and nights in Eastern Europe's most notorious prisons. In a convenient analogy the authorities had considered that they had taken him as a rough diamond and polished him to a fine and often admired stone, and an even finer mentor to the other inmates. They had also created a far more impressive criminal. He had become so resistant to punishment that even the most hardened of guards enjoyed the challenge of ruining his day. It was almost as if he was no longer able to detect pain.

Confined to his cell he would often talk to himself, for he was almost always alone, condemned to a thankfully solitary confinement. To alleviate the boredom, he would invent ways to brutalise people and importantly how to leave no trace of his mastery.

Years later he was able to call on these skills when the couple were brought to him, having been deliberately caught mid-act. They were paraded before him, naked and in the male's case, afraid.

Alex skilfully peeled a pear with a razor-sharp vegetable knife as he spoke in a rational almost friendly tone.

"I recall our conversation about trust. Do you?"

He slid a slice of the white fruit from the blade and into his mouth.

The male nodded, closing his eyes as he did so. It was a fortunate act as the first punch was unseen. The second was delivered swiftly, up and under his ribcage punishing him and forcing the air from his lungs. It was one of his favourite strikes. Remarkably, the male remained standing. A mistake, brave though it was.

The black-haired, tanned and powerful fist that drove down onto his right shoulder caught him off-guard, the deft tap onto the back of his right knee caused him to buckle further and in a second the most trusted member of Alex's team had the male in a carotid hold. His intention was not to choke him to death; that would follow. He simply needed to suppress his ability to fight, and this happened in no more than fifteen seconds.

The surfer was speechless, her mind a swirling fairground ride, colours, sounds, smells, childhood memories, nightmares. She needed more of that pure white ash, more than she needed to see the male survive. It was a drug that created its own egotistic demons.

She tried to cover herself but another of the boss's team slapped her hands away, again and again until she stood, deflated, isolated and cognizant of one fact − that her brief but gaudy life was probably about to end.

He paced around in front of her.

"Was he worth it? So much better than me? Am I not attractive too?" He found a space in his soliloquy to laugh. "Do *not* answer that!"

As the sentence finished, he punched her in the throat and then stepped to one side and kicked her in the stomach dropping her to the ground. He plunged his fingers into her belly-button and ripped the diamond from her stomach, pulling the stud clean out of her skin, causing it to pour with blood.

"This was for you. Worth more than you would ever earn. More than you could ever dream of owning. More than your entire shitty family could ever *wish* for!"

She was sobbing now, interpreting the situation as best as she could.

"Open your mouth."

She did as she was instructed. He forced the bloodied gemstone into her mouth, pushing it past her teeth and holding her jaw tightly until she got the message.

"Keep it in that vile hole until I tell you. Now, bring him here."

The larger of the two employees dragged the naked male across the wooden floor and left him prone before their boss.

"Open his mouth." He turned to the girl. "Now you, kiss him. Go on. Kiss him. I want to see how you did it. But don't lose that diamond. Do you hear me? This is a game!" He clapped his hands together gleefully – apparently enjoying things enormously.

She fought the urge to swallow it as her mouth was arid, it now felt so vast, so valuable, so disagreeable and so obstructive that she retched.

"I said...kiss him!"

She lowered her mouth onto the semi-conscious male's lips until they formed a seal, desperately hooking the stone with her tongue.

"Open your eyes – like you did with me the other day. Enjoy yourself, relax and let your lips taste him. Good? Yes? Don't stop Honey." He laughed as he stepped out of her line of sight.

It was enough to relax her for a split second. He chose the moment with precision, slamming his foot down onto the back of her head and in turn driving her face, her nose and her mouth onto his. Her front teeth, weakened from drug abuse shattered and in turn caused his own to break.

Not content with hearing the hideous collision he did it again. And again. She lost consciousness soon after the fourth blow as her lover began to regain consciousness and immediately began to choke.

"Hold him down!"

The male panicked, alive with pain as his brain fought off the signals that rushed around his frenzied mind. His fight-or-flight mechanisms were in overdrive, no longer caring about his naked state or the girl, he knew he had seconds. The large hand that covered his mouth only shortened that timeline.

"Keep it there."

Alex glared at the male. "Swallow it all. Her teeth, her

blood and my diamond. Choke you bastard and go to hell regretting how you betrayed me."

Stefanescu was wide-eyed now and beginning to enjoy himself. Aroused.

"Swallow!"

The male relented and began to choke on the metallic cocktail of blood-washed ivory and crystalline carbon. And he choked some more, but still they held him down, now a thumb and a forefinger closed his last air supply, gently squeezing his nostrils together.

Alex kneeled at his side and whispered into his ear, knowing that this primary sense would remain until the end.

He kissed him deftly on the cheek and watched the life seep from his eyes.

"Goodnight. I do hope you spread the word in hell that I am not to be trusted."

He had further gained, among a sphere of people with whom morals counted for little, a reputation as a calculated, clinical, creative and cruel man.

On a much broader platform what Alex Stefanescu expected to gain from his team in London was worth so much more than any currency. Intangible to many, it provided him with potentially greater wealth than a hastily snatched collection of hackneyed, felt-lined bags of glistening gems ever could.

It provided him with what he craved. More than a simple article, a headline in a newspaper, or show of grotesque overt wealth, more than any prize, or any girl for that matter. It provided him with a reputation and a chance to hold one, or possibly two ace cards; signed and sealed many days before by a clueless audience, and in this case, the audience was a government and the rewards were potentially immense.

It now sat in a secure Pelican tactical case, along with a few of the finer diamonds, safe from harm. The only problem being he didn't have it in his hands. And one thing he despised was a lack of control.

Nevertheless, when he finally got to reverentially receive it, to run his eyes and hands over it, then he could relax. Then they would listen to *him*.

What would count, would make all the difference, was not if he revealed his hand, but when.

The southern van was rapidly approaching Chatham and minutes away from a rendezvous with the team domiciled at the industrial estate.

The rest of the operators could take the spoils of war and spend them as they wished, at their own risk. The cash from the ATMs was being counted at various locations around the south and west of London. Set out in piles, fresh, virgin notes stacked ready to sweep into holdalls.

"Tell them, they can use it as they wish; cars, clothes, drink, whores, but not drugs. If they buy drugs, I will have them impaled upon something sharp, jagged and rusty – and from a great height. If they are caught and they so much as even suggest that they are part of something larger, the punishment will be a lot worse; a long, drawn out, pitiful existence. Death would be a pleasure in comparison."

Stefanescu recalled his brother's words clearly. He had witnessed his appetite for cruelty first-hand and shuddered at past memories.

"As you say brother, as you say."

The southern van pulled into the yard and was soon behind chain-assisted, corrugated shutters.

The driver left the vehicle first, shook hands with Stefanescu and handed over the black tactical case, then embraced Constantin.

"At last we meet brother. Your advice worked perfectly, the flare set fire to the car in seconds. And the safe...it was like melting butter with a hot knife."

His analogy was slightly flawed but the older male knew exactly what he meant. He grimaced at the thought of the night he had spent in prison and how he had been offered the safe code for the return of a favour or two, both of which had left a vile taste in his mouth. At the time, he hated himself, but now, with the offer of freedom, both financial and physical he deemed it worthwhile. He would soon be home and could start his long journey to redemption.

Hewett was asleep – to the viewing public. But inside his mind he plotted, planned and ran the whole process again and again until he was exhausted. If he managed to drop off for a second he would wake with a start. His every waking second was filled with questions, images, what ifs? And maybes. He could just get up and walk out, what was the worst thing that they could do? Kill him?

'It might actually be a blessing.'

Cade and Daniel sat in the car for a moment, the engine and brakes cooling beneath them.

"Nice view."

The storm had failed to materialise, and now sat on the

seafront at Dover they could see through the outer harbour breakwater and across the busiest shipping lane on the planet, to France, which announced its presence with a series of emerging white and amber glistening lights.

"Now what?"

"Fish and chips?"

Cade ignored his boss's flippant remarks but Daniel had planted a culinary seed. Cade picked up the UHF radio, dialled in channel 30 and called up for the local Special Branch officer.

"Hello Oscar this is Zero Two Mike Papa – Golf Tango are you receiving?"

Gary Marshall the on-call SB officer slid his own newspaper-wrapped meal to one side, swallowed an already luke-warm chip and responded.

"Good evening Golf Tango. Go ahead."

"Thank you Oscar – can we ring you?"

Marshall passed the number over the encrypted radio and waited for the call, forcing a bit more of his meal down his throat before the tell-tale *Ride of the Valkyries* ring tone interrupted him.

"Sir! Welcome to the patch. What do you need?"

"A local set of eyes and ears please Gary. You've got all the info?"

"I have and I've briefed both my local colleagues from Kent Police and the Harbour Board Police too. If a desperate group of criminals arrive at the port, I'll have their balls in a baguette before you can sing a Vera Lynn song boss."

"Lovely woman. I met her once. Anyway, moving on. There is a chance that the group will be arriving at separate ports. We need to be super-vigilant. As it stands we have one image to share with your colleagues – and sadly he's one of our own. You have my permission to shoot him before you place his flaccid wedding tackle onto your crusty bread."

Daniel had driven further along the seafront and turned into a side street, he left the car and walked across the road to a row of shops.

Marshall continued to chat and when Cade was happy that he was dealing with an experienced operator he cleared down and allowed the phone to rest for a while.

Cade considered his recent life-changing events as he gazed across the marina and out towards the sea. Despite the chaos, the losses and the heartache – the physical pain of losing staff and the deep-seated frustration over O'Shea and an unmapped future he nodded when he said to himself that he wouldn't change a thing. Penny, for all her faults, had done him a huge favour.

Daniel arrived back at the car, got in and passed his colleague a package wrapped in white paper.

"Enjoy!"

He did. It had been the first substantial meal he could remember, let alone enjoyed in days.

"Can you believe the events of the last few weeks John?"

"Not at all. What concerns me is that we are sat here having, what can only be described as a rather romantic meal and talking about what we have got up to; chasing people, pursuing cars, impressing bosses, infuriating bosses, attempting to drown folk, recovering bodies, shooting at people, trying to create bodies..."

They laughed before he continued. "Battling with our enemies and a notable few of our managers, and above all the criminal syndicate that is causing us to go grey, or rather greyer. Jesus Jack you've certainly got the Midas touch when it comes to pandemonium, disarray, turmoil and bloody heartache. Who did you piss off in a former life?"

A gull had landed outside the car, its plumage was pristine, gleaming white with deep black wings and a strong, yellow and red beak. It paced up and down, conscious that any moment Cade would lower the window and drop the remains of his meal onto the pavement. They all did. It stared at him with its impassive yellow eyes, rimmed in bright red.

Cade couldn't help feeling that they perfectly resembled his.

In pity he lowered the window and tossed a couple of the smallest chips into the air. The gull had caught them before they hit the floor and had soon flown up into the night sky, its cacophonous cry shattering the peace, causing more of its kin to join in.

"Incredible bird really the seagull Jack."

"No such breed JD, they are gulls that sometimes live on the sea."

"Bloody hell, when did you become an ornithologist?"

"I've always loved birds. Just not the one that liked to spread its wings and legs for all and sundry."

"Ex-wife?"

"Current, I think, I've probably signed something but God only knows what my marital status is at the moment."

"Would Carrie not mind – you know, being the new chapter in your life, all the while knowing that you have an Albatross around your neck?"

"What?"

"Samuel Taylor Coleridge Jack. The Rime of the Ancient Mariner."

"I know what the bloody poem is, just not sure what you mean about Carrie."

"Well, I suspect if she survives, and knowing the girl as I do, in the short time I've known her, she will." He'd lost his way, mid-sentence. "Well, I strongly suspect that she will want you all to herself. So you need to do some serious thinking, in years to come there will be lengthy application processes as the administrators take over. The European job has been offered on a plate. If you take it your career and reputation will be in the ascendency, but you will need to say farewell to her. Or, should you decide to stay then..."

Cade's phone vibrated before ringing, cutting off Daniel's theory.

"Cade. Yes. Understood. Thank you."

Daniel threw the remaining meal out of his own window and caused what could best be described as an airborne riot. He put the window up quickly and waited to be briefed.

"I have absolutely nothing to tell you. Zip. Diddly squat. Bugger all. There's a hint of chaos back at the ranch, some robbery at Hatton Garden but other than that..."

"So he was right then?"

"Valentin? Yes, spot on. He's better placed than we are John. His source must be one of the group. We will have to isolate him as soon as possible, put him through the system but provide him with complete support."

"And Valentin? You've forgiven him for invading your life and harming the girl you so clearly adore"

"Totally. He was just doing his job."

"Aren't we all? I know I'm getting ready for retirement and the unspoiled white beaches of New Zealand. I've had enough of the chase, the thrill is still there but my energy is waning. I could do with some type of work-related Viagra." He laughed at his own comments. "However I've got about eight to go, or as one of my old team used to say..." He mentally calculated, "...ninety six paydays."

Cade had a considerable amount of paydays to go but also felt as if his energy was being sapped. He spent a while, quietly, watching the gulls circle among the powerful flood-lights that serviced the quayside.

"Clever things you know these seagulls."

"No such thing Jack."

"Bollocks. It's a figure of speech. My point is they come and go as they please. No borders. If that one there for example wants to fly to France, he can. He just launches himself off the nearest cliff and as long as he can be bothered to flap his wings he'll get there. And when he gets to his destination, he can start a new life among similar seabirds. Sans frontières as the French would call them – without borders. Given the ability to move around by a greater authority, at their own pace, to come and go as they please. The diplomats of the skies."

Daniel started the car and moved off, driving back along the main road towards the Eastern Docks, the main ferry terminal and the hub of vehicular and foot traffic to the continent. He'd driven halfway along the promenade when he screeched to a halt.

"Greater authority!"

Cade was unsure whether the sentence was complete, so waited, but realised that Daniel had made a statement that was always meant to be just two words. He said it again.

"Greater. Authority."

"I heard you the first time. Care to embellish?"

"Hewett. He's the key to them getting into and out of the UK. He's got the status and governmental position to facilitate it. His recent behaviour, evasiveness, anti-establishment attitude. It all adds up to him turning to the dark side – I sense a great disturbance in The Force Jack. And that smug bastard is none other than our own version of Lord Vader. All we need is the proof."

"Illogical."

"Wrong film."

"I know…"

Further north the activity was equally dynamic.

"OK. Get ready everyone, we go in five minutes."

Stefanescu walked around the unit, looking for evidence of their presence, but found only take away food wrappers in the bin, all of which were due to be transferred to an outdoor makeshift fire and lit as soon as they moved out of the fenced compound.

"You all know the next phase. Van One will head to Dover and board the night ferry. Van Two is heading to Felixstowe already. Vans Three and Four join us soon and Van Five will contain the package. We will head to the tunnel and if God grants it we will meet up with Van Five and our dreams will be rewarded. Make sure that everyone has the correct appearance, like they know what they are doing. Be confident. We have planned for this for many months. There will be no excuses for failure."

He looked at each man again. He smiled broadly, knowing that in their minds the vans would contain cash or gemstones, when in actual fact most would contain nothing.

He approached Hewett.

"You OK? You look nervous. Do as instructed and you will be fine. You are one of us now. Therefore, we will protect you – with our lives. We expect you to do the same in return."

He held out his good hand.

Hewett, sensing a refusal would be insulting and life-shortening gripped hold of it and shook it firmly.

The fire was well and truly destroying evidence as they exited the industrial estate. The keys to the short-term unit were couriered back to the estate agent as arranged. She would ensure that the place was sterile, for what they had paid her she would have done anything and besides, they were her people.

Stefanescu looked in the door mirror and saw the orange flames already dying.

"Let's do this."

CHAPTER TWENTY-FIVE

ALEX STEFANESCU STOOD AT THE OVERLY LARGE PICTURE window in the lounge of his palatial property and watched the fireworks in the valley below, erupting, exploding and temporarily destroying the peace and quiet of a Spanish evening. He knew the fireworks that lit up the sky, with their brilliant reds, and yellows and electric blues were almost certainly being launched into the ether by expatriate Brits, happy to leave their weather behind but never their customs.

"Guy Fawkes was a hero of mine you know. He and his loyal friends. He lived here, in Spain. Fought against the British in the Eighty Years War. He fought for a Catholic rebellion in England, wanted to replace the Protestant King James with a Catholic ruler."

He looked over his shoulder at the girl who was sprawled on his sofa, convinced she was hanging on his every word, he continued.

"There was thirteen in all, conspirators they called them. For many months they sought and gained access to the parliament buildings, then stored gunpowder beneath them, ready for Fawkes to light the fuse, escape across the Thames and then back into Europe where he could live a life of comparative luxury. The comparisons between what he did, and what I have planned are very similar don't you think?"

The girl muttered something vaguely encouraging as she slid further and further off the sofa, half-dressed and less interested.

"But you see there was a flaw in their plan and they were discovered before parliament could be destroyed. Fawkes was tortured and eventually gave the names of some, not all of his co-conspirators. He was, naturally found guilty and condemned to death by being dragged by a horse, backwards, his head near to the ground. As if that were not enough his genitals would be cut off and burnt, before his own eyes and his heart and bowels removed. Then, and only then would they be dismembered and quartered, sent around the land for all to see."

He laughed, took a small sip of his wine before finishing the story. "I can only admire the British for their ability to torture their fellow man. Remind me next time I need to extract the truth from someone, or teach them a lesson to read the tales of the Gunpowder Plot beforehand my dear."

He turned away from the window. The girl had slipped off the sofa and onto the floor. She was, he thought, not the most beautiful creature – he had seen much prettier than her. But she was rather willing. Willing to do anything he asked, without any coercion. But she lacked character, and the drugs that he used to keep her in the mountainside home did nothing for her looks or her entertainment value. She could go tonight. He really needed to find the perfect woman.

He had.

And Cade had made him take her away into the next life, just like the British had done with Fawkes – *'halfway between heaven and earth'*.

"To teach a lesson in good manners and loyalty."

He raised a glass to the vaulted ceiling. "Jack Cade and all who choose to fight with you. May you be hung, drawn and quartered, in a place and at a time to suit me. And may all your acquaintances also meet an untimely and altogether disgusting demise. Next week, next month, in ten years' time. Either way, I will choose my moment to ruin your world as you have ruined mine. And it will be most unpleasant."

He walked over to the prone girl and kicked her in the ribs. She was practically comatose. He could do whatever he wished and she would have no recollection whatsoever the following morning, but she never did and she was way past caring. He was bored with her now and needed a replacement.

"I should travel to London and kidnap your girl Cade. Bring her here to my beautiful home, fill her body with drugs and her mind with horror until she begs to be my plaything. My sweet Nikolina resisted, even with all of her skills and training, but in the end she fell for me too. I am, after all, a very reasonable man. And I am far from selfish. I would share your girl with all of my friends. Carrie O'Shea. Interesting name you have, probably Irish. Clever thing, unconventionally pretty, according to my brother, and quite the feisty little office girl. I should have taken you whilst I had the chance instead of allowing that toothless half-wit to poison you. I should have had you brought to me. For *me* – for *my* pleasure. Chained to the *fucking* wall!"

He threw the glass against the exposed stonework, shattering it in a thousand directions.

"Chained up like a *bear*. To perform for its master *whenever* he clicked his *fingers!* Manacled – deprived of your liberty, as I was in Pazardzhik Prison, all those years ago, left to rot, lying in my own filth. Then we could see the life drain from you, the whites of your pretty eyes turning yellow from the damage caused to your organs, your teeth loosened from abuse and malnourishment..."

He picked a piece of glass off the floor and after examining its edges carefully placed it in the waste bin.

He was strutting now, as a specimen would in a zoo, backwards and forwards. Years of anger and suppressed hatred were surfacing, rising to the surface like emotional magma waiting to spill over the rim of a volcano and down the sides of the mountain towards its many and varied victims, searing their skin, ripping their last breath from their fume-filled lungs.

It had taken years but something, a firework, a glass or two of the local wine, the insolence of the girl – how dare she ignore him? Something had festered, and clawed at his insides and now, for the first time his protracted and intense resolve had finally shattered.

He dialled his brother.

"Pick up the phone you useless bastard."

Stefanescu's younger sibling answered after four rings to be greeted by silence.

"Are you there, brother? Is everything OK? Speak to me."

There was a long pause whilst Alex calmed himself down, breathing deeply, focusing on the purpose of his call.

"Brother. I am having a very bad night. I am feeling a little, anxious. A little, how can I put this? Murderous." He cackled his signature laugh. "I need to vent. To take out my sheer – my total, my complete and utter anger on those people who have betrayed me. I can count them on the fingers of one hand."

He was in the exquisite white kitchen; white floors, white units, white worktops. He opened a drawer and selected a large serrated bread knife and walked back, through the dining area and into the lounge where he found the girl, still asleep and drooling; undignified and worthless.

"The fingers of one hand." He bellowed the last word.

Stefan knew the signs. His brother was reverting back to his former self. For some time he had been balanced, rational and enjoying the spoils of war; cash, jewellery, cars, homes, and women, singularly or in pairs, once even three, all clambering over him like a pack of desperate gluttonous hyenas.

What he could hear in his brother's words were the months of torture he had endured at the hands of the Bulgarian authorities. It was they who had done this to him.

Flashbacks some people called them, catching the unwary when they least expected them. For his brother, Alex, these were subterranean fault lines, waiting to shudder, to collide and tear their counterparts to pieces. It was just a simple matter of when.

"Alex, my brother. Listen to me. We are almost there. I need you to stay calm, breathe like Doctor Petran taught you. Do it with me."

His older sibling matched the timing of his brother's commands and could feel himself calming, the bile emptying from this system and gradually he began to return to what he considered a normal state.

"Thank you Stefan." He hadn't used his name in years.

"It is OK Alex. It is what a good brother should do. A few more days and we can relax, have fun together, up in the mountains. We could ski perhaps?"

"We could. I have to go. There is something I need to do."

"OK but promise me you will remain calm. This is our time. In the years to come you and I will be famous among our people. Two young boys from a broken home who became rich and powerful. It is what you have always wanted. Promise me?"

The reality, and they both knew it, was that the familial home had been broken by Alex Stefanescu. Literally, piece by wretched piece. His younger sibling had spent his life, or at least his formative years wondering whether their parents had indeed died at the hands of the communist government and its expert interrogators, for their passing had been so brutal. The limited investigation stated quite clearly that their bodies had been experimented on so cruelly.

The line was quiet, only a feint hiss could be heard. "Promise."

The older male dropped the phone onto the sofa and picked the girl up, sitting her against the leather sofa. He placed her hand onto the slate floor, spreading out her fingers.

He selected the smallest first, lowered the wavy-edged blade onto the first knuckle. He pressed initially but met with resistance. She didn't flinch. He pushed now but failed to reach his goal. He gripped both ends of the knife and lowered his weight onto the limb until, with a disgusting crunch it separated from its donor.

"The fingers of one hand."

He repeated it with the ring finger until it too gave in, the white gold ring that once adorned it now dropped to the stone beneath and sat in a pool of blood. He picked it up with the end of the knife and examined it.

"Nice, white gold, possibly titanium. You have taste. Pity your fiancé isn't here to claim it back."

He started on the third finger when she jolted and was abruptly conscious again. He dropped the knife and quickly got hold of her feet and dragged her across the chilled stone floor, headfirst, caring not that her bleach-blond skull struck the corner of a cabinet with a dull thump. He was soon in the garage pulling the once-more unresponsive girl behind him.

He first tied her ankles together, then slipped a ten metre-long blue nylon rope through the knot and hooked it onto the tow bar of his Range Rover, a car he enjoyed immensely and one he had left in the garage in case he ever needed to use its impressive off-road capabilities.

He knelt down beside her, reeled off a half metre length of duct tape and wrapped it untidily around her head, covering her mouth. He looked at her for the last time, stroked her hair away from her face and lowered his mouth to hers and kissed her through the semi-gloss aluminium barrier.

He stood, climbed up into the car and with the press of a button one of three garage doors opened smoothly. He turned the key and the V8 engine purred into life. With another button he shut off the lights to his much-favoured mountain home and having engaged first gear he moved off gently, across the manicured lawn and onto the main track that led to his home. He crossed over it, very slowly and entered the more barren landscape that surrounded his house, rocky with shale and tufts of grass, scattered by nature's hand, here and there.

He was wise, even among the rage, to realise that he was potentially leaving a forensic trail. The few fibres that now littered his once-perfect, tyre-tracked lawn could be explained away to the police staff that weren't already in his back pocket. Any other tell-tale evidence, hair, skin, clothing, teeth would soon be scattered over such a wide area that they would be difficult at best to locate, and even sooner the first snows of the Sierra Nevada winter would obliterate the remaining traces of her last moments.

He didn't once look in his mirror. Now off-road and joining a gravel track he accelerated. The girl was awake now, wide eyes focusing on her new surroundings. Was this a dream? A nightmare? Her arms were free but her feet were tied. Ahead of her two bright red lights stood out against the deepest black landscape, only a single blue rope was illuminated, leading directly from her body to the tow bar.

She clutched and gripped and grabbed, grasping for anything that she could to slow her rate of departure down. Her hands scraped along the arid surface, gripping hold, then instantly letting go of foreign objects, a small piece of a plant, a stone, or branches. All she succeeded in doing was to leave her DNA scattered along a half kilometre of the Spanish countryside.

Her arms were raw now and her lower back shredded, the dense, deep muscles that aligned and protected her spine no longer resembled anything human. She was an animal now. Her legs thrashed from side to side, again, desperate to slow the vehicle down. At one point, she somehow found the strength to begin to sit up. She leaned forward and gripped onto her own bound ankles, praying for someone to come to her aid.

For the first time he looked in his door mirror and saw her face, lit up by the red tail lights. She was beyond frantic, this twenty-year-old from northern Spain, not missed by her friends or family and momentarily shown love by a man with more money than she could have ever dreamed of.

Such a pity. But she should have listened to his account of Guy Fawkes. She really should.

He looked away and wrenched the steering wheel from left to right causing his human trailer to whip from right to left. Now he was having fun.

She fell backwards onto the rough track and knew that her time was done. She closed her eyes and willed the pain to stop. As he negotiated a sharp right-hand bend she careered across the track and collided with a larger rock. Her chest took the brunt of the blow, shattering her sternum and caving in her lungs. It was a divine blessing.

Her lifeless torso had given up now. Her heart was almost beating its last. Her arms, no longer mentally connected, thrashed around like a dying fish on a marbled market slab. The hair that he had lovingly groomed only minutes earlier was now stained red; bright, oxygenated red.

Another minute had passed when he pulled over, assured by the fact that he was literally in the middle of nowhere. The dust was reducing now, swirling around in the head-lamps, which also picked out a few small trees and an almost lunar landscape ahead of him.

He walked to the rear of the car, untied the rope from the tow bar and shuffled away from the bumper towards the girl, folding the rope perfectly, as a climber would until he eventually reached her.

He lowered himself down to her side and used his phone display to light up her face. Her eyes were lifeless but as he moved the phone, he detected a flutter of her eyelids. She was, incredibly, still alive.

He stood, grabbed hold of her feet and dragged her towards the edge of the track. He took a moment to get his breath back, breathing deeply, partly to try to rid himself of the sight of her face. He rolled her now, using his foot as one would roll up a rug, until she had reached the edge of the gorge.

He found the end of the tape and unceremoniously stripped it from her face hoping that by the time she was found, if indeed she ever was that the glue would have dissolved, and in doing so taken with it another evidential trace. Her face was such a mess that it hardly mattered, but the almost ruthless attention to detail was typical of his behaviour when dealing with his fellow man.

The last time he had seen such terrified eyes was when he had ordered the submersion of an equally beautiful life, through the ice and into the lake in his home country. She had the same chances as this one – but nowhere near as much fight.

He stood, marvelling at the intensity of the Milky Way, the heart of the galaxy that he chose to exist in. It was such a stunning sight. He craved a cigarette, or an expensive brandy. This was a moment to savour.

He looked down at her, whatever her name was and spoke to her, quietly, as out there in the expansive mountains his voice boomed if he dared to raise it above a whisper.

"My dear, when I tell you an interesting story in future, it would be wise for you to listen. You were so disrespectful. Are you sorry?"

The very last action her brain instructed her head to carry out was to nod, once, almost imperceptibly. But he saw it.

"Good girl."

He pushed his foot against her, and she slipped over the edge. He was in the car with the heater on before she had reached her resting place. If he was lucky, the birds would avoid her and leave the unfolding seasons to blend her into the landscape.

She should have listened.

As he drove back to his mountain home, he felt uneasy. There was a sense of being uncomfortable, he shuffled in the leather seat until he was able to isolate the problem. In the diminished light he looked down and saw that he was holding the girl's ring finger. Strangely, having been the one who had removed it from her it made him feel nauseous. He shuddered and swallowed rapidly, trying to contain the bile.

He opened the driver's window and considered the finger for a second, rolled it between his own, then flicked it out of the car and into nearby undergrowth as one would a spent cigarette.

He arrived back at the driveway of his substantial home, opened the garage door and drove in. He sat for a moment and contemplated his life, not for a second giving the girl a second thought, switched the Range Rover off and got out and walked into the kitchen. He picked up a cloth and some bleach and began to meticulously wipe down every surface that she had come into contact with.

He knew that the authorities would seize on the slightest droplet – telling from one cursory look which way the victim had walked, or in her vile case, had been dragged.

He spent time on the knife. Teasing himself with its sharpness. With each wipe he folded the cloth before eventually placing it into a plastic bag and walking back outside to the outdoor patio fire.

He stood and watched the flames, depriving himself of his night vision. He missed a shooting star which his grandmother had always said was a sign of good luck.

Trapped in a crevice in a cool mountainside location not so far from her own home the girl saw it. Her eyes were vacant a second later.

He shivered and stepped closer to the flames, withdrew his cell phone and dialled.

In Kent, alongside the English Channel Cade answered.

"Mr Cade, how is the weather there? It is rather lovely where I am – a shame I just had to end the life of a pretty and all-too willing young lady. But this is what you have created Jack."

Cade was listening.

"This and everything else I do that society deems to be wrong is entirely your fault. Entirely. You see had you have just allowed me to operate as I wanted to, you and I would never have crossed swords. And, people would not have suffered. All was going well...."

He paused.

"Are you there Jack?"

Cade prayed for the day they were a foot or so apart but for now knew he needed to play the game. "Yes. I am here Alex. I am all ears..."

"Good. For a moment...anyway, did I ever tell you that Guy Fawkes was a hero of mine? He lived here, in Spain. Fought against the British in the Eighty Years War. But you know that, being an intelligent man. What am I rambling on about, eh? Well I like to read history and your history fascinates me. Jack Cade was a rebel too, wasn't he Jack? And yet his modern descendant is a company man through and through. I am offering you one chance, join us if you must continue to be fascinated by what we do, or leave us alone!"

His voice was slowly getting louder.

"Above all, stop interfering or I will plunge my hand into your ribcage and slowly pull your collective hearts out, one, by one. Yours will be the last and the finest moment. Have a lovely evening. Oh, and Jack I actually nearly forgot!"

"Carry on."

"I loved her you know. Truly. And our daughter Elena means more to me than my wealth, even more than my reputation. She is safe for now. She wants for little and as educated as she is she is oblivious to the happenings of the world around her. I will always protect her, to the death. If you or your authorities ever try to take her as you did her mother then I will make the ultimate sacrifice."

"You'd kill your own offspring? Surely that's a trait reserved for animals Mr Stefanescu? You make it sound like you are an insect not a nurturing bear."

"Maybe in your world. But in mine we consider it the actions of a brave man. Go and be a policeman somewhere else and leave me and my...locusts to strip your plentiful fields of all their goodness."

"I will. In the meantime I'm shopping for an appropriate pesticide to eradicate you. No offence."

"None taken Mr Cade. I would say until we meet again but that would be a lie. A famous Hungarian scientist wrote about the six degrees of separation Jack, I cannot recall his name, but it is not important. What is important is that we will never meet until I am ready and when that day comes, it will probably be your last. You will then suffer a degree or two of separation." His cackle filled Cade's earpiece.

"Before you go Mr Stefanescu."

"You have five seconds Jack. Four..."

"The scientist was called Frigyes Karinthy. His theory was simple, brilliant, but simple and suggested that any two people, even you and I, could be connected in no more than six steps. Talking of which, thank you for confirming that you live in Spain."

There was no trademark laughter, just an emptiness that caused Cade to smile. He dropped the phone into his lap before speaking to Daniel.

"John I confess to having enjoyed that, but make no bones about this, this guy is unhinged. This is no longer about money. This is an old-fashioned 'he and I' game and that scares me. People are going to get hurt. This nutcase would even have his own daughter killed to prove a point. Whichever 'path he is, he is that one."

"Sociopath. I've seen his type before. All talk Jack."

He wasn't convinced, and neither was Cade.

"One thing's for sure JD — he didn't like being caught out just then and he won't be in Spain much longer. I made a mistake there. God knows where he'll head now — can we put in a call to our friends in Interpol and see if they have any new notices for him or at worst some local intelligence to suggest where else he may have properties or associates?"

"Consider it done. In a few months you could do it yourself." Daniel waited to see what reaction he would get from Cade, a man he knew was in turmoil over a professional and personal decision that he clearly didn't wish to make.

"I'll give the team a bell. Here you go Jack, you drive."

The two white vans joined the M2 motorway and were joined by two marked vehicles from Kent Police. A highly conspicuous yellow and blue Volvo T5 saloon sat at the rear providing cover whilst its estate version, larger and containing an alert and ever-hungry German Shepherd dog, three staff and an assortment of weapons cruised along at around eighty, its driver watching ahead, knowing that his colleagues were observing the rear.

A total of four Metropolitan Police patrol vehicles had shadowed the procession south and were now peeling away, around the major roundabout and quickly back onto their area in London, just south of the River Thames. Their work was done. They had picked up the vans as directed in a covert briefing, accompanied them to the agreed rendezvous and were with any luck going to be back at base in time for an early finish – and all on overtime at less than eight days' notice.

All the Kent team could see now were three articulated trucks, a rental car and two unmarked Volvos – more of their own team, all armed and standing off – ready. It was quiet but the briefing had informed them of extensive traffic ahead, a consequence of yet another French port blockade and lightning strikes by workers at the port of Calais. Known as Operation Stack it had been a major headache for Kent Police and the Highways Authority for many years – chaos, neatly parked up and packaged as a success.

"So what's your thoughts on all of this then Pete?"

"No idea. The boss mentioned some sort of package. The French have insisted that they collect and deliver in person. Somehow they've been given permission to come onto our patch and pick it up. It's apparently really bloody important so they've come in force. I offered to take them all the way to Paris, but the boss thought I was taking the piss."

"Andy Mahoney gave me the heads up. Apparently it's a secret agreement between the UK and France – a political hand grenade for which only Home Secretary Blunkett has the pin. Some sort of open borders policy they've signed off on, allows more nations to enter our place unimpeded. If this gets leaked early, it could cause mayhem with tens of thousands of folk trying to get into Britain, we'd lose all control of the border and probably never recover. Andy told me not to say anything, or he'd shoot me."

"You're safe there then pal!"

The two laughed like errant schoolboys as the convoy accelerated down Bluebell Hill towards the M20 interchange and a faster route south to the coast.

On board the French vans the police staff chatted in their own language, almost replicating the conversations of their British colleagues, not least about the opportunities that the overtime would bring them.

At Guy's and St. Thomas' Hospital, a new shift had arrived. Fresh and bright-eyed and ready for the night shift that would inevitably leach their energy and resolve until the early shift relieved them, allowing them to head home, grey-skinned and lifeless, the only joy being dropping into bed when their neighbours were heading out into the cold.

A newly qualified junior doctor took a quick look at O'Shea's note and tutted.

"How's this one doing?"

"Honestly? Not good. Case studies say she should be responding but she has shown no signs of recovery yet. We are working with the Poisons Centre but even they are somewhat flummoxed. There's a suggestion she may have ingested something else – unwittingly – but the two have formed some type of cocktail that we don't know a great deal about. Time will tell."

"Any relatives? If so, let's think about getting them here shall we, I assisted on a case like this last year, he was doing fine, then gone. No outward signs that we were about to lose him."

He clicked his fingers to emphasise the speed of demise and picked up a new set of notes.

"Looks good. Good reaction to the drugs and the infection appears to have abated. Let's send him home in the morning shall we?"

In the adjoining wing Roberts was also being readied for discharge. A pile of painkillers, a sling, a doctor's note and word or two about his recovery from a charming nurse was all that stood between him and a few months off work.

The trouble was he was already bored. He flicked through a much-thumbed copy of *Top Gear* and decided on the Porsche. Then changed his mind and chose the Ferrari. He put it back down again and shuffled around the room, sat down and stared out of the window. It was then he saw his phone.

His call was answered almost immediately. "Cade."

"Jack, it's me. How's it going?"

"Christ, it's the Great Train Roberts!"

"Nice. I see what you did there. You took my surname and added it to a historical and somewhat notorious crime to make a pun. So seriously guys come on, how's it going. Are you missing me?" He grimaced quietly, trying to find a comfortable position.

"Shouldn't you be in bed being tended to by stocking-wearing nurses?"

"I have been Jack but to be honest Dennis wasn't my type. What can I do to help? It'll be ages before my wife gets here."

"Go and see Carrie for me. Send her my love and tell her to get well soon. Right now that's the best way you can help me. We are narrowing things down here. We've got some good intel that suggests our people are en route to the south coast. We have every man, his dog and the dog's dog waiting in the wings. You know there was a job earlier at Hatton Garden?"

"Yeah, the guard outside my door filled me in on all the gossip. Sounds exciting, but what's that got to do with our band of merry men?"

"One of three things Jason. Nothing. Greed or a very fine attempt at distraction."

"Why not both? A bit of good old fashioned gluttony and distraction?"

"Indeed. But we are all completely buggered if we can't figure what we are being distracted from."

"I'll do some digging. I've got time on my hands. I'll put a call into my old girlfriend Lucy. She owes me one. If anyone knows the inside word on that toothless lover of hers it's our Lucy."

Suddenly re-engaged, Roberts was dialling her number before Cade realised he had even disconnected.

"Lucy speaking."

Roberts grimaced again, but for different reasons. Knowing he had added his own codename to appease his cross-dressing playful informant he swallowed hard and continued, praying that Cade and Daniel would never find out.

"Harrier. It's Spitfire here. I need your help."

He spent fifteen minutes outlining what he needed and promised to wipe the slate clean and forget about the rather distressing fight that they had once had.

"So, you just want me to phone Constantin and ask him

where he is, what he is doing and why and how he plans to leave Britain? Anything else darling?" he added sarcastically.

"When would be really nice."

"Whenever you are ready sugar."

"Lucy, seriously stop it. I am not your type. I'm far too straight."

Thomas snorted a laugh, "Darling, you married types think you are straight when in actual fact you are the campest of the lot, you thoroughly naughty boy. Anyway, leave it to me. I'll work my magic. Ciao!"

CHAPTER TWENTY-SIX

A text revealed itself on Constantin's cell phone. Although full of flirtatious chatter the key message was clear. Thomas wanted to know where he was. He was sorely missed, it said.

He trusted no-one. But surely, he could trust her? Even his paranoia allowed for that.

I am heading home. One day I will return for you. Keep yourself warm for me. La revedere. C xx

Thomas read the basic response and assumed that 'home' meant Romania. That was the easiest job she'd ever had and the resultant official pardon would be worth its weight in diamonds and pearls.

Goodbye indeed.

She copied the wording and forwarded it to Roberts adding, "Now we are even. Keep in touch. I'm always here for you. X"

Roberts read the data and deleted it. The last thing he needed was his wife to misread the signals and assume that he was being unfaithful with a member of the fairer sex when nothing could be further from the truth.

He wasn't being unfaithful, full stop. But how he explained to his adoring wife that he had been spending quality time with a dubious, undeniably cross-dressing, jelly-wrestling and shaven male prostitute he really was not sure. Roberts wasn't certain what his intelligence source Harrier was anymore, male or female or some kind of weird twenty-first century hybrid – A male Prostitute, perhaps? There were some things he could never explain and many more that he could never un-see.

In seconds the message appeared on Cade's frenetic phone. It only sought to reinforce what they already knew.

"Tango Mike One-Four."

"Mike One-Four."

"Convoy is proceeding south. No issues. Any intelligence updates for us, please. Over."

"Negative One-Four. Be advised that heavy traffic is ahead of you. Operation Stack has been initiated. Expect significant delays as you approach the tunnel."

"Ten four thank you."

Pete French grinned at his partner. "Marvellous. Ah well, think of the overtime."

They both rubbed their hands together and carried on along the major British motorway towards the iconic tunnel.

Ahead and deliberately stuck in the southbound chaos were two of the marked Renault vans belonging to Stefanescu's group. Seemingly part of the serpent that wended its way towards the coast, they were primed. Having joined the traffic queue only minutes before, the varied members were readying themselves.

'Make it simple. Do not over-complicate.'

"Mike One-Four passing Ashford, approaching stationary traffic. Stand by."

"Standing by. Cameras show all three lanes are now static One-Four. Control room inspector has authorised that you use the hard shoulder."

"Yes, yes. Moving towards the hard shoulder now. Convoy is indicating to follow us. All units reducing speed and entering the hard shoulder. Over"

A mile further ahead an articulated truck had limped off the inner line of traffic and onto the emergency lane. With no apparent technical fault it came to a halt just outside the village of Sellinge. With its dark blue trailer and no lights it was barely visible. On a section of the motorway not covered by cameras it simply wasn't there.

The convoy made its way at speed along the hard shoulder, travelling at a pace that was both rapid and safe.

French had been an advanced driver for ten years – he had developed a sixth-sense for trouble and normally this served him well. Like most of his colleagues he had had a few 'bumps' – one at a hundred miles an hour. But he knew instinctively when something wasn't 'right'.

He glanced in his door mirror, everyone was still with him. Looking ahead, he could make out a slowing sea of tail lights, braking and further ahead, stationary. This was the regular consequence of Operation Stack. It happened so often that they had got used to it. Three lanes of one of Britain's busiest motorways brought to a standstill every time the 'bloody French' decided to head out on strike again.

He felt sorry for the lorry drivers, some of whom were lucky and had cabs in their trucks, with basic kitchen facilities and a bed. The others weren't so lucky and had to find comfort in whatever way they could. There were hundreds of them, from as far afield as Greece. Many of the drivers had left their cabs and were tracking down their compatriots; a chat, sharing a story, a hand or two of cards or better still a meal.

At the end of the extensive sound deadening barrier, one of them, a twenty-seven-year-old Greek from Patras had taken the opportunity to walk across the emergency lane and had climbed over the crash barrier, seeking refuge with a group of countrymen on the grassy verge. They smoked, told jokes and generally waited for the signal that the nearby tunnel and seas ports were opening up again.

Sometimes it took days.

They paced around, dancing from foot to foot to avoid the cold, some thinking they would be better off in their cabs. Sephos Christakos had heard enough of the age-old jokes and decided to call it a night. He clambered over the single metal crash barrier and looked back up the carriageway. He saw a set of headlights but knew they would be in the lane next to the hard shoulder and besides they would have to slow down soon.

He turned back towards his peers and wished them a pleasant and hopefully warmer night. He was a metre away from the barrier when he realised that the vehicle had illuminated its distinctive blue lights. It would be the last thing that he would remember and the first that he recalled when he woke with a start three days later in Ashford Hospital.

Despite the narrowing of the roadway and the relative speed of the convoy, French was able to have a reasonably engaged conversation with his partner Shaun Douglas. They did this every day and often at speeds twice as fast.

French was concentrating on the road ahead, as he had been taught. It curved slightly to the left and about a mile ahead of them he swore he could make out an outline but wrote it off as being the overhead gantry that was displaying ironic traffic data – 'Expect delays'.

"No kidding. Bloody French. Oh well, think of the cash Shaun."

French noted a few stray drops of rain on his windscreen and began to reduce his speed, bringing the average pace of the convoy down to a level that was both manageable and safe.

He leaned across and turned on his heated seat, looked back up and then immediately managed to gain some clarity on what had earlier caused him to question his vision and whether all was well in the world.

He saw the rear of truck ahead, the right-hand edge illuminated by the xenon headlamps on his Volvo. The blue strobes flickered and ricocheted off the surrounding traffic, hypnotic but essential.

And then, it happened.

Training, muscle memory and pure adrenaline-fuelled skill took over, his right boot scrubbing off the miles per hour in feet, per second. The tyres were grappling onto the rough surface of the emergency lane but fighting a losing battle. The lane surface was of the same standard as its nearby main carriageway but sustained periods of rubber, oil and motoring debris made it far more hazardous than the average driver could ever anticipate.

Neither officer uttered a word. Neither were average. It

had happened before, all part of the job. What they hadn't anticipated was a pedestrian, standing, staring straight back at them and stood petrified, perfectly in the middle of their lane.

At a little under sixty miles an hour, the front passenger wing of the Volvo struck Christakos. The collision was instant. French had not even seen the driver until he turned to face him, a pitiful owl in the blistering-white headlights.

French braked, hard. With limited means of escape he had no choice but to hit the Greek father of two, who catapulted up and over the bonnet, his right shoulder striking the familiar federal light bar, partially dislodging it from the roof and in turn tearing the rotator cuff to shreds.

With already life-threatening injuries, the long distance driver hit the surface of the carriageway with a sickening thump and then rolled fortuitously into the gutter.

The driver of the first French police van was not so swift to react, seeing the pedestrian at the last moment. He too braked hard but began to lose control. Christakos instinctively rolled himself into the foetal position and prayed to whoever might be listening.

The van missed him but swerved into the inside lane, continuing with the second following close behind as they had been instructed to do.

'Do not stop for anything.'

Ahead and unaware of the developing and unexpectedly chaotic windfall, Stefanescu turned to Hewett.

"The money we paid our countryman to park his truck in the emergency lane was well spent, no?"

It had been a simple aspect of the broader plan. Plan B –

if Plan A – a well-timed swap nearer to the tunnel or in it had not come to fruition.

Plan B was always the riskier option. Cause a block on an already busy motorway and pray that in among the chaos his team could respond as envisioned, over the countless hours in their anonymous industrial warehouse using their own vehicles as props. Again and again, written up on a whiteboard, until just like the jewellery operation in Hatton Garden they could do it in their sleep.

Stefan considered it his finest hour. Not without risk, in fact, his greatest rewards had always followed his most reckless risks. Unlike his brother, he always had a Plan C too. Better to live and tell the tale than die with a story untold. He was convinced that his sibling would do just that one day soon and love and admire him as he outwardly did he also despised him in equal measures.

Either way, he considered his future to be alone – and in no way connected to his big brother. He brought him fortune, but he did not crave the fame.

A fifty year old long distance driver had been offered a day's wages to pull his articulated vehicle off the main motorway and tell the world that he had broken down. 'Of course. As long as no one will be harmed,' he said, 'It would be a pleasure'. And the cash would be rather nice.

"With any luck, the police vehicle will run into the back of the truck and then we can move. The gap we have left will enable us to do what we need to do."

He checked his wristwatch. "Any time now."

French brought his car to a standstill, rammed on the handbrake and ensured that the emergency lights on his car were on for all to see. He grabbed the Maglite from the door pocket and ran back along the hard shoulder.

Douglas was calling the Force Control Room advising them of the road traffic accident.

"Mike One-Four, we have had an RTA. Repeat RTA. We've hit a pedestrian. Ambulance to the scene please, alongside marker post..." He strained his eyes in the now pouring rain. "6993."

"Received, ambulance en route, do you need any other units?"

"Yes over. And get a supervisor down here please so we can deal with the accident. God only knows where our French colleagues are heading, they haven't stopped. Can you try and make contact? Mike One-Five has put in a rolling block behind us if you can get us on camera please."

Blissfully unaware of the situation on the motorway and bored beyond six games of 'I-Spy' Cade and Daniel were now playing a new round of 'Would You Rather?'

"Neither!" said Daniel indignantly.

"You can't answer like that. You have to respond with an option."

"OK, OK. I'd nibble a cherry from a nun's arse."

"Interesting choice. I'd have bashed the bishop. Hang on – standby."

He answered the phone, shoving it under his right shoulder and propping it against his ear.

"Yes. Yep. Aha. Yes. Understood."

Daniel looked at Cade, still disappointed in his heavily imposed choice of clerical-sex options.

"Well?"

"Suffolk Police have stopped a van en route to Felixstowe. Four Eastern European nationals on board and a whole pile of jewellery fresh from Hatton Garden. All hidden away. They had a cracking cover story but the local cops saw right through it."

"Excellent stuff. Hewett or Stefanescu with them?"

"No. Sadly not."

"So now what?"

"I guess we wait. They will come, they have to and meanwhile..."

"No! I am not choosing between intimate acts of lust with a frolicsome walrus or the blowhole on a dolphin. I am just not. OK?"

"Fair enough, JD. But at least if we're caught you could always say you didn't do it on porpoise!"

It was characteristic of the black humour that accompanied police officers the world over.

"Get out Cade and go and fetch me a strong coffee."

"Mike One-Four ambulance ETA is about seven minutes. Sitrep please."

"Received, thank you. One male pedestrian, struck by our vehicle. Has extensive leg and upper body injuries. He's conscious and breathing. Our vehicle is still in situ. One-Five has the traffic stopped now. You had better inform the media, this is just going to make a bad situation worse."

"Received. Any news on the French vehicles?"

"Your guess is as good as mine."

About three quarters of a mile ahead, the French vans had come to a standstill. Their radios were as good as useless and following the briefing to the letter they remained in their vehicles, now penned in on both sides by other traffic. The driver of the first van switched the blue lights off, shrugged Gallically and cracked the window down a notch as he lit up a stereotypical Gitanes cigarette.

He leant out of the window and looked back at his counterpart, who followed his lead. They too were on overtime and were happy to ride out the storm. The fact that their armed guard was now nowhere to be seen appeared not to bother them.

Their instructions were clear. Proceed without the UK Police team only when you have lost communication, you are informed that the plan has changed, or you sense that you are under immediate threat.

"They would be here by now." Stefanescu looked back up the motorway for the British police vehicles, then turned and spoke forcefully into the rear cargo area of his own van. "Go and see what has happened. Come on, quickly!"

Dragos Saban seized the moment. Pulling his collar up and around his neck he left the rear of the van, noticing how cold it had become. He also noticed how many people were milling around what was normally one of the business motorways in the world.

Ahead of him he could make out the two French vans. The officers inside didn't bat an eyelid at the sight of 'one of their own' running along the carriageway and away from them, they were at best disinterested.

He ran back up the road, towards the blue lights that stood like sentinels on the British patrol cars. Shielding his eyes, he stared up the major arterial route and could make out some activity on the ground. A man had been hit. Poor devil.

Saban looked for a spare police officer, but they all appeared to be busy. He knew that this may be his only chance to alert the authorities, but he also knew he was being watched. No one in the group trusted anyone else. It was incestuous, deceitful and greed-laden and possibly the worst combination in a group that already had few friends, and plenty of enemies.

And despite his uncle's advice, he needed the money too, just like the other disparate members of his team.

He walked back, then jogged to avoid the rain. As he ran he made the decision that the financial rewards outweighed the risks. His uncle would despise him, but needs must. And his needs were greater.

He reached the van, pounded on the back door and was let in.

Stefanescu called out to him from the front.

"Well? What can you tell me?"

"It is terrible. A man was run over by a police vehicle."

"Most fortunate. And the vans that were with them?"

"I could not see them. I think they are somewhere ahead in the traffic."

"Then get someone and go back out there and find them. Now!"

Daniel looked down at the foot well and flicked a small stone around with his foot.

"I'm not happy, Jack. There's bugger all happening and like you I'm an active rester. I need the thrill of the chase one last time. Like all good murder mysteries, this one has some clues – and we are missing them. Agatha Christie would have cracked this bloody case weeks ago, the dirty little minx."

Cade did not respond. His mind was focused on other places. Carrie's calm hospital bedside, the chaos that revolved around the Stefanescu family and the reason for that chaos – a wave of greed. He felt like he was the only one pursuing them. And it was getting tiring. His head nodded and soon he was in that hideously indistinct state somewhere between consciousness and deep sleep where the words of his partner could be heard but he was unable to answer them without appearing drunk, his words slurred, punch-drunk and concussed from the preceding weeks.

Daniel turned to Cade, who was now in a deep sleep.

"I said Agatha Christie..."

Cade grabbed Daniel's hand and gripped it tight. "I heard what you bloody said John. If you are that bothered, give her a bloody ring – I'm sure you've got her on speed dial."

Hewett was unsettled. Physically exhausted, he knew that within twenty four hours he could be in a new country, alone and yet potentially free of the shackles of debt and dishonour. He persisted in giving the outward impression that he just needed to put up with the group for a few weeks, then he could escape and flee – anywhere. If his reputation remained intact within European government circles he could start again. If.

'Then you will be a man, my son...' His father's words echoed with the classic Kipling poem.

Dragos returned, shattering the silence, somewhat breathless.

"Up ahead. About a kilometre. The driver of the van is asleep! We should go now!"

Stefanescu broke the silence. "Need I remind anyone

who is in charge here? No? Exactly. We go when I am ready. Not you, or you." He pointed around the van. No one returned his critical stare. "Good. So, are we ready?"

It was Hewett who spoke first.

"I am."

He wasn't – he never really would be, and might never be able to live down the deep sense of current betrayal, but the British government owed him so much more than the apparently lucrative salary they paid him. His historical negotiations and those of his parents before had benefited the nation to the tune of millions in grants and trade deals. His father had worked himself into a potential early grave, his mother had become what could best be described as an upmarket whore – a prostitute of the British government.

And between them in order to live up to the hedonistic lifestyle they had overspent, over-stretched and borrowed way beyond their means. And, as their loving son, he had gambled in secret to try to alleviate their financial misery.

At first it was a means to an end, a logical method of using his classical education, a way of allowing his razor-sharp mind to read the cards and work out the odds – stacked against him though they were.

In the beginning it was also a necessary evil, but he soon found that he left the overt and less apparent casinos with more than he arrived with. And no casino owner ever enjoyed losing.

Above all he wanted a reward, more than anything, more than a sharp suit and a European car. More than a Thames-side flat and a place on the starting grid of the social circuit. And betrayal worked both ways. Those men in sharper suits, scarlet ties and cufflinks, filling their vaulted-ceilinged offices with decadent, bitter cigar smoke. There, in their ivory towers they had hung his parents out to dry all those years ago.

His delightful mother, the doyen of those blissful, semi-tropical, colonial days now spent her days staring out of a window in her French home almost permanently reminiscing about the past, dementia slowly gnawing away at her, piece by painless piece. And he hated that more than anything else.

"Retribution is apparently a dish best served cold Stefan. I am ready."

Stefan made the call. Time to see if the Englishman was as good as his word.

He hung up thirty seconds later.

"OK. Let's go. Remember your roles. Do not take any risks and above all try to avoid attracting too much attention.

The first van edged its way out of the main carriageway and onto the emergency lane that hugged the edge of the motorway. The driver illuminated the front emergency lights and was soon followed, after some skilful negotiation by the second white van its own mesmerising blue strobes flooding the area with cobalt lightning, sporadically rebounding off the stationary traffic and illuminating the miserable, jaded faces of the less fortunate drivers around them.

The abandoned articulated wagon had created the perfect, fortuitous shield which in conjunction with the rain had allowed them to proceed without alerting the British police – who were now hastily reprioritising.

Everyone had changed their plans now. For the Eastern European team, things had become so much easier.

The rain that emptied from the night sky added to the equation. In the back of the lead van Dragos found a sense of well-being in listening to it ricocheting off the metalwork, it was a noise that had settled him since childhood and now as he fought to find a comfortable position he stared down at the van floor – empty, sterile, not a match or cigarette stub. Not even a hair. They all wore gloves, as far as a DNA traces were concerned it was a vacuum.

The best a thoroughly-prepared Scenes of Crime Team could hope for was clothing fibres; the uniforms the occupants wore could only ever be traced back to the French Police. Sometimes having people who were in equally dire financial need and susceptible to a bribe was a hugely positive thing.

In a few minutes, the two white Renaults were as close as they could get to their identical cousins. The crew of the first legitimate vehicle were already waiting, doors unlocked and ready to carry out their own limited tasks. They had been well paid for what might manifest as a few days' work. Negotiations with them, months before, were so covert that not even the most notorious of whistle-blowers would ever be able to divulge the information.

The second team were not so amenable. The front seat passenger ran his hand over his right thigh, cursing the fact that the British had refused to allow them to carry weapons on their soil. He picked up the microphone that was cradled on a stainless steel bracket to the right of his leg. As he was about to speak into it, he noticed that the occupants of the two unheralded vehicles were all wearing familiar police uniforms. He relaxed a little.

He had amassed twenty-two years loyal service in the military and civil police and had been posted around the world where the French had once been a power to be reckoned with; the Pacific, North and East Africa, he had been there, done that.

He shielded the glare by placing his left hand against the

glass and through the cloudburst saw a more senior officer, his coat over his head to avoid the rain.

The officer tapped on the window and perhaps unnecessarily pushed an ID card up against the glass. His name was Charles Durand, a brigadier-chef in the Police Aux Frontières and that meant he was very much in charge.

Confident that he was an ally the passenger lowered the window a fraction, allowing a hurried conversation to commence.

"Hello, sir. Would you like to get in with us? You will be soaked."

"No, it is fine. Thank you, Sargent. I need you to swap vehicles with us, though. I have the papers if you need to sight them." He paused long enough to allow a challenge which never really came.

"Is there anything I need to know, sir? The plans have changed? I wasn't made aware. We were told to wait. We could move out of this jam and make our way. You know, given what we are carrying. But we were told to wait for the British."

"Indeed, Sargent, even a brigadier-chef does not always have the luxury of being fully informed. Your urgent needs have been answered. I am in charge now and the government has decreed that I now have the responsibility for what is in the back of these vans and also for getting it to Europe. The government asked for a senior officer to take over – and that, mon ami, is me. You and your team will take our vehicles...back there."

He pointed back along the rain-soaked carriageway, genuinely trying to shield himself.

"My second team will take the other vehicle. We need to move before our delay causes our government to be concerned – before we embarrass President Chirac himself.

It seems that our militant brothers at the ports have caused this chaos. Civilians!"

He raised his eyes theatrically to the anthracite sky, finishing a masterclass in French which had aroused no suspicion at all.

Hewett signalled to the junior officer. "Follow me. Leave everything in your vehicle. When this traffic starts to move make your way to the tunnel. Forget about the escort from our so-called British friends if you have to. You will be met by the UK authorities and escorted through to the other side. I will arrange this. Our team will pick you up in Calais and from there you can stand down. Thank you for your efforts today."

"Pleasure, sir. Oh, sir?"

Was this the challenge?

"Yes?"

"May I have the key?" Hewett laughed, it was a genuine moment of relief.

"But of course, and don't get stopped for speeding!"

The sergeant shook Hewett's hand firmly. "Is it true, sir? What they say about our cargo? That its contents could be worth tens of millions of francs?"

Hewett wiped the rain from his eyes and smiled his best underpaid government employee smile.

"Possibly even more Sargent. Possibly, in the wrong hands, even more – it could be priceless. Merci, au revoir."

The career sergeant left the van, pulling his collar up around his ears as he ran to the awaiting Renault. He was paid to follow orders, and the orders were clear. Why he could not proceed with the vehicle, he was in was beyond him. However, whether the orders made any sense on a wintry, rain-laden night in a foreign country was not for him to challenge. Rank had its privileges in any nation.

The crews were exchanged as per the plan and in under ten minutes Hewett, Stefanescu and the team were forcing their way onto the emergency lane and heading south.

Hewett sank back into the driver's seat, adjusting his night vision and contending with the rivulets of water that danced across his broad windscreen. With each laboured arc of the wiper blades, he was a step closer to his new home.

Candy from a newborn child indeed.

Cade rang Gary Marshall from Special Branch.

"Anything?"

"Nope. Not a whisper. There's practically nothing moving due to the ferry strike."

"Ah, I thought Dover was always this quiet?"

Marshall laughed "Hardly, this place is the Gateway to Europe. Never sleeps."

"OK, well if someone were to hear of anything let's hope they might ring us, as for now DCI Daniel and I are fed up to our mercury-filled back teeth with playing I-Spy."

About half an hour from the motorway, in a small two-storey control tower a female picked up the vibrating Nokia cell phone whose liquid crystal display lit up the low-light, temporarily depriving her of her night vision and making her curse in her native tongue.

"Yes. I can hear you," she continued to affirm, nodding unseen to the caller who spoke freely in a heavily accented version of the Slavic language.

"Good. You have done well. If you help us as discussed I will personally reward you. You cannot be allowed to rot away in some desolate corner of England when there is such a big world out there waiting for you to discover."

"Thank you. I don't need to impress anyone Mr…"

He cut her off quickly. "We can talk freely, but not that freely. You never know who might be listening. We grew up in the same part of the world, my dear. We should both still be suffering from untold levels of paranoia." He laughed, forcibly. She responded in kind.

"What time will you be here?" A simple, closed question.

"At some point." An open, non-committal answer.

"That does not help. I have things to do."

"So do them. Prepare yourself."

"And if you fail to arrive?"

"Then you will be better off – you won't have to meet my new miserable team member and I will still allow you to keep the money. I am a man of honour. Despised, allegedly cruel, sexist, overly stylish but ultimately honourable. I also reward loyalty."

"Then I cannot lose. See you when you get here. The western gates will be locked. When you arrive turn your headlights off. Then on. Wait ten seconds and flash twice. I will let you in."

"So you are the security guard, the mechanic, the administrator and the pilot? How many in your team?"

"One. I am a team of one."

It was good to hear, less trouble and far fewer lines of evidence if she were to go literally off the radar.

"Mike One-Four from Control. The duty inspector needs a sitrep. Where are the French vehicles, over?"

"One-Four I have no idea over." Douglas was yelling into his microphone to avoid the background noise of an approaching fire engine and the building cacophony of a developing storm.

"Last I saw they were together and heading further down the motorway. We are pretty much marooned now. Can we see if we can get another southern unit to intercept, even a local car – either that or we allow them to continue and hope they have a Plan B – over?"

On board the second van Constantin checked and re-checked his plan, and then his equipment and satisfied he began the more complex task of countering the ever-present irritating inner voices.

'I don't need any. Drugs are a thing of my past.' He meant it, but he also wished the voices would leave him alone and allow him to recover mentally. He picked at his fingers, pulling the dried skin from the cuticles until they bled. Physically he would carry the scars forever but his personal goal – above all others – was to use some of his hard-earned, ill-gotten gains to correct the visible signs of abuse.

He tested the gear that lay before him, each component part tucked into a purpose-made pocket, itself secured inside a green textile roll. He had purposely placed every part where he could find it in any condition, day or night, light or dark, upside down. In the darkest moments in a tepid cell he had pictured this time, cautious not to reveal his plans to an overly friendly British cellmate. It was said there was honour among thieves but he had never found one he trusted; for goodness' sake there were times in the past where he didn't even trust himself.

He looked up, aware that the youngest of the team, a boy barely old enough to be his son was looking at him. He returned his stare with a fractured smile and a simple question.

"Boy. Will you promise me that you will never end up like me?"

The young male nodded, unsure whether to speak.

"It's OK, I don't bite. When the time comes, you will see why Jackdaw chooses to have me on his team."

The male wore an inquisitive look and matched it with a reasonable question which immediately put Constantin on edge.

"Forget it. Forget I mentioned that name, never, please, ever repeat that name again. For your own safety. OK?"

He cursed himself in the half light of the Renault's cargo area as the van sped south, its tyres rhythmically colliding with the brightly coloured cat's eyes that separated the lanes. He must learn to take control of his nomadic mind if his future goals were to be realised. Fool.

"So, have you made the decision yet Jack?"

It was Daniel, using his best interview technique – trying to elicit the truth for once.

"You need to make up your mind soon or the ship will sail. There may never be another opportunity."

Cade felt slightly better for his micro-sleep but was still on edge.

"John, how the hell can I make such a decision when all the planets are far from aligned?"

"I have no idea Jack and right now I can see that you don't know your Mars from Uranus..."

"Puerile at best Daniel. I'm disappointed in you." No sooner had he finished the sentence he started to laugh.

"I hate you John, but it has to be said, publicly that you are good for me. I should make you a friendship bracelet."

"Please don't. Seriously, what are you going to do?"

Cade paused for a moment, exhaled and looked across the harbour, counting the lights on a departing ferry.

"If Carrie recovers, I'll take the job in France. Even if it's only for a year."

"And...?"

"And if she doesn't, I won't."

"You think it's that simple? What if she takes months to recover? What if..."

"She doesn't? I can't actually broach that subject John. She's quickly become a part of my life. I know it will never be normal in the true sense of things but I owe her a lot. If nothing else she's taught me a great deal about myself."

"In such a short space of time?" Daniel seemed sceptical.

"When you met Lynne, you knew didn't you?"

It was enough to stop the conversation in its tracks for a while.

Cade continued to look out of the car window and watch the P & O ferry exit the safe haven of the harbour and head out to sea where small whitecaps danced around its hull.

"For now JD let's just say that if Carrie doesn't come around in the next three to five days, then I'll stay put. If she does, then I can tell her to her face that I'm being advised to pursue the opportunity with Interpol."

"It would certainly open up the world Jack. Think of the opportunities. I hear they have plans to build a centre of excellence in Singapore one day, their HQ in Lyon is growing and it will do your C.V. no harm whatsoever. If I were a younger man..."

. . .

The French vans had split up, one heading south, continuing its journey to the Channel Tunnel, the other across country, south west to an aerodrome. A third was already setting a pace through the Kent countryside and was now driving along the A2 towards one of the busiest passenger ports in the world.

As it slowed at the approach to a roundabout, the driver looked across to his right. A partially floodlit castle had caught his eye. Its Norman walls had seen many battles, and he found himself thinking that if he needed to hide, to shore up his family from invaders that this would be an ideal place.

He was distracted for a second and almost pulled into the path of a yellow, white and blue Ford which had entered the roundabout from his right. The driver, a young constable from the Kent Police shook his head and was about to take it further when he spotted the French police insignia on the door. He waved cordially and allowed the van to continue. Something caught his attention though and like many street-hungry staff the world over it was enough to plant a seed. He had a minute to allow it to germinate.

The van driver looked directly ahead. In the distance, twenty-two miles to be precise lay the French port of Calais, its amber and white lights sparkling on the horizon, differentiating between the land and the night sky.

He waved back, mouthed the word 'sorry' and hoped that he had not aroused any suspicion. But for the obvious interaction at the border they were almost on mainland Europe and the boss had said that whatever they had stolen they could keep. It was a supreme way of engaging staff. The other males on board kept quiet. No one wished to tempt fate.

PC Charlie Harris, a former butcher and still only in his twenties had joined the police to make a difference. It was a superb cliché, but it was the best he could come up with at his interview. The truth was, he had a child on the way, a younger unemployed girlfriend and was genuinely fed up with dealing with blood and guts. He actually considered harming a human to be more palatable. A vegetarian butcher was never going to work.

As he accelerated along the Deal road the seed germinated and bore fruit.

'The badge! The bloody badge wasn't straight.'

In the brief moment that he had observed the Renault he had looked at the driver, a police officer in a French uniform. The van was clean and white. It had a passenger, also in French police uniform. The sight of a foreign force vehicle was new to him but probably not unique in a port so close to France.

"Uniform Two Three Control?" he asked with an inquisitive edge.

"Go ahead."

"Strange question control but are we expecting any French police vehicles on our patch tonight?"

The operator looked around the control room, twenty miles away and shrugged, receiving a similar response from her boss.

"Negative Two Three."

"Yeah received. It was heading down Jubilee Way towards the docks. I'm going to turn around and have a look at it if anyone else is around or nearby."

The controller had got to know Harris well over the last six months and knew he had a keen eye for detail.

"Anything specific that has caught your attention?"

"Not sure control. But worst case I might pick up a French badge for my collection. I'm coming up behind it, speed fifty, just passing the emergency run-off area."

"Received. Uniform Three Three is committed at a domestic in town. Get back to me if you need anything."

In his office Gary Marshall had heard the last and also found new life blossoming in his mind. French Police on mainland Britain. It didn't add up. He dialled Cade's number.

"Boss. It's me. Can you switch to Channel Fifteen UHF and listen in?"

"Pretty sure we can Gary. What's happening?" Cade dialled in the channel as he spoke.

"Not sure yet. Call it the instinct of a young local cop."

Cade navigated his way through the radio channels until he found himself on the local town frequency. As a matter of professional courtesy, he announced their presence.

"Zero Two Mike Papa this is Golf Tango are you receiving?"

"Golf Tango yes R5."

His signals were clear. Now all he had to do was listen and monitor their cell phones. It had been too quiet. A little like fishing; sometimes you could wait all day, all night and not see the float even twitch – other days the float would disappear like a submarine avoiding its hunter.

This was a nibble from an inquisitive bottom feeder.

"Two Three I'm approaching the main roundabout. The vehicle is indicating to turn into the port. I'm going to try and stop it before he gets there."

He illuminated his blue lights and flashed his headlights twice.

On board, the driver had seen the patrol car the second it had reappeared behind him.

"Do we phone the boss?"

His colleague was quick to respond. "No! We are on our own now remember? Just stay calm. He is British, he won't speak French, just put on an accent – tell some jokes about the weather."

"No, if he stops us he will search the van. We need to...go."

He accelerated, turning left and driving along the dual carriageway towards the town centre and parallel to Cade and Daniel.

"What are you doing?" asked the passenger.

"I have come this far, I am not going to get caught."

"Two Three – erm, the French van is failing to stop. Speed four zero towards the town, road conditions are good, traffic is light. I suspect he may be lost, but he's definitely failing to stop."

The control room inspector was now interested. He put down his twice-heated take away meal.

"Ask him why he is stopping the van? And let's find out why we have company. We should have been told about this. Get onto the Frontier Operations Team at the tunnel, see if they can shed any light."

"Two Three – why are you trying to stop the vehicle, over?"

"The insignia on the door. It wasn't straight, like it didn't belong. And the driver. He didn't look French."

The control room staff considered the words of a junior staff member and deliberated about the fall out if there was a crash involving a visiting forces vehicle. One also contemplated what a 'French look', looked like and considered searching for it on the internet.

"Get me an update." The rapid tone of the inspector.

"Two Three – sitrep please."

"Still failing to stop, speed is five zero towards Snargate Street and the A2o. He's hardly Grand Prix material but I'm not sure. Over."

Daniel's battered cell phone buzzed in the centre console, quietly screaming for attention. He missed it at first but took a moment to look down and saw the illuminated screen and the icon indicating that he had received a message.

He opened the phone with an easily remembered PIN number and made a dissatisfied noise – a saddened and frustrated sound that gained Cade's attention immediately.

"Something wrong?" His first thought was O'Shea.

"Yes Jack. Text from Paul Clarke."

Cade knew that Clarke had taken over from Roberts, acting in his position until he was fit for full duties again. He was also painfully aware that Clarke had his finger on the pulse back in the city. Sensing Cade's concern Daniel followed up with a quick and reassuring sentence. It didn't contain many words, but in this case, the fewer the better.

"It's not Carrie, don't worry. Sadly, it's not good news either."

Cade was tired of bad news, it seemed to follow him around constantly. If there was enough shit to stick to a blanket Cade was likely to be draped in the bloody thing.

"Go on."

"Mary-Jane Shipley is unlikely to make it. Surgeons did their best, as did you. Brave girl Jack. She deserved to live, and you deserved to meet her one day. I'll make sure our welfare team make an approach to her family. If it comes to it, we'll get to her funeral."

Cade had a genuine tear in his eye. His efforts and those of a raw and plucky constable were in vain.

"Why is it always the good ones John?" He wiped his eye discreetly before adding, "I am growing to hate this group just a little bit more every waking hour. Poor girl. What a fucking waste!" He slammed his fist onto the dashboard causing his knuckles to suffer more than the padded plastic.

He swallowed the rising bile in his throat and knew that he had to carry on, cleared his mind and called up on the same channel as Harris.

"Hello this is Golf Tango can we be of assistance. Our map shows that we are running parallel to your officer."

The control room inspector nodded his approval.

"Yes Golf Tango. Maintain a safe distance at all times and if the pursuit becomes dangerous to you or any members of the public you are to abort, received?"

"Yes-yes. Received. We are on Marine Parade heading towards your unit."

It was good to be back in the saddle again and for Cade it was vaguely like being home again.

CHAPTER TWENTY-SEVEN

Ten minutes away, as the crow would conventionally fly, a female with glossy black hair was moving deliberately around an aircraft. It was evident to any onlooker that she knew what she was doing and had a familiarity with the machine that suggested that she was either an engineer or more likely, its pilot.

She looked fit too. There wasn't a spare ounce of fat anywhere on her body and she moved in a way that men would either find attractive or intimidating. Below her right cheek she bore a small scar, it hid a tale, or rather the expensive make up she used did. It was her only feminine vice, although she often longed to rid herself of her masculine flying suit and headphones for a Coco Chanel dress, the desire to be airborne outweighed the feelings ten to one.

She had been flying since 1993 and had been just twenty when she had first been told via a very similar set of headphones, and with that familiar two-way radio traffic buzz, that she had control of the aircraft.

She had control.

She had been flying ever since. In 2001 she had moved to France on the promise of a general aviation role at a small airfield near Dunkirk. Gaining a solid reputation as a reliable and skilled pilot she soon found she had made enough money to fund her own aircraft.

She was a skilled negotiator and knew a bargain when she saw one – more likely a man on his knees who needed at worst to achieve a fifth of what his aircraft was actually worth in order to fund credit card debts.

The twin-engine Piper Chieftain could hold up to nine passengers and their minimal luggage. Although twenty years old it was a sturdy aircraft with a sound reputation, could travel at a one hundred and eighty-five miles per hour and had a range of over nine hundred nautical miles. It was capable of landing and taking off on short runways, its familiar Lycoming engines more than a match for most terrain.

For a few thousand Euros the entire aircraft could be chartered by business people and others, most likely criminals, to cross the English Channel.

Maria Anghel was born in Bucharest, the daughter of two state workers who had aspired to what they had achieved, a basic home and an education for their two children, Maria and her younger sister Daniela.

Maria had yearned to travel the world and as soon as she was able she hugged her mother and father, promised to write, left home and never considered returning until on a whim she had arrived in Romania, unannounced, landing at a small private airstrip near her uncle's home.

Her arrival was greeted with almost prodigal scenes as her parents put on a meal fit for a queen and welcomed their dear Maria home once again. She was a success, and many toasts were made, one by her sister who had matured into the most popular girl at school, both in and out of the building. She had her sibling's strong DNA; clear almond-tinted eyes, smooth, gently tanned skin, a perfectly fashioned nose and jet black, gleaming, shoulder length hair.

"I can only stay one night papa." Maria had announced. "I have to be back in France for a charter flight."

"Why did you come all this way my dear?" Her intrigued father had asked her in a quiet moment.

"Because now, I can. And now, I want to." Nine simple words had summarised countless years of missed conversations. Her father didn't express it in so many words but his look told her he was proud.

She had bid her family farewell the next morning, took up the offer of a free ride to the airfield, carried out the muscle-memory pre-flight checks, climbed aboard and took off, setting a course for France. She knew that she would stop once for fuel over southern Germany.

Now, as she completed her pre-flight checks, she considered the information before her – basic, uncopied passport details, like many of the others provided to her, they contained names that she knew were most likely as false as her sister's eyelashes.

It was early days for the UK authorities but they had insisted on clamping down on illegal migration from France and its notorious refugee camps who pumped men, women and children of all ages into a relatively defenceless Britain, and so in a measure seen by some as desperate they had insisted upon passenger names being filed – despite not being able to police the travel movements.

Small groups of apprehensive people, Albanians, Romanians, Iraqi, Iranian and occasionally those people from the smaller Middle Eastern and East African states, all hoping to claim asylum in the land of milk and honey had gathered together the requisite and comparatively low amount to charter an aircraft. In doing so, they had reduced their risk levels considerably, crossing empty borders in Europe was one thing, laying near the French coast for days, hidden in a container or clinging to the chassis of an articulated truck with limited air, food and water was an entirely different prospect.

There were countless sharks hunting in the shallow waters, their dorsal fins gliding above the surface, picking off individuals and families for five times the amount that she would charge, and all with no guarantee that they would even ever get to the chosen place. She may be exploiting them too, but she got them to their destination. As far as the moral high ground was concerned, she could sleep at night.

As a result of the relative safety, small airfields across the south of England had become targets and were extremely vulnerable. The United Kingdom border authorities had publicly acknowledged this, but in truth, with two major airports, a hugely popular sea port and the tunnel, their priorities lay elsewhere.

Those with aircraft, or the ability to charter and fly them had made enough money to live a comfortable life. Some even had the same moral compass, and Maria fell into the camp of only assisting those that she felt truly needed help. But each trip that she arranged, and the damaged souls that she observed, only helped to make her more cynical.

What Anghel did well was to fly above the radar. She found that being overt actually threw the authorities off her scent. In many cases, in her defence, she carried legitimate passengers from Calais to Lydd and vice versa, Lydd being the largest of the lower-level provincial airports in the county of Kent meant she could build up a reputation in the area – she could also easily divert to smaller, private airstrips where cash was the currency of choice for a struggling farmer, willing to mow and preserve a few hundred metres of grassland.

Stood on a non-descript but well-maintained airfield to the west of the channel tunnel she checked her charts, marvelled at the slowly developing stars and looked forward to an event-free trip, cash in hand and with any luck a glass of Cabernet Sauvignon at the end of her day.

It was planned to be a night flight, and she enjoyed those the most as her passengers normally slept and she could enjoy the glittering lights of the coastline and watch the constant stream of maritime traffic negotiating the Strait of Dover, the narrowest part between England and France.

She was ready. All she needed now were the aforementioned passengers and their luggage.

"Uniform Two Three?"

"Go ahead."

"An update please."

"Still Snargate towards the Western Docks. I think they are going to head for the A20, but I have no idea where to from there and why. I'm going to try to get a look at them."

Harris accelerated and ducked down the left of the Renault, trying to see, or better still communicate with the passenger. He looked in his mirror and saw an unmarked vehicle coming up fast behind him.

"Golf Tango to Uniform Two Three – how can we help?"

Harris knew the roads well and could see that getting off the A20 and heading back to Dover was no longer an option

– the endless queue of articulated wagons stacking up and waiting for the ferries to start running had all but closed the motorway. If he could keep the Renault on the main road it would help, would be safer for everyone, and perhaps it might just stop when the driver realised that even the police needed to stop when asked to do so by their colleagues.

"If you can hang back please. Keep any traffic behind us, I'm trying to get alongside and see if I can use my best schoolboy French to tell them to stop."

"Arrête from memory but don't quote me." Daniel had a smug look on his face, recalling his own distant school days.

Cade did as requested and tucked into the middle of the two lanes, holding back anyone with a desire to overtake what was now a three car procession.

"Speed six five, road conditions are good, no risk to any other road user at this time." Harris quoted, almost verbatim, he'd done it so often.

He settled into his seat and waited for the driver to make the next move. His training, basic though it was had taught him never to force the issue unless lives were at risk. It was miles to the next town, so he also positioned his vehicle in the middle of the two lanes and observed and hoped that sooner rather than later someone in authority might bring the convoy to a halt – he was at court the next day so had an early turn around, ideally he wanted to finish on time, such was life in the force, he knew it was now unlikely.

The two males in the rear of the Renault were silent, one, over six foot four and of athletic build was now beginning to show signs of nervousness. His foot twitched repeatedly, and he rubbed his palms together as he knelt and looked out of the tinted rear windows.

"Slow down!" His call to the driver was very direct. He knew now that this had already gone too far, that the

British, with their reputation, would find a reason to detain them.

"What is your worry brother?" shouted the passenger, "We are police officers!"

"Then why do we not just stop. Tell this fool to stop now or I will strangle him with my own hands."

"No. I need to get to the tunnel."

"But we were booked on a ferry. It was all arranged." He ran his hands through his coal-black hair. "It was all arranged."

"Yes brother, it was but now the plans have changed. We have two smoke canisters left. If this doesn't go to plan you pull the pin on one, cover your faces, wait a moment and then open the back door. But let me do my best to get to the tunnel."

The plan, if that was what it was, was ludicrous. He knew it too.

Hewett pulled up at the perimeter fence, bit his lip, prepared himself for the next phase and looked across at Stefanescu who had fallen asleep. He still had an injured arm; one against one he could throttle him with his seat belt or just beat him to death, set fire to the van and somehow get back to London before the morning, present himself to his superiors and pray that his story held water.

'I was minding my own business when a malevolent group of...'

He snorted audibly and reminded himself in his dear mother's words, that he had made his bed and he had no choice but to lay in it. Little did she know?

"Hey, we are here."

He turned his lights off and then on as instructed.

Moments later a figure appeared at the gate, shone a

torch in Hewett's face, then at the passenger. Hewett was unable to make out whether the figure was male or female, in fact he was unable to see at all for a few seconds as the powerful torch had deprived him of all night vision.

Anghel recognised the male passenger and lifting the floor bolts on the large gate, swung it open and allowed them to enter.

She closed the gate behind them and instructed Hewett to drive to the nearby hangar. He did as she asked and entered the dilapidated building, hearing the sliding door close behind him. Once the door was shut she turned on two powerful floodlights.

She thumped the rear door. "OK, you can get out. One at a time."

Stefanescu was first. He eased himself from the van allowing her to see he wasn't a threat. Hewett followed.

Anghel spoke in Romanian.

"Gentlemen. Thank you for your business. I am Maria. You don't need to know anything else. We load up in five minutes. I will not be touching your luggage. Once we are on board, you are to follow all my instructions. It is about seven hundred miles to your destination – about four hours in my plane. Go to the toilet now. Grab some water. There is no inflight service!"

She could sense that Hewett did not understand.

"You speak English?"

"I do. I am."

"Good. Then just follow what he does and do not make a fuss."

She opened a smaller side door and pointed to the aircraft. It was starting to rain, not what she wanted.

"Come, let's get your precious cargo on board before the weather turns." She pointed again, encouraging her passengers. The quicker she got to her destination the quicker she could think about returning.

Stefanescu grabbed her forearm with his remaining and surprisingly strong hand.

"Who told you our cargo was precious?"

"By booking with me and paying cash and providing a passport that was probably false, for a late flight out of a grass-strip airfield in the middle of nowhere? You did, sir. You did."

She had a point. He liked her. If she ever gave up flying, he could find work for her. She was bright, multi-lingual and very attractive. A deadly combination. He was spot-on with the first two observations but way off course with the latter. The only male she had kissed in recent years had been her father. And the only other male to lay his lips upon her face had been a priest from the Eastern Orthodox Church.

Like the majority of her fellow Romanians, she followed the disciplined approach to Christianity – she tried to attend a church whenever she was able to. In reality, she had been only three times in as many years. But she believed that He would watch over her. She just prayed that He would forgive her ongoing transgressions too.

She watched, pretending to feign indifference as Hewett and Stefanescu struggled to carry the three black Pelican cases across to the aeroplane. In truth she wondered what they contained – drugs, probably, and then considered whether she could take off with the cases and not her passengers. She smiled; airlines did it the other way around every day.

Hewett shouted across the mown paddock as he headed back to the hangar. "I just need to visit the gents. I'll be back in two."

Stefanescu waved an uncaring hand and began to strike up a conversation with his pilot who spoke first.

"Sir. I do not ask questions of my customers, and I do not answer any either. I find it is best for everyone." She offered a smile of closure.

"OK. You are the boss lady. But here is my cell phone number. When the day comes that you want to put your skills to good use ring me. I can provide you with enough opportunity to buy a jumbo jet, not this little thing." He indicated dismissively, kicking the tyre.

"Mr Stefanescu. That little thing will get you and your friend into mainland Europe from where you can do whatever it is you intend to do with those cases. Take it or leave it. I don't need your money."

She paused long enough to win a staring contest, noting his striking eyes. He was a handsome man. A pity.

Hewett had three, maybe five minutes before his absence would be noted. He knew that once he stepped onto the aircraft, he was a prison sentence waiting to happen, The British government would not hesitate to cast aside one of their poster boys.

Loyalty was rewarded. Loyalty, and if loyalty didn't work then corruption at the highest level with no chance of discovery.

These were the rules of his founding fathers. He was in so deep that loyalty no longer featured in his lexicon. What had he become? He even had voices in his head. This didn't happen to people like him. It just didn't. He was one of the good guys.

He paced around the hangar looking for a way out. His phone was lying at the bottom of a river. His mind unable to recall even the simplest of directory entries. He could call 999 – yes, that would be wise Johnnie. Just bloody marvellous. Where would he even begin? Why would they even bother to believe him? He was Johnathan P Hewett, Foreign Office; all-round nice guy with the biggest set of bollocks in Whitehall that's why!

'Christ John what has become of you?' His father's words.

Outside and into the mounting wind Anghel called out to him.

"Hey British guy, we have to go."

Stefan was pumping his thumb across the keypad of his phone.

"Heading to our destination. Leave in 2. ETA 4 hours. We have the luggage."

Hewett was walking towards the door when he kicked a screwdriver across the floor. It was black handled and worn but he picked it up nonetheless. Slipping it into his pocket he flicked off the lights, exited the hangar, drew the door shut behind him and ran to the Piper to find his colleague already on board.

"What took you so long? Ringing your mother?"

"Funny. You threw my phone into the river if you recall? No, if you must know I get nervous on planes." He sat, strapped himself in and felt the reassuringly sharp blade of the screwdriver in his pocket. He felt something else too, his second phone.

Up front to the left of the cockpit, Maria Anghel continued quietly to impress her customer. She ran through the drills she had been taught years before, knew how to start the engines, applying the correct mixture of throttle and prop controls in her sleep, and all the while she was verbally running through her emergency procedures. If the plane struck a problem, her life was the most important. Everyone else's depended on her. If it happened mid-channel, it was every man, or woman for herself.

"If we get into difficulties, mid-channel there is a life raft at the rear of the aircraft. Throw it out through the door – it will deploy. Then get to it and ensure we all get on board. I will let you decide whether those bags are worth saving. OK?"

Both men, suddenly feeling somewhat vulnerable looked around and saw the brightly coloured canister. It was marked Ocean Safety 4 Man. Hewett, whose story about flying anxieties was actually true, hoped it would remain firmly in situ and that in four hours they would be safe at their destination. What his plans were when they arrived, he simply had no idea. But with four hours leeway at least he had time to think.

With her equally disciplined avionics checks complete she was ready – however she made no call to a tower or air traffic control. She would fly low and hope to get over the channel quickly. Her worst case would be to announce herself mid-flight and state with a calm and authoritative air that she had encountered radio problems.

She ran the engines up to high power, checking for faults and then, content that all was as she had expected she turned onto the grass runway.

The Piper was now at full power and making its way along the gently undulating path, at about seventy knots and into the wind; she needed around thirteen hundred feet of runway but with a light payload and a developing headwind she was up quickly and without fuss.

Her only issue was taking off on a grass runway in a twin-engine aircraft. There were plenty of people in the avionic world that said it should never be done. But those people sat in ivory towers and had no reason for a covert departure.

She'd only go if the runway was smooth, dry and she had the skill to do it. She was a gifted pilot, but never arrogant, and she had taken off in a hurry from far worse places.

With a climb rate of around a thousand feet a minute she could soon be up at her ceiling, but she intentionally stayed low to avoid watchful eyes – knowing this would make for an uncomfortable journey.

Their instructions were clear: Get us to France. No questions asked.

CHAPTER TWENTY-EIGHT

CHARLIE HARRIS WAS A YOUNG COP WITH AN OLD SCHOOL head on his shoulders.

He had quickly earned the respect of his bosses and importantly, his peers.

He also knew when something wasn't quite right. The good police officers always did. It was a mixture; a blend of gut instinct and sixth sense. A stray look to the side, the almost-hidden nod of affirmation, its owner frantically trying to deny any connection to it or what it concealed and conveyed.

It was the subtle hand across the mouth – thou shalt not speak!

The shifting from one foot to the other. The clenching of the facial muscles.

But mainly, it was the eyes.

Or in the most dynamic of incidents, the fact that the person being questioned had just galloped away as fast as his legs could carry him. And invariably, to set the record straight, it was the male of the species.

This case was different and Harris had no idea why. Conventionally it was a van-load of international colleagues, all with the same broad instinct and desire to lock up the criminals. So why was he now chasing them? And why were they not stopping?

In the van the team were trying to remain calm, trying to stay connected, part of a team. But there were factions starting to build, fractures starting to appear.

Constantin had been sitting in the shadows, contemplating many things. He knew that he had to mine deep into his reserves of control and take over – the unelected leader in a vehicle full of young and adrenaline-fuelled males, now being pursued at the eleventh hour, when everything had seemed to be going suspiciously to plan.

"Right. Everyone shut up and listen. I am in charge."

Silence.

"Good. I am here for a reason and you will soon realise why. You will all do as I say. And that includes you." He pointed to the largest male.

"I need you to help us, you need to use your strength and we may have to fight our way out of trouble. We are heading for the tunnel. When we get there, we will be met. The officer will be wearing a uniform. He will escort us through the service tunnel. We will head down, deep beneath the sea."

He paused not for effect but to imagine what it would actually be like.

"We will drive through the tunnel, away from the public. We are French police officers remember, not a group of criminals with a vanload of stolen diamonds!"

Mumblings of approval echoed around the interior of the vehicle. He knew he now had their interest and support.

"Soon we will change our appearance. But we need to get rid of them." He pointed over his shoulder, back down the road towards the pursuing police vehicles.

"We are almost home brothers. When we get safely into France, we will divide up what we have. Stefan is making his way home with the Englishman; rather him than me. Stefan gave me instructions to divide everything equally. Be careful how you sell these jewels or they will be your downfall. Now I need you to listen, for this is the most important part of our plan. If things go wrong..."

He shouted out the plan, so that everyone heard him. With no obvious lack of understanding, he thanked them all and asked to be left alone.

He unrolled the set of tools and removed a spherical device and held it reverently in his hand. It had taken weeks of part-time work to create it and in a moment it would be history. He placed it to one side where it would be safe but accessible.

He picked up the remaining grenades, commonplace, inexpensive and readily available, they would serve two purposes.

"Accelerate as fast as you can."

The driver responded without question.

"The rest of you – cover your faces."

He nodded to the impressively built male. "You know what to do? Good. Now open the door."

He engaged the Noise Flash Diversionary Device in his left hand so that he could reach around the static door.

His new team mate held the door ready.

"Do not let it fly open. I need about half a metre. When I throw this, you pull the pin on that, and whatever you do, do not drop it!"

. . .

Harris was accelerating now, the red mist slowly enveloping him. As far as pursuits went this was tame, both vehicles heading along a motorway, safe from oncoming traffic – technically this could go on until one or both ran out of fuel. All he needed to do was stay in touch and wait for further back up. He glanced into his door mirror, the Met Police team were still with him.

It was then he noticed the Renault's door opening.

"Two Three. Stand by. Stand by. The rear door is opening."

Cade had 'that' feeling again and began to accelerate too, shifting out to the right, holding back traffic and trying to work out what was happening.

"You see that?"

Daniel responded in clipped tones. He was suddenly twenty years younger and back in harness, transformed; the hound chasing the hare. "Yep. I see it."

Constantin yelled to the driver "Brake. Now!"

He primed the NFDD, or as it was known with global affection a flashbang. He hurled it towards the patrol car trying to land it as close as possible to the windscreen.

His hope was that it would act as a distraction.

The M18 smoke grenade followed.

"Go, Go. Faster!" he yelled to the Renault driver.

Harris was trying to do five or even six things at once; drive, think, commentate, stay safe, keep everyone else safe and somehow do it all within the bounds of the law.

The bang was loud. Very. No one within a hundred metres could miss it. But it could have been a backfire at the speed he was travelling – his vehicle was almost through it before it had any chance to impact. But the flash was blinding and instinctively he swerved, blinked repeatedly and tried to regain control. And now he was heading into a thin veil of acrid scarlet smoke. He was lost.

Cade was braking ferociously, moving further to the right to try to avoid Harris and somehow maintain a view of the rapidly disappearing van.

The noise that greeted Harris next was different, deeper, bass-like and industrial. The front of the car crumpled and collapsed as it struck the crash barrier and pushed the Ford onto its side. Harris was unable to avoid striking his head on the passenger window and lost consciousness, his last defining moment was hearing his temple cracking the lightly-tinted glass and then, in moments, he began the sleep of kings.

He would indeed be late home. But at least he would make it.

Cade locked the brakes in their own vehicle and quietly hoped that the three cars following would do the same. A few hundred metres back down the road the remains of the military smoke grenade drifted across both carriageways and caused a few motorists to panic briefly.

Cade's vehicle came to a halt in the evaporating sea of red.

"Do we stay?" It was meant to be rhetorical, but both men knew that their prime role had now changed. They left the car, its rear blue lights dancing mesmerisingly among the smoke screen and acting as a basic warning to other motorists.

Daniel was already at the Ford's door trying to open it as Cade called up on the UHF channel, confirming the news that their constable, Charlie Harris and his rather-special instinct was right.

"Yes, towards Folkestone or Ashford. Look, we've lost it. Can you notify other units please? Do you have air support? Can we get fire and ambulance here too – ASAP?"

He knew it was a long list – but he also knew that the operator would be triaging as he reeled them off.

"Yes sir, fire and ambulance en route from Dover – about five to ten. Any sitrep please?"

He looked at Daniel and waited for a thumbs up.

"Your man is unconscious but breathing. My colleague is tending to him. We need to get going as soon as possible. Can you get a local unit to take over here?"

"Affirmative. We have a motorway car trying to get through the east-bound traffic to you. We've got Operation Stack running, it's a little chaotic…"

As the operator finished, Cade heard the familiar and comforting wailers approaching, but in the opposing lane. The driver nodded and weaved in and out hoping to get to him as quickly as he could. All that power and nowhere to go.

"JD we need to go." He pointed at the growing crowd who had left their vehicles, wondering how or if they could help.

"Get one of them to take care of him."

It was a moment of callousness from an ordinarily compassionate man. But the red shroud that surrounded him also coursed through his veins and he wanted the occupants of that van. Now.

Daniel found the best of the bunch when it came to first aid and briefed them. Yes, the car was safe, the smell was just the airbag and no, it wouldn't catch fire.

"And don't let go of his neck until someone takes over. We have to go."

And with that they did, Cade accelerating up the westbound motorway, first, second and third, hitting the rev limiter in every gear.

As they passed the small village of Capel-le-Ferne another patrol car joined them.

"Uniform Three Five to Golf Tango. Behind you and in support over."

Cade raised a hand in thanks as Daniel acknowledged on the local channel. "We are banking on them heading to the tunnel."

A few miles ahead the target vehicle had slipped off the motorway and into a large lay-by, normally full of trucks. The port strike had created a great opportunity and the small tree-lined lane offered them the chance to exit the van and carry out the next phase of their plan undisturbed.

Whilst two men pulled the police insignia from the Renault and threw it deep into the undergrowth the others undressed and replaced the police uniform with a different outfit. Carefully bagged, the French law enforcement overalls were also thrown into the snarling, bramble-laden undergrowth.

New insignia was being quickly and skilfully placed onto the front and rear doors and an orange rotating beacon up and onto the roof. The common theme now was altogether different but uniform in appearance: a red semi-circle sat above a blue one and in the middle against a pure white background were black capitals that read EURO TUNNEL.

On the front, a white number plate was being affixed, its combination of five letters and two numbers mirroring the rear, brighter, yellow plate. It was now a British tunnel maintenance vehicle, and it was at home in Britain or France. In three minutes it would be just that little bit closer to the latter.

Cade, Daniel and the solitary Kent Police officer arrived at the outskirts of the Euro Tunnel operation at Cheriton, a hitherto unknown place until the channel tunnel concept had been unveiled for the third, or possibly fourth time in history.

It was an idea first mooted in the late 1800s but thwarted by British fears that Napoleon himself might walk through it and invade England. At least the coffee would have been better, Cade mused.

Daniel allowed the Kent officer to call up the separate Frontier Operations team on their own channel – announcing their presence and asking for help.

The visitors were all soon acquainted with the specialist team from the Frontier team. The duty sergeant Neil Gregory was a strictly 'black and white' character and liked his briefings to be just that, without a hint of grey, but he acknowledged he was considerably outranked with Daniel being on site and saw that as a signal that he needed to elaborate just a little.

Daniel was actually more than happy with brevity. The briefer the better in fact.

Gregory was joined by his section of five constables, all wearing the de rigueur yellow high visibility vests craved in such operationally hazardous environments.

"Sir, welcome to the tunnel, anything you need just shout. Let me recap. If that's possible. We have a group of Eastern European criminals who have been targeting bank machines – I read about that only last night. They've hit the capital and having started to make an impact until your team have come along and stepped on their toes and as a result they've decided to Foxtrot Oscar back to Romania?"

Cade smiled at the use of police phonetics to cover off the obligatory use of swear words.

"And having tried to empty the banks by inserting stuff, covering the machines with realistic templates and then blowing them to bits with oxy-acetylene they turn their hand to more daring stuff – nicking diamonds from Hatton Garden."

He whistled. "We are in the wrong job guv."

"Indeed, we are. Neil, I'll cut to the chase. We need to find these people. Possibly a British Foreign Office staff member too, who may, or may not be part of the group, and, there is something else that we are looking for but that's very much need to know."

Gregory bristled at the intonation.

"Right now this is my tunnel boss and I need to know."

Uncharacteristically Daniel pulled rank.

"Yes, it is Sergeant. And no, you don't. End of." He waited for the nod of affirmation.

"Right can we start looking for our gendarmes please? I take it your French counterparts know?"

Gregory had recovered, he knew when a battle was temporarily lost, but he was buggered if he would let it lie there.

"Yes boss. And we have a small team over the other side too, based at Coquelles. Special Branch staff. I'll assume they have the necessary clearances?"

"I doubt it Neil. Now let it go will you, or do I need to ring your chief constable?" The detective chief inspector held his gaze until he held the higher ground.

The team grabbed car keys and divided up the manpower.

As they walked, Daniel spoke to Gregory.

"Don't think I'm an arsehole who hides behind his rank Neil. There are some things you are better off not knowing."

"Roger that sir." Gregory was happy that in his eyes the DCI had apologised and allowed him to save face in front of his small team.

"Jack and I will remain as one unit, can one of your team escort us Neil?"

"Ken. You go with our guests will you?" He gestured to the remaining Kent officer. "You can come with us."

With the teams created they moved off towards the main vehicle entry points at what was one of the largest passenger facilities in the world. Everywhere Cade looked he saw cars, motorcycles, coaches and heavy good vehicles. And trains. A lot of trains.

The white Renault van swept over the motorway, along the Ashford Road and after a few minutes turned right and onto the service road. The driver was following a set of clearly-defined instructions and they needed now, more than ever, to have the appearance of a team that not only belonged on site but also knew where they were heading. It was all about confidence. Actions would need to speak louder than words.

The same could be said for the sister van and its occupants which had headed straight to the Port of Dover, unwittingly timed to perfection, it missed the chaos caused by its sibling and slipped into the vehicle lane, among other similar vans, cars and coaches, awaiting clearance for the one hour crossing to Calais aboard the *Pride of Dover*. Bearing the emblems of the P&O Line it too would blend beautifully, a vehicular chameleon and just another non-descript van in a row of others, waiting patiently to board.

The third van also cruised along the M20 motorway and arrived into Cheriton, minutes away from the seaside town of Folkestone. It drove along the M20, taking the vehicle exit and three minutes later had stopped on the Vehicle Departure Road. It no longer bore the hallmarks of a French police vehicle – now it was a hired van from Avis, generic, a few battle scars here and there and as anonymous as could be.

In an hour, if all went to plan, all three vehicles would be on French soil, two would head south-east the other west, looping around the Benelux countries before also heading due south and for home.

For now their work was done. They had arrived, quietly, into a foreign country under the leadership of a man they had never met and importantly never would. They had defeated the basic surveillance systems that the British had considered state-of-the art and had set about systematically exploiting the lower-tier banking systems. In doing so, they had been able to work almost with carte blanche whilst the authorities had searched for bigger fish, hoping to land the biggest and most destructive. When all the time, the small bottom-feeding shoals had swept across one of the greatest financial cities on earth and emptied accounts, stolen data and finally, even unbeknown to them had stolen something even more valuable.

They would head home and celebrate, in small teams to avoid detection by the Romanian Police – a highly driven organisation that despised the reputational harm that Stefanescu and his seemingly unconnected team had done to both Britain and in turn Romania.

They would drink Tuica. They would dance, with women

and among themselves. They would be treated as folk heroes. All Constantin Nicolescu wanted, all he needed was a cool bed, perhaps a glass of wine and a safe in which to store his share of the proceeds. That, and quiet, no sounds whatsoever, and no drugs. Chemicals must never pass his lips or flood into his veins ever again, of that he was certain.

His body was a chapter-filled book; injuries, disease and abuse had almost led to his demise. He knew he had one last opportunity to really live – and now he had the financial security that he had yearned for over the years. If he remained loyal to the Jackdaw, his future was bright.

Forget the Tuica! When he was safely home, he would find the dust-laden bottle of Rakia and either share it or drink it alone as he contemplated where his life would take him next. He had proven his worth to the boss and now, feeling worthy again he could finally regain some respect. Already closing the door on his past he broke free from his daydream and looked out and through the windscreen of his current shelter and prayed that they would all make it. Including the group of disparate men around him in his plans was a sign that his normal selfish nature – a by-product of drug addiction – was perhaps ending.

'Close the door on your past. Lock away the demons,' he whispered to himself.

"This way boss?" The driver pointed a finger towards the service tunnel.

"Yes, drive carefully but be confident. We need to appear to know where we are going. You have the card?"

The driver lowered the sun visor and removed the plastic access card from the vinyl pouch and placed it onto the seat between his legs.

"Yes, I do."

"Good." Constantin was enjoying the level of responsibility bestowed upon him. "When we get to the outer door run that card over the reader and wait." He had memorised the instructions which were sent via a text message on a phone long since discarded.

"Once we are in the outer security area we wait. The lights will change to green and we move forward. Then we leave this vehicle in a parking bay and board the rapid transit system. We walk to it quickly, but do not run. We have a friend on board. Get on and sit down and do not speak. We don't have to do anything. We will be safe. Does anybody not understand what I am saying?"

Silence.

The rapid system was designed to carry service personnel through the fifty kilometre long tunnel. It was a gangly love child, the fusion of a coach and car, it's almost toy like appearance, tall and slim, allowed for two of the same vehicles to pass through the tunnel at once.

The police used a smaller version of a Hyundai hatchback to move through as quickly as they could, again, anything larger would prevent seamless traffic conditions. At stages along the tunnel, there were places where a wider vehicle could just about pull over and move out of the way. The vehicle system was brilliant in concept but nothing compared to the overall design of the tunnel itself, some thirty-nine kilometres of which was beneath the water, easily making it the longest undersea tunnel in the world.

The complex had two main train tunnels; the south, carrying trains from France to the United Kingdom, the north from the United Kingdom across to mainland Europe.

In the middle of the two larger tunnels was the Service Tunnel. Along which, at every three hundred and seventy-five metres was a cross passage, guarded by remote control hydraulic doors, linking the two main tunnels and used for maintenance, navigation and in the event of an emergency a way of moving passengers quickly and safely from one side to the other.

There were other smaller tunnels too, but they were rarely visited, let alone used.

Fire was the ultimate fear for any tunnel builder and operator. And the Euro Tunnel organisation feared it as much as any of their peers. In 1996 they had fought such a fire, and it wouldn't be the last, however their systems were state-of-the art. Any trace of a fire would be responded to immediately; subsequent chaos caused by evacuations was a consequence – as long as no one was injured the tunnel team knew how to prioritise, even if it took hours to repatriate people with their cars or even other loved ones.

What saved significant damage and casualties was a fire-fighting system that incorporated pressure. Every two hundred and fifty metres a large duct carried air and extracted the deadly gases emitted from a fire, forcing them up and out of the tunnel. For this reason, each tunnel was kept under constant pressure.

The van pulled up on the large concrete pad, surrounded by train tracks, overhead power lines and a sense of almost constant movement. At any other time, Constantin would have taken time to marvel at its simplicity and admire its quite incredible infrastructure. He put his hand into his backpack and felt one of two reassuring cold alloy cylinders against his clammy fingertips. When the time was ready. But not before.

"OK, let's go. Come on. Like I told you. Smile if you have to but don't engage in conversation. Leave that to me."

The small group left the van keys still in the ignition and walked the short distance to the rapid transit vehicle.

Constantin boarded first. There were others on the vehicle already, so nothing was said, but his discreet nod was enough to gain a reciprocal movement. He sat down and prayed the other younger men would just follow his basic instructions. They did. They were on the way.

Each held onto their hand luggage as if it contained the answer to a brighter future. It did. And in most cases they were prepared to fight for it. In their new leader's case to the death. He had travelled too far, physically and emotionally to give in now. It was only money, only wealth, only obscene and gratuitous greed and he loved it and would cling to it like an infant clings to its mother's hip.

The door closed, and they moved forwards. He stared out of the window, sub-consciously biting his nails, protecting himself from speaking, as he dined on the edges of his fingers and spat out the hardened skin he thought of no one.

It was getting darker by the second. It always did at this time of the year and it was colder outside now, winter was fast approaching. He knew with luck on his side he would be home within a day, to a colder place, where few would probably remember him. His mind wandered once more, thinking about the last few years, the last months and then the preceding forty-eight hours. And then he began to shake quietly. What had he done? He could only recall about a third of the chaos that had surrounded him and that alone was enough to make him heave.

He licked his lips. The top one was cool now and damp, yet he was hot, he needed air. It was all coming back in a wave that he fought to control. He swallowed a mixture of saliva and bile.

'Not now. Please. Haunt me another time. Just not now.'

He pressed his hand against the cold glass and then held his palm against his cheek to try to cool himself down. As he did so he stared out of the vehicle across the wide expanse of concrete and closed his eyes.

Cade, Daniel and their new team mate pulled onto the same piece of road and made towards the service tunnel. Like his Romanian quarry Cade wished he could explore the place, take in the remarkable feat of engineering and perhaps even go abroad, driving a nice car across the continent. He thought of the girl, Nikolina Petrov and her courageous nature, her exquisite beauty.

He pictured them driving through France in a sports car, a bright red Aston Martin Vantage – via Poplar-lined high-ways they were wending their way through small villages, larger towns, awash with history, the palpable scent of heavenly, just-cooked pastries and fresh coffee. Further south, to the Mediterranean, savouring every minute before arriving into a quiet coastal village where they could finally be alone.

He too closed his eyes and thought of the days that had led to this. He could smell the sea now, wild, windswept – the familiarity of ozone fought for primacy as he tried to close out the world around him. And better still, he could taste her flawless lips and breathe in the fragrant scent of her hair. He just needed to keep his eyes closed to maintain the reverie. Just a few more moments.

. . .

Both vehicles were waiting now, parallel and with others, containing a mixture of tunnel staff, border agency officers and a privileged visiting travel writer who was there to report on the continuing success of the tunnel.

She would later write in a provincial newspaper:

'The operation never ceases, not for them the curfew of an international airport. This place could run constantly if it chose to. Ants shuffling from one place to the next; a colony of cars, coaches, trains, people, property, and all underground. Under the English Channel, deep beneath the chalk. The Victorian engineers that first considered the idea would be astounded!'

Cade was almost asleep. The trials and tribulations almost overwhelming him. He could hear Daniel chatting, and occasionally nodded and hoped it was at the right time, in the right place. When this was all over he would sleep for a year and a day.

The rapid system vehicle started and as it did so Cade came to, blinking his eyes back into focus. Across from him, leaning against the vehicle glass a male stared back. He had also woken with a start, his heart now pumping just that little bit harder.

They looked at each other for five, maybe ten seconds. No one was counting, then would look away as humans often do, unless there is a chemistry to bind the senses.

Cade lost the battle and looked away first. He had seen enough ghosts, and the male looked like one, ashen, drained skin and sunken eyes – poor toothless bugger, he was probably as tired as the man who stared back at him in an equal trance, on his way back to France at the end of a shift, no doubt. At least he was on his way home. With Cade's dream broken, he now found himself back at O'Shea's bedside. Shit. How could he forget her? How could he banish her so quickly from his thoughts – replacing her with a half-baked, broad daylight fantasy?

"John. Any news from home?" He meant the team. "How's Jason? And Carrie?"

It felt like months, not just days before that Roberts had been brutally assaulted by the very men they were pursuing. Worst still, it could have been years since he had walked into O'Shea's flat and detected an odour that rapidly had him crawling across her floor, hunting through narrowed eyes, clinging to life. It wasn't many months, but hours ago. And he had already forgotten her, but she would never relinquish her hold on him.

She had failed to gain consciousness and as far as her brutally honest Canadian doctor had stated, she may never do so. 'You should prepare yourselves, gentlemen. Notify her family.' The words were crashing back over him – a wave; massive, powerful, fifth, sixth, seventh, it mattered not.

He shook his head.

"You alright, Inspector?" It was Daniel.

"Yep. Same old horrors. Any thoughts on how we try to coordinate this better?"

He was deliberately trying to distract himself from the chaotic scenes he had left behind. "We've got staff all over the bloody region looking for ghosts, John. Kent are backing us up admirably. Any news from London?"

"Nothing. Most of the team has resumed. A couple of staff are trying to gather evidence still, nevertheless the pressure will be back on. Breaker will soon come to an end, Jack. We both know this."

He did. Operation Breaker was not dissimilar to most police operations – anywhere in the world. They started with a hiss and a roar, if they had the backing of a senior manager all the better, but like a child's favoured toy, once a new distraction appeared on the scene it would be discarded, back in its box, behind a closed cupboard door. Forgotten, a politicised puppet with its strings cut.

Breaker had identified a growing group of males who were undoubtedly working for a brighter, better equipped leader, who in turn was reporting up the food chain to someone with greater influence. He smiled, in one respect it was no different to the scalar principles employed by law enforcement teams. When it was good, it was great. When it was bad, it was diabolical. Whatever the region, whatever the team, shit rolled downhill.

Where Breaker had won initially was in its backing. Bodies appearing in a city, some marked with a familiar tattoo, were enough to pique the attention of even the most battle-hardened commander. Throw in a few gas attacks on banks, a growing cash mountain and a banking system unwilling to disclose it had a problem, and you had a developing issue that needed addressing before the media turned it into a frenzied, one-sided journalistic free for all.

Throw in the blatant armed robbery of a diamond dealer, chaotic scenes on the streets of London and a few compelling bystanders with a tale to tell and you now had the manager by the short and curlies. Start shooting at police staff and you had the same manager by the balls. Adding a sixth degree of chaos, in the form of a Foreign Office member who had become feral, was enough to squeeze the aforementioned testes until the veins bulged and rapidly became purple. The manager was gasping now, nauseous and contemplating life in the body of a eunuch.

"But we haven't got anyone in custody, Jack. And we both know that sooner or later the sponsor we have at the Yard is going to pull the pin. Knifepoint robberies. That's where the political money is, that's where the media want to direct our resources. The public doesn't care much for bank issues. Banks? They can afford it. It's a victimless crime. Some might even say they deserve to be fleeced for all their obscene profiteering." Daniel stopped. He was depressing himself and everyone around him.

The Kent officer stretched his arms out so he could look at his watch. Surely it was time to go home? The overtime would be nice, but by the time the taxman had taken his cut it would hardly be worth it. He grimaced, actually, he decided, the taxman was probably a woman and if she was anything like his estranged and second wife she'd take him for every penny.

Cade did the same with his own watch, but overtly.

"I'm tired, JD. Shall we call it a day? As I said I am sick of chasing ghosts by day, let alone night."

"And miss the chance to see inside the greatest engineering accomplishment since the Titanic?"

He had a point. But that great engineering achievement had sunk.

Their driver started the small patrol car, and they moved forward, tucking in behind the Mercedes rapid transit vehicle. The service tunnel doors opened in front of them, silvered, hydraulic arms sliding apart, pistons easing the large white doors back and into a locked position. The first vehicle edged up to the red stop line and waited.

It entered the airlock, and the doors closed behind it. Constantin and the other occupants felt their ears equalise as they dropped down into the tunnel and waited for the second fire door to open. They were now in the service tunnel and en route to France. He could almost hear the accents changing. They were 'this' close.

The Frontier Operations car was soon in the sterile area. The outer doors closed behind it and once again the pressure altered. Cade squeezed his nostrils together and blew to balance his ears. The larger yellow fire doors slid open and allowed them to see the serpent-like tunnel that lay before them.

Lights ran along the roof as far as the eye could see. Cables lined the walls, neatly tucked into conduits, and a large pipe ran parallel to that. It was industrial in its beauty. Cold, solid concrete sections shaped the tunnel, in the middle of which, on the roadway, was a solitary white line.

Cade could see the transit vehicle ahead. It was moving at a steady twenty miles an hour and soon they were a hundred metres behind it, travelling at the same speed.

Sat two places behind Constantin, Dragos Saban, the young son of Christina and nephew of Valentin Niculcea, shuffled nervously in his seat. He sat alone. Alongside him a dark red back pack contained a cell phone, an apple, a small carrier bag containing cash and a smaller one which held flawless diamonds – not many, but enough to change his life – and to their right, an awkward bedfellow, a revolver.

His briefing had been specific.

'You are one of the few ones with recent military experience. If we are compromised you will protect us so we can escape. Your family will be well-rewarded.'

He believed nothing they told him.

At the bottom of his bag, his hand rested against the icy steel of the aging revolver. He wondered if it had ever been used to kill anyone. He worried whether he had the courage to even pull the trigger, let alone point it at a fellow human being.

The two different vehicles moved along the tunnel. The

uniformed officer asked what seemed to be a stupid question, but it broke the ice.

"Where to, sir?"

Daniel was the first to respond. "France, my good man and don't spare the horses."

CHAPTER TWENTY-NINE

"Seriously JD, where are we heading?" It was a weary Cade, asking an equally ridiculous question.

"I get we are making our way to France, but this is not achieving anything. Would we not be better back up on top, more eyes, scanning the terminal?"

It was a fair point.

"I acknowledge that Jack but honestly, among thousands of people, what are our chances? By heading to France we can be at the right end and hopefully our colleagues might allow us to filter the passengers, and who knows we may just spot Hewett among them."

"You really don't like him now, do you?"

"He's broken the oath as far as I am concerned, Jack."

"But he wasn't a police officer?"

"Correct. But he must have made an oath to Her Majesty at some point. And as far as I am concerned that is treason – and that was a hanging offence until not long ago."

"Are we one hundred percent happy that he's turned?"

"I looked into his eyes, Jack. Those bloody things are the

window of the soul don't forget. The roadmap for any copper. It's never let me down yet. And when I stared into his a few hours ago in that busy traffic, he couldn't hold my gaze and more importantly he couldn't wait to get away."

"Fair enough. I'll go with your gut instinct." He turned to Ken Smith, their driver and tour guide.

"Is there a McDonald's in here anywhere Ken, I could murder a Happy Meal?"

"Sadly not sir. But if there was, may I suggest that the toy would be the McTraitor."

"Possibly too soon, Ken. But nice attempt at levity."

They continued along the seemingly endless concrete tube, France was about half an hour away. At least they might have some decent coffee and a baguette or two.

"What do we do when we find this group of people boss?" It was Ken again.

"Lock 'em up, Ken, and throw away the key," replied Cade, now desperate for sleep and a square meal, actually desperate for a meal of any shape.

"And what if they start shooting?"

"That's what uniform staff are for Ken."

With hindsight, it wasn't funny – and it wasn't that long ago that Cade wore the blue serge. "Sorry Ken, that was uncalled for. We'll push the chief inspector out of the car first, then we can slam it in reverse and make for England. Deal?"

"Deal," he answered but was distracted. "Wait one, sir, the bus is slowing down."

Only a few miles away the Piper Chieftain was level, flying as low as it comfortably could and tracking across the English Channel.

She needed to keep the small aircraft over the sea as long as she could; experience had shown her that this way she avoided attention, especially heading south west, running parallel with the French coastline.

Below them ships passed south west and north east, and between the larger deep water vessels a trail of small, faster ships and boats, bisecting their journeys, all governed by the clifftop Coastguard station at Langdon and its French equivalent twenty or so miles away.

Anyone mapping the area, covering maritime and aviation journeys would be forgiven for becoming confused by the myriad signs of navigation, both on the water and above, in the air. It was, to say the least, a busy part of the world.

Maria Anghel was a supremely confident pilot. She knew the area, and she understood the foibles and quirks of her aging aeroplane. Tonight it sounded as sweet as a nut, perfectly in tune with its surroundings, and she was making good progress.

Had Anghel have filed a flight plan it would have shown a long dog-leg, down the centre of the English Channel, turning south west towards Le Havre and then inland, bypassing Le Mans, Tours and Poitiers.

France, being a genuinely large country, offered many places for them to hide as they journeyed south towards their destination, a small airstrip north east of Bordeaux.

Why they chose this ridiculous place, she had no idea, but they paid well and by the next morning she could be home, or anywhere a full tank took her. For now, anywhere meant the United Kingdom, moving people and commodities back and forth across the channel.

Hewett stared down at the ground, wishing he was alone, wishing he was on the ground, anywhere would do, just on the ground and away from the present company. There, below, a gently lit cottage, fire ablaze, that would suit him. Ideally alone, with his thoughts on how to bail himself out of this utter bloody chaos.

What had he become? A slave to a group of immoral men who viewed wealth as the only indicator of success. To a point he was as guilty. A beautiful car here, a wristwatch there, he admired such things; they didn't have to be classically pleasing to the eye as long as they were well-engineered.

If he had kept his head down and his backside up and worked for another fifteen years, he could have lived a very comfortable life. But instead he chose to gamble, and only gamblers prepared to risk it all ever won.

Below him, he had no idea of the height; the kilometres swept away in a country he actually adored. Whatever the earlier town was, it was gone, and they were now just a distant sound above a densely black area. He formed the opinion that it was forest; he knew there were plenty of them.

All he needed was to get onto the ground; a moment of surprise, the upper hand and a spade. A swift blow to the head and the bastard slumped in the chair next to him would be dead and buried. Gone, out of his life. He would be debt-free again. They would have nothing with which to blackmail him.

Perhaps he should just hand himself in?

Perhaps he was many things?

His head began to nod and soon it was pressed up against the Perspex window of the Piper aircraft. Up ahead and minding her own business, the pilot did what she did best in these situations, busying herself at the helm and ignoring her passengers unless they expressly wished to communicate.

'I bet you really love passengers like this?' Hewett looked at her and deliberated if he could overpower her and take control of the aircraft. He was sure he could land it if he had to. It couldn't be that difficult.

Looking sideways he saw Stefanescu, half asleep, favouring his injured arm. He whispered, "I detest you. Just give me the opportunity and I will end your life..." His words tailed off. It was pointless, he was theirs now and for the near future he just had to accept it.

Minutes later, Stefanescu turned to him.

"Jonathan. When you mutter words under your breath, make sure your intended audience cannot hear them. I am so hurt, after all I have done for you." He smiled and closed his eyes, confident that Hewett had just lowered his opinion even further.

"Get some sleep while you can, my friend. We have a long journey ahead."

Hewett decided upon a different tack.

"I'm sorry. I am afraid. I am loyal to you and your brother. You have to understand I have never been in this situation before."

"And you think I have?"

"Honestly? Yes," replied Hewett, shifting in his seat, trying to alleviate the pressure on his sore legs. It felt like he hadn't rested properly in weeks.

"You need to learn to trust us, Mr Hewett. For we are all you have left. You were classically educated. May I suggest you put that learning to good use? Trusting you is my decision, John. Proving me right? That is your choice."

Hewett took a moment to consider the words. "OK, so I trust you, but it works both ways, I gave you everything, my soul, my integrity and my reputation."

"Johnathan. Your reputation was only paper thin. They

hated you. Despised you. They saw you as arrogant, a government whore prepared to sell his soul – and they were right. It doesn't make you any worse than any of them. Ultimately, we all prostitute ourselves at some point in our lives."

He stared at Hewett long enough to unsettle him. "Letting me down is something that will cause you problems in the future, wherever you choose to hide. I will be a long-term irritant. Let Alex down and you won't have a future. He has a sadistic streak that concerns even me. He harms people for fun. Yet, he would never tear the wings off a fly. In his eyes, that is cruel. But he would happily pull your eyes out one by one, allowing you to see the first one in the palm of his hand. He's kind like that."

Anghel broke the conversation, pointing to the headphones at the side of both men. They slipped them over their heads and heard the familiar buzz of a two-way radio.

"Gentlemen, we are about half an hour away. You will need to be strapped in. Do it now. I hope it has been a smooth flight, the landing will not be so good. A night landing on a grass strip."

She shook her head, unseen to her two passengers.

"When we land I will taxi, the engines will remain running, you will leave, taking everything with you. I will take off again and our paths will never cross. Thank you for paying me Mr Stefanescu. It is quite unusual for men like you to honour your debts."

She flicked a switch and condemned them to radio silence once more. Neither man spoke for the next thirty minutes as the Chieftain reduced altitude and made its approach to Saint Helene, a remote village north west of Bordeaux.

Hewett moved in the seat and felt the screwdriver

against his hip. When the moment arose he was going to plunge it into his new controller's neck.

Valentin pressed the red phone icon on his Blackberry and slipped it into his coat pocket. It was cool outside, even for a region so far south. About six degrees and a clearing sky.

The voice had been clear, concise, a mixture of Home Counties English and formulaic British gentleman.

The voice had also made sure that Valentin knew exactly what he needed to do.

'Almost there, dear chap. Almost. Do what you can for me.' Quite why the bloody British couldn't sort their own problems out was beyond him.

He set the alarms, double locked the door, scanned unnecessarily and walked towards his car, a non-descript off-white Citroen ZX, one of two cars that he kept in a nearby outbuilding. He picked up a box, placed it into the hatchback, started the car and drove towards the nearest town.

Twenty minutes away from Saint Helene, west, towards the striking Atlantic Ocean coastline was where he now called home. A deliberately rundown gîte, on a farm track, at the edge of a large and immature pine forest and accurately described, in any language, as being in the middle of bloody nowhere.

It suited him. It suited those that chose to work with him. As technology progressed he could work from anywhere, but this place, deep in the French countryside, was ideal. He looked like a local, drove like one, and sounded very much like one too. If anyone ever challenged him he said he had spent time overseas. It was an easy lie.

He could get to the nearby towns of Saint Helene or Lacanau. He could walk through the woods, the forests or on the remote beach.

He had chosen the place, or rather, it had chosen him when he placed a ruler on the page of an old atlas. He knew he couldn't go east, or north and south into Bulgaria offered further risk. Looking at a map, he was attracted to the comparative remoteness of the Nouvelle-Aquitaine region. A much-thumbed guide said he could surf. A solitary pastime for a solitary person.

East it was.

He took a detour. He always did. Checking left and right and up. He would have checked down too if he could.

Assume nothing. Believe no one. Challenge everything.

It was his ABC, and it had saved his life, at least twice.

When he left his homeland, he knew he needed to get away from civilisation but also blend in. An Eastern European state was not suitable. His own paranoia would have given him away to someone, watching, waiting, expecting to earn a few extra Leu.

If he ever trusted anyone enough to have a conversation he would have answered the question 'how did you end up here?' with a simple shrug and a descending index finger onto a map.

He had been happy living alone. He missed her terribly. His beautiful wife, Ana. How could they have taken her from him like that when he had offered them so much?

Daniel was busy dialling into the team back in London.

"Any news?"

"Not much boss." Came the reply.

"A few in custody, a few escaped, some with bugger all on

them, others some cash. We've had intel coming in from every man and his canine partner. Seems that this group are bigger than we think, fingers in pies, lots of pies."

"OK. How's Jason? And Carrie?"

"Both doing well, sir. I'll let you know if anything changes."

Daniel knew it was a lie.

He looked ahead. "You are right, Ken, that thing is slowing. Can we get past it?"

"Sure. Stand by to be amazed by the power of this beast."

He changed from fourth to third, eased over the white line and accelerated. As they ran alongside the Mercedes shuttle Constantin turned his head to look. It was an involuntary move, and he hated himself for such a simple mistake. The face that looked back looked as exhausted as his own, a little healthier, but exhausted. And he recognised him immediately. So much so that he looked ahead and tried to shield his features with a subtle movement of the hand.

It was all Cade needed. Tired or not, he spotted the non-verbal signs.

"Yes, you bastard!"

Daniel was alert now. "John?"

"He's on the bus JD. It's our man – Constantin. Ken, stop the bloody thing! Radio in. Tell them we need backup."

JD changed the instructions quickly.

"Ken, get ahead. Give us some distance – we might need it."

Ken Smith, a veteran of the tunnel, knew he had little in the way of options but accelerated ahead, grabbing the radio handset and calling up for assistance.

"Uniform Three Seven – one of the targets has been spotted on the shuttle. We are about half way, we passed the midway point about a minute ago. Coming up to tunnel marker…" He waited to see if he could identify exactly where they were.

"I can't see a marker but we are in Interval 4."

"Yep received, from control, can you keep going, we will despatch French units to you? They are closer."

"Negative. The shuttle has stopped."

Smith came to a halt. The three men turned and looked back at the lone shuttle, now parked in the middle of the tunnel, lights blazing.

The driver, a forty-year-old Frenchman, was doing as instructed. Avoiding his radio and his phone. The other passengers were following suit.

"I don't want to harm any of you. We are leaving now. If you stay on here and don't call anyone, you will all be safe."

Mike Harris, a British father of two, time-served engineer and hued from a buggered-if-I-will-give-in granite mould started to stand up in his seat.

"Now look lads, we don't want any trouble. OK?" He considered his approach to be man in the street, borderless and compassionate. Hand outstretched, revealing an empty palm. No weapons, no threat.

"Whatever it is you have done, we can all turn a blind eye. We've got families and I for one wish to see them again." He was getting bold now, pointing his finger.

"But you can't escape from here, you are stuck. The authorities will capture you. Now, if you work with me…"

Constantin had heard enough. "Stop! Shut up. Sit down." He could feel the adrenaline starting to visit his veins and wished he had something else to pump into them to calm him down.

Harris was now bristling for a fight. He'd always protected the weak. He should have joined the force when he had a chance to follow on in his father's footsteps. Engineering seemed a safer option.

He stepped into the narrow aisle and began to walk towards his captor. It was at that point he realised that the lone man that appeared to be in a hurry to leave held more than one ace.

A younger male, equally dark haired and equally eager to leave, stood too. He placed a hand into his backpack and produced a revolver. It arced up and into Harris' face, the end of worn barrel stopping just underneath his right eyebrow, nestled into the socket and close enough that Harris could smell the metalwork.

He was now quiet.

"OK. Does anybody else wish to stop us?" The six passengers shook their heads and prayed for Harris to sit down, shut up and act like a terrified engineer on a diminutive bus that was previously minding its own business and heading to France without a care in the world.

Cade, Daniel, and their uniformed colleague could make out what was happening. The tunnel seemed to draw their focus straight onto and into the bus. No words were needed to support the actions. A gun, stuck in someone's face, spoke a thousand words.

"Ken, get this relayed, will you? Where are we exactly and what are their options?" Cade was no longer tired. He looked down the tunnel, past the shuttle, looking for a way out. To the left of the vehicle and about fifty metres further down the tunnel, he could see a gap in the endless concrete structure. It must have been one of the many links that he had been told about in the briefing.

He knew back up was perhaps ten minutes away, staff had to get through the airlocks and then drive as fast as possible, but without firearms they were as useless as him.

The nearest armed response team was twenty minutes away at best. He considered using the Hyundai as a weapon but realised he couldn't get beyond the shuttle. If its current position was deliberate, it was clear that this was a planned decision.

On board, Constantin was engaging his team in a simple conversation, confident that none of the other passengers were going to risk becoming a headline on the evening news.

"OK. You all know what comes next? We go in sixty seconds."

____

CHAPTER 30

____

MICHAEL BLAKE SAT IN A COMFORTABLE OFFICE IN THE magnificent Foreign Office building in King Charles Street, London. It was far too late to be in the office, even for one so thoroughly committed to his work. It was often said to very close friends that he and his team had absolutely no life outside the splendidly constructed walls.

Why would they? Their work was everything.

Blake also said that there were far worse places to work, and as organisations went, the FCO was very much in the upper-echelons; there, on a pedestal; polished marble, no doubt.

The FCO had a job to do, and it had chosen people carefully over the years, casting a weather eye back to the regal days of the Commonwealth when much of the colour on a world map was pink, a simple indicator of the sheer might of the British government and its quest for global power. It had a reputation, then and now.

Blake had joined the FCO from university, where he studied politics and law. His first role, in the eighties, was seen as a test – if his resolve and the department's trust in him grew, then all would be well. The role of Deputy High Commissioner in Pakistan had broken many before him, but it was a part he relished and had cut his professional teeth upon.

He flirted with Joint Intelligence Committees and advisory roles, moving from the United States of America to Eastern Europe, and he had risen through the ranks stratospherically. Having guided Prime Ministers and advised on foreign policy he found himself sat in a much-loved leather chair, his hands warming on a cast-iron radiator, staring out through a panelled window and onto a statue of Clive of India – the man who had famously established political and military control of enormous parts of south east Asia.

It was a familiar and regular late-night view for the Director General, Consular and Security, Foreign and Commonwealth Office.

He had majored on national security, consular services, cyber security, crisis, non-proliferation, and it that portfolio was not weighty enough, defence, intelligence and international security. Finally, and importantly for Blake, he maintained the portfolio on Russia, Central Asia and Eastern Europe.

What Blake didn't know about his role, about the influence of Britain on the world stage and foreign policy priorities was, it was said, not worth knowing. His knowledge of Europe as a whole was outstanding. He spent weeks backwards and forwards to Brussels, where he held a post within the United Nations – just another diplomat in a sea of consular advisors and ambassadors.

It was whilst in Brussels he had met her. Whilst she flirted with the Africans he had caught her eye. He knew it. It was that sense of recognition that men and women have when the gaze is held just too long. Neurons, chemicals combine, clash, collide. A second too long becomes disturbing. A second less and the moment is lost – the chemical equation broken.

Patiently waiting for her to finish her obvious charm offensive with the heads of despot Central and West African states, he watched her walk up to the bar. Her evening gown was just above the knee, quite daring for such formal circles. The other women hated her, except one. The US Ambassador's wife Julia had immediately taken a shine to her when she had met her a week or so beforehand and as she also had a personal friendship with Blake, she said it would be her honour to introduce them.

Blake could not believe his fortune. The woman, more of a stunning girl, was eating out of his hand. Able to hold her drink, she didn't appear to need alcohol to reduce her inhibitions. She was the most attractive and best-dressed in the building, and all the other men couldn't take their eyes off her. A white dress and white shoes, dangerously close to lascivious – however the way she wore it was flawless in both conception and reality. Her toned figure allowed the dress to speak a thousand words, most of them quietly uttered in the male minds that surrounded her, watching her, discreetly. Imagining.

An hour later, the same dress was lying on the floor of Blake's bedroom. She had pulled back the dark blue floor to ceiling curtains and allowed them both to be exposed to the sparkling cityscape before taking control and riding him senseless, her perfectly shaped back facing him, arched her hips pulsing as she maintained control. She held him expertly inside her as she watched the city going about its business. It was easier than having to look into his eyes as he reached a shuddering and noisy climax.

They dressed, and she headed back to her own cheaper hotel where she showered for thirty minutes, ridding herself of him. Of the two, she wasn't sure who the professional whore was. But she had got more than she had bargained for from Mr Michael Blake. He was different. The Africans allowed her to explore the avenue of false passports, visas and lines of credit. Blake allowed her a way out − all she needed to do was flatter his ego once or twice, make a breakable promise, maintain a discreet relationship until she could get to London and then cash in her favours.

Married with three children, he lived for the weekends when incongruously he spent most of his time in a beautiful home in commuter-belt Surrey working in a study that almost exactly mirrored his office.

Work aside, he was fit and healthy. He maintained a steady marathon time in the three-hour range and swam every morning, and often, when time allowed in Hyde Park where he was a member of the exclusive Serpentine Swimming Club.

Life was just glorious.

Or rather it has been until he had closed the Intelligence Report marked 'Eyes Only', sliding it to one side in the hope that it might tip over the edge of his desk and into the shredder.

Blake had lost something intensely valuable, from a place that had been chosen by a trusted aide for its apparent security and anonymity. Why didn't he listen and just put the bloody thing in his safe, behind a card-accessed door in another secure part of the building? Jesus, the Queen's bedside drawer would have been safer.

To exacerbate things, he'd also lost a member of staff

that he had trusted and now couldn't help adding two to itself and coming up with four.

And to piss on his delightful parade even further, everyone that was anyone wanted a few moments of Blake's time, and they all appeared to be on top of the pecking order. Foreign Office, Security Service, Police and the government itself. He was being pulled, metaphorically, from limb to limb.

He gazed at the statue of Clive. He even asked a few questions of the old bugger, hoping in vain for an answer.

The first was desperate. "How the hell do I get it back?"

The second was more pleading in nature. "Where the hell is it?"

And the third, inquisitive, was said during a long and restless sigh.

"And, having agreed to pay a king's ransom to get him out of the country, do I really trust Mr Johnathan Hewett?"

The Chieftain was losing height, dropping lower by the second and following Departmental Road number 5 that tracked south west and allowed Anghel to gather her bearings. A street lamp here and there offered a partial map of the ground, but as experienced as she was, she began to have some doubts.

She had little with which to judge her position, with very few terrestrial markers and fewer celestial ones, she was at the very edge of her ability and skill. She relied on her instruments – and luck.

Landing a powerful, twin-engine aircraft during daylight hours in stable conditions relied on skill and often required knowledge of the location and weather patterns. She had the former in bucket loads, but the latter eluded her. From her seat the weather looked as fine as it could, in the dark, with no visible cloud.

The powerful Lycoming engines were a double-edged sword, handled with respect they were a joy to control, but misjudge their power on take-off or landing and the result would be far from envisioned.

She reduced speed further, waiting for the visual reference, the aim point that she needed to put the wheels down and start to decelerate, to brake, in itself a hazardous occupation on a fast, grassy strip – at night.

The words of her flight instructor were repeating in her head.

'What you can't see can still hurt you Maria...never forget that.'

"Where is my aim point?"

Stefanescu was focused now. "Is something wrong, my dear?"

"No. Everything is fine. And if you call me your dear once more, I will deliberately fly us into the ground. You said there would be a marker of some kind. I see nothing ahead."

"Trust me..." He said the words clearly. "They will appear."

In the tunnel, Constantin opened the shuttle doors and prepared to flee. He looked back – he didn't need to produce a special stare. He was menacing all the time.

"If any of you try to follow us, or do anything heroic, I will personally shoot you. That goes for you too." He looked directly at the driver, the only member of the captive group with the potential to harm them.

In truth, he *was* thinking about running them down. How dare they point a gun at his passengers?

The passengers in question said nothing, left their phones alone and kept their hands in plain view. Everyone, including Mike Harris, wanted to get home intact. He had a son in the local police, a fine young man called Charlie and he was desperate to share his story with him. He decided that as soon as he surfaced from his current logistical tomb he'd ring him, regardless of the fact he knew he was on duty somewhere not far away.

"OK. Go!" Constantin felt alive as he ran to the side of the shuttle, away from view.

Cade and his two colleagues were powerless, and their quarry knew it.

"Dragos, you hold them there, shoot at them if you have to. We will meet soon." He placed a hand onto the younger man's shoulder, gripped it quickly, tapped it twice in succession and then ran to the opening in the wall.

Cade was already moving.

"Jack. It's not worth it. They are probably armed and need I remind you, we are not!"

"So what's the option, John? I am not losing sight of that bastard. Now, unless you order me to stay, I'm moving. They can't get far. You coming?"

It was one of those moments. Daniel decided he was too old for this nonsense. And yet he was so relatively young – having joined the police at a young age, it felt as if he had given his life to the job. In reality, that wasn't far from the truth.

"You go. Ken and I will figure out what to do with the guy who's now pointing a gun at us."

It was enough to change Cade's tactical options.

"Give me the keys, Ken."

"But boss, I'll get fired if the car gets damaged."

"Put John's name on the paperwork I'm sure he signed up for damage waiver insurance. Keys!"

Dragos Saban was a relatively young man, with a dream of a bright future. He had promised his uncle he would help him, but at what cost? If he started firing into the tunnel, he could hit one of them and that would change his life, and theirs, forever. He didn't want to harm anyone, but he was a rabbit in a set of rather bright headlamps.

Looking behind him, he could see he was now alone – at least as far as his comrades were concerned. They were running down the link tunnel towards the main train tunnel to freedom. To freedom. Even the word sounded empowering. He was alone, underground, and although in control, he felt helpless.

He stood and raised his hand in the air. The aged firearm was visible and his finger was curled around its trigger.

Cade started the small car, selected reverse and accelerated. He was a little wayward, but the distance was reducing rapidly. What he was going to do when he reached Saban was as yet unplanned. A casual passer-by would have observed that it was courageous, if not a little foolhardy.

He looked back at his small team and as they became more distant, he pondered just what his boss would say when or if they were reunited. Technically, whilst trying to resolve one situation, he had created another – leaving them both completely exposed in what was basically a twenty mile long, well-lit shooting gallery.

He let out an expletive as he reminded himself it was easier to ask for forgiveness than permission and carried on.

He wrenched the steering wheel violently to the right causing the front wheels to respond, in turn throwing the car into a rapid, noisy and decelerative turn within the already compact space. He corrected the car mid-turn, slamming the gearbox into first and accelerating now, into second, then third. The little engine was protesting as it hit its rev limit.

With the driver's window down, the noise was ludicrous, but not so loud that he couldn't hear the much louder report of a firearm.

Cade didn't see the round, in fact he didn't even flinch when the bullet struck the left side of the Hyundai's windscreen, causing a small hole that was fringed by white fractured glass. A super-heated projectile punching through a snowflake.

The round continued through the car and into the bodywork. It was certainly a distraction as it worked out a way of dispersing its energy.

Daniel and Smith were at somewhat of a loss. Chase after Cade and get shot or stand still and get shot. Or, run the other way to France and end up causing a diplomatic row over their arrival with no travel documents.

Or get shot for desertion. In the back. Probably by Cade.

"Come on. Let's go!" Daniel began to run towards the fight. It was what most police officers did, albeit the unwritten rule was subtly different: run to a fire, walk to a fight.

The second round left the chamber, a bright yellow flash and the thunderous sound of black powder detonating in such a restricted space caused all three pursuers to pause for a millisecond. It missed all three of them, ending up God only knew where.

Daniel made a mental note to ask him next time he was at his place.

Dragos' comrades were now well into the complex and making good progress. If they stuck to the plot, they would be in the main tunnel soon and Constantin could carry out the second part of his escape and evasion plan. Simple, straightforward and potentially lethal. A marvellous, old-fashioned diversion.

Cade had never contemplated reducing his speed and was now moving through the tunnel at about fifty miles an hour. Hardly exhilarating, but in the current confines it felt like Monaco; exiting Portier and into the tunnel, foot flat to the floor. Actually, it felt much faster, as a go kart fixes itself low down against a track.

His vision was distorted, but he could make out the male who was now steadying the gun and aiming straight at the windscreen. Cade leaned slightly to his left and readied himself for the collision. At least this way he didn't have to see his attacker's face.

The front driver's side wing caught Dragos Saban's mid-thigh and hurled him up and backwards, straight into the concrete wall. His back hit it with such force that it drove the air out of his lungs and appeared almost to deflate him. The sound was curious, intense and disgusting, not dissimilar to a carrier bag full of water being thrown to the floor.

It felt as if a huge weight had crushed his bones, dropping them from a great height, body meeting concrete.

He slipped down the curved wall section and ended half standing, half prone.

Cade recalled a hanging he had once attended when he was a young police constable. The male had ended his life on an unsympathetic and depressing day, using a dressing gown chord tied to a relentless curtain pole.

Cade had never been able to delete the image from his waking mind, he often recalled it and Dragos looked so similar, it put Cade back there, in a semi-darkened bedroom, in a semi-detached home, part of an anonymous housing estate, in a non-descript corner of Britain, on a miserable Tuesday at a little after eight in the morning.

He remembered every single part of the job.

He had found himself unable to leave, watching the deceased, wide-eyed, waiting for him to talk and praying he wouldn't.

Alone, with a stone-cold, wretched and lifeless marionette.

He shook the vision away and swept the ground for the firearm, seeing it two car lengths away he knew he was as safe as he could be. He called out to the shuttle.

"Are you OK?"

There was a pause. The driver had had a reasonably bad day, and this latest event had just made it worse.

"Yes." Another pause as he looked around and got several nods of approval. His accented English was clear enough as he stammered, "We are OK."

Cade was out of the car and walking carefully towards the young male. He could hear him moaning and knew he would be badly injured.

"Police. Don't move." Not that he could without unravelling more crushed blood vessels and the floodgates to a river of internal bleeding.

Daniel and Smith were alongside him now. The senior man was grabbing lungful's of the eerily still air.

"I need to retire Jack." He looked at Smith, who hadn't missed a breath.

"You alright, pal?"

"Fine boss. You?"

"Superb. What about him, Jack?"

"He'll live."

Cade and Smith lowered Saban to the ground, gently putting him into the recovery position, searching him as they moved.

"Cuff him governor?" Smith was of the once-bitten school of policing.

"No, I think he'll be just fine Ken. Get us some help if it's not on the way."

Cade looked at the young man. He barely looked old enough to shave, let alone stand at the midway point between two countries, hundreds of feet beneath the ocean and shoot at police officers.

"Can you hear me?"

He nodded, carefully.

"I hear you. Please do not kill me." He tried to breathe but torn intercostal cartilages screamed in protest as his buckled right ribcage creaked, his lungs hissing and crackling.

"I was told if I didn't help they would kill my family, and my uncle. He said that when the time came, I should tell the British his name. That he has been loyal to you. That you would help me."

"You shot at me and my colleagues. I think you are far from help my young friend. We'll deal with that another day. There is medical help on the way. Now, what is your name?"

Saban's eyelids were scarlet and filling with tears. He felt as if he had limited time and began to pray and ask for his mother, Christina.

As Cade watched him slip in and out of consciousness, he recalled the last conversation he had had with Valentin.

"OK. What is your uncle's name?"

"Niculcea. Valentin Niculcea."

Cade looked up at Daniel and raised his eyebrows.

"Then you are with friends. Relax, try not to move. But before you do any of that, I need to know where they are heading and what the plans are. And I need to know that right now."

Saban could hear his voice rasping. He was afraid the clicking in his speech was caused by internal bleeding. But as much as he feared death, he also knew he had to help the man kneeling at his side.

"They are heading to France. Constantin is the leader. I sent you a text..."

"Where in France?"

"Just France. Then home to Romania to live as heroes. Jackdaw said they can keep the diamonds."

"Diamonds?" It was new information for Cade and Daniel.

"Yes. We took them from the jewellery company. Everyone had three or four. And the boxes. And some cash." He took a shallow breath, terrified of drawing in too much air.

"They all had some. The group will split up once it gets to the other side. And in a few months we will all be famous, like your Robin Hood. Stealing from the rich, to give to the poor."

He was drifting in and out of consciousness, his eyes closing and his head dropping, snapping his neck backwards in response.

Flashing beacons from the English side of the tunnel gave Cade some hope. A paramedic crew was arriving but had remained a few hundred metres away for their own safety.

Smith called up his own control room, and the police vehicle that had accompanied the medical staff. "It's clear. Get them here ASAP – we've got a serious casualty, accidentally run over by one of our own cars."

Cade was doing his own back-slapping now, firmly tapping Smith on the back as he moved off, via the prone revolver and towards the service tunnel exit.

"I'll leave you with it Ken. Job well done. You coming, JD?"

"I suspect I have little choice. Does that thing have any rounds left?"

Cade carefully handled the firearm. On any other day, he would have taken time to admire the thing – a Russian Nagant 1895 revolver.

He could see that it contained rounds, but struggled to work out how the thing actually worked. It was rudimentary but had effectively drilled a hole through his windscreen so he was cautiously handling it.

He pulled at a rod at the front of the weapon and could see that eventually he would work out how to load it, but with limited time and even more limited ammunition he knew it was futile. What he wouldn't give for a Glock and seventeen fresh rounds.

The revolver was a much-loved, hand-me-down from the former Soviet military. Saban had been handed it, wrapped in an old T-shirt, and told that it was fully loaded. All he had to do lewas pull the heavy double-action trigger and hope it did its job.

In its day it was one of the few revolvers that could be suppressed and with practically no gas escaping and a chamber that retained cartridge cases it was considered an ideal assassin's handgun.

It had been handed to him because it had no serial number and its only known history was in the late 1940s in a best-forgotten, pre-communist Romania. As such, it made it an ideal weapon to leave behind.

They left the scene and made their way down a smaller tunnel, turning right and into another, even smaller one. About two metres in height and a metre across, it seemed claustrophobic in comparison.

It was lit, but only for about thirty metres. They walked quietly, Cade in front, handgun up and in the ready position.

The pathway was damp in places, and in others wet. A sideways glance at the walls made them both realise that they were now in a chalk tunnel. The rock was white, but not pure as one would imagine, it was tainted with green algae and there was a fusty smell, as if they had stepped into a Napoleonic escape tunnel from the early eighteen hundreds. They existed along the south coast of Britain, so it wasn't beyond the realms of possibility.

What they were inside was an earlier tunnel – a trial run that had been aborted and the further they progressed the less they could see, and the more confined it seemed to become. Cade sensed that they were walking in a westerly direction, but slightly uphill. He slowed his pace slightly, aware that he was starting to leave Daniel behind.

"You OK?"

"Yep."

"And the truth?"

"I hate confined spaces, Jack. Goes back to childhood, I

think my mother tried to dispose of me in a forest one night. But let's press on."

"Go back. I can deal with this. Round up the troops and head to France. We can hopefully cut the bastards off at the pass."

"And leave my junior man to fight with them on the way? If you think that, then why are you walking down this tunnel? Surely you would..."

Cade held up a hand. Then placed his index finger to his lips. He didn't need to do another thing.

They stood, trying to silence their breathing, and waited a moment. Without phone coverage and no radio, which might have had the same issues, they were technically up the proverbial creek without the legendary paddle, or in their particular case, hundreds of feet below the channel, in a side tunnel, unarmed and without so much as a torch.

Cade was focused on the task, but starting to question his motives.

Was this in danger of becoming personal? He knew it was a past tense question.

There was a definite noise, somewhere in the distance, but this was a massive operation; a network of tunnels, of engineering, and trains, pumps, fans and hydraulic rams and rods and doors. Noise was a pre-requisite.

What both men heard was human. And it was getting further away.

"Come on let's go." Cade was off again, checking his footsteps, trying to be as quiet as possible but also avoiding the now hazardous path.

Ahead he could make out an opening to the left and another to the right. The place was a warren, and neither had a map. Ten paces into each there was a door.

Cade flipped a metaphorical coin and said in a whisper, "Heads."

He went left.

As he got to the door he realised, even in the half-light, that it was locked. It looked as if it hadn't been opened in twenty years.

Daniel approached the door, a simple green-painted metal panel with a correspondingly modest handle. A white painted code had been templated onto it some years before. As he gently turned the handle, the door flew towards him, its edge striking him to the side of his right eye and scraping the skin away before sending him crashing backwards off the chalk wall.

He was stunned by the speed of the event. For a second he was unsteady and bent double. He tried to grab hold of the person in front of him, but he was struggling to process the incident.

Cade ran to the door expecting to see the back of Daniel's attacker, but what he saw was the face and body of a large male. He had no idea, even as a professional witness how tall the man was, his best description might be 'towering'.

Other than 'very tall and broad' he knew he needed somehow to counter the threat of the man that was now punching Daniel and at the same time struggling to fit in the narrowing passageway.

Two blows had landed. The first to the left side of the head the second a short, sharp jab to the side of his abdomen, forcing air out of his body and later described over a medicinal single malt as similar to being kicked by a distrustful mule that had just found out its partner was having an affair with a far more attractive horse.

Daniel was trying to get back on his feet. Like all police

staff, he knew the worst place to be was on the ground. Get up. Get back on your feet and if you can't work at arm's length then get in close and start causing some pain. It was all very well in training and it had been a while.

Cade was looking for weapons of opportunity. The tunnel was clear. An axe would be nice, or even a lump of rock. After all he was surrounded by the bloody stuff. Nothing.

The problem he was facing was how to get past Daniel. He grabbed hold of him and started to drag him back towards the main passage, hoping that the noise might attract some new arrivals from the police. It mattered not which country they came from – at that precise moment he didn't have a clue whether he was in England or France and more importantly, didn't care, there was language aplenty and none of it Anglo Saxon.

The male continued to strike Daniel, who let out a series of painful exclamations. He had time to hold an internal conversation or two.

'This bastard is rather strong. Now might be a good time for Cade to shoot him, perhaps?'

Whether Daniel had telepathically transmitted that thought would never be known, but it brought Cade to his senses. Here he was scrabbling around for a weapon when all the time he was clinging onto one, there, in his hand. He had even tried to hit the male with it. If it wasn't so ridiculous it would be funny.

He raised the gun up into the aim, wrapped his hands around it, targeted the central mass on the unknown male and pulled the trigger. The male kept punching Daniel as if nothing had happened. And it hadn't. Cade was still pulling the bloody thing, the trigger weight felt close to four ton. Were these Russian troops born with a grip that could arm-wrestle a yeti? It wasn't what he said but with time and a different environment might have been.

He pulled the trigger again. The second attempt was successful, if success can be measured in hitting one of your own. The round pierced the top layer of Daniel's jacket and rammed home to the right of the target's windpipe, scattering itself throughout his upper chest, dragging bone and chaos with it as it frantically sought an exit point.

The unknown offender dropped immediately. There was no theatrical delay, clutching at the wound or staggering back and forth. He just slumped to the side and onto Daniel. He was bleeding heavily from the entry wound, a darkened access point to the inner workings of a previously powerful, healthy young male. His raised heart rate and adrenaline had actually helped to end his fight. A pity he would never see his family again.

Daniel was furious. Furious that he had been shot – although Cade was sure he would later see the funny side of it, but more so because he was now trapped, underground and claustrophobically-clawing at the hundred kilos of solid corpse that pinned him unceremoniously to the ground in his favourite Aqua Scutum suit.

Cade dragged the male away, checked his pulse and knew his actions would lead to an alpine region of paperwork, and an inquiry that would last months. And then more paperwork.

Fortune favours the brave and in his case, despite appearing unprofessional, he was pleased to see that Napoleon had not thought to install cameras and that there was only one other witness. And moreover, the nameless offender broke the golden rule by trying to throttle his friend and boss. You play with fire…

Praying that back up would follow them and locate the body, they moved forwards.

"You OK?"

"You shot me. This is my favourite suit."

"It didn't match the shirt to be fair. Seriously John, there's a hint of blood there, are you OK to carry on?"

"Is the Pope?" It wasn't religious in any way.

Cade laughed. "That's the way, mate. Come on, let's go and cause some havoc."

"I'm sweating like a bullet in a china shop, Jack." The mixed metaphor should have concerned Cade, it was a sign that all was not well with his boss.

CHAPTER 31

Almost eight hundred kilometres south of the tunnel, Valentin Niculcea was hurriedly driving his aging Citroen along the grass runway near the small French village of St Helene.

Alongside him, in the passenger seat, were two large boxes. They both contained chemical glow sticks. The first box green, the second, red.

Each stick was nearly a foot long. He broke them in turn, as he did so the two compartments within released chemical compounds, diphenyl oxalate and a dye to create the colour and in the second compartment Hydrogen Peroxide.

Merely breaking the glass led to the colourful reaction, and the outside temperature, being cold, allowed the chemical process to last longer and thus met his needs.

He drove as fast as he could, the green sticks were dropped to his left, paced as far apart as he could accurately drop them until he reached the end of the strip. He turned and repeated the process, illuminating the left side in bright red.

It was hardly London Heathrow, but it gave the inbound pilot a chance.

Maria Anghel gently banked the aircraft, reduced her speed and scanned the ground. Villages to the left and right of the runway announced their presence, a glowing window here, a street light there. A car, now and then, moving from A to B. In the distance Bordeaux with its modern, effective runway system was teasing her constantly. She wished she could land there, taxi to a remote part of the airfield and lock the plane down, taxi again, this time to a hotel and sink into a deep bath and wash away the stress of the day.

And stress was at the forefront of her mind. What was she thinking?

She was planning to land a twin-engine aircraft onto a grass runway at night. A grass runway that she had never landed at before. In the dark.

Her fear was not her ability, but the stress on the under-carriage and the propeller clearance on the Piper. If the surface was not level, she could easily strike the blades and at the speed she would be landing, it would be at best, disastrous.

She turned to Stefanescu.

"I cannot afford to land my plane here. We need to get clearance to land at Bordeaux. This is not safe."

Stefanescu had been catching up on some sleep. He woke with a start, allowed his heart rate to settle, and then spoke.

"Maria. You came highly recommended. You agreed to take on this task. I paid you more than adequately. I think you should concentrate on getting us safely down, then we can negotiate."

He had the upper hand. In his mind.

"No. That is not how it is going to happen. If I call up the tower at Bordeaux, they will ask questions – and then there will be some explaining to do. But at least we will live. It is down to you."

Hewett was now very much awake too. Never a natural passenger – in any vehicle – he preferred to be in control. He went to speak but was cut off by his associate.

"Then what do you require, Miss Anghel? How much, seeing as though this is no longer about your skill."

"Your psychology will not work. I am still in control here."

"How much?" His voice had changed, more demanding now and not a little concerned about the consequences of colliding with the ground at over a hundred miles an hour.

"Fifty thousand."

"Done. Now land this plane whilst I still find your audacity amusing."

She had to smile quietly to herself. Playing men off against each other was nothing if not rewarding. So far both Stefanescu and the much more endearing Mr Blake had paid her to rid England of the annoyingly handsome Hewett. Oh well, you have to speculate...

She banked the aircraft, scanned the horizon one last time and trusted what her instruments told her and began to reduce altitude.

She pulled back on the throttle and eased back on the control wheel. Her speed reduced. She wanted it to be around 80 knots. Hewett wanted it to be a lot lower, and ideally, now.

"This is not good. We need to get this thing down!"

He leaned forward and removed the screwdriver from his pocket. One swift strike would render Stefanescu immobile, along with his existing injury he wouldn't be able to fight back. He was sure he could throw him out of the aircraft, either during the flight or once they had landed. The latter seemed more palatable. A rapid financial negotiation with the female would enable them to get airborne immediately and fly to Bordeaux where he could hopefully convince the authorities that he had been kidnapped – and somehow build a case for the defence.

"Calm down, Johnathan. Maria is more than capable, you will only make her nervous and that will not be good for any of us. Once we land, you can kiss the ground or jam that screwdriver into my neck or whatever else you have planned – for now just strap yourself in and act like a man. And John."

He looked forlornly at his associate. "Yes?"

"I really wouldn't do the whole airborne flight or fight scene. You are hardly Bruce Willis. And besides, we are allies. I am hurt. How little you think of me, such shallow words back in England."

It was now or never.

He had unbuckled and edged forward. He grabbed hold of Stefanescu by the throat and squeezed until he could feel a strong pulse. His other arm gripped the Romanian's forearm, causing instant pain.

The strength of the Romanian's counter-attack took Hewett by surprise. He held the advantage, being at waist height he had him firmly in his grasp, increasing the grip on his testicles by the second, causing him to cry out in agony. Stefanescu knew they were seconds away from bursting – it was gladiatorial but effective.

Stefanescu hissed at Hewett. "Let go now. You don't

want to do this."

Hewett replied in an equally serpent-like voice, which in any other circumstances would have been almost amusing.

"You betrayed me, you bastard. I gave you everything and you..."

"No. I bailed you out of your family debt. How does that make me...?"

It was a Mexican stand-off and Anghel had heard enough. She jerked the controls sharply, throwing Hewett backwards and into the fuselage, cracking his head against the Perspex window. Stefanescu jolted against the seatbelt and cursed as his arm jarred, opening up the existing wound and allowing it to bleed once more. It seemed like weeks since that idiot Cade had shot at him at the river.

To make matters worse, the black Pelican cases were now free of their location and sliding up and down the aisle. One struck Hewett's foot, slamming it into the seat frame.

"For Christ's sake. Can anything else go bloody wrong today?"

Anghel fought to control both the passengers and her aircraft.

She yelled at them, "You are like children. You should be ashamed. Both of you. Do you want to get us killed?"

Silence.

Actually, she could hear the men breathing, which unfortunately meant that at least one of them was alive.

She pulled the carburettor heat switch out towards her and lowered the landing gear. Ahead she could now see the runway, hardly Charles de Gaulle, but better than an emergency landing in a field with headlights – and having done that once she vowed it would never happen again.

Hewett had gone beyond panic, beyond anger. And he had played his cards too openly too. It wasn't in his nature to run away, but it was even further from the norm to grab the pilot and fly the bloody plane into the ground. Whichever bridge he was on right now, he would need to cross it and hope for the best.

The way the injured Stefanescu was looking at him, the best option didn't bode well at all. And yet there was something that told him that his co-passenger could have caused him more damage, even with one arm tied behind his back. He had stopped first. Why?

It felt like the plane was dropping all the time. It was. She was back in control and now revelling in the moment. She picked a spot on the runway, illuminated by her meagre lighting, adjusted the aircraft's nose, balanced the throttle and allowed the Piper wheels to contact the dry grassy surface. It began to bounce, Hewett gripped onto anything stable and quietly prayed as the French scenery rushed past, bright green markers flashing in his peripheral vision.

Another heavier bounce and the Piper was on terra firma. It just needed the front wheel to make contact. The old adage about any landings being good was probably being recited in Anghel's mother tongue.

She pushed the pedals, braking the aircraft, reducing their speed, but to the passengers it was still too fast. They were used to jets and their rapid deceleration.

Steering it down the runway towards the white car that lay ahead and off to her left, her speed was in fact reducing all the time, but the aircraft was noisy in such a generally quiet rural area. If the locals weren't awake, they were now.

The Chieftain came to the end of the runway. She turned it around and lined it up with the centre line. The Lycoming engines were ticking over and she was ready to discharge her passengers and cargo and leave France as soon as possible. Her relationship with this team was over.

"Welcome to France. I have no idea what this is all about, but it is time for you to leave," she said coldly. "Walk behind the aircraft and make sure you pay me what you owe me." In truth, she didn't care anymore – they had already paid her well for her time.

Valentin left the relative calm of the Citroen and using its headlights for guidance walked towards the men who were already stood by three black cases. One of the males was favouring his arm, a darkened patch of blood obvious to anyone that was stood on a grass runway in southern France at such a ridiculous hour.

He spotted the eyes straight away, so the other one must be Hewett. He looked different in the dark; dishevelled, away from home, from the city and the protective layer provided by the British Foreign Office.

Hewett was rubbing the back of his head and checking for blood. Valentin had no idea what had happened during the flight and didn't care, but curiosity got the better of him.

"Gentlemen. A turbulent flight?" His smile lit up the surrounding area more than his rudimentary runway. It also revealed the pistol in his right hand. He held it with a gentle grip, it was more accurate that way. Both men saw it. So did the pilot.

"I'm going, clear the runway."

As she reached the door to climb back on board Stefanescu called over to her.

"Hey. Thank you. I will recommend your services to anyone. You will be paid what we agreed, no more. However, if you make contact with me soon I will provide you with enough opportunities for a wonderful future. Until then, take care up there." It seemed genuine. Perhaps she would see him again. Most likely she wouldn't.

Valentin watched her fasten the door, take her seat and

start the process all over again, building up the power until she began to roll down the grass runway.

He shouted over the noise. His handgun was more evident now, in the favoured Sul position, held close to his torso but ready to use in a split second.

He spoke in English but looked through his audience.

"You will put those cases in the car. Then we will move to a safer location. From there we will sort out what we do with the one among you who has betrayed the government that I work for, and then, how to get you back into their custody. Local French police staff are travelling to us now. I should not have to tell you that I will shoot first and won't ask questions later."

He looked at the two males who seemed to be oblivious to the fact that the Piper had thundered down the runway and lifted off into the night, heading for a safer local airport with a plausible story in exchange for fuel and a tarmac runway.

With the cases on board and the hatch closed, Valentin continued.

"The British government has asked me to take care of you. It recognises your service, the risks that you have taken, and also for recovering the packages from London."

Neither male spoke back, allowing Valentin to continue. It was Hewett that looked confused, but he was growing in stature. He nodded, affirming he was listening and encouraging the unknown armed male to continue. Perhaps there was some hope? He was speaking in accented English, after all.

"Mr Stefanescu, if you would be so kind." He handed him a set of Speedcuffs and gestured towards Hewett, who looked as if his own mother had betrayed him.

"What? What in God's name are you doing? I am the

one who works for the British bloody government! I am British! I am well respected by the Foreign Office. Just ring them! And who the hell are you to tell me what will and will not happen?"

The handgun was now pointing at Hewett.

"Yes, Mr Hewett, you are British. The rest is past tense. And my name is irrelevant. Needless to say, the British government considers me an ally – and has done since I first played chess with them many years ago."

Hewett was growing angrier by the second, now manacled, he lifted his chin up and spoke in a public school voice, clear and precise.

"I play chess too Mr...?"

"Nice. Old school, but nice. I told you, names are not important, Johnathan."

Sensing defeat, he tried once more. "Then if you won't allow me to know your name perhaps you would be brave enough to outline where exactly he, and you and I sit on the chessboard?"

Valentin pushed Hewett into the back seat, shielding his head from further injury. As I said to another keen player not long ago, "I am the Queen, I move where I want, in any direction."

Valentin got into the driver's seat with Stefanescu behind him, sat alongside Hewett.

"It's OK, Johnnie. Trust me. We had to bring you here, to get you away from London, and importantly my dear older brother. He would just play with you until you gave up every secret of the British government. There is a lot to learn about him. But, as you may have discovered tonight, there is more to learn about me. More than you, or Mr Cade or his devoted team at Scotland Yard can ever know. You see, we all swim in the same cesspool Johnnie...it really depends on who with and how much you are prepared to breathe."

Hewett was exhausted but had reserves that he now called on.

"I have no idea what you are...on about. I work for the British Foreign Office. I was sent to investigate the rise in thefts from British banks..."

Stefan held up a hand until Hewett stopped speaking.

"John. We both know that is not true. Are you telling me you are some sort of double agent? This is the stuff of spy novels. Wouldn't you agree, Valentin?"

The driver smiled and continued on his course to his home in the woods.

"No John, you see the truth is you are in debt, probably to more people than just Alex Stefanescu and not just financially. But you allowed yourself to become a customer of my brother and his. How can I put this, unofficial bank, correct? And in doing so you became a plaything of his – and they normally end up dead. Trust me on this – they really do."

"But you said, back there, that you work for the British? I'm tired but this makes no sense, and won't do when I am rested."

"You expect me to just tell you everything? Naïve at best, my friend. Naïve. No, close your eyes, we have a short drive, then we can eat and all will be revealed."

"Tell me what is going on. Please." Hewett sounded desperate.

Stefan tapped Hewett on the leg. "It is not wise to make war with your brothers in arms..."

Hewett stared out of the car window into a dense forest and began to rewind the previous few days and weeks. Dire straits indeed.

CHAPTER 32

"You must feel better for some food and refreshment, Mr Hewett."

It was Valentin that was speaking now. His English was accented but had a hint of private school. He was entirely self-taught, like most of his skills his linguistics had been honed by years of necessity.

He took a sip of a local red and continued. "There are some things that can never be explained – every government has a need to know policy, as a Foreign Office worker you of all people should know that. In the case before you it is so overly complex that even bite-sized pieces would make an elephant difficult to digest."

Hewett was still cuffed but able to use his hands – to a point. He drank some water, wanting to retain as much of his faculties as possible.

"I am cleared to an extraordinarily high level, there is nothing you cannot discuss with me, if, as you suggest, you are employed by the same government as me." Hewett was digging into his reserves and past training. He was known for his negotiation skills as well as his rather charming manner.

"Not in this case, John. Sorry. Even we only have limited access. What I can tell you is that you have wandered carelessly into a swamp from which there appears no way out of."

"For Christ's sake, will you just spell it out in words of simple syllables – I haven't slept in days and..."

"John, the Clownfish has a special relationship with the Sea Anemone. In exchange for shelter, the Clownfish protects the anemone and preens it of parasites."

Hewett banged his head on the white kitchen table. "Are you not listening? It's all fucking riddles. Tell me how much trouble I'm in and what I need to do to get out of it. Or shoot me now. Please."

"If you would allow my colleague to finish." It was a partly rested Stefanescu, cleaned of dried blood and looking a little brighter for nourishment. "We are the Clownfish Johnathan. The British government is the Anemone. Simple enough?"

"Oh well, thank you both for an enlightening National Geographic documentary on the life of the Great bloody Barrier Reef. I feel I can sleep tonight!"

"Sarcasm becomes you, it really does." Stefan was smiling and forcing more food into his mouth, knowing that it might be awhile before they ate again.

"The bank attacks in London and the English counties?"

"Go on," replied a barely interested Hewett.

"They are my brother's rather elaborate game – a way of luring the other fish out of their safe harbour and into the path of the sharks."

"Do you know what gentlemen, I've heard enough." Hewett pulled at his cuffs and tried to stand, but Valentin simply jammed his foot across the top of Hewett's own. He held his gaze long enough to enforce the point.

Stefanescu waited for silence. "The money was useful, after all, every criminal loves nothing more than cash and it makes the world go around. But he has enough. Obscene actually, he has notoriety too, but what he craves the most is respect. He is surrounded by opulence and whores, and dare I use another marine analogy...leeches?"

He finished off the block of cheese and drained his wine glass. "And you, in a moment of weakness provided him with an opportunity to gain total respect from his own country and yours too. Great Britain with its ceremony and reputation. And you knew the whereabouts of two things that could drag it into the cesspool along with everyone else. Not jewels or inappropriate photographs of a princess, but documents, two to be precise."

Hewett knew that they held the winning hand.

"Your brother gave me no choice."

"No, you had every choice available to a man in your position. All you had to do was say no, or admit to your country that you were in debt. You were such a champion, a rising star, they would probably have given you the money!"

"So now what?" Hewett tried to be resolute, but his limited audience could see he was failing.

It was Stefan who spoke first. "Now, you have to find a way of closing Pandora's famous box. You need to work with us. Johnathan, you have become a link, you could say a degree of separation. I am sure you have heard of the famous Hungarian and his theory of inter-connectivity?"

"Of course, I am quite intelligent you know."

"Absolutely you are. Now, we all need some sleep. But before we do, indulge me, would you?" Stefanescu looked at him through bi-coloured eyes, picking food out of his teeth with his investigative tongue.

"Mr Cade is the first degree. Miss Nikolina was the second. Her daughter the third. A man who is known to you in the Foreign Office, he's the fourth. And I am the fifth which if my rudimentary mathematics allows...makes you the sixth."

"But you have left out one key person in this fool proof equation of yours, Stefan. Your brother."

Stefan laughed. "Hardly. My brother Alex is the seventh. That goes without saying."

"But there is no such thing as seven degrees of separation."

"Oh, trust me, there is now."

Cade pushed forward along the off-white tunnel until he reached another door. He could feel a draught through the gaps, not dissimilar to the last time he was in a tunnel, desperately trying to track down his other partner in crime: Detective Sergeant Jason Roberts.

For a split second, he thought about him and how he was. How O'Shea was. How he has missed at least one funeral and how his arse still burned like crazy from the gravel rash injury he had endured. When was that exactly? The week before, the one before that? And why did it appear that everything happened to him?

Daniel was alongside him now and had broken the chain of thought.

He whispered, "Anything?"

Cade shook his head and eased open the door. He could hear a mechanical noise, a deep, guttural metal on metal sound. The change in air pressure shocked him. The locomotive, a Class 9, built expressly for the Euro Tunnel operation, was immense, more so given he was stood just below the level of the track.

He fell back, almost into Daniel's arms, and then grabbed hold of the ducting that ran through the tunnel. They were in a service door and looking out into the main train network that linked France to England. The train was massive, the tunnel immense. It dwarfed the service tunnel that they had previously been in, and both men felt insignificant.

Cade knew the Eurostar trains could travel at high speed – he thought around one hundred and fifty miles an hour – he was short by twenty, but assumed that in the tunnel the locomotives would have to slow down for safety reasons. They did, to a steady hundred miles an hour. And the one that had just roared past him was about a metre away. He could have easily touched it or been consumed by the airflow and dragged under its wheels.

It banked slightly around a curve. It was then both men heard the first crack, a sound like a shotgun or a demolition blasting cap. In the confines of the concrete tube the noise was heightened. For some reason, call it grass roots policing. They ran out into the tunnel, onto the narrow walkway and allowed curiosity and instinct to draw them along the underground passageway.

The noise was repeated five times. Each sound was the explosion of a track safety device, hurriedly laid on the track by Constantin, who waited ahead with his team. It was the last of his old-school chemistry set that he had carried for days, guarding it for just this occasion.

A sizeable piece of metal had also been draped across the line, and a small cloud of smoke was visible. To the driver, at speed and approaching the hazard quickly, it looked as if the roof had collapsed but he knew this was impossible. He was already braking hard when another series of devices set off additional charges, which in turn initiated smoke. In a tunnel smoke is the first alarm flag, and often where there is smoke, there is fire.

By the time the first carriage had struck the caps, the driver had applied the brakes. He knew there were no engineers working on the line, and a gut feeling told him something was wrong.

The smoke was rising up and encompassing the carriages before he even had chance to radio his control room. He couldn't see flames, but in a tunnel your instructions were clear. Get out and stay out. Let the system do its job.

They had trained for this moment repeatedly. Previous fires in tunnels around the world had caused havoc and claimed many lives and the channel tunnel was no exception when it came to risk. With a clear line of communication to the central control team, the driver edged the train forward, through the enveloping, dark grey smoke until he reached the bright yellow hydraulic door that he knew would lead his passengers to safety.

With alarms activated, the response from both sides of the channel was rapid and effective. Fire, police and ambulance staff were despatched, emergency sprinkler systems and extraction devices were automatically employed and already inhaling the gases as staff implemented the heavily drilled response programmes.

As the first of the four hundred passengers left the train and entered the cross tunnel system, those that were left in Constantin's group mingled and blended, effectively disappearing.

Quickly through the door the passengers entered a clean air bubble and were protected from inhalation and although now in the more cramped conditions of the service tunnel they were safe. British, French, American, Eastern European, there were people of all races and all became one, shuffling to the orders of one man in a high-visibility vest.

Further back down the tunnel a small group of vehicles were parked up, a man lay on the ground with police around him. It didn't appear to be the tunnel company's most fortuitous day.

"Boss, you follow the crowd. I'm staying this side. Call it gut instinct."

Inside the main tunnel, Constantin Nicolescu was regaining his breath. He had been affected by the initial fire and dense smoke, all of it caused by his own party piece diversion. He was back on board the train, invisible now and hiding from the inevitable authorities – and one in particular. Would he ever give up?

Locking himself in the toilet, he leant against the wall and caught a glimpse of himself in the mirror. He looked drawn, grey and in desperate need of food and water. It was a blessing that he didn't crave the drugs that had ruled his life for so long. It had been days now, and he seemed to be coping without the euphoria they provided. How long it would last, he had no idea. He just needed to avoid Cade and his agenda-fuelled quest for vengeance.

He started laughing, adrenaline often did that. Then he held a whispered conversation with himself, still looking in the mirror.

'To be fair, you did damage his colleague. I can still hear his arm snapping when your foot plunged through it. Snap! And what about the others that you shot at? Complete strangers. What has become of you Nicolescu – son of Nicolae?'

He sipped some water from the tap and ran the remainder over his face.

'And then there was the girl. She is probably dead. Probably. Whore deserved it. But why?'

He couldn't remember why he had even entered the Old Queen Street property. Perhaps they were right, those many people who had warned him about the impact of controlled drugs on the human mind.

'Why was I even there?'

It was revenge. Nothing more. To harm his woman is to harm him.

His head nodded, and he slumped onto the seat and drifted into a micro sleep.

Within half an hour the bulk of the passengers had been screened and escorted back towards the train, assured that there were no problems and that the explosions they had heard were errant track warning devices, left in situ by forgetful engineers. With food vouchers and a discount on future travel, all appeared content to be marshalled back through the tunnel and onto the train bound for the continent.

The small police and tunnel team that had arrived to carry out the rudimentary security checks had been briefed. They knew what they were looking for. CCTV footage had supported that two of the group were now technically in the custody of the Kent Police, they just needed to sort the wheat from the chaff and the living from the dead.

Dragos Saban was en route to William Harvey Hospital, under guard and pleading for his freedom and a rapid recovery from the injuries he had sustained, which were somewhat unfairly caused when the Englishman Cade had deliberately driven into him.

The other male from the footage had been identified and was being photographed in situ, bent double in a side tunnel having been shot in the chest. Local detectives were already keeping the scene sterile and gathering what evidence they could of a potential police shooting. On the face of it, with the testimony of an acting inspector and a detective chief inspector, it would appear to be a prima facie case of self-defence.

That left two or possibly three males. Two were found in among the group as they re-boarded the train. Dropping a bag containing a Romanian passport and a handful of diamonds had eased the investigation somewhat. The other, tried just too hard not to be suspicious and in doing so stood out to an exhausted Cade, who even whilst being questioned by his colleagues about the earlier bedlam was able to differentiate between a legitimate train passenger and a sweating, overtly guilty criminal.

He pointed and shouted to a 'black-pyjama' wearing firearms officer. "That's one there. He's your man!"

The fact that two men ran in different directions caused consternation for the combined British and French police staff that were now on scene. It would transpire that the first ran because he knew they were likely to shoot him, the second because he was wanted on a fines warrant at a British magistrate's court and had failed to tell the most important person in the equation, his wife. Of the chaos in the tunnel, he was completely innocent.

A suitably attired police officer with a Heckler & Koch rifle hanging across his chest would later say to Daniel.

"Your man here didn't have a ticket either, guv – so it was hardly twenty-first century policing!"

Cade walked quietly along the concrete safety platform that separated tunnel workers from a gruesome collision with a high-speed train. He was happier that his boss was with other people, and potentially with medics. He didn't look too bright. That said, he knew he should also be with other police staff. Searching the tunnel for Constantin on his own was increasing his risk, but in a way it had been deliberate. He had consciously allowed himself to be separated from the pack. It made it a fair fight.

He used the steel rail to support himself, dragging his exhausted frame along and through what remained of the dense smoke. The system was indeed effective. In only a few minutes, it was clearing the tunnel. Now all that remained was a solitary police officer, thousands of tons of curved concrete, a resting locomotive and, betting his pension on it – the remaining offender.

John "Jack" Cade took a moment to count his friends, recall his last few weeks and the series of events that had injured him and his colleagues, and claimed the lives of people that had tried to make a difference. He stood still for a moment longer, checked the firearm and assumed he had one round left, then climbed up and into the train. There was nowhere else to hide – he had to be on board.

'I'm coming for you, you bastard.'

It was ludicrously late in London when Detective Sergeant Jason Roberts had finally got home. His wife had arrived to pick him up and lovingly tipped him into the passenger seat of their private car.

Before he had left the hospital he insisted on calling in to the guarded side ward, checking on his most valuable staff member O'Shea. He had introduced himself to Tony Hay, the casualty officer who seemed to live at the place.

"Well?" Four letters that replaced a thousand words.

"Pretty outstanding actually Jason." Hay's words had taken Roberts by surprise.

Roberts pulled the doctor to one side.

"I was told she wouldn't make it. You know, call the family, plan for the worst – I can't lose two staff in one month," he whispered, causing the Canadian medic to smile.

"I can bloody well hear you...boss – I haven't even got any fuckin' grapes and you are planning my funeral. I mean what's going on here?" It was an equally quiet sentence, but she was speaking. She was alive. He needed to call Cade immediately.

Cade could feel the vibration in his pocket. He'd forgotten about the phone, he'd actually forgotten about everything 'normal', marooned underground and in a subterranean nightmare.

It rang again. This time he let it go to answerphone – the caller would have to wait. If it was important, they would leave a message, along with the other three hundred that he was sure he had received over the last twenty-four hours. He grunted quietly at the thought of his overtime claim. It was an amused grunt as he wasn't paying the bill.

The phone buzzed once more. The message had come through.

"Jack, it's me, Ginger. No idea where you are. You could

be in bloody Bucharest by now for all I know. Anyway, the missus has picked me up and I'm heading home. I'll be in a cast for a few weeks, I've gone for my team's colours. The doc is happy with the job he's done, says I'll be able to play the violin after all. Right, give me a bell when you've done whatever it is you are doing and Jack, some good news. Carrie is conscious and being really offensive. All for now, bye, bye, bye....bye."

At the Foreign Office in Central London Michael Blake had closed the drawer on his desk, switched the table lamp off and took one last look out across the walkway and out into the great city of London. A text message lit up the screen on his Blackberry and partially illuminated his desk.

'We have the package. It will be released soon.'

A simple message that allowed the senior advisor to the British government to push back, close the door on his office, locking it securely behind him and in minutes head out in to the night air.

'Don't let me down.'

Cade had little idea of the time, the days had blended into one, existing on coffee and take away food he realised that sooner or later he would give in to the tidal pull of sleep deprivation.

The train was still lit but was understandably quiet. He knew that it wouldn't be long before the passengers would be allowed to re-board. There was nowhere to hide. The seats did not allow for places to secrete anything, let alone a body. The only place would be the toilets, or, further ahead, the driver's cabin. But he assumed that would be locked.

The first toilet was showing vacant, but he eased the door open, stepping back and pointing the gun into the space. Vacant indeed. He edged down the carriage and into the buffet area, all polished chrome and wooden highlights. Into another carriage, this one more upmarket.

Nothing.

Through a door and into a standard cabin he could see for about fifty metres. At the end, another toilet cubicle waited to be searched.

Constantin shuddered awake. His heart pumping overtime. He tried to stand but staggered slightly. He forced himself to breathe and waited. Everything told him it was Cade.

Leather soles crept across brown industrial floor covering, step by step. Cade was convinced he was making a noise as loud as the train itself, but each step was tactical, gently onto his toes, holding the weapon in the low-ready.

He approached the door, as he did so it swung open. He grabbed it and tried to push it back, but Constantin was out and running down the aisle towards the next set of doors. He prayed that his instinct was right, that Cade wouldn't shoot him in the back. A British police officer would never do that.

Cade brought the pistol up and into the aim.

"Armed police. Stop or I will shoot!"

He kept running.

Cade started to run after him, cursing conventions. They reached the door between the next two carriages. It was shut and locked.

Constantin started to kick it and punch it with his fists. He stopped and turned around. He was cornered. The mighty lion, now a faded street cat, destined to end his days in prison, lured into depraved acts just to lead an existence.

Not again.

He ran at Cade. 'Shoot me if you must, but do it with one round.'

The aging pistol came up and Cade challenged him once more.

A human can close down the gap on his aggressor very quickly, especially if the aggressor knows he or she is about to end someone's life. There is always the chance that the person with the weapon will freeze, just stare at the target and hope it will all just go away.

Cade waited for Constantin to get within ten metres and fired. The Nagant revolver kicked like a wilful child at bedtime, putting one round straight through the door, before releasing the last of the seven rounds, which left the barrel and in a fraction of the standard muzzle velocity had reached its target.

It had probably last been fired in anger in a war or rebellion long forgotten, but fire it did. The bullet entered Constantin just above his right hip and sounded like a hammer hitting a piece of over-ripe fruit. The weapon pulled to the left and down; Cade had been aiming for his heart.

What shocked Cade was seeing his target running towards him – and angry. He looked over the weapon and fired again. It was empty. Dropping it onto the floor, he prepared for the collision. Constantin hit him hard. Both men were of a similar build, Cade fitter and younger but still surprised at the force used by the wounded animal who had now driven his attacker back and partly into a chair.

The Romanian's arms were wind-milling now, hitting anything, the chair included. The now-familiar, small, bright blue tattoo was visible on the inside of his right wrist. A wave. A simple curved outline.

He landed a few blows on Cade's jaw and neck before the police officer was able to drive a palm strike up and into his opponent's chin. It forced his head back and gave Cade a second to grab hold of Constantin's face and claw at his eyes.

His screams could be heard by the arriving passengers who were being corralled back to the Eurostar train. As if their day couldn't get better they were now witnessing a fully engaged fight between two males. The one in the seat looked as if he was fighting for his life.

"Stay here! All of you." A constable from the Frontier Ops team had seen it too and was running onto the train, CS spray in hand and wondering just what more the day would bring in the way of better work stories.

Constantin was oblivious, and thrashing out at any part of Cade he could reach. He leaned into him and feeling flesh against his mouth bit down and crushed the skin between his decayed and jagged teeth.

The pain was unbelievable. Cade could feel the teeth sinking into his collarbone, almost ripping out the muscle and nerves that it protected. It was then, somewhere in the distance, he heard the familiar racking of an ASP baton. Metal on metal, sliding open and ready to be used.

'For God's sake, man, use it.'

The Frontier officer didn't issue a warning or say a word. Instinct told him that the taller of the two targets was the aggressor and the third man they were hunting for. He swung the baton over his right shoulder and slammed it into Constantin's left arm. Holding the metal bar in place for a split second transferred some of the force and hurt him even more. With the return strike, swinging past his head, the officer struck again, from left to right hitting him on the right side of his neck. It was enough to bring him to his senses. In fact, it was enough to almost kill him, the bar hitting the carotid sinus area with such force that he became momentarily unconscious. Any harder may have caused him to have a stroke or heart attack.

Cade pushed him off and onto the floor.

"I'm on your side!" He yelled as he struggled for footing.

"I guessed that boss. Either that or I'm a terrible judge of character." He handed his Speedcuffs to Cade who was wiping a trace of blood from his nose. The first link snapped onto Constantin's wrist as Cade pulled the unresponsive right one towards him and locked on the second cuff. He didn't bother to double lock them, caring not if his circulation was cut off.

He lowered his head down and spoke.

"I know you can hear me, you piece of shit. If this officer wasn't here, I'd tie you to the back of this bloody train and deliver you to the custody area myself. I hope you enjoy your time in prison. I may even visit one day just to remind you what freedom is all about. I'll be doing my utmost to make sure you die there."

He looked up at the younger officer, six foot plus, triangular upper body and a well-groomed beard.

"Thanks, pal. Nice work with the baton. I'll make sure when I write this all up that I'll say that I feared death or GBH. I owe you."

"No problem, boss. Your mate said you'd be on the train. It was nice to give the baton a run out, to be honest. First time I've used it other than breaking windows."

He put out his hand and helped Cade to his feet.

"Thanks. Been in long?"

"No sir, I haven't. Two years now."

"Good stuff. Call me Jack."

"Dale Barnett. Nice to meet you, Jack."

"Ever arrested someone for murder, attempted murder,

GBH, firearms offences and driving a vehicle with no insurance?"

"Not yet, boss, no."

"Well, you have now. He's all yours. Could make a name for yourself with this one."

More staff arrived and dragged Constantin unceremoniously along the carpeted floor until they reached the door. Paramedics were called to check him over, it was a necessary gesture before they manacled him to a wheelchair and took him through the cross tunnel to a waiting van.

Cade followed them through the air locked system and met up with Daniel, who had coordinated things the other side. He looked up when he saw Cade approaching.

"Don't tell me, I should see the other guy?"

"Funny."

"What happened?"

"I got thrown off the train for not having a ticket."

He laughed, it was one of those too tired not to laughs.

Twenty minutes later a car pulled up at the rear of the convoy, its driver offering the two Metropolitan Police staff a free ride back to England.

"Just before you go boss, you might want to join an elite club."

He handed Cade a black permanent marker and pointed to the wall. It was covered in modern graffiti. Celebrity names, heads of state, they had all left their mark.

"Thanks, nice gesture. I feel privileged."

He thought for a moment, then wrote a few lines from a poem.

'I know I don't deserve a place among the people here, they never wanted me around, except to calm their fear. Anon.'

"Very poignant boss, there's always a place for humour too, you know."

"True. We often forget that. Can I have that pen again?"

He found a place on the honour's wall and wrote, "Detective Sergeant Jason Roberts Met Pol wasn't here. 2004."

"There you go, I doubt he'll ever get down here to read it, but thanks mate."

Turning to John Daniel he said, "Come on, let's go home, or at least find a bed somewhere, it's been a long...day."

Daniel walked with him, back along the tunnel and towards the White Cliffs of Dover.

"Are there seventy-two hours in a day, Jack?"

Valentin and Stefanescu were as tired as Hewett, but knew that one of them needed to maintain a watchful eye on their captive.

Hewett didn't utter a word over the next four hours, but maintained eye contact with Valentin throughout, hoping, waiting for him to drop off to sleep. When he eventually did, he moved carefully across the lounge area, almost without exhaling, picked up the car key and made his way to the driveway, eased the door open and sat in the worn driver's seat.

Willing the handcuff key to still be in situ, he opened the glove box and there it was. It was an amateur mistake, Hewett had spotted its long black handle the day before and had seen Valentin putting it there among some old bits of paper.

Perhaps his luck was about to change?

He struggled for a while, but using one hand and his mouth he was able to insert the key. Pausing, he turned his hand back towards the cuffs and twisted. Thank God they were placed onto him the way they were. If they had been applied correctly, he would never have been able to remove them.

He put them into the glove box, not knowing if he might need them in the future, and slid the worn car key into the ignition and waited for the diesel glow plug to extinguish. A full tank greeted him. Any second now and he could leave. Once the engine was running, he knew he had to drive as fast and as far as he could, towards the Spanish border and the Sierra Nevada Mountains. It was over a thousand kilometres and an eleven hour drive lay ahead of him, avoiding toll roads and Madrid where there would be cameras. He also knew he would have to steal fuel from somewhere, ideally a remote station with little chance of being caught. Another bridge he'd cross when the time came.

The engine fired into gear and away. Hewett turned left and hoped for the best. It would be hours before he could even begin to relax, watching the fuel, praying the Citroen would get him there, travelling at a speed that covered the miles but didn't attract too much attention in a region where cash might be needed to pay for a ticket or pay off a gendarme.

Back near the French village of St Helene, Valentin walked into a small bedroom and handed Stefanescu a cup of strong coffee and a fresh piece of bread.

"He's gone." It was matter of fact and without a trace of drama.

"Good. I couldn't stand another few hours watching him." They clashed their coffee cups together and smiled.

Valentin went to shower, leaving his associate to get out of his makeshift bed and clear his head of dreams, stretch his battered body as best he could and prepare for the day ahead. Within thirty minutes, both men were sitting at the breakfast bar in the restored gîte and watching the blue dot head south. Using a bastardised pre-launch version of Google Maps, Valentin was able to track the car almost anywhere.

Up, inside the same glove box, Valentin knew that a small device was sending a signal back to the unlikely allies in the British Foreign Office who were now talking to the men on a cell phone.

"He should be south of the Pyrenees by now. If your theory is correct, then he is heading all the way to the coast and hopefully our primary target."

"Indeed. Gentlemen, thank you. We owe you a great deal."

It was Stefanescu who spoke first, hands free.

"Yes, Mr Blake, you do. But my rewards are enough. I have given you my word that I will continue to work with you until you recover what it is you seek. Just make sure you keep your part of the bargain and remove my troublesome brother from society's grasp."

"You have my word. It may take some time, possibly years, but we will resolve this situation – ideally within the bounds of the law. Consider your contracts to be long and prosperous. You will need, at times, to do things that may not be comfortable for you, but that is the drawback of working for two organisations at once. Above all, you need good memories."

"Just pay us what you promised and I will continue to support you. I believe I speak for Mr Valentin too."

"Ah yes, before we finish. Valentin, I can never repay you for your services. Allowing you access to our systems, our cameras, it was a risk you know...but a justifiable one. I trust you. You may have saved a life or two, Mr Cade certainly appreciates what you have done. At least if he had half a clue about your role he would." He laughed down the phone, it was the first humorous moment in a dark couple of weeks.

"Be careful with Mr Cade, sir. He is far brighter than you understand. Cornered animals often are."

"Of course." He discounted Cade immediately. He was a small fish in a much larger body of water. "Our goal, our absolute need, is to ensure those bloody documents stay away from the House, from cabinet and critically, the British press. If they get out, we are all done for. Let's keep the degrees of separation to a minimum, shall we, gentlemen? And when Hewett's back in our custody, I'll go to great lengths to discuss the value of loyalty. Good morning to both of you. I trust the sun is shining wherever you are."

It was rhetorical. He knew exactly where they were. In a game of cat and mouse, he considered himself the feline. Typical of intelligence officers the world over, they both did.

Blake picked up the second phone in his office. An older, simpler affair, but actually far more secure.

"Yes. All is going to plan. Cade and his team have managed to run riot throughout London and the south east and were last seen heading west through the tunnel pursuing a bunch on inbred thieves. It was altogether a wonderful diversion. Keep the media happy at any cost. He'll be feeling quite pleased with himself, no doubt. I have made a request that he receives a commendation and that the operation is terminated forthwith. We have no need for them now."

"Thank you, Michael. Job well done, at least it will be if the last phase goes ahead without a hitch. I have your word?"

"You do minister, yes. Have a good day."

Wheels within wheels − in a concrete shelter, protected from any possible intrusion. Hallowed conversations, deep inside the locked and sterile rooms of the Foreign Office.

Where trust was the only thing on the agenda, and ironically not one person likely to be present trusted the other as far as they could kick them.

That is how Blake saw the operation now. 'No more bloody cock ups! Not a single bloody one.'

In Kent, Daniel and Cade arrived back at the Frontier Operations station after a night in a local Travellodge. Hands were shaken and backs patted as breakfast was devoured. At some point in the future, wooden plaques would be exchanged, inscribed, and hung on walls to commemorate the event.

Police custody staff had accepted the offenders and ensured they were processed and delivered to separate Category A prisons; safe, secure and accessible for future questioning.

Cade and Daniel made countless calls, filled out endless paperwork and provided robust statements, at the very least covering off the incidents and offending in the Channel Tunnel. There would be enquiries, and investigations, and a lot of questions. But for now they were done.

"Let's go home. Right now."

CHAPTER 33

LATE THAT AFTERNOON, THE PLAIN CAR TURNED INTO THE car park of New Scotland Yard. Two men stepped out, shivered in the cold and straightened their suits, which looked like they had spent the night wrapped around their owners. It was an entirely accurate observation.

"Afternoon John. You look like shit." It was an altogether sharper Malcolm Johnson, assistant commissioner and long-time friend of Daniel's.

"It's been a fairly busy few weeks, sir. We are both in need of some R&R. Go easy, please."

"Rest and relaxation J.D. You get that when you retire! Talking of which you must go soon?"

"A while yet Malcolm, working with Jack has made me realise just how much I enjoy the noble art of policing."

"Noble art, my arse! I've got a stack of complaints, invoices and God only knows what else to clear thanks to you and the Operation Breaker team."

"Anything in particular?" asked Daniel more out of curiosity.

"Oh, let me see…I've got a new windscreen for a Hyundai hatchback. That bill came from Kent Police. A forensic bill for at least one police shooting – Kent again. A claim for a new Aqua Scutum suit, three meal claims for fish and chips, four million pound's worth of diamonds and a new set of underpants for a channel tunnel bus driver!"

He stepped in closer, a flicker in his blue-grey eyes.

"Keep it within these four walls. We got most of the diamonds back gents. I got a deal on a new windscreen and if the DCI thinks he's getting a new suit out of me, he can bloody well think again. I'll have it repaired. Now go on, piss off and try to make it to your office without causing any more bloody mayhem. I've got a date with a certain Foreign Office colleague. He sounded bloody furious. Fortunately, it would appear that we are not to blame for that state of affairs. Gentlemen, good day to you."

Johnson walked to an awaiting BMW, got in and got straight onto his phone. He stopped the driver before they left the car park. Lowering the window, he shouted.

"Jack. I forgot to mention. The job of Interpol Liaison Officer is yours – or rather if you were to apply there would be no resistance, if you understand my meaning. Your knowledge levels are spot on and we feel that now might be a good time to get out of London, if only for a few years. You know, let the dust settle a little, let us get back to policing how we used to do it before your circus arrived in town. No arguments. OK?" He winked and put the window up before resuming his phone conversation.

Cade looked at Daniel and said, "That's not how I work, John. Not at all."

Daniel exhaled. "No, I understand that, but it's how he does. Best you take the chance while you can. Now, whilst we take the lift to the office, remind me why I agreed to run this team, Jack?"

"As you said to the assistant commissioner, you have found your niche, your reason for enjoying policing again. Shall we take the stairs, better for us? We can chat en route."

By the time they had got to the fifth floor they were both shattered, having tried to continue their discussion about Cade and his apparently seamless transition into Europe.

"I feel that I have no choice, John. But what about the team? And Carrie?" There was that name again.

"You heard the doctor Jack, Carrie may never recover. And, even if she does, what's to say the relationship will still work. It's early days, you are both young, she'll understand. And it's only an hour on a plane."

"OK. But if anyone asks I had no choice, I was pretty much ordered to go. I need you to lie for me if it comes to it." As the words were leaving his mouth, both men knew that it was not what he meant. He was once told he couldn't lie if his life depended upon it. Most men and women who dedicate their lives to unearthing deceit cannot fabricate the truth – integrity and reputation are the bedrock, the mortar that binds together a team and dishonesty the cancerous mechanism that destroys it.

For Cade, his reputation was sacrosanct and Daniel both knew it and respected it hugely.

"You'll be the death of me, Jack, but yes, I will always have your back. Now, are you ready for the debrief session of a lifetime?"

They walked into the office to find that Roberts had arrived back at work – contrary to medical and marital advice. He had even made sure his tie matched his plaster cast.

"Team, look who is here!" A ripple of applause greeted the senior men who walked into handshakes and offers of tea and biscuits – custard creams, not ginger nuts. Someone had been given strict instructions.

Roberts nodded subtly to one of his team who left the office with a set of car keys.

Ten minutes later, the team were all gathered in the Briefing Room. Many were standing. It was a full house.

"After you, Jack."

Cade spoke uninterrupted for fifteen minutes. Having outlined the start of Operation Breaker, the highs and the lows, the gains and losses, he drilled down on the latter part of the operation.

"What we saw was a highly organised team. Controlled out of Europe, with some significant backing too. We also know that Hatton Garden was a smokescreen, quite literally according to witnesses – and all skilfully done on Guy Fawkes Night. As yet, we don't know what this aspect of the operation was about. We may never find out, as this has gone upstairs...possibly even higher. We've heard talk of Foreign Office involvement so it's probably way above our pay grade, need to know, and all that."

He swallowed some tea and finished.

"I said at the start of this that we were dealing with some serious street craft, and balls bigger than space hoppers. I stand by that. The team that latterly call themselves the Seventh Wave certainly announced themselves on our patch. I don't like them but you have to respect these people, they've stolen hundreds of thousands of pounds from the main banks using a relatively simple system that they can replicate anywhere on the globe. But, as I mentioned, the boss and I are convinced there is something we are missing, and it may not be cash or jewels." He let the sentence hang, hoping for a moment of inspiration.

"The good news is we have people in custody and eventually one or two might talk. Anyway, if there are no questions?" He looked around, hoping he'd covered every angle.

"Good. I don't know about you, but I'm ready for a drink. I've got some news to discuss with you and we can do that at The Sanctuary. The first round is on DS Roberts, who's already half plastered."

There was a cheer and someone clashed a pen against a cup. It was a cheap alternative to a cymbal but had the desired effect.

Roberts, Daniel and Cade made their way to the favoured drinking hole, its nicotine-stained walls and ceiling a strangely welcoming site.

"What's it to be gents? Your drinks are on me. It's almost Christmas after all." Roger Walsh greeted them with a rare smile, an open wallet and a reminder that the silly season was only five weeks away.

Was it really that time of year again? With its associated financial pandemonium, Cade couldn't help feeling that the members of the crime syndicate with a simple blue tattoo had missed a golden opportunity in Christmas and the financially exploitable chances it could bring – mass crowds, swift hands and a holiday period to conceal the realities of the offending, It was an ideal hunting ground.

The three found a table, sat down and waited for the team to arrive. They did, in twos and threes until all but two were present.

Daniel stood and cleared his throat whilst tapping a silver pen on a small ice-filled glass.

"Team, I've only been with you for ..." He looked at his watch, "...what seems like days. In that time, I've learned a lot about you. We've had some outstanding successes and, it needs to be said, we've lost some good people. We'll discuss those further tomorrow, but we need to raise a glass to our absent friends."

They all followed the time-honoured toast and thought of their colleague Clive Wood, the brief relationship they had with the spirited Nikolina Petrov and an intensely brave air force officer who was lying in a hospital bed with nothing but her spirit.

Finally, they took a moment to think about their own colleague, Carrie O'Shea – the often deep-thinking, occasional spitfire that had earned her place in the team long ago.

"Absent friends." They all took a sip of their favoured drink.

Daniel continued. "Talking of which…"

He looked at Cade, almost seeking his permission. Cade nodded, unsure whether to advertise the fact that despite everything he had said and done with his new team it was all about to unravel in what some might see as a selfish act. But 'the job' was like that, people came, they either destroyed the equilibrium or got promoted up and out, or, in the rarer cases, they made a real difference and left a legacy. Either way, many managers didn't last long in one post in the modern police force – a square peg in a matching hole was frowned upon.

As Daniel continued to speak, the side door to the pub opened, allowing a breath of cooler air to enter; winter was well on its way. Two people had arrived, coming in off the cold street. One was pushing a wheelchair. It was Dave Williams, Roberts' favourite detective and tonight acting as a hospital porter.

Daniel was in full flow now. "So whilst we are discussing

absentees. I have some good news, for once. Flight Lieutenant Mary-Jane Shipley, who you may have heard about – she was either a foolhardy or brave young lady who chased a few of our targets into the underground system of this fine city and tried to kick merry shit out of them? Well, I'm delighted to say she is alive. She'll take a while to heal and her life is owed very much to this man stood next to me." He shook Cade's hand. It was genuine – there was a real sense that this would be a lifelong friendship and despite where they both may end up Cade knew he could always turn to Daniel as a mentor and professional guide.

"Secondly, Jason, himself a survivor of that frantic day underground, is also healing fast – in fact his wife is already frustrated having him at home! Good to have you back on deck, Jason – just pace yourself."

Another ripple of applause followed before Daniel spotted a gap and continued. "OK. Carrie." He drew in the air he needed to continue, "You will know that things were not good. Cyanide poisoning is often a one-way street. Not good at all. The man who broke into her home has been charged with attempted murder and Carrie being Carrie has belligerently clung onto life, confounding her medical carers. She's a fighter as some of you know all too well. And only last night she reeled off a tirade of abuse worthy of a London Docker when Sergeant Roberts unwittingly spoke about her behind her back. Give her time and she will be back. When she returns support her like only good colleagues can. Thank you."

A buzz of delight echoed around the private room.

"Finally. Have I said finally already? In breaking news, Jack has been offered the role of Liaison Officer at Interpol in Lyon. He has the backing of Assistant Commissioner Johnson and, despite me wanting to hang onto him, he has mine too. Jack will be with us for a few more weeks. It's been a tough call for him to make, but the time is right. And a security assessment has suggested he goes as soon as possible. Jack, the floor is yours."

Cade stood and leant against the sticky wooden bar top. Normally a fastidious man, he was too tired to care about his appearance.

"It's been a long day, again. Thank you team, because we are after all an incredible little team. I arrived here from Nottingham, having caused havoc up there. All of that havoc caused over a female..."

He took a sip of his sixteen-year-old Lagavulin malt whiskey, savoured its smoky flavour and continued. "...who trusted me with her life. Having brought the circus to your town, I was truly inspired by your passion and professionalism, when I asked you to follow me on the adventure that was to become Operation Breaker you did, without question. And boy have we had some success." He smiled a genuine smile.

"It's not over yet, as we speak things are being put into place to finalise the op, here in the UK and across the water in Europe. But for now we need to prepare for the operation to come to an end."

There were sounds that Cade took to be that of disappointment and dismay. The wheel was far from broken – why fix it?

"What I do know is that this group will not go underground forever, all the while they have a leader like Alex Stefanescu and his brother Stefan at the helm they will continue to be influential and profitable. To have followers, you must have a strong leader. As much as I despise the man, he is an effective leader. They can afford to recruit the best and as we know, money talks. And it talks in many languages too. We have learned of betrayal at so many levels." He let the sentence drape over his audience.

"I am leaving soon, but I encourage you to continue with your fight and please know that you will always have a friend in me. One day I hope to return. I also hope to travel the world, like the boss here I've got my eye on New Zealand, it's about as far away as you can get from here before heading home again and you can ski in the morning and surf in the afternoon..."

"Pretty tiring if you ask me!" It was Roberts, as always, providing levity.

"Plagiarist!"

"You can talk, you were quoting Shakespeare earlier!"

Roberts' words had barely finished when Cade stopped. He was about to wrap up his unplanned farewell speech when he looked across the room and saw a female in a wheelchair being steered into a warmer part of the room. It got the loudest applause of the day. People flocked around her.

Once the team had all had their brief moment with a clearly drained O'Shea, Cade walked over to her and pulled up a chair. He held her hand.

"Don't, Jack." It was a gravelly purr. He thought about commenting on its sexiness but knew that not all police conversations had to be smutty – just ninety percent of them.

"Carrie. I was told that..."

"You have made your decision...and I support it." She was struggling to speak. The chemicals had obviously damaged her throat. "You must go, I've been told why." Her eyes narrowed, an indicator of pain. "Just promise that you'll stay in touch." It was glacial.

Cade could feel an island forming in his throat.

Emotions were driving this reaction, not hazardous compounds. He swallowed audibly.

"Now hang on Carrie, if I had known, if the doctors had told me, then..." He stopped, he knew it was pointless.

She let go of his hand. "I need to head back to St. Thomas' Jack – I'm hoping that the ward hasn't noticed I've been kidnapped. You can stay at my place as long as you need to. I have no plans to come back soon. When you are ready to give your key to Jason."

Had she seen him for what he was? A shallow man with his eye on the future, selfish and lacking compassion? Or was it a front, a safety net for her own impending lifestyle changes?

Roberts had tried to use her as a lever. He wanted Cade to stay. Cade wanted to as well. Johnson had been quite clear – 'we decide on your future, Jack, not you.'

He needed to go. He had to go. At least that is what she told herself in her quietest moments – all the while knowing the exact opposite was the truth. Moreover, she wanted to be allowed to love him; just maybe not in this life.

She asked Williams to wheel her back out into the cold and left Cade standing next to the bar, alone with thoughts and an empty glass.

A voice asked if he wanted a refill.

"Why not? I've nothing else planned."

He looked around the busy room and envied the normal conversations taking place, the banter, the thread of policing, along with the endless war stories where one staff member would tell the story of owning an elephant and another, stating with complete authority that he had a box big enough to put it in.

Cade wasn't a part of any of the chatter, couldn't join in comfortably, and already felt as if he had betrayed his team. He was alone with his own company and didn't even like himself.

Further south, twenty hours behind the wheel to be exact and far away from his home in the City of London, Hewett had arrived.

A flashing blue dot on an electronic map, they had followed his journey, broken only by a stop in a remote part of northern Spain, where he was able to convince a solitary female attendant that he was desperate for fuel having been robbed at knifepoint. He looked dishevelled and had injuries. He was also good-looking and plausible. He promised to return and make good his debts. Johnathan Hewett was nothing if not a formidable actor.

The white Citroen climbed up and into the Sierra de Guadarrama Mountains. It was getting cold and the heater was struggling to provide comfort. As well-travelled as he was, Hewett was surprised to see so much snow in a region so close to the Mediterranean Sea. Forty minutes later, after twisting and turning through the foothills, he stopped the car.

He got out and breathed in the clinically cold mountain air, it was electrifyingly clean and offered some much-needed purity to his life. The view, even in the half-light of a fading day, was ethereal, spectacular and worth being alive for.

Cut into the edge of a nearby hill was the property known as *La Najarra*. He had made it.

In the kitchen of the rambling but luxuriously appointed home, sipping on an ancient brandy, Alexandru Stefanescu watched as Hewett arrived on his driveway and stretched out his tired back muscles before picking two items of luggage from the car.

The first was a black canvass bag, the second a more expensive-looking black case. Alex zoomed in on the smaller case and smiled.

"Now that is worth waiting for." He chuckled, although it was more of a cackle, a bird-like noise and one which gave rise to his street name, the Jackdaw.

He greeted Hewett at the door, like long-lost friends, albeit they had never actually met. It was as if, to the onlooker, that Hewett had arrived at the home for Christmas, bringing cheer and gifts from afar.

A brandy was decanted into a crystal glass and offered to the traveller. He put his key onto the island worktop, clinked the glass against his host's and took a long sip. It tasted incredible – as if someone unseen had torn a four hundred-year-old raisin apart and decanted the golden brown centre into his mouth.

It had been a long journey indeed.

"You must be tired. I have made up the guest wing for you. The housemaid had to leave unfortunately – she told me that she found the journey home too painful, so I dispensed with her services."

He pointed to the corridor that led to a subtly lit room. It was surreal, to say the least.

"Please. You must rest."

Hewett found him almost charming, certainly disarming.

"Do you not need to talk? To discuss what I have done, what I have been through? The things I know?"

"No. It is late. That can wait until tomorrow over a good breakfast. As I said on the phone long before you left London, we are associates now and you are part of the team.

You are debt free, Johnnie. Debt free. Listen to that, think of it as you sink into the Charlotte Thomas sheets. They are superb, Merino wool and Egyptian cotton. Devine! I had them made for my most welcomes guests. You learn to appreciate the finer things in life when you have spent night after putrid night awake, lying in your own excrement in Pazardzhik Prison." He drained the glass.

"Sleep well. Tomorrow is a new day. We must lock that case in my safe." He picked it up and walked towards the centre of the house, closed a door behind him and put it onto the floor of the storeroom. He would leave it out of the safe for the night – a test for his visitor – a mark of their unified trust. At least he would once its contents had been removed and placed beneath the floor in a simple but discreet wooden canister.

He *was* debt free. The heavily accented words were still replaying in Hewett's ears three hours later. He had a lot to think about, most of which was complex and finding himself a guest, and a rather well-cared for guest of one of Europe's most wanted men was nothing if not unsettling. He was fully awake now. Waiting.

Alex was also awake, unusually he was alone. The last girl had disappointed him and paid the price with her life, her body a short drive away, decaying. He knew it wasn't the thought of her demise that prevented his slumber. They were coming for him – he could feel it.

When the light in his bedroom went out suddenly he needed no further convincing. The timing was all-too convenient.

The front, rear and side doors all gave in to explosive entries in a coordinated and spectacular fashion. Four teams entered the building, as black as the night sky they had left, rappelling from a helicopter on the other side of the hills that surrounded the Spanish ranch house.

Weapons up and in the aim, night goggles guiding with their familiar haunting glow, the teams rapidly moved through the house, following hours of pre-planning, they knew the layout as well as its owner.

Without a shot fired, Alex Stefancscu was in custody, cable-tied and dragged out onto the front lawn. Hooded and now kneeling with the ever-present black leather Magnum boot of a Tactical Operator from the Spanish GEO – Grupo Especial de Operaciones – tucked firmly into the back of his knee.

He was going nowhere and could only listen as Hewett was brought out next, slammed to the floor and bound in the same way.

Alex knew they would come one day – he had mentioned it to his dear Nikolina. It was one of the last things he had said to her. He had put things in place, for her and their daughter, knowing, arrogantly that whatever sentence a court imparted would only last as long as it took to escape the subsequent incarceration.

Hewett's arrival had accelerated the arrival of the authorities. Alex was matter of fact about it. He couldn't live every day looking over his shoulder. Que sera, he thought to himself as he strained to see through the woven hood that deprived him of his key sense.

They were taken by armoured vehicle to Madrid and placed into custody awaiting a joint British, Spanish and Romanian team to intervene and start to unravel the last few months, trying to add sense to the cat's cradle of criminal chaos.

"I will only be here for a short time. You need to trust

me on this one thing." Alex had said these words to the senior investigator as they led him away to his cell, which he remarked to the guards was like the Hilton compared to his last concrete tomb.

"I could grow to like it here. Such welcoming facilities." He laughed his signature laugh as the guard overly slammed the solid metal door and watched through the toughened glass porthole.

Hewett immediately demanded an audience with the British Consulate who sent a representative from nearby Malaga, and in turn responded to Hewett's further calls for assistance from the Foreign Office. Hewett had provided a simple statement, which he asked the Consular Officer to deliver back to London. It read:

"If my life were ten times dearer than it is and if I could by any means, redress the wrongs of that persecuted land by sacrifice of my life, I would willingly and gladly do so."

The words meant nothing to the staff member, but everything to the female who read them in London.

It was five hours later when the custody staff escorted him to a private room containing a fixed table and grey plastic chairs, a toilet and a phone.

He picked up the worn device and spoke.

"Thank you for calling ma'am."

The voice that responded was attractive; clipped, polished and professional. Her words were delivered in a hushed but confident tone.

"My pleasure. You have led us all on a merry dance, Johnathan. But I at least appreciate what you have done. There are more twists in this bloody story than a Florida theme park. Sadly, not everyone will get to know of your involvement, but please allow me to pass on my thanks and that of the boss. I rather enjoyed your use of the historical quote to confirm it was you. If I am not mistaken they were the words of the last man to be publicly hanged in London?"

Hewett caught a glimpse of himself in the polished steel benchtop. He hadn't shaved for days and the prison suit was hardly Saville Row, but he allowed himself a flick of the eyebrows and a smile.

"Indeed, they were. I was concerned I might be the next?"

The voice continued. "Doing what you did was not without risk. But we will reward you handsomely. And don't worry about Michael Blake, we'll smooth the waters there too. We are sending staff from London down to you as we speak. They will recover you and the package."

Debt free and out of trouble. Johnnie Bloody Hewett. Back in the saddle – if indeed he had ever left it. The only thing he had to do now to gain complete legendary status was figure out how the bloody hell he was going to locate the other half of what everyone was conveniently calling the package. And shave. He needed to shave.

Alex Stefanescu appeared before a local judge who remanded him in custody until his trial.

He thanked the judge for his professionalism. He meant it. He prided himself in rewarding a job well done, as by sending him to where he did and not another prison, it allowed his cellular network to be rekindled in a matter of hours. It was worth the money.

'Pass on the message – Jackdaw is alive and well.'

When he was produced from prison into the Audiencia Nacional – the High Court in Madrid – he initially feigned illness, then in a moment of arrogance tried to talk over the judge.

The judge allegedly found him to be 'an irritating man of shallow morals and a conceited view of life and the rules that surrounded it.' He convicted him without remorse. He told him not to appeal or appear before him ever again, and more to the point told him to expect at least fifteen years in a Spanish prison for his role in high value car crime, fraudulent activities and violence against the person. He also outlined that he knew of many other cases that could have been brought against him and that he would be wise to consider himself fortunate that the witnesses were either unwilling to testify – or no longer able to.

"Furthermore, the defendant should expect that at the end of his sentence to be relocated to Romania, where the local authorities were waiting to try him on several counts of organised crime, drug trafficking and murder."

"Thank you, sir. Most kind. I look forward to my appeal and your... future passing."

As threats went it was veiled, but the authorities took it seriously enough to provide a discreet security provision for the next six months.

The Jackdaw was convicted and received a ten-year sentence without parole and was sent to the notorious Valdemoro Prison. The judge expressed his distaste at only being able to hand down a ten-year sentence, sighting the pressure he was under to reduce prison populations in his homeland. Ten years and one day later his planned release would see him being handed over and into the custody of the Romanian authorities.

It had been the first time that his legal team had failed to release him within a month. And yet he appeared to be able to accept his fate – as if he knew that his planets would soon align – with the aid of a new team of Armani-suited legal experts who had advised him to remain placid, to adhere to all the instructions and be patient. Appeals took a while, as long as they only appealed his sentence and not his conviction they were confident of a victory – of sorts.

'Remember the words of his Honour Judge Varela? Do not appeal his judgement.'

The Jackdaw was many things; unpleasant yet loving, malevolent, arrogant but far from rash and foolhardy. He knew that the old judge was unlikely to live for ten years – he could almost guarantee it. If, or rather when that happened, he would insist that his team appealed the sentence, based upon the doubts that would be sown around the judge's mental capacity at the time.

In an ideal world he hoped that Mother Nature took its course a little sooner – if he could, he would have paid her to accelerate his death. It transpired that even nature had a price. Alexandru was a patient man, it was one of his finer virtues. Twenty-three hours strapped to a filthy bed in a compact cell, without light, being forced to concede that occasional meals of ambiguous contents and ever more dubious origins were better than slowly starving to death, all ensured that if nothing else he was patient. He would wait a lifetime if he had to.

CHAPTER 34

The next morning Michael Blake met with Malcolm Johnson in a briefing room at the Foreign Office. Johnson immediately noted another guest.

"Assistant Commissioner, thank you for attending today. You are familiar with my senior colleague?"

He was. It was Sassy Lane, the Secretary of State for Foreign and Commonwealth Affairs that assumed control and spoke first.

"Let's cut to the chase here, shall we, gentlemen? Both of you have been involved in Operation Vault – unwittingly, as it happens. Malcolm, your team has done a sterling job at keeping the lid on. Do pass on my thanks."

Blake must have looked hurt. "Oh dear, this is not a personal attack on you. And your team too, Michael. Yours, too. Especially Mr Hewett and his legendary prowess. A nightmare to supervise, I suspect?" It needed no answer.

"But what you don't know is that his role is, how can I put this? Complex."

She had their attention. Sassy was a name from her

childhood, her real name was unknown but her nickname suited her. She never struggled to get attention and lived up to her lively and feisty name, particularly among her male counterparts. Shoulder length honey blonde hair, impressive iridium blue eyes and a wicked, razor sharp sense of humour. She had a bite worse than a piranha if anyone crossed her – or worse still, picked on the weak. Bullies were her absolute favourite plaything, and she had a box of tricks likely to make the most hardened operator salivate.

"OK. I'll be brief as I have another meeting and in scissors, paper, rank terms he outranks you significantly, plus, forgive me, but he's really quite a dish." Having deflated the egos of her male visitors, she carried on, measured but eloquent.

"Earlier this year we had some close-held human source intelligence from our good friends in Europe. They ran an electronics job on a small group of criminals; small, but with great intentions. Now, this is where it gets all too complicated for the time I have available, so strap yourselves in gents and let me remind you that this is classified about as high as it gets. Those lovely little letters on the back of your government ID cards are not enough to allow you to know the full detail. One whiff of this outside of these walls and we all head to Newgate."

Blake wasn't a hundred percent sure, but nodded with conviction. Johnson knew exactly what the reference related to – the last public hanging in London took place at Newgate Prison only a short ten-minute drive away.

"The man you know as Stephen Simovich is actually Stefan Stefanescu. Yes, the brother of the man you both have an interest in, one Alex Stefanescu, or as he likes to be known in his own marvellously self-effacing way, the Jackdaw; the leader of the group known latterly as the Seventh

Wave. And Christ what a royal pain in the arse he has become."

She overtly checked her watch before continuing. "You see contrary to what you might believe Stefan hates his dear brother – blames him for killing their parents...we can't corroborate this, but having read Alex's file it is probable. He's what the psych teams refer to as an alienated, disempathetic, dyssocial and occasionally hostile sociopath – in a nutshell he would rather nurture a puppy than a princess, content to throw the latter overboard and watch her drown. And when he's not caring for the said puppy, he's quite adept at extreme cruelty towards his fellow man. Nothing would be beyond the realms of unpleasant." She had clearly researched the varied backgrounds of sociopathy and knew she would not be challenged.

"Anyway, Stefan has worked for the British government as an unpaid intelligence asset for years, all on the promise that one day they will capture his brother, put him away for a very long time and allow him to gain control of his legitimate business empire."

Both men looked at each other. Blake spoke first.

"Legitimate? That man doesn't have a straight bone in his body."

"Oh, but that's where you are wrong. He may be up to his sweetbreads in high value cars, class A drugs and other commodities, but he is a registered diamond trader. And very good at it too. On the face of it, he doesn't touch the business with a twenty-foot pole. No links whatsoever. But if I told you he has interests here in London..."

"Hatton Garden, by any chance?" It was a fair but anticipated guess and laced with sarcasm.

"Yes. And before you ask, yes. The recent raid, by his team, stole most of his own diamonds."

"But..."

"Why? Great question, Assistant Commissioner. It was, and this is the sensitive part remember, a training session for his up-and-coming team. They have plans to steal something more valuable. We are just buggered if we know what that night be!"

"I was told the raid the other night netted millions of dollars of stones. Is that not valuable enough?"

"Short answer? No. And we got most of them back, anyway. So technically he can't even claim on his insurance, which is a sort of 'up yours' by us!" She laughed a carefree laugh, stretching her arms above her head and checking her Raymond Weil watch once more.

"My sources tell me Alex Stefanescu wants power, he's a sociopath, but he also has a soft spot for all things bright and beautiful. Including a rather devastatingly pretty Bulgarian redhead. Whose death, incidentally, he blames upon your team, namely one Inspector John Cade."

"But we are almost certain that his own men killed her. Upon his instructions. Drowned the poor girl in the bloody Thames. He as good as admitted it to Cade in a recorded phone call."

"True. But in his mind he is not responsible. I'm not a shrink, but I'd say our man Alex has a narcissistic personality disorder."

"Great. So we have one brother who is a double agent for the Brits and the Romanians and stands to inherit a fortune in dodgy diamonds and yet we know sweet FA about him, and another, who worships at his own alter and would happily pluck the eye out of one of his victims and feed it to them whilst they watch with the remainder and wonder when the good news is finally going to arrive. Talking of which, do you *have* any good news, Sassy?"

She bristled at the use of her first name.

"The other man, Valentin Niculcea. We are pretty certain he's turned. Works for us now, in deep, and we need to maintain that security blanket around him. He will come into his own as we move forward. Trust him. End of."

"OK, so we end on a high note. But I suspect there is something missing from this little briefing."

"Oh absolutely, I was getting to that. When Alex planned the jewellery raid he was advised by a source, as yet unidentified, that stored in the vaults at Hatton Garden were a number of documents." She looked both men in the eye and allowed them to paint a picture of the scene – also discreetly looking for signs of guilt from her own man Blake – whom she found to be both brilliant and unsettling at the same time.

Whatever analogy she could think of that involved twists, and turns appeared to sum up where the current operation lay. She found herself trusting foreigners more than some of her own senior staff. Greed was a terrible drug. She made a mental note to revisit the whole damned affair and work out who was who in the ever-growing zoo. She was able to think this through whilst formulating her next statement. Sassy by name.

"You may recall that a number of black Pelican cases were taken? Alex knew that one contained a complete set of papers that relate to a super-sensitive meeting last year. It was so ruddy sensitive that we didn't know where to store the minutes. We looked at your place, the Yard, the Bank of England, even burying them in my back garden... I joke of course, as I don't have a back garden. No, you see the problem is they were so explosive in the wrong hands we didn't know which hands to put them in. It was entirely a trust thing."

The two high-ranking men nodded, as if to say, 'And...?'

"And the former Secretary of State for Foreign Affairs suggested the strong room at Hatton Garden. It's a warren of safes, vaults and more safes. Call it an independent hidey hole. He said that no one would ever think to go there for documents that related to the planned dissolution of the British Monarchy."

It was intended to be a line that she delivered quickly – able to move on and ideally without being challenged. It was, in reality, too much to ignore.

Michael Blake's eyes opened as wide as they could go. He was unable to speak. Johnson had the look of someone who had just woken from a rousing sleep to learn that a passing stranger had defecated on his top lip. It was far from pretty.

This wasn't bad. This was too ludicrous for words.

Blake tried to generate a sentence. "But, er. I. Look." He composed himself. "For Christ's sake, Sassy tell me this isn't what Alex Stefanescu has in his possession?"

He paused. "Hewett...he led him to it. It was him, wasn't it?" He was pointing a loaded index finger.

She smiled a disarming smile. "No, Michael. It wasn't. You need to get off Johnathan's back and tie up that high horse. He's actually saved us a considerable amount of money and embarrassment. Think of the cost to Britain, in terms of reputation if this got out. Her Majesty's own government seeking to undermine her, to overrule *her*. Dear God, perish the thought. It would cost billions in lost revenue and trust and above all trade. And heaven knows how much in lost tourism and God himself knows what HRH would do to us. She'd be bloody livid. Off with their heads!"

Blake was confused. Johnson remained quiet, trying to figure out how, for once, the police were not to blame.

"Forgive me, Minister. If he's saved us would you mind explaining how? I was all for releasing the dogs of war and ripping the bastard's throat out." It was Blake who had spoken first.

"Oh, good Lord no Michael, don't do that." It was apparent that she had a soft spot for Hewett. "He has recovered the papers. They are safe. Cast iron, probably buried in his garden."

Blake wasn't in the mood for humour. "I am aware you have another meeting. You say Hewett has the papers, that there is no issue here?"

"Yes. And no. Hewett has the papers relating to the Monarchy. He hand delivered them to Alex at his house in Spain. He had to, to make it look plausible, as if he were on his side. A turncoat, a traitor to the government that Alex blames for killing his one and only love. Johnnie is nothing if not a sublime actor." She unwittingly licked her lips.

"The Spanish authorities recovered the case, which Hewett had personally sealed. They are on the way back to London under very close guard and when it gets here, its contents will be destroyed by two people," she smirked. "I will be one of them, so all is well in the world, gentlemen. Right, I really must dash."

She got to the door, having shaken hands, and thanked the men for their time. Johnson, a career police officer, had that age-old feeling that she was only telling them what she wanted them to know. He was due to retire, so threw caution to the wind.

"Minister. I know you are in a hurry. Please excuse me." She stopped. She knew.

"I believe there is a 'but' to this story that we are sworn to remain secret on. Forgive me, but I feel as the officer with a portfolio for national security and foreign affairs that I have a duty and a need to know."

She closed the door. Her eyes closed for a second. It was thinking time.

"I was rather hoping I could avoid this. In the third case that was taken was a separate set of papers. These were not minutes but a complete cabinet paper, a full decision if you like, set in stone. There was a secret motion to explore the concept of Britain leaving the European Union by 2007. The overwhelming majority was in favour..."

She let the words hang like an autumn fog over the River Thames.

"Yes indeed. You are right to have that look. If word got out, it could destroy us way beyond the Monarchy issue – we have more princes in waiting after all – we would recover. But Europe...think trade, security, travel, identity, pensions, salaries, currency, public opinion, the Stock Exchange...need I go on?"

"Good God. Leaving the European Union? It's outrageous. Any other gems whilst you are purging Minister?"

"A couple – as it happens. We took part in a secret meeting with our trusted EU counterparts this year – the inner six as they are known. The six degrees of European separation. It transpires that by 2007 Romania and Bulgaria will join us as part of Europe, it is considered to be part of what is known as the fifth wave of enlargement of the European Union. It will open up the front door of Britain to millions of people, some legitimate, wanting a brighter future, bringing skills."

"Go on."

"The problem is many of these people will be utilising false passports, out of Albania, Turkey and Syria or further afield. Europe is in a right old mess with immigration and people trafficking and the signs across Europe all point to a worsening situation over the next few years, and Mother England is seen as the dumping ground. Nirvana at the end of the bloody rainbow. And frankly, gentlemen, we cannot cope with an influx in the region of five million people – let alone the security risk that this could bring for the future of Britain. It would be the gift that just keeps on giving."

She had stopped looking at her watch now. "We had to stop it. The decision to leave the Union was made. We would commence our withdrawal next year and complete it before 2007 – start to put the drawbridge back up before we opened our doors and our welfare state to the people of Europe. If word reaches those affected states, the other members, our allies...the general public and God help us, in the year before a bloody general election, the media..."

"So where are *those* papers, right now Secretary of State? And the papers you described as minutes, where are the actual originals?" Blake had recovered.

"Michael. For these walls only. I, or should I say we, have absolutely no idea – OK? There's another issue, even greater. Look, I have to go." She held her index finger in the air. "You speak to no one."

She glided her hands into her favourite goatskin gloves and pulled her coat collar up and around her neck to shield against the cold, then gently closed the door behind her. As she stepped out onto the street, she contemplated the immediate pain of being run over by a bus. It seemed easier in the short term.

Walking to her car, a silver, long wheelbase Jaguar, she saw that her driver was already holding the door open, stood in driving sleet ever the professional, she couldn't help but envy his comparable stress-free lifestyle or avoid the internal monologue that had haunted her for weeks.

'Alex Stefanescu has the copies. I think he knows this – and will exploit the belief that he has the originals. But I'm not sure, he's a good chess player, better at poker, and whilst he doesn't hold the royal flush, I think he knows where it is being held. So one question remains. Who has the originals and what are they worth? And when will they surface again, because as sure as smoking follows sex, they will.'

She sat back in the leather-clad isolation of the government car and asked to head to Downing Street. There were other things to discuss, and for once she didn't feel confident about the subject matter.

Neither man said anything for a while. It was Johnson who decided to swallow hard and clear his throat.

"I guess you have some work to do, Michael, and an apology to give?"

"Oh Jesus. He's going to be unbearable. I could always pretend I don't know."

"I'll leave that one with you. I have my own house to repair. This operation has cost the Metropolitan Police an inordinate amount of money, I've had to send flowers to at least two funerals and attend the bedsides of a few battered staff, assuring their families that we are there to support them through thick and bloody thin, all in the name of greed, and to cap it all I'm losing two of my best people soon. Do you think we will ever get to the bottom of the where the other documents are? Do we have a contingency plan if they turn up – some time, anywhere?"

Blake shook his head in disbelief. "Honestly, Malcolm? No to both questions. It's rare that I'm right on anything these days."

"My old man used to say even a broken clock is right twice a day, Michael."

"Did he? Then he was far wiser than me. I suppose we need to bring Cade and Daniel into this equation somewhere along the line. We need Cade out of London, that's for sure. And retire Daniel early too. Not a bloody clue where along that line we allow them to enter."

"For now, I'd say we start at the beginning, but that would be as ridiculous as the middle. How about the very last part, the bit where we introduce them to a few people and say 'it's not how it looks' and see where we go from there. Thoughts?"

Blake gave a resigned shrug. In theory, it made sense.

"I just need to know where those bloody papers are. If Hewett has something, what exactly does he have? A photocopy? This is dynamite. Bloody hell."

Introducing Daniel and Cade had its merits. As long as Cade didn't put Stefanescu through the nearest window before all could be explained. That would really round off the week in fine style.

"Tomorrow? Ten o'clock. My office?" It was Johnson who set the date and time, knowing that he'd rather keep the peace on police property than somewhere else.

They shook hands, but it was a lifeless gesture.

Secretary of State Lane walked into the Prime Minister's office twenty minutes later and wanted to weep, and he knew, immediately.

"Give it to me in bite-size pieces, Sassy. It's been too big a week to take on the whole elephant in one sitting." He looked at her and nodded encouragement. "Go on."

"We've got a few issues, Prime Minister. A couple you know about – the European papers, the situation with opening up the borders and the perennial thorn in our side in the shape of the Monarchy."

"Yes, I am aware of each and every one of those little darlings. And...?"

"No point in delaying this, Jim. We are royally in the shit."

"Lovely. Just how deep? And why?"

"Waist high. Summary? The royal family have been investing offshore for some time..."

It was the crowning glory to a bitch of a week for James Cole – the Prime Minister and surprisingly pleasant Conservative leader of the United Kingdom.

Cole was just forty. A shade under six foot and prematurely grey. Slate grey eyes were enhanced by blue framed glasses and he was always immaculate. Always.

He was also devoutly single. And she knew it. Had done since they met at university, fell recklessly in love and then went their separate ways.

"Superb. Just amazing. Just...great. Tell me it's OK – that somehow this won't cause the world to collapse around our ears?"

"As individual cases, they are a nightmare. As a collective – it's nuclear. Her Majesty of all people needs to be beyond reproach Jim. All we can pray is that she has a canyon-full of plausible deniability and a great accountant."

"The royals are more stable now since – I don't know, probably since the early eighties when Dianna arrived and gave them all celebrity status. But this..." He exhaled loudly. "This could really get the country in a spin. If the gutter press get hold of it this will make Armageddon seem like a cake judging contest in the Cotswolds."

"I'm sorry, James."

"You knew?"

"For a while. But I hoped it would go away."

"Indeed. Then that is what you need to do. Make it go

away. Gather the main players. Chatham House Rules applies Sassy. Not a bloody word to anyone we don't trust with their lives. We lock this down for at least ten years. Lock it in the Tower. Lock it down, dispose of the key. And tell Her Majesty to do the same. Make an appointment to see her tomorrow.

"Tomorrow? But…"

"Tomorrow." He waited for the response. "Sassy?"

"Noted Prime Minister."

"Good. Fancy a take away tonight? The Spanish Embassy just cancelled their tapas night and I'm buggered if I'm going out to dinner."

Cade and Daniel finished the day early. If they could have done, they would have flagged it altogether. They had both earned at least two days in time off – whether they ever got to cash it in was a bone of contention.

Daniel winced as he removed his jacket. The wound had been cleaned up and butterfly stitched.

"You should take it easy, boss. You are not getting any younger you know."

"To be fair, it's not every day my partner shoots me. I'll see you tomorrow, Jack. Get some rest and make sure you eat. Are you heading to see Carrie later?"

"I thought so, but last night I got the message quite clearly. If I head to France I do so with her blessing, but not with her."

"Give it time. She'll come around."

"I suspect not John. It's a chance I have to take. Send my love to Lynne. I'll see you in the morning, bright and early. We have a meeting with Mr Johnson. Can't wait."

. . .

The morning arrived. Cade had watched the winter sunrise over London. He had his best navy blue suit back from the cleaners, Daniel had rescued another favourite with a subtle red check from the back of the wardrobe and met his second in command on the stairs heading up to the tenth floor. They walked into Malcolm Johnson's large office, side by side, and stopped in step, instantly.

"What the...?" Surprisingly, it was Daniel who had started the conversation.

"Gentlemen. Don't be hasty. Close the door, please. I need to explain." He was speaking in a rapid tone that said, 'I am in charge here, let's not forget that.'

He spoke for five minutes, outlining as best as he could, why a man, previously one of the key targets for Operation Breaker, was now sat in his office drinking coffee and waiting to be attacked, verbally, possibly even physically.

"So you are telling me that *this* man is on *our* side?" Cade asked incredulously. "Actually working *with* us?"

"May I Mr Johnson?" Stefanescu stood and walked carefully towards Cade. He was obviously in pain.

"Mr Cade. Please, allow me to explain my side of the story. I can do it slowly or in a few quick sentences. Either way, I need to be as fast as possible – it's been a long week and I have a need to have an injury tended to. It might be familiar to you?"

"You are lucky I missed. I was aiming for your head."

"I judged the boat height just right." He smiled, but it was his eyes that fascinated Cade. He suspected he would never forget them.

"I don't trust you, Stefanescu, despite what the assistant commissioner says. You've done too much and it will take a long while to allow that to evaporate from my memory. I hold you responsible for the death of one of my team, the near death of another, and in connection with the death of a female who was working with us."

"There is so much I would like to tell you, Mr Cade..."

"I bet there is. Why don't we start with two females found at an out-of-town rubbish dump near the Romanian city of Craiova, naked with their throats cut, their eyes surgically removed and left hanging on their cheekbones. Ring any bells, Stefan?"

His head bowed slightly. "It does Mr Cade, yes. But sadly, I am forbidden to discuss this with you. It has been a traumatic time for us all. Can we at least shake hands and make a pact to hunt for the group that my brother created? You know, take them down as they say in the films."

"All the while you have that tattoo on your wrist I'm going to struggle. No point in lying. I'd much rather these two gents left the room for ten minutes so we can get properly acquainted."

"I am sure you would. The two girls you mentioned? It wasn't me. My name was connected, like it is with many atrocities in my home country, but please, you have to understand I am not an evil person despite what the Interpol files say. I must not lie to you, I have done some things that I am not proud of. Some of those events have been very carefully calculated to cause harm – but with limitations. It is very difficult to explain in such a short amount of time. I am not as evil as you suggest. If, on the other hand, you wish to find the psychopath in my family, then you need to look at my dear brother and not me."

"Thank you, Jack. I think we need to press on." Johnson had heard enough. "I also need to mention Valentin Niculcea briefly. This is a name you are both familiar with?" He knew the answer.

"Valentin has been working with us for quite a while. We

gave him higher level access in a number of areas and he was able to steer us along a set of paths, particularly in relation to the bank attacks. Plus, I suspect he was instrumental in guiding you towards Miss O'Shea at her time of need."

"And where is he?" It was a fair question and one that Daniel wanted an answer to.

"He is in France, and he will stay there. He needed neutrality, and we were happy to support him. For now, he is unable to return to Romania, and you have seen to it that he cannot enter Britain either, he is somewhat nomadic through no fault of his own."

"But he walked into Carrie O'Shea's bedroom and almost slit her throat all in the name of making a name for himself. He told me that he had probably killed people – that he is an assassin, trained by the Romanian government? Is this a lie too?" Cade needed answers.

"I doubt it is Jack. His country has yet to forgive him completely for what he did, after it is alleged they killed his wife. He is a very capable man, John – but he hasn't killed for fun. There is a difference. Keep your friends close and all that."

"Whilst we are in eradication mode, you know, clearing the slate, is there anyone else you both feel I should know about?"

It was a heavily loaded question. And both Blake and Johnson were aware of the answer.

Hewett's timing was exquisite. As his name was mentioned he was ushered in by Johnson's executive assistant. He was surprisingly upbeat.

"Gentlemen. Good morning. Apologies for my current state, not really the British Foreign Office way I realise." He sat in a chair and crossed his legs, trying somehow to disguise the soiled paper custody suit he had travelled in, the

Spanish authorities having destroyed his clothes upon arrival at their major prisoner handling centre.

"You also need a shave and a shower" said Blake who was still unconvinced. How could one of his best people operate at a level even higher than his? It was like Goering telling Hitler how to run the Luftwaffe.

"There is so much to tell. Another time perhaps, another chapter in the book." Sitting cross-legged with his hands on his knees, he looked at Daniel and Cade.

"John, Jack, I am personally sorry. It was very much a need to know – and I understand you now do – or at least a smattering of it. No hard feelings?" He poured a coffee and forced a scone into his mouth, desperate for sugar and caffeine.

Cade stood and spoke. "I have no idea what the hell is going on here. This is six degrees of separation at its best or worst? I don't know whether to shake your hand or dance on your grave. You have some explaining to do – if you are able to?"

Hewett picked at another scone and drained a second cup of coffee.

"All fair, all justified, Jack. One hundred percent. But it's not six degrees, more like seven. We are all connected by those six stages, so they say, but in this case there is one extra, the untold story, the unforeseen ally or enemy. We have a long road on which to travel, but we will get there. You have only a limited idea of what I have been involved in. For the record, it's a hundred percent accurate, and ninety percent true. It's the best I can offer – you will not be hearing any more from me on this subject."

He brushed some crumbs from his palm and held out his hand.

Cade looked at him, then Daniel and lastly Johnson. He

shrugged, "To be honest, I have no idea who is doing what, with whom, or why."

He stepped forward and took the olive branch. Daniel followed suit. Stefanescu was cautious at best, surrounded by men who were clearly capable of causing him harm. He wasn't sure whether he preferred their company or that of his brother – a man who tortured and humiliated people for a hobby.

The answer was easy. He just needed to work with this new team and convince them he was trustworthy. It might take a while, but if it took ten years, then it was a worthwhile investment. The problem was he needed to maintain a level of subterfuge and that meant deceit and in the world of organised crime it meant hurting people, just to stay alive. In a dog eat dog world, Stefan Stefanescu needed to remain close to the top of the canine food chain.

Hewett was intensely relieved to be back in the upper reaches of the same chain. Somehow he had played the ultimate game of cat and mouse, to a point where not even his own manager was aware of his role. The British government had cultivated him – and he in turn them. He had also manipulated them.

It was an exquisitely managed example of double bluffing. He had been selected for a job that required his skills and knowledge, to save the face of both the government and the monarchy. It required guile and balls of a magnitude that rarely existed in a central government team that normally used other, better-qualified people to take such risks.

His mission was simple: 'Get the packages back on British soil but make it look as though a common thief had removed them. To do this, you will need to give up everything that you have strived for – at least on the face of it. Immerse yourself, convince them of your worth in future attacks on the financial quarter of Britain and above all remove the temptation to sell British secrets to the highest bidder.'

It was reasonable to expect or anticipate that a bidder that could come from any quarter of the European Union or further afield, even a wealthy individual looking to make a shrewd investment. Blackmail by any other name.

The fact that he had only partially succeeded was still hailed as a success, for now the truth had been locked down and Hewett was once more the poster boy, adored by the Foreign Minister and potentially the royal family too. It could hardly have been more wonderful. If they knew where the remaining papers were they could all relax. They weren't in the possession of the group called the Seventh Wave, that much was obvious, or Alex would be using them to barter – the subterranean chatter would have been frenzied. His younger brother had no need for them. The entourage that adored and followed the Jackdaw certainly did not have them in their possession and frankly if they did it was unlikely that they realised their real worth.

As far as Johnnie Hewett was concerned his involvement was over. His immersion was complete, his alibi had been cast iron, even down to the escape from London and the off the radar flight, across the channel to France. All designed to get him out of the country and add weight to the story when he finally met with Alex Stefanescu, a man, it was once said that trusted no one, not even his own mother. Which may have explained why he chose to end her life.

Hewett had known he had to leave in a light aircraft, below the radar – leaving no footprint. Any normal border crossing was destined to fail and France was a large country where he could slip into the approaches to southern Europe and work without interruption or risk of being found.

The fact that his boss, the charming Miss Lane, did not know that both Stefan and Valentin were working for the British government was his only concern. If she was supposedly in the inner sanctum then why was she not aware – or was she a supreme actress too? Was Blake really as naïve as he appeared? A stack of questions – some of which might never be answered.

The most incredible aspect of the whole operation was actually the one that wove itself around John 'Jack' Cade, a police officer who left his acrimonious home for a new life and ended up in the right place at the wrong time. Over the course of ten years he would be drawn into an unforeseen web but allowed to escape – many times.

A chance meeting at an airport? A stunning redhead – that story, the one where a woman's fury was put on display? Was it woven out of the truth, or an elaborate multi-jurisdictional operation designed to create a smokescreen and allow the termination of an ancient monarchy and the insidious destruction of an economic powerhouse?

Who to trust?

The drop-dead pretty girl that had sat in an interview room at East Midlands Airport and sobbed through her story had been incredibly plausible. Nikolina Petrov, daughter of Simona and mother of Elena, had arrived to escape from her sociopathic husband and start her own new life. She offered a series of facts that were potentially useful at a time when the United Kingdom was experiencing the viral nature of Eastern European crime.

She was heading for London when Alex's hired team had found her, taken her against her will and without the timely intrusion of an alert and enquiring police officer would have been abused, maimed and eventually killed.

Safely in the custody of the British, her task was simple; take the documents from their secure location and hide them, then make it look like a delightfully brilliant burglary, where the thief had found more than they had bargained for.

And she had.

Her training had shone through. She really was as good as her masters had predicted.

In a few hours, during a normal business day when the Breaker team had all been consumed by chaos, she had slipped out of Scotland Yard, and, as they had trained her to do had concealed her identity, navigated her way across the city to the place where the charming British official had told her she would find the documents. He assured her he would be distracting the secretary; it was his duty to.

The briefing was simpler than the task: 'Remove the documents quickly, make a mess by all means, and leave no trace, not even one hair. Then get out, get back to the Yard and smile that sweet, sweet smile.'

She recalled the next part with such clarity. 'Post one set to your daughter. Ensure she understands their importance. The other can go in my safe deposit box. I will reward you in ways you cannot imagine, more than just physically. Money. Yes, a lot of money so that you and your daughter can one day be reunited, away from his grasp. Are you OK with this Niko?'

She was completely engaged and working for two controllers, enjoying the challenge which was both physical and mental – the perfect scenario for a blue-flame, rising star of the Bulgarian Intelligence Service. As she had listened to the final element of the briefing, it became apparent that this was more than a test. Create a smokescreen, they had said. She would ensure that she would create a forest fire. For her government, and the people of Bulgaria, this was a chance to hold the ace and its three sisters. It provided them, her people, with the lever that they might need should their seemingly endless and patronising wait to join the European Union fail at the first hurdle.

Having waited so long for the chance to prove herself, she had carried out the operation to the letter. One set of the documents had been posted to her daughter, the other, as time was against her, she had retained, slipping into a bag to be delivered later to his secure deposit box. Almost as arranged. And all was heading along the path to perfection when they had taken her; enraged at being made to look foolish and abandoned by the mother of his child, Alexandru Stefanescu had issued strict instructions.

'No one ever disrespects me this way. Find her – have fun with her – let me have a few last words with her – then kill her in the way I am about to outline. Only in this way or you will go the same way.'

It had shocked even his most trusted stalwarts.

She should have killed him when she had the chance.

It had all been going so well. If the British detective hadn't had exposed her to danger in the safe house, they would still have found her, sooner or later. It was only a matter of time. Not even Cade could protect her forever. She had trusted him. She liked British men, men in authority, and if they were as disarming and handsome as him she knew she could learn to live again. A new life in a new country. Her contact at the Foreign Office had said he would make it happen. New life, new name, new identity. She was surrounded by men who were incapable of denying her.

"Just do this one thing for me, Niko and we can begin to

create that new identity. You can even help to choose your name. How exciting would this be?"

He was patronising at times, but powerful. Above all, he was the key to her future, to getting her daughter back and living a life where checking the reflection in a shop doorway was no longer an essential pastime. He was doing what he had planned for greed, for his future financial portfolio – in a way they were not dissimilar. Her needs though were not financial, but she had a hunger too. They were an unforeseen team, Nikolina Petrov, the girl prodigy of the Bulgarian Intelligence Services and the British man they called Michael Blake.

Shaking his head, clearing his mind of the last few days, Hewett knew that life had changed for the better. He often had his greatest successes when he took risks. He was debt free. Financially, at least. His family name would remain disagreeable to a certain self-proclaimed master criminal who had lost nearly half a million pounds in the bargain. Hewett was able to live again, but he knew he would always have to look over his shoulder at those same reflections, a car door closing rapidly, footsteps. Was now the time? Had they come for him?

The hardest part of his life, moving forward, would be identifying his enemy. He contemplated heading overseas – he had the requisite visas to enter any country, he just needed to ask. He had the financial backing, and he had a reason to get out of Europe for a while. But where? With half a million pounds and a small bag of diamonds, he could easily set up home in any of the four corners of the world.

The first thing he needed to do was to visit his mother, tell her that he was fine but moving onto a new role. She of all people would understand – the old fox was probably connected to his world far more than he could ever have realised as a young and impressionable boy.

Then after putting a roof over his head, he needed a new car and a watch. In that order. The watch would take longer to choose. He had lost his somewhere along the way. He surmised that it was probably sitting on the wrist of a twenty-something boy from a city further east. Either that or in a bag in a custody facility with an onlooker declaring it to be of dubious origins. Real watch, fake owner.

The new replacement watch had to be right. Stainless steel, clinical, cold, with a coal-black face and sweeping second hand and a trademark cyclops lens over the date. It had to feel as if it were hewn from a solid ingot of steel.

Oh, and a new wardrobe, a must, an absolute must. A call to Anderson & Sheppard should resolve his issues. Three suits. One navy blue, one light grey and a charcoal pinstripe. Not brown, it just didn't work. White shirt, blue shirt, pink shirt, two each of those. Belts, two. Matching socks and handkerchief and shoes, Loakes, polished, classic brogues, one black, one brown. After all, he could hardly convince the old, or potentially a new country, to take him seriously in a stained paper prison suit, could he?

More importantly, he couldn't return to his old apartment. He had stripped it and put everything into storage, assuming that he might not return from his soiree with the Stefanescu brothers. He had left instructions and the key with an old friend – a sassy lady indeed who knew how everything worked.

If only he had known that Stefan was actually an ally. What was it that was said? More twists and turns than a Florida theme park? He wouldn't know, Disney was hardly his thing.

. . .

The drive back to Scotland Yard was quiet. Daniel and Cade were both pensive, but for different reasons. Suddenly they both spoke, followed by a round of 'after yous'. Cade went first.

"I don't get it John. You were convinced that Hewett was bad to the bone. I trusted Valentin, and I was right to, but Stefanescu. I'm still not sure. He has a lot to gain by getting rid of his brother, and who's to say we aren't just being used to act as a massive bloody lever? He's got blood on his hands."

"I think I agree on all counts, mate. To be honest, I'm ready to jack it all in, sell up, head to New Zealand and start that café by the beach. You should come too, Lynne and I are heading their early next year for a recce. Do you good to experience the place. Somewhere far from anywhere. I hear the locals are friendly and you never know you might meet the girl of your dreams one day. I can picture it now, you are sat in a bar on a stunning waterfront somewhere warm...and in walks a girl!"

"I should be so lucky." Cade was smiling for the first time in days.

He didn't realise it but Daniel had sown a seed that would take years to germinate.

They took the lift, turned right and walked into the main office. It was the usual mix of phone conversations, tapping keyboards, one-to-one chats and an underlying wave of banter. It was, in that respect, no different to any other police station the world over.

Roberts was given the rundown on Stefanescu and Valentin and lastly, Hewett.

"I don't know which one I'm least pleased about. I'll go

with Stefa-bloody-nescu. One of that bastard's men broke my arm. I'll never play the flute again."

Once again Roberts had brought some of his much-needed light-hearted repartee into the office, an office on the tenth floor of one of modern policing's most iconic buildings. The Yard, as it was known with affection, was due to close at some point, so rumour had it, and another story that was circulating among the team was that their current operation was coming to an end.

It fell to Detective Constable Del Murphy to ask the question.

"Guv. We've heard that Breaker is coming to an end. Is this true?"

Daniel looked at Cade. "Do you want to answer this one?"

"Del, team, the answer is yes, but only because we have been so incredibly amazing. And I mean that sincerely. We've hunted them down, recovered sizeable sums of cash and diamonds and now something worth more than gold – of which, sadly I can't discuss. But the time has come for us all to move on, and me with it. It's been a blast. I know I will return here one day, Mr Daniel too, possibly on holiday, as I know he is looking at heading to the Land of the Long White Cloud to start a new life with Mrs Daniel."

He took a moment to reflect.

"I can go knowing the team is in great shape, with some good people. You know Maori in New Zealand have a saying, I won't try to pronounce it, but essentially it asks, what is the most important thing in the world? And the answer is, the people, the people, the people. It means a lot to me to know that I had you all alongside me. Without a doubt, the best team I've ever worked with. But I must bid you farewell."

The team took it in turns to shake Cade's hand and wish him well for his next chapter. He walked over to O'Shea's desk, took a letter from his jacket and placed it in between the buttons on her keyboard.

Roberts joined him. "Alright mate?"

"I've had quieter stations to work at Jason. And I wouldn't change a thing."

"You know what I'm talking about. JD filled me in. She'll miss you."

"And me her. But I'm told I have to leave, and she needs calm, not the chaos I seem to attract – Carrie O'Shea does not need me in her life at the moment. I'll come back for her one day."

"I'll be sure to let her know."

"It's in that letter, Jason. The ball is lovingly placed into her court now."

"So now what?"

"Pack up here, clear my things from her flat, head back to Nottingham, do the same up there, make sure I visit Penny and let her see how happy I am, probably visit a few old friends and acquaintances and then...and then head to Lyon and see what order I can bring to Interpol."

"You stay in touch. That's an order, one day I'll outrank you so consider it one for the future. I'll miss you too, you know. It's been superb. Painful at times – we won't mention Harrier and *that* incident – but fun, it's certainly been fun. Now go before I get emotional."

Cade shook Roberts' hand and then pulled him in towards him for a heartfelt hug. "Thanks, pal. I owe you. Send me an invite and I'll return one day."

"You don't need an invite. Part of the team, remember?"

He walked back to O'Shea's desk, recovered the letter and then walked out of the office. He got to the main door, stopped, waited for a sizeable audience, then turned to call back to Roberts.

"Oh, Sergeant Roberts. Mallory St John called. It's pronounced Sinjun, apparently. He runs the alternative gentlemen's club on the Embankment. Anyway, he wanted you to know he's waiting to hand your ID back. Reckons he'll whip you into shape. Says he can't wait to take your cuffs but leave your wife at home."

Cade winked, his azure blue eyes were lacking their normal sparkle, but they were still blue – as deep as an ocean on the other side of the world.

As Cade left, Roberts was theatrically berating him and his abilities, but it all was for show – he rated him highly and wondered what it would be like Monday morning without him.

An hour later, Cade was at O'Shea's Old Queen Street address. He walked into the flat and looked around, lowered some flowers into a vase, added water and placed the envelope next to it – he aligned it twice, knowing that the owner would want it just so.

He walked through each room, checking that there were no obvious signs of the event that had nearly killed her, then. He took a moment to look around the lounge, recalling what might have been, wondered how things had changed so quickly then placed his access card on the kitchen worktop, clicked the latch on the door and walked out, down the stairs and quickly onto the street.

His phone throbbed in his coat pocket. It was Roberts.

"You missing me already, dear?"

"Ha ha, very funny. I was just ringing to say I got my driving licence back. My good lady dropped me off at The

Rack. All very amenable. The facilities there are great, they've got a gym with ropes and restraints, even a sort of pommel horse with a large rubber handle."

"Jason, tell me you are not being serious. I worry that three minutes in the vice-like grip of Harrier the transvestite hooker has rendered you liable to be sucked in by our Mr Sinjun and his band of merry men."

"Ooh, Mr Cade, is that a euphemism."

"No, Sergeant Roberts, it's not. Clean your licence in bleach, you never know where it might have been, used to cut cocaine or involved in some type of crack at the very least." He didn't give Roberts time to reply.

"Good night."

He pulled his coat up and around his neck and tucked his scarf up and under his chin. Winter had arrived in London. The buildings were grey, the people too, the trees skeletal and the sky charcoal. The river dark and brown, ever-flowing to the sea, carrying his dreams and nightmares.

In New Zealand it was summer. He hailed a black taxi cab.

"Where to governor?"

"The nearest travel agent, please."

He leant back in the seat, metaphorically waved goodbye to everything that had been a part of his recent life and began a mourning process that would last for years. His promise to Roberts was not a shallow one. He would be back. One day.

CHAPTER 35

London, December 2014

CADE WAS A MAN OF STRONG MORALS AND INTEGRITY. HE believed wholeheartedly in keeping a promise.

Having left Scotland Yard in the summer of 2014 and finishing an unpaid stint as an advisor to the Dedicated Cheque and Plastic Crime Unit, he had headed offshore. It had been a series of events that had driven him away. It was nothing personal, and not a single crossed word had ever occurred with his old team. He just knew. He knew that he needed to keep moving and more to the point that he had to step away and let Jason Roberts lead the team.

In the ten years that followed the success and ultimate demise of the Operation Breaker team, Roberts had been promoted to detective chief inspector – taking Dave Williams with him as his detective sergeant.

Cade had visited the team after what was supposed to be a sabbatical, a series of jaunts around the world and ideally finding a new life in New Zealand. Unfortunately, the ghost of Christmas Past had come back to haunt him. He had once led the team to great success, from the front and at the expense of his own health, but there were too many spirits pursuing him. He still had the dreams – often at the most inappropriate times.

That summer of 2014 would be cathartic. He had arrived back at the Yard. Another set of circumstances had forced him to abandon his new life, board a plane to London and regroup with his old team saying a brief goodbye to his now retired boss, who practically pushed him onto the aircraft.

In the immediate aftermath of the event, in which a well-organised team of criminals had visited a small and exquisitely beautiful part of New Zealand and unleashed hell via a targeted series of attacks, Cade had found himself back in the thick of operational policing, in his mind it was 2004 and he was knee-deep in organised crime. He was still an operational police officer.

Where his years of experience and skill had failed him was quite simple. He had allowed the mind and body of a forty-year-old to be captivated, captured almost, by a pretty girl, ten, twelve years his junior. She was there for a reason; he knew that now. Her journey had commenced with two things in mind, two separate pieces of information that needed clarifying and dealing with.

The first was genuine and heartfelt, to find Cade and thank him for caring about her mother, for showing her in a few tempestuous days that human kindness did still exist – and without agenda.

The second task was to carry out her mother's wish – to furnish Cade with one half of a powerful document. A document so damning that it would potentially set back relations and financial success ten or twenty years. It was a document that had been missing, presumed sold for many years.

Sadly, her cover as a tourist, who happened to be travelling in the same region as Cade now lived was poorly planned and Saptelea Val – the Seventh Wave – as they had become over time – were able to easily identify and locate her. Their goal was to kill her, recover the files and flee, all within the realms of what would look like a simple vehicle crash, involving a tourist in a far-flung corner of the world, where their criminal group were not known to operate.

They had failed to anticipate a love struck former British officer.

Cade was so blinkered that even with his extensive policing experience he had missed it – missed the plot, literally, the act and the links to his past. Why was it not calling from the rooftops? If it feels too good to be true, it probably is. How many times had he said that to potential victims?

Most of the old Op Breaker team had moved on, but a few remained, loyal to Roberts and the fight against crime syndicates. They held one such group as a standing order item on their monthly briefings – that group was known simply as the Seventh Wave or when time was of the essence – Seventh.

Roberts took every opportunity to drive home the issue of bank ATM offending which had spread, becoming more technically savvy and lucrative. There were new methods coming online too, some so advanced that the police were yet to see them in action, let alone understand them.

It lwas a rare event to catch anyone in the act. It was even harder to calculate just how much damage had been caused to the financial sector in ten years. Millions were always a good start in any conversation.

Having watched the team perform, Cade had offered his

services as an unpaid advisor. John Daniel had told him there was no such thing, but Cade, who had recently put the word Consultant on his simple business card, was still financially independent and able to travel around the world, picking up work when he chose to. He lived a pleasant lifestyle that was funded by that word consultant, the interest from his savings and the profits from the best restaurant in the ocean side town he had learned to call his second home.

He had propagated a series of seeds sown over fifteen or so years that were now bearing fruit – and he was in demand. And it felt very agreeable indeed.

He would never forget the damage that Alex Stefanescu had done to him and a select few people, some of whom he liked, one he was sure he probably would have grown to love. Equally, he couldn't forgive himself for the harm he had caused to her.

He had spent weeks, probably months hunting for the group, in the great city of London, across the south east of England and ultimately into Europe.

Alex had been arrested without incident by a specialist unit in Spain. His brother Stefan, had, much to everyone's disbelief turned up at the Foreign Office headquarters with a get out of jail free card and an explanation that Cade, nor Daniel were able to accept. Valentin Niculcea, a man none of them had met, became an ally, and a family of females with the surname Petrov disappeared into Bulgarian folklore.

There were others out there. Some had managed to escape, others had lay in waiting, sitting back and watching, waiting for the moment their leader initiated what he called the third phase. The first was to target the banks, their machines and their accounts. The second was to advance things a little – raise the ante – steal jewels and a set of documents. The third was still future state, pending the return of the Jackdaw. It was already planned – target a Major event and use it as a smokescreen for something far more lucrative. All it needed was the man himself. For now, no one knew where he was. He had the financial networks and reputation to make a call and go to ground until he was safely able to re-emerge. On that score, the clock was ticking and the pages of the calendar falling to the ground. Any day now.

The middle name of 'Bloody' had ceased to be used when people were referring to Johnathan Hewett – Foreign Office darling and poster boy for the British government. He had somehow pressed reset on his life, burying the skeletons firmly underground, somewhere. Cade thought he envied him, but deep in his own closet he kept returning to the mistrust that Daniel had cast upon him. And if John Augustus Daniel, Detective Chief Inspector, Metropolitan Police said something was not right, then frankly, it bloody well wasn't.

The Seventh Wave: Cade even hated thinking the name, let alone saying it audibly, and he certainly despised their bright blue tattoo and their arrogant and at times cruel methods. Their strength had not been in their numbers, but their networks. Allowing themselves to collaborate with other equally Machiavellian groups had been wise, long before others had even contemplated the idea. Sharing the profits from across Europe into North Africa and the Middle East had been inspired.

Cade missed the job – that of a streetwise police officer.

But times had changed and so had he. He was stood now, watching younger staff, knocking out intelligence reports with one hand and updating their social media pages with the other. He felt old, but in his forties was far from it. A look in the nearest mirror reminded him that grey, or as he fashionably called it, titanium, was the new black. The girls loved it, the women more so. With a flash of marine-blue eyes and a year-round, natural tan, he felt he still had the ability to charm the birds from their safe haven.

He had blended into the background at the office of the DCPCU, watching the afternoon develop. His old partner Roberts had covered off the word of the day and the daily occurrences and having completed the online quiz had finished on a good news story. He always did. Cade wasn't sure where he found half of them, but good news travels fast in a police station. Never as fast as bad news, mind you, Cade thought out loud.

Roberts sported a light blue suit, white shirt and a hand-kerchief in his jacket pocket. As always, he wore black, rather superb Oxford brogues, and his ensemble was finished off with a garish and broad tie. The tie had a double Windsor knot and sat almost halfway up his chest in homage to a bygone era. In that regard, nothing had changed.

Today's offering was lime green, as bright as the lurid paintwork on the Lamborghini Gallardo that had just driven past the Yard, turning left and out onto Broadway.

"So how have you been me, old China?" Roberts was ebullient as ever.

"Really average mate. Actually, that's not fair, I've been great. I left you and trawled around the UK and Europe. Haven't had the courage to return to New Zealand yet. JD's got it all in hand. I left behind a lot of a mess. He sees to it that my lawn gets mowed now and then, collects mail from the post office and slags me off to anyone that knows me. I haven't been back since..."

"I'm sure my friend, but head back you must. Remember, you can ski in the morning and surf in the afternoon!"

"Must be tiring." They both laughed. "Talking of which, Jason, did you ever learn to play the banjo?"

"I never did Jack. Truth is, I never could."

"No, seriously? I would never have known."

Roberts placed a hand on Cade's back. "Come on pal, let's head to The Sanctuary, it's still there. I'll buy you a lemon fruit tea or whatever it is you kiwi types drink. They've done it up. Really swish it is."

"Really? I'm shocked. What have they done?"

"Changed the beer mats!"

There was genuine laughter now. Cade relaxed and walked towards the door, knowing from muscle memory where to head next. "Hang on, mate. Just wait one?"

He walked back across the office to O'Shea's desk. She saw him coming and started to rotate a pencil through her sharpener.

"I hope you've got a licence for that thing, Miss O'Shea?"

"I have Inspector Cade." She smiled. "How are you, Jack?" She was more sincere than he expected.

"I'm fine. One hundred percent."

"That's good."

It was painful. Cade had two choices.

"Carrie, we are heading to The Sanctuary. See you there in twenty?" He recalled that she sometimes liked it blunt, delivered without prose.

"Only if you are buying and promise to be good."

Cade inhaled and grinned "I'm nothing if not predictable. See you there."

He walked back towards Roberts. O'Shea removed the pencil and slid it back into her drawer. It didn't need sharpening, anyway. She located a small bottle of Chanel No 5 in her desk drawer and applied some to her wrists and neck, stood, locked her drawers and made towards the lift. As it arrived, she walked in and stood in a group of six people. She'd lost weight. She looked good. She couldn't jump for joy but would have done if the lift had been empty.

The late afternoon became the evening and along with the newer members the old team had made a pact to remain in touch and do whatever they could to put every last member of the Seventh Wave team in a prison cell, for some were still out there, carrying on the dream of their beloved leader. Their leader, the man who referred to himself as the Jackdaw and who, to everyone's frustration, anger and amazement had been released from the Romanian prison he had been transferred to in 2006.

When the Spanish and British authorities had questioned the decision, the response was simple, it was easier to release him than manage the chaos that he caused inside the high security prison, and to be rational he had only committed lower level offences in Romania that they knew of and were able to successfully prosecute.

The Spanish judge had sentenced him to ten years for his role in being part of an organised criminal group – it was ambiguous at best. Yes, there were probably unsolved murder cases, people trafficking and a smorgasbord of other cases, but with witnesses either hostile or missing each case collapsed or was withdrawn, leaving one of the most wanted men in Europe with a surprisingly small list of convictions.

. . .

Cade made his excuses – he knew that he needed to play a longer game with O'Shea. On paper she had probably forgiven him for walking away, but she had a pachydermic quality and hadn't yet forgotten or forgiven completely. Time would tell.

"Good night team. Carrie, you OK to get home?" She still had a slight limp, a legacy of her attack in 2004 when something concealed deep inside her physical make up had shifted, permanently.

"I'm a big girl, Jack. But thank you."

He knew when to quit. "As you wish my lady. I'll perhaps see you tomorrow? I leave soon."

"Perhaps."

He walked out of the pub and stood. Left or right? Right took him towards O'Shea's place and he had long lost the rights to enter there. Left ended up down by the river near the Houses of Parliament. Why not, he'd never walked down there at night, as a tourist, when in Rome and all that.

Although it was relatively late the streets were well lit and Cade felt safe. He'd once chased a gunman down this same street, had been forced off the road by a vanload of men hell bent on killing his passenger, and had crawled in subterranean passages, up to his neck in river water and sewage. He had literally lived the metropolitan dream. So yes, for Jack Cade, nomadic police officer, the streets of London felt safe.

He turned when he heard the familiar growl of an Audi V10 engine – sat somewhere in the body of a flouro-green Italian thoroughbred. 'Nice, but not that practical' thought the man who then recalled that somewhere, twelve thousand miles away he had his own mid-life crisis locked in a garage, covered in a dust sheet, the only dynamic aspect of which was a ticking clock.

He crossed the road and began to walk towards Westminster Bridge. He was amazed at the size of the crowd when he got there. A group of tourists had bolstered the ranks of twenty to thirty other sightseers, busy snapping photographs, two fingers respectively showing to the cameras in every pose.

His pocket was buzzing, that familiar feeling that someone wants you. He pulled out the phone and checked the screen; it was Roberts. 'Bless, he misses me already.'

He enjoyed the fact that Roberts had to make up something minor in order to ring him. He was a good man – one day their paths would cross again. Of that Cade was sure. For now, he pressed the red button and condemned Roberts to an answerphone message.

He shuffled into the crowd and stepped to one side to avoid a jogger. She was running at speed and looked quite impressive, and he envied her. He knew her gender as it was clearly a female from the build. He resented that she could leave her home at this time of the day, wherever that may be, and run through the streets of the iconic city unencumbered by the trials of life.

The runner did that thing where she diverted onto one foot and then the other. He mirrored her moves. She was wearing a hood to combat the cold and woollen gloves, but the rest of her clothing was pure athlete, Lycra, wrapped around an obviously honed body. For a thousandth of a second, he locked onto her eyes. Jade, perfectly shaped and alluring. He took it all in. A slender pink scar over the left brow, slightly tanned, almost olive skin. It was all going in subconsciously.

A collision looked inevitable, but the female managed to swerve around Cade, brushing against him, spinning him one hundred and eighty degrees, stumbling slightly, righting herself before she blended into the building line and headed up the road towards Parliament Square. The very place that Cade had chased Constantin all those years before.

He wondered what had become of him. Not for long, but he wondered nonetheless. He involuntarily favoured the collarbone where the bastard had sunk his teeth into him, ripping a piece of flesh that had never recovered, leaving a dark red and hollowed out reminder every time he looked in the mirror.

He shook his head and muttered to himself, 'You need to let it all go John Cade. You need to let it all fade away.'

He heard the car again, knowing that the engine note belonged to the German V10. It was accelerating away from him, shifting rapidly between the gears.

'Nice. Very nice.'

He continued walking. It was cold, so he increased his step. As he passed an office on Storey's Gate he cursed, remembering that he still had a slightly creased envelope in his jacket pocket. It was a Christmas card which he intended to post weeks before, early enough to get there among the thousands of others trying to beat the annual postal deadline.

Addressed to a small property in a semi-rural location near the town of Whitianga, on the Eastern Pacific Coast of New Zealand, it was a simple greeting to an old friend to whom he owed his life. Inside, double-sealed to stop pilfering, he had placed a cheque for a thousand dollars, a door key and an inscription. It read:

"To my warrior friend. My home is your home. I'll be back at some point in 2015. Use my place over the festivities and have a great time. The drinks cupboard is full – empty it.

The keys to the car are on the hook just inside the garage. Don't break it. Kind regards, always. Manuia le Kerisimasi / Merry Christmas. Jack."

It was already stamped and ready to go. He slipped it into the letterbox and nodded. It was a good thing to do in the season of goodwill, for a man who worked tirelessly, living off the land where possible and trying to shape his life once more. He had very little but the genuine love of his family. In a strange way Cade envied him out there on his favourite beach, collecting seaweed and harvesting the shoreline with just the waves and the call of the oystercatchers for company.

The temperature had tumbled. Ten paces up the road and back up to speed, he put his hands back in his pockets. It was starting to snow and as fast as his pace was, he was still feeling the effects as the large flakes began to drop from the sky, bringing a sense of silence to the ever-busy streets.

His hand stopped on a piece of paper. It immediately felt extraneous. Running his fingers over it he became curious so he removed it, slowly unfolded it and used the nearby streetlight to help him read the words. He brushed a few of the beautifully symmetric flakes from the white paper and read it twice.

'Catseye Lodge – Whitsunday. 17/01/2015.'

He cast his eyes over the words once more, turning to see if anyone was watching him, trying to understand how the note had got there. Perhaps it had been there for a while?

Perhaps, it wasn't for him? The date meant nothing, the location even less, although he knew of its reputation as a breathtakingly pretty place, tucked into the Great Barrier Reef off the east coast of Australia. But it was in the middle of bloody nowhere. Why would he go there? Too many questions. He folded the paper back into a neat square and resisting the urge to throw it away put it into his jacket, started walking towards his apartment and decided to revisit the situation the next day.

As he walked, he sent John Daniel a text message. Simple and to the point. 'I'll be home in January – get the barbie cleaned and the wine in the fridge. Love to you both. All is as well as it can be.'

It was three the next morning when he woke with a start. The female on the bridge. *She* had put the note in his pocket. It had to be her. Of course it did. No one else had the opportunity. It was obvious, unless you were exhausted and your mind lacked the capacity to absorb so much as another word.

He sat up, turned on the bedside lamp. She had woken him from an unbroken sleep. She had invaded his subconscious mind.

It looked like her. She had her eyes, of that he was certain. The more he thought back to the scene, the crowd, the girl, the skill it would have taken to deposit the note without him realising, the more he knew.

It was her. And she was alive.

ACKNOWLEDGMENTS

In the acknowledgements section of my first thriller *Seventh* I said that there were countless people I could thank. That was true, of course, but the reality is I have to thank people in order.

In 2014, I took special leave to fly halfway around the world. It was a trip that was awash with adjectives. It was cathartic like no other journey and above all it was uplifting, heart breaking and final.

On a late spring afternoon in the County of Kent, England, I sat in a hospice, reading aloud from my first ever book, my autobiography, *Actually, The World Is Enough*.

I had been putting off writing it for years until the momentum to complete it was spurred on by the unwelcomed and devastating news that my dear old dad was terminally ill.

I sat next to him for days as he lay, with incredible dignity, waiting to die. I read page after page to him as he continued to charm the nurses and make outrageous offers to anyone that would listen to him whilst he held court. Why not? He had nothing to lose.

At one point he stopped me and with tears in his eyes he said, "You know son, that piece right there, the story and the way you tell it should be a complete book. It deserves to be told. Do it for me?"

Flying home, I had a whole day to contemplate life. In truth, I spent most of the journey crying and sleeping and thinking; staring out of the window, holding my wife's hand, looking down at a landscape I neither knew nor appreciated.

The moment I got home, I started the *Seventh Wave* trilogy. Three years later, *Seventh* was published and now only six months later its sequel *Seven Degrees* has gone to print (and for our many friends who inhabit the paperless world – Kindle!).

I must also thank Claire. Without divulging any more information, Claire is one of those six degree, lifetime, tectonic friends. Our paths crossed many years ago when as complete strangers we helped a mutual colleague who needed defending at a time of crisis. Claire was 'ex-job' – retired early with injuries sustained on duty and frankly far too good to be ignored as a source of information and literary debates over the ludicrous and infinite potential of the female mind.

To Mum. For your support and love when times were really tough. We got there in the end, didn't we? I always knew we would.

My children, Stephanie and Andrew, growing up so fast that I didn't quite spot that they were both in their late twenties. Where would I be without you two – and where has that time gone? You complete the perfect family; with your combined menagerie of wonderful animals and delightful children you support me totally. I simply cannot find words to say how much I appreciate you both and how proud of you I am. The only way I could do it was to offer you both cameo roles in the series and these books as a legacy.

Amanda. My first, my always. Watching you read *Seventh* in four days, whilst in paradise, under an island sun was both intriguing and bloody nerve wracking. You are indeed my greatest critic, but for all the right reasons; for saying the things I need to hear (and keeping those other lesser thoughts to yourself). Thank you for caring for me. A veritable tower of strength. I love you more.

To my early readers; that sounds so pretentious. Your feedback and genuine warmth is truly humbling. I hope that one day you can be among the elite who can sit back and say, "I knew him when he was awful *and* unknown."

To the characters in the series. You know who you are. Some of you are still propping up the thin blue line so require an air of anonymity; some have moved on, but with each of you there is a bond stronger than many could ever imagine. You are the mortar in society's brickwork. Thank you for your support, your love and your dedication and above all thank you for allowing me to craft a character out of you. It's never easy. I hope they meet with your approval!

Finally, 'Mr Russell'. I saved you until last. What can I say? Your seven series logos deserve to be seen around the world. Simple but clever at the same time, it could be argued, a lot like us.

Anyone that can put up with my myriad editing disasters deserves recognition. "Seriously, you should never be allowed near your book again!" was the low point. Helping you with your own work of art helped to ease my burden somewhat. If you love football and want to read a heart-warming tale of

one man's obsession with a second-tier football team, read
Dell Boy.

As this sequel heads to the presses in time for Christmas, I know I have to start the final leg of the journey –
either that or my best-selling series will be a two book trilogy. New characters, a continuing story and the possibility
of a new, standalone novel. Whether I write it is down to
you, my sanity, and if I am gifted with enough time – for
that is one commodity none of us should take for granted.

Thank you for supporting me in everything I do.

ACKNOWLEDGMENTS TO NEW EDITION

It would be a travesty if I did not mention two wonderful
people, once strangers and yet now friends, confidantes and
mentors, occasionally humble students, sounding boards,
passionate, eager, energetic and so supportive, they are
Rebecca Collins and Adrian Hobart, the directors of
Hobeck Books.

I feel we discovered each other when I was about to call
time on my hopes and aspirations to finally be recognised as
a genuine author and Hobeck were seeking new talent.

The planetary alignment was completed with a shooting
star that lit up a velvet sky. I am so thrilled to be working
with them and the other members of the Hobeck team.
Thank you. x

Lewis

ABOUT THE AUTHOR

Lewis Hastings is a pseudonym. He was born in 1963 (a by-product of the long, harsh winter of 1962) in Kent, the Garden of England.

By virtue of his father's role as a prison officer he became somewhat nomadic, moving from county to county during his formative years. As quickly as he made friends, they became a distant memory.

His school life was a heady cocktail of fun, misery and abject failure which explains why he decided not to pursue a university career. Having successfully taken the entry exam, military history cruelly prevented him from a chance of a career in the Royal Marines.

Regretting the decision not to wear the Green Beret, he forged out a highly unsuccessful and miserable career in sales; a way to pay the bills and provide a home for his growing family. In 1988 a cathartic event changed his approach to life and he spent two frustrating years trying to forge a new career as a police officer. By doing this he would in fact continue a family tradition stemming back to the early 1800s.

His career commenced with the Nottinghamshire Constabulary at a time of enormous change and he was soon posted to some of the most beautiful and dangerous locations in the county where he learned the noble art of policing including community, intelligence and vice work (the latter, whilst challenging, at least offered a secondary income).

In 2003, wearing a different hat, he found himself in New Zealand, soon realising that the age-old maxim about excrement, locations and days of the week still rang true. Considered a subject matter expert in border related matters, Hastings brings absolute accuracy to all of his plots – having instigated the real life investigation into an international syndicate he can say with authority that this story is very true.

This is his third book. The first, an autobiography, *Actually, The World Is Enough* has attracted positive reviews for its ability to make the reader laugh and cry, often in the same sentence.

Hastings' second book, *Seventh* is a crime thriller and the first part of a trilogy called *The Seventh Wave*.

Seven Degrees has authenticity, dark humour and diverse characters which allow it to standalone in a sea of crime thrillers written by current and former law enforcement officers.

Hastings is married with two children, a lake-loving Labrador, and lives in a house.

ALSO BY LEWIS HASTINGS

The Angel of Whitehall

Twelve women hunted by a deadly enemy

A young African woman's body is found slumped in a London side street. Her stomach slashed open, a single diamond hiding within.

A shameful secret that must remain hidden

Former British police officer, Jack Cade, is the only man who can help unravel the mystery. Piecing together the fragments of information that an old man's fragile memory reveals, Cade unearths a people trafficking conspiracy with links to the heart of the British Establishment.

They want his source silenced. Cade is the only person who can protect him. But who can Cade trust?

————————————
READER REVIEWS
————————————

SEVENTH

'Emotions run high reading this thriller and I feel totally spent now.'

'Expect adrenaline surges, plenty of testosterone, comradory, deceit, empathy and extreme hate in this intense journey that is full of tension, suspense, action, drama and intrigue.'

'Clearly written from the heart.'

'I literally could not put it down.'

'Every page is a delight to read and the story takes you through an amazing journey.'

'A real page turner, I couldn't put it down.'

'This book is a must read.'

SEVEN DEGREES

'A fast paced crime thriller with enough twists to keep readers guessing.'

'...gripping...'

'If book 1 of this trilogy blew me away, then this one blew me harder.'

'...edge of your seat stuff...'

'Fantastic.'

SEVEN OF SWORDS

'Twists and turns in every chapter.'

'Had me gripped from the start...truly magnificent writing.'

'I didn't want it to end!'

'WOW what a read!'

'I implore you to pick up this trilogy.'

'Read it, this will not be a disappointment to you.'

THE ANGEL OF WHITEHALL

'I would recommend this book unequivocally with no reservations, my one issue is that it will ensnare you and leaving it will not be an option until the last page. This is a story destined to be remembered as crossing a threshold of this specific genre. It is that good.'